SKYWARD FLIGHT

THE COLLECTION

BOOKS BY JANCI PATTERSON

A Thousand Faces

A THOUSAND FACES
A MILLION SHADOWS
A BILLION ECHOES

The Skilled (with Megan Walker)

SINKING CITY
DROWNING CITY
RISING CITY

SKYWARD FLIGHT

THE COLLECTION

SUNREACH · REDAWN · EVERSHORE

BRANDON SANDERSON
AND JANCI PATTERSON

DELACORTE PRESS

Text copyright © 2022 by Dragonsteel Entertainment, LLC
Interior illustrations by Charlie Bowater and Ben McSweeney copyright © 2022 by Dragonsteel Entertainment, LLC
Jacket art © 2022 by Charlie Bowater

All rights reserved. Published in the United States by Delacorte Press, an imprint of Random House Children's Books, a division of Penguin Random House LLC, New York.

Delacorte Press is a registered trademark and the colophon is a trademark of Penguin Random House LLC.

Reckoners®, Mistborn®, and Brandon Sanderson® are registered trademarks of Dragonsteel Entertainment, LLC.

Visit us on the Web! GetUnderlined.com
Educators and librarians, for a variety of teaching tools, visit us at RHTeachersLibrarians.com

Library of Congress Cataloging-in-Publication Data is available upon request.
ISBN 978-0-593-56785-2 (hardcover) — ISBN 978-0-593-56827-9 (lib. bdg.)
ISBN 978-0-593-56786-9 (ebook)

The text of this book is set in 12-point Apollo MT.
Interior design by Ken Crossland

Printed in the United States of America
10 9 8 7 6 5 4 3 2 1
First Edition

For Cortana Olds, my first reader.

For Kenton Olds, who makes me laugh every day.

For Darci Cole, who let me borrow her faith
for a while.

—J.P.

CONTENTS

SUNREACH

FREYJA MARTEN

CALLSIGN:
FM

1

The day the delver came, I stood staring up at the stars.

Even after all these months, I wasn't accustomed to living in the sky. I'd grown up underground, in a cavern so deep it could take hours to reach the surface. I'd felt safe there, buried beneath kilometers of rock, other caverns forming a buffer above the one where I lived—down where nothing could reach us.

Now everyone called me FM, but my parents named me Freyja, after the warrior goddess of my ancient heritage. I was never much of a warrior. Everyone expected I'd take the pilot's test and hoped that I'd graduate, but after that I surprised them by continuing to fly. As a full pilot, I could have had any job I wanted in the safety of the caverns. Yet I'd chosen to move from the surface of the planet— open and foreign and exposed—up to one of the enormous platforms that orbited above it, sheltering the surface from the sky. My father had taken to saying I was skysick, but it was the opposite— the sky terrified me. It was so big and wide I could fall into it and be swallowed up.

Above me, the other platforms that dominated the skies crossed over each other again, blocking my view of the eternal blackness dotted with the strange white stars I'd only heard of before I joined the Defiant Defense Force. My alarm went off—the beeping alert from my radio that my flight was scheduled for immediate take-off. It was normal for flights to be called up at random—I'd been responding to sirens at a moment's notice since my first day as a cadet.

But today, half of my flight was missing. The rest of us had assumed this would afford us some unofficial R&R; while our flight-leader, Jorgen, was planetside, surely we'd be called up last.

Apparently we'd guessed wrong. When I reached the landing bay, I immediately understood why. It wasn't only our flight that had been called up. Every fighter was readied, the maintenance crew working their way through preflight checks at double speed while pilots ran for their ships and jumped into their cockpits.

I looked for the rest of my flight. Without a flightleader, we couldn't take off until we knew who was in command. There were four other members of my flight currently in residence on Platform Prime: Kimmalyn, who was part of my original flight, and our three newer members: Sadie, T-Stall, and Catnip. Nedd and Arturo were planetside with Jorgen, so Kimmalyn and I were the most likely to be given command, but I didn't want it, and I knew Kimmalyn didn't either.

I didn't see any of my flightmates at the moment, but my friend Lizard from Nightmare Flight waved at me from the open hatch of her cockpit. Lizard had bright blue eyes and waist-length black hair. I didn't know how she kept it so long—mine started to bother me if I let it grow to shoulder length. Lizard's real name was Leiko, but like me she went by her callsign almost all of the time.

"FM!" Lizard called. "They're combining your flight with ours. Nose said to wave you all down as you came in and tell you to set your radios to our channel."

Thank the stars. I would have followed any flightleader, of course, but I'd flown under Nose before, and a lot of the members of Nightmare Flight were my friends. Lizard was close to my age—she'd been in cadet training right before me. The sophomore class tended to be hard on the newest pilots, but Skyward Flight was something of a legend thanks to our flightmate, Spin, which earned us respect most newly minted pilots could only dream of.

"Any idea what's happening?" I asked Lizard.

"No clue," she said. "But Nose is already in the air. We'd better get up there."

"Thanks, Lizard," I said. I ran for my fighter and found Kimmalyn already in her cockpit across the way. As soon as I climbed into mine, I saw the light blinking and switched my radio to her private channel.

"FM," Kimmalyn said as I readied my fighter. "Do you know what's going on?"

"No idea," I said. "An attack of some kind?" We often dealt with small groups of Krell fighters, though only a really massive attack would justify calling us all up at once.

"I don't know either," Kimmalyn said. "But I just saw Spin. She's back."

I blinked, my hands pausing on the controls. Spensa had managed to use her strange psychic powers to leave our doomed little planet and run some crazy spy mission, trying to steal hyperdrive technology from the enemy. Until we had that technology we were marooned here, fish in a growth vat waiting to be speared. Spin had been gone for weeks, and I knew Jorgen and Admiral Cobb were worried she'd never return.

"Did she bring us a hyperdrive?" I asked.

"I don't know," Kimmalyn said. "But I doubt it's a coincidence we're being called up now. I'm guessing she brought trouble with her. Like the Saint always says, 'Trouble follows its own.'"

Kimmalyn was probably right. As glad as I was to hear Spensa was back, I didn't think it was a good sign for any of us. If disaster struck, generally Spin was right there in the middle of it. Not that she *caused* it necessarily, but it did seem to follow her around.

I engaged my acclivity ring, then boosted out of the landing bay to join the mass of other ships in the air. The platform itself was high above the planet, part of the massive layers of platforms and debris that shut out almost all view of the sky from the surface below.

Scud, there were a lot of ships up here. Whatever trouble had followed Spin home, Admiral Cobb was sparing no one to stop it. If this was the day the Superiority had chosen to destroy us, we were going to have to show them exactly how dangerous we were.

I tuned in to Nightmare Flight's channel, and Kimmalyn and I flew to the coordinates Nose gave us, a pocket between some of the nearby platforms. Most of the rest of Skyward Flight was already there, including T-Stall and Catnip—cool guys who were a blast to hang out with, but a little lacking in the common sense department—and Sadie, who had been flying as my wingmate in the weeks since Spin had left.

"Welcome to Nightmare Flight," Nose said to the five of us. "Quirk, you'll be Sushi's wingmate today."

"Understood," Kimmalyn said.

"We're all here," Nose said. "We're going to follow our nav path out of the platforms and cut across to the right flank of the battlefield. Sound off."

One by one the members of Nightmare Flight called in, giving their ship numbers and callsigns. We'd switched numbers in Skyward Flight several times. I was Skyward Five currently, and the members of my flight kept our Skyward numbers, sounding off in order after Nightmare Flight finished.

We flew at Mag-3 in a line astern formation, weaving between the layers of platforms, and then Nose gave us a heading on the far side of the battlefield. We loosened our formation, flying in a wide V away from Detritus's autonomous gun platforms and then cutting across the curvature of the planet to approach the incoming ships.

As we did, I could see the two battleships that had been watching us for the past several weeks out in the blackness of space—monstrous, looming shapes totally unlike our sleek fighters, clearly not made to deal with atmosphere and air resistance. We didn't have anything like that on Detritus. Our biggest transport ships didn't carry more than a few dozen passengers.

Beyond them I could now see another long, boxy ship—newly arrived. It was hard to make out against the black, but there were smaller ships out there as well, congregated in a cluster. Probably approaching us at high speeds, though it was difficult to tell at this distance, even on my monitors.

"Our orders are to come up the right flank and engage the enemy," Nose said. "They're fielding a lot of drones, but also fifty piloted spacecraft."

Fifty? We were used to fighting large contingents of drones with a few enemy aces, but not *fifty* piloted ships.

"Flight Command says they have intel that the piloted craft aren't enemy aces," Nose said. "But we also don't know *what* they are, so we're to engage, drawing as many as possible away from Platform Prime."

Some of the other flights congregated just outside the reach of the gun platforms, waiting for orders. This first approach would be an experiment then. If Command didn't know what these craft were, they'd need to study their behavior before they could commit their entire force. It made sense from a strategic point of view.

But it was a lot less comforting being the subject of the experiment. The cavern where I'd grown up was home to a research facility that tested everything from new toothpaste recipes to the effects of toxic chemicals. Some of my Disputer friends talked about raiding the place someday and releasing all the lab rats, whose lives were sad and often short. I saw one once that had escaped. It had chewed off most of the fur from its hind legs, which were covered in boils from some chemical reaction. Not, I hoped, from the toothpaste.

Sometimes I identified with those rats.

As we made our sweep above the platforms, my wingmate, Sadie, called on a private channel. "What does Nose mean, they don't know what these things are?" she asked. "How do they know they're not aces then?"

"I don't know," I replied. "But I think we're going to be among the first to find out."

Sadie's channel went quiet, and then a moment later the comm light for her channel brightened again. "I wish the others were here."

"By the others, you mean Spin," I said. I tried not to tease her about her obvious adoration of Spensa. The others, especially Nedd, tried less.

"I mean, she's an incredible fighter! Don't you think our chances would be better if she were here?"

"Quirk said she saw Spin right before we were called up. So she probably *is* here."

But not flying with us. What did *that* mean?

"Really?" Sadie said. "That has to increase our chances, right?"

Sadie had done some fighting with us, but we'd seen fewer and fewer Krell attacks lately, especially since the battleships arrived. "Probably," I said. "But our chances increase a lot more if we don't think about them and instead focus on what's in front of us."

"Right," Sadie said. "Focus. That's what Spin would do."

"Also shout graphic and violent things at the enemies. So I suppose you could try that."

"That's right! Down with you, vile . . . space-dwelling . . . ships of . . . vileness! May you all die painful, fiery deaths! How was that?"

"That was definitely something," I said. "Did it make you feel better?"

"A little. I think I need to practice. May you all explode in big fiery explosions, approaching not-ace ships of whateverness!"

"Uh, Sentry? Maybe practice on your own and just share the highlights, okay?"

"Oh, right," Sadie said. "Sure thing."

The radio went quiet, leaving me alone with my thoughts. What

I said to Sadie about focusing was true, but I'd always been better at dispensing advice than following it.

"Ready, flight?" Nose said.

"Skyward Five, ready," I responded. I listened to other voices over the radio doing the same. There were more of us than usual, but it still felt strange to be missing Jorgen, Nedd, and Arturo.

I didn't think any of us—aside from maybe T-Stall—were stupid enough to believe the official excuse for their absence. You didn't send the flightleader *and* his two assistants for R&R at the same time unless there was a very good reason.

As we approached the right side of the enemy formations, several ships broke off and headed straight for us.

"Sentry, FM," Nose said on the general channel, "take point and engage the enemy, then move to evasive maneuvers. T-Stall, Catnip, follow up. See if you can draw them into a bait and switch."

Sadie and I broke out of formation, launching toward the enemy on overburn. Immediately four ships chased after us as we led them along the outside of the platforms surrounding the planet.

Sadie and I began evasive maneuvers, weaving about so the ships behind us couldn't get a clean shot with their destructors. I checked my proximity sensors. Of the four ships following us, two were drones and two were piloted ships, the ones we usually assumed were enemy aces.

"FM and Sentry, hold course," Nose said. "Quirk, pick them off."

"Yes, sir!" Kimmalyn said, and a few seconds later the ship following me the closest took a hit and veered off to avoid Kimmalyn's fire.

"We're about to pass a gun platform," I said on a channel to Sadie. "Let's see if we can get Quirk a little auto support."

"I'll cover you," Sadie said. She moved into position, with me closest to the planet, soaring above the many platforms and hunks of debris that covered Detritus like a loose fragmented shell. I continued my erratic course, dodging bursts of destructor fire. With each bank toward the planet I moved a little farther in, using the readings on my dash to gauge exactly how close I was edging to the gun platform. Most of those platforms were autonomous and would target us the same as the enemy. The Engineering Corps hadn't yet been able to break into the systems to bring them under our control. The enemy ships—drone and pilot alike—knew enough to avoid the gun platforms, but sometimes when we engaged them in enough of a chase we could get them to—

There.

One of the ships tailing me banked too far to the right, and the gun emplacement on the nearby platform fired, the ship disappearing from my sensors in a silent explosion. Kimmalyn fired on the other drone, while Sadie engaged the final ship in a smart series of maneuvers to shift it out in front of me. I shot it with my lightlance, then catapulted myself around it, using my momentum to send it sailing into range of the autoturrets. The platform fired, and the ship burst into fragments, air tanks igniting in a fiery blaze.

"Nice work," Sadie said.

I was pretty sure it was *passable* work, but I wasn't going to say that to her, not in the middle of a battle. She might take it as an insult, and she needed to keep her morale up.

"Thanks," I said. "You too."

"You did most of it."

Sadie was a better pilot than she gave herself credit for, but I wasn't going to have that conversation in the middle of a battle either.

We made a sharp turn and accelerated back toward our flight and the right flank of the battle. Other flights were now engaging the enemy ships, and from the look of things the battle was going well.

If this was the best the Superiority had to send against us, maybe we stood a chance after all.

Sadie and I flew toward Nose and her wingmate, assisting them in shaking a couple of tails. Sadie soared in close to one of the

8

enemy ships and used her IMP to take out their shield, then cut away toward the edge of the battle while I pressed forward, firing my destructors at the now-defenseless ship.

"Quirk, can you cover Sentry?" I asked Kimmalyn over the general channel.

"Quirk's busy," Lizard said. "I'm on it."

The ship in front of me lit up with an explosion above its acclivity ring, and with no air resistance to slow it down, the wreckage continued sailing in the direction it had been going. I cut away, flying out to join Sadie and Lizard, reaching them just as Sadie reignited her shield.

"Nice work," Nose said over the general channel. "Skyward Flight, it's always a pleasure."

I smiled. We worked well as a group, though we didn't fly together regularly. Before I joined the DDF, I hadn't understood the mentality that pushed people to fight as one, to keep doing so even as their friends died around them. I'd never felt that violence was the best way to solve problems, though I understood that violence was the *only* solution that kept us alive when the Krell kept trying to bomb us out of existence. Still, I'd found the rhetoric about glory disturbing, the way the National Assembly seemed to justify anything they wanted by saying it would help us fight the Krell. I had thought pilots were sheep. Skilled, determined, well-respected sheep who did what they were driven to do because they didn't know any better.

Now though, I understood the glue that held us together, and it wasn't stupidity. It was the bond shared by people who faced death together. It was a sense of belonging, of being a piece of something bigger, something important, though I still wasn't convinced everything about it was good. I'd never felt that I needed a military to tell me my place in the world before, and I still didn't.

But there was something about knowing that without me my friends would be worse off that kept me flying even when it terrified me.

"New orders," Nose said over the general channel. "We're to move to evasive maneuvers *only* and then turn off our comms."

Excuse me? "Nose, did you say turn *off* our comms?"

"Those are the orders, FM," Nose said. "All comms off. Do not turn them on under any circumstances."

That couldn't be right. Without the ability to communicate, we couldn't work together as a flight. We'd end up scattered across the battlefield. Good pilots are good communicators. I learned that from Cobb. Without the ability to talk to each other—

Well, it wasn't *exactly* like flying blind, but it was a hell of a lot closer than I liked.

"Are we going to retreat?" Lizard asked.

That would be more manageable. If we could head back beyond the gun platforms we could at least hide, or make our way to Platform Prime under the shelter of the rubble belt.

"Negative," Nose said. "Comms off. Maintain evasive maneuvers. Try to keep the ships busy and await further instructions."

"Instructions?" I said. "How are you going to give us instructions if our *comms* are off?"

"Pilots, we need to go dark," Nose said. "The order comes straight from Admiral Cobb. Stick with your wingmate. If you get stranded, find another member of the flight and stay together. We'll reassemble on the flip side. Nose out."

Scud. "Sentry," I said over a private channel. "You heard Nose. We'll have to stay close together." I had no idea what Command was up to, but Cobb wouldn't give an order like that without a good reason. "Follow my lead." I was the senior pilot. It was my job to keep her alive.

"Oh—okay," Sadie said. She sounded close to panicking, and I couldn't blame her. Terror crawled its way up my throat as I put my hand over the comm button.

And then I turned it off.

2

The world went silent except for the hum of my instruments. The ships around me made no sound as the battle raged on. For the first time I envied Spensa her AI-equipped ship. It chattered like Kimmalyn after too many desserts, but at least it wasn't . . . silent.

Sadie and I flew in close formation so we didn't lose sight of each other. The battle in front of me fractured; ships that had been flying together broke off into wingmate pairs, while the enemy formations stayed mostly the same, chasing our fighters in groups of three or four. They outnumbered us, but we flew better, leading them around in circles.

Sadie would be waiting for my lead. I needed to think of a plan, figure out how to use these new orders to our advantage and communicate it by the way I flew, since we couldn't talk.

But stars, I couldn't take this silence.

I reached around to the belt loop of my jumpsuit. I never used my transmitter while I was flying—Jorgen wouldn't be happy if I transmitted unnecessary noise over the comm. My transmitter didn't emit a ranged signal, but it did something even better.

It played *music*. Handheld transmitters were expensive and rare. My father had given it to me when I made pilot—I used it more than he did when I lived at home. Today I wanted something peppy, something that definitely couldn't be played at my funeral by some three-piece band.

So I turned on one of my favorites, a song my father said was classified as "big band," though many of the other songs featured far more instruments. I thought I understood: the band wasn't big because of the number of players (which was still more than ever played together in the Detritus caverns), but because of the sounds they made, loud and punchy, like the music itself was trying to swing you around and toss you.

I tapped my feet against the floor, listening to the beat as I flew around the outskirts of the battle, watching and waiting for my move. Our orders were to stick to evasive maneuvers, but there were plenty of tricks we could pull that would do damage to the enemies while still being considered evasive.

I found my opening when three ships peeled off the mass of the main battle and bolted toward us. I darted out front, my head nodding to the rhythm of the drums, and the ships chased after me, leaving Sadie behind to shoot with her destructors. She still overused those—Cobb hadn't taught her as a cadet, so we'd had to give her some extra coaching after she made pilot to get her up to speed.

The destructors wouldn't do much while the Krell had their shields up, but there was no way I could use my IMP and still claim I was being evasive. The IMP would take out my shield along with the Krell's, and I didn't dare do that with my comms down—there was no way I'd be able to call for help if I got myself into real trouble.

We were supposed to fly defensively, but that didn't mean I had to let these ships shoot us out of the sky. I bobbed my head to the beat and circled around to some debris that floated above the platforms, out of reach of the gun emplacements.

I grabbed one of the enemy drone pilot ships with my light-lance and fired my thrusters in its direction, dragging it after me toward the rock. Sadie dashed ahead, kiting the other two ships after her as I raced toward the debris. Then I rotated my thrusters and cut the light-lance at the last moment, propelling myself downward beneath the debris while the Krell ship crashed into the rock above me.

I overshot. My GravCaps maxed out and I was struck by g-forces that forced blood upward toward my head. For a moment my vision went red, but I reduced my speed and managed to maintain consciousness, though the music warped in my ears and the lights on my ship controls swam before my eyes.

I began to recover, my head still swimming, and found Sadie flying toward me, the other two ships no longer on her tail. I didn't know if she'd lost them or taken them out while I was distracted, but I was glad either way. I lifted my finger to call her to tell her so before I remembered.

Silence. We were flying in silence.

And I still didn't understand *why*. Sadie and I swung around as the music crashed toward a crescendo, and we soared toward the main battlefield again.

My proximity sensors beeped over the music, warning me of incoming ships headed straight for me at high speed. I didn't dare turn the music up any louder, though I wanted to. I adopted a weaving pattern, moving in rhythm with a trumpeting horn—and the first enemy ship matched my flight pattern, almost as if it wanted to run right into me. I went into a dive, Sadie following after me—

And pulled out right as one of our own fighters passed in front of my nose.

Nightmare Seven. Lizard's ship. Four Superiority fighters followed after her, only one of them breaking away to pepper me with destructor fire.

Scud. Where was Lizard's wingmate? She'd flown so close to get my attention, because she couldn't radio in for help. I pivoted my boosters, veering off in Lizard's direction. Behind me, Sadie launched a barrage of destructor fire at the lone ship near us, the blasts seeming to shoot in time with a snare drum. Sadie executed an Ahlstrom loop to turn herself around and follow after me. That ship might chase her, but I had to trust her to deal with one tail.

With four ships behind her, Lizard was in much bigger trouble, and she needed help. We were better trained, but the Superiority forces had always had more powerful destructors and stronger shields. I accelerated to Mag-4 to catch up with the ships. Ahead of me, Lizard spun in a rolling twin-scissor, trying to shake her tails, but they stuck with her. This group were all piloted ships, and they were working together better than the Krell drones we usually fought. As Lizard pulled out of the scissor, one of the Krell pegged her with a destructor shot.

We had to help her. She still had a shield, but it was weakening. Lizard knew what she was doing—she was already headed toward the gun platforms where we could push the ships close enough to take fire. We were too far from them though. She wasn't going to make it.

My whole body jittering to the syncopation of the music, I opened fire on the nearest Krell, forcing the ship to take evasive action and lose its bead on Lizard. Sadie caught up to me and then pulled ahead, speeding forward.

She was making herself a target, giving me an opening to take care of the other ships while she and Lizard took the destructor fire. It was a risky move—even though Sadie still had a full shield, the Krell destructors could quickly destroy it. If I'd had my radio, I would have yelled at her to pull back and stop being so reckless. Jorgen would never have approved that maneuver.

But I couldn't. I couldn't tell her anything. Instead I followed after her, darting forward to engage one of the other Krell fighters.

We were approaching the gun platforms now as one of the Krell fighters took the bait and went after Sadie instead. Sadie executed a perfect twin-S, dodging the destructor fire.

I missed with the light-lance, and the other two ships bore down on Lizard, both unloading their destructors on her at once.

Lizard evaded many of the blasts, but not enough. With a blink of light, Lizard's shield went down.

I put my hand over the comm button, then pulled it back. We were on our own. I hit my overburn, speeding out in front of Lizard and trying to draw away the Krell fighters. If they followed me, I could evade them while Lizard escaped and got her shield up.

It didn't work. The Krell maintained their focus on Lizard, and a destructor blast hit her boosters, sending the ship spinning toward the planet. I watched helplessly as Lizard's ship spiraled into range of the gun platforms and exploded in a fiery burst. A crash of cymbals seemed to punctuate the explosion.

"No," I whispered. *No.*

Sadie's ship pulled close to mine. Lizard was gone, just like that. She'd never again tell me my boots looked stupid with my jumpsuit or challenge Nedd to a tower-building contest with algae strips. Nothing was going to change that.

I couldn't even call in to Nose to let her know. We wouldn't be able to retrieve Lizard's pin—a ship destroyed like that in the vacuum wouldn't even be good for salvage. She would get only a symbolic ceremony, not a real pilot's funeral.

I focused on the music, though it was now nearing the end of the song, the music building up, the drums punching in an off-kilter syncopation. The ships that took out Lizard were turning around now, though Sadie seemed to have shaken the one that was after her. Together Sadie and I wove back and forth until the ships gave up on us and went to seek easier targets.

The song ended, and silence echoed in my ears.

Lizard was gone. I'd never hear her voice again. I reached for my transmitter, starting another song. I chose a haunting piece played by an instrument my father called a piano. He'd shown me an image of one from the records, but I couldn't imagine how a large bench with buttons made notes like the ones in the song—nimble and lilting and all working together like a well-tuned machine.

This music was much more sedate than the big band music, but I'd suddenly lost the desire for pep. I pulled ahead of Sadie, leading her away from the battlefield. I needed a moment to clear my head. A lack of focus would get us both killed. I could grieve later—now I had to concentrate. I had to keep Sadie alive. I had to—

Suddenly, the blackness of space seemed to *shift*. As if the layers of space itself were being pulled apart, the whole of the battle before me rippled, one layer separating from another, distorting in waves and bends. I shook my head, afraid for a moment that the g-forces might have had some delayed mental effects. What would I do if I had an emergency out here? I couldn't radio for help. I couldn't request to retreat.

And so, even with Sadie flying at my wing, I was still completely and utterly alone when the deep shadow darkened the blackness of space, passing over it like a shroud. In the distance, beyond the circling ships, a mass appeared—another ship maybe, but unlike any I'd ever seen. A core with spires jutting from it like the head of a mace, enormous—perhaps as big as Detritus, but far enough away that it was difficult to tell. The mass was immediately obscured by clouds of dust and shapes that didn't exist—*couldn't* exist— that undulated as the folds of reality seemed to separate and reform across the battlefield, rippling out into the vastness of space. The piano music rose and fell, providing an eerie soundtrack.

Scud, what was *that*?

My finger hovered over the comm switch, trembling. The explosion of Lizard's ship played over and over in my head, even as I tried to banish it. Was I losing my mind? Was this some kind of trauma response? I had to talk to *someone*, didn't I? I had to report what I was seeing, though as I watched the reactions of the other ships in the battlefield, I became increasingly certain I wasn't hallucinating.

I wasn't the only one faltering. Ships that had been engaged in maneuvers flew off course, scattering. The battlefield widened as many ships skittered away from the main fight, probably trying to avoid being shot down while they reconciled themselves to what they were seeing.

Or tried. I didn't know that there was any way to reconcile

myself to *this*. It couldn't be real—the colors and shapes were too maddening, too impossible.

It had to be a hologram, or an illusion like the one that had fooled Spensa's father, convincing him to attack his own people. Except those tactics were supposed to only affect cytonics, people with defects—or assets, we were starting to learn—in their minds that let them travel and communicate across the vastness of the universe. Those shouldn't be able to affect everyone.

And if this was a hologram, it was scudding *big*. What would be projecting that? The enemy battleships? They hadn't done anything like that in the weeks they'd been parked above Detritus, and besides, the vision seemed to be having the same effect on Defiant and Superiority ships alike. I fired my destructors once and watched the dust ripple around the path of the blast, reacting to the force.

The dust at least was real. But what was it, and where had it come from?

I startled as Sadie's ship shot out in front of me, then dropped back. She was flying dangerously close, near enough I could look out my window and see through the glass of her canopy.

Sadie looked right at me, eyes wide in terror. I didn't know what to do—I couldn't talk to her. Instead I simply shook my head. I didn't know what was happening. From the looks of it, *nobody* knew what was happening.

And then with no preamble, the folds of space seemed to ripple, and the strange phenomenon vanished. The battlefield reformed once more, clear and crisp, all the dust moving away as if sucked into the cracks in reality from whence it came.

My finger shook above my comm switch, but then I dropped my hand, gripping the dash. I'd been ordered to turn off my comms, and I hadn't been ordered to turn them back on.

For a moment the ships seemed to regroup, both enemy and friendly drawing back together, like they were all remembering we were supposed to be fighting each other.

And then the enemy force turned, almost as one, and started to withdraw toward the enormous carrier ship. Generally when the enemy withdrew, we didn't chase them, but we also didn't withdraw without orders.

Was it safe to turn comms back on? I scanned the battlefield, looking for other members of our flight, and found Nose and her wingmate hitting overburn, bolting toward us. When she got close, she reversed her thrusters to slow down and pulled up next to me, T-Stall and Catnip following behind her. Nose frantically waved a hand at me, pointing at her own radio.

I switched off my transmitter and flipped my radio on. "Nose?" I said. "What the *scud* was that?"

"Command says delver," Nose said. "I don't know what that means, but I've heard rumors."

We'd all heard the rumors. Kimmalyn and some of the other members of Skyward Flight had been there when the engineers managed to break the encryption on the footage of what had happened to the people who used to live on our forgotten planet. I'd missed the footage, but I'd heard about it. Some giant thing had materialized in the space outside the planet and devoured everyone and everything who lived here. I'd expected it to be more . . . substantial, I guess. More material. That had hardly seemed like a creature at all.

If *that* was what this had been, why were we still alive?

"Nose," I said. "Lizard went down over by the gun platforms. The Krell got her. We tried to save her, but—"

"Copy, FM," Nose said. "You're sure she didn't survive?"

I swallowed. "Affirmative. She spiraled into range of the gun platform. Her ship was annihilated."

The radio was silent again. Nose was Lizard's flightleader. I'd failed to save Lizard, but Nose hadn't even been there.

She'd feel as responsible for her loss as I did, maybe more.

"FM? Nose?" Sadie said, only now getting the message it was safe to turn her radio back on. "What just happened?"

"I'm sure we'll know more soon," Nose said. "Orders are to

regroup, hold until we know the enemy is leaving, then head on back to base."

That made sense. We couldn't abandon the battlefield if they intended to rally and keep fighting.

The concern turned out to be unnecessary. The Superiority fleet gathered at the carrier ship, and then the carrier ship blinked out of existence as if it had never been there at all.

"They had a hyperdrive," I said to Kimmalyn on a private channel. "Maybe we should have been trying to steal it."

"Spin might have found us one," Kimmalyn said.

I hoped she had, because the confusion of this fight made it clearer than ever that we were completely out of our depth. Yeah, we were better pilots than the enemy, and we had gained some ground by taking the fight into space. Platform Prime was a convenient place from which to fight, but it was also vulnerable to attack. It was one small step, barely meaningful if we didn't find a way to get off this rock—if we couldn't find a way to take the fight *to* our enemy rather than merely defending ourselves.

In general, I found self-defense to be a much more admirable pursuit than invasion, but a fish could only live in a vat for so long before it was fried.

We were trapped on Detritus, while the enemy could travel anywhere in the universe, had every resource at their disposal. We needed more. More resources. More pilots. More help. More than we could muster with only what remained of the Defiant fleet after it crashed here almost a century ago.

We lost Lizard today; we were dwindling one by one. I was a pilot. I could follow orders. And my team was the best there was, even when pieces of it were missing. But I also wasn't stupid.

I might not have Cobb's experience or Spensa's vision, but I knew if we didn't figure out how to change the course of the war soon, humanity wasn't going to survive.

3

Four days after the battle, I wandered toward the mess hall on the labyrinthine Platform Prime. I didn't know what this structure had been built for, but whoever constructed it obviously hadn't felt a powerful need to be able to get anywhere quickly or easily without a very detailed map.

I was still in something of a daze. The battle had been labeled a big success by basically everyone because the delver had not, in fact, wiped us all out of existence. But that merely made us *lucky*, a whole lot luckier than all the people who'd died the last time a delver visited Detritus—when it had destroyed the entire civilization that had lived here before us. And while we didn't really know why it had come here or why it had left, we were alive, and hadn't been completely annihilated by it or the Superiority. I should have been happy.

But we weren't *all* alive. Lizard wasn't the first friend I'd lost in battle, and she wasn't the first I'd blamed on myself, even though logically I knew neither Bim's nor Hurl's death had been my fault. The delver had gone, but it could reappear anytime. The Superiority forces had fled, but they too might come back without warning. And when they did, my friends and I would be out there fighting back. We were pilots. We were the only things standing between the last of our species and total extinction.

I knew the *reason* for what we did—and I believed in it, much as I hated what it had done to us as a people. It seemed like that should make me feel better.

But I didn't feel better. All I felt was empty.

After Hurl's death, our whole flight had been given mandatory leave. No one had been given leave this time—not Nightmare Flight, not us, not anyone. That meant Command was worried that the delver would return, that the Superiority would attack. And yet Jorgen, Nedd, and Arturo were still on their mysterious trip planetside. Spensa had disappeared again when the delver did, and Kimmalyn said even Cobb didn't know where she'd gone this time.

Which was why, when I first heard the soft trill of Spensa's pet, Doomslug, I thought I was imagining it.

The sound came from up the corridor, just around the corner in the opposite direction of the mess hall. Before Spensa left on her secret mission, Doomslug used to turn up all over the base here on Platform Prime. I once found her hanging out in the women's room near the cleansing pods, sleeping on one of the heat vents. She liked to perch on my shoulder to listen to music from my transmitter through my headset, and if I offered her flatfish caviar, she'd stay for over an hour.

My parents probably would have been horrified that I fed their expensive gift to a slug, but Doomslug enjoyed the caviar, I enjoyed sharing, and my parents didn't know about it—so everybody won.

I turned the corner and there was Doomslug, curled up by the ventilation grate, warm air blowing the bright blue spines that ran down her back.

"Hey, girl," I said, kneeling down next to her. The slug turned toward the sound of my voice—I wasn't sure if she could *see* or only sense—and I pulled my hand back.

This slug had blue markings down the sides of its face that

almost looked like gills, while Doomslug's face was all yellow. It wasn't Doomslug, but another slug of the same kind.

I blinked down at it. I'd never seen one of these slugs before Spensa brought hers up to Platform Prime. She'd found it in the surface cavern where she'd stayed when she was denied permission to live on Alta Base with the rest of our squad of cadets.

What would *another* of those slugs be doing *here*?

"Hey, buddy," I said, extending my fingers and letting the slug examine them with its bulbous face. The truth was, I had no idea how to determine the sex of a slug, if they indeed had one at all. I wasn't sure if Spensa had actually discerned Doomslug's sex, or arbitrarily decided to refer to her as female.

I slipped my fingers down under the slug's chin—it had more of a fleshy bulb than a head, having no bone structure at all, but it did have a little point of flesh where the chin *might* be. The flesh withdrew slightly at my touch, and then the slug slid forward, leaning in as I scratched its leathery skin. "What are you doing here?"

"Here," the slug trilled softly. Doomslug did that too—repeated words and sounds. This one had a quieter voice, or maybe it was in a quieter mood.

The slug flinched slightly as bootsteps pounded down a nearby corridor. The bootsteps came closer, and the slug slipped back against my knees, hugging its body to me, though it was a bit too large to conceal itself entirely. Jorgen Weight, my flightleader, came barreling around the corner. Jorgen and I grew up in the same cavern and went to the same primary school, so we'd known each other tangentially since we were kids. Jorgen had deep brown skin and curly black hair, and right now was sweating like he'd just run laps around the orchard outside Alta Base. He skidded to a halt and put his hands on his knees, breathing hard. "There it is," he said, looking down at the slug. "That's the last one. I think."

"The last one?" The slug huddled against me, and I scooped it up into my arms, keeping my fingers away from its face. Its mouth wasn't visible, but Doomslug had opened an orifice there when she devoured the caviar. I'd seen her rows of sharp-but-flexible teeth, and while I didn't know if these things were prone to biting, I didn't want to find out.

"Yeah," Jorgen said. "Those devils are slippery. I don't know how they keep getting out of their crate."

Huh. "Collecting more pets for Spensa?" I asked. That seemed a little pathetic, even for Jorgen. He and Spensa had been drooling over each other since before we left Alta. I was pretty sure Jorgen thought it was a well-kept secret.

"Not exactly," Jorgen said.

"Seriously, though, where have you been?" There had to be an explanation beyond what Command had told us.

Jorgen sighed. "Come on. If you can get that thing back into the crate with the others, I'll fill you in."

I looked down at the slug, and its face pivoted docilely toward me. I wanted to know what Jorgen and the others had been doing planetside, and getting the slug into a crate didn't seem like a monumental task. I knew a good trade when I heard one.

"You got it," I told him, and followed him down the hallway into a mostly empty room with two large crates stacked in the center and more piled against the wall. On top of the stack in the center sat Nedd, one of our assistant flightleaders. He was tall and broad-shouldered, and made me feel small beside him, something few people could do. Arturo, our other assistant flightleader, leaned against the wall by the door. He was several inches shorter than me, with tanned skin and dark hair.

"FM!" Nedd shouted, much louder than was necessary. "It's good to see you!"

"You too," I said, with much less gusto, while Arturo gave Nedd a look.

Nedd was an expert at not taking hints. About a month ago during leave, he'd cornered me and asked if I wanted to go out. I'd been aware of his interest for a while; Nedd is cute and all, but not really my type, so I'd finally told him outright that I'd rather be friends. He'd taken it pretty well, but ever since then he'd been overly friendly to me, like he wanted to prove how not-weird the situation was by making it . . . more weird.

Which was exactly why I had ignored his interest to begin with.

Jorgen motioned for Nedd to climb off the knee-high crates. "Do we have them all now?"

"I don't know," Nedd said. "I thought maybe if I sat on them they would stay put—but the lid was closed all the way here, so I don't know how we lost them to begin with."

"They're slippery," I said. Though they weren't, not literally. As I ran my hand down the slug's back, it felt more like petting a well-polished pair of leather boots. "Doomslug used to get out of Spensa's room all the time, even with the door locked." I turned to Jorgen. "But I think you owe me an explanation."

"Not until the slug is in the crate," Jorgen said, pulling off the lid and pointing inside.

"Crate!" a couple of slugs trilled, their voices echoes of each other.

I still didn't see what the big deal was about putting the slug in the box, but I gave its head one more scritch and then nestled it in the crate—

With so many other slugs that they filled the box, all crawling over each other. There were several yellow and blue ones, but also other colors I'd never seen—some purple with orange spines and others red with black stripes.

"Where did you get them?" I asked. "And why are they here?" I was guessing Cobb wasn't starting some kind of pilot support-animal program—not that I would have minded having a slug for myself. For creatures that looked so inhuman, they were remarkably friendly and comforting.

Or maybe I'd been starved for the comforts of home for far, far too long.

"I don't know what Cobb told you about where we went," Jorgen began.

"That you were on leave for R&R," I said. "*All three* of you. Simultaneously. Which I don't believe for a moment."

"Good," Nedd said. "Because if that trip was supposed to be restful—"

"We went looking for something down in the caverns," Jorgen said. "Something that makes the same vibration that Spensa heard from the stars."

I stared at him. "You went searching for something that makes a vibration no one can hear but her?"

Jorgen looked nervously down at the floor.

"*Oh,*" I said.

"Yeah," Jorgen said. "I have the defect, same as Spensa."

"I'm telling you, you shouldn't call it that," Arturo said. "If you can move yourself across the universe with your mind, that's not defective. It's *awesome.*"

"*Theoretically* I can travel across the universe," Jorgen said. "In practice, I have no idea how to do that. Spensa's done it, but she's not here to explain. And the vibrations I felt came from . . ." He looked dubiously at the crate full of slugs. "These."

I smothered a snicker. "So Spensa talks to the stars, and you talk to . . . slugs."

Jorgen looked like he was already sorry for telling me this, so I kept talking, trying to make it better. "I mean, they're cute slugs. And you have a whole crate of them, so that's—"

"Good," a voice said from the hallway. Cobb filled the doorway, wearing his admiral's uniform and regarding us all with a stern expression. "That's very good." Cobb limped into the room followed by Rig, who had been part of our flight when we all started school together, but had since joined the Engineering Corps. His real name was Rodge, but our flight all referred to him by his callsign, same as they did with me. Rig was almost as tall as Nedd, lanky with pale skin and bright red hair. He was cute in a nerdy sort of way. Everyone said he was basically a genius. I wished we'd had a chance to get to know each other better before he'd left Skyward Flight.

Cobb stared into the crate at the slugs. "Apparently these things are called taynix. Why are they all different colors?"

Jorgen looked horrified at not having an answer to this question. "I don't know. I assume they're different kinds? Why do we have different colored hair, sir?"

"I'm sorry I asked," Cobb said. "But they're all cytonic? You're sure?"

"We found them all in that same area," Jorgen said. "The caves where I heard the . . . sounds. It's harder for me to hear one or two of them at a time, but the whole crate sort of . . . vibrates. It's difficult to describe."

Rig looked at them thoughtfully. "It could be that only the one kind is cytonic in nature—or it could be that the colors are incidental, and they all have the same natural affinities."

Huh. That was definitely the most words I had ever heard come out of Rig's mouth at one time. Apparently he wasn't some kind of mostly mute genius.

"I have no idea what kind of affinity that would be," Jorgen said. "But I brought them back so you could experiment on them."

"*Experiment* on them?" I asked. "You're not going to hurt them, are you?"

"No," Cobb said. "These creatures are far too valuable to waste. They're hyperdrives."

We all stared at him. Well, all of us but Rig, who apparently already knew. Rig looked around at all of us, but when he met my eyes he suddenly developed an interest in his fingernails.

"Sir?" Jorgen asked. "The slugs are hyperdrives? How do you know?"

"Spensa told me," Cobb said.

"Spensa's back?" Jorgen asked. He sounded so adorably hopeful that even Nedd, socially clueless as he was, had to have noticed.

"She *was* back," Cobb said. I was ninety-nine percent sure that Cobb also knew about Jorgen and Spensa's mutual crush-fest, but chose not to say anything about it. Or maybe he did say something about it, just not in front of the rest of us. "She showed up right before the Superiority fleet, and then left with them. She was unable to steal the hyperdrive technology, but she did learn that these things"—he gestured to the crate—"are the key."

"She left," Jorgen said. "Where did she go?"

"We don't know," Rig said.

Jorgen's face fell instantly, and Rig looked sympathetic. He and Spensa grew up together. They were close, and I'd always suspected Rig had a crush on her, because he followed her around like a puppy. I wondered if Spensa talked to him about what was going on between her and Jorgen. It was hard to imagine Spensa talking about her feelings . . . ever.

"I love Spin as much as the next guy," Nedd said, though I was pretty sure he didn't. "But are we not a little more concerned with the fact that we're sitting on a crate full of hyperdrives?"

"You're not sitting on it anymore," Arturo pointed out.

"And it's a good thing, because if it's true, these slugs are worth more than all the ships in the DDF combined!"

"They certainly are," Cobb said. "But these things are worth nothing if we can't figure out how they work."

That was true from a tactical standpoint, but I didn't like that he thought of these living beings as pieces of equipment that had no value unless they were useful. I really didn't like the idea that they might be experimented on like the lab rats back home.

"I don't know," Rig mused. "It's possible the Superiority is somehow extracting the cytonic organs from them and using *those* to build hyperdrives. But M-Bot's hyperdrive was in a box. Maybe it's the cage they used to house the slugs before using them to transport?"

"Hey Jorg," Nedd said, "where do you suppose you keep your cytonic organs?"

"Shut up, Nedd," Arturo said, probably because Jorgen was way too reserved to tell Nedd to shove it in front of Cobb, though Cobb didn't blink an eye.

"The slugs are actually pretty intelligent," I said. Doomslug mostly parroted sounds, but one time I taught her how to say "please" before I gave her each bite of caviar. It was adorable. "They're definitely not *things*."

"Things!" one of the slugs said from the crate.

"You are not helping yourself," I told it.

"I don't care if they're geniuses," Cobb said. "We need to figure out how to use them to get off this planet before the Superiority comes back with a force we can't handle. They already did that once. If they hadn't turned around and left on their own, that might have been our end. Is that clear?"

"Yes, sir," Jorgen said, and the rest of us echoed him. The truth was, it wasn't my decision. Like with my friends, there was very little I could do to protect these slugs.

"Rigmarole and Jorgen, I'm putting you in charge of the investigation."

"Sir?" Jorgen said. "I don't know anything about animals—"

"The Assembly wants us to put our focus on defending ourselves, and I can't blame them for that. So, the Engineering Corps is busy working on the platform defenses. They're lending us Rig because he has the most experience with this technology through his work with M-Bot. And you're a cytonic, and the slugs are a cytonic . . . *thing*." Cobb waved his arm in the direction of the slugs, somehow managing to sound authoritative even though he didn't know the right term. I wasn't sure there *was* a right term. This was entirely new territory for all of us.

"Sir, I'd like to help," I said.

Cobb looked me over. "Fine. FM will also help. I want a report on your progress in twenty-four hours."

Rig paled. "I'm not sure we'll have results in—"

"Just a report of what you've learned. I know you and your pals in engineering would like a month to poke around and design experiments, but we don't have that kind of time. Do I make myself understood?"

"Yes, sir," Rig said.

"First, we need to figure out how to prevent them from escaping," Jorgen said. "They keep getting out of the crate."

"I hope you'll have something more for me by tomorrow than whether you were able to keep an animal in a cage," Cobb said.

"You don't have experience with these animals, sir."

It was weird how they kept escaping. The crate *looked* pretty secure, and I didn't think the slugs were strong enough to lift the lid. Certainly not with Nedd sitting on it. Even Nedd would have noticed *that*.

"Do you think they're hyperjumping?" I asked.

Jorgen and Cobb blinked at me, and then we all looked down at the slugs. One of the purple and orange ones climbed on the back of one of its friends, its bulbous face crinkling at us speculatively.

"Doomslug used to escape from Spensa's bunk all the time," I added. "And has anyone ever seen these things travel around? They just seem to . . . *appear* places."

"Yeah, that would explain it," Jorgen said. "The one FM found sure got away fast."

"If that's the case," Rig said, "maybe we *don't* try to contain them, and see what we can observe."

Cobb clapped Rig and Jorgen on their shoulders. "I'll leave that to you."

"Sir?" One of Cobb's aides stood in the hallway, peering into the room. "You have guests waiting for you in the command center."

"What guests?" Cobb asked.

The aide looked around at the rest of us, as if she wasn't sure she should say. "The National Assembly sent some representatives to talk to you about the defense effort, sir. Jeshua Weight is with them."

We all looked at Jorgen. His mother was a famous pilot who'd fought in the Battle of Alta alongside Cobb. She was a legend, even among pilots. Now she mostly worked with her husband, Jorgen's father, who was a leader of the National Assembly.

"Did you know your mom was here?" Nedd asked.

"No," Jorgen said. "I've been with you for days, remember?"

"I dunno," Nedd said. "Didn't Spensa's grandmother say she could, like, read people's minds?"

"I can't do that," Jorgen snapped. He sounded more upset with himself than irritated with Nedd, as if being a cytonic should have come with a manual.

This was Jorgen. He probably *did* think being a cytonic should have come with a manual.

"I'm not going to keep her waiting," Cobb said. "I expect that report by tomorrow." And he strode out of the room, leaving us all standing around the crate full of slugs.

"All right," Jorgen said, nodding purposefully. "Rig wants to observe the slugs to see what happens when they escape. Nedd, Arturo, and I will get these crates to the engineering bay, and then Rig can set up his equipment."

"What am I going to do?" I asked. I wasn't going to *complain* if I wasn't asked to carry boxes, but I definitely wasn't going to let Jorgen leave me out.

"You can be in charge of keeping the slugs in the crate," Jorgen said. "Finding them if they escape, maybe tagging them all somehow so we can keep track of them."

He looked at Rig. I assumed he was making things up when he talked about Rig setting up "equipment," but I didn't know much about what they did in engineering, so I wasn't going to point that out and reveal my own ignorance.

Rig looked suddenly uncomfortable. "That sounds great."

He didn't seem like he thought it was great. He seemed like he thought I might be too incompetent to babysit the taynix. But Jorgen nodded as if nothing was amiss.

"All right. You heard Cobb. Let's get moving." Jorgen counted the slugs in the crate. "Scud, we're missing one again."

They all looked at me. It might have been easier to be assigned to carry the boxes. "I'll go look for it, I guess."

"We'll probably want to have her put a marker wherever she finds the slugs," Rig said. "So we can get a reading on their habitual distances."

"*She* is standing right here," I said. "And if you give me a marker, I'll leave it when I find one."

"Oh—okay," Rig said. He looked abashed, but still refused to meet my eyes.

Apparently my interest in getting to know him wasn't returned. That was a shame—there was a serious dearth of cute nerdy guys my age to hang out with up here on Platform Prime. Especially ones I hadn't spent the last few months watching have contests to see how many callsigns they could utter in one belch.

I told myself it didn't matter. I had work to do, so I spun around and stalked out, off to find myself a taynix.

4

Over the next few hours, I became certain that the slugs were teleporting out of the box. The yellow and blue ones would periodically disappear, regardless of whether the lid was on or off. Sometimes I'd find them slithering around some other part of the engineering bay. Sometimes I'd find them out in the hall, or down the corridor. A few times I had to venture all the way up to the command center or out to the landing bay to find the slugs chilling on someone's chair or on the wing of a ship.

There didn't seem to be any way to stop them from doing this, but only the yellow and blue ones had a penchant for wandering. The others remained in their crate, crawling over one another. The teleporting slugs seemed to leave less often when I played them music from my transmitter, so I left it looping a slow melodic song next to the crate. The slugs trilled along, echoing the notes. If the music bothered the engineers, they seemed to accept it as a necessary part of the scientific process, because they didn't ask me to turn it off.

I returned to the engineering bay with my most frequent traveler, the slug with the blue gill-like markings. The slug shivered slightly—a lot of them did that after I found them, especially if I did it quickly. They'd startle when I approached, like they were frightened of something.

Retrieving them from all over the platform wasn't my favorite pastime, but it kept my mind off of Lizard, so I was grateful for it.

"Well," I said to Rig, "at least you've got a lot of data about how far they go."

Rig sat at his desk, looking over what I assumed was an array of said data, though it could have been something else for all I knew. He didn't even glance up. "Yeah," he said. "Thanks."

I scowled at the back of his head. Since Jorgen had gotten called away to talk to his mother shortly after we arrived in engineering, Rig was back to talking in single-syllable sentences.

Maybe I wasn't the most scintillating person around, but it still stung that he seemed to barely notice I was here. Or worse, he did notice and wasn't happy about it.

I scritched my most recent escapee—who I had named Gill for obvious reasons—on the head, and then counted the slugs. I had all of them again—or at least all that had been there when I took over responsibility for them. They'd been disappearing with greater frequency over time, and I thought I knew why.

"I think it's time to feed them," I said to Rig, not taking my eyes off the slugs. I was still waiting to catch one of them teleporting away, which they never seemed to do while I was looking. "Do you know how we do that?"

Rig did look at me then, but only to give me a wide-eyed look of terror, similar to Jorgen's when Cobb asked why the slugs were different colors.

"Do you know how to feed them?" I asked again. "I think they're wandering away faster because they're hungry, and I don't have enough caviar for all of them."

"Caviar?" Rig asked. "Why would you—"

"There're mushrooms in one of the crates," Jorgen said, and I turned around to find him standing in the doorway. "We assumed that's what they eat because there were a ton of them in the cavern where we found them. They seem to like them well enough." He walked over to one of the other boxes and pulled off the lid. Sure enough, it was filled with wide-capped mushrooms in various shades of cream and brown.

Gill trilled eagerly. I gave him the first taste and then dropped several more mushrooms into one of the slug crates. The slugs migrated toward the mushrooms, all clustering together. Hopefully that would motivate them to stay put for a while.

"How was the thing with your mom?" I asked Jorgen.

"Complicated. Apparently the National Assembly was frightened by the appearance of the delver, and now they want to have more say in what the DDF is doing. Cobb doesn't like it."

I understood why—it wasn't like the National Assembly had any practical experience with the Superiority, let alone a delver.

Then again, neither did the rest of us.

"There's more," Jorgen said. "The assembly has been able to monitor some of the information on the Superiority datanets. They say *Spensa* was the one who turned the delver away from Detritus. Then she apparently turned it on *them*."

Rig and I both gaped at him. "Do you think that's true?" I asked.

"Maybe," Jorgen said. "If anyone could figure out how to wrangle a space monster, it would be her."

That was fair. Spensa was a little mythic in the things she pulled off. If I didn't know her well, I would have thought she was something better than human.

"If so," Jorgen said, "we need her back. The Superiority doesn't seem to know where she went. They do seem to know she's not here. They're reaching out to all their people, telling them they need to mobilize and destroy us while our cytonic is gone."

"They don't know we have you," I said.

A shadow passed over Jorgen's face. "And I'm no good to us unless I figure out how to use my powers. Or we learn how to use *these*."

"Is that what your mother wants?" I asked. "To oversee the development of the hyperdrives?"

"She wants to oversee *everything*," Jorgen said. "Or the Assembly does. I think they decided since my mom was in the DDF for so long, she'd be a good liaison as they begin negotiations."

"And you don't agree?"

"I think it makes sense," Jorgen said. "But she's . . . less happy I admitted to Cobb that I have the defect. It's supposed to be a family secret."

I understood why they'd kept the secret this long. After all, the Superiority had taken advantage of Spensa's father, using his powers to turn him against his allies. That . . . couldn't happen to Jorgen . . . could it? "But you can't keep it a secret now, can you? You're basically our only hope."

"Spensa was a better hope," Jorgen said. "I think my mom's worried about what's going to happen to me if I start experimenting with my powers."

That also made sense. I wondered if Jorgen's parents were behind the move to keep the engineers focused on defense and away from hyperdrives, which would put Jorgen in more danger.

"Spensa will find her way home," I said. "She did it before, and she'll do it again."

Jorgen gave me a suspicious look, like he wondered why I was trying to comfort him about Spensa. If Rig hadn't been sitting right there, I might have told him I knew how he felt about her. Rig was watching us curiously from his desk—I think this was the longest he'd ever bothered to look at me at one time.

"Of course she'll be fine," Jorgen said. "And Cobb and the National Assembly will figure out what to do. We just need to learn how to turn these slugs into hyperdrives."

"No pressure," I said. We both looked down at the slugs, which had finished their mushrooms and were slithering around the large crate, looking for more. I tossed a few more in the box, and they set about devouring them while I fed the other crate of slugs as well.

Jorgen sighed and turned to Rig. "What do we know so far?"

"Not a lot," Rig said. "I've gathered the data FM generated with the trackers. The slugs don't tend to go far, the farthest distance being about two hundred meters, but most went less than twenty."

"But we think they're hyperjumping," Jorgen said.

"I don't know how else to explain it," I said. "Unless they suddenly move *really* fast when we aren't looking. And probably invisibly. And can open crates and close them again."

"Okay," Jorgen said. "So if they already hyperjump, we probably aren't going to need to cut them up. We just need to figure out how to get them to do it over bigger distances and to go where we want them to."

"And to take you with them," Rig said.

"Right."

"How would you get it to go where you want?" I asked. "It's not like you can give it directions." The slugs were smart enough to mimic basic words and get themselves out of small spaces, but I wouldn't exactly want to give one a map and then sit back and trust it to send me across the universe.

"When Spensa left for Starsight, the alien girl Alanik put some coordinates into her mind," Jorgen said. "She did it cytonically, I guess. The way that Spensa's grandmother said she could hear Spensa talking to her all the way from Starsight. I don't know how to do that—but if we could give them to the slugs . . ."

"Too bad we can't ask the alien girl," Rig said, and Jorgen nodded.

Alanik had been shot down by the gun platforms upon arrival, and was still in the medical bay, unconscious. I think the medtechs were hoping she would heal on her own, since they didn't know enough about her anatomy to do much besides keep her medically sedated and wait.

The slugs finished their second round of mushrooms and snuffled around for more. We would clearly have to send a team to harvest more. Hopefully there were a lot of these to be had somewhere in the caverns. The slugs seemed to have been surviving down there okay.

I grabbed a few more mushrooms out of the crate and saw the layer of mushroom below it . . . moving. When I lifted it up, I found two more yellow and blue slugs, looking fat and happy and lying on an extra-large half-eaten cap.

"Well, aren't you clever," I said. If the slugs were going off looking for food, at least some of them had found it. I pulled out the two slugs—one of which had an especially long blue comb down its back, which flopped over to one side as it snoozed—and placed them back in a slug crate.

"So," Rig said. "I've constructed a box out of the same metal used in the one M-Bot indicated was his hyperdrive."

Jorgen looked the thing over intently. "What does it do?"

"Nothing," Rig said. "It's just a box."

"Okay," Jorgen said. "So what was its purpose in M-Bot's design?"

"My guess," Rig said, "is that it's supposed to contain the slug so it doesn't zip all over the ship, or teleport outside the hull and die in space. Even if they can survive without atmosphere, a pilot could get stranded if his slug wandered away from him mid-flight."

Rig was all chatty again, now that *Jorgen* was here. Had I done something to offend him? I had no idea what that could be.

"Okay," Jorgen said. "So the slugs can't hyperjump out of the box."

"That's the theory," Rig said. "We'll have to put some in it to make sure. I also think the box may cause the slug to take the ship with it when it hyperjumps, but I'm not sure how."

"So we don't know how to make it move," Jorgen said, "but if it decided to, it might teleport the whole box?"

"Possibly," Rig said. "We'll have to try it and find out."

"Great," Jorgen said. "FM, grab a couple slugs and put them into Rig's box."

"Yes, sir," I said. It came out more sarcastic than I intended. I *had* volunteered to be the slug handler, after all. Jorgen gave me a sharp look, but I ignored him and lifted two more blue and yellow slugs out of the crate. These two were less skittish than some of the others, and let me stroke them for a few moments before I placed them into Rig's box and fastened the dark metal lid.

Both Rig and Jorgen stared at it.

"I think we'll notice if the box hyperjumps away," I said. Which it might have been more likely to do if I hadn't *just* fed them. I decided not to bring that up.

"Good point," Jorgen said.

Rig looked nervously at me, and then at Jorgen. "Maybe you should try to make one of them move on purpose. Even if you don't know any coordinates, could you try to figure out how to communicate with it?"

"You want me to talk to a slug." Jorgen stared down at the slugs in the crate.

"I talk to them," I said. "You don't have to make it sound like it's crazy. It might be easier with one of the ones you can see. That way you can get to know it."

Jorgen gave me a look that said he thought maybe I *was* crazy, but he still leaned over the crate, considering the slugs. The red and black slugs had finished with the mushrooms the fastest, and were now lounging about trilling softly. The way they sang almost sounded like music, though it was lower and deeper than the trills of the yellow and blue ones. The purple ones' tones were somewhere in between. Their voices all together were calming, in an eerie sort of way.

"Anyone have a suggestion as to how I should do this?" Jorgen asked.

"You could start by befriending one," I said. "Maybe give it a name?"

"They aren't my *friends*," Jorgen said. "We're not naming the test subjects."

"I already did," I told him, pointing to one of the slugs. "This

38

one is Gill. And I'm thinking those two"—I pointed to the extra-fat slugs I'd found in the mushroom crate—"should be Happy and Chubs."

Rig smiled, and both his cheeks dimpled adorably. He was really cute when he wasn't snubbing me.

Focus, FM. "Your turn," I told Jorgen. "You name one."

"Really?" Jorgen said. "This is supposed to help me figure out how to talk to the slugs *with my mind*?"

I put a hand on my hip. I understood that he liked to study everything out before he did it, but he was being a baby. "Do you have any better ideas?"

He groaned, but reached in and picked up one of the purple and orange ones. It gave a shrill squeak.

"You're squeezing it too tight," I said.

"I don't think I'm doing any irreparable harm to it."

"No. But if you were a little bit more gentle with them, they might like you better."

"I don't care if they like me!" Jorgen said. "I only want to figure out how to use them so we have the tools we need to fight against the Superiority."

I narrowed my eyes at him. Usually I thought Jorgen was a really good commander. A little too stiff, a little too interested in running things by the book, but he cared about the pilots in his flight, and he went out of his way to make sure we were all okay even when it made him personally uncomfortable to do so.

But Spensa had nicknamed him Jerkface on our first day as cadets, and at this moment I felt the callsign was well deserved.

"It's okay," I said to the slug in his hand, mostly to bother him. "That's how they treat the rest of us here too."

"All right!" Rig said. "So, Jorgen, do you feel anything? Like, that vibration you were talking about earlier?"

"I don't know," Jorgen said. "I mean, I can hear the mass of them . . . humming, I guess. Singing in my mind."

"Can you hum back to it?" I asked.

Jorgen glared at me, even though it was a perfectly reasonable question.

I held up my hands. "We're supposed to be experimenting with them, aren't we? You could at least try."

"Fine, but I'm not naming it."

"Fine!" the slug trilled at Jorgen.

"I think maybe you just did," I said. "Fine."

"Fine!" the slug enthusiastically agreed.

"Okay, *Fine*," Jorgen said. "Be quiet now. I'm going to hum to it."

Jorgen squinted at Fine, then closed his eyes. He kept them closed for a moment and then he started to hum, a noise I would have described as off-key if it wasn't so completely tuneless.

Kimmalyn appeared in the doorway. "Is he constipated?" she asked. Probably Nedd and Arturo had mentioned to her what we were doing with the slugs, so she'd stopped by to check it out.

Jorgen's eyes popped open and he dropped Fine into the crate—a good two feet down. The slug gave a low, grumpy trill. I reached in and scritched its back in apology on Jorgen's behalf, though Jorgen didn't seem the least bit apologetic.

"No," I told Kimmalyn. "He's trying to commune with the slugs. Cytonically."

"Close the door!" Jorgen said. "We don't have to announce that to everyone."

"Did the humming seem to do anything?" Rig asked.

"It made me feel stupid," Jorgen said.

"It's like the Saint says," Kimmalyn added, " 'I feel, therefore I am.' "

Jorgen squinted at her, but Kimmalyn just smiled at him innocently.

Jorgen sighed and looked over at the hyperdrive box. "What about those slugs? Are they still in there?"

I opened the lid and peered inside. "Yes. Both of them. And

they appear to be asleep." One of them made a soft wheezing sound with its comb that I thought might be a snore.

Jorgen looked down at the crate. "Maybe this would be easier if there were fewer of them. I can't focus on this many at once. FM, pull out three of them, one of each color."

At least I was more gentle with them than he was. Rig brought me a cardboard box and I gingerly picked up purple Fine, yellow Gill, and one of the red and black slugs who was as yet unnamed.

"I'm going to hum at them," Jorgen said. "And you all are going to keep your comments to yourself. That is an order."

"Bless your stars," Kimmalyn said.

I bit my lips to keep from snickering. Jorgen's hum sounded like a wounded animal.

Finally Jorgen sighed. "This isn't working. Maybe I should have some time alone with them."

"I still think you should try treating them nicer," I told him. "Bond with them."

Jorgen rolled his eyes. "I don't see how that's going to help."

"Spensa has a bond with her slug, right? Maybe that's how she found out it was a hyperdrive."

"We don't have any idea how Spensa found out Doomslug was a hyperdrive."

"I'm just trying to help," I said. "You're the one who appointed me slug welfare specialist."

Jorgen stared at me. "What?"

I thought what I'd said was obvious. "Slug welfare specialist. I'm here to take care of the slugs."

"FM," Jorgen said, "you don't know any more about these slugs than we do."

"I do so," I said. "I was friends with Spensa's slug."

"You were . . ."

"*Friends*," I repeated. "With Doomslug. You remember her?"

"Of course I remember her," Jorgen said. "That thing was

supposed to stay in Spensa's bunk, but it would show up all over the platform. I found it in my cockpit once, and I couldn't get it to leave! Every time I tried to catch it, the thing kept shrieking 'Jerk-face' at me. I swear Spensa trained it to do that on purpose."

"See?" I said. "Clearly you have no experience handling these animals. But Doomslug and I had a *relationship*. She used to sit on my arm and purr while I fed her caviar."

Jorgen looked at me like I'd lost my mind. "The slugs *purr*?"

"I mean, they *trill*, but it was a purr-like trill—"

"And you fed her *caviar*? Where did you even *get* caviar?"

"My parents send it to me, okay?" I said. "The bottom line is that without Spensa, I'm the next best person to help you handle the slugs. And I think if you make them comfortable—"

"We're not trying to make them comfortable. We're trying to develop *hyperdrives*. Spensa said these things—"

"They are animals, not things."

"—these *animals* are the key to getting us off Detritus. And in case you didn't notice, we need to develop them as quickly as possible, because we were just visited by a *delver*, and it might return at any time to destroy us."

"I don't think it's coming back," Rig said.

We both looked over at him.

"You said Spensa drove it off, right?" he said. "She'll have figured out a way to keep it away from us."

Yeah, okay. He definitely had a crush on Spensa. Which was fine. It wasn't like I was trying to date the boy—that wasn't a pressing concern, what with the Krell on our doorstep—but a conversation would have been nice.

Jorgen sighed. "Maybe. But even Spensa can't keep the Superiority away from us forever. These slugs are our most important lead."

"Exactly," I said. "So we need to make sure we're treating them with the respect they deserve."

"I simply think," Jorgen said, "that we shouldn't let your affection for the slugs get in the way of our progress."

"I wasn't aware you were making progress," I said.

"Maybe we *would* be if we were focusing on the slugs instead of having this conversation," Jorgen said. "We selected a box of three slugs—"

"Two slugs," Rig said.

Jorgen blinked at him.

"Technically," Rig clarified, "there are only two slugs in this box."

Jorgen looked into the box, where there were in fact only two taynix—Fine and the red and black one.

"Clearly the slug welfare specialist isn't doing her job," Jorgen said. "You were supposed to get them to *stay* in the *box*."

"Fine," I said.

"No," Rig said. "Fine is still here; it's the other one."

Kimmalyn laughed. Maybe Rig did have a sense of humor after all. But when I grinned at him, his cheeks grew pink, like he'd messed up somehow by joking with me.

Had someone *told* him not to talk to me?

I looked around, but Gill appeared to have hyperjumped out of sight. "All right, I'll go find him, but—"

"Hey!" Jorgen said. I looked down to find that the red and black slug had eased its way out of the box and was now carefully sampling Jorgen's bootlace. He reached down to pick it up, squeezing it too tightly again.

"Jorgen, you need to be more—"

"FM," he said, raising his voice, "I've *got it*—"

"*Got it*," the slug trilled.

Jorgen looked at the slug with a long-suffering expression.

And then the slug exploded.

The slug itself stayed intact and unharmed, but something *pushed* out of it, like it sent the air itself spinning in all directions.

Jorgen dropped the slug and jumped back as ribbons of red opened up on his forearms and cheeks and across his nose. Rig startled, and even Kimmalyn looked terrified. The cuts weren't particularly *deep*, but there were many of them, like they'd been opened by the soft touch of a dozen razor blades.

We all stared at Jorgen. The slug crawled placidly across the floor.

"Are you okay?" I asked.

"I think you should name that one *Boom*slug," Kimmalyn said.

"I think you need to go to the infirmary," Rig added.

Jorgen pressed his fingertips to his nose, smearing blood in a streak across his face. "FM, do you think you can get the slug back into the crate?"

"Sure," I said. I bent down and let Boomslug inspect my hand before gingerly lifting it into the crate with the others.

"Good," Jorgen said. "Meeting adjourned." And then he strode out of the room with little rivulets of blood still running down his skin.

5

After I put Fine back in the crate and replaced the lid, I followed Jorgen to the infirmary. I had no idea what that slug had done to him—Doomslug had never done anything similar that I was aware of—but Jorgen was stressed out enough *before* being cut to ribbons. This couldn't help.

When I arrived in the doorway, the medtechs were applying tiny bandages to his cuts and questioning him about what happened.

"It's classified," Jorgen told them.

I supposed that was true—and it meant he didn't have to explain he'd been cut because he'd startled a slug. I looked through the glass into the room across the way where the alien girl lay asleep on a stretcher. She was humanoid, though her skin was a pale violet color and her hair was an unnatural white, matching the color of the growths that protruded from her cheeks. She looked so strange, with high cheekbones and a wide forehead that were almost human, but also definitely *not*. The effect was disturbing, even in her sleep.

"You can tell Command he'll be fine," one of the medtechs said to me as they left the room. It made sense they thought I was waiting to report back, but Command wasn't aware there was a problem yet.

With Jorgen's face all bandaged, that wasn't going to last long, and I worried about what it meant for the slugs.

I turned to look into the room. Jorgen was still sitting on the cot alone. "Are you okay?" I asked.

"Yeah," Jorgen said, looking at his reflection in the glass window. "Fantastic." One corner of his mouth turned up. "Though clearly I should have listened to you about not squeezing the slugs."

"I didn't expect it to hurt you though," I said. Doomslug had hung around Spensa enough to be startled a time or two, and she'd never exploded. Then again, only the yellow and blue slugs seemed to hyperjump, so maybe only the red and black ones . . . exploded?

"I don't know if that's all there was to it," Jorgen said. "I was still trying to focus on that vibration, you know? The one I can definitely *not* approximate by humming."

"That much is clear."

Jorgen's smile grew more genuine, though it pulled a bit at a cut on his lip and he winced. "But I feel it in my mind. It's hard to pinpoint one of them at a time because the vibration is so soft, but I was trying to get it to . . . talk to me, I guess. Like you were saying."

That sounded incredibly difficult. No wonder he was frustrated. "So you think when you talked to it, you convinced it to explode?"

"Sometimes I have that effect on people. Just ask Spensa."

I laughed, and Jorgen joined me. Despite what people thought of him, Jorgen did have a sense of humor. He was simply too uptight to let it out most of the time.

"I do think it would help if you built a relationship with them," I said. "They're not machine parts. You can't expect to plug them in and make them work. They're living creatures."

"So says the slug welfare specialist."

"That's right. And speaking of their welfare . . ." I sighed. "Do you think this will put them at risk? If people think they're dangerous . . ."

Jorgen shook his head. "It won't matter. If the taynix are really the secret to intergalactic travel, then we have to continue to experiment with them, no matter how dangerous they are. Though I may wear gloves next time. And a face mask."

"Maybe Cobb could find you some full-body armor."

"That might be nice."

"It's possible only the yellow ones are hyperdrives," I said. "The different colors might indicate different powers. Doomslug never exploded."

Jorgen nodded. "That's a plausible theory. We have enough of the yellow kind to work with those first. We can worry about the other kinds later." He looked up at me, fixing his dark eyes on me like he saw right through me. "Why are you so worried about the taynix anyway?"

I shrugged. "I'm not."

"You appointed yourself slug welfare specialist, but you're going to tell me you don't care?"

"*You* appointed me slug welfare specialist."

"FM, I told you to keep them in a crate. That makes you a slug *location* specialist. You made up the welfare part all on your own."

I crossed my arms and leaned against the door frame. "I just think we shouldn't treat them like they're machines. If they can get us off this planet before the Superiority succeeds in destroying us, we have to do everything in our power to make that happen. But they're living creatures. We don't have to be monsters while we do it, do we?"

"Of course we don't." Jorgen winced. "And if I'd listened to you, maybe I wouldn't have gotten my face sliced up. Tell me the truth. How bad is it?"

"The medical people said you'd be fine."

"Right, but I look ridiculous."

He had little pieces of plastic tape holding his face together, so it was kind of true. "Hey, girls like scars, right?"

Jorgen closed his eyes.

Right. There was only one girl whose opinion he cared about, and she wasn't here to appreciate them.

Though, now that I thought about it . . . "I mean, really, if there was ever a girl who was going to appreciate a scar, it's Spensa, am I right?"

Jorgen gave me one satisfying look of shock and horror that I'd called him out before he recovered and turned the conversation back on me. "I think we were discussing your sudden obsession with animal rights."

"I think we were discussing your face, but if you want to talk about animal rights—"

Jorgen's eyes caught on something behind me, and I turned to find one of Cobb's aides standing in the hallway. "Admiral Cobb needs you in the command center," she said to Jorgen. "Should I tell him you're indisposed?"

Jorgen groaned. "No, tell him I'm coming. He's going to hear about this eventually."

"What do you think it's about?" I asked. "It's too early for your report."

"Come with me and find out," Jorgen said. "You can help me explain what happened to my face. Since you're the slug welfare specialist and all."

I still needed to hunt down Gill plus any others that had liberated themselves in the meantime. But I wasn't going to pass up an opportunity to find out what Cobb's plans were. I followed Jorgen down to Cobb's command center, which was a large room with a wide table and a holoprojector at the front.

Cobb was seated at the table with two of his aides on either side of him. Across the table from him was a woman with dark skin and black hair that matched Jorgen's, though she wore hers in twists along her scalp.

Jeshua Weight, Jorgen's mother, was one of the most decorated pilots ever to retire from the DDF. Her political power had only increased when her husband joined the National Assembly. She had two other people with her—I guessed from their expensive clothing they were either minor politicians or other liaisons sent to speak on the National Assembly's behalf.

Rig stood with one of the other engineers at the head of the table, fidgeting nervously. "We think we're close to getting the planetary defense systems working," Rig said. "The encryption is tough to crack, but we've broken some of the code, and we're trying to make sense of what we're looking at. It's much more complicated than any of the programming we use in the caverns, and we're not exactly sure what a lot of it does."

Rig was apparently also capable of speaking in Cobb's presence, though I could tell he was nervous. People tended to assume that anyone who passed the pilot's test would be comfortable with public attention—or at least accustomed to it—but I didn't think that was true in Rig's case. At least he wasn't trying to pretend *they* didn't exist, even if he looked like he wished *he* didn't.

"Presumably the code is what causes the gun platforms to shoot ships from the sky, yes?" Jeshua said in an even voice. "So if you can crack it, we would be able to use those guns in our favor. It would help us a lot to be able to use those turrets the way we use the antiaircraft guns around Alta."

"That's the hope," Rig said. "We're also working on reviving an old shielding system that might help us to protect the planet from future attacks. A lot of it is still a mystery to us, so we can't promise anything."

Jeshua didn't look pleased about that, though Rig and the other engineers were clearly doing all they could.

"Thank you for your report," Cobb said. He looked over at

Jorgen and me standing by the door. "Son, what in the North Star's Light happened to you?"

Jorgen winced. "We had a little incident with one of the taynix. Apparently they need to be handled carefully."

Jeshua looked alarmed. "You didn't tell me these creatures were dangerous," she said to Cobb.

"They're hyperdrives," Cobb said. "I'd imagine they're very dangerous."

This did not seem to make Jeshua feel any better. "Perhaps someone more *qualified* should be conducting these experiments." She eyed Jorgen with a look of disapproval. Jorgen somehow managed to stand at attention and appear like he was shrinking into himself at the same time. Which made sense—his mother had basically announced that he wasn't capable of doing his job.

It wasn't exactly my place to speak in this meeting, but Jorgen had asked me to help explain. "The slug reacted poorly when Jorgen tried to communicate with it cytonically," I said. "But we're working on some theories to keep it from happening again."

Jeshua narrowed her eyes at me. "Who are you?"

"She's one of the pilots in Jorgen's flight," Cobb said. "She's helping Jorgen and Rig with the slug experiments."

"FM has some experience working with the taynix," Jorgen said. "She's helping us figure out how best to handle them."

Jeshua looked over Jorgen's patched-up face and made a tsking sound. "She's obviously not doing a very good job."

I bristled, but kept my mouth shut.

"It's not her fault," Rig cut in. "It's the nature of the scientific process. We have to try things out, or we won't get results."

Huh. Apparently Rig didn't hate me, if he was willing to defend me to the brass. He was clearly more comfortable talking about things he understood, and none of us understood the taynix and the hyperdrives very well. Maybe if I found a minute to ask him about his other work, he'd stop treating me like a pariah.

"We don't have a report for you yet," Jorgen added. "We're still working on it."

"That's fine," Cobb said. "That isn't why I called for you. There's something I need you to hear."

Cobb nodded to one of his aides, who pushed some buttons on the holographic projector. Instead of a hologram though, an audio recording began.

"Admiral Cobb," a voice said. It was strangely accented and oddly even, like it might not be entirely real. "This is Minister Cuna. I'm sorry our earlier communication was interrupted. I was betrayed by the same people who sent the delver to your planet and am no longer able to hyperjump. I have information from your agent, Spensa. She asked me to come to your planet to offer aid, but I have been attacked by our mutual enemies and am unable to reach you as planned. Instead, I must ask for your help. My people and I are marooned on the abandoned outpost at Sunreach, and the radicals in control of the Superiority government are hunting for me. I fear we have very little time. If you can reach us, I offer you all the help I can give in return. We are located at—"

The voice read a few coordinates, but then the recording cut off.

"Is that it?" Jorgen asked.

Cobb nodded. "Even if we had the full location, I don't know how to reach them without a functional hyperdrive. We were wondering if you felt anything from it. Any of those vibrations you keep talking about?"

Jeshua's face darkened when Cobb asked Jorgen about his cytonic abilities, but she didn't interrupt him.

"No," Jorgen said. "Should I?"

"My previous communications from Minister Cuna came via radio," Cobb said, "but this one came through the platform's old communications systems. They're probably using some kind of faster-than-light communication device. If it uses cytonic technology, we thought there might be some component only a cytonic could hear."

51

Jorgen shook his head. "I'm sorry, sir. I didn't feel anything."

"How did we receive it?" I asked. "Do *we* have an FTL communicator?"

I probably didn't have the authority to ask that question, but Rig answered it anyway. "Not that we know of," Rig said. "But there are a lot of things the platform systems are capable of that we haven't been able to figure out yet. The message was routed through one of the receptors in the communications system."

"So we received it," Cobb said, "but we don't exactly know how. Engineering is trying to figure out if we have the ability to respond."

Interesting. If we'd been able to get up here and investigate the platforms surrounding the planet years ago, we might have been better able to figure out how to defend ourselves.

Which was probably one of the reasons the Superiority had been so intent on keeping us in the caverns below the planet's surface.

"What are we going to do if we can answer?" Jorgen asked.

"We don't know for certain what this person's intentions are," Cobb said. "It might be a trap. Alternatively, it might be our only lead on an ally, and stars know we could use a few of those right now."

"If this person is indeed a minister," Jeshua said, "perhaps we could use their connections to reach people higher up in the Superiority government, to find a way to reach an agreement."

An *agreement*?

Jorgen's shock echoed my own. "You're going to try to *talk* to the Superiority?"

Jeshua nodded. "We've been fighting this war for too long. Continuing the way we are will only result in our extinction. Now that we know more about the forces we're facing, the National Assembly believes we should start considering the political implications of the situation, along with the military ones."

In principle I agreed, but I hadn't seen any evidence that the

Superiority wanted to negotiate with us. Especially if they'd been the reason for the delver's appearance.

Cobb cleared his throat. He had to hate this, but he was too good at his job to betray that on his face. "We'll try to respond, but getting those coordinates does us no good if we can't *get* there, and we can't do that without a hyperdrive." Cobb focused on Jorgen. "Spensa felt coordinates in her mind, and then she was able to travel to them. I was hoping that recording might do something similar for you, but if not, we're going to have to go through with our other plan."

"Other plan, sir?" Jorgen said.

Jeshua nodded. They'd obviously already discussed this. "Yes," she said. "The alien who crashed here is the only one among us who might be able to produce coordinates that would allow us to reach this person. We're going to need to wake her up."

6

The next morning, I was paged to the medical bay almost immediately upon waking. I found Jorgen standing outside, looking into Alanik's room through the glass. The bandages on his face were new and clean, but still numerous. "They say her wounds have mostly healed," he said. "They've been keeping her sedated, but now they're bringing her around. Cobb suggested that I talk to her since we're both cytonics. I could use your help. You're . . . better with people than I am."

"Of course," I said. That was quite the admission for Jorgen, who never liked to appear less than perfect. But this was a delicate situation—Alanik had been unconscious for weeks now, and we didn't know much about her. "Will we be able to speak to her?"

Jorgen held up a pin. "Rig says this is a translator. Spensa took the one Alanik was wearing when she crashed, but the engineers found more in her ship. It should make it so we can understand each other."

That would make things a lot easier. "Any particular tactic you think we should use to talk to her?"

"No idea. Do you have a suggestion?"

"I think maybe we should try to convey that we're friends first. Help her feel like we're all on the same side." I didn't know much about what had gone on between Alanik and Spensa. "We are, right?"

"I hope so," Jorgen said. "That sounds like a good tactic. Thanks."

One of the doctors stepped out of the medical bay and nodded to Jorgen. "She's waking. She may be disoriented at first, so don't be surprised if she has a hard time talking."

Jorgen gave the doctor a crisp nod and then we walked into Alanik's room, stopping at her bedside.

The yellow overhead lights cast eerie shadows over Alanik's strange features. With her cheeks oddly pronounced, her skin that strange shade of violet with white growths protruding from her skin like crystals, she was beautiful in an unnerving sort of way. She stirred, murmuring something softly, and then opened her eyes.

They looked human, except for their violet color. I'd never seen a human with eyes quite that pale and arresting. She looked up at us in confusion.

Jorgen glanced at me. He wanted me to take point on this.

"Alanik," I said. "My name is FM. I'm glad you're awake."

Jorgen held the pin awkwardly between us, and it translated the words into a lilting language I'd never heard. Maybe I should have used my real name, but I had become accustomed to everyone using my callsign. Besides, to an alien, "FM" probably wouldn't seem any more strange than "Freyja."

Alanik squinted at me, still confused. If she was alarmed by the many bandages on Jorgen's face, she didn't show it. Probably a lot of things here looked strange to her, so what was one more? "Human," she said. "Where is . . . the other one."

"Spensa," I said. "She left. You gave her coordinates, and she went to take your place."

Alanik closed her eyes for a moment. When she opened them again, she looked more focused. More alert. "Where am I?"

"In a medical facility," I told her. "On a platform above a planet called Detritus. You were shot down by autonomous platforms. That wasn't my people. We can't control them. The guns shoot at us too."

Alanik nodded. "Humans," she said again. "How have you survived?"

"With difficulty," I said. "We've been defending this planet against the Superiority for years."

"We were allies once," Alanik said. "My people were punished for working with you. The Superiority . . . they say they want peace, but in truth they oppress us. Their peace is only control."

"Yes," I said. "And they want my people dead. We need your help."

Alanik's eyes narrowed slightly. "I need to contact my people," she said. "The other one . . . Spensa . . . may have already arrived at Starsight. They are expecting me to check in, and I will need to tell them what's happened."

Jorgen and I exchanged a glance. Alanik thought it was still the same day as when she'd arrived. "About that," I said. "You were injured in the crash, and our doctors have been trying to help you, but they didn't know much about your physiology. They've been keeping you in a coma, giving you a chance to heal."

Alanik looked at me in horror. "How long?"

How long? I looked to Jorgen. "About nineteen days," he said.

"That long?" Alanik struggled to sit, though the tubes and wires attaching her to the medical monitor got in her way. She grabbed at them with her slender hands, and I noticed her nails were made of the same white substance that protruded from her cheeks. They were sharp and pointed, almost like talons.

"We need your help," Jorgen said again. "We're all trapped here."

Alanik stared at him. "You aren't trapped," she said. "You are cytonic, same as Spensa. Can you—"

Jorgen shook his head. "I can't do anything," he said. "I've only just learned about my powers, and I don't know how to use them.

I need you to teach me, so we can get my people off this planet. I need your help."

He looked at me, but I didn't know what to say beyond that. He'd made a pretty good case. "Please," I added. "You said we were allies, right? Well, we need allies now, and it sounds like your people do too. We have a message from someone in the Superiority, a faction that wants to help us. But we don't know how to reach them—"

"Don't trust them!" Alanik said. She pulled at the tubes on her chest, tugging them free. Thankfully they seemed to only be sensors, though she had a needle in her arm hooked up to an IV. As she shifted it, a spot of dark blood formed on the bandage that held it in place. "You can't trust them. They say they want to help, but they don't. They only want control. You can't—"

She broke off as a shadow darkened the window to the hallway. I turned and saw Cobb standing there with Jorgen's mother. They were speaking quietly enough that we couldn't hear them through the glass, but Jeshua Weight did not look happy.

"Okay," I said, trying to hold Alanik's attention. I reached down and took her hand, hoping this wasn't some sort of cultural taboo to her people, but she didn't pull away. "We can't trust them. This is why we need your help. You know more than we do, so we need you to guide us. We don't know how to use the powers, but we do have ships, and resources. We can help you in return."

"FM," Jorgen said. He gave me a warning look, and I knew I'd gone too far. We couldn't promise her resources. That would be up to Command and the National Assembly. I might have just lied to her. It could be a tactically sound decision to make promises to Alanik's people, but I didn't have the authority to do that.

Jeshua knocked on the glass and gestured to the door, which I'd closed behind me. Jorgen sighed, set the pin down on the edge of Alanik's bed sheet, and walked to the door, stepping out into the hall to talk to his mother.

Alanik was still holding my hand. Her lavender skin looked so strange against mine, but the anatomy of her hand was human. She was a person, same as me. Alien, but familiar. She was far from home, alone and frightened. I could imagine what that would feel like.

"What were you going to do when you reached Starsight?" I asked her.

Alanik hesitated. "I am a spy for my people," she said. "We need their hyperdrive technology. Without it, they isolate us on our planet. They deny us passage on their ships. They control our imports, our economy, our ability to progress. We need to know their secrets."

"So the hyperdrives," I said. "You don't know how they work."

"No," Alanik said. "That was what I was going to learn. But if it has been weeks, the opportunity may have passed."

It had—Spensa had taken her place, pretended to be Alanik. Sharing the information Spensa had discovered—the very secrets Alanik had intended to steal—might go a long way toward building goodwill between us.

But I definitely didn't have clearance to do that. I glanced out the window and found Jorgen talking to Cobb and his mother. From the look of it, Jeshua was doing most of the talking.

"Are you also a prisoner here?" Alanik asked.

I looked down at her. "You're not a prisoner," I said. "We were trying to help you."

Alanik shook her head. "All of you. You are prisoners on this planet, dependent on the Superiority."

Oh, that. "More than your people, I think," I said. "They don't trade with us. They've attacked us for years, making us fight them to survive. We live underground, using only the resources of this planet and the means we had with us when our ships crashed here—that was generations ago."

"So you are desperate," Alanik said. "You will do anything to escape."

It was true, but I didn't like the way she said it. "We want to work together," I said.

"You want to speak with the Superiority," she said. "To respond to their message."

"We have a message from someone," I said. "If you would listen to it, maybe you could help us figure out if that person is—"

"You will make a deal with them," Alanik said. "You will do it because their false peace is better than your war."

That was startlingly similar to what Jeshua Weight had said the National Assembly wanted to do.

"Have other planets tried that?" I asked.

"Yes," Alanik said. "My people were punished because we fought alongside yours. Some on my planet think it is better to go along with the Superiority. To accept their peace. But their peace is a tool to maintain their power."

"We don't want that kind of peace," I said. The decision wasn't up to me, so I was surprised by the strength of my response. "They've murdered my friends, our people. They tried to wipe out our entire planet, and I'm still not sure why we survived. I don't want to work with them, Alanik, and I don't think others will either. We aren't a peaceful people. We will fight."

That should have been the opposite of what I wanted. It was the opposite of what my Disputer friends stood for.

Maybe my time in the DDF had changed me the way they all said it would. Several of them had tried to talk me out of taking the pilot's test. They said the DDF would make me see things their way, compromise my ideals. I thought becoming a pilot would give me more authority to speak up for those ideals, so I did it anyway.

And here I was, arguing for war instead of peace.

Alanik had it right though. Not all peace was of equal value. I wasn't going to trade one cage for another. I hoped that in the end, the warlike nature of the Defiant League would protect us from that kind of prison, even if it certainly also had its downsides.

Alanik's eyes met mine, staring at me intently. And I thought for a moment that she believed me.

The door opened, and Jorgen motioned to me. "FM," he said, "Command wants to talk to her."

Alanik looked at me, as if gauging my reaction, so I tried not to look alarmed. I squeezed her hand and then stepped away, but I didn't leave the room. I wasn't going to leave unless Cobb ordered me to.

He and Jeshua strode into the room, and Jeshua stared at Alanik with obvious disdain. I glanced at Jorgen, who hovered by the door, and he shrugged. He couldn't do anything about this, and neither could I.

"It's Alanik, is that right?" Cobb asked.

Alanik narrowed her eyes at him. "Who are you, and why have you kept me here?"

"We were trying to help you, Alanik," I said. "We were just—"

"We need to know who you are," Jeshua said. "And where you come from."

Alanik sat up straighter. She'd removed all the sensors except the needle in her arm, but she appeared to be growing stronger and more alert the longer she was awake. Hopefully she'd healed enough that we weren't putting her in danger by overtaxing her. "I am Alanik of the UrDail," she said. "And you are?"

"I am Admiral Cobb," Cobb said. "And this is—"

"It does not matter who we are," Jeshua said. "We need you to tell us what you know about hyperdrives and the Superiority's faster-than-light communication."

I closed my eyes. I was pretty sure from my conversation with Alanik that we knew more about hyperdrives than she did. I looked over at Jorgen. We should have coordinated before this conversation, made a plan.

He shook his head. We couldn't stop this from happening.

"I am your prisoner, then," Alanik said. "You intend to use me."

"We only want to exchange information," Cobb said. "We have a mutual enemy."

"This isn't an exchange," Jeshua said, cutting him off. "Tell us what you know, and we'll let you go."

Alanik straightened up further. "You'll let me go," she repeated. "You think you can hold me here?"

"We have your ship," she said. "We will negotiate for your release if you will cooperate with us."

Did Alanik need her ship to transport herself to her planet? The slugs clearly didn't need ships to hyperjump.

"Mom," Jorgen said. "I think—"

"You know nothing," Alanik said.

Jeshua straightened to her full height—which wasn't especially tall—and looked down her nose at Alanik. "You're not doing yourself any favors here."

"Mom—" Jorgen said. Alanik looked over at him and Jorgen cried out, squeezing his eyes shut and putting a hand to his forehead between the bandages. I took a step toward her—I didn't know what she was doing to him, but she was obviously an accomplished cytonic. We barely knew what they were capable of.

"What are you doing to my son?" Jeshua said, grabbing Jorgen by the arm.

Jorgen collided with the doorframe, opening his eyes wide.

And then Alanik disappeared. One moment she was there and the next she was gone, leaving the bandage and the IV needle to fall against the sheets, the dark stain of her blood spreading onto the white fabric.

"Seriously?" I said. "Why did you do that?"

"FM," Cobb said. His tone held a warning—I obviously wasn't supposed to speak to Jeshua Weight that way—but at the moment I didn't care.

"I was making progress with her," I said. "She might have helped us."

Jeshua was still focused on Jorgen. "What did she do to you?"

"She was talking to me, that's all," Jorgen said. "Speaking in my mind."

"What did she say?"

We all stared at him, and Jorgen hesitated. "Not much," he said. "Just that she didn't trust us."

Cobb raised an eyebrow at him. Jorgen wasn't a particularly good liar, but if he decided to withhold information from his superiors, he must have a scudding good reason for it.

"What are we going to do now?" I asked Cobb. "She was our only chance at communicating with Cuna, wasn't she?"

"What did she say when you were talking to her?" Cobb asked me.

"She said we shouldn't trust anyone from the Superiority. She said they would lie to us, that we would trade away our freedom to them if we tried to make peace with them."

"We need a full report of everything she said to you," Jeshua said. "We'll send it down to the National Assembly, so they can decide what we should do."

"We'll make that report," Cobb said. "And then I will decide what to share with the National Assembly." Jeshua scowled at Cobb, but he kept talking. "FM, Jorgen, let's head up to the command center for debriefing."

He stalked out of the room and Jorgen and I trailed after him, leaving Jeshua behind.

7

When I left the command center, I headed toward the engineering bay to check on the taynix. I'd told Cobb everything I remembered from my conversation with Alanik, but Cobb had interviewed Jorgen separately, so I still didn't know what Alanik had said in his head. Jeshua hadn't been in on either of the meetings, which I was sure had angered her.

I didn't have a lot of sympathy for her. I was furious that Alanik was gone—and with her our only chance to communicate with Cuna and to train Jorgen in more advanced cytonics. Spensa's grandmother had helped some, but her knowledge was limited.

The National Assembly was so used to ordering people around and having everyone do what they said. I was glad Jorgen had taken me to talk to Alanik—but it highlighted a huge weakness in our government. We didn't have diplomats. We weren't used to cooperation. The Assembly wanted to treat this as a political situation, but they were scudding *bad* at it. We were supposed to be Defiant, but what good did that do us if all we did was defy other people to our own detriment?

I had no way to know what Alanik was going to tell her people— our former allies—about the humans of Detritus, but I guessed it wouldn't be good.

I stopped short at the end of the corridor that led to the engineering bay. Rig's metal slug box, based off M-Bot's supposed hyperdrive, was resting in the middle of the floor.

No one else was in sight, and I guessed that Rig hadn't left it there. I knelt down and opened it, and found the two yellow taynix inside, snuffling around like they were hungry.

If one of them had hyperjumped, it had brought the box and the other slug along with it. Rig must have missed its disappearance, or he would have gone looking for the box and found it as soon as he opened the door to Engineering.

I didn't know how much it would help, but at this point any news felt like good news. I dropped one of Rig's location trackers on the floor, picked up the box of slugs, tucked it under my arm, and opened the doors to the engineering bay.

A couple of people from Rig's team were working on a hunk of metal and wires that looked like it might have come from one of the platforms. Rig was nowhere in sight.

"Have you seen Rodge?" I asked them.

One of them waved a hand at me. "He's at the platform controls in Charlie Sector."

My instinct was to feed the taynix in the box first. But if their hunger made them teleport more, I'd wait a little longer and see if we could catch them in the act.

I carried the box with me to Charlie Sector to find Rig. As I passed a series of exterior windows, I looked up at the platforms above ours. I wasn't exactly sure how they'd been built originally, but the technology of the people who lived here before us was far more advanced than ours.

Until they'd been destroyed by the delver, each and every one of them wiped out, leaving the planet barren and alone.

I didn't really understand why humans had chosen to live on Detritus to begin with. I'd been born in the caverns, but the stories we told of other planets spoke of green trees and vast oceans, fertile land to grow food instead of vats hidden away in caverns. The surface of Detritus was a craggy wasteland of debris both natural and mechanical. We'd managed to scrape together enough fertile soil to grow orchards near Alta Base, but I didn't imagine Detritus had ever been a paradise to live on. It seemed strange to me that people with such superior technology chose this place to call home.

If we did manage to use the taynix to escape Detritus, I wondered where we would go. How would we find a place to go, and if we did, how would we know if we'd be safe? Detritus was inhospitable, but it was also familiar. The idea of living somewhere with an ocean like Old Earth seemed mildly terrifying. How did all that water not consume the land around it?

I looked up at the platforms above, imagining the stars beyond— white lights burning brightly against the black. Some of those would have planets around them, planets we could visit in the blink of an eye with FTL travel. But if the Superiority controlled all of them, would we really be able to escape? Would we be able to run far enough, or would we merely be looking for a better battle position?

Alanik seemed to agree with the basic philosophies of the DDF. She didn't trust peace, and was afraid that we would accept another set of chains for a false promise of safety, and the National Assembly seemed to be leaning in that direction.

I stood by what I said though. I knew my people. We didn't trust peace any more than Alanik did. In fact, I was afraid we'd never be willing to set down our weapons. A wasteland could feel more comfortable than a paradise, if that was what you were used to. Though I agreed with the Disputers who yearned for peace, I didn't know that I would be able to trust it.

I reached Charlie Sector and wove between the long rectangular blocks that held a lot of the machinery keeping the platform running. Power matrixes hummed with life, and a water pump churned, supplying our indoor plumbing. Most of the rest of the devices I couldn't identify. I found Rig standing at the side of one such block. He'd pulled the paneling off the side, revealing a set of wires and circuit boards beneath. The ground around him was littered with pieces of machinery.

Rig's boss in the Engineering Corps, a woman with long pale hair—whose name I thought was Ziming—stood to the side, looking over the rubble.

"I've got Thadwick picking up your work on the platforms," she said. "We're close to getting those gun emplacements working. Do you have anything more on the encryption?"

Rig shook his head. "I'm sorry. I've been working on the hyperdrives, so I haven't had time."

"We'll keep at it," Ziming said. "At least we're into the shield system now. There are still too many questions to run a test yet, but we're getting closer. Keep up the good work."

Ziming strode past me, and I nodded to her. Rig was still looking into the tech behind the panel like it was a difficult problem.

"Rig?" I said.

Rig jumped, and then stared at me wide-eyed. "Hey," he said. "Hey."

That was not only a one-word utterance, but the same word twice. Not an auspicious beginning. "I found this in the hall." I lifted the box for him to see. "So unless you left it there, I'm thinking the slugs teleported it."

"Oh!" Rig said. "Oh, that's good. Are they still in there?"

"Yeah," I said. "It's been most of a day since they've eaten, so they're probably hungry, but I thought I'd leave them that way for a bit so we could see if they'd do it again."

"That's great!" Rig said. He rubbed his palms on the pants of his jumpsuit. "Thanks."

He blinked at me like he wasn't sure what I was still doing there, and I sighed. I hadn't trekked all the way out here just to turn around and go back. "Did you hear about what happened with Alanik?"

"I heard she disappeared," Rig said. He winced. "I guess maybe we should have been more delicate about interrogating a cytonic."

"I tried to be delicate," I said. "But I didn't have the rank to insist others do the same. I got to talk to her a little bit, and I think her people are also being oppressed by the Superiority." Though evidently the Superiority wasn't shooting at them. That must be nice.

Rig looked away from me back to the wall he'd been tinkering with. There were a *lot* of wires in there, and several blocky widgets similar to the ones he'd already removed. Layers and layers of circuits and machinery, extending deep into the unit. I wondered if there was any way to get inside this one, or if it was just a massive block of technology.

I'd meant to catch him at a moment when I could ask him about his work, and this seemed like a good time.

"What was your boss saying?" I asked. "You guys are close to getting the gun platforms working?"

"Not close enough," Rig said. "The encryption on the gun platforms is a lot heavier than on most of the other platform systems. Which makes sense. If someone is going to hijack your water system, that's bad. If they hijack your gun emplacements, that can be much worse."

"I guess so," I said. "Though I'd rather have working water than working guns."

"Depends on whether there's something you need to shoot at in a hurry," Rig said. "The water will keep you alive in the long term, but it won't matter if you don't live through the moment."

"What did she mean about the shields?" I asked. "It's something experimental?"

Rig sighed. "Experimental would suggest that we've experimented with it. Some of my colleagues managed to hack into the planetary shield system. We're not entirely sure what a lot of it does, but some of it was clearly intended to turn parts of the debris field into a shield against orbital attacks. But we don't have a projection of what the shield is supposed to do, let alone confirmation that it would work."

I smiled. That was a lot of words all in a row. Coherent words, even. This was definitely progress. Maybe he'd never had an issue with me at all. Maybe he was just *that* socially awkward.

"What are you doing now?" I asked.

"Trying to find the communicator," Rig said. "We received that communication, which means we must have some kind of hypercomm. If it can receive, it was probably once designed to send as well—so if we can find and examine it, we might be able to make it work."

"Did you find it?" I asked. "How did you know where to look?"

"I followed the path of the alerts we received in the main system," he said. He glanced at me self-consciously. "How is probably boring, but the trail led me here. I think the communicator is somewhere in this block, but I don't know what a lot of this is." He glanced at the mess around him. "I don't want to break the thing in case Cuna sends us another transmission, but if we could get it working, we could respond. And that might be the only way for us to get in touch, now that . . ."

"Now that Alanik was scared away," I said. "It really wasn't my fault."

Rig looked horrified. "I didn't say that it was! I mean, I didn't think it. I mean, I'm sure—" He blushed. "I'm sure you did a great job talking to her. Look, I'll probably be working on this for a while, so you can take the box back to the lab. Or leave it here and I'll watch it! Either way is fine."

He turned back to the machinery, unplugging some wires and then pulling out another block and setting it to the side, inspecting what was beneath it.

I set down the box with the slugs in it. I'd thought we were making progress, but now I was being dismissed. "Is there something I can do to help?"

"No!" Rig said. "I mean, you're supposed to be watching the slugs, right? I wouldn't want to keep you."

Yeah, definitely trying to get rid of me. I was getting really sick of wondering what was going on with him. "What's your problem with me?" I asked.

Rig looked at me, wide-eyed. "I don't have a problem with you."

"Really? Because you obviously don't want me to be here. You barely talk to me, even when we're supposed to be working together. You seem to like Jorgen just fine, but you won't even speak to me. What did I do to make you dislike me so much?"

Rig pushed a hand through his hair, closing his eyes. "I don't dislike you, FM."

"Then what?" I demanded. I probably should have been more reasonable, but the *last* person I'd tried to be reasonable with had disappeared into thin air, probably fleeing across the universe to get away. And while I knew she wasn't fleeing from me personally, it still didn't feel good.

At least Rig couldn't hyperjump away.

"No," Rig said quietly. "I . . . scud, Spensa didn't tell you?" He looked at me plaintively, like he was begging me to have any idea what he was talking about. I was starting to have the creeping sensation that I was missing something enormous.

Rig sighed. "I guess she didn't. I didn't mean for you to think that I didn't like you, when the truth is I—"

Oh scud.

Oh SCUD.

I *was* missing something, something so obvious I clearly should have seen it.

Rig wasn't afraid of me. He—

"—kind of, um, like you," he mumbled.

"That— *Oh*." My face went hot. I was being as bad as Nedd right now. I did not see this coming. I'd known Nedd was interested in me, of course, and about Jorgen and Spensa, but none of them had acted like *this*. I normally thought I was pretty good at reading people, but—

"Why would Spensa have told me that?" I asked.

"I asked Spensa to ask you if you were interested," Rig mumbled.

"I thought probably she did, and you weren't, and neither of you ever wanted to tell me, which was probably for the best. But I guess she never mentioned it at all? She must have been distracted by saving the world and everything. I get it."

He didn't sound like he got it. He sounded hurt. "No," I said. "She never said anything. I had no idea. But . . . aren't you interested in Spensa?"

Rig choked. "*Spensa?* Do I seem like I want to torture myself?"

I would have laughed if I weren't in a state of shock. Rig and I stared at each other, the longest he'd ever made eye contact with me at one time.

Rig grimaced. "I'm sorry I made you feel like I disliked you. I was embarrassed, that's all. We don't ever have to talk about this again, and I'll try to act less like I hate you and not die of embarrassment, okay?"

"Okay," I said. My face was still flaming, and Rig was bright red, and I probably should have done us both the favor of preserving what was left of our dignity by walking away. I felt like a complete idiot for confronting him when he'd obviously been trying so hard to avoid it. Nedd had done the same thing to me, and that had become all kinds of awkward the minute it was out in the open.

Except I didn't want to go. I'd *wanted* to get to know Rig, and I still did, even if it was awkward. Rig was worth wading through the awkwardness for. "Are you sure I can't stay and help?" I asked again.

Rig looked at me like I had lost my mind, and maybe I had. "You really want to help?" he asked softly.

"Yeah," I said. "I mean, I want to help you figure out how to answer that message."

"Of course." Rig somehow managed to look even more dejected. Obviously that wasn't the answer he wanted. I wasn't even sure it was the answer I'd meant to give him.

Between this and my experience with Alanik, I was clearly much worse at dealing with people than I thought I was. "And I'd

70

like to talk to you some more," I said quickly. "Do you think we can manage to act like human beings while we do that?"

Rig looked a little horrified, but then he smiled tentatively. "Maybe? I mean, if this conversation is any indication, I'd say it's unlikely."

I laughed. "Yeah, okay. Do you think we could act like freaks, but not freaks who hate each other?"

"That sounds a little more achievable." He squinted at the next panel. "If the schematic I looked at is correct—not that I completely understood it, mind you—I think the hypercomm should be somewhere in this block. Want to help me lift this off?"

"Sure," I said. I stepped around some of the mechanical bits he'd already removed. "I have no idea what any of this is."

"And I have only vague ideas," Rig said. "To be honest, it will probably take a lifetime to sort through all the things that make this platform run. Don't get me wrong—it's fascinating work. I just wish we were doing it under better circumstances."

"Don't we all," I said. Rig unplugged a couple of cables, and then he lifted half of the panel and I hoisted the other half. Together we lowered it to the ground.

Rig brushed some grease off his hands onto his jumpsuit. "That was really unmanly of me, wasn't it? Asking you to help me lift that thing. Nedd would have done it one-handed just to show off."

"Yeah, well, I'm not interested in Nedd," I said.

Rig looked at me, and there was something so sweet and vulnerable about him that it made me want to reach out and touch him.

I stood frozen to the spot. I'd tried not to think about guys since I'd joined the DDF. Something about all the fighting and dying made dating seem ridiculous, like it had about as much place in flight school as the fancy dresses people wore to parties back home.

But I was thinking about one now, and I didn't really want to stop.

"Is there someone you *are* interested in?" Rig asked quietly.

He looked like he was bracing for bad news. I wanted to say

yes, but I didn't want to give him false hope. I liked him, yeah. But could it really go anywhere? What future did any of us have with things the way they were?

Not one we could bank on, that was for certain. "I don't know," I said.

"Yeah, okay," Rig said. "No problem."

He'd taken that as a rejection, but I wasn't sure it was.

Rig cleared his throat and turned to look at the machinery behind the panel we'd just removed.

"Oh," Rig said.

There, amid the wires and circuits and foreign devices, was a box identical to the one Rig had built based on M-Bot's design.

"That's how they did it," Rig said, and I nodded.

We had an FTL communicator.

But it required a taynix to make it work.

8

"So you're sure," Jorgen said, "the FTL communicator is designed to house one of these slugs?" He was sitting on one of the metal chairs in the engineering bay with Fine, the purple taynix, stretched across his lap. Jorgen had fewer bandages on his face now, the remaining little white pieces of medical tape standing out in stark contrast to his dark skin.

Jorgen ran his fingers absently through Fine's orange spines, and it shimmied slightly, like it was happy about it.

"Pretty sure," Rig said. "FM discovered that the slugs do bring the box with them when they hyperjump. If the box in M-Bot's ship was built to house a slug, the box in the FTL communicator probably has the same purpose."

"But you wouldn't want the slug jumping away with the communicator," Jorgen pointed out.

"Our theory," I said, "is that the different kinds of slugs have different cytonic abilities. The purple slugs and the red slugs don't escape the way the yellow ones do, so the yellow slugs are the teleporters."

"Right," Rig said. "And the red one did that . . . exploding thing. It's possible that the purple ones have a third power."

"A communication power," Jorgen said. "Like the way Spensa communicated with Gran-Gran from light-years away."

Rig smiled. "Exactly." He turned and looked at me—which he seemed able to do a lot more after our conversation. This time I had to resist looking away. I wasn't entirely comfortable with the way I felt when he paid attention to me—like my heart was skipping beats. It made me nervous and worry about hurting him, which was stupid, because I already had, hadn't I? He seemed to think I'd let him down easy, and maybe I had. Now I just needed to leave well enough alone.

But I still felt unsettled, and more than a little disappointed.

"But why would you build the same box in the ship and the communicator?" Jorgen asked. "If you're not going to teleport the communicator around, and the purple slugs can't escape, you don't need the same sort of device in the communicator as you do in the ship. Not if the purpose of the box is to make sure the ship hyperjumps with the slug."

"That's true," Rig said, "if the only purpose of the box is to send the ship with the slug." He pointed to a piece he'd pulled out of the device before we found the box. "But I think the inside of the box might have a second function. This is a holographic projector. It's not as advanced as the one on M-Bot, but it's *more* advanced than the ones we use. I think it might have been used to project an image on the inside of the box."

"Shouldn't M-Bot's box have one of those too, then?" Jorgen asked.

"M-Bot's technology allows him to project holograms on almost any surface," Rig said. "So he would have been able to project onto the inside of the box without a dedicated holoprojector."

"And the purpose of the projector is to tell the slugs what to do," I said.

Rig smiled at me. His cheeks dimpled, and my heart did that skippy thing again. I definitely needed to figure out how to get that under control. "That's the idea," he said.

Jorgen nodded. "And if we have the slugs, the box, and the projector—"

"Then we should be able to do the same thing."

"Okay," Jorgen said. "That's good work. I don't suppose getting the communicator to work is as easy as putting a purple slug in it?"

"I tried that," Rig said. "The slug sits there, and maybe if we waited long enough it might send a communication somewhere . . ."

"But we need to be able to direct what it says," Jorgen said. "How do we do that? Do we even know where to send the message?"

"I think so," Rig said. "There's some metadata that came with the communication from Minister Cuna. I think we might be able to use it to respond. The communicator has some hardware similar to Alanik's translation pin, and I think that might send a specific message through the taynix even if the taynix doesn't actually *understand* the message. What I haven't figured out is how to get the slug to participate in the communication."

"It probably has something to do with cytonics," Jorgen said. "Boomslug exploded while I was trying to talk to it with my mind. So maybe I have to"—he gave me a side-eye—"*ask* it to send the message?"

"Or induce it to somehow?" Rig asked.

"What were you thinking about when Boomslug exploded?" I asked. "You said you were trying to talk to it. What were you saying?"

Jorgen rubbed the back of his neck. "Nothing much. You said I should befriend it, so I was trying to . . . empathize with it, I guess."

"Empathize with it," Rig said.

Jorgen groaned. "Yes, okay? FM said I should bond with it—"

"And you told me that was stupid—"

"Because I *thought* it was stupid. But nothing else was working, so I thought it would be worth a try. I told it I was sorry that I ripped it out of its home and was now invading its mind and talking to it through that creepy place with all the eyes. Okay?"

75

"Wait," I said. "The eyes?"

"Yeah . . ." He trailed off, and looked at the slug.

"The eyes," Rig said. "You said they're creepy, right? And you're afraid of them?"

"I'm not afraid of them," Jorgen said. "But yeah, the times I've seen them, they're . . . unnerving. It's uncomfortable, all of them staring at me. It makes me self-conscious."

"Self-conscious," I said. "Otherworldly, all-powerful beings that could snuff your life out in an instant—along with the rest of the lives on our planet—stare at you, and that makes you *self-conscious*."

"Yes, okay?" Jorgen said. "It's not like I *choose* how I feel about them. It's hard to explain if you've never experienced it."

"But the slugs have," Rig said. "And when you thought about those things, Boomslug was frightened."

"Maybe," Jorgen said. "So when I thought of the eyes, the slug used its cytonic abilities. I suppose we could try again, to confirm . . ." He felt at the bandages on his face. "Maybe we should try one of the other varieties, like the teleporting ones. Perhaps I could . . . *scare* the slug into hyperjumping."

"It seems like a good thing to try," Rig said.

They both looked at me, like they wanted my opinion.

"Um," I said. "I don't love the idea of terrifying the slugs, but since it's the only lead we have, it seems worth trying."

"Right," Jorgen said. He gingerly lifted Fine off his lap and put him in the crate. "Maybe we could use one of the slugs in the metal box. You said they already moved it once, right?"

"Right," I said. I turned around to grab the box from where we'd left it next to the slug crate.

The box was gone.

"Well, we've proven they hyperjump with the box then, right?" Jorgen asked.

"Yes," I said. "*Where* they took the box is another question." I glanced out in the hall, but the thing wasn't there.

"We can use a different slug," Rig said, "and find the box later."

I retrieved Gill from the crate.

Jorgen took Gill in his hands and looked him in the face. "Do you think I should try to . . . bond with it first?"

"I'm not sure how that will help you scare it," Rig said. He looked at me like he expected me to argue.

"Yeah," I said. "I don't think bonding it is necessary here." I didn't *want* the slugs to be miserable, but befriending them might actively make them more comfortable and less likely to move.

"Okay," Jorgen said. "I'm not going to hum this time."

"That seems like it would be to everyone's benefit," Rig said.

"I don't know," I added. "If our goal is to terrify the slug, your humming might help."

More dimples.

Scud, I was in so much trouble.

"Here goes," Jorgen said. He closed his eyes, and nothing happened.

Rig and I looked at each other. The trouble with experimenting with cytonics was that the majority of the time we had no idea what was happening.

Then, without warning, Gill disappeared.

"Oh!" Jorgen said. "Hey! It worked."

"Yeah," I said. "Um . . . where did Gill go?"

We all looked around, but he wasn't in the immediate vicinity.

"It's occurring to me now," I said, "that if you're successful at this, you create more work for me."

"Hey," Jorgen said. "You volunteered for this job."

I did. I headed out into the hall, searching the surrounding rooms for Gill. I found the box with the other two yellow taynix in it in an adjoining room, and brought it back and set it inside the door. There was no sign of Gill in the surrounding halls though, or the corridors beyond that.

I was about to give up when one of the aides from Command came up the hallway holding a canvas bag that emitted a fluting sound. "Admiral Cobb sent this for you," he said. "Apparently it materialized in the middle of his holoprojection."

"Thanks," I said, lifting Gill out of the bag. "You can keep the bag in case you see any more of them."

"Okay," the aide said, looking at the taynix warily.

Gill shuddered a little, trembling under my touch, and I reached into my pocket, pulling out a little tin of caviar and offering a bite to Gill. Even my parents would have to approve of this if they knew the slugs were the secret to saving the lives of everyone on Detritus.

"Okay," Rig said when I returned. "We have an idea for another experiment. Is Gill ready?"

"Hasn't he been through enough?" I asked.

"We know he's frightened of the eyes," Jorgen said. "And we want to see if we can get him to move the box."

Rig had already removed the slugs who had been hanging out in the metal box. I went over to the crate and gave the slugs a couple of mushrooms. If we weren't relying on starvation to motivate them to teleport, there was no need for the poor things to go hungry.

"Okay," Rig said, handing Jorgen the box with Gill loaded into it. "Hold on to the box, and we'll see if we can get it to take you *and* the box with it wherever it goes."

"Wherever it goes?" Jorgen said. "We have no idea where it's going to go, and we want it to take me with it?"

"That tactic could have its uses," I said, "like for getting fighters out of trouble when they're being tailed by Krell. But it's not useful for going to meet with Cuna." I was still nervous about trying that—what if Alanik was right, and Cuna was merely another tool of the Superiority looking to control us?

Without Alanik though, Cuna was our only option. If Alanik's people didn't want to be our allies, we were still going to need help if we expected to escape from the Superiority.

"I don't think it's going to take you far," Rig said. "None of the taynix have left the immediate vicinity. You're not going to get carried off the platform."

"So getting them to travel across the universe is its own problem," I said.

"Right," Rig said. "But one thing at a time."

"Fine," Jorgen said.

"Fine!" Fine piped up from over in the crate.

Jorgen drew a deep breath, holding the metal box in his hands. Nothing happened.

After a really long silence, Jorgen opened his eyes. "It's not working."

"Maybe it's not scared anymore," Rig said. "You showed it the eyes and nothing happened. If someone showed me the same scary image over and over again, I would stop being frightened of it."

"Good point," Jorgen said. "Maybe we need to think of something else that scares them?"

"Or use another slug," I said. I reached into the crate and pulled out Happy. "Let's try this one."

With Happy secured inside the box, Jorgen closed his eyes again.

And then, without warning, he disappeared.

"Owwww," Jorgen said, and Rig and I spun around to find him lodged inside one of the cubbyholes filled with rolled-up design schematics. The rolls of papers were all crushed to the sides, and Jorgen's body was folded with his knees up to his chin. The box with the slug in it was jammed in front of him, and he pushed it out, shoving it onto the floor with a clang. Jorgen swore.

I giggled, and Rig snickered and then started to laugh.

"It's not funny!" Jorgen shouted.

"I think the evidence is against you there, Flightleader," I said, though he was right. Sure, him being crunched up in that cubbyhole was amusing, but what if the slug had hyperjumped somewhere more dangerous, or smaller? The slugs were used to finding spaces for their own body mass, and we didn't even know if they were perfect at that.

I think Rig had the same thoughts at the same time, because he crossed the room and helped Jorgen extract himself. Jorgen rubbed one of the bandaged cuts on his elbow.

"I don't think we should test it like that again," I said.

"Agreed," Jorgen said. "I wonder if the slugs have more awareness when they're teleporting an entire ship. It seems like bad design to use a creature to teleport that wants to crunch you into a tiny space."

Rig nodded. "I'm still impressed we managed to make it work at all."

"We did," I said. "But what's the point?"

"The point?" Jorgen asked. "Of learning to use the slugs as hyperdrives?"

"Of having hyperdrives that only teleport cytonics," I said. "If it requires a cytonic to use a hyperdrive, and cytonics themselves can teleport without hyperdrives—"

"Maybe it comes back to the projections," Rig said. "They project something frightening onto the inside of the box, and then a cytonic isn't necessary. My team can work with the projector to see if we can get it to project inside a box we can install in a ship."

"Besides," Jorgen said, "*I* am a cytonic and I don't know how to hyperjump. If I can make the slugs do it, we're still up from where we were, even if there are easier ways out there."

That was true, but something about it still bothered me.

Rig considered for a moment. "You might be right that the slugs are more aware of their size when they're taking a whole ship with them. M-Bot might also have had some way to deal with being placed in a small space, though I'm not sure what it would have been."

"So what do we do now?" I asked.

"We don't really have a choice," Jorgen said. "Dangerous or not, we need to try this out in a ship."

9

We all agreed it would be best if Jorgen didn't try to use the hyperdrive for the first time while piloting a ship. Cobb granted us the use of one of the two-seater Dulo-class fighters, which had pilot and copilot seats side by side. The cockpit of the Dulo was still narrow, with the fuselage only a little wider than a Largo class. Even so, as I climbed in, the cockpit felt smaller than normal, like the fuselage was squeezing in on me.

Rig had bolted his metal box under the dash between the instruments and the floor, so the slugs couldn't hyperjump without taking the rest of the ship with them. He was already working on some duplicate boxes, in case we got this to work.

At least this time we weren't flying out into the black. The Krell hadn't pierced the debris belt in months, so chances were good I wasn't going to have to watch any of my friends get shot out of the sky today.

Didn't make it any easier to be in the pilot's seat again.

"You're sure we're ready for this?" I said to Jorgen as we climbed into the ship.

"No," Jorgen said. "But I don't think we can afford to wait. The engineers are working on the defenses, but they say they have no way to know if they'll ever be functional."

Jorgen settled in the copilot seat, shoulder to shoulder with me. This was going to take some getting used to; I was accustomed to having a bit more space from my flightleader while I was flying.

Jorgen checked on the slugs in the box. We had Gill and Happy in there, plus a couple other yellow slugs. We all agreed we needed to bring more than one, in case something went wrong and we lost some of them in transport.

"All right," Jorgen said beside me. "Let's do this."

I put on my headset and turned on my radio, setting the channel for Command, which in this case connected me with Rig.

"We're ready," I told him.

"Copy," Rig said. "Skyward Flight, you are cleared for departure."

I engaged our acclivity ring, and several other ships lifted out of the landing bay alongside us. We hadn't gathered the entire flight, but Sadie, Kimmalyn, Nedd, and Arturo were all accompanying us in case we got into trouble. Jorgen jumped on the channel we shared with them—he was still flightleader, even if he wasn't technically flying.

"Skyward Flight," he said. "Descend to 100,000 feet and meet at coordinates 334-1280. Quirk and Sentry, you two fly ahead to scout the area for unexpected debris fall. Amphi and Nedder, follow us in point formation."

Our flightmates sounded off, and then I accelerated. We flew at half a Mag until we'd slipped down through a gap in the belt of platforms, soaring beneath the lights that illuminated the planet from the debris layer.

Jorgen fidgeted nervously with the bandage beneath his chin. "You worried this won't work?" I asked him.

"Yes," he said. "I'm also worried that it will."

That made sense. We needed to be able to get off Detritus, but I didn't envy Jorgen being the key to it all. We knew how to hide on this hole of a planet and fight for our lives. Everything else was a great unknown.

"What did Alanik say to you?" I asked. "When she spoke in your mind right before she left?"

Jorgen was quiet for a moment, and I expected him to say it was classified, but he didn't. "She said I was powerful. That I shouldn't let other people control me."

Huh. "Is that it?"

"Yeah, that's it."

"Why did you lie about it?"

Jorgen sighed. "It didn't seem like a great thing to say in front of my mother. But I told Cobb the truth when he debriefed me."

"Why do you think she said that?" Alanik seemed to have issues with authority, which made her fit right in with the Defiant League. She didn't trust *us* either, though. Not that I could blame her.

"I don't know," Jorgen said. "Maybe on her planet the cytonics are in charge? It might feel foreign to her that people who can teleport across the galaxy on a whim would listen to a chain of command."

"You don't agree with that though," I said. Jorgen was the champion of the chain of command. He knew protocol forward and backward, better even than Cobb did.

Jorgen shook his head. "It's one thing to have power, but if you don't direct it you can end up making huge mistakes and hurting people. There's a reason Command is in control."

"And the National Assembly?" I asked. "Do you think they should take command power away from the DDF?"

Jorgen shrugged. "I think they have a point. Our military shouldn't head up diplomacy for the Defiant League."

I gave him a look.

Jorgen sighed. "Neither should my mother, okay? They sent her to be the liaison to the *military*. She isn't a diplomat."

"Do we have people like that on Detritus?" I asked.

"I don't know," Jorgen said. "You did pretty well at it."

I snorted. "I don't have training as a diplomat."

"No," Jorgen said. "But no one here does. You're a scudding better diplomat than my mother, that's for sure."

That wasn't a comforting thought. We had a system for training pilots, for fighting the Krell. We'd spent generations perfecting it.

What would we do now that circumstances suddenly demanded different skills, skills we hadn't valued as a people?

"We're going to have to figure it out," I said. "Quickly, if this works."

Jorgen looked at the instrumentation. "We're getting close to our heading. I'm going to focus on the slugs now."

"All right," I said. "Just . . . try not to hyperjump us anywhere dangerous, okay?"

Jorgen didn't respond. He still didn't know how to relay cytonic coordinates, which meant he'd have no control over where he sent us.

There was a lot more debris down here to crash into if the slugs decided to teleport us into a tight space the way they did with Jorgen in the engineering bay, but we didn't dare try this experiment outside the atmosphere where the remaining Superiority outposts might observe us.

Still, the slugs had only teleported meters away in the lab. None of them had left Platform Prime—I'd always been able to find them again. They weren't likely to choose this moment to take us light-years away. If they did, we'd still have a hyperdrive; we could figure out how to get back.

Except Spensa left with the same intentions, and now no one knew where she was—another reason Jorgen shouldn't try to hyperjump in a ship by himself.

I didn't think the *two* of us being lost in space was a huge step up.

As we reached the area we'd designated for experimentation, Kimmalyn and Sadie shot off ahead, canvassing the area in their sleek scout ships. I liked flying scout-class ships better than the heavier classes, and I was going to miss that maneuverability if we needed it.

"Call Rig," Jorgen said, his eyes closed behind his visor. "Tell him we're ready."

"Rig," I said over the general channel. "We're ready to begin."

"Everything's clear out here," Kimmalyn added. "No debris, no transport ships, nothing."

"Jerkface, you ready for this?" Arturo added.

"Tell them I'm ready," Jorgen said. But he was gripping the edge of his seat like he was terrified. I didn't think that was a personal affront to my flying.

"Jerkface is concentrating," I said. "He says he's ready."

"Try not to crash into us," Arturo said.

"She said Jerkface was concentrating," Kimmalyn said. "Like the Saint always said, 'A silent fool is a stealthy fool.' "

"Who are you calling a fool, Quirk?" Nedd asked.

"Not you," Sadie said. "You're never silent."

Nedd grunted. "Good thing I'm too dumb to know if that's what she meant."

"Tell them to cut the chatter," Jorgen said.

"Guys, stay off the channel," I said. "And track us on your proximity sensors. We may not move far, but we'll need to prove if we *did* move."

The channel went quiet, and I glanced at Jorgen.

"You look like you're going to throw up," I said. "Don't do that in my cockpit."

"I'll try not to," Jorgen said. "Do you think we're doing this too soon?"

"No. I think we're doing what needs to be done. But if you don't relax, you might scare that slug enough to hyperjump us a lot farther than we want to go."

"Maybe," Jorgen said. "I don't know if that's how it works. I'm trying to relax."

85

"You could hum again."

Jorgen opened one eye and glared at me.

I was joking, but that gave me another idea. "Here," I said, reaching for my transmitter. "Maybe this will help."

I flipped on the transmitter and chose a slow, beautiful piece, played by only a few string instruments. We had banjos and fiddles on Detritus, but the sounds that came out of those were pale shadows of the long, melodious notes soaring from my transmitter.

Jorgen opened his eyes, and his shoulders did relax a little. "Where did you get that?"

"From my father," I said. "Isn't it beautiful? This is the one I listen to when I'm nervous."

Jorgen took a deep breath. "It's wonderful."

It was so sad that while we had this music, we didn't play it publicly. On Earth, music used to play over the radio all the time. Tune in to an FM channel and you could listen to anything you wanted. It was incredible to me that the air used to be filled with these waves. That was why I picked FM as my callsign: it thrilled me that the initials of my name—Freyja Marten—were the same as the term for music that used to be so widely available.

"Are you ready?" I asked.

Jorgen nodded. He did seem a little more relaxed.

I flipped on the radio again, not bothering to turn off the transmitter. "Rig, are we cleared to hyperjump?"

"Cleared, FM," Rig said. "When you're ready."

"Scud, here it goes," Jorgen said.

For a moment the music ascended, but nothing else happened. I tightened my grip on my controls, looking out over the barren surface of the planet. We were too high up to see the craggy patterns of the surface, and too far from the debris belt to distinguish more than the largest platforms and pieces of debris. Suspended in the middle, flying at Mag-1 so I'd have more control if we needed to fall into evasive maneuvers. Beside me Jorgen breathed in deeply, and the music dropped into a series of quick, low notes that aligned with my heartbeat.

Maybe this wasn't working. Maybe something was wrong. Maybe—

I blinked, and a chunk of metal debris appeared in front of my ship, bearing down on us.

No. We were bearing down on *it*.

I pulled up, narrowly missing the debris as I slipped into the crack between two large chunks of metal that spun freely in the debris belt—remnants of the systems up here that had long since started to disintegrate. Beside me, Jorgen snapped his eyes open and gasped in surprise as I slipped around the debris and shot downward—at least I thought it was downward; I'd lost all my bearings when we teleported.

"Look out!" Jorgen shouted, and too late I saw the chunk of rock our boosters had destabilized spinning toward us. We rammed straight into it, cracking our shield, and I rolled the ship to the side to avoid colliding into another piece of debris.

"FM!" Rig said over the radio. "You guys okay?"

Jorgen grabbed the radio. "Rig, where the scud are we?"

"I've located you in the debris belt. You're deep in an unstable area. I'm trying to find the best heading for you to get out."

"Scud!" I said, slowing our speed as I wove between large pieces of debris that looked like a platform broken apart at the seams. "Tell him to do it quickly."

"Now, Rig," Jorgen said. "We need that heading now!"

I swept between two pieces of the platform, but they moved toward me instead of away, folding in on each other as if on a hinge. I accelerated, but Jorgen put a hand on my shoulder.

And then suddenly we materialized just past the edge of the folding platforms. I watched on my monitors as the monstrous shapes clapped against each other behind us.

"What did you do?" I asked, swinging us around another chunk of debris.

"I focused on the space where I wanted us to go," Jorgen said. "I think I can give the slugs an instruction for where to run, as long as I can see the space I want them to run to. I might be able to do it if I can visualize the place and it's somewhere they recognize. We'll have to experiment with that though."

The section of the debris field in front of us was a little looser, and I continued to weave through the debris as the music swelled in long, slow swoops. *Calm*, I thought. *Focus.* I found a portion of the debris belt with wider, more open spaces and circled around and around while Rig worked on that heading.

"We could experiment now," I suggested. "You could visualize the space over Platform Prime and see if the slug will take us there."

Through his visor, Jorgen grimaced. He didn't respond.

"Jerkface," I said, "you okay?"

"Yeah," Jorgen said. "But I think—I think that second time something heard me."

"Heard you?" I asked. "Like, cytonically?"

"Yeah," Jorgen said.

My heart dropped. "A delver?"

Jorgen shook his head. "I don't think so. It was like—like it was surprised. It heard me reach out to the taynix, and it was shocked I was there. Like I opened a door and startled the person on the other side."

"If it wasn't a delver, and it wasn't a taynix—" The only other cytonic on the planet that we knew about was Spensa's grandmother, though she knew about Jorgen, so she shouldn't be surprised. "Are there more of you? Because we could use—"

Jorgen shook his head. "I don't think it was us," he said. "I think it was *them*."

Oh. The Superiority? We knew they had cytonics, and it made sense that there would be one or two assigned to the battleships parked near Detritus, especially if they used cytonics to run their hyperdrives. "If they heard you—"

"Then they know what we're doing," Jorgen said. "They might

have sensed what we did just now. I don't know that I want to try it again right away with them listening."

That did seem unwise. If they knew we were developing hyperdrives, what would they do to us?

"Okay," Rig said over the radio. "I've got coordinates for you. You're going to need to move away from Platform Prime to a more stable part of the debris belt you can cut through to come back down." Rig gave us some coordinates, and Jorgen put them into the nav system. I accelerated a bit more and swung around chunks of debris that were almost as big as Platform Prime, but twisted and battered.

Jorgen switched the radio to the general channel, and I lowered the volume on my transmitter, but didn't turn it off.

"Amphi?" Jorgen said. "Nedder? You guys okay?"

"You're alive," Arturo said. "Scud, Jerkface, you just *disappeared.*"

"That's what he was trying to do, wasn't it?" Nedder said.

"Right, but I didn't expect him to actually *do* it. Where are you guys?"

"Up in the debris belt," Jorgen said. "I'll send you the coordinates where we expect to emerge, and you can escort us to Platform Prime."

"Did you really hyperjump?" Sadie asked. "What was it like?"

I flipped on my radio. "Like being in one place and then suddenly being in another."

"Um, guys?" Rig said. "The command center is filling up. I think they're going to take my channel soon."

"Take your channel?" Jorgen asked. "Why?"

"Hang on. Let me find out."

Jorgen and I looked at each other.

"We got those coordinates," Arturo said. "Moving your direction."

Through the chunks of metal below us, I caught sight of the surface of the planet.

"Skyward Flight," a familiar voice said over the radio. Cobb, taking over from Rig. "I'm going to need you all to report back to Platform Prime immediately."

"Why, sir?" Jorgen asked over the radio.

"We've got movement from the battleships," Cobb said. "It looks like they're pulling their largest ship into position, the one with the planetary weapons."

Stars. "The *what*?" I asked.

"Sir," Jorgen said. "Did you say *planetary* weapons?"

"Affirmative," Cobb said. "We knew from the chatter on the datanets that they had missiles they could use to bombard the planet. They hadn't shown any sign of using them, but they're moving into position now."

"Do you think that's because of us?" I asked Jorgen.

"I don't know," he said. "But it seems like too much of a coincidence not to be."

"Better tell Cobb then, yeah?" I asked.

Jorgen nodded. "Sir, we were successful in our mission, but when we were, I think the Superiority cytonics heard us."

There was a pause, and in it I imagined Cobb swearing up a storm. "They may have decided it's time to annihilate us. Can you use the taynix to get any of us off the planet?"

"Negative," Jorgen said. "I think I can teleport to places I can see or maybe remember, but that's it."

"Copy, Flightleader. Get back here as fast as you can."

I swallowed and resisted the urge to turn up the music again.

We weren't ready. We couldn't run, not without full control over the hyperdrives, and the Superiority wanted to destroy us before we got that far.

If they attacked at full capacity now, would any of us survive?

"We're on our way," Jorgen said to Cobb as I broke through the edge of the debris belt. Arturo and Nedd both fell in behind us in flanking position, with Kimmalyn and Sadie leading the way to Platform Prime.

"There has to be some way we can use the hyperdrives to our advantage," I said to Jorgen.

Jorgen nodded. "Admiral," he said over the radio, "we can't use the hyperdrives to flee, but I think we could bring them to bear in the battle."

Cobb was quiet. "You're too valuable a resource to risk," he said finally.

"Maybe," Jorgen said. "But if we don't make it through this, it won't matter what we hold back, will it?"

It was a good point, if a sobering one.

"All right," Cobb said. "Tell me what you have in mind."

10

When we arrived at Platform Prime, the landing bay was in chaos. Much like before the battle where the delver arrived, pilots raced for their ships as they received last-minute instructions, an air of nervousness permeating it all. I brought my ship down next to Skyward One, Jorgen's usual ship. Rig and two of his fellow engineers were standing around it with the canopy open, and Rig motioned to them furiously.

Jorgen opened the hatch and hopped out.

"Cobb said you were switching to your own ship," Rig said. "We took the interference module out of Alanik's ship and installed it in yours. If the information we took from her databanks is correct, it'll stop the enemy from projecting illusions into your head. You also have five yellow taynix in a box under your dash. It isn't pretty, but it's bolted in place, so the slugs won't teleport without you. Will you be okay with no one to help you with them?"

"I'll be all right," Jorgen said. "We need you to fly with FM in the Dulo."

Rig looked at Jorgen with terror. "I'm not a pilot, Jorgen. I barely started flight school."

"And you're not piloting today," Jorgen said. "We're going to try to use the hyperdrives to launch a surprise attack on the ship with the planetary assault cannon. The goal is to disable their cannons so they can't destroy Platform Prime or hit the surface of Detritus. The thing is, we don't know exactly how these weapons work. We don't know how to destroy them, or if we can. But if we send you in there, and you get a good look at the guns—"

"Then maybe I can help figure out how to disable them." Rig nodded.

"Command won't let me do it myself," Jorgen said, "but I can feel the slugs in my mind from a distance. I don't need to be right next to the slugs to communicate with them. So, we're going to send you in with FM. You won't be up there alone—they're willing to let me command Skyward Flight to back you up because I'm going to have to see where I'm sending you. Also, I'll be able to use the hyperdrive to pull you out if things go wrong."

I wasn't thrilled about the plan myself—once I was in there, theoretically Jorgen should be able to teleport me out if something went wrong. But it was all *very* theoretical. This wasn't a suicide mission, but it was the closest thing I'd ever done.

I wasn't Spensa. I didn't enjoy running headlong into danger and figuring things out as I went along. But I also wasn't going to let my entire planet be destroyed because I wasn't willing to do what needed to be done. I was a pilot. I signed up for this. I was going to do the best I could to make sure that as many people came out of this alive as possible, even if I wasn't among them.

Taking Rig with me was another matter entirely.

"He can't order you to do it," I said to Rig. Rig knew that of course, because he wasn't in Jorgen's chain of command, but it seemed like a good moment for a reminder. "And Cobb hasn't ordered you to do it either." Cobb understood the reasons a pilot might have for not getting into a ship again. Cobb had done it when he felt he had to, but he wasn't going to make that decision for someone else. He hadn't ordered *me* to do this either—it was too experimental, too volatile.

Rig nodded. "I know. I'll do it."

"Are you sure?" I asked.

Jorgen gave me a sharp look. Rig had just agreed, which was obviously what we needed.

But I didn't feel good taking someone up into battle with me on a mission this dangerous unless they were sure they wanted to be there.

"Yes," Rig said. He motioned to a box next to him. "We have one more taynix, in case we need it." He hoisted the box into the Dulo, with Chubs looking contemplatively over the edge. Rig climbed into the copilot seat beside me. He squirmed a little, scrunching himself up on the side of the seat farthest from me, even though I wished he'd sit closer. He put on his helmet.

Scud, I hated this. He'd dropped out of flight school for a reason, and he hadn't ever wanted to come back, not like Kimmalyn or Nedd. If I got him killed, that was on me. In my mind I saw Lizard's ship exploding, the wreckage spiraling toward the planet.

Not Rig. I didn't want that to happen to him. I couldn't let it.

It didn't feel like a comfort to know that if he died in this fight, I was likely going with him. "You really don't have to do this," I said. I *hoped* he would back out, even though I needed his help.

This was exactly why having complicated feelings for someone in a situation like this was a bad idea.

"I know I don't have to," Rig said. "But Jorgen is right. You shouldn't be working a hyperdrive alone, especially since you don't actually have control over it."

"We'll be fine," I said with a confidence I didn't feel. "I have a perfect record of not dying in combat."

Rig laughed, but it sounded forced. He was avoiding my eyes again. At least this time he was clearly terrified of the combat and not of me.

"I'm going to do my best not to get you killed up there," I said. I would. I *had* to.

"I believe you," Rig said. "But it's not always under your control, is it?"

Of course it wasn't. I could never guarantee that I was going to return from any mission, much less that I could keep anyone else safe.

That was what worried me.

Next to us, I could see Jorgen checking his ship, getting ready to take off. Kimmalyn, Sadie, and the others were hovering in the air, waiting for rendezvous coordinates. T-Stall and Catnip had joined them.

"This new planetary weapon," I said. "Isn't it the kind of thing that shield you're working on is supposed to defend against?"

"It could be if the shield worked," Rig said. "But we haven't tested it. If we turn it on, maybe nothing will happen. Or parts of the system might come online, but others might be too damaged to function. The debris around Detritus is in bad shape. The system might fail. Worse, it might short out, making it harder to use in the future."

"And at worst?" I asked.

"I don't know," Rig said. "We haven't had time to map out all the ramifications. If there are shorts on important platforms, there could be considerable damage."

"To Platform Prime?" I asked.

"I don't know," Rig repeated. "That's why it's too volatile to try until we have time to work up the likely scenarios. But we've given a full report to Command about what we know and what we don't. It'll be up to Cobb to decide what to do with it."

Jorgen had a point about the command structure. It did make sense for power to be organized so it could be used efficiently. But then everything depended on the decision-making of the person at the top. Cobb I trusted. Jeshua and the Assembly, less so.

Jorgen's ship lifted off, and I engaged my acclivity ring, lifting up beside him.

"Skyward Flight," Jorgen said over the radio, "our orders are to engage the fighters protecting the battleships. We cannot let them destroy Platform Prime or penetrate the debris field to hit the surface of the planet."

"Skyward Five, ready." I said over the radio.

When the rest of the flight had sounded off, we followed our navigation track through the maze of upper platforms.

"We're going to be in the center of the battle today," Jorgen said. "Our orders are to hang behind Victory and Valkyrie Flights as they punch up toward the battleship." Jorgen wasn't going to talk about the other part of our mission over the radio, where there was even the slightest chance the enemy might be able to intercept the message. "FM is in the Dulo today with Rig."

"Wait, *Rig* is flying with us?" Kimmalyn said. "Welcome back, Rig!"

"Tell them thanks," Rig said.

I pointed at Rig's radio controls. "Tell them yourself."

He switched on his radio. "Thanks, Quirk," Rig said. "I'm um . . . not totally against being here."

"From Rig, that's a resounding endorsement," I said, and he gave me a weak smile. He relaxed in the seat a little, so our shoulders touched, and that at least was a comfort.

"I do intend to keep you alive," I said to him.

"We're flying toward a bunch of aliens who intend the exact opposite," Rig said. "Especially once they realize we have a hyperdrive, even if it's not a very effective one, and that we're there to destroy their cannon."

"Rig, FM, you have the device ready?" Jorgen asked over a private channel as we cleared the platforms and shot out into the black.

Beside me, Rig opened up the box and looked at the taynix.

"Do you know which one Jorgen already used?" he asked.

"I don't," I said. "Maybe swap them all out?"

"Yeah, I'll do that." He pulled out the four taynix already in the box and swapped them for the one he'd brought with him. Happy stretched out across his knee, trilling softly. I reached over and scritched him behind his frill.

"Ready," I told Jorgen over the radio.

"That's an overstatement," Rig muttered beside me. "But we're as ready as we are right now."

I laughed. That felt both profound and terrifying. I put a hand on my transmitter. "How do you feel about music?" I asked.

"I liked that song you were playing before in the lab. Do you have any others?"

"Yes," I said, and I turned on my transmitter, flipping through the short list of pieces before selecting one.

This one was heavier than the one I played for Jorgen. I had no concept of what instruments could possibly make these sounds. There was a melody buried underneath a lot of shouting in a language I didn't understand. But the beat was clear and the sounds were oddly engaging, even as loud and angry as they seemed.

Rig listened for a moment and then wrinkled his nose. "Is that music? Are you sure?"

"It is," I said. "It just takes a refined taste to appreciate it."

The flight accelerated together, moving toward the battleships in a standard V formation. My proximity sensors began to pick up ships—lots of them, though not yet as many as we'd faced when the delver arrived.

More alarming, the larger ships were now moving toward Detritus. Up to this time they'd stayed in place—a waypoint, not a danger themselves.

The music continued its relentless march as we continued to accelerate up to Mag-8. Outside the debris field, there was so much, well, *space*. The ships loomed in the distance, but even at high speeds it took us a long while to approach.

A while in which I was increasingly aware of Rig sitting next to me. Our arms were touching now, from shoulder to elbow, warming my whole body. Scud, this was not what I was supposed to be thinking about when I was heading into combat. It was like I told Sadie during the last fight: I had to *focus*. I wasn't used to having anyone in the cockpit with me during a fight, let alone a guy who liked me.

He did still like me, right?

"I'm not sure this music is getting any better," Rig said.

"Fine," I said. "I'll turn it off."

"No, you don't have to," Rig said quickly, but I'd already reached for the dial, searching for another song. I didn't share my music with many people, which was probably selfish. It wasn't that I wanted to keep it all to myself—more that I didn't want to share it with anyone who wouldn't appreciate it. It was the one thing that connected me to who we used to be, before our people crashed on Detritus and were reduced to nothing but survival.

I probably shouldn't have chosen one of the weirder pieces in my collection to share with Rig. So I decided to pick something a little easier to appreciate.

I chose a choral piece, also in a different language, one my father said had fallen out of use long before humans left Earth. Dozens, maybe hundreds of voices all blended together, singing with different tones and pitches, loud and yet somehow soft all at once.

"Oh," Rig said. "Stars, that one's beautiful. Are any of those instruments?"

"I don't think so. Just voices."

"Wow." Rig petted Happy absently on his knee, and the slug began to trill along with the music, adding another high-pitched tone to the voices. Gill edged his way over, nuzzling my thigh.

"You have to like this one," I said. "Even slugs appreciate it."

Rig narrowed his eyes at me, and I laughed and smacked him on the hand.

I wished I had the guts to do more. I wished the battle wasn't coming up so fast. Scud, another carrier ship had arrived, and more fighters poured out of it. It seemed incredible that they'd gotten here so fast, but the Superiority had working FTL communicators. They had hyperdrives that went where they told them to go, and the ability to call up their pilots and transport them across the vastness of space in moments.

We'd made progress, but we were still so scudding far behind it made me want to cry.

Not now. This wasn't the moment to lose my composure. My flight was depending on me. Rig was depending on me. Detritus was depending on me.

The ships splayed across my proximity sensors as we rapidly approached the battlefield. This time we'd brought the fight to them.

I wished I thought that would give us enough of an edge for the victory to be decisive.

"We're as ready as we are right now," I said.

Rig nodded. "No more, no less."

Several of the enemy ships broke away from the pack, heading toward us.

"Here we go," I said, and we streaked toward them through the black.

11

Our flight cut up through the center of the battlefield in the wake of Valkyrie and Victory Flights, who were both tasked with getting us close enough to the gunship for Jorgen to see a clear path to it. Jorgen needed a visual on the place he was going to send us to be sure we'd actually arrive.

The enemy ships fanned out, intercepting our fighters as they moved toward the gunship. There had to be a way to take that thing down, or the Superiority forces wouldn't be so determined to defend it. We didn't need to destroy it, only disable the orbital weapons before they had a chance to damage Detritus.

I soared with the lift of the music toward the incoming enemy ships and peppered them with destructor fire. I immediately picked up a couple of tails, and Sadie and Kimmalyn fell into position behind me, ready to fire after I took down the enemies' shields.

I reversed my boosters, slowing me down. In atmosphere, the drag of air resistance did this work for me, but up here I had to do it myself. The other ships quickly caught up and I did a barrel roll to avoid their destructor fire, though some of it crackled across my shield.

"Scud," Rig said, gripping the dash. "I forgot how disorienting this is." Still, he leaned over the proximity monitor, scanning it

100

quickly. "Roll right," he said. "They've got a friend joining them. If you pass between the two you can get all three of them with your IMP."

"Done," I said, and I rolled to the side and then engaged my boosters to send my ship backward through the enemy fire. My shield cracked further, but it didn't matter. I hit my IMP, dropping my own shield as well as the shields of all three enemy ships. Sadie and Kimmalyn opened fire while I used a series of defensive maneuvers to avoid the enemy destructor fire.

Beside me, Rig squeezed his eyes shut. "Yep, don't miss this part," he said.

"It's probably worse when you're not in control," I said.

"Oh, no," Rig said. "I'd much rather you were in control than me."

"Flight," Jorgen said. "Converge on the gunship. Victory and Valkyrie have cut us a path."

I reignited my shield, and we fell into an M formation as we worked our way up the battlefield. "Incoming," Arturo said, and I glanced at my proximity monitors to see five ships coming in to break up our path. The enemy wasn't stupid. They knew we were trying to get close to the battleship to destroy it.

Though if they sent all their reinforcements into the fray to fight us, they wouldn't have any to defend the guns once we reached them. Skyward Flight broke formation, falling into evasive maneuvers.

"Amphi, Nedder," Jorgen said, "lead those ships away from the rest of the flight. T-Stall, Catnip, back them up."

"It's working," Rig said, scanning the monitors. "They're not holding anything back to defend the gunship. Why would they do that if they know we have a hyperdrive?"

"I don't know," I said. "Maybe because they don't use their hyperdrives this way. Can you imagine what would happen if they hyperjumped in a lifebuster and detonated it over Alta Base? And yet they never do."

"Cobb says they're careful with the technology," Rig said. "They don't trust it to individual fighters, for fear of losing control of the secret to FTL travel. Once people know how it works, the smaller planets will be able to use it, and the Superiority will lose control."

If that was so, control came at a massive cost. There had to be a way we could use that against them.

But first we had to survive.

The battleship loomed larger in the distance, and Jorgen opened a private channel with me. "Okay, FM," Jorgen said. "I can see the area in front of the battleship well enough now that I think I can direct the device. Are you ready?"

"Ready as we are right now," I said.

"I don't know what that means," Jorgen replied.

"I'm ready, sir," I said. The right answer, even if it wasn't strictly true. There was no "ready" for this.

"Okay," Jorgen said. "I'm focusing on the device on your ship."

Happy vanished from Rig's lap.

Scud.

Jorgen got the wrong slug.

"Sorry!" Jorgen shouted over the radio, just as one of the ships the others had distracted turned and fired its destructors toward us. The arc of fire closed in, and Rig squeezed his eyes closed.

And then suddenly a battleship loomed directly in front of me, so close I had to roll to the side to keep from sailing right into it.

The ship was boxy, and clearly not designed to be flown in an atmosphere. Two massive doors across the front rolled to the side, revealing a round, glassy cannon inside.

"I'm thinking that thing is the planetary weapon," I said to Rig. "Any idea where I should start shooting?"

"Not at the cannon itself," Rig said. "It's built to take fire. Your destructors won't be enough to destroy it. The cannon controls will be much more vulnerable, but they won't have those mounted on the outside of the ship where they can be easily shot. Try flying around the front again so I can get a better look."

"FM?" Jorgen said over the radio. "Status?"

"Jump succeeded, Jerkface," I said. "Evaluating target now." I swung around and headed toward the fore of the ship, avoiding the area directly in front of the cannon. I didn't know how quickly the thing could shoot, and I didn't want to find out by having my ship blown to bits by a projectile designed to destroy a planet.

"Uh, FM?" Nedd said over the radio. "Where did you go?"

"Busy, Nedder," I said.

"FM, you have incoming," Jorgen said. "A bunch of Krell turned around and are flying straight toward you. Victory and Valkyrie are nipping at their heels."

"Permission to give chase, sir?" Kimmalyn asked.

"Permission granted. Keep as many of those ships away from FM as you can."

"There," Rig said, pointing to something on the monitor. "Below the gun, there's a shield to deflect incoming fire. I don't know if it's the cannon controls—could be the ship's acclivity ring, if they have one, or propulsion systems."

"Let's find out," I said. I dove down below the front of the ship, skimming the underside where Rig had indicated he'd seen the shield. Predictably, there was no big red button labeled "To Destroy Cannon, Press Here."

But there was a hatch about the width of my wingspan with the door closed tight, and I blasted it with destructor fire. The shield held for a moment, and then broke, and the door blew off, flying into the cavity beyond. I didn't get a good look inside the wreckage before more destructor fire came sweeping in from my six, and I ducked my ship under the door and circled around again, bobbing to avoid being blown to bits by the incoming enemy.

"Well, they found us," I said. "So much for our lead."

"They're still at a disadvantage," Rig said, scanning his monitors. "They're scrambling to protect the ship and you just blew a hole in it. Can you get a look inside?"

Destructor fire sprayed toward me as I wove around toward the front of the ship. An eerie blue energy was collecting around the cannon, so I gave that a wide berth as I flew beneath it again.

And encountered an immediate barrage of destructor fire. There *must* be something important down there, because three enemy ships were circling the damage, defending it as the cannon charged up to shoot toward the planet. Several fighters from Valkyrie and Victory Flights flew in and surrounded the enemy ships, forcing them to scatter or have their hulls torn to pieces.

"FM?" Jorgen said. "The enemy forces are turning around on you. We're doing the best we can to keep them off you, but we're outnumbered. Let me know when you need me to pull you out."

"Not yet," I said. I joined the other fighters in scattering the enemy ships while Rig reached down and unlocked the box, pulling out a quivering Chubs, clearly rattled from making the hyperjump. I took Chubs from him and set him on my shoulder. That was when I realized I had no idea where Happy had gone.

Stars, was the slug wandering around somewhere in the vacuum? Some things could survive without atmosphere, but I had no idea if taynix were one of them. The idea of poor Happy lost and alone in the black made me want to cry again.

Which I still did not have the luxury of doing right now.

The choral piece was a long one, the music still wafting out of my transmitter. I circled toward the broken hatch again, destructors firing, dodging around enemy ships. I could see some machinery in the wreckage of the blasted door, though I had no idea what it was for. "Rig?" I asked.

"No clue," Rig said. "I say shoot it."

I opened fire. The bottom of the ship lit up, some of the blasts glancing off the hull and ricocheting out into the battle while others tore through the tech behind the hatch door.

Destructor fire cracked my shield, and I pulled an inverse backpedal, trying to get away from my pursuers. Three enemy ships had me in their sights though, and they followed me as I darted away from the bottom of the ship.

It had only been a matter of time before their command identified the ship with the hyperdrive. Two more ships joined them, and I launched into a complicated series of moves that kept them from frying my shield entirely.

This was it though. "Jerkface," I said over the radio. "I need to retreat."

"Copy," Jorgen said.

Another blast obliterated my shield. One more, and we were gone.

The glass of my windshield abruptly went black.

Rig swore. "Are we dead?"

Sparks, thousands of them, all stared at me. Not eyes, but beautiful white stars, worlds away. "Not dead," I said. Having caught my breath, I reignited my shield and then scanned the proximity monitor. We might be too far for Jorgen to bring us back, especially with our exhausted slugs. The DDF would come after us if our fuel ran out, but only if there was a DDF *left* after this latest attack.

And my flight. What would happen to them?

"There," Rig said, pointing on the monitor. I fired my boosters to turn the ship around at his direction. *There.* We were close enough to see the battle, though we were now *behind* the battleships, farther out in space.

A flash of yellow, and a taynix appeared on the dash. Happy.

He'd returned, alive and unharmed.

"Hey buddy," I said, reaching over and scratching him under his spines. "Glad you're okay."

Chatter resumed over the radio.

"I got him!"

"T-Stall, Catnip, help Sentry shake her tail."

"On it."

"Stars, there are more of them!"

"Has anyone heard from FM?"

That last from Jorgen. "We're here," I said. "Coming up on the rear flank of the battle in—"

"Two minutes," Rig said.

"Two minutes."

"That far?" Jorgen asked. "I directed the slug to send you toward the platforms, but I guess it didn't work."

"No," I said. "It sent us in the opposite direction." That was worrisome, though I guessed we should have expected it from creatures who were reacting in fear.

"Glad you're okay," Jorgen said. "We'll head to you. You might encounter resistance on that flank. Flight, disengage and skirt the left side of the battlefield to wrap around and meet with FM. FM, give us a bearing."

Rig read one off over the radio, and the rest of the flight affirmed they were coming in our direction.

"Sitrep?" I asked Jorgen.

"Not good," Jorgen said. "The battle has split into two. One contingent of enemy ships is protecting the battleships and the other is cutting through our forces, heading toward Platform Prime. The other flights were unable to disable the cannon, and—"

He cut off as a beam of hot white energy erupted from the gunship and hit one of Detritus's gun platforms. Debris scattered out from the rubble belt, destabilized by the impact.

"They're firing on the planet," Rig said. "Our existing defenses can't stop that."

"Scud," Jorgen said. "Cobb's calling the retreat. All forces are to abandon the fight and return to Platform Prime."

Was there going to *be* a Platform Prime to return to?

"Um," Rig said, studying the monitor. "Looks like there are five ships headed our way. They may know we hyperjumped to get here."

"We're coming for you," Jorgen said. "FM, evasive maneuvers until we get there. We're not going to leave you behind."

"Understood," I said. Then, to Rig, "How long until those ships reach us?"

"Not long," Rig said. "They're moving fast."

I reversed my boosters, slowing down to dogfighting speed.

Five ships. I couldn't outrun or outgun them, and there wasn't a lot of terrain to work with this far out. Under normal circumstances, I could speed away and hope they wouldn't consider me worth following, but if the enemy knew I'd hyperjumped, they would assume I was a cytonic and pursue me relentlessly.

"Incoming," Rig said. "Scud, they're piloted ships, every one."

"Hold on," I said. I performed a Barrett sequence, a complex set of dodging loops that made me nearly impossible to target. Rig groaned and grabbed the dash. I might have apologized if I wasn't currently saving our lives. I thought for a second that he might throw up, and I apparently wasn't the only one. Happy slid over onto Rig's lap and cuddled up against him, trilling softly.

I broke out of the Barrett and immediately went into a twin-scissor as all five Krell ships bore down on me, the space in front of me alive with destructor fire. One blast hit my shield, weakening it.

"Jerkface, how long until you get here?" I asked.

"We see you on the monitors," Jorgen said. "Hold on."

I couldn't engage my IMP, not with this much heat on my tail. Destructor fire rained over us from all directions. The enemy had figured out a formation to make it nearly impossible to dodge the fire. I could tell by the way they flew that they weren't as good as I was. But there were more of them. A lot more. Another blast hit my shield, then another. I went into a barrel roll, but it wasn't going to be enough.

We weren't going to make it out of this.

Suddenly, ships came flying in from my left—Nedd and Arturo, who used their IMPs to take down the enemies' shields. One of the enemy ships continued to tail me as the others broke off to deal with the new threat. Kimmalyn picked off the ships with their shields down in two clean shots.

"Told you we were coming," Nedd said over the radio. T-Stall and Catnip took out my last tail, then turned around and helped Jorgen chase down one of the last two ships. Jorgen moved in on it to get within IMP range—

And then Jorgen's ship suddenly jerked to the side.

I tried to open a private line to him, but Jorgen didn't pick up.

"Jerkface, you okay?" I asked over the general channel.

Nothing.

The enemy took advantage of Jorgen's apparent distraction, and turned and scored a direct hit. By the way his shields crackled, they were dangerously low. But at last he reacted, starting into an evasive pattern, and managed to lose his opponent.

"Skyward Flight, go defensive," Jorgen said finally. "FM, cover me while I reignite my shield."

"Sure," I said, and followed on his wing as Jorgen slowed his ship and fell into a defensive position. The rest of the flight chased down the last two ships, then fell in with us while we waited for Jorgen's shield to reignite. He was still headed away from the planet, when our orders were to go the other way. Something had clearly gone wrong with him, and he still wasn't responding to my private hails.

"What's going on with him?" I asked Rig.

"No idea," Rig said.

Finally, Jorgen's shield reignited and his voice returned over the general channel. "Sorry," he said, though I wasn't sure what he was apologizing for. "Skyward Flight, reverse direction. Time to return to Platform Prime."

We all reversed direction, flying back with Jorgen at the center. "Cobb says the gunship has blasted holes through the debris field big enough to reach the surface," Jorgen said. "Another hit could destroy the apparatus and bury the caverns. All flights are to retreat below the platform belt—they're going to engage the planetary shield. I don't know what that means. Rig?"

"It might not work," Rig said. "But if it does, the platforms should move into position to protect the surface of the planet from bombardment."

I looked back toward the planet. There were two more large destabilized areas in the debris field now. While I'd been distracted, the battleships had continued firing.

"What about Platform Prime?" I asked. "Won't that still be vulnerable?"

"We don't know," Rig said. "But Platform Prime controls some vital planetary defense systems. Cobb said it wouldn't be good tactical strategy to install that on the outside of your shield."

"Regardless," Jorgen said, "they're relying on the gun platforms to defend Platform Prime while they get the shield up and running, and we are to head home at full speed."

I accelerated to Mag-9, and the rest of the flight kept pace with me. We were in this together.

And we watched together as suddenly, all throughout the debris field, the platforms began to move.

"Stars, is that happening?" Kimmalyn said.

"Looks like it," Arturo responded.

As far out as we were, we had the perfect view as the platforms began to rearrange themselves, edges extending toward each other. They spread out over the surface of the debris field like ships with wings stretched in all directions, and a crackling blue glow formed over them like a thin film.

"What the scud is that?" T-Stall asked.

"Energy field," Rig said. "There aren't enough platforms to cover the entire atmosphere. The energy field stretches between, filling in the gaps. It's also covering the platforms to protect them from—*that*."

As he spoke, the battleship lit up its gun again, and the white energy hit the newly forming shield.

It bounced off, scattering in all directions. No debris flew off this time.

"It held!" Rig said. "By the North Star, it *held*."

"Uh, guys," Nedd said. "How are we going to get *through* it?"

Scud. As we flew closer, I scanned the planet. There were areas where the platforms were clearly damaged, non-functional, or missing. That made sense, given the amount of debris that had fallen out of the atmosphere and landed on the surface over the years. But the energy shields stretched over those areas, covering the gaps. The next blast from the battleship focused on one of these areas, but it didn't crack through the shield.

"It's working," I said.

"Trust me," Rig said. "No one is more surprised than I am."

"Rig, what happens if we make contact with the shield?" Jorgen asked.

"Um," Rig said, "I would not recommend that. At best it would interfere with your instrumentation, maybe make your controls malfunction. At worst, the energy might fry you."

"Okay," Jorgen said. "So how do we get inside?"

"Um," Rig said, "our exhausted hyperdrives maybe?"

"Guys?" Nedd said. "What are we going to do about the large force of enemy ships still hanging out right where we're headed?"

I could see them on my proximity monitors, still trying to fire on the planet, chasing down the few ships that had been left outside the shield.

"I just heard from Cobb," Jorgen said. "We're going to run and hide."

I supposed that was the only option we had left.

12

Jorgen gave us a heading to a cluster of space rock that had been too far out for the gun platforms to blast from the sky, but which was large enough for us all to hide within.

"Cobb agrees that we're going to have to use the hyperdrives to get on the other side of the shield," Jorgen said. "He can't afford to drop the shield as long as the gunships are parked there. The engineers are working on how to turn off individual sections of the shield, but that will take time."

"It might take *months*," Rig said. "We could starve to death waiting for that, if we don't run out of fuel and freeze to death first."

"Right," Jorgen said. "And we want several fresh taynix before we try, so we don't end up getting stranded or stuck somewhere the Superiority can get to us. So we're going to have to wait for all the slugs to . . . cool down, I guess? Calm themselves? We have time, because Cobb is sending our coordinates to the other ships caught outside the shield. The slugs bring everything that's touching their box with them, so we'll all huddle together and touch wings and try to hyperjump beneath the shield without losing anyone."

"It would be easier if we had some way to interlock," Rig said to me. "Like the Defiant Fleet ships used to do before they crashed here. When this is over, my team should work on that."

I picked Happy up off his lap and scooped him into my arms. "Jerkface," I said over the radio. "You should probably try to comfort your slugs. Might make them ready to use again faster."

"*Comfort* them?" Jorgen said. "How do you want me to do that? Tell them a bedtime story?"

"You could try to hum again," I said, mostly because I knew it would bother him.

"Don't," Rig added. "You wouldn't want them deciding they'd rather face the vacuum of space than stay in there with you."

"Very helpful," Jorgen said. "Remind me to thank you."

"Pick them up," I said. "Pet them. Make them feel comfortable."

We clearly should have brought some mushrooms with us, but I did have some caviar with me, which I pulled out of my pocket and scooped onto my finger, offering it to Happy. Gill trilled excitedly down by my knee. He crawled up the seat to sit on my armrest, lifting the front part of his body into a begging position. I laughed and offered him a scoop as well.

"I feel I should tell you," Jorgen said over the radio, "that I now have a slug on each shoulder and three on my lap, all seeming vaguely uncomfortable that I'm touching them. I blame you, FM."

"Be more gentle," I said. "Quit squeezing them."

"I'm not squeezing them! Have *some* faith in me."

"You could always try that bedtime story," Sadie added. "I could use one of those about now."

"I'll tell you one," Nedd offered.

"Don't," Arturo said. "Nedder's stories always end with everyone getting eaten by space monsters."

"Hey!" Nedd said. "All the best stories end in people getting eaten. Isn't that right, Sentry?"

"Um, I'll pass, thanks," Sadie said.

"Anyone else?" Nedd offered. "Quirk? FM?"

"Thanks, I'm good," I said.

"Bless your stars," Kimmalyn added.

I leaned back in my seat. According to the proximity monitors, the Krell hadn't located us here. They'd no doubt be looking for the cytonic ship that escaped, but since they knew we had hyperdrives, they'd probably expect us to have escaped beneath the shield by now.

"I think we're actually going to survive this," Rig said. He sounded surprised.

"So little faith in my flying," I said, smiling at him.

Rig smiled shyly, and I found myself paying far too much attention to his lips.

He'd been an asset today, even without much pilot training. I should probably tell him so, but instead I opened a private channel to Jorgen. "Jerkface?" I said. "What happened? After your shield dropped in that last skirmish? It seemed like your ship malfunctioned."

Jorgen was quiet for a minute. "I saw Spensa."

Rig and I exchanged a look. "What?"

"I saw Spensa, in a reflection in my dash. But it wasn't a reflection. It was *her*. I could feel her, same way I feel the eyes. Same way I found the slugs under the surface."

"Seriously?" I asked. "Where is she?"

"In the nowhere," Jorgen said. "In the place we travel through when we hyperjump. She's stuck in there, and she says it's supposed to be impossible to get out."

Beside me, Rig closed his eyes.

"She'll escape," I said to Jorgen, for both their benefits.

"That's what I told her," Jorgen said. "And I believe she will. But I wish she were back already."

"So do I," I said, though I imagined it was for very different reasons. "But it's Spin. She'll survive."

"I sure hope so," Jorgen said, and he closed the line.

Rig and I sat there in silence for a moment. My arm felt warm where it touched his, and the heat radiated through my body. Finally Rig muttered, "I can't believe you thought I was into Spensa."

I laughed. "You guys are close, right? So I just assumed—"

"We grew up together. She's like my *sister*. Not that I ever had a sister, but if I had one who was, like, *terrifying*, that's how I think it would feel."

"Okay, fine," I said. "I shouldn't have made that assumption."

Rig blushed. "Can we listen to that song again?" he asked, probably to change the subject. "The one with all the voices?"

"Sure," I said, turning my transmitter back on. The chorus filled the cockpit again, and the slugs began to trill along in perfect harmony. I ran a hand down the fringe on Gill's back, hoping this was helping him to relax.

So we could scare him again. That still made me feel like a monster. These creatures were saving our lives, maybe were going to save our whole civilization.

And what did we do in return? Terrorize them.

In the copilot seat, Rig had two slugs stretched across his lap, and another particularly long one draped over his shoulders.

"I think we should name that one Drape," I said.

"I like that," he said, running a hand down the stomach of the thicker one on his knee that had rolled over for a belly rub. "I think this one is Twist."

"Nice."

"Hey," Rig said. "You kept your perfect record of not getting killed. I appreciate you not making an exception this time."

I smiled. "Thanks for your help. We made a good team up there."

"Yeah." Rig smiled, though he looked a little wistful, and I thought I knew why. "I'm glad we're friends," he said quietly.

I'd never told him that I only wanted to be friends. He'd assumed, and I supposed that was fair.

It just wasn't true. "It's definitely better than you ignoring me," I said.

Rig winced. "Yeah, sorry about that."

"You don't have to apologize. I get it."

"Still. I shouldn't have made things weird. It's not a big deal if you're not interested in me."

"Interested in me!" Happy trilled helpfully.

"Thanks, Happy," Rig said.

Scud, should I say something? I obviously *was* interested in Rig. I liked how competent he was, how confident he got when talking about something he loved. He was kind and quick-thinking, and we did work well together as a team.

And that smile. Stars, I could stand to see that smile every day for a long, long time.

No, it wasn't a lack of interest that held me back. It was the situation, the knowledge that any day I could fly out on one of these missions and never come back. It had almost happened today— it could happen anytime. I depended on my flight and on the other pilots. I didn't know yet who we'd lost today, but I was betting there had been casualties in this battle, people I knew and liked. People such as Lizard, who would suddenly be gone, blinked out of existence like dying stars.

I didn't know if I was ready to form any deeper attachments than the ones I already had. I wasn't sure how Jorgen handled it, knowing Spensa would always be charging off into danger. If Rig hadn't been sitting right here, I might have called Jorgen and asked him.

Rig leaned back, closing his eyes and listening to the music. He wasn't sulking. More . . . *sad.*

I didn't like causing him pain, especially when he had the wrong idea. But was I ready?

I'm as ready as I am right now, I thought.

Maybe in this dangerous existence, that was as close as I was ever going to get.

"I didn't say I wasn't interested," I said finally.

Rig's eyes snapped open. "Really?" he said. He sounded doubtful.

"Yeah," I said. "I said I didn't know."

"Yeah, okay," Rig said. He continued to stroke Twist on the belly, and the slug took the high soprano part while Drape trilled alto from Rig's shoulders. He was so gentle with them, so sweet.

I'd have to be an idiot not to give this a chance, whatever the circumstances.

"Maybe I have a better idea now," I said. And then I reached over and took Rig's hand.

Rig's sharp intake of breath nearly made me let go, but then he relaxed, smiling. His cheeks turned a bright pink, but he didn't let go either.

We sat there listening to the swell of the music, neither of us speaking. A quiet peace overwhelmed me, and I closed my eyes, savoring it.

Maybe it wasn't just the slugs who had needed comforting.

Finally Jorgen's voice returned over the radio. "Cobb says the shield is holding and the gunship has stopped firing for now. Four other ships are going to catch a ride with us when the slugs are ready. They're currently hiding on the other side of the rock cluster and I've invited them to this channel."

The pilots all called in, two from Ivy Flight, and one each from Riptide and Ranger, a scout flight we'd worked with before.

Stallion, assistant flightleader from Ranger Flight, piped up. "What's the plan out here? Command said you were going to take us home. Are we finding a hole in the shield?"

"Negative," Jorgen said. "We're going to use a hyperdrive."

There was silence over the line. "Repeat, Skyward One?" Stallion said. "Did you say a *hyperdrive*?"

"Affirmative," Jorgen said. "We have a hyperdrive on board, which we will use to get inside the planetary shield."

He sounded more confident about that than he probably was, given our adventures with the hyperdrives so far. Still, with the shield blocking entry to the planet, it was this or wait for our ships to run out of power for our life support.

"What's the matter?" Nedd asked. "Never used a hyperdrive before?"

"Ummmm," Stallion said.

"Where have you been?" Catnip added. "I use hyperdrives all

the time. Used one on my way to the cleansing pods this morning, didn't I, T?"

"Totally," T-Stall responded. "I thought everybody had hyper-drives these days."

"All right," Jorgen said. "That's enough."

There was silence on the line for a bit, and then Stallion said what the other pilots all must have been thinking. "But seriously? A *hyperdrive*?"

"He's being serious," I said.

"If you say so," Stallion said.

I smiled. "I do."

Jorgen reopened our private line. "FM, how are your slugs doing?"

Gill looked a bit affronted that I'd stopped petting him when I took Rig's hand, but other than that they seemed relaxed. "Good," I responded. "Maybe ready? You could try and see?"

"I think we should use one of yours. Mine all seem pretty dis-gruntled."

"Stop squeezing them."

"I'm not! I swear!"

I laughed, and Rig joined me.

If we were preparing to hyperjump soon, I was going to have to let go of his hand. I mean, my elbow was kind of aching from being at an awkward angle on the armrest and my palm was sweating. But I still weirdly didn't want to.

That probably meant something, but I was more comfortable with the idea of attempting a hyperjump than I was with thinking about that.

I let go of Rig's hand, stretching my fingers. "Let's try to put them all in the box, so Jorgen doesn't get the wrong one again."

"I'm a little worried they're going to start expecting the scare the moment they're put in the box," Rig said. "I wonder if we should be keeping them in similar boxes when they're off duty to acclimatize them."

Much as I didn't want the poor slugs consigned to living in dark boxes for their entire lives, his logic made sense. And I did like that he referred to them as being off duty instead of out of use, like they were creatures rather than objects.

"Let's hope they haven't totally made that connection yet," I said. "Because I don't know that we have time to acclimatize them to it now." Rig and I wrangled the five slugs into the box, shutting them in.

"Okay," I told Jorgen. "We're ready."

"Skyward Flight," Jorgen said, "And . . . guests. Come join us up by the . . . curvy formation at the top of this rock. We're going to need to get our ships close enough to touch wings."

I looked out through the canopy to see what Jorgen was talking about—a wicked hooklike protrusion on the top of this piece of space rock. I engaged my acclivity ring to lift us up toward it, and the other ships clustered around us. Jorgen's ship pressed close on our right until our wings touched, and I could see slugs perched precariously on each of his shoulders.

"They do look uncomfortable," Rig said.

Kimmalyn used her boosters to scoot up next to us on the left, giving me a bright smile and a thumbs-up through the glass.

"All pilots, confirm you are in position for hyperjump," Jorgen said.

Everyone confirmed, though the new pilots sounded significantly less confident that we were in fact about to hyperjump.

"Skyward Five, we are a go," Jorgen said.

And then the stars disappeared.

13

Jorgen managed to get the slug to hyperjump us within a few kilometers of Platform Prime, which was several layers below the shield—a crackling, glowing net that stretched across the spaces between the platforms over our heads. We were greeted in the landing bay by Cobb and Jorgen's mother, who looked happy for once. She ushered Jorgen off, telling him they needed to debrief.

"I can handle getting the slugs into their crates," I told Rig. "I'm guessing you want to go talk to your friends in engineering about the shield."

"You sure?" he asked.

"Yeah, I've got it." The rest of my flight headed to the mess hall to wind down from the battle, but I waved them off too.

Usually I liked companionship after a battle, but today I wanted to be alone.

"I don't know what's wrong with me," I said to Gill, who rode on my shoulder while I toted the rest of the slugs toward Engineering in a box. "I should be happy."

"Happy!" Happy said from the box.

"Yeah, exactly," I said. No one in my flight had been hurt, despite several close calls. Rig and I were . . . something, though I didn't know exactly what. I didn't regret holding his hand—

I wasn't sure I'd ever be able to regret that. We'd gotten the hyper-drives to work, sort of. Not enough to change the outcome of the battle, but enough to give us some hope.

But that was exactly it, I realized. I wasn't sure what came next. We didn't have a cytonic to teach Jorgen how to give coordinates to the slugs. We had a shield that was working for now, but there was no way it would hold up indefinitely. We had potential allies we still couldn't reach, and a whole lot of enemies sitting on our doorstep.

We'd survived, but we were just as trapped on Detritus as we'd ever been—maybe more so. For a while we'd been able to reach into the expanse of space—and if our freedom had been measured in kilometers rather than light-years, it had been ours.

Now we'd lost all that, and the only way out was to rely on the whims of creatures who, while adorable, weren't easy to control. Jorgen could only do so much by himself. Even if engineering could replicate the holographic technology to outfit every ship with a functional box, there had to be a limit to how many hyper-jumps he could track at once. The slugs had generally gone where he'd asked them to, but on that one jump he'd sent me in the opposite direction. That had worked out fine, but we couldn't guarantee that it always would.

And it would only be a matter of time before the Superiority figured out how to target and kill Jorgen. Without him we'd be lost.

We had to do better. *I* had to do better.

When I reached Engineering, I found Cobb in a meeting with Ziming and several of the other engineers. Rig waved to me, but one of Cobb's aides ushered me out, showing me to the room next door.

"We've decided to give the taynix their own space," she said. "We've been using this room to build boxes for the ships, but Rig said you wanted to start keeping the slugs in those full-time. You can start with the ones we have, and we'll build more as we go."

I stepped into the room, finding it filled with metal boxes the size of the one installed in the Dulo. The crates of slugs and mushrooms had been left in the middle of the floor, with the tools and materials for box building spread out around them. We were probably going to need to find a way to hold the boxes down so we weren't picking them up from all over the platform, but this would work for now.

"Thanks," I told the aide, and then I set the box of taynix on top of their crate and closed the door behind me.

"Thanks," Gill trilled on my shoulder.

"Thank *you*," I said, reaching into my pocket for my tin of caviar. It was almost gone, but I'd put in a requisition request to Cobb for more, and he'd said he would speed that along. I wished I had enough to reward every taynix who helped us today, but I felt like I should conserve what I had left until the requisition order arrived.

What I could do, however, was feed them. I opened the crates and offered Happy, Twist, and the others some mushrooms. More of those were also supposed to arrive with the requisition order, though the mess hall had sent over a box of algae strips to try in the meantime.

I pulled one out of the package. "What do you think?" I asked Gill. He nudged the strip with his face, but didn't open his mouth, instead nuzzling my finger for more caviar. "Yeah, that's what I thought." I offered Gill a mushroom and then sat down, watching the slugs happily eat, prolonging the time before I had to shove them each into a dark box to become comfortable in hard, cubic containers.

Trapped until they were useful to us, without even an apparatus to build spacecraft to fight back.

I sat down and leaned against the side of the crate, the tears I'd held back before burning at my eyes.

It was stupid to worry about the plight of the slugs. There were human beings who would continue to die—people I knew, people I loved. Unless we figured out a better way to use the hyperdrives, they would all be lost, the slugs taken away by the Superiority to be used in their ships.

The tears escaped from the corners of my eyes.

Maybe that was the problem. I wasn't only worried about the slugs, or only about my people. I was worried about *all* of us.

"I'm sorry about your part in this," I said to Gill.

"This!" he repeated enthusiastically.

The door opened, and I startled, wiping my face with the back of my hand. Rig saw though, and he came in and closed the door behind him.

"You okay?" he asked, sitting down on the edge of a table near the crate.

"Sure," I said. "Fine. Great."

"Fine!" one of the red slugs piped up with its deeper trill from the crate behind me.

"My team took Fine up to the communicator," Rig said. "Cobb wants to try scaring the slugs into sending a message to Cuna, now that we know how it should work. They're prepping Jorgen for it now."

"Fantastic," I said. It didn't sound like I meant it, and I wasn't sure I did.

Rig looked at me sympathetically, which I should have appreciated, but instead it made me want to hide. That was what I was doing in here originally, I realized. Hiding from my friends, from Command, from everyone.

"Want to talk about it?" he asked.

I shrugged. "I don't know what there is to say."

"I'll start," he said. "That was terrifying today. The hyperdrives worked, and the politicians are thrilled about that, but that's because they weren't in a ship being teleported right to the heart of the battle. That was scudding scary."

"Sorry," I said. "I didn't mean for you to get caught up in that."

"We're *all* caught up in it," Rig said. "And I'm not sorry I was there." His cheeks went pink, so I didn't think that was merely because he wanted to help with the war effort.

"It was scary," I said softly. That wasn't something I would usually admit after a battle. The flight liked to gather together and reenact our successes with dinner rolls and algae strips as stand-ins for ships. Except on missions when we lost someone, we all put on a brave face, mocked each other, and laughed about it until our nerves faded away.

That was probably what I should be doing now. So why didn't I want to?

"Do you need me to keep going?" Rig asked. "I can list a lot of things I think are scary."

"Is that supposed to help?" I asked. "Making a list?"

"Talking about it might help. If you're not ready, I'll continue. I'm terrified for Spensa. Being stuck in the nowhere seems like a really bad thing, and even though we all say Spensa will get out, can we guarantee that, really?"

"No," I said.

"No," he agreed. "And a few days ago there was a *delver* on our doorstep, and I'm still not sure why it didn't kill us all or when it will be back."

Rig had insisted it wouldn't be back if Spensa could help it. I wasn't surprised that was mostly bravado. "Did the delver look as freaky on the monitors down here as it did out there?" I asked. "Because I had never seen anything like that, and I hope that I never do again."

"It was horrifying!" Rig said. "I nearly crapped my pants."

I laughed.

"Okay, your turn," Rig said. "What are you afraid of?"

"Not coming back," I said. I hadn't realized how deep that fear went until I said it out loud. I felt it in my bones. "Dying in battle. Ceasing to exist. Being the scar my friends won't acknowledge or talk about." I paused. "And the opposite of that, being the last one left."

"Yeah, that's enough to give you nightmares."

I nodded. "No wonder it's so hard to keep it together."

"Seriously?" Rig asked. "You seem like you *always* have it together."

"Is that what you like about me?" I asked. "Because I don't have it together. I just don't talk about it."

"Clearly you should," he said.

That wasn't an answer to the question, and I found myself suddenly self-conscious. I crossed my arms, leaning back against the crate.

Why did I care what Rig liked about me? I didn't usually give much thought to anyone's impression. I showed up and did my job and tried to protect my friends; if people didn't like me personally, so be it. Maybe it was better that way. The closer I got to people, the worse it felt when I lost them.

Had I always felt that way? No, not before flight school. Not even after. This was recent. A defense mechanism, I guessed.

It wasn't one I particularly liked.

"Is that why I like you?" Rig said. "I don't know. Maybe a little. I like how steady you are, how confident. I'm always so anxious about everything. I've wondered what it's like to be, well, *not*."

"Are you disappointed to realize I'm not really like that?"

"No," Rig said. "More relieved."

I stared at him.

"What?" he said. "You think I want you to be some emotionless robot? It's *good* to have feelings, FM. It's good to express them. And it's kind of nice to know that I'm not the only one who's terrified."

"You're not," I said.

"I know. But we all show it in different ways. Spensa picks fights and threatens to murder you. Jorgen gets all tangled up in his rulebook. You pretend to be fine."

"Fine!" Gill trilled.

"Yeah, okay," I said. "What about you?"

"I stress," Rig said. "And I work on hard problems and try to fix them. When Spensa disappeared the first time, I spent a full week trying to deconstruct a navigation system we found in the planetary defenses. I think it's supposed to interface with the ship nav systems so everyone can coordinate better during flight."

"But you didn't figure it out?" I asked.

"No," Rig said. "There are too many pieces we don't understand yet. It kept me sane for a while, but then I just felt like a failure."

"You're clearly not a failure. You figured out how to improve our ships based on M-Bot's design. You're the main reason we were able to use the hyperdrives at all, even if they aren't perfect yet."

"We all worked on that," Rig said.

"Still. Not a failure."

"I know," Rig said. "I just always feel like I should be doing more. If I could figure everything out faster, more lives would be saved. Every time someone dies in combat, there was more I could have done to prevent it."

Huh. I felt that way, but I hadn't thought about the people who stayed here on the ground feeling responsible for our deaths. "You're doing the best you can though. No one can ask more than that."

"Right. Does that make you feel better when your friends don't come back?"

"No," I said.

"Exactly."

"Exactly," Gill agreed.

"You're certainly being chatty today," I said, offering him another mushroom. I looked up at Rig. I wished he'd sit closer, but I wasn't sure I was ready to suggest it.

He was right. It was good to talk. But the more I did, the more exposed I felt, like he could see right through me.

I didn't like anyone seeing what a mess I really was, least of all him.

"Did you feel like a failure when you dropped out of flight school?" I asked.

"Not really," he said. "It was Spensa's dream, not mine. I felt more . . . directionless. Like I wasn't sure what I wanted to be, but I knew it wasn't a pilot."

"Today probably reaffirmed that."

"Yes and no," he said. "It was more like a window into everything I gave up, you know? The engineering crew is a team, but it's not the same. You guys . . . you depend on each other to survive. And everyone is still nice to me, though I'm not part of the flight. It was nice to experience that again, even if I know I did the right thing by dropping out."

"We depend on you to survive," I said. "It was engineering that saved us all today, not the pilots. But I know what you mean."

The slugs were slowly wandering out of the crate, since I'd left it open. Twist perched on the edge and trilled until Rig reached out to pick her up.

"For what it's worth," I said, "I don't think the rest of the flight sees you as a dropout. Most of *them* dropped out of flight school too. Jorgen and I were the only ones who graduated."

"How did that feel?" Rig asked.

"Lonely," I admitted. "Cobb told us on our first day that most of us wouldn't make it. I felt guilty that I did and the others didn't."

"Didn't stop the rest of them from flying though," Rig said. "Just me."

"Do you regret it?" I looked up at him, and was surprised to see him considering the question. He'd said he knew he'd done the right thing, and it was clear to me that his calling was in engineering.

I also didn't hate that on a normal day he wouldn't be in nearly as much danger as the rest of us.

"No," he said. "Doesn't stop it from hurting sometimes." He looked down at me. "If you had it to do over, would you still become a pilot?"

"Yes," I said. I was surprised at how easily that answer came, even after all we'd been through. "If I wasn't, I wouldn't be able to protect my friends, you know? They'd still be up there flying, but I wouldn't be there."

Rig nodded. "Is that why you became a pilot? To protect people?"

"Ultimately, yeah," I said. "I didn't intend to stay in the DDF forever. I don't like the way the Defiant League acts like war is the most glorious thing ever, the way they make violence seem wonderful, when really it causes so much pain. But I thought if I was a pilot, I'd have the authority and respect to talk about that, you know? That I could stand up for people no one else would defend, and people would have to listen to me."

"People do listen to you," Rig said. "I've always respected that about you. When you talk, everyone listens. Not because you're a pilot. You command respect by being who you are."

My face got warm. "I don't feel like that," I said.

"Yeah," Rig said. "I guess none of us really believe the good things about ourselves, do we?"

"Spensa maybe," I said. But no, that wasn't true. Even Spensa was insecure sometimes. It just made her louder and more threatening.

"She wishes," Rig said. Gill butted up against my elbow until I rested my hand on his head, petting him gently.

"What I wish," I said, "is that I could guarantee these guys a life where the primary goal isn't for us to be able to scare them as many times as possible. I wish there was another way."

"It would be good if we could find something," Rig said. "Because if it takes longer and longer between scares, we're going to need more slugs, or be really limited in how often we can use the hyperdrives. The Superiority has a galaxy worth of planets they could have mined for slugs. They probably have breeding programs. So far, we have the population of one cave."

"If we figure out how to use them more efficiently, we might be able to get an edge on the Superiority." I cringed. Now I was the one talking about the slugs like a resource. "It would improve quality of life for the taynix as well. If they could be *convinced* to hyperjump, even though it's scary, then we wouldn't have to rely on their primal impulses."

"It's a good goal," Rig said. "We could design an experiment, see if we can find anything."

I looked up into his eyes, which were a deep and clear blue, and had some primal impulses of my own. "Fine by me," I said.

Rig stood off the table and offered me his hand to help me up. When I stood, I didn't let go.

We were about the same height, so our faces were close without either of us having to lean. I clearly surprised Rig, because he stuttered a bit, but he didn't move away.

I took that as a good sign. The slug on my shoulder, on the other hand, appeared incapable of reading the room. "Fine!" Gill said.

"Hush," I told him. And then I leaned forward and brushed my lips against Rig's.

"Fine!" Gill yelped, and then teleported away. Another escapee I was going to have to track down. *Later*.

I smiled against Rig's mouth. "Better than fine," I said.

Rig laughed. "So much better."

Maybe the slug could read the mood after all.

14

When Rig ran an experiment, he did not mess around.

It took us most of the evening to design something up to his standards, even though the experiment itself was only comprised of a couple of boxes set up across the room from each other.

The next morning, we were ready to start gathering data. We'd sorted the slugs, isolating the red and black ones, since we weren't ready to deal with them yet. Our new idea was that in the absence of coordinates, we could teach the slugs to hyperjump to a familiar place on command. It wouldn't immediately help us to reach Cuna, since the slugs had never been to wherever Cuna was, but Rig said that big breakthroughs had to be broken down into smaller steps. Getting the slugs to do *anything* without scaring them would be one important piece. Then, if we could learn how to give them coordinates, we'd have another means to motivate them to go.

If the experiment worked, of course.

"Okay," Rig said. "I think we're ready for phase one."

I pulled Chubs out of the crate. We'd kept all the slugs in the closed box while we set up the experiment, so they couldn't watch us. I wasn't sure how much they would pay attention anyway, but Rig insisted that could invalidate the results.

I opened one of the boxes, showing Chubs a scoop of caviar sitting in a dish on the bottom. "Home," I told him.

"Home!" Chubs trilled.

I let him eat the caviar, then put another small scoop into the dish where he could see it before finally closing the door on the box. Then I took Chubs across the room and put him into another box facing away from the one with the caviar. This box was made out of wood and had a clear front so we could observe him inside and see when he left. Chubs wouldn't be able to reach the caviar unless he decided to hyperjump.

Chubs crawled around the box, his face crinkling at me through the clear plastic.

"He's not doing anything," I said.

Rig stood over me with a clipboard, writing notes. I didn't know what he was writing, because nothing was happening.

"Still nothing," I said.

"This is how science works," Rig said. "Nothing, nothing, nothing. Maybe something! Oh, no, that was also nothing."

"I don't know how you stand it," I said.

"Are you kidding? It's fascinating."

"Really? *Nothing* is *fascinating*?"

"Sometimes," Rig said. "Depends on the nothing, I guess. Try giving him the keyword now."

I pressed my finger to the plastic, getting Chubs's attention. "Home," I said to him.

He didn't move.

"Home," I said again. "Go home and get the caviar, would you? You're making me look like an idiot."

"Home," Chubs trilled, his voice muted by the plastic. "Home, home."

"Try looking away," Rig suggested. "They don't seem to like to hyperjump while we're watching."

"Okay, fine," I said, turning around. "I'm not watching."

A moment later, a slug nudged my ankle. There was Chubs, looking up at me expectantly from the floor.

"I think he sees you as the source of caviar, FM," Rig said.

"FM!" Chubs said.

"Not me," I said, carrying Chubs over and giving him a second look inside the home box. Then I brought him back to the observation box and shut him behind the transparent door.

"Home," I said, and I turned around.

Rig studied his clipboard. When I glanced back at the observation box, Chubs was gone. I found him in the "home" location, chowing down on the caviar.

"Hey!" I said. "Good job! Home."

"Home!" the slug trilled happily.

"Okay," Rig said. "So he went to find the food because he knew where it was. Now see if you can get him to do it without seeing the food first."

I waited for Chubs to finish his caviar, and then took him back to the observation box and put him inside. "Home," I said to him.

"Home," he replied.

And then he disappeared and reappeared in the "home" box, sniffing around for caviar.

"Hey, it worked," I said. I pulled out my now almost empty tin of caviar and gave a scoop to Chubs.

"Okay," Rig said. "Now try it with another slug."

When I turned around, Drape had already climbed onto Rig's shoulder, nuzzling his cheek.

"Looks like Drape volunteered to join the experiment." I scooped Drape up off Rig's shoulders. Standing this close to him made my skin tingle, and I wasn't alone; when Rig blushed, even the back of his neck turned red.

Then the door opened abruptly, and we jumped apart.

Jorgen stood in the doorway, holding Gill and looking at us curiously. "Hey," he said. "Everything okay in here?"

"Fine!" Rig said, too loudly.

"Fine!" Gill said from his perch in the crook of Jorgen's arm.

"Don't start that again," I said to Gill, taking him from Jorgen. "I'm glad you're here. You're just in time to participate in our experiment."

"I don't think I have time for that," Jorgen said.

I shrugged. "I wasn't talking to you."

Jorgen looked at me like I'd lost my mind, but at least he didn't comment on how close Rig and I had been standing when he'd walked in.

"I was actually coming to tell you two that they're almost ready to try using the communicator to reach Cuna," Jorgen said. "They're going to use the holoprojector to power the communicator, but Cobb still wants all of us present, since we've been working with the slugs. Thadwick wants Rig to consult with him on the communicator, and then FM and I are supposed to report after that."

"Sure," Rig said. "FM can show you what we've been working on." He hurried out of the room more quickly than normal. I hoped he was looking to get away from Jorgen and not me.

Probably it wasn't me.

Jorgen cocked an eyebrow at me. "Working? Is that what you were doing in here?"

"Yes, *actually*," I said. "We designed an experiment."

"Is that what they're calling it now."

"Shut your mouth," I told him.

Jorgen smirked at me.

"Would you like me to mock you about Spensa now?" I asked. "Because if that's fair game, let me just say—"

"Forget I said anything," Jorgen said quickly. "Show me this experiment."

"Thought you'd never ask." I handed Jorgen Rig's clipboard, though he didn't look anywhere near as cute carrying it. "You take notes."

Jorgen squinted at Rig's notes while I used the last of my caviar running both Drape and Gill through the experiment. Drape didn't teleport into the box no matter how many times I showed her the caviar, but Gill did so right away, trilling "home" happily at me.

"Huh," Jorgen said. "Maybe some of them are more motivated by food than others?"

"Probably," I said. "But even Chubs took a while to follow the command. I don't know if this will be a reliable way to get them to hyperjump or not, though they do seem to be able to do it over and over again without having to wait for us to scare them."

Jorgen consulted his watch. "We're due up at Command," he said. "I see what you're doing here FM, but I don't know that it's any better than what we have."

"Not yet," I said. "Rig says science takes time to yield results."

"That's my point," Jorgen said.

He didn't have to elaborate. We both knew time was one thing we didn't have.

The command center was crowded with members of the command staff, the engineers, and a few more people from Jeshua Weight's retinue sent by the National Assembly. Jorgen shouldered through to stand behind his mother, and I shadowed him, feeling out of place. I felt better when Rig joined us, coming over from a discussion with several of the other engineers.

"Fine is loaded in the communicator," Rig said. "And we've got the holoprojector hooked up. Cobb has recorded a message and we've set up the data in the communicator to align with the metadata from Cuna's first transmission. It's all very theoretical and I wish we'd had more time to test it, but it should probably work."

"Do you ever get used to it?" I asked. "Always having your projects thrown into service before you feel comfortable with the amount of testing you've done?"

Rig wiped his palms on his jumpsuit. "I definitely haven't gotten there yet."

"All right, quiet now," Cobb said from his place at the front of the room. "We're going to send the message." He nodded to Ziming, who pressed a button on a control panel, and then Cobb spoke into his headset. "This is Admiral Cobb, human from the planet Detritus. Minister Cuna, please confirm receipt."

Ziming pressed another button. "Did it work?" Cobb asked.

"I think so," Ziming said. "It sent, but I don't know if it was—"

"Admiral Cobb, human of Detritus," a voice said over the loudspeaker—the same eerie, even voice we'd heard in the first message. "I confirm receipt. Thank you for your response."

Cobb nodded, and Ziming resumed the transmission. "Minister Cuna. We would like to meet, but are unable to discern your location. Our cytonic is untrained, and our hyperdrives primitive. Any assistance you can offer to help us reach you would be welcomed. Please advise."

"I am afraid time is running short," Cuna responded. "The Superiority has sent forces to bombard my location, and while our minimal artillery has kept them at bay, we expect them to send for reinforcements at any moment."

"How many ships?" Cobb said over the communicator.

There was a pause. "Twenty fighters. We hear over the datanet that the Superiority forces are spread thin. I fear they will soon mobilize on your planet."

"They already have," Cobb said. "We're holding them off for the moment."

"Twenty ships," Jorgen muttered. "We can handle that. If we can get there."

"I am routing coordinates through my hypercomm," Cuna said. "Please interface your cytonic with your communicator to receive coordinates."

"Interface our cytonic?" Jeshua said. "What in the North Star's light does that mean?"

Most of the room looked at Jorgen, who stuttered. If there was one thing Jorgen hated, it was not having an answer.

"Maybe he needs to interact with the taynix," I said. "The one we used to send the message."

"Fine," Rig said. "He's in the communicator in Charlie Sector."

"You shouldn't have to touch Fine, right?" I asked Jorgen. "You could scare the slugs at a distance, so you should be able to—"

"Hold on," Jorgen said, closing his eyes. "I'm working on it."

"You do that," Cobb said, pulling the microphone closer. "This is Admiral Cobb," he said. "We're working on interfacing our cytonic now."

"Well?" I asked Jorgen quietly.

"I'm trying," Jorgen said. "Maybe if I—" Jorgen jerked back like he'd been slapped in the face. "I've got it. Admiral, I've got the coordinates. I know where they are. Stars, that's painful." He rubbed his temples. His mother watched him with concern.

"We have your position," Cobb said. "We're going to send a flight to defend you. Jorgen, take Skyward Flight and—"

"We should contact the National Assembly," Jeshua said. "Let them make a decision before we send away one of our cytonics. We don't know if they'll be able to return."

Cobb looked at Jorgen.

"That's true, sir," Jorgen said. "I'm not sure I can find Detritus again on my own. The slugs might be able to return instinctively from that far of a distance, but I can't be sure. But these aliens, they understand the hyperdrives better than we do. They might be able to teach us how."

Cobb turned to Jeshua. "You want to be able to communicate with our enemies. This is the only alien force that has ever offered to talk with us. We have to take this chance."

"I agree with you," Jeshua said. "But it's up to the National Assembly to decide—"

"Sir," Jorgen said. "The coordinates are fading. It's slow, so we have a little bit of time, but it's like it was with Spensa. I don't know how to hang on to it."

"Take your flight," Cobb said to Jorgen. "Go now."

Jeshua scowled at him.

Jorgen hesitated for a moment. Then he nodded. "Yes, sir," he said, and I followed Jorgen out of the command center. Together we ran for the landing bay.

15

The rest of our flight met us at our ships. T-Stall was still munching on a handful of fried algae strips from the mess hall, and Catnip was zipping up his jumpsuit, but Kimmalyn and Sadie were already climbing into their cockpits.

"What's happening?" Arturo asked, meeting us by Jorgen's ship. "It's just us this time?"

"We're going to rescue a defecting Superiority minister," Jorgen said. "Just our flight, but we need to hurry. Minister Cuna is already under attack. I have coordinates to hyperjump there, but we're still figuring out how we're going to get back."

Arturo looked alarmed at that news. "Those are our orders?"

"Those are our orders," Jorgen said. "Let's get everyone in the air."

Arturo nodded and headed for his ship, yelling at Nedd on the way to do the same.

Rig ran up with a box full of slugs, which he thrust into my arms. Gill was in there along with Happy, Chubs, Drape, and Twist. "Cobb wants us to keep the holoprojector attached to the communicator," he said. "That way we'll be able to communicate with you when you get there, because we'll have one and Cuna has one."

"You might not be able to scare Fine again," I said. "You'll have to try another purple slug. Though we received more than one communication from Cuna out of the same one, so maybe the connection lasts for a while after it's established?"

"I'll check on that as soon as you leave." Rig bit his lip, looking like he wanted to say something but thought better of it.

"I'll help you load the slugs into Jorgen's ship," I said, looking down at the slugs. There was another purple slug in there and I thought it had gotten mixed in, but when we reached Jorgen's cockpit Rig put him in the metal box beneath the dash with the others. "I think you should take a communication slug with you," he said. "I don't know for sure how many taynix Cuna will have. Technically, Jorgen can communicate cytonically without a slug at all, but I think you should have every resource we can spare with you in case—" His voice broke, and he took a deep breath.

I got it. I was going and he was staying, and he was scared. Probably for all of us, but I liked to think that he was sparing a little extra for me.

"I'll come back," I said. "Perfect record of not dying, remember?"

"Yeah," Rig said. "I remember."

I wanted to take his hand, but Jorgen was already climbing into his cockpit.

Time to go.

"We haven't had time to set the ships up with interlocking pieces," Rig said to Jorgen, "so you're going to have to do it the way you did last time, all touching wings."

"Got it," Jorgen said. "We'll make it work. FM, let's go."

Rig reached out and squeezed me on the arm, and then hurried away. I ran for my regular Poco and climbed in, immediately engaging my acclivity ring and boosting away. As my ship rose toward the ceiling of platforms between the sections of crackling blue energy holding the shield together at the seams, I looked back and saw Rig watching us go.

I'll be back, I thought at him. Saying it wouldn't make it more or less true though. It wasn't a promise any of us could make.

Maybe I shouldn't have started anything between us, put him in a position to hurt even more if the worst happened. Or maybe I was making too much of it. Maybe none of us mattered, not really. What did it change when any of us were gone? The DDF still churned out more cadets. If they ran out, they'd lower the age to take the pilot's test and bring them in younger and younger. We'd keep sending groups on missions like this, never knowing if they'd come back, because our survival as a group mattered more than the individuals. I didn't disagree with that; I saw the logic to it.

But I still wondered: if we didn't matter as individuals, then what were we saving the group *for*?

I joined the rest of the flight less than half a kilometer from the platform. Through a gap between platforms I could see the crackling net of the shield. As frightened as I'd been of the stars—feeling like I could fall off the face of the world—I missed them now that they were gone.

I supposed I'd be seeing them again soon enough.

"Skyward Flight," Jorgen said, "move in together. All ships need to be touching, or some of you will be left behind."

I maneuvered my ship between Sadie's and Kimmalyn's with a gentle touch. The metal of our wings rubbed against each other, and I could see Sadie looking over at me through her canopy. I tried to give her a reassuring smile. I remembered what Rig said: *You seem like you always have it together*.

I *wanted* to seem that way, I realized. Spensa lost her temper, Jorgen got frustrated, Rig could talk about fear like it was his best friend.

And me?

There was safety in being the one everyone else looked to. I felt everything, but I didn't want anyone to know it.

"All right," Jorgen said. "That looks good. Initiating hyperdrive."

I closed my eyes. We were about to hyperjump many, many times farther than we ever had. I wondered if it would take longer. I wondered if—

"Stars!" T-Stall said over the radio. "Are you guys seeing this?"

"Yes," Jorgen said. "I think—I think that's our destination."

I opened my eyes and stared out through the glass of my canopy at the expanse of black in front of me. The light of the nearest star was behind us, illuminating an object in the distance—a large rock that was dominated by dozens of white tentacles protruding from it like petals on some wildflower.

Or, well, it was impossible to tell by sight *how* large or distant it was. I'd never seen anything I could compare this thing to. I widened the scope of my proximity monitors, trying to get a sense of it.

"We're a hundred and fifty klicks out," Arturo said, beating me to it. "That *thing. That's* where we're going?"

"I'm getting a communication," Jorgen said. "Hang on."

We hung on. Our ships had drifted a little since we'd jumped, so we were no longer bumping into each other, but none of us had engaged our boosters to move far.

My radio made a little flickering noise, and I reached out to adjust the dial. This wasn't the time for the thing to fritz out.

And then Cuna's smooth, alien voice came over the radio. "Skyward Flight," the alien said. "Thank you for coming to our aid. Your leader has given me permission to address you. As you can see, my crew and I are stranded on the old Superiority outpost of Sunreach—an abandoned research facility built here to study this rare species of mammoth starpod. You'll want to avoid it. It's nearing its molting cycle, which makes it especially hungry."

"It's *hungry*?" Catnip said. "Jerkface, what does she mean it's *hungry*?"

"I understand you humans have not often encountered other species," Cuna's voice continued. "My species is referred to as *they*, because we do not conform to human genders. Diones are—"

"Jorgen?" Nedd said. "What is the alien talking about?"

"They're saying don't call them 'she,'" I said. "But maybe we could deal with the formal introductions when we get there?"

"Right," Jorgen said. "Um, thank you for the . . . etiquette lesson. My team will do our best to learn what language you prefer. For now, can you tell us how to reach you? Are you saying that giant star . . . flower . . . *thing* is going to eat us?"

"Yes, the mammoth starpod. It generally prefers minerals and other space matter, but the feeler tubes on its limbs can't distinguish the metal in your ships from more nutritious varieties, so you might get past its mandibles before it realizes it has captured you in error. I recommend avoiding the limbs entirely by flying around the back side of the . . . Oh, *that's* unfortunate."

Beyond the mammoth starpod, several objects soared toward us. Ships, from the look of them on the proximity monitor, probably the ones waiting for backup from the Superiority. Except they must have noticed us, because they weren't waiting anymore.

"Please," Cuna said. "*Hurry*."

"Skyward Flight," Jorgen said. "We're going to fly around to the . . . side of this rock that doesn't want to eat us. Anyone *not* clear on which side that is?"

"The one without the pretty space monster," Kimmalyn said. "Got it."

"Right," Jorgen said. "Avoid the enemy ships, but if one shoots at you, shoot it back."

"Always solid advice," I said. "Formation?"

"Double V," Jorgen said. "Orient so the giant space monster is on top of the . . . giant space rock."

Without a planet nearby to orient which way was down, I supposed it made sense to agree on it in advance.

"Why on the top?" Nedd asked. "Couldn't the tentacled monster of death be on the bottom?"

"Because flowers grow *up*," Sadie said. "Even giant death flowers. Everyone knows that."

"She's got you there, Nedder," Arturo said.

"Less chatter," Jorgen said. "Let's keep an eye on what we're flying into."

We quieted down and fanned out, rotating so that the starpod bloomed upward into the dark sky, then accelerated toward Sunreach in wingmate pairs, Arturo and Nedd taking point on one side with Sadie and me on the other. With my proximity monitor still zoomed out, I could see ten enemy ships closing in on a location near the center of the underside of the rock. Another ten ships were closing in on us now. They outnumbered us, but we were used to it.

"FM and Sentry," Jorgen said, "draw off as many as you can. T-Stall and Catnip, back them up. The rest of us will try to punch through to the other group of ships. Divide and conquer."

Dividing the team into two groups also weakened us, but it seemed like a good choice, all things considered. If we spent too much time on the intercepting force, the remaining ships had more time to kill or capture Cuna.

"Understood," I said, and Sadie and I sped toward the incoming ships. When we drew closer, we pivoted our boosters to slow down to dogfighting speeds. Sadie would follow my lead, which meant the specific shape of this maneuver was up to me. The smarter thing for these ships to do would be to refuse the bait and keep a perimeter to prevent us from getting close to the base where Cuna and their team were sheltered. I had to make it look like I was trying to punch past the ships instead of trying to distract them from their mission, and hope they saw me as enough of a threat that it worked.

"Cover me," I said to Sadie.

"I've got you," Sadie replied.

I kicked into a complicated sequence of evasive maneuvers, the kind that would have made Rig turn green. I slipped past the enemy ships through a shower of destructor fire. Several pivoted, their lines of red fire following me. I took a hit, but it glanced off my shield. I sped toward Cuna's location, gathering tails as I went.

"Nice going, FM," Jorgen said.

"We've got you covered," Catnip added.

Now it was time to fake panic. I let my evasive maneuvers grow wider and sloppier, not so much that I gave the enemy too wide of a target, but enough that they might interpret it as me losing control. Then I reversed my boosters, feeling the sharp drag as the g-forces overwhelmed the GravCaps. I switched direction, darting back toward the enemy ships in a way that was impossible to do in atmosphere but worked beautifully in a vacuum. I roped one with my light-lance and used my own momentum to execute a turn, then flew off to the side, letting the ship go once I was past.

It worked. Half of the ships followed me as I shot off toward the side. T-Stall and Catnip joined Sadie in firing on the ships from behind, adding to the adrenaline of the chase. The enemy ships raced after me, destructor fire surrounding me, weakening my shield. I sped up—I wouldn't be able to outrun them, but they'd become less accurate at high speeds, and out here we had all the space in the world.

"Well done," Jorgen said. "Moving in toward the base now. Amphi and Nedder, take point. Quirk and I will cover you."

"They're on to us," T-Stall said. "Peeling away and coming your direction, Jerkface."

It was true. Two of the ships were still hot on my tail, but the other three were making a wide loop and heading back to chase down the rest of the flight.

"Sentry and I can handle this if you want to follow," I said to T-Stall and Catnip. They both readily agreed, circling around to go after the returning ships.

I continued my evasive maneuvers, trying to hold the interest of my two tails. I couldn't keep it up forever though.

"Ready to take care of these guys?" I asked Sadie.

"Ready and willing," Sadie replied.

"You take the one on my left wing," I said. "I'll take the one on the right."

"You got it," Sadie said, and I abruptly cut speed, slowing myself with a reverse of my boosters. The enemy ships shot past me and I engaged my IMP, dropping their shields.

Both Sadie and I opened fire, ripping the enemy ships apart against the dark sky.

"Good work," I said to Sadie. "Let's help the others." We paused while I reignited my shield and then we reversed course, now far enough out that I couldn't get a visual of the others against the dark expanse. I listened as the others exchanged orders over the radio, engaging with the enemy ships.

"Jerkface, they're headed for you."

"I've got them. Cover me."

"Jerkface, I've got a clear shot. Can you bring down their shields?"

"On it."

Sadie and I accelerated as I found the others on my monitor. It was scudding hard to take down a Krell fighter without bringing down their shields first, but these ships were too good—all enemy aces, not the less-skilled drone pilots we'd been fighting. Our team needed backup.

"Jerkface, you've got three ships on your tail," Arturo said. "Don't bring down your shields."

"I see them," Jorgen said. "I'll jump out right after. Engaging IMP."

Sadie and I soared closer, and I finally spotted Jorgen's ship against the backdrop of space just as his shield went down.

Half a second later, he disappeared. I immediately zoomed out my proximity monitors, searching for his ship.

Jorgen reappeared on the other side of the rock, up near the mammoth starpod and its dangerous tentacles.

"Jerkface, what are you doing?" I said over the radio.

"I overshot," Jorgen said. "I think the slug misunderstood me."

"Get out of there!" I said.

"I'm on it," he said. "I'm going to go evasive and try to fly out. If that fails, I'll engage the hyperdrive again."

On the monitor, the arms of the starpod moved slowly, like they were swaying in a breeze.

"Um, guys?" Nedd said. "What is the enemy doing?"

I watched on my monitors as several of the ships near Cuna's base—and all of the ones we'd been dogfighting—sped out around the edge of the rock and upward toward the tentacles of the starpod.

They knew more about this creature than we did. If they thought they could survive flying through the tentacles, they probably could.

But Jorgen couldn't take all those ships. Not by himself.

"Humans," Cuna said over the radio. "Our analysis of the enemy flight patterns suggests that their primary focus is now to kill your cytonic."

"You don't say," Nedd said.

"Jerkface," Arturo said, "they're coming for you. Get out of there."

"Engaging hyperdrive," Jorgen said.

"We're on our way," I said, accelerating to follow the other ships up and over the rock.

Scud, the starpod was *enormous*. This rock was far smaller than a planet, much closer to the size of one of the larger platforms around Detritus. But the arms of the starpod reached many times farther than the diameter of the rock, each tentacle many wing-spans wide and several kilometers long. They were whitish in color, with a smaller purplish stalk growing up the middle of each arm giving the illusion of a purple racing stripe. If the starpod was using those feelers to catch debris out of the space around it, it could almost certainly grab and hold a starship. As if attracted to my motion, one of the arms began to lean slowly in my direction, and I rolled my ship out of the way to avoid it.

Up ahead I could see Jorgen's ship near the center of the creature. The enemy ships raced toward him, opening fire, as the tentacles of the starpod slowly swayed in their direction.

"Engaging hyperdrive," Jorgen said. His ship blinked out—

And back again, this time *closer* to the body of the starpod.

"Scud, the slugs aren't listening to me," Jorgen said. "I think they're trying to get into a smaller space."

I steered my ship up to get a better view.

And stared into the scudding maw of the creature. Rows and rows of long ivory protrusions jutted from its center like teeth, but these were clearly flexible, waving about like the much-longer tentacles.

Tongues. This creature had a thousand tongues arranged in circles around its pink, cavernous mouth. And at this moment, all of them were reaching for Jorgen's ship. The enemy ships continued to move toward him and I followed, Sadie at my wing. Jorgen pulled up, clearing the tongues, then evaded a tentacle that undulated down, looping toward him. The enemy reached him, destructor fire raining everywhere.

"Get out of there!" I said to Jorgen.

"Engaging—" Jorgen said.

His shield cracked.

"Hyper—"

His ship jerked to the side, like he was trying to avoid the fire for one more moment to give himself enough time to frighten one of the slugs. One final movement, and then his shield broke.

"Scud—" Jorgen said over the radio.

And then his ship ripped apart, torn to bits by enemy fire, the pieces floating backward as the creature licked toward them eagerly with its tongues.

16

No.

I pulled my ship up, then ducked down again to avoid a tentacle that swung toward me and the enemy ships with a broad stroke. The enemy avoided it as well, but I wished a fiery death upon every one of them.

Jorgen had a ship full of hyperdrives. He should have been able to get out when his shield dropped. But if he did, the slugs would have teleported him somewhere out into space. If Jorgen wasn't dead yet of depressurization, he would soon asphyxiate.

No.

"FM? Sentry?" Arturo said over the radio. "What's going on up there?"

"Um," Sadie said. "Um, Jerkface—"

I wasn't going to make her explain this. "Jerkface is down," I said.

"FM?" Arturo said. "Say again?"

"Jerkface is down," I repeated. I didn't know how I could sound so dispassionate. My voice was foreign to my own ears. "His ship was destroyed. Salvage irretrievable."

Silence over the radio.

Finally, Kimmalyn was the one who spoke. "He got out, right? He had all those slugs. He must have gotten out."

"FM?" Arturo asked.

"I don't know," I said honestly. I didn't explain what the likely outcome was if he had. My friends already knew.

"All right," Arturo said. "Mourn later. We have a mission."

"Amphi—" Nedd started.

"Mourn *later*," Arturo said firmly. He was first assistant, now our flightleader. "Flight, regroup. We're going to make a run for the base, try to take out the remaining ships on the way."

"Humans?" Cuna said. "I have lost contact with your commander."

"This is Amphisbaena," Arturo said. "I'm in command now." His voice was tight, clipped. He was clearly struggling to follow his own orders, and I didn't blame him. "We're still coming to get you and your people out of there."

"That would be appreciated," Cuna said. "The ships are firing on our location, and our shield has been breached."

Sadie wove among the tentacles of the starpod, headed for the edge of the creature where we could dive to the underside of the rock again. The enemy ships followed, and Sadie and I performed a double scissor, avoiding their fire. As one of the ships tried to chase us, a starpod arm slapped it from beneath. The ship stuck to the stalks and the tentacle carried it away down toward its mouth.

If ships weren't nutritious, the creature clearly hadn't figured that out yet.

"Status, FM?" Arturo asked.

"We're on our way, Amphi," I said. "Don't wait for us."

"Copy. All pilots, move toward Cuna and destroy the enemy ships."

I rolled away from another tentacle as it arced toward me, shooting over the edge of the creature and plummeting down the side of the rock. Sadie followed right behind me, finally out of the starpod's reach. My flightmates coordinated with each other over the radio as they engaged the enemy. I knew we had to join them—we were still outnumbered, and the more of us got involved in the fight, the greater chances we'd get out alive.

Though I wasn't sure what the point was. We'd lost Jorgen, our only cytonic. Without him, what were the rest of us going to do? We'd be as stranded here as Cuna, waiting for the Superiority to send reinforcements to finish us. Cuna probably had a slug and a projector for their communicator, but without a cytonic we couldn't use those to get home.

We'd lost. We'd gambled and we'd lost.

And so—despite my absolute agreement with Arturo that the time to mourn would come later—I felt tears forming in my eyes. Hot streams of them ran along my cheeks, and I pushed my ship faster, almost welcoming the g-forces as they overcame the Grav-Caps.

We were approaching our flight now, and as we did a shape popped into existence on my dashboard, causing me to jump.

Gill sat there, nuzzling my arm.

Had he tried to save Jorgen? If his body was lost in space somewhere, we wouldn't be able to bring him home.

Gill slipped off the dashboard and onto my lap, quivering up against me like he wanted to comfort me. I didn't blame the slugs for what happened to Jorgen. I was glad Gill had gotten out, and hoped the others had as well. Maybe Jorgen had opened the box at the last moment, realizing he wasn't going to make it out, giving the slugs the chance to escape. The communications slug couldn't hyperjump, so it had likely been consumed by the starpod.

Without cytonic abilities or a holoprojector, I couldn't make Gill hyperjump, so his presence wasn't useful to me. We were still in far too desperate a situation for me to feel relieved.

I couldn't help but be glad that he was here though. I ran one hand up his back as I engaged my destructors with the other, distracting a ship that was tailing Kimmalyn. As if he could sense my distress, Gill cuddled closer, tightening around my waist like a leathery belt.

And then everything changed. My ship disappeared, my monitors, the whole of space. I was plunged into darkness.

And landed with a thud onto a cold concrete floor.

"Ouch!" I shouted, cradling my shoulder where I'd landed. Gill dropped off my waist, rolling over on the floor. I couldn't see anything, but I was definitely not in outer space anymore. Or in my ship, as I lay on a slab of cracked concrete. As my eyes adjusted to the dark, I could see a shadow up ahead, and I crawled toward it with one arm out.

My hand met wood. A doorframe, I realized, and there was the door, which moved on squeaky hinges. Gill had hyperjumped and taken me with him, though I didn't know where or why. Technically we could be anywhere in the universe now, but the taynix didn't tend to go far without specific instructions.

I stood, pushed the door the rest of the way open, and stepped into a shadowy corridor. What little light there was came from a thin band of tube lighting that ran along the ceiling, and I followed it, moving up this corridor and then down another. The air was warm, I realized. There was atmosphere for me to breathe and gravity to hold me down and heat to keep me from freezing to death. Wherever Gill had brought me, it appeared to be somewhere relatively safe.

And then I felt the explosion. It reverberated through the building, the stone trembling beneath my feet. This might be the source of the cracks, I realized. This building was under attack.

I had begun to suspect where I was, and so I was only slightly astounded when I reached the end of the corridor and stumbled into a room filled with creatures unlike any I'd ever seen.

A tall, slender humanoid with bright blue skin stood at a control panel of some sort, flanked by two similar creatures, though one of them had skin that was entirely red. They had ridges over their eyes that were similar to Alanik's, though without the crystalline growths, and cheekbones too prominent to be human.

Next to the slender blue alien was Jorgen, looking out the glass window at the stars.

"Jorgen!" I said, and launched myself across the room to throw my arms around him. I overshot a bit, running into him and knocking him off his feet and into the console. I ended up mostly hugging his shoulder as I tried to keep from falling over.

Not my most graceful move, but given that Jorgen was alive and not currently suffocating in the vacuum, I could accept it.

"FM," he said, "what are you—"

Sadie's voice cut him off, crackling over the radio. "—her ship was empty, Amphi. I got a good look before it crashed. She wasn't there."

"Where in the stars did she go then?" Arturo answered. "She can't have just *disappeared*."

"She's here," Jorgen said, pushing a button on the radio. "She's attached herself to my arm in a very awkward fashion, but FM is here and very much alive."

I let go, taking a step back.

"How did you get here?" Jorgen asked me.

"Gill," I said. I left him in the corridor, I realized, and he was just now catching up, lying on the floor by the doorway. I ran over and scooped him up, giving him a hug for good measure. He'd teleported me out of my ship in the middle of a fight, and it had apparently crashed into the rock, but he'd clearly been trying to help.

"Glad to hear it," Arturo said over the radio. "Sentry, help Quirk. She's got three tails. Scud, they're firing on you again—"

The radio cut off as another explosion rocked the bunker where we stood.

The blue alien closed their eyes, then turned to Jorgen. They were wearing one of those translator pins, like the one we used with Alanik. "Our defenses won't last much longer," they said. I recognized their voice from the transmission. This must be Cuna. "They are targeting our life support generators. When those fail, so will the artificial gravity, the air field, and the heat producers. If we don't go now, we may be out of time."

Jorgen glanced over at me.

And all at once, I realized what Cuna meant.

"You're not thinking of *leaving* them here," I said. "Our flight. Our *friends*. We can't go without them."

"Cuna has the coordinates from their communicator," Jorgen said quietly. "We have the ability to get home with Cuna and their staff. Those were our orders, FM."

He didn't sound happy about it. *Of course* he wasn't happy about it. Jorgen didn't want to leave our flight here any more than I did. "Can we get out of here?" I asked. "Do we have a slug that hasn't been scared?"

"We have Gill and Chubs," Jorgen said, gesturing, and I found Chubs sitting in the corner in a strange disk-shaped chair. "I don't think I used either of them when I hyperjumped. I definitely didn't use both. We should be able to use them to jump to the Detritus coordinates. It'll take us to the location of our communicator on Platform Prime."

I knew the right answer. The needs of the group outweighed the needs of the individuals. We were pilots. We signed up to protect the lives of the citizens on Detritus. We were willing to make this sacrifice, every one of us.

I would have been willing to die to save the lives of my friends, no question. But could we really just leave, sacrificing their lives for ours?

Rescuing Cuna was the mission. That was exactly what we were expected to do.

"Nedder, help Sentry," Arturo said. "She's overwhelmed. Quirk, do you have a line on that ship on my tail?"

Cuna slipped their thin fingers up onto the dash and pushed a button. The radio went quiet.

They were turning off the voices, trying to make this decision easier. It could have been a kindness, but it felt like a slap in the face.

Another explosion rocked the base, and the lights flickered out.

"We can't leave them here," I said. Stars, this was why I never wanted to be in command. I didn't have the stomach for it.

"We'll come back," Jorgen said. "I'll jump Cuna and their people out and I'll *come back*—"

"You think they're going to let you?" I asked. "You think they're going to let their *only useful cytonic* come jumping back to probably *die* here? Will you really *do* that?"

Jorgen looked at me, and I could see the weight of the decision in his eyes. This wasn't his fault. None of it was. We were all of us in a terrible position.

But it was our team that was going to pay the price.

"Fine," I said. "I know you're only doing what has to be done."

"Fine!" Gill said in my arms.

"Not now," I said to him. He'd saved my life bringing me here. I should have been grateful. But what I wanted was to be out there in my ship, fighting alongside my friends.

Gill must have sensed my despair, because he disappeared.

Jorgen closed his eyes, and I could see the grief on his face.

"All right," he said to Cuna. "Prepare your people to go."

Cuna put out a call for the rest of their team to converge on the control room, then Jorgen took control of the radio. "Flight," he said. "Abandon the mission."

"Say again, Jerkface?" Arturo said. "Abandon—"

"We are taking Cuna to safety," Jorgen said. "All units pull back in a full retreat, delta formation. Go on full burn on a heading Arturo chooses, and we'll try to come back for you once the minister is safe."

He glanced at me. "I'll come back for them," he said. "I'll bring a ship. I'll get the coordinates again, fly back here, and *bring them home*—"

He was pleading with me to tell him I believed this was possible. Maybe it was. Maybe he was right.

But I worried that the politicians would overrule Cobb, if he was inclined to allow it. No way were six pilots worth risking our only cytonic. I didn't even blame them, really. I understood the math.

But I hated it all.

"Fine!" Gill's voice said. I turned around to find Gill in the doorway with Fine, the communications slug that had been in the communicator at Detritus.

Right there on the floor.

"What in the stars—" Jorgen said.

"Fine!" Gill said, sliding toward me and trilling louder, like maybe I hadn't heard him. "Fine!"

He'd gone to retrieve Fine, all the way from Detritus. He'd done it because he thought that's what I wanted. No one had to scare him into it. He'd done it for the same reason he'd taken me out of my ship. Because I was upset, and Gill was trying to help.

Help.

I grabbed Jorgen by the arm. "Send him an image of Sadie," I said.

"What?" Jorgen asked.

"With your *mind*," I said. "Send Gill an image of Sadie, like you do with the eyes, and with the locations you want them to travel."

"Why would I—"

"Now!" I said, squeezing his arm tight enough that he winced. Bullying the flightleader wasn't my finest moment, but we didn't have the time for me to explain.

"Fine," Jorgen said.

"Fine!" Gill replied.

"No, Sadie," I said. "Go get *Sadie*."

Jorgen closed his eyes.

Gill disappeared.

"FM," Jorgen said. "We can't send the slugs off. We need them to—"

Another blow rocked the base, and I felt the atmospheric production system go offline. My ears popped as the room began to depressurize. Two more of the strange aliens appeared in the doorway, stepping over Fine and moving into the room.

"We're all here," Cuna said. "It's time."

I shook my head. "Wait. Give Gill a moment."

"FM—" Jorgen started.

And then Sadie appeared. She materialized a few feet off the floor and landed with a thump, her knees bending, arms stretched out to keep from falling over. Belatedly, she screamed.

And I gave my second awkward hug, throwing my arms around her and nearly bowling her over. "Jorgen!" I said. "Tell Gill to get the others. Send the images to Chubs too. We can pull them out. They *want* to help." I scooped Gill up off the floor. "I'm going to give you a whole *case* of caviar when we get back," I said. "Go *get our friends.*"

Jorgen blinked at me, but he must have done as I said, because both slugs disappeared.

"Commander," Cuna said. "With all due respect, we need to *go*—"

Another blast made the floor shake, and Sadie and I clung to each other to stay upright.

"What's happening?" she asked me.

"I'll explain later," I said.

This most recent blast must have hit the system that created the false gravity, because suddenly my feet were no longer stuck to the floor. Arturo appeared beside me, and then Kimmalyn. Chubs and Gill came with them, and then Twist appeared with T-Stall, and Drape with Catnip. Happy blinked in a moment later and Nedd appeared up by the ceiling, floating. The rest of our flight looked at each other in confusion.

"That's everyone," Jorgen said. "Huddle together!"

Another blast from the ships cracked the window, which fractured in a spiral pattern. T-Stall reached up and grabbed Nedd by the wrist, pulling him down with the rest of us, and we held on to each other. Cuna and their staff crowded in as well, linking hands. I let Sadie hold onto my waist and grabbed Gill in one hand and Chubs in the other and tossed them to Kimmalyn, who caught them while I gathered the rest of the slugs in my arms.

"Don't scare them," I said to Jorgen.

"FM," he said, clearly exasperated. "What in the—"

"Home!" I shouted. "Home! Take us *home*."

"Home!" Chubs and Gill trilled together.

Glass rained down over us as the ships above opened fire.

And then the entire world disappeared.

EPILOGUE

We appeared in the room where the slugs were housed on Platform Prime, all bunched together in a group and about four feet off the ground. We landed in a tangle of limbs both alien and human, with a chorus of groans and ouches and Nedd yelling, "Get the scud off my neck!" My knees were bruised and my neck tweaked, adrenaline still pumping so hard you'd think I'd faced a firing squad.

But I laughed. I laughed because we were somehow, all of us, *alive*.

As my flightmates on the edges extracted themselves and began helping the aliens to their feet, I sat in the center of the floor laughing my head off, until Gill came and tucked himself up under my arm. "Home?" he said uncertainly.

"Home," I said. "Home, home, *home*." And I hugged the slug tight to my chest.

"Um, FM?" Jorgen said. "I don't think you're supposed to squeeze them like that."

"Shut up, Jorgen," I said. And then, right in the middle of laughing, I also burst into tears.

That was what I looked like when the door to the room flew open and Rig stood there, gaping at all of us, Cobb right behind him looking like he'd seen a ghost.

Rig watched me sitting there, laughing and crying, and came over to kneel next to me. He looked up at Jorgen. "You broke FM?" he asked.

"Apparently," Jorgen said.

Cobb shook his head. "I thought Spensa was the only one who pulled scudding stupid stunts like that. You realize you left your scudding *starfighters* behind, don't you? I can't turn my back on any of you for a moment."

I wiped away my tears and stood. The ships were a loss, no question, but I could tell from the way he looked at us that this wasn't Cobb's primary concern. He'd been as worried for our team as I was. "Apparently not, sir," I said.

Cobb looked up at the aliens then, cleared his throat, and held out his hand.

"Minister Cuna, I presume?" he said. "I'm Admiral Cobb. Pleasure to make your acquaintance."

Cuna stood to their full height, which was taller than Cobb, and bared their teeth at him. Cobb looked worried for a moment.

"It is a pleasure," Cuna said. "Thank you for sending your team to our aid. We look forward to repaying your trouble."

Out in the hallway, Jorgen's mother cleared her throat. Cobb's face darkened briefly, and then he stepped to the side. "Minister Cuna," he said. "May I introduce Jeshua Weight, our emissary from the National Assembly. She's eager to speak with you."

I exchanged a look with Jorgen. His mother had barged in and scared away our last diplomatic opportunity. I didn't know where Alanik had gone, but I doubted very much that she was ever coming back.

"Of course," Cuna said, gliding elegantly out of the room, their teeth still bared, their retinue following after them.

Scud, was that supposed to be a *smile*?

"The rest of you," Cobb said, "come up to the command center for debriefing."

"Sir," I said. "I'd like to get the slugs settled, if you don't mind."

"Fine," Cobb said.

"Fine!" several of the slugs replied.

"Stars, those things are annoying," Cobb said, and he led the rest of the team up the hallway.

Only Rig stayed behind.

"Hey," he said.

"Hey," I said back. "Were you listening over the hypercomm to all of that?"

"Some," Rig said. "It sounded pretty dire."

"It was," I said. "I thought Jorgen had been eaten by a giant space monster, but the slugs jumped him out."

Rig gaped at me, and I felt a bit of hysterical laughter welling up again. "A *space monster*?"

"Mammoth starpod, specifically. You should have seen it. It was bigger than Platform Prime. And then Gill took me to find Jorgen, and for a while we thought we were going to have to leave the rest of the team there to die."

"Gill took you," Rig said. "Of his own accord."

"Kind of," I said. "He thought I wanted him to. These things are a lot smarter than we assumed." I found Gill wrapped around the leg of the table and scooped him up, running my fingers through the fringe on his back. "We need to figure out how to *communicate* with them. Once they know us and care about us, they want to help us out. We don't have to scare them. We can . . . *ask* them."

"Like a partnership," Rig said.

"Like a partnership." I set Gill down on the table and looked up at him.

Rig stood awkwardly with his arms crossed like he didn't know what to do with them.

Scud, that boy was cute. "I'm sorry to have worried you," I said.

"Yeah, well," he said, scuffing his toe on the floor. "I should have known you wouldn't break your perfect record."

"Not if I can help it," I said.

I didn't know if I'd always be able to help it, not really. There was always the chance that I'd go out on a mission and never return, like Lizard, like Hurl and Bim before her. Like so many others we'd lost. We weren't done. The hyperdrives gave us hope for the future, but things were only going to get more dangerous from here, not less.

Maybe it would have been safer to protect myself. Maybe it would have been kinder to Rig not to let either of us get attached.

But I reached out a hand, and Rig took it. His fingers laced through mine.

It wasn't enough to survive for survival's sake. I wanted to *live*. I leaned in and kissed him, slowly and tenderly, like we had all the time in the world. And by the stars, I hoped we did.

"Help it!" Gill said, and I turned around to see all of the slugs we'd returned with gathered around a stack of goods that must have been brought in from requisitions in our absence. Several boxes of algae strips, some vacuum-packed mushrooms.

And an entire tower of jars of caviar.

"All right," I said. "You guys have earned it."

I cracked several jars open and let them eat their fill.

ReDAWN

ALANIK

1

I stood at the edge of a balcony on one of the branches of the Stadium tree, watching the games play out in the enormous hollow below. This particular tree had been chosen for its shape—branches reaching out horizontally and then curving up and inward like the sides of a massive vase, large enough that the spectators on the far side appeared to be nothing more than rows of rippling dots. Twelve ships soared across the widest part of the hollow, six painted Independence blue and the remaining in Unity yellow.

Dim light filtered through the red and purple miasma in the sky above the canopy, and enormous spotlights hung on cables from the branches above, illuminating the ships jetting about. Above the spotlights, just beneath the huge sweeping branches, a hologram enlarged the skirmish, and I watched as one of the Independence ships broke away from the pack, dodging a barrage of laser fire, and slipped through the hoop marking the goal.

Cheers rang through the stadium, and the mining corps that sponsored this match lit off a round of fireworks in Independence blue. With three goals so far, the Independence team was winning.

At least we were winning at *something*.

Beside me, Rinakin—my advisor in the cytonic training program—half-heartedly waved an Independence pennant: a twig with a blue fabric leaf attached at the top. While most in the stadium wore garments of yellow or blue, Rinakin dressed entirely in black, though at least his jacket had a blueish sheen. He was taller than me, and his skin had a slightly rosier tint to it, both traits that indicated his ancestors came from Reaching tree. In the days before ship travel, the denizens of each tree only intermixed when the trees bumped into each other across the miasma.

Now that Rinakin had lost his Council seat in the wave of Unity appointments, we were more or less equals—him as the leader of the Independence Party and me as a cytonic. That felt strange; he was many seasons older than me and much wiser, yet here we were, now essentially the same status even if I didn't have his experience.

"It is good to have you home, Alanik," Rinakin said. "I was worried about you."

"It is good to be home," I said. "Even if it means I failed."

"Many of our people have failed between these branches," Rinakin said.

That was true. I remembered a time when failing in the games had felt like a tragedy. The stakes here were personal—members of the winning teams of even the junior league championships could expect to secure top spots as transit and cargo pilots or appointments to the air force, not that ReDawn had seen actual combat for generations.

I'd skipped over all that when my cytonic powers had manifested—I'd jumped from the junior leagues straight to the upper echelons of the fighting corps. As one of only five living Ur-Dail cytonics and the only capable teleporter, I was theoretically invaluable to my people's survival.

Not that I'd done them much good during my last mission.

I sighed, leaning back against the wooden seat carved into the branch of the tree. The island trees floated in the miasma of ReDawn, their roots planted in large chunks of naturally occurring acclivity stone. The trees grew thick layers of bark, deep enough that entire rooms could be excavated beneath its surface without reaching the living parts of the tree near the base of the branches. Here, higher in the branches, one might be able to reach new wood by digging in six feet or so—plenty of room to carve smaller structures without harming the tree. This balcony and all of its seating had been meticulously carved into the bark, making it a part of the huge living stadium. It was good to be back beneath the familiar branches, but . . .

"I was supposed to bring back the secret to hyperdrive technology," I said. "Instead, I gave the opportunity to the humans. They'll try to make peace with the Superiority—make the same mistakes we have made."

"Perhaps," Rinakin said. "I'm more concerned that *we* will make the same mistakes we have made."

Given the number of yellow pennants flying in the stadium, the fear was reasonable.

"Besides, we have information now," Rinakin said. "Not the information you left to retrieve, but important information all the same."

Much less important, in my mind, but Rinakin had a point. Many of my people believed the humans had been exterminated for their refusal to capitulate, for their stubborn insistence on fighting for freedom instead of assimilating into the Superiority. Humans were a cautionary tale, a justification for the appeasement policies that gave the Superiority more and more control over ReDawn.

If it became known that the humans were alive, that they had somehow managed to resist all this time—indeed, that they were beginning to break free from the Superiority's forced imprisonment— it would be a huge blow to the Unity movement. A weakness I hoped we could exploit to drag some kind of success from my failure.

Which was why I wanted to keep the information from Unity for as long as possible. We needed to figure out how to use it before they did.

Below, the teams lined up for another bout. As per the rules, the

Unity team would now appoint a new stringer—the ship whose job it was to cut across the battlefield and make it to the opposing team's hoop without getting tagged by the lasers. Each pilot had to take a turn as a stringer until everyone had had a turn, or until the other team could no longer catch up in points. A team couldn't rely on one strong player—the tree was only as healthy as its weakest branch.

Unity selected their stringer—Havakal, one of their strongest offensive players. Independence had started with their best players in the hopes of building momentum—it was easier to perform at your best when you already felt like you were winning. Unity had saved their better players for last.

"They're hoping to prey on our overconfidence," I said. "But the Independence team will know that's what they're doing."

"Yes," Rinakin said. "But it may still work."

I looked around at the cloud of blue and yellow pennants waved by the thousands of spectators gathered on their balconies. The colors were about even, which should have been a comfort. But they hadn't been even in the Council balancing, when Unity swept the Council seats, demolishing the Independence majority. I'd been gone for nineteen sleep cycles—missing the balancing entirely.

I'd left hoping to discover the secret that would free my people from Superiority control. If I had succeeded and returned before the balancing, the wind might have swept in our favor, but I'd returned with nothing, only to find us closer to bondage than ever.

I glanced over at Rinakin. He'd intimidated me at first, but though he expected a lot of me, he was never discouraging, only intense. In fact, there was an intensity about him even when he was relaxed. Rinakin wasn't a cytonic himself, though he'd mentored most of the UrDail cytonics as we'd come into our powers.

The other cytonics were all working with Unity now. And because the Superiority designated us as "dangerous," they'd agreed to use their cytonic abilities only under Council supervision.

We *were* dangerous to the Superiority. I would give them that.

Rinakin kept his focus on the hologram above. I'd attended games with him before, but when I'd been in training there had always been some lesson I was meant to learn, some larger goal.

Today we were here to keep up appearances. To prove I wasn't hiding from the Council and their questions since my return four sleep cycles before.

Even though I was.

The private balcony did afford us an opportunity to talk out of earshot of others. That was a luxury on the populous trees of Re-Dawn. "At least people are still flying our flag," I grumbled.

"Yes," Rinakin said. "But most of them have forgotten this is more than a sport."

"They remembered when they cast lots in the last Council balancing."

"That too is a sport," Rinakin said. "They vote for their team, and some switch sides when their current team is losing."

He was right, depressing as that was. Even most of my own family had switched sides in the balancing, voting for Unity instead of Independence. "But that doesn't make any sense. If enough people change their votes it *causes* the other team to lose."

Rinakin's bone ridges arched. "That's politics," he said.

It *shouldn't* be. The decisions of the Council determined everything, and when the balance of representatives shifted, so did the policies. The current Council was a Unity majority, with only a few Independence delegates remaining, so Unity chose the delegates who negotiated trade agreements with the Superiority.

The Superiority set the terms, of course. The Superiority always set the terms. But at least when the Independence were in control of the Council, they didn't grovel at the feet of the Superiority hoping to be treated like favored pets.

Unity scored, and the hologram switched to a series of messages from sponsors—a transportation company showing off the interior of their new luxury ships, and the vineyards on String with a new limited juice flavor they hoped we would try. At the end of the endorsements, a familiar face dominated the air at the center of the branches.

Nanalis, new Council President and Unity High Chancellor. Her booming voice addressed the crowd from the speakers built into the floors of the balconies.

"Greetings, citizens of ReDawn," Nanalis said, her voice proud and confident.

"What is *this*?" I muttered to Rinakin. "*Unity* is taking out endorsements now? That's not allowed, is it?"

"They're supposed to give us equal time," Rinakin said. "But the Council recently decided to waive that requirement so long as the message isn't overtly political."

I wasn't sure Nanalis was capable of a message that wasn't overtly political. She continued to speak—no doubt this message was prerecorded. Many Council members attended the games to see and be seen, but the Council President was often too busy.

Nanalis thanked the pilots for their hard work and preparation. "You represent the best of us, and it is because of you that our future is bright."

I supposed it wasn't out of line for the Council President to congratulate athletes. But then she went on.

"We call ourselves Unity and Independence, but we all enjoy the benefits of both freedom and peace. The real enemies are those who seek to divide ReDawn, who threaten our peace, who put the prosperity of all denizens in jeopardy."

Unity was always calling us divisive for disagreeing, as if they weren't doing the same by disagreeing with *us*. But of course, as they liked to say, the opposite of division was Unity. As if their choice of a name left us no other option but to fall in line with them. "She called us the enemy," I said. "How exactly is that apolitical?"

"That's why I argued against this in the last session," Rinakin said. "Who is to determine what is 'overt' and what is not?"

As Nanalis made her final remarks, pennants waved all around the stadium, both blue and yellow. Everyone seemed to agree with her, Independence and Unity alike.

Everyone but us.

"Progress for ReDawn!" Nanalis declared. "May her enemies be swiftly silenced for the good of us all."

Hairs rose on the back of my neck as voices sang out from all around the stadium, joining in a great rumbling chorus. They were cheering for pretty words that would destroy us.

Progress for ReDawn. It was what we all wanted, of course.

But some of us thought it mattered what we were progressing *toward*.

I knew which enemies she meant to swiftly silence. "I didn't realize the miasma had gotten so thick," I said.

Rinakin stared up at the hologram, which had cut away to feature the ships as they lined up for their next bout. "The wind has shifted," Rinakin said. "I fear it grows more toxic all the time."

The ships flew across the field for the next bout, but all I could see were the waving blue pennants, each one representing a person who should have been ready to fight for our planet, for our *home*, but was instead allied with Unity, who wanted to give it all away.

"I think we should leave the match now," Rinakin said. "I don't know how many will believe we are the enemy, but I would rather not be caught in the crowd."

Cheers went up again, and yellow fireworks filled the air—Unity was gaining on us now.

I didn't want to watch the match turn on us. "Yes," I said. "Let's go."

We stepped onto the stairs that wound down the branch, passing more private balconies and some larger ones crammed with families—children riding on parents' shoulders, waving yellow flags. When we reached a crook in the branch we followed it down the stairs to the platforms around the trunk, descending beneath the playing field to Rinakin's small transport ship, made of dark metal mined from the core of the planet.

I was still bitter about the loss of my own ship, which had been effectively stolen by the humans. I'd put in a request for another, but the order was taking time to process. Normally I would have been granted one instantly due to my status as a cytonic. But the Unity officials must have wanted something to hold over my head until I told them where I'd been and what I'd learned while I was gone. By law, they couldn't force me. I would have been happy to report to the previous Council, but now I would be facing a room full of Unity officials with very few friendly faces.

I guessed they were growing tired of me putting them off.

I climbed into the copilot seat, preferring to sit beside Rinakin rather than on the cushier seats behind us. Rinakin flew us away from the Stadium tree through the purple and red swirls of gas in the miasma. Somewhere far below us was the core of the planet, noxious and uninhabitable, visited only by the mining corps in heavy protective gear. We were in a day cycle—and still a few sleep cycles away from the fall of night—so the ambient light was fairly bright.

We flew into the atmospheric bubble of Industry, one of the largest of the trees, which housed nearly a quarter of the population of ReDawn. The branches of Industry reached horizontally away from the trunk of the tree in all directions, and towers stretched into the space above them, while shorter buildings were suspended downward from beneath. Several kilometers from the trunk, the branches reached for the sky, with structures built in spiral patterns winding up the branches all the way to the tips. The air was thinner here, as the tree processed the toxins out of the atmosphere and produced the oxygen we needed to breathe.

A voice reached into my mind unbidden, though I wished I could ignore it.

Alanik, it said. *You and Rinakin left the match before I could speak to you. We would like to meet with you in the Council chambers immediately.*

"What is it?" Rinakin asked.

"Quilan," I said. He was one of the Unity cytonics, the closest to my age, though he was a few seasons older. "He wants us to meet him at the Council tree."

If he'd noticed we'd left the stadium early, he'd been watching us. Probably planning to move on us in the stadium, where it would be harder for us to refuse an escort. Where if we resisted they could accuse us of making a scene, turn public opinion against us.

As if the wind weren't already blowing that way.

2

"I'm not going to meet with them on their terms," I said. I could hyperjump from almost anywhere on ReDawn, but the Council tree—the capital of ReDawn—was home to the other four cytonics. Working together, they could create a cytonic inhibitor, a field from which I'd be unable to escape.

They could all come to me, of course, but it would be much easier for them to catch me if I agreed to walk right into their jaws.

"Offer to meet them in a neutral location," Rinakin said.

"I don't want to," I said. "Too much risk. They'll bring the other cytonics."

Rinakin pressed his lips together. I was right and he knew it.

Alanik, Quilan said. *Please respond.*

I will not be meeting with the Council at this time, I answered. *I will let you know when I am next available.*

I'm sorry, Alanik, Quilan said. *But your attendance is required.*

"He's not asking," I said. "He wants us to believe we don't have a choice." Though of course we did. As long as we could escape from them, we would always have a choice. To believe otherwise was to hand over our own power, the way they wanted to hand ReDawn over to the Superiority.

"Soon we may not," Rinakin said. "The Council voted to consolidate the military. Many of the Independence bases are already submitting to the Council's control."

I stared at him. ReDawn had maintained two air forces since the end of the last war. We competed and drilled against each other, with the understanding that if ReDawn faced a common threat we would work together to fight it. The division kept us sharp, each side trying to maintain an edge against the other.

"They're getting ready to move against us," I said.

"Yes," Rinakin said. "And they're doing it in the name of peace."

There hadn't been real fighting on ReDawn in almost a century, and both Unity and the Superiority promised peace and cooperation. Never mind that the Superiority had kept us contained here all this time, punishing us for rebellion. Never mind that if we accepted their peace, we also had to accept their control over every aspect of our technology, our travel, our behavior, our culture. They'd already made us paupers, withholding advanced technology from us because we rejected their rule. Now they would make us beggars as well, stripping us of our dignity and our heritage in the process.

And so many of my people accepted it. A prisoner could be convinced that they lived in a paradise, if the prison was pretty enough.

"Is there anyone left who will fight with us?"

"The base on Hollow refused to unify," Rinakin said. "I sent my daughter and her family there. But I'm afraid they won't be able to hold out long."

My brother Gilaf was stationed at Hollow. He and his flightmates helped supervise the lumber work there. Unlike the rest of my family, Gilaf wasn't going to swallow Unity lies.

"If the other Independence bases see that there are holdouts, maybe they'll reverse course," I said.

"That is my hope, but I expect Unity will mobilize their forces quickly to bring them in line."

It was hard to imagine my people firing on each other, but

Unity always seemed more willing to strike out at us than at the Superiority.

"How can they do that and claim it's for peace?" I asked.

Rinakin didn't answer that question. I already knew the answer anyway.

It was easier to believe the story they were told than to awaken to the reality of our oppression.

"What we need," Rinakin said, "are some allies who have not forgotten that we are at war."

I tapped my sharp nails on the dashboard of the ship. "I know," I said. When Rinakin originally suggested that I answer the call to join the Superiority military, I'd been excited. Finally, something I could *do*. All anyone on ReDawn ever seemed to want to do was *talk*. Even though I hadn't made it to the tryouts, discovering that our old human allies were still alive and fighting should have been a victory.

But then those former allies kept me unconscious for weeks, woke me only when they needed something, and then treated me like a prisoner.

Still, I remembered the desperation of the woman who spoke to me first. *They want my people dead. We need your help.* She at least seemed to understand the gravity of the situation.

And the other one—Jorgen, the male cytonic. He was clearly untrained, to the point that he didn't know how to communicate properly. But I did get a bit of emotion from him through his cytonic resonance, enough to know he wasn't happy with the direction things were going.

He was *scared*.

But at least the humans knew what it was like to fight back.

"The humans are facing the same problem we are," I said. "Their leaders are looking for a way to end the war. If we appeal to them for help, they could side with Unity."

"I don't think that will happen," Rinakin said. "The Council has received a directive from the Superiority. There's someone new in charge apparently, and they're demanding we turn over the humans we're harboring."

I stared at Rinakin. "We're not harboring humans, are we?"

"No," Rinakin said. "But a human took your place and infiltrated the Superiority. How are the Superiority to assume that happened?"

By the branches. "They think I was working with the humans."

"They think *we* are working with the humans," Rinakin said. "And now they've issued an ultimatum. Turn over the fugitives—"

"Or they will very politely destroy us," I said. "Which isn't aggressive at all, I'm sure."

"They'll justify it," Rinakin said.

They justified everything. And more than half of my people would parrot the justification as if it made sense, simply because the Superiority said it.

"You think I should return to the humans and ask for help." In hindsight I should have stayed longer, tried harder to discern their true intentions. But I'd been disoriented, alarmed at how long I'd been unconscious, how much I might have missed.

And I *really* did not like that nasty government woman.

I'd thought the myth of human aggression was propaganda spread by the Superiority. Now I wasn't so sure. And if they were as aggressive as the Superiority said, they could be good allies to have right now.

They also could be twice as dangerous if they turned against us.

"The Superiority controls us by dividing us," Rinakin said. "That's why they wanted us to think the humans were eradicated. They're afraid of what we can do together."

That sounded like a Unity argument, but I saw his point. From what little I'd seen, we had more knowledge of cytonics and politics, while the humans had real fighting experience, something no one on ReDawn had anymore.

"I don't know how strong the human military force is," I said. "Or how many ships they might be willing to send our way." If any. My last meeting with them had gone poorly—I hadn't endeared myself to their leadership, nor them to me.

"Then perhaps they would take us in as refugees," Rinakin said. "We could begin to build a resistance from their planet, the way they once mounted a resistance from ours." He glanced over at me. "If the humans joined us, it might grant us the most important resource. Hope."

I didn't like relying on flighty emotions, but Rinakin was right. The humans might be our best option.

They might be our *only* option.

"Or, we could use your knowledge of the humans to buy us time," Rinakin said. "If we seem like we're cooperating, Unity might leave us alone a while longer."

He didn't sound any more excited about that prospect than I was. "If we give the Superiority what they want, we're playing right into their hands."

"Yes. But the Superiority might not be our most pressing concern."

"I don't want to tell Unity I found humans," I said. "We should be using that information to discredit them."

"I agree," Rinakin said. "That's why I think you should return and ask the humans for help, while I go to the Council and try to reason with them."

"They won't *see* reason," I said.

"They might," Rinakin said. "Most of Unity's supporters are blowing their way because they don't see any other choice. If you bring the humans to our aid, you give them another option, another path. Remind the humans of our old alliance, and our potential as current allies. If you succeed, someone is going to have to advocate for that option with the Council. Will it be you?"

I sighed. We both knew I wasn't a diplomat. Rinakin wasn't a Council member anymore, but he was the High Chancellor of the Independence. The members of the Council listened to him—those left on our side, at least.

Still. "You can't cooperate with them," I said. "That is their way."

"Cooperation is not evil, Alanik," Rinakin said. "It depends entirely upon who you are cooperating *with*."

"It's evil to cooperate with *them*," I insisted. "They want to work with our oppressors."

"We all want the same thing," Rinakin said. "Peace for ReDawn."

"But the way they're going about it is *wrong*."

"It is. And someone has to continue to tell them that, so they can't forget there's another way."

Rinakin exited Industry's airspace and turned toward Spindle, a smaller tree where we both made our homes. An alert flashed on the panel—the color indicated that we were ordered to stop at the nearest landing bay for inspection by a government vehicle. Normally this alert was used for traffic violations, though we were flying at regulation speed through open airspace.

Alanik, Quilan said in my head. *We've come to escort you to the Council chambers. Please ground your ship.*

I dug my nails into the plush armrest. "It's Quilan," I said. He wasn't a teleporter, but he did have access to cytonic skills I hadn't yet been able to access—including concussion bolts and mindblades. Last I knew, he wasn't strong enough to use the mindblades effectively, making him as dangerous to himself as he was to others. "He wants us to land so he can escort me to the Council."

"You can flee to Hollow," Rinakin said. "But they'll come for you there, and you won't have enough people to defend yourselves. We simply don't have enough pilots to resist them."

Rinakin turned the ship toward the nearest landing bay, a loading dock for one of the lumber yards. We cruised over a lot filled with old bark that had been stripped away. It would be turned into remanufactured wood in a pressing facility nearby and used for buildings that couldn't be hollowed from the branches.

The ship following us pulled up over our left wing to escort us down into the landing bay. Rinakin turned off his boosters and lowered his altitude lever, bringing us down onto the smooth, shaved wooden surface.

As he did, Quilan's voice reached into my mind again. *I'm here in peace*, he said. *This doesn't have to get aggressive.*

I dug my nails harder into the armrest. His words made me want to scream. There was nothing quite so frustrating as soft words being wielded like clubs. At least a straightforward attack was honest; everyone could see it for what it was.

Later, when the Council discussed this, Quilan would testify that he was perfectly docile and reasonable, and I was going to look like the problem.

My fingers pierced through the armrest. I was going to owe Rinakin for repairs, but I wasn't sorry. It felt *good*.

If that made me aggressive, so be it.

"I don't like leaving you here," I said. "You could come with me."

"Our branches fork here," Rinakin said. "But we're still connected at the root."

Pretty words that meant there was no convincing him otherwise.

I reached across the negative realm, searching for that strange planet, the rock with the eerie, clear atmosphere surrounded by orbital platforms and a thick layer of debris.

I found it, but as I tried to form the coordinates in my mind, the surface of the planet felt slippery. Empty. Blank.

They had a cytonic inhibitor. When had *that* happened? That hadn't been there when I'd left them. I didn't think they had enough cytonics or enough knowledge to form one—this was probably more similar to the ones used by the Superiority, especially because it seemed to cover the entire planet.

I scanned over the area searching for a gap, but I found none. Instead I sensed a mind hovering in their atmosphere—Jorgen. His abilities were still active, otherwise I wouldn't have been able to find him.

Superiority cytonic inhibitors operated with a key—a set of

impressions that allowed a cytonic to bypass the inhibitor. That made the inhibitors particularly nasty, neutralizing all cytonics except for those the Superiority sanctioned. I didn't imagine the Superiority had handed the humans one—they must have somehow found one on their own.

At least I could speak to Jorgen, even if I couldn't hyperjump to his location.

Rinakin released the ship doors and stepped out with his hands held clearly in front of him. "Quilan!" Rinakin said. "Thank you for escorting me. I was going home to prepare, but since you've gone to the trouble I'd be happy to come with you now. Alanik has business of her own to attend to, so I'm afraid she's going to have to request an extension—"

A flare of cytonic energy blasted from Quilan—a concussion bolt that sent Rinakin to his knees.

3

Rinakin knelt, looking up at Quilan, who remained in his ship. He'd been stunned by the bolt—a mindblade cut through physical material, but a concussion bolt passed right through it, bouncing around inside your skull. Quilan had surprised Rinakin, hit him dead on. He'd be stunned for a few minutes at least, and would probably have a headache for days.

Two security guards stepped up on either side of Rinakin, each taking him by an arm. They weren't rough with him, but they placed their hands on him firmly and hustled him into the hold of the ship.

I thought this didn't have to get aggressive, I sent to Quilan. *He was going to come with you.*

We welcome your cooperation, Quilan said.

I had to get out of here, but if they were going to hurt Rinakin, I was bringing him with me whether he liked it or not.

I couldn't let them take him, not to hand over to the Superiority. I could hyperjump to him—one touch and I could take him with me as I escaped. I reached toward the ship, past Quilan, who stared at me with a hard look on his face. Into the back, where I could see the bone ridges of the top of Rinakin's head, where he sat sandwiched between the two guards.

My mind hit a pocket of dead space.

No. They had a cytonic inhibitor on board, creating a space behind Quilan that I couldn't reach with my powers, even though Quilan could obviously use his.

Cytonic inhibitors required cooperation from multiple cytonics, but if Quilan had brought everyone he would have surrounded the ship to keep me from escaping as well. Beyond Rinakin and the guards, I spotted two diones with bright blue skin. This was Superiority technology, run by those diones because the Superiority would never entrust something that powerful to a "lesser species."

Unity was already working with the enemy, trading away ReDawn's autonomy for the ability to destroy the Independence.

Alanik, Quilan said. *Step out of the ship, if you would.* He sounded so reasonable, which only made me angrier.

I wasn't coming with him. I reached into the negative realm toward his mind, ready to tell him so, when I caught a bit of cytonic communication coming into his ship.

—have them yet? someone asked.

Not yet, Quilan responded. *—picking them up—*

—getting impatient . . . wants humans, but we don't have them . . . they will have to do. We need to make the offer before—

I paused, my hands on the altitude control. Quilan's ship hovered over my wing, but if I engaged my boosters, I could shoot out from under his wing and then ascend. I'd flown with Quilan in the junior leagues. I knew I was a better pilot.

But what was *that?* The Council was getting impatient. They didn't have any harbored humans to turn over, so instead they were going to make an offer.

What were they offering?

Rinakin and me?

I wasn't going to be their next bargaining piece. But Rinakin— they were going to give up the leader of the anti-Superiority movement as an offering to appease them.

You're going to give us to them? I asked Quilan.

Your cooperation is appreciated, Quilan said.

This wasn't happening.

I couldn't hyperjump in there. I couldn't save Rinakin.

The only thing I could do was run.

I twisted the dial that fired the boosters.

The ship roared to life, but it only jerked forward a few inches. I twisted around to look and found that Quilan had used a light hook to hold my ship in place. He climbed out of his ship, walking with a brisk step. He might want to convince me that he came in peace, but he also didn't want to give me time to escape.

As long as I didn't let him get me in the back of that ship, he couldn't keep me here.

"Alanik," Quilan called. He was no longer speaking to me cytonically, possibly trying to distract me from anything else I might hear. "Come with us, and we can get this all worked out." He slowed as he approached the door to the ship.

I was going to have to leave this ship behind, but I might be able to get a new one at Hollow. I reached through the negative realm, forming the coordinates for the base on Hollow in my mind. If that base was the last holdout, I could take shelter there while I made contact with the humans. I'd also be better positioned to get my people out if things went wrong.

"I'm sorry, Alanik," Quilan said. "I thought you might still see reason." He sent a concussion bolt flying into the ship. I felt it coming and ducked just in time, missing most of it, though my ears rang and my vision swam.

I ripped into the negative realm, hanging there for a gut-dropping moment, staring out at thousands of white eyes that all focused on me. I felt lost here as I always did, slack and untethered like a streamer torn free of its post, floating for a moment before fluttering inevitably downward into the dark. The eyes regarded me as a trespasser—

And then I returned to myself. I stood in a vestibule in the Independence base on Hollow, a tree even larger than Industry, though far less populated. This tree was dead, and was now used mostly for lumber harvesting.

Through the enormous window comprising one wall of the vestibule, I could see Wandering Leaf—an abandoned military platform similar to the ones that had shot me down when I first visited the human planet—drifting in the miasma. The platform was slowly migrating closer to Hollow, though if it had to threaten any of our trees with its autoturrets, at least it was a sparsely populated one.

The base around me was silent, the hallways empty. That was odd—there were usually a hundred people in residence here helping with the lumber transportation, keeping an eye on Wandering Leaf, and monitoring the trec itself for signs that it was becoming unstable.

"Secure the area," a voice said at the end of the hall, and I pivoted to see several people approaching. They were wearing Unity pilot uniforms, yellow leaves emblazoned on their shoulders.

They'd already taken the base. So where were the Independence pilots? I ducked back into the corner, hiding in a recess until the Unity pilots had passed me by.

Motion through the window caught my eye. I looked down to see a Unity ship hovering just under the branch, outside the base's landing bay. It would be dangerous to hyperjump again so soon, especially if I wanted to bring my brother or some of the other Independence pilots with me when I jumped out again. I'd never done many jumps so close together before—the more times I hyperjumped in quick succession, the more I would draw the attention of the eyes. Being a teleporter was considered one of the most hazardous of the cytonic skills, because we traveled physically through the negative realm.

We didn't always come back. But the risk would be worth it if I could get us all to safety.

When I reached into the negative realm, the surface of that ship felt smooth and impenetrable—blank, like the inside of the ship that had taken Rinakin.

Another Superiority inhibitor.

Unity wasn't going to turn us *all* over, were they?

Alanik, Quilan said in my mind. He'd found me again, though he was still near Industry and he couldn't hyperjump after me. *Come back so we can discuss this.*

So they could capture me was more like it.

Rinakin was right. We needed allies who knew how to fight. If I could convince the humans to side with us instead of the Superiority, maybe we could remind my people of our heritage of resistance, remind them of what we were capable of.

I reached through the negative realm toward the human planet, finding Jorgen again.

I need to speak with you, I sent to his mind. *Can you give me the code to return to your planet?*

Alanik? Jorgen said.

Yes, I answered. *I would like to return to speak with you, though I need the code to your inhibitor.*

Our what?

I closed my eyes. He didn't even know he had the code. Those leaves were the same color as the ones I'd seen when I met him.

Boots marched down the hallway toward me. I might be able to hide here a bit longer—

Alanik, Quilan said. *You're not going to find any friends on Hollow today.*

I took a deep breath. Quilan knew where I was. He could easily send a hypercommunication to the Unity officials here. They'd be looking for me. I reached into the negative realm, and sure enough I could hear his chatter.

—catch her— Quilan was saying. *—convince the Superiority— worth more than all of them combined—*

I shook my head. Quilan and the others were trying to prove their value to the Superiority. They'd accepted aid to contain us in the form of those ships, but if they didn't do the work themselves, they wouldn't earn any favor.

And I was the rebel cytonic, the biggest prize of all.

I had to get out of here.

You have a code in your mind, I sent to Jorgen. *It lets you use your cytonic powers on your planet. I can't return unless you give it to me.*

You used cytonics here before, he replied.

I did not have time for this. *You have an inhibitor now*, I said to Jorgen. *And you know that code, even if you don't know that you know it.*

Um, I'm not sure how to give you that. Let me go talk to Command, see if they'll—

I'm in kind of a bind here, I said. *There's no time for that. There's an impression in your mind. Try to think about allowing me to come there. Try to will it to me.*

I mean, I think you're welcome to come back. I'm sure Command would like to speak with you again.

The words didn't come with an impression. They were useless to me.

"Find her," a voice said from down the hall.

The impression is in there, I said to Jorgen. *How do you access your cytonics? Do you have exercises?*

I meditate, Jorgen said.

Try that, I said. *Do it fast.*

Hang on, I'm trying. I could feel Jorgen's cytonic resonance growing stronger as he deepened his connection with the negative realm. He was welcoming me into his mind, giving me access to his deeper thoughts.

More footsteps. One of the Unity pilots turned a corner, stepping into view.

Alanik? Jorgen said. *Is it working?*

I reached into his mind as he reached into mine.

There. An impression, like a cytonic key. I copied it, embedding it in my own thoughts, and reached toward the human planet, which took shape again, feeling solid. Accessible. I focused on that place, forming the coordinates.

The Unity pilot's bright eyes fixed on me. "She's here!" he said.

Quilan's voice filled my mind. *This is a mistake, Alanik*, he said. *You can't run from us forever.*

We're going to find out, I said.

And then I pulled myself into the negative realm and left my people behind.

4

When I emerged from the negative realm, escaping from the ire of the eyes, I stood in the infirmary room I'd fled when I left the humans. It was empty, the overhead lights turned off.

The first time I'd hyperjumped to Detritus, I'd been shot down by the automated weapons that guarded their planet. My wounds had mostly healed while they kept me unconscious here—not that I was inclined to thank them for keeping me in a coma. I was still technically supposed to be taking it easy, and felt twinges in my abdomen if I overdid it.

Thankfully, hyperjumping wasn't physically strenuous.

I pressed my back against the wall by the window so I wouldn't be visible from the hall, then reached out, trying to find Jorgen. The building around me buzzed with a surprising amount of cytonic energy. At first I wondered if the humans had far more cytonics among them than I'd previously supposed, but no, these minds felt different, their energy more subtle—like the difference between a large fruit and a tiny seed.

Potential cytonics perhaps? If the humans had this many, they'd be formidable allies indeed.

I found Jorgen's mind, with two of the smaller resonances hovering near him.

I made it, I said. *Thank you for your help.*

Oh, good, he said. *I lost track of you, and I thought maybe something bad had happened.*

Several bad things, in fact. *I need to talk to you*, I said. *Can you come alone?* He'd wanted to alert his commanders to my presence, and maybe he already had. But I wasn't eager to speak with them again until I had someone on my side, given how poorly things had gone last time.

Where are you?

He couldn't locate me, then. That wasn't a surprise. He was untrained, and of all the cytonics on ReDawn, I was by far the best at picking out locations and individual cytonics in the negative realm. I sent him a picture of the infirmary room.

Jorgen paused. *Can I bring FM?*

That human woman. I'd liked her. *Yes, but only her.*

On my way, Jorgen answered.

I wished I'd been able to choose someplace with more space, where I might be able to get a look at the humans before they found me. But I had the key to their inhibitor now, so they wouldn't be able to stop me from leaving again if it came to that.

But if I left, I'd be no better off, with no way to help retake our base and no leverage to inspire the rest of the Independence military to do the same.

I tracked Jorgen as he moved through the building, first away from me, and then closer. The door to the infirmary opened, and Jorgen and FM stepped in, shutting the door behind them. FM's hair was lighter, similar to an UrDail's though it had an odd golden quality to it, while Jorgen's was dark and tightly curled. The cuts on his face were almost healed, the bandages gone. FM drew a curtain across the window, and they left the lights off.

They weren't any more eager to be caught by their commanders than I was.

"Alanik," FM said. She had one of the translation pins they'd found in my ship, though it barely changed the sound of my name.

I spoke fluent Mandarin, which was a human language still in use on ReDawn, but these humans spoke English, and I only knew a few words of that one. "You came back! We didn't think you would." FM smiled. Her face looked so strange, all naked skin with no protrusions, like the bone ridges had been filed off. "It's good to see you again. How are you feeling?"

It took me a moment to realize she was referencing my injuries. Last time she'd seen me, I'd been in a hospital bed.

"I'm well," I said. "And you?"

"Um, we're fine," Jorgen said. "We're glad you're back, but—what are you doing here?"

Straight to the point then. I liked that, but it was the opposite of what my espionage trainer, Finis, had taught me before I'd left for Starsight. Many species were suspicious of direct requests. They saw them as too aggressive. I wasn't much of a spy, but I was the only cytonic who could answer the summons by hyperjumping in my own ship, and who could have the chance to hyperjump back out again if things went wrong. I'd failed, and these humans had succeeded in my place.

If they wanted to be aggressive that was fine by me, but I hadn't forgotten everything Finis had taught me.

"I need help," I said. "And I'd like to offer assistance in return. Your people are in a poor position with the Superiority."

"That's an understatement," Jorgen said. He was about to go on when two brightly colored animals appeared on his shoulders—sluglike creatures with bulbous heads and spines running down their backs. One was yellow with blue spines and the other red with black stripes, and each emitted one of the smaller cytonic resonances I'd felt before.

Had those animals just *hyperjumped*?

"Jorgen!" the yellow one said.

I took a step back into the corner.

They also talked?

"Hi, Snuggles," Jorgen said. The pin translated "Snuggles" as a cuddling action, but the slug looked too spiky to cuddle with to me. Jorgen shot an irritated glance at FM. "I thought you were working on that stay command."

"We're *working* on it," FM said. "Gill is getting pretty good, but—"

"Gill!" the yellow slug said, and then it disappeared and reappeared again on the floor by FM's feet with a second yellow and blue slug in tow, this one with blue markings framing its head.

"Yes," Jorgen said. "I see that Gill is great at it."

"To be fair," FM said, "that wasn't his fault."

"Gill!" Snuggles said triumphantly.

Jorgen sighed, and FM pulled a fabric sling out of her pocket, wrapping it over her shoulder. She picked up the slug from the floor and tucked it into the pouch, petting it on its spines.

I stared at them all. "What is that?" I asked.

"It's a taynix," FM said. The creature leaned toward me out of the sling. Its body was long and thin, like the wood leeches that sometimes infested the bark of the trees back home.

I was familiar with several alien species, but not one that looked like this. "Are they intelligent?" I asked.

"Yes," FM said.

"Sort of," Jorgen corrected her.

"Not as intelligent as humans," FM allowed. "They don't actually talk. They repeat things we say."

"Things we say!" Gill said.

"Yes, like that," FM said. "Thanks, Gill."

"And they hyperjump," I said.

Jorgen closed his eyes. "Yes. So much for not revealing all of our secrets immediately. Thanks a lot, Snuggles."

"Snuggles!" Gill repeated.

This was officially the strangest meeting I'd ever had, but at least I'd already learned something. "The creatures are cytonic," I said. "I can feel them in my mind."

"Yes," Jorgen said. He peered around the side of the curtain, like he was afraid we would be overheard. "But don't try to communicate with this one." He indicated the one riding on his shoulder. This taynix was red with black stripes down its sides and black spines running down the center of its back. "He's . . . temperamental. I can't go through that again."

"Again!" the red slug said. Its voice was deeper than the others, and somehow more disconcerting.

"But you're not here to talk about slugs," FM said. "You said you needed help? I'm surprised you'd come to us, after the way you were treated last time."

"I don't want to judge your whole people by the actions of a few," I said carefully. "I would not like it if you judged my people by the actions of some that I know."

FM smiled. "I'm glad you feel that way."

They both watched me expectantly. We'd certainly been through the small talk portion of the conversation that Finis recommended, even if we'd been talking about teleporting slugs, which was definitely not part of my espionage primer. "Some of my people have decided to align themselves with our common enemy," I said. "I think both our peoples could benefit from an alliance."

FM and Jorgen looked at each other. "I agree," Jorgen said carefully, "but I don't have the authority to make one."

I'd been too aggressive. Maybe humans *were* more like the peoples Finis had prepared me to address. "But you are a cytonic," I said. "Surely you have *some* sway in what your leaders decide."

Jorgen and FM exchanged another glance. "Is that what it's like on your planet?" Jorgen asked. "The cytonics are in charge?"

"Not in charge," I said. The Unity leaders weren't cytonic, and neither was Rinakin, though he was the highest ranked Independence official. "But we are respected for our powers."

The Unity leaders respected the cytonics who sided with them, at least.

"Things are different here," Jorgen said. "Our people are afraid of cytonics. The Superiority has used them against us in the past."

Of course they would, if given the opportunity. "So you see that the Superiority is not to be trusted."

"Yes," FM said. "We've been fighting them for decades. You said you were afraid we would trust them, but they haven't even offered us peace. We are looking for allies though, and there's a former Superiority Minister in residence here who—"

"They are here?" I asked. The Superiority sent representatives to ReDawn of course, under the guise of checking on our progress as a people. They were like squirrel keepers checking the cages. They never came too close, in case we would bite.

"Cuna isn't in good standing with the Superiority," FM said quickly. "The Superiority tried to kill them, and we rescued them. We're not looking to join the Superiority, Alanik. And we do need allies against them."

That was good. If this Cuna had turned against the Superiority, they might have information my people could use. "Is Cuna cytonic?"

"No," Jorgen said. "Aside from Spensa, we only have two cytonics. Spensa's grandmother and myself."

That was important information, and he probably shouldn't have given it up so easily. I needed to keep them talking, see what else I might learn. If they decided not to send help, at least I'd be armed with more information. This was going much better than our last conversation, when that angry woman threatened to keep me as a prisoner.

"Spensa still hasn't returned from Starsight?" I asked.

Jorgen took a deep breath. "She did. But she's . . . gone again."

"How did she go there without drawing attention to herself?" I asked. "She sent a message to my people saying she was pretending to be me, but her ruse should have been discovered immediately. How was she able to disguise herself?" I'd been in shock and in pain when I'd given Spensa the coordinates. I'd never been clear on the details of how she'd managed to use them.

"We had a ship with advanced holographic technology," Jorgen said. "Technology even the Superiority doesn't have. Spensa was able to use a hologram to make herself look like you."

"That is clever." A resource like that could be used to walk right onto the Council tree and break Rinakin out without the use of cytonics.

"It was," Jorgen said. "But the ship didn't make it back from Starsight. We can't use that trick anymore."

Another broken branch.

"What are you hoping to gain from an alliance with us?" FM asked.

I set my shoulders. This was the opening Finis had taught me to look for. A direct inquiry to my intentions, an invitation to announce what I needed. Time to get to the point, to beg them to send a military force back with me. Quilan wanted to capture me first, but he wouldn't wait forever before he transported the rest of the resistance to the Superiority. I didn't know what they would do with us.

I also didn't want to find out.

"Your people know very little about cytonics," I said. "I don't know everything, but I could offer more instruction than you have now. As for what I need—the Superiority already believes that my people are working with yours, because Spensa was discovered to be a human disguised as an UrDail. They've demanded we turn in our human co-conspirators, but of course we have none, so instead our government wants to turn me and other resistance members over to them instead."

"They're going to turn over their cytonics to the Superiority?" FM asked. "That seems unwise."

"They've already captured our faction's High Chancellor, who champions independence for ReDawn. By turning him over to the Superiority, those who seek unification will find themselves unopposed."

"They're trying to use the Superiority to take out their political enemies," Jorgen said. "Because that can't go wrong."

FM shook her head. "Two birds with one stone, the saying goes."

The pin didn't have a direct translation for that first part. "What's a bird?" I asked.

"A flying animal," FM said. "We don't really have them anymore. They were a thing from Earth. You don't have birds on Re-Dawn?"

"We don't have creatures that fly," I said. "Anything that strays too far from the trees without an atmospheric generator will choke on the miasma."

Both Jorgen and FM blinked at me.

They clearly had no idea what I was talking about, but it was also beside the point. "As for what I hope to gain, I'm hoping that your people would be willing to help me defend mine against the Superiority."

"We can't promise you anything," Jorgen said. "But if you'll come with us to talk to our admiral—"

"Is this the woman who tried to interrogate me?" I asked. "I'd hoped to avoid involving her."

"You've met Admiral Cobb, but he didn't get to say much," FM said. "He's . . . much more reasonable than Jeshua Weight, the woman you ran from. But yes, she will probably be there, especially if you want to meet with Minister Cuna."

I doubted Jeshua Weight was going to want to work with me. I knew her type—always reaching for power, never wanting to extend any in return. "And if your leaders refuse an alliance?" I asked.

Jorgen and FM exchanged another look. "There's nothing we can do for you without their permission. That's not the way it works here."

"Here!" chimed the red slug on Jorgen's shoulder.

"Not now, Boomslug," Jorgen said.

"Boomslug!" sang both yellow slugs, and they hyperjumped onto Jorgen's shoulders with the red slug. All three slid off and rolled onto the ground at his feet.

The pin translated "Boomslug" to mean a mollusk that explodes. That was ominous.

Jorgen shook his head. "We really need to get them to only do that when they're given the code word."

"Rig and I are working on it," FM said. "But I think they like each other more than they like caviar, so it's slow going."

I had no idea what that meant, but I didn't think these two were going to help me unless I spoke to their leaders. At least this time I was in a better position. They knew I wasn't their prisoner, and an alliance would be advantageous to us all.

I'd come this far. I wasn't going to go home without trying everything.

"All right," I said. "I will speak with your admiral."

"Good," Jorgen said. "I really think we can all benefit from working together. I could use some coaching in cytonics, if you haven't noticed."

"I noticed," I said. All cytonics had slightly different capabilities, but I could show him the basics at least. At some point, we all had to figure out the nuances of our powers on our own.

"So that's settled, then," FM said. "I can wait here with you while Jorgen sets up a meeting, if you want."

"Please," I said, and Jorgen returned Gill to FM before leaving to talk to his leaders.

I hoped my meeting with them went better this time, because otherwise I had come a very long way for nothing.

5

It didn't take long for Jorgen's admiral to agree to a meeting. FM and her strange slug kept me company in the infirmary while we waited for Jorgen to send word that they were ready for us.

"What are you doing with the taynix anyway?" I asked her.

"Bonding," FM said. "I shouldn't say too much, but it's a new program the pilots are trying out."

The pilots were bonding with creatures that could hyperjump. After one of their own had infiltrated the Superiority in my place, trying to find the secret to hyperdrives.

The humans, as it turned out, had found it.

"You can use them to hyperjump," I guessed. "Even if you aren't cytonic?"

FM winced. "I really don't have the clearance to tell you that."

"You didn't tell me," I said. "Your slugs revealed it."

"Yeah, we really do need to figure out how to get them to only do that on command. It gets really confusing when they want to buddy up every time we mention their names."

I stared at the taynix, which was tucked back in FM's sling, nuzzling the crook of her elbow. If those things were the key to Superiority hyperdrives, I would need to take at least one with me if I had to flee.

A radio attached to FM's belt made a beeping noise, and then Jorgen's voice spoke. "We're ready," he said. "FM, can you bring Alanik to the command room?"

"We're on our way," FM said, and she smiled at me in a way that was probably meant to be reassuring.

FM led me through the stark metal hallways. My body felt lighter, my steps bouncier than expected—the gravitational pull of Detritus had to be slightly less than ReDawn.

Everything on this platform was so flat, the ceilings so low, not like the buildings at home—which would wind up the branches of the trees, filled with ramps and stairs on the inside and the outside. On some of the wide lower branches, where flat horizontal ground was easier to come by, a building might have a wide first story, but then it would soar upward, making use of the space above it, or spiral around the branches with lower floors built on the bottom side of the branches.

Who wanted to live in a building that was so . . . squashed? I felt like the ceiling was pressing down on me, closing me in.

Before we reached their command room, we passed beneath a large skylight through which I could see the other platforms that traveled above. They looked a lot like Wandering Leaf, though there were so many more of them.

"Was this an outpost during the last human war?" I asked. "Is that how you became trapped here?"

"No," FM said. "The technology here is a lot older. Our people were travelers with a small fleet of ships. We crashed here and were imprisoned by the Superiority after the war ended."

I wondered if there were more humans hiding in pockets across the universe. The people here had been resourceful enough to survive.

As we walked, I caught glimpses of an electric blue barrier stretching across the sky between the platforms above. "What is that?" I asked.

"Our planetary shield," FM said. "It protects us from the

Superiority gunships. Jorgen told me we apparently have a cytonic inhibitor? I guess that must have activated around the same time we put the shield up. We still don't really understand how all these systems work."

If I had more information about that, I could have used it as currency, but most of this technology was foreign to me as well. Jorgen had the key to the inhibitor in his mind, but he hadn't known it existed. I wondered if being born here attuned him to it somehow. That would also explain why the slugs could use their abilities as well.

FM led me to a room with a slightly higher domed ceiling. Several humans with a variety of skin tones, all in shades of beige and brown, sat around a large table. I wondered if those tones revealed their places of origin like with us, or if they were indicative of something else.

The woman I'd fled from—Jeshua Weight, FM had called her—glared at me. The meanings of facial expressions varied from species to species, and Finis had made me memorize many of them before I left for Starsight. But I was pretty sure that glare meant the same thing in every humanoid culture.

At the far end of the table sat the only other non-human in the room, a dione with blue skin. This would be Minister Cuna.

"Alanik of the UrDail," they said. "Welcome." They, like everyone in the room, had a translator pin perched on their shoulder. I hadn't had this many in my ship, so Cuna must have brought a large number as well. Jorgen offered one to me, and I pinned it on.

"Yes, welcome," said a man in a white uniform. I remembered him vaguely now—he'd accompanied Jeshua the first time we spoke. "I am Admiral Cobb, and this is Minister Cuna." Admiral Cobb had hair growing from the space below his nose—a big white bush of it. That had to be impractical when his nostrils cleared. Or maybe the bush existed to collect the contents. That was a disgusting thought.

I wasn't supposed to judge other cultures' practices—Finis said we had to be open-minded about the customs of other species if we wanted them to be open-minded about ours. I understood that in theory, but it didn't make it easy.

Admiral Cobb went around the room, introducing Jeshua Weight and several people who seemed to be her attendants, though I didn't understand the significance of their titles or manage to remember their names. Finis would have been disappointed. A good spy, she'd said, always paid attention to detail.

Unfortunately, I was distracted by Snuggles, who slipped off Jorgen's shoulders and onto the table, meandering over to Cobb.

"Is it necessary for those things to be here?" asked a man to Jeshua's right.

"Yes," Cobb said. "The pilots have been instructed to carry their taynix with them at all times."

"Could we at least get rid of that one?" the man asked, pointing at the red and black slug. "We all heard what it did."

"Boomslug isn't going to hurt anyone," Jorgen said. "I'm working with him."

"Perhaps the pilots could step outside then," the man said. "Since this isn't the place to discuss the taynix program." He looked meaningfully at Jeshua. While I didn't know enough about human expressions to deduce the full meaning, I could guess.

"I know that the taynix are hyperdrives," I said.

Everyone in the room looked at me in alarm, including FM and Jorgen, though I wasn't going to reveal that they'd given it away. "We UrDail are not as ignorant as the Superiority assumes."

"Your species shows great promise," Cuna said. "That's why you were selected from among the lesser species to try out for our military exercise."

I tried not to bristle at the term 'lesser species.' This wasn't the time to split twigs.

"That military exercise showed up on our doorstep and tried to kill us," Jeshua said. "So let's not make it sound like such an honor to be invited."

Ah, so the Superiority was gathering a military force to destroy the humans. That made sense. Perhaps it was a good thing then, that I'd avoided recruitment at Starsight. Now I knew the secret I'd meant to glean there, *and* I hadn't made an enemy out of the humans.

Jeshua continued to glare at me.

Most of the humans anyway.

"Let's get to the point," Jeshua said. "Why have you returned, Alanik? What do you want?"

Cuna leaned back and their eyes widened—a dione gesture of discomfort, I thought. FM stepped back against the door where she still stood, while Jorgen tried unsuccessfully to get Snuggles to return to him.

I would have written Jeshua's direct question off as human aggression, but it seemed not all the humans accepted it as normal.

Interesting.

"I returned because I think we can help each other," I said. "The Superiority is also the enemy of my people."

"The Superiority is not the enemy," Cuna said quickly. "Winzik, the current leader of the Superiority military, has taken a hard line against the humans, but the Superiority itself is not a monolith. It is a sprawling amalgamation of diverse peoples and perspectives, none of which can be summarized with a single creed or—"

"Yes, as you've said," Admiral Cobb cut in. "But whatever you want to call it, its military is trying to exterminate us. And that makes us enemies."

"I think the more immediate question," Jeshua said, "is what the UrDail have to offer us."

I stood up straighter. Like FM, I had not been given a seat at the table. I didn't know anything about human customs. Finis would want me to reserve judgment, to allow that perhaps in the human culture being left to stand was a gesture of respect.

But it obviously wasn't. Any idiot could see that.

"I can teach your cytonics," I said. "My skills are more developed, because I've had knowledge and training that your cytonics lack. If we were allies, we would share information with you. We have knowledge and experience with the Superiority that you don't have here in isolation."

I shot a look at Minister Cuna, who certainly had far more experience with the Superiority than I had, but they didn't argue with me.

Besides, experience cooperating with the Superiority wasn't the same as experience resisting.

Jeshua hesitated. They did need help with cytonics, and they knew it.

Admiral Cobb cleared his throat. "What exactly do you want in return?" he asked me. "An alliance between our governments?"

That wasn't something I could officially offer, not with things the way they were. "An alliance between the humans of Detritus and the Independence faction of ReDawn," I said. I might not have that authority either, but Rinakin did, and he'd sent me. "I need help to defend my people and to inspire others to fight. Once we've secured our military base, we could formalize the alliance, build a plan to resist together. Your people and mine resisted together in the last war—"

"And we lost," Jeshua said. "That's how we ended up in this fix to begin with."

I didn't like the implication that the UrDail were at fault for that.

"We were allies for generations, not only in the last human war. And now my people are in trouble," I said. Unity tried to suppress the history, but I'd read the books Rinakin had on the subject. "A rival faction is rounding up those who want to maintain independence from the Superiority, and they're going to use us as leverage. If we first work together to rescue my allies, we can then build a coalition to fight back against the Superiority together."

"So you're asking for help," Jeshua said. "Not offering help to us."

"I think Alanik is saying that an alliance between your peoples would be mutually beneficial," Cuna said. "And I concur. The UrDail are still somewhat aggressive, but if that aggression can be properly channeled—"

That was enough. "We aren't aggressive," I said. "We are *defending ourselves*, same as you are. And together we have more resources—"

"We are using all our resources to help ourselves," Jeshua said.

"It seems like a good offer," Cobb cut in. "If we share knowledge and resources, we'll all be better positioned to fight back."

"Maybe," Jeshua said. "But if we align ourselves with rebels, we might lose the opportunity to bargain with the Superiority. They are the ones with the real power."

FM and Jorgen both looked at me. The last time they'd talked about bargaining with the Superiority, I'd reacted poorly. That clearly had been the wrong tactic. Finis said a good spy was level-headed, measuring her reactions.

"If you bargain with them," I said, "you will always find that your wood returns to you rotten."

"Regardless," Jeshua said, mostly to Cobb, "We can't send our starships away. We need them to defend Detritus."

"The shield is defending us now," Cobb said. "This might be the *best* time to send some of our ships away, to strike out instead of hunkering down here and waiting for the Superiority to devise a new way to come at us."

"This isn't our decision," Jeshua snapped. "An interplanetary alliance should be voted on by the National Assembly."

"That depends," Cobb said. "If it's a military operation, then the DDF should make the call."

I didn't know enough about human politics to know who was correct, but I did know enough about politics in general to guess that everyone would interpret the law in the way that best suited themselves.

I reached out to Jorgen's mind, hoping he wouldn't react visibly. *Do you agree with them?* I asked him.

Jorgen stared at his unruly taynix, who was lying on the table just out of his reach, fluting softly.

I don't know, Jorgen said. *It isn't my call.*

I know it isn't your call, I responded. *I'm asking what you think.*

We don't have a policy for this. There's no precedent.

That wasn't an opinion either. Were these humans not even allowed to *think* for themselves? How had they managed to outlaw *that*?

"Perhaps you could offer Alanik some quarters while you discuss it," Cuna said.

"Yes," Jeshua said. "I think that's an excellent idea."

I didn't. "My people are in danger," I said. "I don't know how long they have before they're turned over to the Superiority."

Aside from FM and Jorgen, only Cobb looked sympathetic. The rest merely stared at me like my problems were none of their concern.

Still, my only choices were to wait them out or return home empty-handed, with nowhere to run and no way to help my brother, or Rinakin, or the rest of the resistance.

"But I would appreciate that," I said, trying to sound like I meant it. "Thank you for your hospitality."

If they took too long, I'd have to come up with another plan. I couldn't leave my people in Unity's hands for long.

But I couldn't save any of my people on my own.

6

Because Cuna professed to be some sort of ambassador to "lesser species," the humans allowed them to escort me to a low-ceilinged room with strange rectangular furniture. At home we carved our furniture from wood, and even basic inexpensive pieces would have designs carved into them. The more upscale furniture would be soaked and bent, the chair arms and headboards molded into swirling shapes. I stood in front of an armchair that consisted of a fabric cushion stretched over a metal frame, every piece forming a square angle.

I sat down on it. It was more comfortable than it looked, I would grant them that.

Cuna assured me that they would speak to the humans about my offer and then left me alone in the room. They weren't gone more than a minute before there was a soft knock on the door. I could feel a congregation of cytonic resonances on the other side.

Jorgen and his slugs. "Come in," I called, and Jorgen opened the door. FM stood on the other side with him, holding a basket of something green and flaky. They both stepped in and shut the door behind them.

"Cobb said we could bring you food," FM said. "But we didn't know what your people eat. Cuna said that algae wasn't toxic for your people, so we brought some for you to try." She pushed the basket into my hands. I knew what algae was, but I'd never thought to *eat* it. It grew beneath the surface bark sometimes, and could form in our atmospheric water generators if we weren't careful to keep them clean. "Cuna also told us that you were more likely to eat fruits and tree nuts. We don't have any nuts, and this was the only fruit we could find." She shoved a small object into my hand. "Detritus isn't the best place to grow things." The fruit was red and roughly round and had a small brown stem at the top. It was much smaller than the fruits that grew on the trees at home, more similar to one that might grow on a vine on one of the farming branches.

"Thank you," I said. I moved over to a small table—also square, with straight-angled legs. The conference table had been the same. These humans were *very* fond of right angles.

"I'm sorry about my mother," Jorgen said.

"Your mother?"

"Jeshua Weight. She's . . . a lot to deal with sometimes. But she means well."

FM looked like she wanted to argue, but she didn't. At home it would be considered rude to comment on the failings of someone else's family member unless one was specifically invited to. Possibly humans were the same.

There was another knock on the door, and Jorgen opened it. Three more humans stood there, each with a yellow taynix tucked into a sling across their chest. The humans all wore the same clothes—flight suits, with the same patch affixed to their shoulders. One was a woman with brown skin and long, curly hair that hung halfway down her back. It still surprised me that all of the humans had hair and skin in various shades of bark colors, like they'd been drawn in different tones with the same pencil.

All except the last man who walked in. His hair was a shade of red nearly as bright as the stripes on Boomslug, and it contrasted against his pale skin. I wondered if that color was natural, or if humans sometimes dyed their hair the way my people did.

"We heard Alanik was back," said the girl with the curly hair. "We wanted to see for ourselves, and Cobb said it was okay as long as we didn't help her escape."

I hoped he said that in jest. "I don't need anyone's help escaping," I said. "I'm here of my own free will."

"Of course you are," FM said. "This is Kimmalyn, Rig, and Arturo."

The one she said was Arturo—a man with brown hair—stood by the door staring at me. The humans had done that less than I would have thought, really. The only reason I could keep from staring at them was because there were so many of them.

This didn't feel rude though. More like he was sizing me up. I stared right back at him to let him know I was up to the challenge.

He seemed more puzzled by that than anything, so maybe I'd misread the situation.

Kimmalyn came over and sat down next to me. "Are they feeding you algae strips? They could at least have brought you some dessert."

"Cuna said the UrDail don't artificially sweeten their food," FM said.

Sweeten it? Most of the spices that grew on the vines were flavorful, but not particularly sweet. Which was good, because some of the fruits we grew were too sweet for my taste, especially when they were raw. "This is fine," I said. "Thank you." I lifted the fruit, testing the skin, which was thin and crisp.

"You can just bite into it," Kimmalyn said. "You don't need to peel it or anything. Unless your species doesn't like peel. We could bring you a knife—"

I bit into the fruit, which had a satisfying crunch to it, not unlike pitchfruit back home. It wasn't nearly as sweet though—it had more of a brisk flavor.

"Is it awful?" Kimmalyn asked.

"No, it's good," I said. "Thank you."

"You don't have to say that if you hate it," FM said. "We don't have a lot of fruit, but we can find you something else."

They were being kind, but I wasn't here to discuss culinary habits. If their politicians refused to help me, I could at least collect more information. "Why are people afraid of your taynix?" I asked Jorgen. "You called it Boomslug?"

"Yeah, he did," FM said, and Kimmalyn and Rig both snickered.

"Are we talking about that?" Rig asked. "She definitely doesn't have clearance."

"She already figured out about the hyperdrives," FM said.

"My apologies for announcing that in front of your superiors," I said.

"It's okay," Jorgen said. "Thank you for making it sound like you already knew."

"But Boomslug—" I said. Boomslug seemed to recognize its name, because it descended Jorgen's arm and slid across the table toward me.

"It exploded once," Jorgen said. "Right in my face." He rubbed one of the cuts on his cheek self-consciously.

I leaned away as it approached. "It *exploded*?"

"Watch out for your algae strips," Kimmalyn said, and sure enough the slug began to sniff them speculatively.

"This explosion," I said. "It was cytonic? Energy pushing out from it and slicing your face?"

"Yes," Jorgen said. "How did you . . ."

I stared at the slug in alarm. "That *taynix* can use mindblades?"

"What's a mindblade?" Rig asked.

Mindblades were an advanced cytonic ability. If this creature could produce them, then it must be a powerful cytonic lifeform.

Though the idea that it could produce a mindblade when I couldn't was frankly a little insulting.

"I've only seen them once," I said. I could have kept this information to myself, but I didn't see how they could use it against me—and giving it to them might make them feel comfortable giving more information to me. "Only one of the cytonics on ReDawn can produce them. They are . . . energy from the negative realm pulled into ours with fantastic force." I watched the slug carefully as it gripped the edge of my algae strip with its mouth and slowly retracted the strip from the basket. "They are tremendously difficult to produce."

FM smiled. "So Boomslug is an overachiever."

"I would like to see it in action," I said.

Jorgen scooted his chair away from me. "Not with us sitting right here."

The slug slowly drew the algae into its mouth, watching quietly.

There *was* something ominous about it. Especially now that I knew what it did.

"Are there other types?" I asked. "Communication slugs? Inhibitor slugs, perhaps?"

"We have slugs that power hypercomms," FM said. "So far we haven't found a good use for those without a full hypercomm, so the pilots aren't trying to bond to them. I don't know about inhibitor slugs though."

"Are inhibitors powered by a cytonic?" Jorgen asked.

"Power," Boomslug said.

That was also unsettling. "Sometimes," I said. "It takes a great deal of power, and generally cooperation between multiple cytonics to accomplish. But the Superiority has hyperdrives that work without a cytonic present. If they are using taynix to power their hyperdrives, perhaps there are inhibitor slugs as well."

"If it takes multiple cytonics," Rig said, "I wonder if it requires multiple taynix. We've only begun to learn what they can do when they work together."

Boomslug continued to munch placidly on the algae strip. The idea of this thing collaborating was even more terrifying.

"What can you tell us about hyperjumping?" Rig asked. "Obviously you know how to do that."

I hesitated. Jorgen and FM and their friends were sharing information with me. I wondered if this was the game—freely give up what they knew so that I would share what I knew with them.

"She's not going to tell us anything yet," Jorgen said. "That's her bargaining chip. She wants help from the DDF in exchange for that information."

"Oh," Rig said. "Sorry."

Apparently that wasn't the game.

"It's all right," I said. "I would like to teach you what I know, if you're willing to work with me."

"I'd like to," Jorgen said. "But it's not our decision."

"About that," I said. "I asked you for your opinion earlier, but you never gave it to me."

Jorgen sighed. "I don't know who should make the decision about an alliance with your people. I think the assembly has a point when they say diplomacy is a political matter, not a military one. But the military has been making decisions for the assembly for so many years, it seems like a bit of a power grab for them to reverse course on that now."

"It's because of Cobb, I think," Kimmalyn said. "Some of the people on the assembly say he's not fit to make these decisions."

"Are they really saying that?" Rig asked.

"They are," Arturo said. "The assembly has been in conflict with the DDF for years, wanting more say in operations. They were too afraid to take power from Ironsides when the war was so close to the surface, but now that the fighting is farther away, people aren't as scared—even though our situation is worse. The assembly is starting to think about how to take power away from the DDF, trying to find other ways to deal with the Superiority, now that we know more about them."

"Are all of your assembly dealings so public?" I asked.

"No," FM said. "He knows because his girlfriend's mother is a National Assembly Leader."

Arturo suddenly looked uncomfortable, but he didn't deny it.

The pin translated "girlfriend" as "potential mate." I wondered if humans got embarrassed discussing such pairings before they were finalized. Some did on ReDawn. It depended on what tree you were from.

"I went home to see my father a couple of days ago," he said. "But neither of my parents would listen to me. They think I've been spending too much time with Cobb."

"They do have a point about the Superiority," FM said. "Finding other methods to deal with them seems like a good idea. It's not healthy for us to think of everything that moves as a target to shoot at." She looked at me like she already knew I would argue.

She wasn't wrong. It must be tempting to think that way after years of fighting, but that was the same attitude that led my people right into the Superiority's trap. The humans' military had experience we on ReDawn could only read about in books. But it was useless without the will to fight. If they fell for the Superiority's lies, then I couldn't rely on them to help pull ReDawn out.

"Some forces can't be reasoned with," I said. "They can only be opposed."

"The DDF would agree with you," Arturo said. "But the assembly is starting to think otherwise."

"Otherwise," his taynix said.

"Which is why I don't know who's right," Jorgen said. "You say we shouldn't talk to the Superiority, but I see the appeal. If we could strike an accord with them, lives could be saved."

"It depends on what you mean by saved," I said. "If you live, but give away your autonomy, your ability to make decisions for yourselves, to be treated as equals . . ."

"Do we have autonomy if all we can ever do is fight for our lives?" Arturo asked. "No one from the Superiority has ever treated us like equals. They treat us like insects."

"They're *afraid* of us," FM said. "And the assembly wants to convince them that they don't need to be, but the DDF keeps doing things that escalate the situation."

"Like turning on the shield," Rig said. "And developing hyper-drives. The better we get at defending ourselves, the more we convince them they'd better bring everything they have to destroy us."

"But if you don't do those things, they will enslave you," I said.

"Is that what it's like for your people?" FM asked. "You're slaves to the Superiority?"

I hesitated. There were so many on ReDawn who didn't see it that way. "No," I said. "Because we have maintained our autonomy. Instead of killing us, they isolated us, denying us hyperdrives and mostly leaving us alone."

The humans all stared at me.

"That must be nice," Kimmalyn said finally.

I looked down at the table. These people had been on the front lines, fighting people who wanted them dead. Our squabbles on Re-Dawn must look so easy to them by comparison. "I'm not trying to compare our situations," I said carefully. "But the Superiority keeps us all in cages of different kinds. They control us and call it peace, but it isn't peace when we don't have a choice."

"That's fair," FM said, but none of the humans would quite meet my eyes. This all clearly weighed heavily on them.

I'd misjudged them, I realized. It wasn't that the humans couldn't think for themselves. It was that they had fought for so long with so few resources—but only for survival, not for any particular ideal.

They were desperate and confused, so they were striking around in the dark making confused, desperate decisions.

That was something I could offer them, I realized. Hope. A goal beyond mere survival.

"Our peoples were both autonomous once," I said. "And Jeshua Weight is right. We lost that war together. But before that we worked together for *centuries*. Cytonics from my planet made contact with yours long before either of us were spacefaring. You inspired myths that we still treasure, and your people wrote about mine in their own mythology. One of your ancient writers even preserved bits of our language, so that when we began to travel across the universe, some of your people could speak to mine." I'd never read the book, though now I wished I had. There were still a few copies on ReDawn. Something about a ring. "We don't have to let the Superiority tell us we're *lesser species*. We can return to our ancestors' fight. We can pick up our old alliances. We can remind the Superiority why they were so afraid of us to begin with, and maybe this time we could *win*."

"Or maybe we'd lose," Kimmalyn said quietly.

"Maybe," Jorgen said.

"If you're losing now, would that outcome be so different?" I asked.

Before anyone could answer me the door opened, revealing Admiral Cobb in the hallway.

"Is this a social visit?" he asked to the room.

Jorgen startled. "No, sir. I mean, we brought Alanik some food, and we were talking, but—"

"At ease," Cobb said, though he was the one who looked uneasy as he checked behind him in the hallway and then closed the door. He limped toward us, leaning on a cane.

"Any word from the assembly?" FM asked.

"Yes," Cobb said. "They've granted permission for Alanik to remain on Detritus as a refugee."

"I didn't ask for that permission," I said.

"I'm aware of that," Cobb said. He scowled at Boomslug, who had started on a second of my algae strips. I hadn't tried them yet, and I wondered if the humans would find that rude. I picked one up with my fingers. It was dry and crumbly, like some kind of wafer. Cobb focused on me, and I held the wafer still. "Jeshua has been conferring with NAL Algernon Weight and the rest of the assembly over the radio. Your petition for military aid has been denied—for the moment at least. The assembly is willing to continue debating the issue, and they say they'll revisit it at a later time."

"But I need help now," I said. "My people are going to be given over to the Superiority—"

"So you said," Cobb said. "They're right that committing so many resources to your cause right now would weaken our position, especially after losing a flight's worth of starships."

FM and Jorgen exchanged guilty looks. I wanted to ask how they managed to lose multiple starships, but I'd lost two so far myself, so I supposed I couldn't judge.

I should have asked that my ship be returned to me, I realized. That would have to be my next request. I stuck the end of the algae strip in my mouth, sampling it. It tasted like bittermoss, deep and earthy, with an even sharper aftertaste.

"It's better dipped in custard," Kimmalyn said. I didn't know what custard was, so I would have to take her word for that.

"I think they're also concerned that sending away starships would spoil their current negotiations," Cobb said. "NAL Weight has been talking to one of the Superiority ministers, trying to negotiate a peace deal."

I nearly spat out the algae strip. "They've made contact with the Superiority?"

"Using the hypercomm," Cobb said. "And they want to have all of our resources available to bargain with."

"They're going to want your cytonics," I said.

Jorgen's eyes widened. "Is that true, sir?"

"I haven't heard their exact demands," Cobb said. "They're trying to keep me out of the meetings, saying that this is a political discussion and not a military one."

"But sir," Jorgen said, "if they're planning to bargain with military resources, doesn't that concern the DDF?"

Cobb went on as if he hadn't heard him. "I don't imagine that the Superiority is going to be fond of us keeping our hyperdrives."

FM's hand went protectively to Gill in her sling.

"Our hyperdrives," Gill said.

"We're not handing the *taynix* over to the *Superiority*," FM said.

Doing so would be incredibly foolish, but of course that was what the Superiority would demand. Perhaps the humans were closer to agreeing to help me than I'd thought. They did have resources they wanted to defend.

"I don't think we should hand over a single hyperdrive to the Superiority," Cobb said. "But right now my hands are tied." He eyed me. "Tell me, would it be of any help to your people if we could send a single flight of ships?"

It would be far less help than an entire military fleet. But with one flight, I might be able to assault the ships that were holding my brother and the others from the resistance. I could rescue Rinakin. He was still respected by many, even though he'd lost the election. He might yet be able to sway others to our cause if we could show that we had human allies. "I would take any resources you could give me," I said, "and make the best use of them that I could. My people want freedom. We've held out for it for so long, but my people have lost hope that they can grasp it. If we could begin to gain ground toward that goal, I believe others would join us."

"What exactly would you do with them?" Cobb asked.

That was a very good question. "To start," I said, "I would liberate the remaining outpost of my faction's military. My people are being held on a Superiority ship and the base has been forcibly taken from us. If I could restore it to our control, the other Independence bases might feel empowered to fight back."

Cobb nodded. "That's good to know. Unfortunately, my hands are tied."

I narrowed my eyes. Why ask if I could use a flight of ships if he had no intention of sending me one?

Cobb stood a bit straighter. "I've been specifically forbidden to order any starships to ReDawn to aid Alanik's people. I can't command Skyward Flight to go. I can't command you to give Alanik the aid she needs in exchange for help learning how to use your cytonic abilities. I can't order you to make an alliance with Alanik's people, and I can't order you to bring some of those resources home to help us here as soon as you can."

FM and Rig exchanged a glance.

"We understand, sir," Jorgen said, looking down at Boomslug morosely.

Cobb raised an eyebrow at him, like he didn't understand at all.

I wasn't an expert in human communication, but that seemed like an oddly specific list of things they were *not* being ordered to do. Cobb looked up at the ceiling and sighed, clearly disgruntled about something.

"You can't order them to do it," I repeated.

"Correct," Cobb said. "I have been absolutely and expressly forbidden from ordering you to do what clearly and obviously needs to be done for the good of Detritus and her people."

"That's really unfortunate, sir," Jorgen said. Cobb looked like he was ready to whack him with his cane.

FM smacked Jorgen in the arm with the back of her hand. "He's saying he can't *officially order* us to go," she said.

"I heard him," Jorgen said.

"Heard him!" Snuggles said.

"We're all going to ReDawn," FM said to Jorgen. "That's what's happening."

Jorgen finally seemed to realize what was going on.

"Like the Saint says," Kimmalyn said, "whenever you get there, there you are."

Jorgen looked up at Cobb for confirmation, and Cobb rolled his eyes. He gestured toward the door.

And then all the humans climbed to their feet. Jorgen scooped Boomslug off the table, half an algae strip still hanging from its mouth.

I paused in front of Admiral Cobb. "Thank you," I said. I wasn't going to call him sir. He wasn't my commander. But he was the only reason I had hope for Rinakin and the rest of my people, so I owed him my respect.

"Don't thank me," Cobb said. "I'm just the bearer of bad news."

I nodded to him, and then followed the others out of the room.

7

We hurried down the corridor in the direction of their landing bay. "Is my ship in your hangar with the others?" I asked.

Rig fell back to walk briskly beside me, looking sheepish. "I'm sorry," he said. "But we kind of . . . took it apart."

"You *what*?"

"We were figuring out the differences between your engineering and ours," he said. "I can put it back together, but it will take me time."

"We don't have time," I snapped at him. I was sure my people would have done the same with a human ship, but that didn't change the fact that I needed to get in the air *now*.

"We'll set you up with one of our ships," Rig said. "Some of the controls are different, but it's the best we can do under the circumstances, unless you want one of the others to take a Dulo and you could ride copilot."

"No," I said. The idea of being at the mercy of one of the humans as we returned to ReDawn was stifling. I could steal a ship there of course, but I'd rather come in with my own set of wings. "Give me one of your ships. I'll . . . figure it out."

"You should take a comms slug with you," Rig said to Jorgen. "In case you need one to contact us."

"Good idea," Jorgen said. "Snuggles, take me to Fine."

"Fine!" Snuggles said, and Jorgen disappeared, and then reappeared a moment later next to FM with a purple and orange slug tucked under his arm.

"Fine!" Snuggles said again.

"Good job, Snuggles," FM said, and she withdrew a tin from her pocket and offered it a pinch of some sticky substance.

Interesting.

"Are you coming with us?" FM asked Rig over her shoulder. "Because if not, you should get back to Engineering. You don't want to be associated with what we're about to do."

Rig hesitated. "I think I should stay here, but . . ."

He didn't seem happy about it, possibly because his friends were all running off into danger and he didn't know when they would be back.

"It's okay," FM said. "If we need you, we know where to find you."

"Yeah," Rig said. "I won't be able to say the same for you."

FM looked like she was about to say more, but she glanced at the others and stayed silent. Rig gave her a sad wave and then turned to go. She watched after him over her shoulder, though I couldn't read the expression on her face.

There was clearly a subtext I was missing there. I'd have to ask her about it later, when we weren't about to steal a flight of starships.

I followed Jorgen out a side door and along a narrow path between buildings to the landing bay. Jorgen breezed past two humans who were working on one of the control panels of a partially disassembled ship.

"We're on orders to take our ships up immediately," he said. "Sorry for the late notice."

One of the ground crew followed on his heels, staring at me in alarm. "Didn't you hear?" she said. "There's a mandatory muster— you're all expected to be in your quarters for a surprise inspection."

217

Jorgen looked relieved. Cobb had obviously done that to cover our tracks, and possibly so he could claim later that we'd used the muster as cover without his knowledge.

"These orders supersede those," Jorgen said.

"We weren't notified," she said. "We can start working through the preflight checks—"

"No time," Jorgen said. "We'll do it ourselves. You can radio to Admiral Cobb directly. He'll authorize it."

Or fail to answer his radio, more likely, to maintain deniability.

"Alanik is going to take one of the spare Skyward ships," FM said.

"There aren't any spare Skyward ships," the ground crew member said. "We've only now got *any* Skyward ships again, and we're definitely not authorized to put an alien in—"

"Do you want to be responsible for us being delayed?" Jorgen asked.

"I am responsible for getting you in the air, and I can't do that without—"

"The shield is going to fail," FM cut in. "There's some debris on a trajectory to destroy the controls, and if we don't get up there and shoot it down, the sky is going to be open to the Superiority again. Do you want to be responsible for that?"

The ground crew person hesitated, and Jorgen shot FM a grateful look.

"Come on," FM said to me. "We'll get you into a ship."

On the way across the landing bay we passed my own ship parked among a few with obvious damage. It was similar in design to the human ships, but made from darker metal. It didn't *look* disassembled from the outside, but when I peered through the canopy, I found that they'd taken *everything* apart. My instruments were in pieces, the navigation module disassembled and left on the seat.

"Not flying that today," FM said. "Rig can fix it for you later. Come on."

I wasn't sure whose ship she brought me to, and when I climbed into the cockpit I had even less idea what I was looking at. The instrumentation was all arranged differently.

"Can you fly it?" FM asked.

"I can hyperjump with it," I said. "Flying might be a bit more of a challenge."

FM pointed out some of the more vital systems, and I began to acclimate myself. I found the eject lever on the side of the seat, in the same location as ours. Not everything was different from our starships. "These are the radio controls," FM said, flipping a toggle and spinning a dial. She handed me a helmet. "I'll set you to the flight channel. Remember what you say over the radio isn't secure. I'm going to get myself in the air, but if you have any questions . . ."

I had a lot of questions, but that ground crew tech was probably trying to reach Admiral Cobb right now. Through the canopy I saw Kimmalyn running across the landing bay with three men following her. Trailing after them was a short girl with blue hair.

"We're all here," Jorgen said over the radio. "Skyward Flight, let's get in the air. Go!"

I scanned the ship controls, trying to remember what FM had told me. I found the lever to engage the acclivity ring—those controls weren't very different from my ship. The throttle lever and the control sphere were the same, though the one in my ship was smaller, and this one felt unwieldy in my hand.

I made sure to remember the location of the button for the destructors—I didn't want to set those off by mistake. I engaged my acclivity ring and rose in the air, and managed—mostly accidentally—to remember which were the dive controls as my ship pitched forward, nose pointed at the ground.

"You okay, Alanik?" FM asked.

"Fine," I said, righting myself. I *could* fly. I only *looked* like I couldn't.

I piloted the ship out of the landing bay and then climbed in altitude until I pulled even with Jorgen. One by one, the ships in Skyward Flight followed us into the air.

"Skyward Flight," Jorgen said over the radio. "Sound off when ready. Alanik, we're going to make you Skyward Eight for the moment. You'll need a callsign eventually, if you don't have one."

What was a callsign?

Then Jorgen called out, "Skyward One, callsign Jerkface,"

Jerkface? My pin translated that to something akin to "rude visage," which didn't seem like a nice thing to call anyone.

The rest of the flight sounded off, and I recognized a few of their voices, though many of them used different names. Kimmalyn was "Quirk," I thought, and FM was still FM. I didn't think I'd met Nedder yet, and I had no idea which of the men I'd seen were Catnip, T-Stall, or Amphisbaena, though I thought that last one might be Arturo, and the girl with the blue hair must be Sentry. My pin didn't even offer a translation for some of them. I didn't fully understand the purpose of the callsigns—perhaps to conceal their identities from the enemy?—but this wasn't the time to ask.

"Skyward Flight," Jeshua Weight's voice said over the radio.

"All ships converge above the landing platform," Jorgen said, ignoring her. "Alanik, we can't use the hyperdrives to reach your planet. Are you prepared to hyperjump?"

"Yes," I said. "But I can't bring you all unless our ships are touching."

"We're going to interlock using light-lances," Jorgen said. "We've tried other things, but that's the fastest way. We'll attach to you, so you don't have to worry about the controls."

Kimmalyn's ship drew nearer to mine, and then a line of light, similar to our light hooks, beamed out from her ship, connecting it to mine.

"Skyward Flight," Jeshua tried again. "You are grounded. Land your ships immediately or you will face court-martial."

The others began to converge around me, moving closer than I was comfortable with as they connected their ships to mine. I tried to adjust my position by manipulating my control sphere, but it was more sensitive than I was used to, and I ended up jogging unintentionally to the side.

"Jorgen!" Jeshua said, shouting into the radio now. "Ground those ships!"

"Sorry, Mom," Jorgen said. He did sound sorry, and more than a little stressed out.

"Um, Jerkface?" Nedder said over the radio. "They're readying ships. You don't think they're going to shoot at us, do you?"

"If you leave to fight for the UrDail without permission you are defecting," Jeshua said. "Ground your ships immediately."

"Scud," Nedder said. "Do you think she'll do it?"

"I don't know," Jorgen said. "Let's get out of here before we find out."

"I'm ready when you are," I told him, and reached into the negative realm, feeling across the abyss toward ReDawn. I reached for Hollow, sensing its familiar branches hanging there, a solid point on the other side of all that nothingness.

"Jerkface," Arturo said. "Stardragon Flight is starting to launch."

"This is Robin from Stardragon Flight," an uncertain voice said over the radio. "Awaiting orders."

"Where is Admiral Cobb?" Jeshua said.

"She can't tell them to shoot," Arturo said. "She doesn't have the authority."

I wondered if that was the only thing stopping her; if she'd really give the order to shoot down her own son.

Jorgen didn't respond. I peered past Kimmalyn's ship to Jorgen's. I could see Boomslug perched on his shoulders, though I couldn't see his face, shadowed as it was by his helmet.

"Alanik, we are a go to hyperjump," Jorgen said.

"Jerkface?" Robin said again. "What are you—"

I reached across the negative realm to Hollow, and I *pulled*.

8

I'd never dragged so much mass through the negative realm before, but I was met with no more resistance. We cut through easily, like a knife through whipped whiteberry jam. For a moment we all hung suspended, the eyes staring down at us. A force, massively big and wide, reached for us like it wanted to smother us all. I felt Jorgen and the many slugs around me, all staring up at them. I could feel fear from the slugs, and something else from Jorgen—shame perhaps?

And then the eyes disappeared, and we hung in the miasma in sight of Hollow. We were still on the day side of the planet, the sky bright. I immediately checked our proximity to Wandering Leaf to ensure we hadn't emerged in range of the autoturrets. The platform was a shadow floating off to our right, not close enough to fire. Hollow's corpse reached upward toward the sky, a hazy outline against the miasma.

"Saints and stars," Kimmalyn said. "Does that thing eat people?"

"The tree?" I asked. "No, it doesn't eat people. Have you never seen a tree before?"

"I've seen a tree," Arturo said. "It wasn't much taller than Nedder."

"These can grow up to fifty kilometers tall," I said. "They float in the miasma, and our cities are built on them."

"Scud, that's creepy," Nedder said.

"And beautiful," Kimmalyn added.

"What is all this in the air?" Arturo asked.

"Gases," I said. "Most of the trees have clear patches of air around them, but Hollow has fewer because the tree itself no longer produces oxygen. There's still a bubble of breathable atmosphere from the plants that grow here and from the atmospheric generators installed by the lumber corps, but it's much thinner and we'll have to be more careful."

I scanned the area quickly with my cytonic senses, but I couldn't find any cytonics besides us.

"I'm seeing a ship on my long-range sensors," Jorgen said. "Looks like a transport ship. Is that our target?"

"Yes," I said. I found the controls to expand my own sensors and took a look. I'd brought us in on the far side of the tree, about a five-minute flight out, not sure if the holding ship would even still be here. It had been a few hours, and they could have taken them somewhere else by now.

But the ship was still hovering outside the base. Either they'd subdued the people inside, or my people were too afraid to fight.

We were going to show them how it was done. The Unity fighters wouldn't be expecting us, so even if they'd seen us arrive, we should have a few minutes to prepare while they readied their starships.

"There are civilians still living on the tree," I said. "Some small settlements, plus the lumber mining facilities. I don't want to fire on those or on the transport ship. My people are being held there, and we're going to need them to join the fight."

"Understood," Jorgen said. "What can you tell us about the ship?"

"Not a lot," I said. "It's a small Superiority transport. It's not a fighter, but it has a cytonic inhibitor, so I can't jump in and get people out. The last ship like that I ran across was manned by diones but piloted by an UrDail cytonic. This time there're no cytonics here but us, unless they're in the hold of that ship."

"Do you know if they have a hyperdrive?" Jorgen asked.

"I doubt it," I said. "They'd never give us that technology, for fear we'd figure out the secret."

"That sounds about right," FM said.

"If they can't hyperjump," Jorgen said, "then we can put pressure on them, try to get them to land. Do you know how many fighters we'll be facing here?"

"No," I said. "However many starships were stationed here, plus the number of fighters Unity brought with them when they took the base. They might not have enough pilots to fill all the Independence ships though."

"All right," Jorgen said. "Our primary objective is to get the transport ship to land and free the imprisoned UrDail inside. Secondary objective is to retake the base. Skyward Flight, detach and move toward the . . . tree thing."

"Its name is Hollow," I said.

"Scud," Sentry said. "Even its name is spooky."

All around me, light beams retracted as the flight let each other go. I didn't see any Unity fighters moving toward us yet.

"Alanik, there should be a button flashing on your radio panel," Jorgen said. "Press it?"

I did so, and his voice continued over the radio.

"This is a private channel," Jorgen said. "The rest of the flight can't hear us. Do you see the dial to switch from channel to channel? You might want to note mine so you know how to reach me specifically if there's something you need to report that you don't want everyone to hear."

"If I have something I need to report," I said, "I could speak it into your mind."

"Oh, that's right," Jorgen said. "I need to work on that. I can do it with the slugs, and it probably works the same? I also need you to show me how to hyperjump without a taynix."

"You might not be able to," I told him. "Not all cytonics can."

"Do we have different abilities?" he asked. "Like the taynix?"

"Not exactly. More like strengths and weaknesses. And some cytonics are stronger than others."

"Figures," Jorgen said. "If it's possible for Spensa to show me up at something, she always will."

He didn't sound bitter about that. I was no master of human intonation, but to me he sounded more sad than anything.

"Where is Spensa?" I asked. "You said she was gone again. Was she taken by the Superiority?"

"No," Jorgen said. "She's lost, somewhere in the nowhere. The . . . place you pass through when you hyperjump. The place with the eyes."

"The negative realm," I said. "What do you mean, she's *lost* there?"

"She went there to escape the Superiority," Jorgen said. "And she hasn't been able to find a way out."

"The negative realm isn't a place you go," I said. "It's a place you . . . slip through. You can't *remain* there." At least you couldn't as far as I knew.

"Yes, well. You don't know Spensa. She does a lot of things that ought to be impossible."

She seemed like a good person to have on your side, though less so if she disappeared.

"Did you want to pick a callsign?" Jorgen said. "We don't usually use our real names over the radio, but I don't know if your people have the same custom."

"We don't," I said. "And I wouldn't know what to call myself."

"If you ask the flight, you'll get lots of suggestions. But you might not like them."

"Why do they call you Jerkface?" I asked. "Is it because of the wounds on your face?"

"No, unfortunately."

"Are you unattractive by human standards?"

"What? No!" Jorgen stuttered a bit. "You think I'm *ugly*? It's not about my face. Jerkface means, like, a jerk. A rude person."

"Oh," I said. "So you are disliked, then."

"I am *not* disliked! Or, I was. By Spensa. Anyway, it's a long story."

I could have stopped trying to figure this out, but I was too amused by Jorgen's defensiveness. "So you and Spensa are enemies then. Because she is always showing you up."

"Um, no," Jorgen said. "We're not enemies. Not anymore. We never really were. It's . . . complicated. Oh, look! The flight is trying to reach us on the general line."

The button for the private channel stopped flashing as Jorgen's voice went quiet.

We started flying toward Hollow. My ship moved haltingly as I figured out how much pressure to apply to the boosters, but by the time we neared the tree I was starting to fly more smoothly.

As we drew closer, the transport ship moved away from the base. The pilot had spotted us, because a flight of Unity ships was now headed our way.

"Skyward Flight," Jorgen said. "Engage those ships. T-Stall, Catnip, FM, and Sentry, keep the fighters occupied while the rest of us cut through to the transport ship."

"Copy that," FM said. We accelerated toward the enemy ships. There were ten of them in total, so we were nearly evenly matched in number. As we approached, Skyward Flight opened fire, forcing the Unity ships to break formation or risk losing their shields.

We used similar techniques when we drilled against each other, but we used lasers, not destructor fire. In this battle there were no tag outs, no warnings. The humans weren't playing a game.

Neither was the Superiority, and it was about time my people caught up to speed.

"Alanik," Jorgen said. "You don't have a wingmate, so you can stick with me and Quirk."

As the enemy ships broke formation, two pairs of human ships darted after them, chasing them in circles. I smiled. The Unity fighters had to be terrified.

Arturo and Nedder took off through the gap left by the broken enemy formation, and Jorgen and Kimmalyn followed. I stayed close to them—none of these Unity fighters were cytonic, and since I was in a human ship they hadn't figured out which one I was in. They wouldn't be able to see through the canopies unless their ships got very close, and even then it would be difficult to discern faces beneath helmets.

I scanned for hypercomm signals and didn't find any, though I might have missed Unity's call to Quilan, or they might have done so over the ordinary radio. They were probably wondering where I managed to get a full flight of unfamiliar ships within a couple of hours, and that confusion could only be to our advantage.

We accelerated, tearing through the miasma toward Hollow. The silhouette became clearer against the crimson sky. Destructor fire followed from behind me.

I banked to the side, executing a swivel-turn, and opened fire on the two ships targeting me.

"Amphi, Nedder," Jorgen said. "Alanik's got some tails. Give her some support while Quirk and I push through."

"On it," Arturo said, before I could even tell them I didn't need help.

Nedder shot past me, drawing the enemy fire, while Arturo did a swivel-turn of his own, pivoting to catch the ships in the crossfire. One of them executed a banking roll and fled in the direction of Jorgen and Kimmalyn, while the other lost its shield and took a direct hit in the left wing. The pilot ejected, a parachute opening and slowing their descent. Their helmets and flightsuits would allow them to survive in the miasma. The pilot would put out a distress beacon as they descended toward the core, and would probably be picked up before they reached it—and if not, shortly after.

We all turned, moving toward Jorgen and Kimmalyn, though Nedder and Arturo beat me to the ship that was chasing them, making quick work of it before I could even get off a shot.

I was going to have to step up my game if I wanted to keep up with them. I didn't appreciate being treated like a novice. *I can handle two ships,* I said to Jorgen. *Just because I don't have combat experience doesn't mean I don't know what I'm doing.*

I didn't mean to insult you, Jorgen responded. *I would have done the same for any one of us.*

Really? They *all* felt like they needed to buddy up just to take down a couple of ships? Yes, I knew what we were doing was a lot more dangerous than the games, but for supposedly hardened warriors . . . it seemed so . . . spineless.

Nedder and Arturo shot out in front of Jorgen and Kimmalyn and then slowed, taking point again. Jorgen didn't say a word about it. Rather, he let them ride out in front of him like he *wanted* them there.

The others must have been doing a good job chasing off the other ships. We were nearing the tree now, passing by the thickest branch of Hollow and into the thin bubble of clear atmosphere. A few small towers wound around the edge of the branch.

The transport ship wasn't going to get away. Even if we hadn't had the ability to hyperjump, it wasn't designed to move at fighter speeds in atmosphere. It seemed to have realized that, because it had stopped moving away from the tree and was now headed toward it, quickly disappearing from view.

"Alanik," Jorgen said. "The ship we're after disappeared into the tree. Is there a hangar down there you're aware of?"

"No," I said. "The base with the hangar is in the upper branches. But they call it Hollow for a reason."

"Okay," Jorgen said. "Let's follow that ship. Alanik, since you know the terrain, take point."

It was a good plan, though I wished taking point didn't put me out in front when I was struggling with my ship's controls. Thankfully I had the maneuvering down, so I didn't look like an idiot as I led them around the thick trunk of Hollow and down toward the chasm in the crook of the tree branches.

"FM," Jorgen said over the radio. "Sitrep?"

"We've got them running," FM said. "They're headed in your direction though."

"Took 'em long enough to catch on," Nedder said.

"They had to know why we were here, didn't they?" Arturo asked.

"They did," I said. I remembered what Rinakin said. Just because they understood our tactics didn't mean they wouldn't work.

I flew my ship through the gaping mouth of Hollow and into the depths of its trunk. It was dark in here, though daylight did shine in patches through knotholes in the sides of the trunk, some of which were as much as a kilometer wide. Spindly buildings stretched up the inside, carved and constructed against the interior of the tree. Lumber mining facilities, cutting out the dead wood to be shipped to other parts of the planet. The chasm went deep down into the trunk, partially formed by the natural rotting of the dead tree and then expedited by mining.

We spotted the transport ship heading toward the mining facilities at the bottom of the chasm. "We've got limited time before those ships arrive," Jorgen said. "Alanik, plan for forcing the ship to land?"

"You can't shoot it down," I said. "And they're not going to land willingly. Do you have light nets?"

"We have light-lances," Jorgen said. "We can use them to grab the ship, but we wouldn't be able to drag a ship that big without taking out its boosters first."

"Will it be cornered down there?" Arturo asked.

"No," I said. "There are exits near the lumberyard for exports."

"It's bigger than a fighter, isn't it?" Kimmalyn asked. "Could we take out the boosters without hurting the prisoners?"

"I doubt it," I said. "The boosters are right below the hold. My people are practically on top of them."

"Let's get closer," Jorgen said. "Quirk can take a look, see what she thinks."

We approached the transport ship. UrDail transport ships weren't equipped with weapons, but this Superiority ship had a shield and some basic destructors.

And they said *we* were too aggressive.

"Boosters are no-go, Jerkface," Kimmalyn said. "No way I can hit those without damaging the hull. Cockpit is possible though. I'm guessing the pilots aren't our friends?"

"Not friends," I said. "But you can't shoot out the cockpit without hurting my people in the hold . . . can you?"

"Quirk?" Jorgen said.

"I think I can get it," Kimmalyn said.

"Be sure," Jorgen said.

"Ummmm."

Below us, the transport ship was moving across the top of the lumberyard buildings. It was a medium-sized craft, designed to move maybe thirty people. If they had fit everyone from the base inside, they'd be packed in tight.

The transport ship cruised toward the exit shaft. They probably guessed we were here to rescue their captives, and that we weren't willing to shoot the ship down.

They guessed right, on my part at least.

"We'll have to get the shield first," Jorgen said. "Nedder, go in close, get it with your IMP. Alanik and Amphi, ping them with your light-lances."

"Where is that, exactly?" I asked. FM had told me, but I couldn't remember. It wasn't in the same location as my light hook.

"The buttons on the sides of your control sphere," Jorgen said.

I found them. "Got it. I didn't hear Quirk say she was sure she could do this."

"Um, Jerkface?" FM broke in. "We can't figure out how to get to you."

"We're inside the tree," Jorgen said. "Entrance is where the branches meet the trunk."

I still couldn't tell several of the humans apart, especially when they all started to chatter together.

"Say again, Jerkface? Did you say you're *inside* the tree?"

"What's the matter, Sentry? Never flown a ship inside a tree before?"

"Shut it, T-Stall."

"We're on our way, Jerkface," FM said, "but you have incoming."

"We need to do this now. Quirk?"

"I can do it," she said. "I don't want it to take me more than one shot, but I can do it."

"Nedder," Jorgen said, "catch that ship before it leaves the tree."

"Jerkface?" Arturo said. "If we chase it outside, we'd have more space to catch it in an uncontrolled descent before it hit the ground."

"Are you talking about *chasing* that ship full of *my people* down toward the core?" I asked.

"Um, maybe?" Arturo said.

"In here is better," Jorgen said. "We have incoming. Nedder, get it done."

"Copy," Nedder said, and he dove toward the ship as it headed into the mouth of the shaft that would lead out of the tree. When he got close, he hit his IMP, dropping the ship's shields.

Arturo dove directly behind him, and I jerked my ship to the side in my attempt to keep up. I wished I had my own ship— I looked like an idiot in this thing, which wasn't going to help them think of me as a capable member of the team.

"Scud," Jorgen said. "Enemy ships, on top and closing. Nedder, help me hold them off." I focused on following Arturo as we neared the transport ship.

Kimmalyn's ship darted over our heads. She had to get ahead of the transport ship to get a clear shot. The transport ship aimed its destructors at her and fired, but she dodged and turned her ship around to face it.

"Ready," she said.

"All right, Quirk," Arturo said. "On my mark." He soared over the transport ship and shot it with his light-lance. I aimed and fired as well, grabbing the ship by the other side.

"Scud," Nedder said. "They're coming in hot."

"Fire!" Arturo said.

Kimmalyn's destructors fired, and the cockpit of the transport ship exploded in a shower of sparks.

9

"Quirk!" Jorgen shouted over the radio. "Report?"

"Successful, I think?" Kimmalyn said. "Cockpit annihilated. Hull is intact."

That was a seriously impressive shot. Kimmalyn would have been a star, even in the professional leagues.

"Alanik? How's the inhibitor?"

I scanned the area through the negative realm. The hull was a giant blank space. "Operational," I said. I held one half of the ship by my light-lance and Arturo had the other. The ship's acclivity ring also seemed to be operational, so we didn't have to adjust our boosters to keep it in the air. Without the cockpit controls, I didn't know how much longer that would last.

"What about the pilot?" I asked.

"Um, dead?" Kimmalyn said. "Copilot, too, if there was one."

I blinked down at the ship. I didn't have a clear view of the cockpit from this angle, but—

"Well done, Quirk," Jorgen said, like it was nothing.

She'd just *killed* people, and they thought of it as *nothing*.

I shook myself. What did I think was going to happen in an actual military firefight?

"We're here to help," FM said, and I looked up through my canopy to see the rest of the flight descending on the remaining ships. They seemed to have it handled for now, and the light-lance would be sufficient to hyperjump us all.

"We need to jump this ship to the base," I said. "Where the pilots can board Independence ships and help us."

"You can take them anytime, Alanik," Jorgen said.

I didn't need his permission, but at least we agreed on what had to be done.

"That base will be crawling with the enemy, won't it?" Arturo asked.

"Probably," I said. "Drop your line if you don't want to come with me."

I gave Arturo a few seconds to decide. With the ship's acclivity ring still functional, I didn't need him to hold the ship, but I could use the backup when we arrived. When he didn't release, I reached through the negative realm up to the airspace in front of the Independence base and pulled us all through.

The eyes were wrathful as we passed beneath them, but no more than last time. Hopefully it had been long enough since my last jump that I wasn't putting us all at too much risk. Especially because I wasn't confident that I was going to get out of this battle without needing to hyperjump again.

"Alanik," Arturo said over the radio, "confirm, personnel in that hangar are the enemy, correct?"

I had to turn my ship to the side to see what he was referring to. There were Unity soldiers inside the hangar, some staring in confusion, others running for cover.

"Affirmative," I said.

"Copy," Arturo said. He opened fire as we approached the hangar, and the remaining Unity people began to flee.

"Do we need to secure the area?" Arturo asked.

"My people can do it," I said. At least, I hoped they would do a better job of it than they did the first time. We flew into the hangar and deposited the transport on the ground, our ships still hovering above it. My people poured out, including my brother, Gilaf, who turned around and stared up at us. There weren't more than fifty of them—I wondered if some of the Independence people had defected to Unity.

I pulled off my helmet and waved at Gilaf. He waved back and joined a group of Independence pilots already heading to the remaining ships. They'd get in the air and join the fight, putting us ahead in numbers.

For now.

I searched again for hypercomm signals. Far out in the miasma, I heard the buzz of a communication.

—at Hollow. Bring her in alive—other cytonic interference—not sure what to expect—

I smiled. Quilan could sense Jorgen and the slugs, same as I could. A group of humans with hyperdrives would be low on his list of possible explanations.

"More enemy incoming," I said over the radio.

"Do we know how many ships?" Arturo asked.

"No idea," I said. "Depends on how many Quilan can muster in a hurry." And how much of a threat he thought I was.

Ships couldn't move as fast through the miasma as they could in the vacuum because of the air resistance. Quilan would probably head straight up out of the atmosphere and then skirt the planet in the vacuum. He'd call up units as close to us as possible—which meant they could be here long before he was.

I widened my sensors, searching for the incoming ships. They were coming through the miasma on the duskward side of Hollow. They'd pass by Skyward Flight before they got to us. "They're coming up fast. Duskward side."

"What's that?" Jorgen asked.

Oh. "The side where the sun sets. On the . . ."

The enemy split into two groups as the ships approached the tree.

"We use time on a clock," he said. "Like, directly behind me is six o'clock, straight ahead is twelve . . ."

I had vaguely heard of this—an old-fashioned way of telling directions, probably from the days when we were allied with the humans. "We don't use that notation anymore. Here." I sent the direction to his mind so he could see what I meant.

"Scud," Jorgen said. "I see them on our sensors now. They *are* coming up fast. Looks like about twenty of them."

"The pilots we rescued are getting in their ships now," I said, "so we'll have backup."

The remaining Unity soldiers seemed unwilling to step into the hangar to be shot by our destructors, which had given the Independence pilots plenty of time to get in their ships. Arturo and I could now go back and help the flight without risking that my people would be overrun.

"We're on our way back to you," I said to Jorgen. "Maybe we can make a stand inside the tree and keep the enemy ships occupied."

"Affirmative," Jorgen said. "But if things get too hot or they try to skirt us, we'll implement bounce protocol."

I didn't know what that was, but I had to trust they would handle themselves. I found the Independence radio channel and broadcast to the ships. "Independence pilots. Allies are fighting Unity forces near the lumber mine operations. Hold the base, and we'll be back to support you as soon as we can."

"Alanik," my brother said over the radio. "Who are your allies?"

I wasn't going to announce that over the radio. "I'll explain later." I flipped to Skyward Flight's channel and followed Arturo as he turned his ship toward the entrance at the base of the branches.

Quilan's reinforcements beat us there. I could see half their flight entering the shaft that led to the lumber mine, while the others flew into the larger upper opening ahead of us. They'd split up to come at Jorgen and the others from both sides. Arturo opened fire as we chased them in, and some of the ships flipped around, returning fire.

"You've got company down below," Arturo said over the radio. "We're keeping them busy up top."

"Copy, Amphi," Jorgen said. "Flight, star formation. Crossfire positions. FM, Sentry, cover our six."

Jorgen had said six was behind him, hadn't he? I was glad that if he was using that terminology, it wasn't addressed to me. I dodged fire from an incoming ship as Arturo and I sped past, leaving them to follow us down into the depths of the tree.

We approached Skyward's formation from above, firing at the ships that had them pinned down near the bottom of the tree. The ship I targeted lost its shield, and I pegged it with a destructor blast right in its boosters. The pilot ejected, joining several other pilots drifting down into the mining facilities while their ships crashed into the wooden wall on the dawnward side.

Skyward Flight flew in a loose sphere with Jorgen and Kimmalyn at the center, all with their acclivity rings rotated to point their noses upward at different angles. They filled the air with destructor blasts, each line of fire crossing over another. This formation was similar to one I'd learned in training, though we used laser guns. If you had an obstacle at your back and enough ships clustered together, any enemy that tried to get through to you risked getting tagged in your crossing lines of fire.

Arturo took up position next to Nedder, and I dodged past the ships between us, flying through to join Kimmalyn and Jorgen at the center.

"What are you doing?" I asked Jorgen over the radio. "You're the leader. Shouldn't you be out front?"

"What?" Jorgen said. "No. If I'm out front I can't watch and give orders. And if I'm in trouble, who's going to make sure the rest of the flight is safe?"

Safe? "But you're not getting any of the action," I said. "How are you going to prove yourself?"

"*Prove* myself?" Jorgen said.

"Quirk, incoming!" FM said. Kimmalyn pivoted her ship to point down, opening fire. It took me a second longer to get my ship turned the right way, and then I joined them.

Kimmalyn especially was a good shot—she got several blows to the enemy shields before they peeled off to the sides and swung around again.

Two more ships broke past FM and Sentry below us. These got close enough that they deployed their light hooks—two from each ship, the streams crossing each other to form a kind of net. They pulled apart, trying to fly alongside Kimmalyn to capture her ship, but she rolled to the side, avoiding the trap. "Scud! What is that?"

"Light nets," I said. "It's a capture tactic. Their orders are to bring us in alive." Or me anyway, now that Quilan knew I was here. Though if these pilots got close enough to recognize the humans under their flight helmets, their commander would quickly realize having humans to turn over to the Superiority could only work in Unity's favor.

Not that I was going to let that happen.

The ships turned their nets toward Jorgen, and I fired at one with my destructors. The pilot tried to maintain the net a moment too long, and I landed enough hits to take down the shield. The ship turned, breaking the net, but Kimmalyn got the final shot and the ship went into an uncontrolled spin. The pilot ejected, and instead of flying off to the side like the others, the ship spiraled into one of the mining buildings below.

At least there wouldn't be many people living in here, though there would be some civilians present. I hoped they'd taken cover when the fighting began.

"Jerkface," FM said, "we have incoming."

She was right. My sensors identified a whole fleet of air force ships, many more than we'd been chasing around this tree, and all of them would be equipped with light nets. They were still a few minutes out, but they were coming for us.

"We can't fight all those," Jorgen said. "How defensible is the base? Does it have ground support?"

"Like guns?" I asked. "No. It's never been attacked, not in almost a century. Maybe not even then."

"Scud," Jorgen said. "We need to get out of here. Skyward Flight, bounce protocol. Fall back to the base. We're not leaving without Alanik's people."

Leaving? We were supposed to take and hold the base. If we left now, how would we inspire the rest of the Independence air force to fight?

I could see the incoming ships on my sensor screen though. There *were* too many of them. We wouldn't be able to hold the base against so many, even if they didn't have a cytonic with them.

FM and Sentry immediately disappeared, though I saw them reappear outside the tree through one of the knot holes. They'd used their hyperdrives to escape. The Unity pilots clearly weren't expecting this, and I could hear snatches of confused exclamations over the radio through the negative realm.

"Alanik," Jorgen said. "We don't want to leave you behind."

As if they could. "I've got it," I said.

"Right. Quirk. Ten o'clock. Here we go."

"Copy, Jerkface," Kimmalyn said, and then both their ships disappeared.

10

I still wasn't sure which way ten o'clock was, but I guessed which tree gap Jorgen was referring to and reached through the negative realm, pulling myself out on the far side. This was my third hyperjump in a shorter space of time than I would have liked, and the eyes seemed more fixated on me than normal, but I emerged from the negative realm half a kilometer from Jorgen and Kimmalyn, who were much closer together.

How do you do that? I asked Jorgen.

I send the slugs an image of a location. And then we ask nicely.

You ask nicely?

It's not the only way, Jorgen said. *But it's ours.*

I couldn't argue with their results.

We had a moment to reposition while the enemy shot out of the holes in Hollow. I tried to track the battle on my sensor screen. Independence ships were in the air now, defending the base. I wasn't sure how many Unity personnel were still inside, but we could deal with them in a minute. Hopefully once we'd won this skirmish they'd surrender.

Skyward Flight scattered, leading the enemy ships in circles around the tree and heading toward the Independence base. Jorgen and Kimmalyn hung back as Jorgen gave instructions to the others.

I still didn't understand it. If a leader did that in the junior leagues, or in air force training, they would be immediately replaced. You didn't raise your shooting averages or your evasion scores by hanging back, and if your stats weren't impressive enough you couldn't advance. Watching Jorgen work made me wonder if I'd made too much of human aggression based on a few verbal arguments and the willingness to shoot out a single cockpit.

Four Unity ships charged up the branches toward us and I pivoted my ship, showering one of them with destructor fire. The ship dodged around one of the branches, flying close to the structures hanging beneath, using them as cover.

That was a cowardly move. I wasn't going to fire at the ship while it passed over civilians, but I also wasn't going to let it get away. I kept pace right over it, readying more fire. The ship twisted around the branch, winding up in a spiral pattern, and I followed. I waited for a clear patch of branch with no civilian targets, and then opened fire. The ship tried to dodge, but Kimmalyn flew in from the side, her destructors blocking off the path of escape. The ship's shield went down, and Kimmalyn's shot hit one of the boosters, sending it spinning away from the branch.

The Unity pilot ejected but missed the tree, floating down below Hollow's jagged acclivity stone.

Alanik, Quilan said in my head. *I don't know where you found another cytonic, but you're only making this worse on yourself by resisting.*

I almost retorted that he was only making this worse on himself by fighting us, but I held myself back. He wasn't worth it.

"Amphi, Nedder, Sentry needs support," Jorgen said. I followed Kimmalyn back to Jorgen. Down by the base of the tree, I could see Sentry's ship being cornered by three ships that had joined their light hooks into a net. They closed in, one of them speeding ahead and cutting her off, catching her ship in their light net and hauling her along behind them. FM was hot on their tail, destructors blazing.

"Sentry," Jerkface said. "Want me to pull you out?"

"Affirmative," Sentry said. "Cheeky's ready."

Sentry disappeared out of the net. The ships wavered for a second, probably wondering what had happened, and then reversed, trying to catch FM in their nets. Amphi and Nedder shot two of them down while FM danced away.

"Um, Alanik?" Jorgen said. "Who is this voice in my head that isn't you?"

"Quilan," I said. "He's on his way."

"He wants to know who I am, but I'm not answering him."

"That's for the best," I said. "Trust me."

We'd shaken most of the first wave of ships, but the second wave bore down on us. They'd be here in moments.

"Jerkface," Arturo said. "We can't take all those ships. Do we have a plan?"

"Unless we have some way to defend the base," Jorgen said, "we're going to have to evacuate."

I'd hoped to have more time to reach the other Independence bases, to call more fighters to join us. If half the fighters *here* had abandoned us, we had even less support than I'd hoped. If Detritus had sent more of their military, maybe . . .

I'd told Cobb I would make use of what he was willing to send, and I intended to do it. We'd rescued my people. That was still an improvement. If the humans were willing to work with me, we could press forward together from there.

"Let's do it," I said.

"Where will we go?" Arturo asked. "Can we hyperjump home to Detritus?"

"Already?" Nedder said. "We were just starting to have fun."

"No, we can't," Jorgen said. "I got a message from Cobb on the hypercomm. He said the assembly has arranged a meeting with the Superiority. He's had to order our arrest upon our return to convince my mother to keep him in the loop. He's worried about the

242

concessions they're making. If we bring Alanik's people to Detritus now, he's afraid they'll end up as bargaining chips."

"That's not happening," I said.

"Scud, those ships are coming in fast, Jerkface," FM said. "We can't pull everyone out with one hyperjump. We'd make too big a target of ourselves trying to connect everyone together."

"FM is right," Jorgen said. "We'll have to use the hyperdrives, and that means it needs to be somewhere the slugs know, or somewhere I can see, at least for the first jump."

"The platform," I said. "Wandering Leaf. You can use your hyperdrives to get beneath the autoturrets. The Unity cytonics can't teleport. They can't come after us there."

At least not unless Quilan could convince his Superiority friends to send hyperjumping cytonics to extract us. He wouldn't want to do that if he could help it; he was trying to prove how useful and cooperative he could be. He'd lose his leverage if he made the Superiority do all the work.

"That might be our best option," Jorgen said. "We'll bring as many of the UrDail with us as we can. Alanik, can you communicate with them?"

"On it," I said.

Quilan's reinforcements were arriving now, destructor fire raining through the branches above. Skyward Flight met them in front of the Independence base, Jorgen giving orders for his flight to defend the airspace out front. I switched over to the Independence channel. "Independence fighters," I said, "there's a fleet incoming, and the force is overwhelming. We need to flee. Who is your commander?"

"Alanik," my brother said, "our captain was injured in the blast. I can speak for the group. Where would we go?"

I was sorry any of them had been injured, but I was glad Gilaf wasn't among them. "We're going to abandon the base," I said, "and retreat to Wandering Leaf."

A long silence followed. "To Wandering Leaf," another pilot said. "The platform that *shoots at us*."

"Exactly," I said. "Stay together in the airspace in front of the base. Have someone land and tell those without ships to gather inside the damaged Superiority vessel." That might be the only way to retrieve Rinakin's family and our other noncombatant allies, in addition to any wounded. "We're coming to get you. Our allies have some . . . unconventional methods, but we're not going to leave you behind."

"Will do," Gilaf said, though he sounded dubious.

"Hold on," I said. "We're going to get you out of here."

"We've got your back," Gilaf said.

"And we've got yours." I switched back to the channel with the humans. "The civilians are gathering inside the broken ship. We should be able to use a light-lance to bring that with us, correct?"

"Yes," Jorgen said. "Quirk and I are headed toward Wandering Leaf. I'll send Quirk in first, and then the rest of our ships can jump to hers. It might take us a couple of trips to get everyone."

I hoped their hyperdrives somehow helped them evade the eyes. They must, since the Superiority felt safe using them as often as they did.

"If you get a chance, I'd appreciate a ride from one of your hyperdrives," I said. I didn't want to risk taking another jump so soon, not if I didn't have to.

"Okay, sure," Jorgen said. He sounded confused, but he didn't question me. "Help us defend the base, and then we'll pull you out when we're done."

I followed him and Kimmalyn on the sensor screen as they approached the platform. They flew through the miasma at close to Mag-9—a speed that must have threatened to rattle their ships apart.

These humans meant business.

"Careful not to get too close," I told them.

"We have experience with these things," Jorgen said. "We'll keep our distance."

I leaned on my throttle, catching up to the humans in front of the base. Enemy ships tore through the airspace, trying to run the humans off, but they fought in tandem, harassing the enemy enough to keep them from landing and arresting my people.

I swept down toward the entrance to the hangar, taking up a defensive position near the broken Superiority ship. Even from this distance I could see people pressed up against the glass at the back of the hold, looking up at us, probably wondering what was about to happen.

At least they'd listened to me. I wouldn't have been able to get them out otherwise.

"All right, I have visual on the surface of the platform," Jorgen said. "Quirk, you ready?"

"Ready," Kimmalyn said.

I watched on my proximity sensors as Kimmalyn's ship disappeared from the sky.

"Quirk, status?" Jorgen said.

"I'm fine!" Kimmalyn said. "Near the surface of the platform, underneath the autofire. Looking for a hangar entrance now."

"We can't wait," Jorgen said. "Skyward Flight, you are a go to bounce."

"Copy, Jerkface," Arturo said. "We're on it."

In the airspace directly above, I felt Quilan descending from his reentry into the atmosphere. *Alanik*, he said. *Stop this before someone gets hurt.*

Too late, I said back. I fired on an enemy ship, shaking it off FM's tail, and FM pegged one of the Independence ships with her light-lance.

Then they both disappeared.

All over the battlefield, the humans disappeared with Independence ships in tow. A moment later FM's ship appeared again, so close to Jorgen's that they nearly collided.

"Sorry!" FM said over the radio. "We really need to work on their sense of space when we're in the air!"

Several of the other humans' ships also reappeared, and I left my post by the base entrance to provide some covering fire while Jorgen did his best to dodge his own reappearing flightmates.

"Why are they doing that?" I asked Jorgen over the radio.

"We're using Quirk's slug as an anchor on one side and mine on the other," Jorgen said. "It's a new tactic. We're still working out the kinks."

The humans made another lap, taking more of the Independence fighters up to the platform.

"Amphi," Jorgen said as Arturo reappeared. "Get the Superiority ship."

"On it," Arturo said as I flew in front of the hangar, drawing the fire of the nearby ships and then twist-rolling over the top of the base to evade them. I didn't see Arturo jump out with the damaged Superiority ship, but when I returned the hangar was empty. A ship closed on me, destructors blazing.

Stand down, Alanik, Quilan said in my mind. *Your force is dwindling and you have nowhere to run.*

That wasn't precisely true, but I gathered Quilan hadn't figured that out yet. I led him away from the base, and from Jorgen. I didn't want any of the human ships getting caught in the crossfire if he decided to—

A current *ripped* through the negative realm by my left wing, and I sent my ship into a roll.

If Quilan was willing to throw mindblades, he must have gotten better at them recently. Last time I'd trained with him, he'd have cut himself out of the sky trying something like that.

"How many ships are left?" I asked Jorgen.

"Not many," Jorgen said. "One more trip should do it. How's everything on your side, Quirk?"

"Found a hangar," Kimmalyn said. "Looks like the inside has working atmospheric generators."

That was good. I'd assumed there wouldn't be much of use on the platform, because if it were still useful the Superiority would have dismantled it long ago. Sometimes scavengers and thrill seekers risked the trip beyond the autoturrets, but that was about it.

Alanik, Quilan said, *you can't hide from us. Surrender immediately.*

Or? I asked. *Didn't the Superiority want me alive?*

Yes, Quilan said. *But if you insist on resisting, arrangements will have to be made.*

And with that, Quilan and two other ships behind him opened fire.

I threw my ship into a defensive sequence, but it wasn't as deft or as immediate as it would have been in my own ship where the controls were second nature. I tipped my nose in the direction of Wandering Leaf and hit overburn, shooting out in front of Quilan and the others. My ship shook like it might fall apart and my gravitational capacitors absorbed the g-forces, but a moment later I could see Wandering Leaf through the swirling red mist—the autoturret platform was as big as one of the larger branches of Industry.

Quilan was catching up to me rapidly, and I kept my mind open to the negative realm around me so I could dodge as he sent two more bursts of mindblades after my wings. I couldn't catch a ride with one of the humans and their hyperdrives while Quilan was on my tail, not without putting them in danger. I was going to have to risk one more hyperjump, and hope I came out the other side.

"Alanik," Jorgen said. "Can you get out of there?"

"Working on it," I said. I'd need to hyperjump under the automated weapons, but to arrive in a position that exact—below the autofire zone but above the platform so I didn't crash—I'd need to be able to see where I was going.

"I think that's the last of them, Jerkface," Arturo said.

"Got it. We're pulling out. Alanik, do you need assistance?"

Quilan could tear the human ships to bits with those mindblades. The only one who could see them coming was Jorgen, and I didn't have time to explain what to watch for.

"I've got it," I said, reaching through the negative realm to the space above the platform. There was a ripple behind me, and I dodged too late. A concussion bolt hit my mind, throwing off my focus and wiping out my vision so all I could see were stars. I nearly lost consciousness.

Fire hit my shield in rapid bursts, depleting it. I didn't have time to reorient myself. I reached into the negative realm and pulled myself and my ship through to the platform on the other side.

I could barely see the eyes, though I could feel their hatred. They were reaching for me, searching for me, ready to tear me apart if they found me—

I emerged, my vision returning, but in my confusion I'd targeted a space too high in the air above the platform. One of the enormous guns pivoted in my direction and opened fire. I dropped immediately toward the platform—

Too late. Gunfire hit my booster, and my ship shuddered and shook. The gun fired again—

I targeted a spot closer to the surface of the platform and yanked myself into the negative realm. Thousands of eyes watched my ship as it coughed and skipped, and then I was back, skimming toward the surface of the platform. I tried to pull up, but I was losing altitude fast.

"Alanik!" Jorgen said over the radio. My sensors showed Skyward Flight and the Independence fighters farther behind me. My ship sputtered, the miasma parting as my nose dove toward the hard surface of the platform.

11

"**E**ject!" Jorgen shouted at me over the radio.

I scrambled for the eject lever on the side of my seat, and my seat destabilized, still attached to the ship.

Scud, that wasn't the eject lever.

Where is it? I shouted at him through the negative realm, and an image formed in my mind, perfectly clear, of a lever directly under my knees. My ship shuddered toward the surface of the platform—

And I hauled up on the lever, my canopy exploding outward and rockets beneath my seat propelling it into the air. I prepared to hyperjump again if the ejection shot me up into the path of the auto-turrets, but I flew through the air below them, and then my parachute opened, yanking me back and dragging me along the surface of the platform. I rolled to a stop at the base of one of the auto-turrets.

I unstrapped from the chute and ran along the metal platform in the direction of my wreckage, the miasma clinging to my flightsuit.

The autoturrets fired above me, warding off Quilan and his people. They were peppering the platform with destructor fire, though their shots went wild because they couldn't shoot accurately from beyond the range of the autofire. I ducked under the metal roof that stretched around the autoturrets, working my way toward the hangar entrance Kimmalyn had found. Skyward Flight and the Independence fighters had all parked their ships on the empty hangar floor. Both humans and UrDail had already climbed out of their ships and removed their helmets, staring at each other.

Jorgen popped his canopy open, looking around at the other ships.

Counting them. Making sure his people were all right, seeing how many of the Independence ships we'd rescued. There were about two dozen of them, plus the broken Superiority ship. I recognized Rinakin's daughter among several other people peering out of it.

I pulled off my helmet. Kimmalyn was right; the platform was still generating atmosphere. I wondered if scavengers had maintained the generators to make their jobs easier. Getting past the autofire was difficult and dangerous, but not impossible if you had enough drones to distract the autoturrets. Those who had been here would have had to be well funded, in addition to crazy. We could only claim the second.

"We made it," Jorgen said. "Alanik, your ship—"

"It's gone," I said. There might be something we could salvage, but it wasn't going to fly again.

"I'm glad you're okay," Jorgen said. He didn't say a word about the destruction of their property.

My brother climbed out of one of the Independence ships and approached me slowly, eyeing the humans like he was afraid of them. When he reached me, he embraced me. "Alanik," he said. "I worried they'd captured you."

Leave it to Gilaf to worry about me when *he* was the one who'd been captured.

"I'm glad you're okay, but—" He looked around the hangar. "*Humans?*"

I hadn't told anyone in my family what had happened on my mission to Starsight, only that things hadn't gone as planned. "They are willing to ally with us against the Superiority."

I saw several of the other Independence pilots looking at each other, trying to make sense of this news. Inin, Rinakin's daughter, stepped forward. She wore a fitted maternity jacket over her round stomach. I remembered now—she was expecting a baby in a few sun cycles. When she'd first announced it, Rinakin had said he wished he could retire from his position to help care for the baby, but of course the political situation made that impossible. "My father was worried the Superiority would come after you," she said. "Do you know if he's—"

I wasn't going to spread jam over this news. "They took him," I said. "We need to find him before he's turned over to the Superiority. Quilan is trying to gather us together to use as leverage. Rinakin and me—and the rest of you—in exchange for better trade terms, more advancement." I didn't know exactly what they were asking for, but . . .

"Progress for ReDawn," my brother said with disgust, and I heard murmurs of agreement throughout the group of pilots.

Inin looked to Jorgen. She didn't have a pin to translate, but Jorgen did. "You're here to help rescue my father? To help us turn the wind to our favor?"

"Um," Jorgen said. "We're here to make an alliance." He looked at me. "We're stronger together, in theory, but we're in a bit of a spot here. This isn't exactly a strong position from which to mount a counteroffensive."

"That's true," I said. "But we saved my people, and for that I'm grateful."

Gilaf smiled at me, but he looked worried. All of them did.

With good reason.

FM looked up through the skylight of the hangar, scanning for ships. "Can they get to us here?" she asked.

I searched for Quilan in the negative realm, and felt his mind hovering out in the miasma. "I don't think so," I said. "They don't have any cytonics who can hyperjump. They could try to bring drones to distract the turrets, but they wouldn't be able to get many ships in that way, maybe one or two, so we'd have the overwhelming force."

By a large amount, with the Independence fighters here. Quilan would have to fall back and regroup. Given his current position, he knew it.

If the Superiority was really bent on collecting me, they'd show up eventually. But even Quilan didn't have Superiority cytonics at his beck and call—and especially not if he expected to prove himself to them—so we'd bought ourselves some time at least.

"Can you hear their communications?" Jorgen asked. "Are they making a plan?"

I didn't hear any hypercomm transmissions in the area, but Quilan would know I'd be listening for that. He might have switched to radio. "Can you try to find their channel?" I asked Jorgen.

"Sure," he said. He reached for his radio, disconnecting the headset so we could all hear. He flipped through silence and static, and then a voice projected from his dash.

"—people of ReDawn, with bipartisan support, we are greatly pleased to announce—"

Gilaf swore, and I almost echoed him. The voice belonged to Nanalis.

"Leave it there," I said, and Jorgen pulled his fingers away from the dial.

Nanalis addressed the audience imperiously. "—our collaboration to elevate the UrDail onto the galactic stage."

"Who is that?" Arturo asked, drawing closer.

"Council President," I said. "Elected leader of ReDawn. Currently, anyway."

Inin folded her arms and leaned back against the Superiority ship. Her father had been opposing Nanalis at Council for years.

"Thank you," a familiar voice said, and Inin's eyes widened. "This is Rinakin, High Chancellor of Independence." It *was* Rinakin—I recognized his voice. "We may have our differences, but one thing both Unity and Independence agree on is that we want the best for ReDawn, and for her people."

"Is that the person we were here to save?" Jorgen asked.

I nodded, though all around the room I could feel the Independence pilots tensing. Our side wasn't supposed to talk like that, particularly not while Unity was in the middle of a military coup.

"It is time to set aside our differences," Rinakin continued, "in the name of progress for ReDawn. I would like to announce a bipartisan cooperation with the Superiority."

That was rotten wood. Rinakin was using nearly the exact words Nanalis had used in her announcement during the game. Jorgen looked at me.

"They're making him say this," I said. "They have to be." Inin's face hardened, and she nodded.

"I will be working with Nanalis and the Council over the coming days," Rinakin said, "to ensure the future of both Unity and Independence, and—first and foremost—progress."

"Progress," Gilaf said. "That's what they say, but they're selling us out. All the other outposts gave in. All of them but us."

"There is one matter that concerns me as we move forward with the coalition," Rinakin said. "Alanik, if you are out there, turn yourself in. It's not too late to be part of the solution. Thank you."

The broadcast ended, and Jorgen switched off the radio.

12

I stared straight ahead, trying to make sense of it. One of the humans I hadn't met yet scratched his head. "I'm not the smartest guy around," he said, "but that sounded a lot like a vote in support of the Superiority." I recognized his voice from the radio—this was Nedder, who flew with Arturo.

"They got to him somehow," I said. They must have threatened him. Bribery would never work on Rinakin. He was too principled for that. But everyone had something they were afraid of. Everyone had something they weren't willing to sacrifice.

I didn't know what that thing would be for me, and I hoped I never had to find out.

"My father would never capitulate to the Superiority," Inin said.

"That's true," I said, mostly for the benefit of the humans. Because it was true. Rinakin believed in debate, in discussion, in continuing to advocate and work with Unity. He believed in persuading people to see reason, but he always stayed true to his principles. There was no way he'd flipped sides in a matter of hours. And even if he *had*, he would never have called me out like that.

He *sent* me away. He told me to get help. He wouldn't do that and then announce to the entire planet that I was a fugitive.

"That was his voice though," I said. "They might have told him they'd captured his family, threatened to torture them."

Gilaf squirmed, and I saw several of the other Independence pilots looking at me in alarm. The idea that Unity might torture someone seemed too violent, too aggressive, even for them.

But given that Quilan had just tried to *kill me*, I wasn't feeling so charitable.

"It's possible," Inin said. "In that case, we need to rescue him." She looked at Jorgen. "You saved us. Are you willing to help us with this as well?"

"Rinakin sent me to the humans to begin with," I told Inin. "This alliance was his idea." This last operation hadn't gone as well as we would have liked, but we had more fighters now and there was still hope.

"We did come to help," Jorgen said, and I could practically hear him sorting through his orders, trying to figure out what he was authorized to do. "It's obviously terrible that your leader is being used against your movement."

"But," Arturo said, "we don't *know* that he's being threatened, do we? How do we know that he hasn't changed his mind?"

Inin's eyes narrowed, but I spoke before she could. "He hasn't. He wouldn't."

Arturo and Jorgen exchanged a glance.

These humans didn't know Rinakin at all. They didn't know *me* well enough to trust my judgment on this, and they knew the rest of my people even less. In their position, I'd doubt me too.

"We need to think this through before we do anything," Arturo continued.

"Yeah," Nedder said, "wouldn't want to defect on bad information or anything."

"We didn't defect," Jorgen said. "We were ordered to go."

"We were specifically *not* ordered to go," FM said. "Remember?"

"Cobb phrased it that way because he had to," Jorgen said. "They were still orders, even if they were . . . not-orders. That means it wasn't defection. Right?" He looked around at the others for confirmation, and they all stared at him.

"Bless your stars," Kimmalyn said.

Jorgen swore.

The girl with the blue hair—Sentry, I'd guessed based on the process of elimination—stepped up to me. "We haven't met," she said. "I'm Sadie. And that's Nedd."

Nedd. At least that would be easy to remember.

Sadie indicated the two men leaning against one of the ships. "And that's T-Stall and Catnip. Their real names are Trey and Corbin, but no one calls them that. They just go by their callsigns."

I had no idea which one was T-Stall and which one was Catnip, but I didn't ask.

"This is my brother, Gilaf," I said. "And Rinakin's daughter, Inin." I didn't know the names of everyone else, and no one seemed to feel that this was the time to require the humans to remember them all.

I turned to Gilaf. I needed to convince the humans to mount an offensive against Unity from here, and that would be easier to do without the rest of my people standing here listening. "We're going to need to map the facilities here," I said. "Figure out what we're working with. Can you take the pilots and try to find somewhere safe for Rinakin's family and the others to rest?"

Gilaf glanced at Inin's pregnant belly, and Inin glared at him. She plainly disliked being treated like a baby simply because she was carrying one.

"I'm *fine*," Inin said. "But it does seem wise to make sure we're safe here. Your captain is injured, and will need someplace to rest."

That was right. I stepped up to the exposed interior of the Superiority ship. Several civilians sat inside, along with the Independence captain, who lay on the floor with a medic attending to a wound in his leg.

"Does he need further aid?" I asked. I could hyperjump him to a hospital if it came to that, but if it wasn't necessary I didn't want to risk it.

"We can manage here," the medic said. "Though he'll need time before he can return to duty."

"All right," Gilaf said. He turned to Jorgen. "Thank you for coming to our aid. Though that thing you did, moving us from place to place—are you *all* cytonics?"

Jorgen looked alarmed, like he wasn't sure if he should give up their secrets. The humans had all left their slugs in their ships, and I didn't want to anger them, but knowing what assets we had on our side would only inspire my people. "They have hyperdrives in their ships," I told Gilaf.

"Shake the branches," Gilaf said, and I heard more murmurs of shock and relief from the other pilots. "We look forward to our alliance." He moved into the ship, helping the medic lift their captain, and together the group of pilots moved through the vestibule that led deeper into the platform. Inin and the other civilians followed them.

I hoped the area wasn't too dangerous, and that any scavengers were long gone. But Gilaf and the others had training. They could handle themselves and protect the others.

I turned to Jorgen and the other humans. We'd come a long way, and I needed to convince them to stick with me a little longer.

"What do we do now?" Jorgen asked. "We don't know if your friend Rinakin wants to be rescued. And these people . . . are they the only UrDail we can expect to be on our side?"

"Rinakin *is* on our side," I said.

"Yes," Jorgen said. "But he's speaking publicly against you, and he's only one person."

Lots of people would listen to Rinakin, which made him one very important person. But given what we'd just heard, that worked against us at the moment.

"You're a fugitive," Jorgen said. "And now *we're* fugitives for helping you."

"We're not going to escape court-martial if we go home," Sadie said. "Are we?"

"Jorgen might," Kimmalyn said. "Is your mom really going to put you in prison for defection?"

"Maybe," Jorgen said. "But it doesn't make me feel any better knowing they're willing to do that to the rest of you. *Scud*. What do we do?"

"You could call Cobb," FM said. "See what he wants us to do."

Jorgen shook his head. "Cobb said he'd be in touch, but I can't call him. He's trying to maintain the illusion that he had nothing to do with our departure, so my parents don't shut him out of the loop entirely."

"Can they do that?" Kimmalyn asked.

"Maybe," Jorgen said. "There aren't a lot of specific codes on the books for how intergalactic diplomacy should be handled, which gives them some leeway."

"Diplomacy is a mistake," I said. "You're no better off there than you are here, not as long as your government is considering capitulation."

"If both our governments are moving in the same direction, what are *we* going to do about it?" Jorgen asked. "We're pilots. We don't have control over things like that."

"There are plenty of people on ReDawn who will do the right thing when they can see it clearly," I said. "But they're being deceived. Unity talks like we can all get along, but we can't do that with people who want to oppress us." I looked around at the others, gauging their reactions. I was in a precarious position here. If they decided not to help me, the other pilots and I would be in it alone.

The humans all looked at each other. They seemed resigned, which in this case was a good thing. I just needed to give them a reason to believe there was hope.

"Rescuing Rinakin will make a difference," I said. "He's beloved by many of my people. If Unity is threatening him and we get him to safety, then he can speak the truth, tell people what Unity is really up to. They've taken over the military, captured our people. If people hear that news from Rinakin's mouth, more of them will turn to our cause."

Jorgen sighed. "Okay. We're committed. Let's make the best of it." He looked up through the skylight at the giant autoturret, which had stopped firing. Through the negative realm, I could feel Quilan moving farther away. "What exactly is this platform doing here?"

"It was a battle platform," I said. "Abandoned after the second war, centuries ago. I think it used to move through the miasma at will, but now it simply drifts."

"We should take a look around," Jorgen said. "The platforms on Detritus are similar, and they have all kinds of capabilities besides the autofire. Maybe it will have a shield we could get working, or something else that might help us rescue Rinakin." Jorgen turned to me. "Is there a reason you don't hyperjump in and pull him up here? Is it because you don't know where he is?"

"If he keeps broadcasting, it will be easy enough to triangulate his location," I said. "But some of the Unity cytonics have the ability to inhibit, so they won't leave Rinakin unguarded. The Superiority also granted Unity some cytonic inhibitors. More than the one in this ship." I gestured toward the wreckage.

"Is the inhibitor still on board?" FM asked.

It was a good question. The ship's inhibitor had stayed active, even after the cockpit was obliterated. It wasn't working now, but the technology should still be on board. I stepped into the empty hull, examining what was left of the ship.

Rows of passenger seats were mostly still intact, and at the end of the aisle was a panel with instrumentation—and a box set into the side of the ship. I moved up the aisle with FM right behind me.

"That's a taynix box," FM said, and she squeezed past me and knelt down next to it. The other humans crowded around the hole in the hull, watching.

"There isn't a slug in it," Jorgen said. "We'd be able to feel it if there were."

He was right—the box felt empty to me. But when FM unlatched it and pulled it open, a pale blue taynix with bright green spines stared up at us out of the box.

"Hey, baby," FM said, reaching in gently and pulling the slug out. She looked at Jorgen over her shoulder. "No slug in the box, huh?"

"I can't sense it in the negative realm," I said. I couldn't even touch the area where it rested in FM's arms, though the area had been too small for me to notice before. "It's . . . inhibited itself."

"It's *adorable*," Sadie said.

FM ran a hand down its spines, and it hummed quietly, as if nervous.

"I guess that answers the question about how they do it," Jorgen said. "And now we have one. Maybe we could figure out how to use it to inhibit the platform."

"Can't you just ask it nicely?" I asked.

"We can try," FM said. "But it might need a little more instruction. Working with the others took time."

"Time," the slug trilled softly.

"Still," Jorgen said. "If we can harness the platform's capabilities, we could buy ourselves some. That would also give us some time to determine Rinakin's location."

FM continued to hold the new slug, and she didn't seem eager to let it go. Technically this slug should belong to my people, because it was recovered on our turf, but I didn't know what to do with it, so for now it was probably better off in her hands. "I expect they'll be keeping Rinakin on or near the Council tree. That's where the Unity cytonics live."

"More trees," Nedd said. "Do you really live on those? Not down on the surface of the planet?"

"ReDawn is a gas giant," I said. "There is no surface, except the core. And the atmosphere down there isn't breathable. We only go down there for mining."

"This is your home planet?" Sadie asked. "Like, your people lived in trees even before you had starfighters?"

"Yes," I said. "We've always made the trees of ReDawn our home."

Sadie made a little squealing noise. "That is *so cool*."

"And kind of terrifying," FM said. "What if you fall?"

"Do you often fall off your platforms?" I asked.

"No," FM said. "But we don't really *live* on those. It's a military base. The civilians on Detritus all live underground. There are no children on Platform Prime."

"We learn young how to be careful," I said. "We don't walk on the edges of the branches without safety equipment. We have walls and railings and nets. A few people fall every year, but those deaths are mostly due to equipment failures, like having a cord break when rubber-jumping."

They all stared at me like I'd lost my mind.

"All right," Jorgen said. "Let's do some poking around and see what we can find on this platform."

I nodded. I wasn't sure what there would be to work with, but at least the humans weren't talking about fleeing anymore.

"Alanik," Jorgen said. "Why don't you try the radio while we look around? See if you can find any more broadcasts that might give us a clue what the people who took Rinakin are planning."

The humans probably wanted to conference without me, but I couldn't stop them from talking to each other. Trying would make me look desperate. "Okay," I said.

FM carried the blue slug out of the ship, and the humans moved toward the doorway that led deeper into the platform. I climbed out of the Superiority ship and moved to Jorgen's cockpit to fiddle with the radio. There was a box bolted beneath his dash, similar to the one that had held the inhibitor slug. I popped the door open, and Boomslug peered out at me expectantly, like I might provide more algae strips.

He was about to be sorely disappointed.

The humans hadn't been gone for more than a few minutes when someone approached the open canopy. Arturo walked toward me with his yellow and blue slug in a sling across his chest. He must have come back to retrieve it from his ship.

I moved to stand, but Arturo held up a hand. "Alanik," he said. "Can we talk?"

"Yes," I said.

Arturo looked over his shoulder, like he was afraid we'd be overheard. The slug in the sling regarded me quizzically. "I was thinking about what you said on Detritus, about the Superiority wanting you to turn over the humans you were working with."

I hadn't said that to him, so I guessed Jorgen must have told him. "We weren't working with any humans," I said.

"Right," Arturo said, his face grim. "But you are now."

Oh. I'd been so focused on getting help that I hadn't thought of how that would look. Clearly I shouldn't have told Jorgen about that particular demand.

"We were just fighting the people who want to turn you over to the Superiority together," I said.

"Sure," Arturo said. "But shooting at a few ships doesn't mean you aren't planning to betray us in some other way."

That was true, and nothing I could say would prove otherwise. "So you believe I'm lying to you."

"I don't know," Arturo said. "I'm not sure what your motivations are. Jorgen believes you do want to make an alliance with Detritus, that you're going to teach him how to use his powers."

"Use his powers!" his taynix added, as if for emphasis.

"Easy, Naga," Arturo said, petting its spines.

"I will," I said. "I would be happy to, because we're working together. You all risked a lot to be here."

"We did," Arturo said. "So I hope you didn't come to Detritus looking for humans you could use to appease the Superiority."

I bristled. "I would never work with them. Their wood is rotted all the way through."

"I want to believe you," Arturo said. "So does Jorgen. That's why he didn't tell Cobb about what you said."

He should have, obviously. Their commander had made a decision without all the information. "Jorgen suspects me of deceiving you," I said.

"No," Arturo said. "Jorgen is too busy worrying about whether he disobeyed orders. *I'm* worried you might have deceived us." He looked me straight in the eyes. His were dark and deep, not clear and bright like most UrDail. "Can we trust you?"

"You already have. You did it when you left your planet with me." I'd fled when I'd first met them, not willing to offer them my trust, yet they'd come to help me anyway. I wouldn't have done the same, but I was glad that in this way they weren't like me.

"We did," Arturo said. "Because the potential benefits outweigh the risks. We need allies, same as you. And we may be clueless when it comes to galactic politics, but we're not helpless. If you turn on us, we will fight back, you understand?"

Arturo presented the threat calmly and evenly, like it was nothing more than a fact.

These humans possessed hyperdrives, had found the secret where I had failed. They'd also survived for nearly a century in the face of Superiority hostility.

"It would be a very serious mistake to underestimate you," I said.

"I'm glad we agree on that."

"And I have no intention of betraying you or your people."

Arturo kept watching me, his face thoughtful, evaluating me. It bothered me that I couldn't read in his eyes what it was that he saw.

"Thank you," Arturo said. "I hope we can keep this between us."

And then he turned and walked confidently back in the direction Jorgen and the others had gone.

I watched until he was out of sight. I hadn't baited the humans here with the intention of trading them to the Superiority, but I did want to use them, in a sense. Unity used the specter of human extinction to terrify my people into submission. If my people saw humans fighting on our side, they'd see that resistance was possible, even against terrifying odds. Their *existence* was a weapon I could use against my enemies.

Given the circumstances, I would be foolish to do otherwise.

13

I could only wait in the ship for so long before I set off to find Jorgen and the others. It wasn't hard to find Jorgen at least, because I could feel his mind and follow in that direction. The passageways here were smooth and sterile, similar to the ones on Detritus, though these were structured more like large tubes than square halls.

Jorgen seemed to shift for a moment, and I wondered if he could sense me coming toward him.

And then— *Alanik?* he said in my mind.

Yes, I replied. *You were able to establish contact.*

It's . . . similar to communicating with the slugs, but also different. It's easier when Spensa establishes the connection first.

Have you spoken with Spensa recently? I didn't know if she'd be able to communicate out of the negative realm the same way we communicated through it.

Yes, twice. Both times she kind of . . . appeared. But she wasn't really there. Not like a hyperjump.

There was a kind of sadness that accompanied this. A wistfulness maybe.

You and Spensa are close, I said.

Another emotion joined the sadness. Embarrassment perhaps.

Oh, I said. *You and Spensa are a mate pair?*

A what? A . . . no, not a mate pair. I mean, there is no mating involved. I mean—

I laughed, and Jorgen's voice disappeared from my mind. I thought he'd withdrawn intentionally, and if so that was good. He was learning even without my instruction. I'd found that was the best way, with cytonic powers. They weren't learned directly so much as experienced and guided. Your mind knew what to do intuitively, if only you could get out of your own way and let it.

I caught up to some of the humans outside a room filled with instrumentation panels. Jorgen and Kimmalyn leaned in the doorway, watching FM as she pored over them.

"Did you find anything useful?" I asked.

"Maybe," Jorgen said. "I don't suppose you happen to be an engineer?"

"No, only a pilot," I said. I approached and glanced at the buttons and switches FM was examining. "Do any of you have expertise?"

"Rig does," FM said. "He might be able to tell us if any of this would activate a shield, or connect to a cytonic inhibitor."

"Any of those would be useful," I said.

FM looked over her shoulder at Jorgen. "As much as I'd love to ask Rig, I don't know that dragging him into this is a good idea."

"I wonder if we could get him out without anyone noticing," Jorgen said. "If we had one of the slugs take us H-O-M-E . . ."

The pin translated that last bit as a set of letters, but I had no idea what they spelled in the human's language. "What does that mean?" I asked.

Jorgen sighed. "It's the word for the place where you live. FM accidentally made that the keyword for the slugs to take us back to Detritus."

"It wasn't an *accident*," FM said. "It was a *logical choice*."

"And we're trying to get them to only do it if we say their names first as a command," Jorgen continued. "But sometimes they mess up and someone says something like, I miss H-O-M-E, and their slug takes them to the engineering bay on Platform Prime. Which is only an inconvenience if they were, say, in the mess hall or something."

Kimmalyn sighed. "But it's a lot more annoying if you were about to climb into a cleansing pod, naked as the day you were born."

"Not that she would know," FM said.

"Bless the stars of those startled engineers," Kimmalyn added.

"So now we're reduced to spelling basic words," Jorgen said. "When we could have picked something more unusual for the code word."

"So you say the word," I said, "and the slug hyperjumps with you? That's convenient."

"When it works it's awesome," Jorgen said. "When it doesn't it's annoying at best."

"Humiliating at worst," Kimmalyn said.

"It could be *life threatening*," Jorgen insisted.

"Hey," FM said. "You and Rig were the ones who said we should stick with the same word when we trained the rest of the slugs for simplicity's sake."

"We're still working with them," Jorgen said. "We only had a short time with them before you arrived. But so far they will all go H-O-M-E when they're asked. Some of them will also take us out a couple of kilometers if we tell them to J-U-M-P."

"I don't know what that means, either," I said. "I don't think the pins know how to spell."

"It's the word for leaping up in the air," FM said. "Also the second half of hyperjump, which they don't seem to recognize as a command, thank goodness. They're all a little better at only doing that command when we say their names first."

"Probably because they'd rather go H-O-M-E than hop somewhere random," Kimmalyn said. "Wouldn't we all?"

"Are those the only commands they answer to?" I asked. The humans were freely giving up the details on how to use their hyperdrives, but I wasn't going to point this out to them.

"If you want to do anything else," FM said, "you need a cytonic. Jorgen can ask the slugs to hyperjump anywhere he can see, or anywhere he can visualize that the slugs can recognize. The rest of us are limited to verbal commands, which we have to drill beforehand. The slugs pick it up pretty quickly, and they understand some basic abstract concepts like danger. We're working on a bonding program. That's why we keep them with us in slings—though engineering is working on a backpack as well. The idea is that even if the pilot can't give a command, the slugs are attached enough to their pilot partners that they want to pull us out of danger, and are familiar enough with us to understand what might be helpful and what won't."

"That seems like a lot to ask of a slug."

"Slug!" Gill trilled softly.

"It is," FM said. "But they're doing great at it. Aren't you, Gill?"

"Gill!" Kimmalyn's slug said, and immediately appeared on top of the dash in front of FM, extending itself up to peer at Gill in FM's sling.

"Good girl, Happy," FM said, reaching into her pocket and pulling out a tin of a slimy-looking substance. The taynix eagerly ate it off her finger, despite Gill's best efforts to nudge its way in and take some.

"That's the other command they know," Jorgen said. "They can recognize each other's names and go find each other, regardless of distance. So even if Alanik didn't want to go to Detritus to get Rig—"

"Are we learning how useless we are without the engineers again?" Sadie asked, walking up behind us with the others. "I thought we knew that already."

"You'd think," T-Stall—or Catnip—said. "But it turns out there is no limit to the number of times we have to learn obvious things."

"Speak for yourself," the other one said. "I knew it already. I was simply waiting for the rest of you to catch up."

Arturo followed behind them with Nedd. He didn't acknowledge me at all, as if our conversation had never happened.

It was entirely reasonable for him not to trust me. But it still *bothered* me that he didn't, though he was justified—smart, even—in thinking I might betray them.

"Does anyone else feel . . . heavier here?" Nedd asked.

"Yes," I said. "Our planets have a slight gravitational difference. I noticed that on Detritus. I don't think it's enough of a difference to matter."

"It matters to my quads," Nedd said. "I feel like I've been doing laps around the orchard at Alta." He blinked at me. "You probably don't have orchards, since you live on trees."

"We do, actually," I said. "We graft smaller trees into the branches of the large ones. They also grow naturally in places where the bark has disintegrated into debris."

FM handed Kimmalyn's taynix back to her. "I was hoping looking at the tech might spark something, since I've spent a lot of time listening to Rig talk about this stuff. But no. Still don't know enough to be useful." She looked over at Jorgen. "It's possible that Command doesn't know Rig was in on us leaving. I don't want to get him in trouble."

"We could try to bring him out and then return him without anyone knowing," Jorgen said again. "We might need Alanik's help for that, though. If we use the H-O-M-E position to hyperjump in, that will be obvious. My mom might even have people staking it out, waiting for us."

"I want to go," FM says. "I can explain the situation to Rig."

"Any of us could explain the situation to Rig," Nedd said.

"Yes," FM said slowly. "But he trusts me."

"He trusts all of us, doesn't he?" Nedd said. "Except maybe Alanik. No offense, Alanik."

"Why would I take offense to that?" I asked. "It's factual."

"See?" Nedd said. "I knew I liked you."

Arturo gave Nedd a look I couldn't quite read.

"Alanik could go get Rig," Jorgen said. "And FM could go with her to explain the situation. Is that all right with you, Alanik?"

Was I willing to take someone with me when I walked onto a platform full of people who now probably considered me a criminal? "Yes, of course," I said.

"I can jump straight to Rig on my own though," FM said. "Gill is really good at finding his slug."

"I still want you to take Alanik with you," Jorgen said. "We *think* Gill will be able to get back easily, but I don't want you stranded on Detritus, facing court-martial."

"Wait," Nedd said. "Why is Gill really good at finding Rig's slug?"

"Because we've drilled them so many times," FM said. She looked a little pink, and sounded defensive.

"Okay," Nedd said. "But we've practiced with all the slugs. We've practiced so many times that I think maybe *I* could find these slugs in the nowhere—"

"You couldn't," Jorgen said.

"Leave it, Nedd," Arturo said.

"But I'm just saying—"

"I hear what you're saying!" FM said, too loudly.

Everyone stared at her.

She sighed. "Our slugs are really good at finding each other because Rig and I are dating, and we use the slugs to visit each other so we don't have to deal with awkward questions, because we weren't ready to tell everyone. There. Now you know."

"Oh," Nedd said. He always seemed to have something to say about everything, but now he seemed abashed. Based on the reactions of the group, I guessed that Jorgen and Kimmalyn already knew, and T-Stall and Catnip didn't care.

"Are mate-pairs taboo in your culture?" I asked. "You all seem very embarrassed to talk about them."

"Not taboo," FM said. "But . . . personal." She looked at me. "Do the UrDail always speak openly about these things?"

"Fairly openly," I said. "It's definitely nothing to be embarrassed about. It can depend on your family culture, but most families are thrilled by mate-pairings, because they welcome children."

"None of us are thinking about children," Jorgen said, quickly.

"Can you imagine?" FM said.

I didn't understand. "Because you're at war? You were all born during the war, weren't you?" Unless I drastically misunderstood human aging patterns, they would have had to be.

"Because we're too young," FM said. "And we're pilots on the front lines. Not a life conducive to raising kids. A lot of our parents were pilots, but most of us had at least one parent who wasn't flying."

"Wait," I said. "You're raised by your *parents*?"

The humans all looked at me like this was a very stupid question. "Yes," Kimmalyn said. "Who were you raised by?"

"My grandparents," I said. "We're encouraged to find a mate-pair young, so we can have children while our parents are still young and healthy enough to raise the children. Parents have to work to support their families. They don't have time or energy for childcare. Besides, we only have *two* of them, when there are at least four grandparents involved, so the odds of one of them being able to care for the children is so much higher than with parents."

"Huh," Sadie said. "I guess that does make sense when you put it that way."

I was trying to picture how human parents must handle having babies while—to use FM's example—still of age to fly in the air force. That sounded like a terrible system.

"Okay," Jorgen said. "I think the lesson here is that none of us want to talk about relationships or plan to have children in the near future, except maybe Alanik."

"I'm not going to have a child," I said. "I'm not in a mate-pair.

But it doesn't bother me to say so. It's not shameful in my culture either way."

"Well, I feel shameful," Nedd said. "Everyone is coupled up but me! FM has a boyfriend, and Arturo is basically engaged—"

"I am *not*," Arturo said.

"And Jorgen and Spensa—"

"Shut up, Nedd—" Jorgen said.

"Kimmalyn, do you have a boyfriend?"

Kimmalyn looked suddenly uncomfortable. "Um, *no*."

"But seriously, it's bad enough that I have to hang around while Arturo and Bryn are making kissy faces at each other—"

"You won't have to do that anymore, trust me," Arturo said.

"What?" Nedd said. "Why?"

"Because we broke up."

Now everyone stared at Arturo. He usually had a confident air about him, but now he withered a bit.

Okay. Humans definitely got unreasonably embarrassed about relationships. It was amazing their species managed to survive.

"Seriously?" Nedd asked. He seemed much more concerned now. "When did that happen?"

"A few days ago. She wrote me a letter. But I thought we established that none of us wanted to talk about relationships. Can we please change the subject?"

"Stars, please," Jorgen said.

"The question is," FM said, "do we think Rig's help with the platform will be beneficial enough that we're willing to ask him to risk a military trial with the rest of us?"

"If it was a military trial, we'd be cleared," Jorgen said. "Because Cobb is our military leader, and he told us to go. It would have to be a civil trial for us to be convicted, and they can't try us civilly because all we did was disobey orders, which isn't a violation of civilian law."

"And we stole starships," Kimmalyn reminded him.

"Which are military property!" Jorgen said. "Also should be tried by the DDF. No defection, no grand larceny."

Everyone looked skeptical, including Jorgen, but if it helped him feel better I didn't see any harm in leaving him to his faulty logic.

"You disobeyed your mother," Nedd said. "What do you think she's going to do to you for that?"

"I don't know," Jorgen said. "But at least the rest of you are off the hook there."

"I'd like my ship," I said. "Otherwise we'll have one fewer pilot in the air. If we brought it here with Rig, could he finish reassembling it?" After my last experience in a human vessel, I'd take my own ship back as long as it flew.

"I bet he'd do it," FM said. "He felt really bad that he'd dismantled it and then you needed it."

"I think the biggest question," Arturo said, "is what are our *other* options?"

Everyone was quiet.

"Okay," Jorgen said. "The rest of us will stay here and see if we can find a place where the platform is built to interface with the taynix."

"Interface with them?" I asked.

"If this platform has hypercomm or hyperdrive technology, it will probably have taynix boxes," FM said. "Like the one in the broken Superiority ship."

"We'll look for the boxes while you're gone," Jorgen said, "and then Rig can help us figure it out when he gets here."

I hoped we wouldn't be gone long enough for them to do much searching. Going to get Rig and my ship should be an in-and-out kind of mission.

But these things rarely worked out that simply.

"All right," I said. "Are we ready?"

FM scritched Gill on the head. "Let me take us," she said. "Gill needs the practice."

I was a bit leery of jetting around the universe at the whims of a slug, but the humans seemed certain this would work. Besides, I'd wanted to learn the secrets to hyperdrive technology. This was my chance to see one in action.

"Okay," I said. FM stood beside me and put a hand on my shoulder.

"Scud, I hope he's not in the shower or something," she said.

"Or in a meeting with Command," Jorgen said.

"Or that. Gill," FM said. "Take me to Drape."

"Drape!" the slug trilled cheerfully.

It took all my concentration not to fight the pull of the negative realm as I was sucked into it by a force completely out of my control.

14

I was unprepared for how it would feel to hover in the negative realm while the eyes fixed their penetrating stares elsewhere. Normally I had their full attention, but this time I was beneath their notice. It was a relief to hide, but it also felt a little insulting.

We emerged in a hallway of the humans' platform immediately in front of Rig, who screamed.

"Scud!" he shouted. "That is *terrifying* when I'm not expecting it."

"Shh!" FM said, and she grabbed him by the arm and pulled him into the nearest room. I took a look up and down the empty hall, then followed them. Into a storage closet from the look of it. There didn't appear to be any alternate exits, but I supposed we could hyperjump out if we needed to.

"I thought you said you do that a lot," I whispered at FM. "I didn't expect him to be so *loud*."

"Usually we arrange it beforehand," Rig said. "Also, you *told* her we do that a lot?"

"It was Nedd's fault," FM said.

"Um, okay," Rig said. "Well, hi. You should know there's a warrant out for your immediate arrest. I could be held in contempt simply for talking to you."

I'd *thought* Jorgen's justifications sounded like a stretch. FM gripped Rig's arm, and they stood close together. And I stood unfortunately close to them, because there wasn't a lot of room between the shelves of . . . packaged algae strips, it looked like. We must be near their kitchen facilities.

"We need your help on ReDawn," FM said. "We found something. A platform that used to move around the planet but now is in disrepair. It seems similar to the ones we have here, but we don't really know what we're looking at. Or how to use it."

"So you decided to pop into the middle of the hallway? In a place where you're *wanted* for *desertion*?"

"Is it only desertion?" FM asked. "We were worried they'd charge us with defection."

"Also grand larceny," I said. "For stealing eight starships."

"Nine," FM said. "Including yours."

"I'm not sure they've *decided* what they're going to officially charge you with. But it seems like a problem for you to get arrested for *any* of it."

This was all beside the point. "Are you willing to come to ReDawn to help us with the platform?" I asked.

Rig blinked at me. "Am I willing to—"

"Come with us to look at the platform," FM said. "If no one sees us leave, you might be able to come back without anyone knowing you were helping us."

"Except I'd also like to take my ship," I reminded her.

"Right," FM said. "Well, you could tell them we kidnapped you or something."

"And add that to our list of crimes," I added.

Rig stared at us with wide eyes. "I'll help you. But you should know, there's a lot going on here too. Cobb and Jeshua met with some representatives from the Superiority."

That was right. Cobb gave that as his reason for not wanting us to return to Detritus with the Independence flight. "Have they returned?" I asked.

Rig nodded. "It was a quick meeting. They used a hyperdrive to meet at a ship right outside the shield and exchanged terms. Then they came back, and they've been discussing what they want to do. I think they might be talking over the hypercomm to the Superiority people now."

"Hold on," I said, reaching into the negative realm, searching for nearby voices.

—*understand your concerns*— said a voice I didn't recognize. —*danger to themselves and others—learn proper safety measures to prevent disaster—send your cytonics to us for training*—

"They're asking your leaders to send your cytonics to the Superiority," I said. "They've tried to get us to do the same thing on ReDawn, first by asking, and then by threatening us. I think Quilan believes he'll have proven himself if he delivers me personally, and that if he does the Superiority will leave him and the other cytonics alone."

"Jorgen's parents aren't considering that, are they?" FM asked Rig. "Turning their *own son* over to the Superiority?"

"My own parents argued I might be *better off* being trained by the Superiority," I said. "You'd be surprised what people will believe."

"Is it possible that *would* be better?" Rig asked. "We're in the dark when it comes to cytonic potential. You can obviously do a lot more than Jorgen can, and the Superiority cytonics might know even more."

"They do," I said. "But they aren't going to help you, no matter what they say."

"I can see the assembly considering it though," FM said. "Believing that trading a couple of lives to end the war would be an acceptable sacrifice. Risking a few to save so many. That's what we all signed up for, isn't it? They might see it as no worse than letting their son join the DDF, and the potential for peace . . ."

I held my breath. I'd told them over and over what I thought about making peace with the Superiority. They already knew what

I had to say. As I listened, I picked out another voice over the hypercomm. Jeshua Weight. —*assurances that no harm will come to them*—

—*valuable,* the alien voice said. *Never be so aggressive as to*—

—*aggressive enough to exterminate us*—

—*work with us, you have nothing to fear*—*turn over your hyperdrives, and*—

"The Superiority representatives say they won't hurt the cytonics," I said. Which might be true, but sending them away was still a terrible idea. "And Cobb was right. They want you to turn over the taynix too."

"We can't do that," FM said. "Right?"

"Right?" Drape said, and Rig put a hand on his spines.

"They're trying to imprison you here," I said. "It's what they do. Keep you isolated on your planet unless you play by their rules."

"That's what they've always done to us," Rig said. "Ever since our fleet crashed here."

"But this time we have the power to leave," FM said. "We can't give that up without risking that they'll go back to trying to exterminate us. The shield stops them for now—"

"But not forever," Rig said. "That's true."

"And we're not giving up the taynix," FM said. "No matter what."

—*negotiate. We would of course need assurances that*—*if we are to cooperate*—

Human or UrDail, politicians were all the same. "It sounds like they're thinking about it."

"I meant *us*," FM said. "*We* aren't giving them up. The politicians will have to come to ReDawn and *take* them from us."

I smiled. "I'd climb that tree with you."

"I imagine Cobb will too," Rig said. "He can't be in favor of this."

—*your generous offer*— another voice said over the hypercomm.

Admiral Cobb, I thought. *—need time to collect the taynix—transport them to you and continue our negotiations—*

"Um," I said. "It sounds like he's also considering it."

"Seriously?" Rig said.

FM shook her head. "We should get more of the taynix out while we still can."

"We can't take them if we aren't ordered to," Rig said. "We'd need to talk to Cobb."

"Cobb says he's in favor of sending them to the Superiority!" FM said. "If that's true, he won't help."

"He might be saying that for optics," Rig said. "Maybe he'd be glad to have an opportunity to send them away so they *can't* be turned over."

"He can only do that so many times," I said, "before your politicians will catch on."

"That's true," FM said. "Maybe we should take them ourselves, without asking."

Rig looked at FM in alarm, but he didn't argue with her.

"Where would we find them?" I asked.

"The ones that can hyperjump are all over the platform," Rig said. "We have most of them partnered with pilots. Some of the hypercomm and mindblade slugs are kept in Engineering, but it's crawling with people right now."

So we wouldn't be able to pull them all out without alerting people to our presence. "I think we should get my ship and get out of here as soon as possible. Is it capable of flight?"

"Not right now," Rig said. "I'm sorry, I haven't had time to—"

"Can you fix it on ReDawn?" I asked. If not, we'd need to take another human ship. When it was time for us to make our move, I wanted all the Independence pilots in the air with us.

"Yes," Rig said. "Given a few hours, I could put it together again."

"What else is the Superiority saying?" FM asked.

I'd been distracted from the transmission, but I focused on it again.

—*meeting to assure you of our intentions—do what is best for your species and the intergalactic interests—*

"They're setting up another meeting," I said. "Probably to turn over taynix, I'm guessing."

"What about Gran-Gran?" Rig asked.

"Who?" I said.

"Becca Nightshade. Spensa's grandmother. If the Superiority is really asking them to turn over the cytonics, she might be in danger."

"Would you like me to contact her?" I asked.

"We should at least warn her," FM said. "Maybe we should take her with us."

I paused, reaching toward the planet below. *Into* the planet, beneath the surface, through the underground caverns where the humans lived.

A voice reached out to meet me.

Alanik? it said.

So she'd heard of me. I spent so long unconscious on this platform, it made sense.

Yes, I said. *Your government is considering a deal to turn their cytonics over to the Superiority. Do you need us to rescue you?*

What followed wasn't words exactly, but a strong sense of reluctance. *Detritus is not our home*, Gran-Gran said. *But these are my people. I won't abandon them.*

Jorgen left to help me, so I felt the need to defend him. *Jorgen didn't abandon them*, I said. *He's gone for help. You could come with us.*

I didn't know Gran-Gran, but I wasn't about to let an old woman to be given over to the Superiority. Besides, we could use another cytonic. The more we had on our side, the more we evened the playing field with Unity.

They are coming for you, Gran-Gran said. *You need to go.*

Who? I asked. Quilan and the other UrDail cytonics couldn't hyperjump, but the Superiority cytonics could.

Did they know we were here?

Go, Gran-Gran said. *A warrior fights. She does not yield, and she does not abandon her people.*

I nodded. "She wants to stay here," I said. "She knows they might try to use her as a bargaining chip, but she won't abandon Detritus."

"Is that a good idea?" FM asked.

"If it's Gran-Gran's idea, you won't talk her out of it," Rig said.

"I can respect her decision," I said. "But she says they're coming for us. I don't know who, but we need to go."

"I still think we should try to get more of the slugs out before we go," FM said. "There are dozens of them here with the other pilots."

"The entire military isn't going to desert," Rig said. "We'd only put ourselves in danger trying to convince them."

"Jorgen can get them to answer him, right?" I asked. "What if I called them to come to me? Do you think they'd do it?"

"Depends," Rig said. "They might be attached enough to their pilots to stay. They'd be more likely to come if you promised them something like caviar."

"I have a little," FM said. "Not enough to feed them all. If you promise them caviar and we don't deliver, that's bad for their training, but not as bad as being *given* to the *Superiority*."

I grabbed a large box of algae strips on the shelf. "We could bring these. The people on Wandering Leaf are going to be getting hungry, so we should probably bring some for them anyway."

"Good idea," Rig said, and he picked up a jug of a white substance.

"Custard," FM said. "Kimmalyn will be happy."

"If I'm going to try to call the slugs, it'll draw attention," I said. "We should do it from the ship, so we can leave immediately afterward."

Rig looked at FM, as if to ask if we were actually doing this.

"I think you should," FM said to me. "I don't feel good about leaving them here, even with their pilots, when we don't know if the other flights will defend them."

"They probably won't," Rig said. "The assembly has come down pretty hard on you guys for what you did, and Cobb has had to go along with it."

"All right," I said. "I can jump us to my ship in the landing bay."

I pulled us through the negative realm beneath those strangely distracted eyes. We were only going a short distance, but space didn't work the same in there. If we were dealing in relative distances we should have spent a much shorter time in the negative realm compared to when we jumped from ReDawn, yet we hung there for a moment and then emerged out the other side in the large hangar next to my disassembled ship. Through a large skylight, I could see the platforms above and snatches of the sparkling shield that encased the planet.

"You're sure you can make it fly again?" I asked Rig quietly.

"It'll take me a bit," Rig said, "but yes, I can."

"It's got a better chance of working than the one you left with last time," FM added.

"Last time!" Gill trilled, and FM shushed him.

"Wait, what happened to that one?" Rig whispered.

"They're here somewhere," a voice said from the edge of the landing bay. "Find them."

FM and Rig huddled closer together under the wing, the containers of food tucked up by their knees.

"That's Cobb," Rig whispered.

And so it was. Had Spensa's grandmother alerted him? She hadn't wanted to abandon her people, but she'd sounded like she wanted us to keep fighting.

No, it was probably the Superiority. One of their cytonics might have warned them of our arrival and then noticed us hyperjumping to the landing pad.

"Alanik," FM whispered. "The slugs."

We might be able to count on Cobb to cover for us for a moment, but not for long. Whatever cytonic was watching would be able to feel me calling for the slugs, but if I hyperjumped out fast enough they wouldn't be able to stop me.

I gave FM a sharp nod, pressed my back to the lower part of my fuselage, and reached out across the base.

There were a *lot* of those tiny minds. Dozens at least. As I reached toward them, they turned to me as if curious.

I could work with that. I wasn't sure how much language the slugs understood, but in the negative realm all communication was reduced to thoughts, which anyone could understand. Still, I didn't want to get too complicated. *Friend*, I sent to them. They obviously understood that concept, given how attached they were to each other and to their pilots. And this was a concept every living being responded to: *Food*.

I could feel them answering me, some of them hungrier than others, all of them searching for a social connection like it was the thing they longed for most. These things had relationships with each other long before the humans captured them, I realized, but they saw the humans not as kidnappers but as a joyous addition to their family.

Many of them didn't want to leave.

Footsteps approached as Cobb's people spread out across the hangar. It wasn't going to take them long to find us here. I didn't have much time.

More family, I told them, sending them images of Rig and FM and Jorgen.

That intrigued them. They knew and liked all three of them, and wanted to see them again.

More boots clicking on the metal surface of the platform. Movement over the edge of the wing, and then . . .

"We have to go," Rig whispered.

Come, I called to the taynix.

And then Cobb appeared, several paces away. His eyes fixed on us under the wing.

And half a dozen taynix popped into existence at our feet.

FM and Rig reached forward, grabbing the slugs, while Cobb's jaw dropped.

"They're here!" he shouted.

No. Not covering for us. The opposite of that. We probably should have expected that, given that we were stealing his military's hyperdrives without permission.

More slugs appeared—maybe as many as a dozen now.

Cobb strode toward us, like he was about to yank us out from beneath the wing.

It might have been for show, but he didn't *have* to alert them to our presence, did he?

I wasn't going to stay here and find out. I reached into the negative realm, toward Wandering Leaf and the rest of the humans. With the ship to my back and my shoulder pressed against FM, I *pulled*, and the landing bay disappeared.

15

We emerged from the negative realm in the hangar on Wandering Leaf, which was empty of both humans and UrDail.

"That never gets less terrifying," Rig said.

"And disorienting," FM said. "And we don't even see the creepy eyes."

"Be glad for that," I said. I reached out again, searching for Jorgen's mind. I found him and the taynix belonging to the other flight members. They hadn't gone far.

"Why did Cobb come after us like that?" FM asked. "He didn't even try to talk to us. Maybe Jeshua is watching him too closely?"

"Maybe," Rig said. "Cobb played along with everything they said after you left. If I hadn't been there when he gave you the order to go, I never would have thought he'd done it."

"Done it!" one of the slugs said.

Cobb was far away now, and whatever Superiority cytonic had been tracking us either couldn't or didn't follow.

That felt more ominous than anything.

"At least we saved these guys," FM said, cuddling the slugs. "Though I don't imagine their pilots are happy with us."

"Happy!" one of the slugs trilled. And then several of them disappeared.

We all climbed out from beneath the wing, FM and Rig hauling the case of algae and the jug of custard with them.

"This way," I said, leading FM and Rig toward the others.

We found them several sections down from the hangar, gathered around an arched open doorway. Most of the flight sat outside with two crates open in front of them. Jorgen was inside, while Arturo leaned in the doorframe, watching the others dubiously.

"Rig!" Kimmalyn said, waving furiously. Several of the new slugs were gathered around her and Happy.

"Hey, everybody," Rig said.

"Look!" Sadie said, waving a half-wrapped wafer bar at us. "We found their old food supplies!"

"The *centuries-old* food supplies?" I asked.

"I don't think so," Nedd said. "I can't read the labels on these, but there's no way this stuff is that old. We took some to your friends, and they said thank you. They wouldn't have done that if we were offering them two-hundred-year-old food, would they?"

I approached, looking at the boxes. "I think you're right. That looks like some salvager's food stash." The wafer bars were individually wrapped, and the outer box did bear the date of origin. "Looks like they're only five years old."

"Delicious," Arturo said.

"This one *is* delicious!" Sadie said. "It has some kind of nuts in it." She looked at me wide-eyed. "Those aren't poisonous to humans or anything, are they?"

"I have no idea what humans find poisonous," I said. "Though your people used to live among us on ReDawn and ate our food, so most of it is probably safe to eat. The nuts are called udal nuts. They grow on bushy plants that live in the crevices of the branches. They're quite good, though I can't vouch for these bars." I pulled one out and unwrapped it. It was more crumbly than usual, probably owing to its age, but at least it hadn't molded.

"Maybe we should have been more careful," Sadie said, scowling at her nut wafer as she set it down.

"It's all right, Sadie," Nedd said. "I'm on my third bar. If you die, I'm going with you."

Sadie did not look comforted.

"We brought you food," FM said, lifting the case of algae strips. "So you don't have to rely on scavenged nut bars."

"Oh, custard!" Kimmalyn said, taking the jug from Rig. "Thanks!"

"You also brought more slugs," Jorgen said, joining Arturo in the doorway. "Why?"

"It's a long story," FM said.

"How long could it be?" Jorgen asked. "You were gone ten minutes tops."

"They were only gone for ten minutes," Sadie said, "and we *still* managed to find the taynix boxes while they were gone." She and Catnip—or T-Stall? I really needed to figure out which was which—slapped their palms together in what I assumed must be a human gesture of celebration.

"Seriously?" FM said. "You found them that quickly?"

"It wasn't hard," Kimmalyn said. "We found a station map of the platform in that engineering room written in English. The control room was labeled on it."

"Shhhhh," T-Stall or Catnip said. "You could have let them think we were *amazing*."

"We *are* amazing," Sadie said. "Amazing at reading maps."

"I want to see this," Rig said, and FM set down the box of algae strips at Sadie's feet and followed Rig and me into the room with Jorgen. The new blue taynix sat on the control panel, and trilled at FM when she walked in.

One wall was dominated by panels and levers and switches, with a wide window above the panels looking over the edge of the platform into the miasma. All around the room, mounted against the walls, were metal boxes like the one in Jorgen's ship.

"Do they all have holoprojectors?" FM asked. "Because if so we could strip those, since we don't need them for the slugs anymore."

Rig knelt down and looked at the wires beneath the panel. "Looks like it's been looted already. But most of the wiring is intact. The wires themselves must not be worth much on this planet."

"Why would they be?" I asked. "They're wires."

"Depends on whether you have the resources to mine the right metals," Rig said. "Some of those are valuable on Detritus."

That made sense. The core of ReDawn was rich with metals, which was why the Superiority bothered with us to begin with. They wanted our resources, and we traded them away for the barest recognition of our dignity, instead of remembering we were in the position of power.

"Taynix are valuable too," Jorgen said. "Seriously, where did those come from?"

"We brought them with us," FM said, "because the Superiority wants to take them."

"Did you talk to Cobb?" Jorgen asked.

"No," FM said. "Cobb and Jeshua were talking to the Superiority over the hypercomm. They've already met with the Superiority once, and the Superiority was asking for them to turn over our cytonics and our hyperdrives."

"FM," Jorgen said. "Please tell me you didn't steal the taynix."

"We didn't *steal* them," FM snapped. "We *rescued* them. Alanik called to them and they came of their own free will."

"They're hyperdrives!" Jorgen said. "Not people. Cobb ordered us to come here, but he *didn't* ask us to take the slugs that were commissioned to *other pilots*—"

FM narrowed her eyes. "Sometimes you have to do the right thing, Jorgen. Even if Command says to do something else."

"*Okay*," Jorgen said in a low voice. "But you were gone *a few minutes*, FM. You didn't think this through. You didn't talk to Cobb, and for all we know he has a plan that depends on the hyperdrives! You can't do this." He looked from me to Rig. "Why did you help her?"

"Um," Rig said.

I didn't have any more of an answer. Arturo was watching me, and I wasn't about to admit that having more hyperdrives on ReDawn seemed like a good idea to me. Arturo wasn't an idiot, and neither was Jorgen. They were probably already putting that together.

"It needed to be done," FM said. "Even if they weren't *living beings* that have *feelings*—"

"The other pilots are *human* beings," Jorgen said. "And you left them without a tool they could use to *survive*, FM. Besides, the fact that the slugs *let* you do this is not good. If they'll respond to Alanik, who they *don't know*, it means enemy cytonics could use the same tactic against us."

"And clearly we need to train that out of them," FM said. "But this time it was a good thing because—"

"This is not a good thing!" Jorgen said. "Coming here when Cobb gave us sort-of orders to do so was one thing, but this is entirely out of the chain of command, *and* you didn't think it through *or consult me* before you did it. You could have had Alanik contact me. We could have had a *conversation* about it—"

FM closed her eyes and drew a deep breath. "You're right, okay? It was rash. But we're not sending them back. Not while *your mother* is considering taking them to the Superiority. That doesn't even make good *tactical* sense, Jorgen, and you know it."

"But *you* don't make the tactical decisions," Jorgen said. "You don't know what the bigger plan is."

"The bigger plan may be to give the taynix to the Superiority!" FM said. "I'm not going to let them do that. And if *you* are, then you are not my flightleader."

Rig and Arturo both stared wide-eyed at FM, like she'd said something horrific. FM looked down at the floor, her hands shaking. "I didn't mean that," she said quietly.

Jorgen stared at FM, his mouth set in an angry line. Rig and Arturo exchanged a concerned look, and outside the control room the rest of the flight had fallen silent.

"Fine," Jorgen said, setting his jaw. "We'll keep them here for now. Though I imagine there are going to be a lot of pilots who are *not thrilled* with us for *stealing their taynix*."

"We'll return them when the situation is safe," FM said through gritted teeth.

Right. Of course they would. They had no intention of sharing with *us*.

I couldn't let the humans leave here with all the slugs. Even *one* could change everything for ReDawn. But they weren't making noise about leaving now, so this wasn't the moment to worry about it. Not when I still had hope they might help me.

"Okay," Rig said. "If the taynix are staying, maybe we should figure out how they interface with this platform."

FM looked like she wanted to flee the room, and Jorgen looked like he wanted to punch someone, but they both nodded.

"Good idea," Arturo said.

"All right then," Rig said. He squeezed FM's shoulder and then moved over to one of the boxes on the wall. "The boxes themselves weren't stripped. Makes sense, if the people here don't know the secrets to hyperdrives."

"We found something weird on that map," Arturo said. "There was a control room and the autoturret systems, of course. But no engines and no navigation systems. Alanik said this platform used to move, but there doesn't seem to be any way to move it, at least not on the schematics we found."

"Interesting," Rig said. "Maybe it requires a hyperdrive to move? Get me something to stand on so I can get a look above the boxes and see how they're interfaced with the platform."

Everything useful in this room that wasn't screwed down appeared to have been looted, but T-Stall and Catnip hauled in a chunk of metal that was tall enough for Rig to boost himself up. While they did, Kimmalyn slipped into the room with us and linked her arm through FM's. She and Jorgen were both still silent. Jorgen leaned against the wall opposite FM with his arms crossed, and FM actively avoided looking at him. It was an improvement over the yelling. The more they fought, the more I worried they'd decide Re-Dawn wasn't worth the trouble. Though if that happened, perhaps I could convince FM to stay and keep the taynix with her. Jorgen was their cytonic, so he could influence the slugs to go with him.

But as we'd discovered, he wasn't the only one.

Rig stared at the debris as Catnip and T-Stall deposited it on the floor. "Is that a piece of a starfighter wing?"

"Yep," one of them said.

"Is it a piece of one of *our* starfighter wings?" Rig asked.

"I had a little trouble with the landing," I said, and the other one snickered.

Rig looked at me like he wondered how I was still alive. "We'll tell you all about it later," Jorgen said. "Right now we need to know what the taynix can do if we interface them with the platform."

Rig boosted himself up on the wing, first knocking on the wall and then swinging open a panel to reveal a circuit board.

"This all looks like it's intact," Rig said. "Either it's not valuable, or the salvagers didn't know it was here. The holoprojectors would have been much more recognizable." Rig climbed down again. "These boxes are labeled underneath, but not in English. Alanik?"

I had to lean over the control panel and crane my neck upward to see the labels. They were in neither English nor my own language, but Mandarin. "This box says it's for the weapons system," I said. "But that doesn't make sense, does it? The weapons systems aren't cytonic."

Rig and Jorgen exchanged a look.

"The autoturrets aren't," Arturo said. "But the map had those facilities in another location. Are there . . . cytonic weapons systems?"

"Maybe," I said. "I've never heard of that."

Still, while the writing on the boxes was a bit antiquated, the meaning was clear. The next few boxes were for the comms system. On the opposite wall I found one with a different label. "This one is for the navigation system."

"So it does have a hyperdrive," FM said.

Rig nodded. "There's only one spot for a navigation slug, and several for the hypercomm. Probably so you could have comm-links open with many people at once. It only takes one slug to move the platform."

I examined the boxes along the third wall. "These are for the defense systems."

"Could be a shield like the one back home," Rig said. "That would be useful. Though I don't know how that would work, because on Detritus the platforms combine to become the shield, and the shield mechanism doesn't require a taynix." He turned to me. "Do you know how this platform was used in the past? Was it part of a larger system?"

"I don't know," I said. "The Superiority doesn't like us teaching the details of our military history. Rinakin taught me some things, but most of our education is limited to being told we were wrong to fight."

"You don't believe that though," FM said. "Why not, if that's what you were taught?"

"Do you believe everything you're told?" I asked.

"No," FM said. "But it's hard for most people to ignore the dominant messaging sometimes, especially when no one is willing to speak against it."

"Oh," I said. "No, the official curriculum is tailored to make us look good for the Superiority, but there has always been turmoil on ReDawn as to whose ideas are the best. There is no shortage of differing opinions here."

"That must be so confusing," Rig said.

"Sometimes," I said. "But it's also liberating. With so many different ideas, it's easier to choose what to believe. Unity would like us to all unite under one set of beliefs, one agreement about what is best. But that takes away our knowledge, reduces our ability to decide what's right and what's wrong."

"So you need each other's ideas to really be free," FM said. "I like that idea."

I didn't feel like we needed Unity, but maybe that was true. Maybe if Independence won we'd do the same, simplifying what we taught to make us always in the right. Maybe the tension between us was what truly allowed the conversation to happen.

If we wanted to maintain that tension, I needed to make sure the Independence survived.

Jorgen still stood to the side with his arms folded. I couldn't tell what he thought, and I didn't think he'd appreciate being called out in front of the others after his confrontation with FM.

You disagree with this idea? I asked in his mind.

No, Jorgen said. *But I agree with Rig that it sounds confusing.*

"Let's try the cytonic defense systems now," Jorgen said to Rig. "If we can inhibit the platform or turn on the shield, we'll buy ourselves more time."

Rig nodded and extended his hand to the blue slug, who seemed to sniff it even though it didn't have a visible nose. After giving the slug a moment to acclimate to him, he picked it up and set it gently into one of the defense systems boxes and closed the door.

Nothing happened.

"What are you supposed to do now?" I asked. "Ask it to do something?"

"I don't know what to ask it to do," Jorgen said. "I can't give it an image of an inhibitor. It doesn't *look* like anything."

"Maybe you could try to show it an image of a cytonic approaching us, let it know what we're afraid of."

"We're not going back to scaring the slugs into submission," FM said.

"Right," Rig said. "But there's a difference between frightening them and communicating with them. You could, like, *explain* the situation?"

Jorgen looked doubtful, but FM nodded and went back to staring at the floor.

"All right," Jorgen said. "I'll try to . . . explain." He closed his eyes, and I listened in the negative realm, trying to hear what he was communicating.

There were no words here, only ideas. Jorgen showed the slug his own fear, and then a picture of a cytonic emerging in the control room. I could feel the slug's own fear—it didn't like the way it had been treated by cytonics in the past.

By the branches. These things *were* intelligent.

Still, the slug didn't do anything.

"Can you ask it to protect us?" I asked. They said the slugs understood abstract concepts like danger . . .

Jorgen sent an image, almost like a request. An impression of the platform being shut off to outside cytonics.

Arturo's slug made a squeaking noise and then the universe around me stopped vibrating, as if the whole of it had suddenly died. It was gone—my ability to reach out, to find the others, to reach the whispering voices that told me I wasn't alone. Maybe that was what Jorgen meant when he said Spensa could hear the stars. It wasn't so much stars I could hear, but all the matter in the whole of space and time.

And now they were gone.

Jorgen looked as disoriented as I felt. Boomslug had his face buried beneath Jorgen's arm, and Snuggles lay deflated in the sling across his chest. Gill huddled around FM's shoulders.

"I can't hear them anymore," Jorgen said. "It worked, but—if we can't use our own powers, we can't keep track of the enemy, or listen in on them." He turned to me. "How did we do that on Detritus? Some kind of impression?"

"There should be a code that lets us use cytonics while we're within the inhibitor. I don't know how you got it back on Detritus, but you did. Maybe because your powers manifested there, you grew up with the code in your mind?"

"That would explain how the taynix got it too," FM said.

"There might be a key here somewhere," Rig said. He leaned over the control panel. "There are some recordings in the database, but they seem to be blank."

"Play them," I said.

"Sure," Rig said, and he fiddled with some of the buttons.

An impression pushed into my mind like a key being slipped under a door. I concentrated on it, committing it to my memory, and the world began to vibrate around me again like a chorus of insects beginning to chirp again after a windstorm.

"Stars," Jorgen said. "That's better."

"Better," Gill and Boomslug both agreed, their voices forming a strange harmony.

I reached out, finding the minds of the slugs farther away on the platform, and I offered the impression to them. I could feel each of their relief.

"That should give us some cover," Rig said. "I can work on getting the shield up and spend some time fixing Alanik's ship so she's battle ready. Then we can try out the weapons systems and the hyperdrive."

"All right," Jorgen said. "That seems like a good plan."

"We think we can use the slugs to move the platform," Arturo said. "But what will we do with it if we can?"

"It's a large and powerful tool," I said. "But not the stealthiest, to be sure. If we start moving the platform around, Unity will take notice. We need to figure out a way to use the distraction to save Rinakin."

"We're assuming he wants to be saved," FM said. She turned to Rig. "We want to rescue her friend, but we heard him over the radio saying he was defecting to the other side."

"Wonder what that would feel like," Rig said.

I imagined they felt very similarly, having their commander try to capture them after sending them away. I hoped there was a reasonable explanation.

FM looked nervously at Jorgen. "There's more," she said. "Cobb sent people after us when we went to get Alanik's ship. They knew we were there somehow, and Cobb saw us himself. I thought maybe he'd cover for us, but he didn't. He called the people who were with him right to us."

"Maybe he did that because he knew we'd escape anyway," Rig said. "He knew Alanik could get us out."

"Still," FM said, "he could have given us a few more seconds."

"He might have noticed you were 'rescuing' taynix," Jorgen said.

"Yeah," Rig said. "That probably didn't help." He looked down at the instrumentation and sighed. "As for how we could use the platform, I want to take a look at these other systems and get a better idea of what we're dealing with. Then we can talk about ways we might use it."

"That will all take some time," Jorgen said, stepping away to peer out the window into the miasma. "It's getting late. At least, it is on Detritus. What time does night fall here?"

I wasn't exactly sure. I looked out the window at the angle of the sun through the miasma. "In about three sleep cycles, I think."

"Interesting," Rig said. "You sleep multiple times in a day?"

"Yes," I said. "One day is equal to nine sleep cycles at this time of year on the tree where I live. Sometimes it will be less or more, depending on the location of a given tree in the miasma. I'm not sure what it'll be here, but judging by the angle of the sun that's my estimation."

"So a day here is about a week," Jorgen said. "We grew up underground, so our days are manufactured as well. Even if it isn't going to get dark we still need to sleep, and eat something that won't kill us." He looked grudgingly at FM. "Thanks for bringing the algae strips."

"It was Alanik's idea," FM said.

"It's a good thing Nedd gorged himself on those nut bars," Arturo said. "Might be some algae strips left for the rest of us."

"Though I hope he doesn't keel over," Kimmalyn added.

"I'll get to work," Rig said. "We can rest and then return to the plan."

"Sounds good," Jorgen said, and he stalked out, leaving the rest of us behind.

16

As Jorgen left the room, FM appeared to deflate.

"You okay?" Kimmalyn asked her.

"Yeah," FM said. "I really shouldn't have said that to Jorgen."

"Definitely not," Rig said. "But I understand why you did."

"I need to walk," FM said. "I'll show you that other control room. There might be systems for the shield in there." She and Rig left, heading in the opposite direction from Jorgen. Kimmalyn followed them, telling the rest of the flight that they needed to check in with the Independence pilots and see if they'd found somewhere we could all be comfortable for the night.

They wandered off, taking most of the slugs and the food with them. Arturo remained behind.

"Are they always like this?" I asked.

"FM and Jorgen?" Arturo said. "No, not like that."

That wasn't much of a comfort, but as they all seemed committed to seeing this through, I supposed I should leave their internal politics alone.

Arturo watched me quietly.

I sighed. "You still think I'm going to betray you?" I asked.

"I hope you aren't," he said. He didn't seem upset about it either way. Merely uncertain.

"You could also betray *me*," I insisted. "You could promise the Superiority you'll bring me in, use me and my people as a bargaining chip to get yourselves a better position the way Quilan is doing."

"We could," Arturo said. He seemed surprised, like he hadn't thought of that.

I hadn't meant to give him any ideas. They'd be heroes, enough that their commanders might forget about their court-martial. Their admiral could claim this was his plan all along. That was what our Council would do in such a situation.

"But we won't," Arturo said. "We've come all this way to secure an alliance. Those are our orders."

They were not-orders, as I recalled. But I wasn't going to mention that.

"Thank you," I said. Arturo nodded, but we both watched each other uneasily.

I waited for him to leave, but he kept standing there. Did he not want to leave me alone in this room? Did he think I would *sabotage* it somehow? "You don't have to watch me every minute," I said.

"I know," Arturo said. He seemed surprised again, like the idea hadn't occurred to him. "I was just wondering why you're doing this."

I blinked at him. "Trying to rescue my friend?"

"Fighting the Superiority," he said. "When you described it back on Detritus, it sounded like your lives are good here."

"They are," I said. "And I'd like to keep it that way."

"So if your people joined the Superiority, what do you think would be worse?"

I opened my mouth, then closed it again. It was hard for me to imagine exactly what that would be like. Giving in to the Superiority felt like the worst thing that could possibly happen, but on the surface I could see how it would look attractive to the humans after the years of war and terror.

"I don't think they'd try to exterminate us," I said carefully. "If they were going to do that, they would have done it years ago, after we lost the last war."

"Okay," Arturo said.

"But I think they would oppress us."

"And they're not oppressing you now?" Arturo asked.

"No, they are," I said quickly. "They withhold the secrets of hyperdrives from us, try to control how we use cytonics, tell us what aspects of our culture are 'lesser' or 'advanced.'"

"Do you really want to fight a war with them just because they're critical of you and refuse to share?"

"It's not that," I said. "They actively try to stop us from learning. They tell us that wireless technology is dangerous, that cytonics are dangerous—but they became a powerful civilization through the use of those same resources. By denying us access—it's not only that they won't help us, it's like they walked through the door and then locked it behind them."

Arturo nodded. "Still," he said, "what do you need that technology for, if you want nothing to do with them? Wouldn't that be the only reason you'd need it? To interact with them?"

"We need it to *fight* them," I said. "Because we don't want to be under their control. Because we're not 'lesser.' We're intelligent, and we have a right to direct our own lives and our own future. We're not trying to take over from the Superiority. We only want to exist without their interference and their . . . *judgment*."

Arturo nodded. I got the feeling he wasn't arguing with me. He was trying to understand. "And that's worth it to you," he said. "To risk war, to risk them deciding to exterminate you after all. To risk your life and the lives of everyone you love, the lives of your whole *people*. To avoid being judged by them."

"It's not only that they judge us," I said. It was so hard to define, but I felt the resistance to everything the Superiority stood for like it was a part of me. "It's that they judge us and find us *wanting*. And if we cooperate with them, it's like we're admitting they're right. That we *are* lesser. And we're *not*. We are equal beings who deserve to be treated as equals. And I would rather risk everything than capitulate, because I can't deny that to myself. It would kill me to do it."

Arturo met my eyes, and he nodded. I thought . . . maybe he respected that answer. At the very least he accepted it.

"What about you?" I asked. "Why are you here?"

"I was ordered to be here," he said.

"You were not-ordered," I said.

"Right, but Jorgen is my flightleader and I followed him."

The way I remembered it, the rest of them dragged Jorgen along until he caught up to the idea.

"So you disagree, then. You don't think you should have come."

Arturo hesitated. Maybe he was worried about expressing disagreement with his superior, but he seemed to have a more familiar relationship with Jorgen. I thought there was more to it.

"Do you wish you were back on Detritus?" I asked. "Helping your people to broker a peace deal?"

He was quiet for a moment, staring out the window into the miasma. "No," he admitted. "I think we're doing the right thing, helping you."

I nodded. "Yes. You are."

"Maybe not the *smart* thing," he said. "I worry we've chosen the losing side on both your planet and mine, and I'm afraid that this is going to go terribly wrong for all of us. But I don't like the idea of bargaining with the people who've been murdering us for generations. I don't like the idea of peace talks with the beings who've been keeping us in a cage."

I smiled. He understood then. "Giving in to them feels like deciding to die slowly."

"I don't know about that," he said. "But you're right that it feels like admitting we're lesser. Like we're saying we deserved the way they treated us, and we're willing to simply forgive and forget."

"The Superiority likes that idea," I said, "so long as we're always the ones doing the forgetting."

Arturo nodded, staring out at the miasma again. I liked the way he thought about things. The fact that he *did* think about them, while so many people on both his planet and mine were willing to swallow the easy story without worrying about whether it was a true one.

"Did you choose to be a pilot?" I asked. "Your people are at war, but you can't all be fighters."

"No," Arturo said. "They say we're all part of the war effort no matter our job, and maybe that's true in a way. But being a pilot gets you a lot of respect. A lot of disadvantaged people want to pass the pilot's test for the opportunities it affords them, but for me it was expected. My parents have a lot of connections, a lot of . . . social power, I guess. And to maintain the empire, I had to be a pilot."

"That makes sense," I said. "You have to prove you are the best."

"They didn't want me to stay and prove it," Arturo said. "I nearly got killed when I was a cadet. My parents pulled strings, got me my pin early so I wouldn't have to keep flying."

"But you are flying."

"Yeah," Arturo said. "My parents weren't happy about it. Neither was my girlfriend. They all felt like I'd done my part. But I hadn't, you know? I hated the thought of slinking back to the caverns and benefiting from the deaths of my friends, people I knew and liked. It felt like cowardice, hiding when I should be out there fighting." He shook his head.

"Is that why your . . ." Jorgen didn't like it when I used this word. "I don't think there's an exact translation for it in my language, but your mate—"

"My girlfriend," Arturo said. "Yeah, that's why she broke up with me ultimately. I think she wanted to for a while, but didn't feel like she could. Like, it doesn't feel good to give up on someone who's fighting for the future of humanity, but she'd always thought I was going to come back a few months after flight school. And then I didn't."

"I'm sorry," I said.

"It's okay. I think we're both better off, honestly. She said I'd changed, that I didn't care about the things I used to." He shrugged. "She was probably right."

Given how deeply he seemed to care about his people's freedom now, I thought that could only be a good thing, but I wondered if he would agree.

"We're on the same side," I said. "As long as you want to fight the Superiority, you don't have to worry about me."

"Same to you," he said. "Jorgen gets hung up on rules, but he doesn't want to play nice with them any more than you and I do."

I believed him. I couldn't be absolutely sure he was telling the truth, but he had the same problem with me.

Regardless, once we got everything in order, we were all going to find out.

I worried it would be uncomfortable to sleep on the platform, but my brother and the Independence pilots had found the bunk rooms from when the platform was inhabited. There was an entire block of them—more rooms than we could possibly need. The Independence pilots took up residence in one, and Rinakin's family and some of the other refugees spread out over a few more. The rooms had obviously been used by salvagers in recent years, because the old cushioning had been replaced on all but the top bunks, where it was mostly disintegrated. The other bunks weren't as soft or as clean as I would have liked, but they were better than sleeping in the cockpits.

The human men all settled into one of the sleeping rooms and the women into another, where they invited me to join them. In one of the adjoining common rooms, Kimmalyn and Sadie divided the algae strips and custard so that everyone got a portion for dinner. I passed on the algae—since we knew the nut wafers were safe for me to eat, I choked a couple down.

I could have gone to eat with my brother, but instead I stayed with the humans. I needed to make sure they didn't have any second thoughts about what we were doing here, and besides that I was starting to enjoy their company.

"You can have a cup of custard to dip those nut bars in if you want," Kimmalyn said, pushing the jug of liquid in my direction.

I peered at the cloudy white substance. "What is it?"

"It's milk," Sadie told me. "But like, old milk. I think? I'm not totally clear how they make it."

"Human milk?" I asked.

"Ew, no," Sadie said. "Cow's milk, I think."

That sounded disgusting. "I'm all right," I said. "Though I think Happy will take my portion."

The slug was leaning out of Kimmalyn's sling, dangling down like it was going to dip its face right into the jug.

"Happy!" Kimmalyn said. "Yours is over here." She pulled the slug out of the sling and deposited it with the others, who were happily chewing algae strips.

Jorgen approached. FM and Rig hadn't joined us—last I'd seen she was sitting with Rig in the hangar while he worked on my ship, both of them speaking in low voices.

"Can I ask for your help with something?" Jorgen asked me.

"Yes," I said, and we walked out into a hallway with a long window looking out into the miasma.

Jorgen pressed his fingers to the glass, watching the miasma swirl against it. "Since we have a minute, I was wondering if you could teach me something about cytonics."

"Of course," I said, and I took a seat on the floor of the hallway, my back opposite the window. The outline of Hollow was dimly visible, its dark branches reaching up toward the red sky.

"Gran-Gran taught me how to meditate," Jorgen said, sitting down facing me. "To listen to the stars. It helped, but I didn't end up hearing the stars. I heard the taynix instead."

"That sounds ultimately more useful," I said.

"It probably was. But Spensa was able to hyperjump all the way to Starsight."

"Technically all cytonics have every power," I said. "I'm not clear on how many there are. We're only able to manifest some of them deliberately after a lot of training. And some we may never be able to use. Of the five cytonics on ReDawn, I'm the only one who has been able to hyperjump."

"Which is why the other cytonics weren't able to follow us here immediately, even before we got the inhibitor up," Jorgen said. "And if I'm never going to be able to learn—"

"That's what I'm trying to tell you," I said. "There are other valuable types of cytonics. Mindblades are supposed to be the most difficult. I've never been able to manifest those."

"You said those are like little bits of the nowhere that cut like razorblades?"

"Yes," I said. "Like your Boomslug."

"Boomslug!" Boomslug said from Jorgen's shoulder.

"I haven't been able to do that either," Jorgen said.

"Let's start with what's already working," I said. "You know how to find my mind and the minds of the taynix. Can you do it now?"

Jorgen absently stroked Boomslug on its spines. He closed his eyes, and I could feel his mind reaching out toward mine.

"Good. Now reach out farther. Stretch yourself over the space of the planet. See if you can find the Unity cytonics. Now that you have the key to the inhibitor, you should be able to find them."

"It's easier when I'm closer to the source," Jorgen said. "When I heard the taynix below the surface of Detritus, there were so many of them, so it was louder—"

"Try, Jorgen," I said. "Stop focusing so much on what you aren't able to do, and *try*."

I felt his presence in my mind as he reached out. *I hate this*, Jorgen said. *I can't do enough.*

"There you go," I said. "You can reach me. Now try to find

others. And be quieter while you do it. They don't know yet who you are, and we don't want to give them that information unless it benefits us to do so."

"You heard that?" Jorgen said. He sounded embarrassed. "I didn't mean to send what I was thinking—"

"You have to be careful not to broadcast when you're making contact," I said. "But now try the meditation you learned before. Instead of reaching for my mind, reach out into the negative realm that surrounds us, out across the planet."

Jorgen was quiet for a long time, while Boomslug tucked itself in the crook of his elbow and snored softly. After a while I thought Jorgen might have fallen asleep sitting up.

"I can feel the other taynix," Jorgen said finally. "I can't find any other cytonics—and there's a space somewhere in the distance, a space that feels . . . solid. Like I can't reach into it."

I followed him across the miasma. Yes, there it was. On the far side of the core, on the side of the planet in a night cycle.

"The Council tree," I said. "Inhibited by the other cytonics." I wondered if they'd done that as a precaution once our inhibitor went up. They wouldn't be able to maintain it all the time, but they must be worried about what we had planned.

They wanted us to believe they were in control, but they were still afraid of us, which meant they weren't. Not entirely.

"I need to learn how to make those inhibitors," Jorgen said.

"You learned how to find a place that's been inhibited," I said. "You might be happy for that first."

"It's not enough," Jorgen said.

I understood what he meant. It would never be enough until the fight was over and his people were safe. "Focus on what you have," I said. "We can work on it more, but I think you should sleep first. Tiring yourself out will only make you more frustrated. And when you're frustrated, it's much more difficult to learn." And dangerous, if you started manifesting things like concussion bolts and mindblades.

Jorgen didn't argue. "That makes sense. Thanks, Alanik."

Now *I* felt inadequate. Jorgen and his team had risked everything to help me, and I'd hardly shown him anything.

It's not enough, he'd said. I felt the same.

"Get some rest," I said.

"Good night," Jorgen said, and he left me staring up into the red-violet glow of the sun against the miasma above.

17

I had a hard time following my own advice, and so I spent a good portion of the sleep cycle lying awake, listening. Sometime while the humans were all asleep, I caught a communication traveling through the negative realm.

—everything in hand— Quilan was saying. *—give us time— retrieve Alanik—*

—give us the rogue cytonic and her allies—if that proves difficult for you—set up a government who can.

I drew a deep breath. Quilan was still trying to pacify the Superiority, but he had a storm in a bottle, and any moment the glass might break. He was holding them off for now, but if they grew tired of waiting we were going to pay the price.

We had to make our move tomorrow, with whatever resources we had to work with.

I woke in the morning unsure of how much sleep I'd actually gotten, though I was still glad we'd taken the time to rest. Tired pilots were sloppy pilots, and sloppy pilots lost matches. Or in this case got themselves killed.

While the humans were eating, I used the radio in Jorgen's ship to check the frequency Nanalis had used to broadcast the message from Rinakin. It was a Unity channel, one they often used to send messages to their people, despite Superiority admonitions that we keep wireless communication to a minimum. I wondered how long that would last once they gave the Superiority more influence over ReDawn. I wondered if they would regret it.

There was no broadcast now, but there was a repeating message about an upcoming special conversation between Rinakin and one of the most popular Unity orators later in the morning.

That was good. If Rinakin was broadcasting, I could use that signal to find his location. They would unintentionally lead me right to him.

When everyone finished eating, I followed the humans to the control room with the taynix boxes. Rig, Jorgen, FM, and I gathered in the room while the others waited outside.

"None of your people died in the night," I said to Jorgen. "So I suppose the udal nuts weren't toxic to you."

"You only say that because you didn't have to share a room with Nedd last night," Jorgen said.

"All right," Rig said. "I've finished reassembling Alanik's ship, and I found this platform's shield systems. They're similar to the ones on Platform Prime, so I was able to get them working. I don't think it's *as* effective as the planetary shield, because we don't have hundreds of other platforms to form a barrier. But look."

He gestured out the window at a blueish tint now coloring the miasma.

"That's something," Jorgen said. "Good work."

I wondered how much sleep Rig had gotten, but he didn't complain. "We expect we know how the comms and navigation systems work," he said. "They should be similar to the hypercomms and hyperdrives we already use. But we want to check out this unknown cytonic weapons system, and then make a plan for how to use the platform to fight back."

"Rig and I were thinking that Boomslug might be the right type to put in a weapons system," FM said. "Given what we've seen him do."

Jorgen knelt to gently pick up Boomslug, who was lying in the doorway to the control room. "You ready, buddy?"

"Buddy," Boomslug said in his deep voice.

"Okay," Rig said. "It would be really nice to have a weapons system we can control."

FM took Boomslug from Jorgen and put him into the box. "I am going to give you so much caviar if this works," she said.

"If we have to experiment on him," Jorgen said, "I'm glad he's inside a metal box where he hopefully can't hurt us."

I was pretty sure mindblades could pass through most substances and do damage as they went, but I didn't tell Jorgen that. If the former inhabitants of this platform had put a taynix in this box and then used it to power weapons, presumably they hadn't cut themselves to ribbons in the process.

"All right," Rig said when the box was locked. "Let's see what he can do."

"What am I going to ask it?" Jorgen said. "Please attack . . . nothing?"

"Go boom," FM said. "You remember what that felt like, right?"

Jorgen winced. "Too well."

"Can you aim the gun?" I asked. "We're a long way from Hollow, but we don't know exactly how far this weapon can reach."

"She's right," Rig said. "The Superiority had planetary weapons. This could be one of those. I didn't see anything on this platform as big as that was, but I didn't exactly perform an exhaustive search, and—"

"I'll try to focus away from the tree," Jorgen said. "Out in the miasma. The same way I do when I direct them to hyperjump. Anyone else have any concerns?"

We were all quiet.

"Okay," Jorgen said. "Here goes."

I focused on the mind of the slug, trying not to make enough contact that I would distract it from Jorgen's message, but just enough that I could feel the change.

I didn't need to though. The whole platform quivered with the reverberation, like a weapon had fired with incredible force. Out the window, the miasma in front of us shifted, swirling in eddies around invisible projectiles.

"Scud!" Nedd shouted from outside. "What was *that*?"

"Mindblades," I said. "Did they aim where you wanted them to go?"

"They did," Jorgen said. "We still have no idea how powerful that weapon is. It moved the gas clouds around, but that doesn't mean—"

"A well-placed mindblade can cut right through a ship's hull," I said.

"That seems like something we can use to defend ourselves," Rig said. "Though I worry we'll have already drawn attention by using it."

A plan began to form in my mind. "Drawing attention might be a good thing though," I said. "If we were to move the platform and activate the weapons, Unity would want to stop us."

"That's true," Jorgen said. "They'd send forces after us."

"But they wouldn't be able to get past the autoturrets quickly," I said. "That kind of operation requires a lot of drones and a lot of patience, and that's *if* they could get through the shield. They'd want to send Unity's cytonics to stop you."

"What good are cytonics if we have an inhibitor up?" FM asked.

"They'd still be able to affect us," I said. "The inhibitor prevents cytonics without the key from using their powers *within* the field. The other cytonics could still surround us and put up an inhibitor field of their own, preventing us from using the cytonic weapons or hyperjumping out, essentially trapping us."

"We'd still have the autoturrets and the shield to defend us," Jorgen said.

"Yes," I said. "But they can also magnify each other's abilities. Quilan can use his cytonic powers to knock people out with a concussion bolt. It's what he did to me before I crashed your ship.

The other cytonics can help him amplify it, creating a concussion field, similar to the way they join their minds together in an inhibitor. They've done it before during political protests." They said they were quelling riots, trying to keep things peaceful. But knocking people out en masse always seemed violent to me.

"Why haven't they done that to us already?" FM asked.

"I imagine they're planning to," I said. "But it wouldn't let them get inside the shield, and it's not easy to do. They'd have to surround the platform and maintain more or less the same positions while they do it. It's not very applicable in an actual battle, where the enemy ships can chase you out of formation."

"So we'd need ships in the air," Jorgen said, "making sure they can't get into formation to inhibit us or use the concussion field. We could tempt the other cytonics away from Rinakin, which would make it easier for you to rescue him."

"Right," I said. Even if they had Rinakin inside a taynix-powered inhibitor, I'd still have a better chance of rescuing him without the other cytonics to contend with.

"What exactly are we going to do to get their attention though?" FM asked. "It'll take more than just firing the hyperweapon into the miasma."

"Is there some Unity base we could fire on?" Jorgen said. "We don't want to hit civilian targets, but if we could hit a military one—"

The idea of actually firing a mindblade weapon, even at a Unity target, was horrifying to me. "I don't want to kill anyone unless we have to," I said.

"Sure," Jorgen said. "We could wait for them to fire first."

"But there will be a lot of Unity people on their base who *aren't* firing at us," I said. "And I don't want to shoot at them."

The humans stared at me for a moment, like they could accept this but didn't quite understand it.

They'd been at war their whole lives and were willing to make sacrifices I wasn't ready for. I acted like I was hardened to the consequences, but I'd never killed anyone. I'd mostly shot people with tagging lasers—most of my time in starships had been spent playing games.

"What if we moved the platform into the miasma outside the Unity headquarters on Tower?" I asked. "It's a tree with a huge population, so I don't want to fire on it. But just *being* there would feel like a threat to Unity, more than any other tree but the Council tree. We can't threaten that one, because we need to draw the cytonics farther away so I can go and get Rinakin if they leave him behind. But you don't have to shoot at the tree. Just hyperjump there, maybe fire a warning shot with the hyperweapon into the miasma."

"That's a better idea," Jorgen said. "You're right. We don't want to hurt anyone we don't have to."

"Good," I said. "Meanwhile I could go in and get Rinakin, since he'd be relatively unguarded."

"Unless they bring him with them," FM said.

"They might," I said. "But if they bring him to us, we can pivot the plan and I can come back to rescue him from their ships."

"You shouldn't go alone," Jorgen said. "There are too many things that could go wrong with that plan, and you'd need backup."

"I'll be stealthier alone," I said.

"But we work as a team," Jorgen insisted, sparing a glance at FM. "You need someone there if things go wrong. At the very least that person could engage their taynix to come back here and tell us what's happened to you, so we can organize a rescue effort."

It was a good sign that they would consider rescuing me if something went wrong.

"I'll have to stay here to communicate with the slugs in the platform," Jorgen continued, "and Rig will need to stay too, but—"

"I'll go," Arturo said from the doorway.

I looked at him. Yesterday it had seemed like he was starting to

313

trust me, but here he was volunteering to come along and babysit me. To make sure that I wasn't going to have his people make a spectacle out of themselves and then grab Rinakin and run.

I could do that, I realized. Arturo's presence wouldn't stop me. But the whole point of going to Detritus in the first place was to find allies. Even if the rest of their people were making a different choice, these humans were still willing to work with me. So far, anyway.

Jorgen nodded. "That makes the most sense. Maybe you should take Nedd as well."

"Alanik is right," Arturo said. "The more people we bring, the less stealthy we are. But if we're going into combat with a ship with a cytonic inhibitor, we'll want at least two of us. If we find that it's being guarded by a whole fleet, we can hyperjump back and regroup, but at least we'll know more than we know now."

"All right," Jorgen said. "We're going to need to get everyone together and talk this through. Alanik, would you go talk to the Independence pilots? See if they'll join us? We could meet in the hangar. It's the only space we've found so far that's big enough to fit all of us together comfortably."

I nodded.

I didn't like putting any of them in danger, but if we succeeded it would be worth it.

18

An hour later, Rig, Jorgen, and I gathered in the control room again to use the hyperdrive. The other pilots—both human and UrDail—were all ready in their ships to be transported out to defend the platform. Rig had pulled the radio out of the wreckage of my ship and installed it in the control room, so he'd be able to talk to us once we were in the air.

"Here we go," Jorgen said as Rig deposited Drape in the navigation system taynix box. "At least we've used hyperdrives before. Do we think this works the same way as the ones in our ships? I just send it a location and the whole platform will move?"

"The Superiority moves massive ships with hyperdrives," I said. "So this platform shouldn't be a problem."

"I only know how to send the slugs to places we both know," Jorgen said. "I don't know where we're going."

"I can give it coordinates," I said. "If we're going to Tower, I want to be sure we're out of range of the tree so the autoturrets don't fire on it." I wasn't going to be responsible for that many civilian casualties, and not just because it would be impossible to convince my people we meant well after something like that.

"Could you move the platform yourself?" Rig asked me. "It seems like you could do it without the help of the taynix."

"Maybe," I said. "But I'd rather not risk it."

"Plus, we should test it with the hyperdrive," Jorgen said. "That way we know if it works, in case I need to pull us out after Alanik is gone." He turned to me. "Do you know what kind of range the guns have?"

"I'm going to overestimate it," I said, "just to be safe. We want the guns shooting at the people who come after us, not at Tower. We can always move the platform a second time if we need to."

I searched out across the planet, reaching past Industry and Spindle—where I lived—to Tower. It was far from other trees at the moment, leaving many branches of space out in the miasma to move the platform to. I needed it close enough to Tower that Unity saw it as a threat, but not so close that anyone got hurt, even aircraft that were passing through the busy airspace around the tree.

Better to be too far out than too close. I chose a place farther away and impressed the coordinates into my mind. And then, reaching out for Drape, I fed them to him.

Nothing happened.

"Why isn't it working?" I asked.

"He's not listening to you," Jorgen said. "Probably because he doesn't know you."

That made sense. Most of the slugs back on Detritus hadn't come when I called them either. And those that had only did so because I'd promised them food and friends.

"That's a good thing," Rig said. "It means not all the slugs can be used against us in combat."

"You're going to have to give him the command," Jorgen said to Rig.

Rig bent down, speaking through the metal door of the box. "*Go.*"

There was the slightest hesitation.

And then that horrible loss of control again as I slipped into the negative realm without pulling myself through. I came back to where I was standing before, in the center of the control room.

The window facing the miasma suddenly went dark.

"Um, guys?" Kimmalyn called from the direction of the hangar. "You need to come see this."

We all crowded out the door to the hangar. Pilots sat in their ships with their canopies open, looking out the enormous windows through the swirling miasma at the reaching branches of Tower, so named because it was the tallest of all the trees—long and lean, with branches that soared nearly straight upward into the sky. Here there were almost no horizontal buildings, only spirals built into the sides of the branches, all illuminated with hundreds of thousands of city lights. The intricacies of the architecture were too tiny to see from this distance, but the overall effect was still impressive. I felt a little bit of pride at the way the humans gaped at it.

"That's incredible," Rig said.

"I thought that other tree was impressive," Arturo added.

"Hollow is a ruin," I said. "*This* is UrDail civilization."

All around, I could see the Independence pilots sitting taller.

I was glad to see that I'd managed to place the platform far enough from the tree that the turrets weren't shooting at it. But we were close enough to be visible from the branches, so people had to be taking notice.

Jorgen moved to his ship and fiddled with the radio. He picked up a channel talking about the weather patterns in the miasma, and then an air traffic control channel.

"—obstacle in the airspace on the duskward side. All flights avoid—"

"Yeah," Nedd said. "They definitely noticed us."

"What about the other cytonics?" FM asked.

Jorgen closed his eyes, and I waited while he reached out across the negative realm around ReDawn. "I can feel one of them," he said. "Your friend Quilan?"

I followed his reach. He was right. Quilan was moving toward us. He'd moved so fast, he must have already been in a ship before we hyperjumped.

"We've got their attention," Jorgen said. "All ships, time to get in the air. We'll fly out of the hangar together. When we're all ready, we'll hyperjump everyone beyond the range of the autoturrets."

Canopies lowered and ships lifted off the landing pad. Nedd hung back, pulling his taynix, Chubs, out of its box. We'd agreed that I should take a hyperdrive with me, in case Arturo and I were separated, and Naga would be able to find Chubs instantly. It would leave Nedd without a hyperdrive in the battle, so he'd have to rely on his flightmates to pull him in and out with light-lances, just like the Independence pilots.

"Okay, buddy," Nedd said. "You're going for an adventure with the nice alien lady."

"Nedd," Arturo said, like he thought he might offend me. But when Nedd handed over his taynix—a *hyperdrive*, a creature so valuable most people in the universe would kill for it—I couldn't feel anything but awe.

They were really going to let me *take* one. And yes, I knew it was only because they thought it would help them follow me if I tried to escape them—and it probably would.

But still. I'd risked everything to find out the secret to these creatures. And now I was holding one in my hands.

It looked up at me, its face quizzical. "Alien lady!" it trilled.

"Get to your ship," Jorgen said to Nedd. "Let's *go*."

The rest of the flight was already maneuvering their ships out the hangar doors and onto the surface of the platform. I set Chubs down in the space behind my seat, but moments later he was nuzzling my ankles down by the pedals. I didn't relish the idea of his obstruction getting me shot down by the autofire, so I scooped him into my lap.

"How do they stand flying with you?" I asked him.

"Flying with you!" Chubs said. The taynix sounded like simple mimics, but they must understand at least some of what they said if they could learn each other's names and then find one another through the negative realm.

Rig waited outside my ship while I checked the controls.

"We removed that thing that was intercepting signals as they came in," Rig said. "We thought it might help Jorgen not be susceptible to cytonic interference."

"No, my ship doesn't block cytonic interference," I said. "I think what you removed was an encryption device, but I won't need that today anyway."

"Oh," Rig said. He looked embarrassed, but he didn't need to be. He'd done a good job getting my ship back in flying condition, from what I could tell.

"Thank you for fixing this for me," I said.

"Of course," Rig said. "I'm confident about the damage repairs. Those were all completed ages ago. All I did last night was finish the reassembly. You should be fine in the air."

He backed off, and I engaged my acclivity ring, lifting off the landing bay floor and flying out to meet the others in formation around Jorgen.

I let one of the humans hit me with their light-lance and hyperjump me beyond the autofire with the Independence pilots. I didn't know how much hyperjumping I was going to have to do, and I wanted to keep the number of jumps to a minimum when I could. Jorgen jumped us way out, giving the autofire a wider berth than we probably needed.

I checked the frequency Rinakin had been broadcasting from. His program had begun, and I could hear him opining about how the rift between our factions was the *real* problem for ReDawn. According to my ship's frequency locator, the signal was coming from the Council tree, exactly as expected.

That was good. I reached out with my cytonic senses, searching for Quilan, and found him closing on our location. I scrambled with my radio, trying to find the flight's general channel to let Jorgen know, but by the time I found it he was already giving the flights the bearing of the incoming enemy. "We're going to slow to point-five Mag," he said, "and fly toward Tower, away from the enemy."

The ships immediately followed his order. By putting our people on the opposite side of the platform from Quilan, Jorgen ensured that Quilan would have to pass around the platform to get to them. Jorgen would be able to fire the hyperweapon at him without worrying about clipping his own people in the blast.

The Independence flight joined us as we flew away from the platform toward the tree, slow enough that Quilan would easily catch us. He had to know we were up to something, but he wouldn't know what.

"Rig?" Jorgen said. "Do you have a visual on the enemy flight?"

"I do," Rig said. "They're closing on the platform."

Flying in the opposite direction, I couldn't see the incoming ships—which Quilan must have called in from the reinforcements at the Council tree—except on my sensor screen. But I *felt* the disturbance rippling through the negative realm as Jorgen contacted Boomslug in the platform control room and directed him to fire on the flight as they skirted the other side of the platform. I scanned radio channels, catching bits of their transmissions as pilots screamed and swore and called their intentions to eject.

I didn't know if they all made it, but as Jorgen directed us to pivot around and fly below the platform again, I did see several pilots descending through the miasma with parachutes. Two of the ships collided with the far side of the platform.

A few more ships cut toward us, having avoided the mind-blades. Unfortunately, Quilan was among them. *Alanik*, he said in my mind. *What are you doing?*

If this distraction was going to work, Quilan had to believe I meant business. *I'm doing what has to be done. Look what that did to your flight. What do you think it will do to your people on Tower?*

You've lost your mind, Quilan sent back.

That was good. I needed him to believe that I had.

"FM, Sentry, take point. Engage the enemy ships. T-Stall, Catnip, Nedder, back them up."

Five ships shot out in front of us, meeting with the enemy ships as they skirted around the platform outside the autofire zone. A number of Independence ships joined them.

I reached into the negative realm, checking on the Council tree. Nearly a quarter of the way around the planet, I could feel the dead space fading away, the area around the Council tree no longer covered by cytonic inhibitors.

Quilan had called in the other cytonics, realizing that the only way to stop the platform was to inhibit our ability to use cytonics in the area or lay down a concussion field.

"Jerkface," I said over the radio. "We are a go."

"Copy," Jorgen replied. "Do it."

"Don't forget about me," Arturo said. He flew close on my wing, like he wanted to be sure I remembered he was tagging along.

As if I could forget.

When I reached out for Naga's mind, I realized that Chubs had snuggled around my waist and fallen asleep.

In a starfighter. In the middle of a battle.

I was glad *someone* had been able to find some peace. It wasn't going to be Naga, as I reached out for its mind, giving it cytonic coordinates near the Council tree, but far enough away we wouldn't be immediately spotted.

"Tell Naga to go," I said to Arturo over the radio.

"Naga, go," he said.

Arturo's ship blinked out of existence, and I followed.

19

We passed through the negative realm and back into our reality, staring out into the purple darkness of the night sky. There were no stars peeking through the miasma, not this deep. Merely a cloudy darkness with patches of violet and red, like someone had put a multicolored blanket over the sun.

It was nearly dawn on this part of the planet. The Council tree stood out in the distance, the walkway lights of the city pathways blinking through the reddish cloud between us.

"Stars, I'm never going to get used to how strange this is," Arturo said over the radio.

"It's beautiful, isn't it?" I said.

"So scudding beautiful," he agreed. "They make our trees look like infants. Those used to seem impressive to me. Most of our plants grow in vats."

I reached out toward the Council tree. Quilan would know I'd disappeared, of course. He'd guess what I was doing. But the other cytonics were moving away from us now in the direction of Tower. They'd boarded ships in a hurry. Quilan was worried.

He was right to be. I'd left a group of humans with a super-weapon outside one of ReDawn's major population centers.

"The other cytonics are leaving," I said. "Do you think Jerkface will keep his promise not to fire on the tree?" I was proud I remembered to use the callsign over the radio, though I still didn't quite understand the purpose.

"He will," Arturo said without hesitation. "Do you worry he won't?"

Yes, I did. But admitting it felt like weakness.

"Your callsign," I said. "It's . . . Amphi?"

"Amphisbaena," he said.

My pin didn't translate it. "What does that mean?"

"It's a dragon from Old Earth mythology. I picked it because it's fearsome and it flies."

"If I need a callsign I'd like something that flies," I said. "That seems logical."

"It doesn't have to be something logical," he said. "It can be anything you want."

That seemed more difficult though. To pick from *anything*. "We don't have creatures that fly on ReDawn. They wouldn't survive the miasma."

"Yeah, well, we never had real dragons either. There are other things that fly though, real or not. Like eagles. Or angels."

"I've heard of those!" I said. "Flying humans from your old religions. When my people first met yours through the negative realm, some of them thought we were angels. Others thought we might be devils. Like angels but evil, right?"

"That's true. But you're more of an angel though, right? I don't like thinking we've made a deal with the devil."

He said it jokingly, but it was the kind of joke that had the bite of truth to it. "An angel then," I said. "Definitely."

"It suits you," he said. "An angel with a great big sword, coming down to exact justice."

I wasn't sure that was what I was, but the idea of wielding a sword of justice against the Superiority was appealing, so long as it was a metaphorical one. I had no desire to get into an actual fight with such a crude weapon.

"One moment," I said. "I'm going to check on Rinakin."

I tuned my radio to the channel he was broadcasting from. He was still there, talking with one of the Unity orators about the trade benefits of capitulating to the Superiority. I ran the signal through my ship's location device, then switched to my channel with Arturo.

"Rinakin is still broadcasting from the Council tree," I said. "The signal is coming from the area of his old residence. His primary residence is far from here, but he has a place where he stayed when he was on the Council, before he lost the election."

"What are we flying into?" Arturo asked. "Do they have gun emplacements? Other defenses?"

"No," I said. "Putting weapons around the government head-quarters would be far too aggressive. They're trying to convince the Superiority that we're peaceful. And Quilan and the others will have taken most of the in-residence air force with them as well."

"Finally the Superiority has done us a favor," Arturo said. "I'll take it. Are we flying in or hyperjumping?"

"We shouldn't get any closer in our ships," I said. "Let's stop our ships and leave them. We can leave Chubs behind as well. That way we'll both be able to get back here if something goes wrong."

"Last time I hyperjumped out of my ship, I left it on the other side of the universe," Arturo said. "But you're the flightleader on this mission. And I'd rather your friends down there didn't see us coming."

"Agreed," I said, reaching out to Naga. I wound my way through the negative realm to the Council building, forming the coordinates in my mind. I'd traveled via hyperjump to Rinakin's residence be-fore, so I knew exactly where I was going.

And then I called Naga to follow as I jumped. The eyes fixed on me and I could feel their ire, like they wanted to swat me out of the sky. That was two hyperjumps in quick succession. I hoped I wouldn't have to make many more.

We emerged in Rinakin's study, next to the wide barkwood table. The room looked pristine, nothing like the mess it had been when Rinakin was working in here regularly. The shelves were empty, the table polished and clear.

Through the arched doorway I could hear a voice.

I grabbed Arturo by the arm and pulled him behind the door. Naga squirmed in her sling, trying to twist around to look up at me.

"Thank you, Cessil," Rinakin was saying. "You don't need to return for the tray. I'll hold it until morning."

"Of course," another voice responded. "If you need anything, don't hesitate to call."

Rinakin was no longer broadcasting. I scowled. He was being treated like a guest, not a prisoner. Maybe Nanalis wanted to keep that a secret from the staff as well, and Rinakin had decided to go along with it. But that seemed so . . . spineless. Rinakin wasn't the type to back down, even if they were threatening his family.

I heard the clicking of a spoon in a metal-lined cup. Rinakin was apparently taking *tea*.

Behind me Arturo was silent, but I could feel his breath against my neck. Every part of me was suddenly aware of him, standing so near. Goosebumps broke out over my skin.

"How do you want to play this?" Arturo whispered. The pin read his volume, translating his words so softly I could barely hear them.

The spoon clicked against a table, followed by silence.

"Wait here," I whispered back.

Arturo nodded. I was glad he didn't feel the need to keep me in sight every second. I didn't need him tending me like a child.

But I hesitated. He could jump away in a moment and leave me behind. I could follow, of course. I could jump right back to their planet and give them a piece of my mind, so it wasn't being left behind that frightened me.

It was losing their trust, I realized. It was being alone.

It was discovering that I always had been.

"You ready?" Arturo asked. He was watching me quizzically, like he didn't understand why I was hesitating.

"You'll be right here," I said.

He looked surprised. "Yes," he whispered, his voice barely a breath. "I'll be right here if you need me."

I was a cytonic. With the inhibitor gone, I was in power here. I didn't need some human watching my back.

But somehow it made me feel better anyway.

"Okay," I said, and I stepped around the door and into the hallway beyond. The corridor opened up into Rinakin's living space. It wasn't the most lavish place—Rinakin preferred function over ostentation. He sat on a cushioned chair formed with branches that twined together high above his head. He had a wooden cup pressed to his lips, and he looked up at me in surprise as I approached.

I glanced around. If Rinakin was secretly a prisoner, they might be recording and monitoring him rather than posting obvious guards. I put a finger to my ear. *Are they listening*? I mouthed.

Rinakin shook his head and set down his cup. "We're safe here," he said. "Alanik, I'm so glad you've come back."

"I can take you out of here," I said. "I got rid of the other cytonics."

"It isn't safe," Rinakin said. "Alanik, I've learned so much since I've been here. There isn't time to explain, but you're in terrible danger."

Obviously. We were *both* in danger. "You need to come with me," I said. "I'll explain everything, but let me take you out of here before the Superiority realizes I'm here."

"That's just it," Rinakin said. "*You* have to come with *me*. I have a ship we can use. I'll tell you everything on the way."

I blinked at him. Had he used the exact line on me that I'd used on him? And why didn't he seem at all concerned about whether or not I'd rescued his family? "I really think we should have this conversation somewhere else."

"Of course. As I said, I have a ship—"

Hairs rose on the back of my neck. Something was wrong here. "Rinakin," I said. "Where did I go when I left?"

"What?" Rinakin said.

"Where did I go?" I asked. "When I left here. Where did you tell me to go?"

"You went to get fighters, and you brought them to rescue our allies at Hollow," he said. "I heard all about it. You've done very well."

"Okay," I said. "Where'd I get the allies, Rinakin?"

"Alanik," Rinakin said. "Time is of the essence—"

"I know," I said. "So *tell me where you told me to go when we last spoke.*"

Rinakin sighed, and then he moved one of his hands to a device on his wrist. I took a step back, afraid it might be a weapon.

But he simply depressed a button.

My cytonic senses abruptly stopped, like I'd gone instantly blind. I was lost, alone, isolated, unable to reach out for the company of the endlessness of *everything*. Rinakin had a taynix box here somewhere. He'd activated a cytonic inhibitor.

"You're not Rinakin," I said, mostly for the benefit of Arturo.

The person who was not Rinakin smiled.

20

"You're not Rinakin, but you look just like him," I said. "How are you doing that?"

He smiled at me again and leaned back in his chair, like he wasn't worried at all about what I was going to do next. That meant he probably had backup on the way, perhaps alerted by the inhibitor, or by another button on his wristband. From there they'd be able to drag me off to their ship, and then to the Superiority.

I hoped Arturo would stay silent. If they didn't find him, at least he and Naga would be able to return to the platform if I didn't find a way out of this. I didn't expect them to mount a rescue, but at least—

A crash sounded from the office behind me, and I closed my eyes.

Not-Rinakin stood. "Did you bring someone with you?" he asked. He edged around me, keeping his back to the wall as he moved down the hallway so as not to turn it on me or the source of the noise.

I should try to make a run for it—

But I couldn't leave Arturo to be taken. I followed not-Rinakin down the hall. Maybe we could surround him. Maybe we could—

Not-Rinakin turned into the doorway to the office, where little bits of a piece of one of Rinakin's decorative vases lay in fragments on the floor. Not-Rinakin had barely taken a step into the room when he took a punch to his knee and an elbow to his gut, and went flying onto his backside on the hallway floor.

I moved toward him to kick him while he was down, but not-Rinakin lifted his hands in surrender. "Human! So aggressive! Stop, please!"

Arturo stood in the doorway, shaking his hand. "*Ouch,*" he said. "That scudding *hurt.* How did Spensa make it look so easy?"

"Easy!" Naga added.

Not-Rinakin tried to scramble to his feet, but Arturo raised his fist, and he sank to the ground again, protecting his face. I grabbed his wrist and pulled off his bracelet.

With a click of a button the inhibitor was gone, and the universe came to life around me again, like it had suddenly burst into song. With a second click the image over not-Rinakin's body dissolved, revealing a dione with bright crimson skin.

"Oh, scud," Arturo said.

This time I kicked the dione. Hard. They moaned and clutched their side.

"Where is Rinakin?" I asked. We didn't have much time, but with the inhibitor down we could get out much faster.

"You won't find him here," the dione said. "They took him away not long ago."

Oh *no.* I put a hand on Arturo's shoulder and sent Naga the coordinates of the cockpit of my ship in the miasma. She was either getting used to me or was very aware of the danger we were in, because she went without Arturo's permission this time.

"Ouch," Arturo said. He was squished in the cargo space behind my seat in the cockpit, his head pressed against the roof. "This is not ideal."

"Better than being taken by the Superiority," I said.

"Taken!" Naga said from the side of my seat.

Chubs sat on my dash, looking at us curiously.

"Think you can return me to my ship?" Arturo asked.

I gave Naga a clear picture of Arturo's cockpit. His ship had drifted away a bit, but I could still see it through my canopy, floating off to the side. Arturo and Naga disappeared, and a moment later the ship started flying toward mine. Chubs settled on my lap.

"Are you okay?" Arturo asked.

"I'm fine," I said. "How's your hand?"

"It's all right, though I think my ego is bruised. Nedd always said we ought to have more training in hand-to-hand combat. I guess he was right."

"It did the job," I said. "Superiority operatives apparently *really* don't like it when you punch them. I still have no idea how he managed to look like Rinakin." I still had the bracelet in my hand, and I set it on the floor next to my seat to be examined later.

"About that," Arturo said. "Spensa had a ship she found on Detritus. It had holographic technology that let her pretend to be you."

I remembered FM and Jorgen saying something about that. "And the Superiority stole it?"

"I think they must have gotten their hands on her ship. They already knew she'd been using a hologram to look like you, so they would have been searching for it intentionally."

That was a terrifying thought. Though it was also startling to learn that Spensa had technology even the Superiority didn't know about. They always seemed like they knew everything.

"Poor M-Bot," Arturo said. "I'm kind of surprised he didn't self-destruct or something. Spensa is going to be *pissed*."

"She's not the only one," I said.

"I'm checking on the others over the radio," Arturo said. "Scud, their situation sounds hot."

It would be. We'd sent all the cytonics Unity had to offer right at them. I hadn't heard from Jorgen. He said it was easier for him to contact me when I was near, but I hoped he could manage it even across the distance. I reached out to him now—the Unity cytonics had reached them, but they hadn't managed to get the field up.

Status report? I asked him.

We're holding out, Jorgen said. *We've kept the cytonics out of position so far, so they haven't been able to get up their inhibitors or that concussion thing. They're too busy not getting shot down. Did you find Rinakin?*

Working on it.

Jorgen fell silent, probably fully occupied dealing with Quilan and his people.

"We have to hurry and find Rinakin," I said. "If they just left to take him to the Superiority, he could still be in transport. Let me see if I can find their ship."

I closed my eyes, reaching across the miasma around the tree. It was easier to find a huge field of cytonic inhibition rather than one ship across the whole of the planet.

"Angel?" Arturo said. "We have incoming."

I opened my eyes and scanned my proximity sensors. He was right. A contingent of ships was headed right for us. Either they'd scanned and found us, or Quilan had reported our whereabouts.

I needed to focus on finding the ship holding Rinakin. "You want to take point on this one?"

"Gladly," Arturo said. "Evasive maneuvers."

"Copy," I said, mirroring Arturo's movements as he cut a path away from the incoming ships. I tried to focus on the negative realm, reaching out with my senses, canvassing the area for dead spots.

There. Above the reaching branches of the tree, kilometers up in the miasma, was a tiny spot I couldn't feel, like a dead nerve on an otherwise healthy patch of skin.

"Found it," I said to Arturo. "Closer to the tree and *up.*"

"You want to take the lead now?" Arturo asked.

"Yes." I accelerated and shot out in front of him, veering sharply upward so fast that my gravitational capacitors engaged, taking the brunt of the g-forces. The incoming ships changed course a moment later, following and gaining on us.

"I don't know what kind of maneuvers you're used to," Arturo said. "And I'm sure we call them different things. So I'll follow you and we'll try not to get shot, okay?"

"Yes, that," I said, and the ships behind us came into range and started to fire. Off my left wing, Arturo rolled his ship and pulled a tight series of dodging maneuvers I'd never seen before. But I had tricks of my own. Three ships came at me, destructors all firing at once, and I cut to the side, weaving between the projectiles, and then rolled upward again, still aiming for that dead patch in the sky.

"*Nice*," Arturo said. "You're going to have to teach me that one."

"Same to you," I said. The varsity leagues would die to get their hands on moves none of the other teams had seen before. Maybe *that* was how I was going to sell this alliance to the rest of my people. If they couldn't see the sense in saving themselves from the Superiority, they could always be counted on to want their team to win.

"On your right!" Arturo said. I dodged before I saw the destructor fire, and it narrowly missed pinging my shield.

"We're coming up on that dead spot," I said.

There it was. The ship Quilan had used to take Rinakin. An UrDail ship with a cytonic inhibitor inside.

"They'll have taynix in there," I said to Chubs. "Should we collect you some new friends?"

"Friends!" Chubs said, hugging my stomach like he was enjoying the warmth.

If the taynix couldn't hyperjump out of those boxes, he wouldn't be able to go in and get them anyway. We were going to have to disable the ship and then grab it with my light hook to pull it in.

The ships behind us must have alerted it though, because it was flying away at high speed. "Accelerating," I said to Arturo.

"Right behind you," Arturo said, and we shot off after the escaping ship, the others close on our tails. I admired the way Arturo somehow managed to pull the most elaborate maneuvers, all while staying near enough to back me up when it got too hot.

I was every bit as good at evasive flying as he was, maybe better. But Arturo was something I'd never been—a real team player.

I closed in on the ship with the cytonic inhibitor, matching its speed. "I need to be sure he's in there," I said. "I'm going in close."

"I'll cover you," Arturo said, and he did, blasting one of the ships on my tail with his destructors.

I cut a path toward the ship, pulling even with its left wing. The miasma turned my canopy into a blur of violet, but I held my ship steady. At this close range and at such high speed, it would be easy to collide and knock us both out of the sky.

The ship was much larger than mine, with a wider canopy. There in the pilot's seat was another dione, recognizable by the bright blue skin under their flight helmet. I pulled farther forward as destructor fire rained over us—the ships behind us were apparently more interested in taking me down than they were worried about hitting their allies. The larger ship cut to the side, trying to evade me—

But not before I caught a glimpse into the hold, where a second dione sat next to Rinakin, who was bound and gagged.

"He's there," I said to Arturo. I followed as the ship turned a wheel roll to try to shake me. I stayed firm on its tail.

"Orders?" Arturo asked.

"Hang on," I said, and I fired my light hook at the spinning ship, trying to grab it.

My hook connected, but the other ship's momentum pulled me to the side, right into a line of destructor fire. My shield took a hit, and I felt the impact in my bones.

"Angel," Arturo said, "I've got three on my tail. I'm going to have to pull away to shake them."

"Do it," I said.

"You've got more on you," he said. "Watch out—"

The destructor fire continued, and I was forced to drop my light hook and take a dive beneath the diones' ship to avoid losing my shield. "I lost them," I said to Arturo.

"Stay alive," Arturo said.

I had to ground that ship, but I couldn't do that way out here away from the trees. And certainly not with so many ships on our tail.

"I'm going to take them on," I said. "Don't let them get away with Rinakin." I pulled one of my favorite maneuvers from the junior leagues, a tight turn where my ship pivoted and my gravitational capacitors groaned and the weight of the universe seemed to bear down on my body—

And then it lifted, and I opened fire right in the faces of the enemy ships. They dodged to the side, but I pegged the shield of one and then caught another in a long burst of fire. It rolled, trying to avoid me, but its boosters went up in smoke and then the ship exploded, blooming like an opening flower.

The ship started to drop, beginning an uncontrolled descent, still flying forward with the force of its momentum.

The pilot didn't eject.

I'd killed them.

"On your right," Arturo said, and he opened fire, driving back two ships. "Rinakin's ship is just ahead."

Right. Focus. I gripped the control sphere much tighter than I'd been trained to do, trying to ignore the panic rising in my throat.

I killed someone.

They were alive before, and now they were dead.

I did that.

Me.

"There it is," Arturo said. As if he sensed my hesitation, he flew past me, chasing after the ship. "Plan?"

Bile rose in my throat. I had to get out of here. I had to get out of the sky before—

Destructor fire shot over my left wing, and I startled. I slammed forward with my boosters, picking up speed, joining Arturo.

That was enough. I had to end it now. I gained on the ship holding Rinakin and shot at it again with my light hook, which connected, wrapping around the fuselage.

With my light hook in place, I did the only thing I could think of to do.

I reached into the negative realm, called to Naga behind me, and pulled.

21

We ripped out of the negative realm and skidded across the metal surface of Wandering Leaf. Our momentum died abruptly in the negative realm, but our boosters propelled us forward anew as we emerged again. I cut their power, keeping my eyes on the ship that held Rinakin as it skidded toward the base of one of the autoturrets and crashed to a stop.

My ship skidded a bit, grinding the landing gear against the metal of the platform, but it didn't sustain too much damage. I scrambled out, tucking Chubs under my arm in case I needed to hyperjump. I didn't know what the diones would do with Rinakin, but I guessed if they were his guards they'd be less averse to violence than not-Rinakin had been.

Sure enough, the canopy opened and one of the diones pointed a pistol at me and fired.

I lunged away behind the wing of their ship. They weren't going to mess around, so neither would I. I grabbed coordinates for the spot right behind the dione's seat and sent them to Chubs.

We appeared directly behind the dione with the gun, and right in front of the other very surprised dione, who let out a shriek.

Arturo's ship had slid farther than mine, and he climbed out and

336

raced toward us, but before he could arrive I put a hand on each dione and sent Chubs the coordinates I knew best.

We appeared moments later in the living area in my home on Spindle. Several Unity operatives looked up at me from where they were playing a card game. They could do nothing but watch as I shoved both diones forward and then slipped into the negative realm again, directing Chubs to bring us both back to the surface of Wandering Leaf.

I ducked into the hangar to find Arturo staring at me wide-eyed. His voice was muffled by his helmet, but still audible. "I was going to try to punch them again."

"Thank the wind it didn't come to that," I said, and climbed into the back of the ship, searching for Rinakin.

The oxygen generators were still working in here, so thankfully he hadn't gotten a whiff of the miasma. Rinakin looked up at me in shock, though he must have assumed I was the one chasing down his ship. One side of his head was red and swelling, possibly from the impact on landing.

I grabbed the gag and pulled it off of his mouth.

"Tell me something so I know it's really you," I said.

"Our first lesson in cytonics," Rinakin said. "I tried to teach you to meditate, and you told me you thought it was a waste of time."

That was true. I still got impatient with it, but now at least I saw the purpose behind it. Rinakin looked over my shoulder at Arturo. "Did you do it? Did you truly make an alliance with the humans?"

"I'm working on it," I said. "Come on. We need to go check on them."

I helped him forward and untied his wrists. He was favoring one of his arms, though I didn't know if that was from the impact or rough handling by his captors. Arturo stepped to his other side and helped me guide him through the hangar and down the tunnels toward the control room. As we passed beneath the skylights

I scanned the sky for ships, but it was too dark for me to see any. As we neared the control room the platform shuddered and the miasma parted off to the side, the mindblade weapons slicing the miasma into ribbons.

Rinakin stared in the direction of the fire. "I think I've missed a few things."

"You have," I told him. "There was someone pretending to be you, making speeches about how you were joining the cause of progress."

"That I did know," Rinakin said. "My captors played the broadcasts for me. That was . . . unpleasant to listen to."

"I don't have time to explain everything," I said as we reached the control room door. "I need to get out there and help the humans."

"You're back," Rig said, turning from the main control panel to look at us with surprise.

"This is Rinakin," Arturo said, helping him inside. Rinakin slid to the floor next to one of the defense system boxes, holding his arm.

"Jerkface," Rig said into his headset. "Alanik's mission was a success."

"Good to hear," Jorgen said over the radio.

"Way to go, Alanik!" I could hear Nedd say.

"Did anyone follow you?" Rig asked.

"No," Arturo said. "Alanik took care of them."

He meant the diones. I hadn't killed them. I'd simply marooned them. Not like that ship I shot out of the sky. It would have reached the core by now, crashed there, entombing the body of the person who'd burned alive inside.

Arturo put a hand on my shoulder, pulling me outside. "Are you okay?" he asked in a low voice. "You're shaking."

My whole body was trembling, and though I tried to get a grip on myself I couldn't make it stop. "I'm fine," I said.

"The hell you are," Arturo said. "What's wrong?"

He didn't know. I'd shot someone out of the sky and their ship *exploded* before they could eject and I *killed* them and he didn't think anything of it. Probably more people had died in the battle here at the platform. I could hear Rig talking to Jorgen over the radio inside. We needed to get up there.

The world seemed unstable though, like the platform was wobbling in place.

"Talk to me," Arturo said.

"We need to go—"

"And we will. But first tell me what's wrong."

He was probably worried I knew something he didn't, that I had some plan I was hiding from him. "I swear, I'm not going to betray you."

"I know," he said. "I believe you."

He seemed like he meant it, but he was still looking at me with concern. If he didn't think I was going to betray them—

Arturo's grip tightened on my shoulder. "Alanik—"

"They didn't eject," I said. It felt good to say it, like I was confessing some sin. "I shot down that ship and the pilot didn't eject."

"Oh," Arturo said. He looked down at the ground. "You'd never killed before?"

"No," I said. "We play *games* in our ships. We tag each other with *lasers*. I don't know what I'm doing out there! And I *shot* someone down, and I *killed* them. And it shouldn't matter, because they were the *enemy*, but—"

"I used to think like that," Arturo said. "Before we knew who the Superiority were, when they were still a faceless evil. It didn't hurt to kill them. Scud, it felt *good*. But now that I've seen their faces, some of them anyway—" He shook his head. "I don't know. It's not as easy anymore. Maybe it never should have been."

"Easy seems better," I said. "When the enemy shoots at you, you have to shoot back."

"Then what you did was justified," Arturo said. "But it *feels* terrible."

"Yes," I said. "It does."

339

Saying that out loud steadied me a little. Arturo dropped his hand from my shoulder. I wished he hadn't, because that was steadying me too.

"Can you fight?" Arturo asked.

If I didn't, and some of my allies didn't make it, I would never forgive myself. "Yes," I said. "Yes, I want to help."

Arturo leaned against the doorframe to the control room. "Jorgen needs to give the order to get back inside the platform. We got what we came for and now we need to *go*."

"They're working on it," Rig said. "But a new flight of Unity ships showed up that's doing a better job protecting the cytonic ships. If they don't keep the enemy moving, the cytonics are going to get the inhibitor up and then we won't be *able* to leave. They could use your help."

The humans could hyperjump, but it would take precious minutes for them to collect all the Independence ships. They'd helped us do this, and we couldn't leave them behind.

"Come on," I said to Arturo. "Let's get to our ships."

We ran through the tunnels and the hangar. Arturo followed me to my ship, checking the damage to the landing gear as I climbed inside. He leaned on my canopy and put a hand on my arm again. "Are you sure you can do this?"

If he were anyone else I would have shaken him off, but Arturo wasn't being condescending. He was genuinely concerned.

"I'll be fine as soon as I'm in the air," I said.

He nodded. I thought maybe he respected that answer. "Good. Let's get up there."

Another burst of mindblades ripped through the space around the platform. I didn't want to teleport us into the path of that, so I turned on my radio as Arturo and I hovered off the platform.

"—got 'em," Rig was saying. "Jerkface, the enemy is circling around to your position."

"Copy, Rig," Jorgen replied. "I see them. Sentry, FM, head them off. I'll ask some of the Independence pilots to help you."

"We're back, Jerkface," I said. "This is Amphi"—I still couldn't remember the rest of his name—"and . . . Angel."

"Ooooh," Sadie said. "Angel. That's pretty."

"Told you," Arturo said.

I smiled. "Where should we jump to?"

"Welcome, Angel," Jorgen said. "Come out on the treeward side. Your friend Quilan is over there with a bunch of Unity ships protecting him. The cytonic ships all seem to have gotten into position now."

Which meant we needed to get out there immediately or we could be trapped.

"Copy that," I said. I picked a spot between us and Tower, and beckoned Naga along with me as I hyperjumped.

I realized too late that I should have used Chubs. The malevolence of the eyes felt stronger than ever. We were angering them, drawing their wrath. They struck a chord with something primal that told me they meant me harm, and someday they were going to snatch me out of the sky and exact vengeance.

Arturo and I emerged from the negative realm in the airspace between the platform and Tower, and several ships immediately turned toward us.

Alanik, Quilan said. *Surrender your humans and I can argue for your pardon.*

They'd figured out who I was working with. I wondered if they'd gotten close enough to get a look, or just deduced.

No, I told him. *But I'll accept your surrender anytime.*

Why would we offer a surrender when we're winning?

"Cover me," I said to Arturo.

"On it," Arturo replied. I went into evasive maneuvers, diving past several of the ships as they came at us, pushing toward Quilan.

I reached into the negative realm to retort, and caught snatches of his voice.

—have your humans— Quilan was saying. *—to the Superiority— come and get—*

By the branches. He was going to turn us in *right now*. He had his bargaining chip—me, Rinakin, and our human allies—all out here in the open. He must have decided that was enough.

"Jerkface," I said over the radio. "Quilan is calling in the Superiority. I don't know how fast they can get here, but—"

—holding out on us— the person Quilan was talking to responded. *—measures, effective immediately—should have been more forthcoming—*

Quilan's voice sounded panicked as he answered. "*—just found them—told you everything we—have been perfectly loyal—*"

"I don't think it's going the way Quilan anticipated," I told Jorgen. "But I don't think it's going to turn out well for us either." At least if he was talking mind-to-mind he wasn't concentrating on the concussion field, though they might not need him for the inhibitor.

"It rarely does," Jorgen said. "Any idea what we're facing?"

"No," I said. "But—"

Alanik, Quilan said. *This is your fault. You brought this down on us. Surrender now, or—*

Shut up, I told Quilan, and he did, though I couldn't shake how *frightened* he felt out of my head.

What had the Superiority threatened him with that had him so shaken?

At that exact moment the universe went silent again. Tucked around my waist, Chubs let out a whimper.

"They've got the inhibitor up!" I said. "We need to get them out of formation or we can't hyperjump out of here." We could leave the platform, I supposed, and run for our lives. But we'd still need time for the humans to light-lance all the Independence ships. We might not all make it.

"Jerkface," Nedd said over the radio. "We lost another one of the Independence ships. Kimmalyn had to fall back to reignite her shield, and we couldn't keep them from—"

"Boomslug can't fire the hyperweapon as long as that inhibitor is up," Rig said. "I don't know what else to do to help."

The longer we let them maintain that formation, the longer Quilan would have to concentrate on getting a concussion field over the area, knocking out the Skyward and Independence pilots so they could be picked out of the air one by one.

And then on my sensor readout, something enormous appeared in the sky above us. I tilted my ship upward to get a better look through the canopy.

It was a Superiority ship. A battleship, judging by the enormous cannon pointed right at us.

At me and my allies. At my *people* on Tower.

"Jerkface?" Nedd said. "Are you seeing this?"

"I'm seeing it," Jorgen said.

"Is that the one from Detritus?" FM asked.

"Looks like it," Jorgen responded.

"I think so too," Rig said. "That means those are planetary weapons."

"What does *that* mean?" I asked.

"It means ReDawn is in serious trouble," Jerkface said. "Unless we can figure out how to take that ship out. Rig, do you think the mindblades are up to the task?"

"I don't know," Rig said. "We can't use them with the inhibitor up."

"We need to get those cytonics out of formation *now*," Jorgen said.

"T-Stall and Catnip are trying to run one off," Nedd said. "They need backup."

Getting just one of the ReDawn cytonics out of position would disturb the inhibitor. I couldn't sense them anymore through the oppressive silence. "Where are the cytonic ships?" I asked.

"I see them," Arturo said. "Follow me."

"Copy that," Jerkface said. "All Skyward pilots are clear to provide backup."

Arturo took off beneath the platform and I followed. The Superiority wasn't going to extract the humans. They were going to shoot them down, right here near a population center. I didn't know how much damage that cannon could do.

And I didn't want to find out.

"Guys," Rig said over the radio. "You're going to want to listen to this."

Rinakin's voice came over the general channel. "People of Re-Dawn," he said. "You've all been deceived."

"Is that broadcasting generally?" Jorgen asked.

"Yes," Rig said. "He's broadcasting to the planet."

"This is a dark day in our history," Rinakin said. "Unity operatives kidnapped me and then had a Superiority agent take my place, giving you a message I myself would never give. The Superiority has turned on us, and now a battleship threatens Tower. But we will not give in, and we are not without support."

Oh. I saw what Rinakin was doing. I held my breath, following Arturo as he sped away from the platform out into the miasma. I could see the ships ahead now, T-Stall and Catnip contending with a group of Unity fighters.

"For today marks the historic reunification of our alliance with the humans," Rinakin said. "They've come to help us in our hour of need."

"Um, Jerkface?" Rig said. "Rinakin wants me to put you on—"

"On the radio?" Jorgen said. "What does he want me to— scud, okay, do it."

Above us, the cannon started to glow with an ominous blue light.

"They're going to fire on us," FM said. "We don't know how long the shield on the platform will hold, so we'd better be fast."

Arturo and I reached the ships and joined T-Stall and Catnip in a barrage of destructor fire. The other ships returned fire, while another ship darted away toward the platform.

That would be the ship with the cytonic, then. "This one," I said to Arturo, then flipped back to the general channel.

"It is my pleasure to introduce to you Jorgen Weight, human of the planet Detritus, whose people have long struggled under Superiority oppression."

"Um," Jorgen said. "Hi. That's me."

An alert blinked—Arturo trying to get me on our private channel. I switched over. "Let's split up and come at them from either side," he said.

"Done," I said, and we veered away from each other, still rocketing toward the ship with the cytonic.

"How long have you been fighting for your lives against the weapons of the Superiority?" Rinakin asked.

That was good. Put an emphasis on their violence. Pull the curtain back on their false peace.

"My whole life," Jorgen said, sounding more sure of himself now. "Three generations, in fact. They beat us back, made us live underground. They've been trying to exterminate us. But we're still here, and we're still fighting."

"Yeah, Jerkface!" Nedd said.

The Superiority ship let loose a blast from the cannon. The shield around the platform sputtered and sparked, but it held—for the moment at least.

"ReDawn is with you," Rinakin said.

"Let it be so," I said to myself.

"Let it be so!" Chubs repeated.

Arturo and I both opened fire on the ship with the cytonic. They dodged, but we wove with them, catching them with one blast, then two, then three. Their shield blinked out and I fired off one last hit—

And missed as I dodged a torrent of destructor fire coming at me from the side.

Quilan. *They're going to destroy us all, Alanik*, he said. He had the key to speak inside the inhibitor, but I couldn't answer because I didn't. *And it's your fault.*

He fired on me and I dodged again. I'd lost track of the first cytonic ship, so I hoped Arturo still had it in his sights. Quilan bore down on me. He was bound and determined to blow me out of the sky.

But I wasn't going to let him best me. I executed a swivel turn and unloaded my destructors directly at his cockpit.

His shield fizzled and dissipated. His ship continued flying toward mine, so close that I could see him through the canopy as I fired the final shot. He pulled his nose up—

But he was too late. The destructor blast took off the nose of his ship and cleaved the cockpit in two. His ship plummeted out of the sky.

He didn't eject. I didn't think he could have survived that blast, but even if he had he wouldn't survive the fall.

He was the enemy. It should feel *good* to kill him.

It's not as easy anymore, Arturo had said. *Maybe it never should have been.*

I pulled up just in time to see Arturo, T-Stall, and Catnip all firing at the ship with the cytonic. Both the pilot and the cytonic ejected, and the ship fell out of the sky.

The universe buzzed to life around me.

The Superiority ship fired again. The shield around the platform blinked out of existence.

One more shot and it would be gone.

"Hyperweapon is back online!" Rig said. "Jerkface, should we hyperjump out?"

"If you do," I said, "can you be sure the Superiority ship won't fire on the tree?"

"Alanik is right," Jorgen said. "We need to finish this if we can, for ReDawn."

For ReDawn?

"For ReDawn!" Chubs said.

They were going to stay and help us. Even at so great a risk.

"Hang on, Rig," Jorgen said. "I think we need to get the cannon closer."

"You're going to put the platform *closer* to the enormous gun?" FM said. "Isn't that giving them an easier target?"

"I don't want to miss," Jorgen said. "Is the hyperdrive ready?"

"Ready," Rig said.

And then the platform disappeared and resurfaced up in the sky, blocking my view of the battleship. The autoturrets fired.

"Weapons system ready," Rig said. "Scud, they're charging the gun again, Jerkface, so make it quick. I don't think the turrets are going to be enough." I lifted my nose and shot up through the atmosphere, cresting the edge of the platform just in time to see the mindblades ripple through the battleship, cutting the metal into long, thin strips. The cannon shattered apart, the energy it had been building crackling back on itself.

"Scud! Someone just landed outside," Rig said. "I think we must have lost our inhibitor when the shield went down."

"Jerkface?" FM said, sounding terrified.

"All ships, converge on Wandering Leaf," Jorgen said. "Bounce protocol."

I didn't wait for him to send in the others. I sent an invitation to Naga and then prompted Chubs to hyperjump inside the hangar.

Another ship had landed ahead of me and I jumped out and followed its pilot toward the command room. It was a varvax—a crustacean species I'd learned about when I was preparing to go to Starsight—but it looked so strange out of its ship, walking in some kind of armor apparatus that looked like it was made from different types of stone.

I ran toward it, though what I was going to do against a creature in armor I had no idea. I knew less about hitting people than Arturo did.

The creature reached the doorway, far ahead of me.

"Boomslug, help!" Rig called from inside.

A torrent of force emanated from the command room and cut the armor of the varvax into pieces. The creature inside the armor scuttled out, and then disappeared into the negative realm again.

"I can't believe that worked," Rig said. He reached the doorway of the command room and knelt to pick up Boomslug. "I am going to get you a whole crate of caviar, Boomslug. I promise."

Boomslug nuzzled Rig, looking quite pleased with himself. And then FM came running up and threw her arms around both of them, knocking them hard against the doorframe.

"Don't squeeze the slugs!" Jorgen said, running up right behind me. No one listened to him.

Arturo came up beside me, staring up through a skylight at the battleship that was breaking into pieces above us.

"Jerkface," Sadie called from her ship. "We have incoming!"

I looked out through the entrance of the hangar and I could see them—numerous UrDail ships painted a bright blue.

More Independence fighters coming to our aid.

"We did it," I said. The Superiority would surely come after us again, but we weren't alone anymore.

22

"I don't know if we need the backup," Jorgen said, looking over Sadie's shoulder at her sensor screen. "The Unity forces are re-treating."

"Thank the stars," Arturo said.

I concurred. From inside the command center, I could hear Rinakin resuming his broadcast about the strength of ReDawn and her ability to resist. He seemed to be using the word progress a lot. I bet Nanalis was going to love that, but Rinakin's broadcast would make certain that blame for the Superiority's appearance fell squarely where it belonged.

"He's going to want to parade you around at the Council tree," I said to Jorgen. "You're the hero of ReDawn now, apparently."

Jorgen looked horrified, and I laughed.

"Hey," Nedd said, coming up and slapping Jorgen on the back. "If you want, you can tell them I'm Jorgen Weight. I've always wanted to be in a parade."

Jorgen looked like he might consider it. "We need to report to Cobb," he said. "Tell Command we've been successful here. After that, hopefully we can go home. If I can talk some sense into my parents, maybe they'll even send an official diplomatic coalition instead of a flight of pilots."

Actual aid, and a renewal of our old alliance. I'd gone to the humans looking for help—but until this moment I don't think I'd let myself believe help would actually come.

"Thank you," I said to Jorgen, "for not abandoning my people to the Superiority when the inhibitor went down."

Jorgen looked confused. "Of course," he said. "That's what an alliance is. It means we protect each other."

So many of my own people backed down at the first sign of inconvenience that I'd expected the same of the humans. They could have left and waited out whatever that ship would have done to Tower in retribution. They'd risked their own lives to save *my* people. They'd done it again and again.

I'd misjudged Jorgen. He was an incredible leader, and it was a privilege to fly with him.

"Yes," I said. "That's what an alliance is."

Jorgen still looked confused, like this was so obvious it didn't bear saying. "I'm going to try to reach Cobb on the hypercomm," he said. "We need to warn them about what the Superiority almost did to the people who were supposedly working with them." He ducked into the command center.

"I told you he wasn't going to turn on you," Arturo said. He leaned against the corridor wall, watching me.

"You did tell me that," I said. "But you also said you thought *I* was going to turn on you."

"I said I *didn't* think you would," Arturo said. "But that it was a possibility."

"I seem to remember you being very threatening," I returned. "And quite concerned."

Arturo grinned. "Fine. Maybe neither of us is a perfect judge of character."

"If I'd really believed you all weren't trustworthy," I said, "I never would have asked for your help to begin with."

"That's probably true," Arturo said. "Though did you have other options?"

"Not good ones," I admitted. "So thank you."

Arturo's expression grew serious. "You shot down that other cytonic," he said. "You knew him?"

I could still see Quilan's face as he bore down on me, destructors firing.

"I did," I said. "He was going to kill me, and I got him first."

"Right," Arturo said. "That seems like it should make it easier, doesn't it? But I've never had to shoot down someone I talked to. Someone I knew."

I wanted to say the world was better off without Quilan in it, but I wasn't sure that was true. My people had so few cytonics. We needed every one.

Maybe Rinakin was right. There was a place for persuasion. Quilan's death was a waste, of a leader as well as a cytonic. Killing him had been necessary, but everyone would have been better off if we could have persuaded him to change his mind to fight for our side.

Now he could never change his mind, and there was a kind of tragedy to that.

"I'm not glad he's dead," I said, "but I'm glad I'm still alive. I wish it had all gone differently, but I don't know what I would have changed, or if I even had the power to change it."

"You had the power to do something really good for your people and ours," Arturo said. "Does that make it feel better?"

I thought about that. "I don't know," I said. "But I don't regret it, I know that."

Arturo nodded. "Yeah. Neither do I."

He held my gaze for a moment, and something about the way he looked at me was thrilling and terrifying all at once. I followed after Jorgen into the control room.

Rinakin was finishing his broadcast. He slumped against the control panel, looking exhausted. His daughter stood by his side, urging him to come rest in one of the bunk rooms.

"We need to get him medical attention," she told me.

"I know," I said. "If the Independence medic can't care for him, we'll take him to a hospital soon." Rinakin's injuries didn't look life threatening, but he should still receive treatment.

Jorgen leaned against the wall by the hypercomm. The purple and orange slug from his ship was now in there, and he tapped his fingers on the control panel, waiting.

"Admiral Cobb will speak to you now," someone said, and then Cobb spoke through the hypercomm.

"Jorgen," he said. "It's about time you reported in."

Jorgen frowned. Cobb had told him *not* to call, hadn't he? Because he was trying to stay in good with the politicians, and not let anyone know he was involved in Skyward Flight's desertion.

"We've been successful here," Jorgen said. "We were able to save Alanik's people and establish an alliance with them."

FM and Rig appeared in the doorway. Rig's hair was a bit messier than normal, probably due to some human mating ritual. I was still fuzzy on the details of all that, but humans were clearly uncomfortable discussing these things, so I wasn't going to ask.

Arturo at least had been open to talking about his former girlfriend when we spoke before. Though the idea of asking *him* about human mating rituals felt . . . disorienting.

"That's good," Cobb said. "I'd like you to return as soon as possible for a full report. And bring some representatives of the UrDail with you, if you would. We'd like to begin official talks with them."

Jorgen looked over at me. "Is it safe, sir?"

"Of course. It's perfectly safe. The shield is holding fine. You have nothing to worry about. I have new orders for you as soon as you can get your people back here."

FM and Rig exchanged a glance.

"You said before that the UrDail should stay away," Jorgen said. "Because you worried they might become a bargaining chip in the negotiations with the Superiority."

"Oh," Cobb said. He sounded surprised, like he'd wanted to

pretend he'd never said that. "No, the negotiations are at an impasse. If you return immediately, I can—"

Jorgen pushed the mute button on the hypercomm. "Something's up with Cobb," he said.

"Is your mother in the room with him?" FM asked.

"Maybe," Jorgen said. "But why would he respond to my call if my mother was right there?"

"Maybe he got the message that you'd tried to reach him in front of her," Rig said. "So he didn't have a choice."

"Or maybe it's not him," I said.

The three of them stared at me.

"What?" Jorgen said.

They didn't know. We hadn't had time to tell them. "The Superiority stole the holographic technology from Spensa's ship. The Rinakin who was working with Unity was a fake—a Superiority plant. If they did that to us . . ."

"Scud," Jorgen said. "You think maybe this *isn't* Cobb?"

"Cobb didn't behave like himself when we saw him last," FM said. "I assumed there must be an explanation."

"I think Alanik just gave us one," Jorgen said.

"Jorgen?" Cobb said over the hypercomm. "Are you still there?"

Jorgen turned on the microphone again. I'd missed the last thing Cobb had said, and I didn't think he'd paid attention to it either. "I'm here, sir," Jorgen said. "I'd like to speak to my mother, if that's all right."

That was a good move. Jeshua might not be helpful when it came to diplomacy, but she'd surely be on our side if she knew she was dealing with a Superiority fake.

"You'll have to be sure she's not also a plant," I whispered, and Jorgen nodded.

"You can talk to her when you return," Cobb said. "I need you here immediately. That is an order."

Jorgen muted the microphone again. "This has to be a trap."

"It sounds like it," I said.

Jorgen swore and turned on the microphone again. "Sir, I'm ordering our people to prepare to return," he said. "It may take us a bit to gather the UrDail delegation together."

"Get here as soon as you can," Cobb said.

"I will. Thank you, sir." Jorgen turned off the microphone. "I need to communicate with my mother somehow. Warn her and the assembly that the Superiority has infiltrated the DDF."

"What do you think they did with real Cobb?" FM asked.

"They probably replaced him when they met for peace talks," Rig said. "Right after you left for ReDawn. We worried it might be a trap, but Cobb and Jeshua went anyway because the offer to negotiate a truce was too good to refuse. And they didn't want to let them *inside* the shield because that could potentially be worse."

"That sounds like the Superiority," I said. "They pretended to talk about peace and used the opportunity to undermine you."

"So Cobb has been in their custody for a while," FM said. "Do you think they'll hurt him?"

"I wouldn't put it past them," I said.

"I can't contact my mother directly," Jorgen said. "She's not cytonic."

"We could contact Spensa's grandmother," I said. "She might know something, since the Superiority is demanding your cytonics. They might have collected her by now."

"Yes," Jorgen said. "That's true."

I was already reaching out through the negative realm, finding Detritus and canvassing the planet. I found Gran-Gran's mind far enough from the planet that she had to be in a ship.

That wasn't a good sign.

Gran-Gran, I said, *It's Alanik. Are you all right?*

These vat-suckers are looking to trade me for their own freedom, Gran-Gran said.

Who's trying to trade you? I asked.

354

Some bottom-feeders from the National Assembly, Gran-Gran said.

Is Jeshua Weight with them?

She is, Gran-Gran said. *War hero my wrinkled behind. They've brought that blue alien too, and the alien isn't happy about it.*

Cuna was a defector from the Superiority, so it made sense that the Superiority would also want them turned over. Gran-Gran seemed to understand what was happening at least.

Where have they brought you? I asked.

They've got us on a ship taking us to some delegation, she said. *They're dressed to the nines too, like they're meeting royalty.*

Oh no. "They've got Gran-Gran and Cuna on a ship en route to some delegation with the Superiority," I said. "Your mother is there, and some people from the assembly."

Jorgen swore. "That has to be a trap too. Tell her to tell them to turn around."

Of course. *Tell them it's a trap. The Superiority isn't going to work with them. They've replaced Admiral Cobb with a Superiority operative using a holographic disguise. They offered progress to my planet and then turned their guns on them instead. Tell them nothing will come of this but ruin.*

I'll tell them, Gran-Gran said. *But they didn't listen to me before and they aren't going to listen to me now.*

"She says she'll tell them," I said. "But she doesn't think they'll listen."

"She's probably right." Jorgen squeezed his eyes shut in frustration. "Do they have a hypercomm on board?"

I searched the area near Gran-Gran. I could sense taynix, all clustered together like they were trapped in some kind of container. "They have a box with slugs in it," I said. And another one alone, sitting a few feet from the others. I probed at its mind, trying to send it coordinates to talk to our hypercomm, and it felt receptive, like it understood the message.

I did the same with the slug in our hypercomm. "Try it now," I said. "I think you'll be able to talk to them."

"Mom?" Jorgen said into the hypercomm.

There was a beat of silence, and then, "Jorgen?" Jeshua Weight said.

"Mom," Jorgen said. "You have to turn the ship around. You're walking into a trap."

"*We're* walking into a trap? You *fled* the *planet* against orders. Where are you?"

"ReDawn," Jorgen said. "We negotiated that alliance. We have people willing to work with us against the Superiority."

"Then you're undermining everything we've been working for here," Jeshua said. "We've met with the Superiority, and they want to arrange a treaty."

"I don't think they do—" Jorgen said, but his mother cut him off.

"I think they're being sincere," Jeshua said. They always did—that was the problem. So many people couldn't taste the poison past the sweetness of the tea. "We can't keep fighting like this. We've been losing the war for years. If there's a chance we can save our people's lives, we have to take it."

"Mom, they replaced Cobb," Jorgen said. "He's a Superiority operative wearing a hologram like the one Spensa used to infiltrate Starsight."

Jeshua was quiet for a moment. "Are you sure?" she asked. "You saw this?"

"No," Jorgen said. "But they used the same trick on someone here, and when we talked to him something was off about him."

"Jorgen, I've been with Cobb for the last two days. He's tired like we all are, but it's him."

Jorgen hit the edge of the control board with the heel of his hand. "It *isn't*, Mom. You can't go to that delegation. You're walking into a trap."

A man's voice came over the radio. "Jorgen," he said, "I know this is all hard for you to accept. We raised you to hate the Krell. We've hated them all our lives. But son, if we keep fighting them you're going to die up there some day. That's what we're trying to prevent. The Superiority is offering to *train* you. This is a huge opportunity, and you need to try to accept it."

"They tried to kill me today," Jorgen said. "They're *lying* when they offer us peace."

"You should never have gone to ReDawn." Now Jeshua was talking again. "Can't you see we're trying to keep you safe?"

Jorgen muted the mic again and swore, covering his eyes with his hands.

Arturo appeared in the doorway. "Everything okay?" he asked.

"No," I said. "The Superiority replaced Cobb, same as they did Rinakin, and Jorgen's parents are taking Gran-Gran and Cuna to a meeting with the Superiority right now."

"Scud," Arturo said. "We have to stop them. We can't let them walk into that."

In my mind, Gran-Gran and the tiny slug presences stopped moving, as if they'd arrived at their destination.

"I think they may already be there," I said.

"We need to go now," Jorgen said. "We're taking the whole platform. We'll come back to finish the alliance with Alanik's people, but for now we may need the air support."

"Agreed," I said. "Let's go."

Rig was already putting Drape back in the hyperdrive box.

"Alanik," Jorgen said. "Can you give him coordinates near where Gran-Gran is?"

"Yes," I said, and I stretched myself across the space between galaxies, pinpointing her location and then sending it to Drape.

"Ready," I said.

"Drape," Rig said. "Go."

We slid into the negative realm beneath the distracted eyes, which then shifted into glittering stars as the entire platform came out the other side in the airspace around Detritus.

A small human passenger ship was docked at the outside of a boxy Superiority transport ship a couple kilometers away. The transport ship wasn't nearly as big as some I'd seen arrive at ReDawn, not even as big as Wandering Leaf.

"You're going to need backup," FM said. I didn't think FM and Jorgen had really resolved their issues with each other, but that didn't seem to matter to either of them at the moment.

"We are," Jorgen said. "I want the rest of you in your ships, ready to fight in case we need additional air support. It doesn't *look* like they brought fighters, but they could hyperjump them in at any moment."

"Okay," FM said.

Jorgen turned to Arturo. "You command the flight while I'm in there. Make sure everyone's ready to go on my signal."

Arturo looked at me, and I thought maybe he'd been planning to volunteer to go with us to the Superiority ship. I wished he would. "Got it," he said, and he spun around from the doorway, moving toward the hangar. "Skyward Flight," he yelled, "everyone to your ships!"

The flight scattered. "I'll get Boomslug back in the weapons system," Rig said.

"Good," Jorgen said. "Alanik, you don't sense any cytonic inhibitors on that ship, do you?"

"No," I said. "Not yet."

Rig handed him Snuggles, and Jorgen slipped him into his sling. "Alanik," Jorgen said, "can you give Snuggles directions to the command room on Platform Prime?"

"Yes," I said. "But I can't jump us into the Superiority ship afterward. I'm not familiar with it, so I could end up materializing us in the middle of a wall."

"The taynix seem to be able to avoid that," FM said. "You said they took some of the taynix with them, right? Could you hyperjump to them?"

"We'll have to try it," Jorgen said.

"It would probably be the ones issued to the other pilots," FM said. "The ones who didn't come with us. Try Corgi or Snide, or maybe Waffle or Pipsqueak."

Jorgen blinked at her. "I'll . . . try to remember that."

"You'd better," I said. "Are you ready now?"

Jorgen closed his eyes, like he was steeling himself for battle. "Ready," he said.

I put a hand on his shoulder and sent Snuggles the coordinates for the room where I'd met with Cobb and Jeshua.

23

We emerged next to the conference table where Jeshua Weight had turned down my offer of an alliance. The room was empty, and Jorgen strode out the door, moving with purpose. I followed behind him as he walked up the hall—he knew where he was going better than I did.

A man sitting behind a desk looked up and visibly startled.

"I need to talk to Cobb," Jorgen said. "I'm to report to him immediately. Is he here?"

"Of course," the man said. "Hold on a moment." He went to the door behind him and knocked, then opened it. "Jorgen Weight to see you," he said.

Admiral Cobb shuffled to the door immediately, looking over the shoulder of the receptionist at Jorgen and me. "Stars, I'm glad you're back," Cobb said.

I could see Jorgen scrutinizing him. This man had Cobb's cane and his limp. His voice sounded the same to me, but so had Rinakin's.

Jorgen closed the distance between them, and I stayed close. I wasn't going to be left behind. Jorgen put a hand on Cobb's arm and slid his sleeve up just enough to reveal the bracelet on his wrist. It was identical to the one not-Rinakin had been wearing.

"What are you—" fake Cobb began.

"Snuggles, take us to Corgi," Jorgen said.

"Corgi!" Snuggles said.

A moment later we materialized in front of a very startled-looking pilot who was lying on a bunk with his jumpsuit half off, taking a nap.

Oh. Apparently Jeshua hadn't taken *all* the slugs we'd left behind with her.

"Hey—" fake Cobb shouted, but Jorgen didn't give him a chance to finish.

"Snuggles, take us to Snide!" he shouted.

"Snide!" Snuggles said.

We passed beneath the eyes, and then suddenly we stood in a storage room on an unfamiliar ship, next to a box containing several small cytonic minds.

I could feel Gran-Gran moving away from us. There were a few other taynix on this ship in other directions, probably powering Superiority hyperdrives or hypercomms.

Fake Cobb recovered enough to wrench himself away from Jorgen and move toward the doorway, but Jorgen caught him by the back of the neck, shoving him to the ground and then twisting his arms behind his back.

"You aren't going anywhere," he said.

"I'm your commander," fake Cobb said.

Jorgen didn't even bother responding.

"They took Gran-Gran in that direction," I said, pointing.

"I think my parents' ship must be docked nearby," Jorgen said. "Let's split up. I'll find my parents and prove to them that they've walked into a trap. You retrieve Gran-Gran and then hyperjump to me." He opened the crate of slugs and handed one to me. "I think that's Snide," he said. "If we stop being able to find each other, we'll know the other got caught in an inhibitor and come help. Does that work?"

"Yes," I said. I moved up to the door, peering through a small window to see if there was anyone there. The hallway was empty, so we moved out of the storage room, heading in two different directions.

This whole ship made my skin crawl. I wished I didn't have to do this alone. The taynix—Snide—snuggled into the crook of my elbow, as if it felt the same.

Gran-Gran and whoever was moving her away from here had to be ahead, but I didn't see or hear evidence of anyone else. The ship was eerily empty, like it had only a skeleton crew aboard. If they really believed the humans were so aggressive, why hadn't they brought more forces?

Gran-Gran, I said through the negative realm. *I'm here on the ship, coming toward you. Where are they taking you?*

To a holding cell, they say, Gran-Gran said. *I spat in one of their eyes. I don't think they liked that much.*

I smiled. The more I got to know Gran-Gran, the more I liked her. *How many of them are there?*

Two diones, she said. *One with me, and one with Cuna. But I'm hoping they'll take me to Cobb. I think I can hear him.*

Cobb was here? I'd assumed they would have transported him away already. *Hear him?* I said. *Through the negative realm?* That didn't make sense. Cobb wasn't cytonic. It shouldn't be possible for her to find him. I searched over the area where she was headed myself, but I couldn't feel anything except a couple of taynix.

Yes, I'm sure it's him. He's just up ahead. Not like those other voices, the quiet ones. Are they your people?

My people? What voices was she hearing? I knew she was an old woman, but had she lost her mind?

Yes, those voices. They're asking me for help.

I don't know who those are, I said. *You probably shouldn't answer them, just in case. I'm coming to get you, but they might have inhibitors on this ship. Those will cut off the use of your powers. You may want to get out now.*

I'm certain Cobb is there, Gran-Gran said. *I want to bring him with me. I don't know if I can travel the way you and Spensa do, but some things feel so real in there—I think I can try.*

It was a risk, but I could hardly blame her for that. *I'll follow until you're out. And then return to help Jorgen. If you can't manage the hyperjump or you get inhibited, I'll come to help you.*

Thank you, Gran-Gran said. *I can tell by your spirit that you have the heart of a warrior like my granddaughter.*

I felt oddly touched by that, even though I barely knew either of them. I continued to move down the hall, peering around corners to make sure no one was there.

The ship continued to be empty, which made me more and more uneasy.

We've reached the holding cells, Gran-Gran said in my mind. *Cobb is here. Stars, he looks bad.*

But he's alive? I asked.

He's alive. I don't know what they've done to him, but—

Gran-Gran's voice cut off as a section of the ship ahead went dead in my mind. I couldn't reach Gran-Gran anymore—she'd disappeared beneath an inhibitor cloud.

I needed to get there quickly and see if I could disable it. I hurried around a corner—

And then ducked back at the sound of voices. There were people ahead, though I wasn't yet close to the inhibited area of the ship. I didn't understand much of the dialect they were speaking, and they were too far away from me for my pin to translate. But I did catch a few words I recognized.

Ready. Hurry. Leaving.

These people *were* leaving. Running in the opposite direction, away from the center of the ship.

What were they trying to get away from so fast?

I needed to get to Gran-Gran, Cobb, and Cuna, but something was very wrong here and I wanted to know what it was. *Did you find your parents?* I asked Jorgen.

Not yet, Jorgen said. *Took a wrong turn. Moving toward them now. Fake Cobb is dragging his feet, slowing me down.*

I wanted to suggest that he break fake Cobb's legs, but that probably wouldn't help them move any faster.

I know where Gran-Gran and real Cobb are, I said. *Cuna is with them too. Will get them in a moment. Need to check on something first.*

Copy, Jorgen said. *Keep me informed.*

I moved in the direction the fleeing people had come from. At the end of a short hall, I found a door with a heavy handle that was closed and locked. I listened; no noise came from inside and no light was visible under the door.

I reached through the door, feeling the space beyond through the negative realm, and then hyperjumped through.

I emerged in a dark room and immediately felt the wall for a light panel. The room lit up, and there in the center of the large room was a taynix box with wires and equipment mounted to the outside.

I took a step toward it, and then paused. The device was hooked up to a large tube with a wide-open end aimed at the wall. It looked suspiciously like a cannon—

And in the box attached to it I could feel the tiny cytonic mind of a taynix.

Oh *no*. The Superiority operatives had said something was "ready" and they needed to "hurry" and get away from it. They had a mindblade weapon, and instead of aiming it into the sky to shoot us down they had it aimed toward the *center* of the ship itself.

It was a *bomb*, and it was rigged to explode.

I was out of my depth here, but I knew where to go for help. *The ship has a bomb on it*, I sent to Jorgen. *I'm going to get Rig.* I gave Snide the coordinates for the control room on Wandering Leaf.

Rig let out an undignified scream, which the slug in his sling promptly echoed. "Scud!" he said. "I will never get used to you doing that!"

I wondered if FM got that reaction when she and Gill snuck around to see him. There wasn't time to talk about it now. "Come with me," I said, and reached for his arm, then directed Snide to take us back.

We appeared again in the room next to the taynix bomb.

"I want to tell you to warn me before you do that," Rig said, squeezing his eyes shut. "But I suppose you did."

I gestured at the device. "We're in the Superiority ship," I said. "This is a bomb, isn't it? Can you defuse it?"

"Can I *what*?" Rig looked over the equipment, and I watched his face contort in horror as he came to the same conclusions I had. "I don't know anything about bombs! I'm not qualified to deal with this."

None of us were qualified, but I couldn't let the Superiority blow up the ship with people inside. "What if we break the box?" I said. "If we remove the taynix—"

"The box is rigged to prevent tampering," Rig said, looking it over. "I don't know how it works, but I can tell that much. Alanik, I'm sorry. I can't fix it. We need to get off this ship immediately."

I understood. There was nothing he could do. "Can you get yourself back?" I asked. "I'll go for Jorgen and the others."

Rig nodded. "I'm sorry."

"Go," I said.

"Drape, take me to Gill," he said.

"Gill!" Drape said. And then Rig disappeared, back to Wandering Leaf.

I tore off down the hallway in the direction of the cytonic inhibitor while simultaneously reaching out to Jorgen. *You need to get out of here. Can you get to your parents?*

Working on it, Jorgen said. *The Superiority people took them into a room, but it's locked. I'm moving around to the other side, trying to find an open door. Fake Cobb is not helping.*

Near Jorgen, I could feel a new patch of dead space—another

inhibitor had been turned on near him, probably in the room with the human politicians. Even if I left Gran-Gran, Cuna, and real Cobb to join him, I couldn't jump in and get them.

Work fast, I said. *We have to get out of here.*

I raced past closed doorways to a side hall ahead, and found a series of rooms with windows in the walls. Cuna was in one and Gran-Gran and Cobb in another, but as soon as I moved close to them the sounds of the universe quieted.

Cobb looked awful—he had bruises down his face, and he sat slumped against the wall like he was having trouble holding himself in a sitting position. Gran-Gran knelt over him, and Cuna stood in the other cell, motioning to me.

"Alanik!" they yelled through the glass. "I don't know what Winzik plans to do with us—"

"He plans to blow us up!" I yelled as I moved by. "We're working on it." I hauled open the doors at the end of the hall, searching for the inhibitor. I found a custodial closet and a room with a couple of old broken chairs. At the end of the hall was another door, this one locked.

I stepped back and kicked it with all my might. The handle snapped on the third blow, and I tore it off and dragged the door open.

There, inside, was a taynix box. I opened it, and a blue and green slug tumbled to the floor.

The cytonic inhibition faded. *Alanik*, Jorgen said in my mind. *I can't get to them. The Superiority people all fled, and you disappeared, and I can't—*

On my way, I said. I didn't waste time running down the hall again. I hyperjumped back to the room with Cuna and grabbed them roughly by the arm.

Get Cobb out, I sent to Gran-Gran. She must have already been prepared to do so, because they disappeared before I even finished the thought. So she *could* hyperjump. That was good. One less thing for me to do in the unknown time before this ship exploded.

"Snide, take me to Drape," I said, and Cuna and I passed beneath the unseeing eyes as we jumped to the control room on Wandering Leaf. I deposited Cuna at the feet of a somewhat-less-surprised Rig, and then Snide and I hyperjumped back to the Superiority transport ship, this time to the storage room where we'd landed originally.

I took off at a run toward the area of the ship where I could sense Jorgen. I could feel his panic even before I reached him. He stood in a narrow observation room overlooking a tiered meeting hall that was clearly designed for a large assembly of people. Fake Cobb seemed to have escaped from Jorgen, because I didn't see him here. There were a dozen or so humans on the other side of the window, including Jeshua Weight, who stood right against the glass. One of the other humans—a man who looked like an older version of Jorgen—hefted one of the chairs and threw it at the glass.

It must have been some kind of reinforced plastic, because it didn't break.

"Humans of Detritus!" a voice said. It was coming from a loudspeaker inside the room, but was loud enough that we could hear it even from here. "For your years of resistance, you have been judged too aggressive to live. You will meet your end for the good of all. In our graciousness, we will end your lives swiftly. Your pain will be brief. Your deaths will be broadcast to your planet, so that they may mourn you. You may have a moment to say your goodbyes."

"How benevolent of them," I said.

Jorgen beat his fists against the window. Inside the room, I could see the politicians starting to panic.

As they should. We couldn't get them out of there. The Superiority might be satisfied with merely enslaving my people, but the humans?

Them they were going to destroy.

"We have to find that inhibitor," I said, and Jorgen nodded, moving toward the doorway.

I tore down the hallway in the opposite direction. But there weren't many crevices in this part of the ship—and all the other inhibitors had been *inside* the zone they inhibited, not outside of it. While there was a door on every side, they were all locked, and reinforced far better than the closet.

I ran the circle around the meeting room until I met up with Jorgen, and then we double-checked the areas we'd each checked before.

None of the doors would give, no matter how hard we beat on them.

When we reached the viewing room again, Jeshua still stood at the glass. She turned around, glaring at Jorgen.

"Look for a box," he shouted through the glass at her. "A box with a taynix in it!"

Go, she mouthed at him.

Jorgen shook his head, beating on the glass with his fists again.

"Go!" Jeshua yelled through the glass at Jorgen. Her voice was faint, but I could make out what she said next. "Do better than we did."

We weren't going to be able to save them. There was nothing more we could do here.

I put a hand on Jorgen's shoulder. He still had Snuggles in his sling. He didn't need me to pull him out.

"She's right," I said. "We have to go."

"No!" Jorgen shouted. There were tears running down his cheeks now.

He wasn't going to leave, but I couldn't let him die here.

I didn't take chances with the slug. I reached through the negative realm to the hangar on Wandering Leaf, and I pulled.

Through the negative realm, I heard a scream.

EPILOGUE

The wrath of the eyes bore down on me as I floated beneath their ever-present glares. But I could barely feel it, consumed as I was by the full force of Jorgen's pain, his anger, even his resentment of me for tearing him away from there. I choked on it, feeling every ounce of it down to my bones.

We fell out of the negative realm and the feeling faded, but the echoes of it lingered, as if I'd just watched my own parents die.

The members of Skyward Flight were climbing out of their ships, moving toward the windows near the entrance of the hangar to watch the Superiority ship as it tore itself to shreds, its hull ripped apart, its engine systems exploding in silent clouds of dust and smoke. Cuna stood off to the side, staring out at the remains of the Superiority ship as they scattered across the backdrop of stars.

Jorgen made a strangled sound and most of the flight turned around and saw us there, shock and relief reflecting across their faces. Arturo closed his eyes, like he'd been sure we were both gone and had to steady himself for a moment. Rig hurried down the tunnel from the control room behind us. "I'm sorry," he said. "I didn't know what to do with it, I—"

"It wasn't your fault," I said. And that was true.

This was the Superiority's fault. Every bit of it.

Jorgen stared out at the pieces of the ship as they spiraled outward, shrapnel spreading in every direction. His face was like a statue, though I'd felt the grief he was holding in.

"Did Gran-Gran—" Rig asked.

"She got out," I said. "So did Cobb. I saw them." I scanned over the planet, searching in the negative realm for another cytonic mind, but I couldn't feel one. I reached out farther, searching for Gran-Gran—or even for Cobb, who Gran-Gran said she could feel in the negative realm though I'd been sure he wasn't cytonic.

I couldn't find them. They weren't here. And there were no dead spaces left that would hide them.

"They made it out," I said. "But . . . I don't know where they are."

"At least they weren't here," FM said. She put a hand on Jorgen's shoulder, but he shook her off.

"We're going down to Platform Prime," Jorgen said.

"Okay," FM said, "but I think you need to stop for a minute—"

"*Now*," Jorgen said. "I'm sorry, Alanik. We'll be a little late returning to ReDawn." He turned and looked at the floating pieces of ship, the place where both his parents had died. "There are some things we need to take care of first."

EVERSHORE

JORGEN WEIGHT

CALLSIGN:
JERKFACE

PROLOGUE

"Jorgen, are you ready?" my father asked, standing in the doorway to the parlor. He looked over my graduation uniform—admiring it I thought, but also searching for anything out of place.

"Yes," I said. I stood in front of the glass case filled with my mother's medals. She was one of the most decorated pilots the Defiant Defense Force had ever seen. At the center of the case was a pewter figure of a Sigo-class fighter—the ship my mother used to fly. As a kid I used to stand here and stare at that ship for hours, imagining what it would be like to be a pilot someday, fighting the Krell: all thrill and heroics and glory. I never took the figure out of the case—my mother would have killed me—but in my mind I flew in that ship to the stars and back.

I could see my reflection in the glass, my dress uniform crisp and fitted. After today, I'd be a full pilot.

"I hope you know how proud we are of you," my father said. "So many cadets begin flight school, but graduating is a real accomplishment."

My father was right. I'd started with what had to have been, in my estimation, the finest flight of pilots the DDF had ever seen. They were incredible people, every one of them. I couldn't have asked for a better team.

And of all of us, only two remained. We'd lost some amazing people in the months of cadet training.

Rig, Bim, Morningtide, Nedder, Amphi, Quirk, Hurl.

Spin.

We needed them, but none of them were graduating today, and the DDF was poorer for it.

That didn't feel like an accomplishment. It felt like a tragedy—one that was mostly on me. What use was I? A leader who couldn't bring his team with him?

My mother came down the stairs in her own dress uniform. She wasn't officiating, but she'd still be there in all her regalia. She crossed the room to the case and opened it, pulling down her medals and pinning them on. She looked up at me, taking in my uniform, though it didn't feel like she was looking for imperfections the way it had with my father.

I felt like she was seeing herself.

"This is an important day," she said. "You've done every bit as well as we hoped you would."

"Thank you," I said—because it was the right answer, not because I felt it. I'd earned the pilot's pin more than I had the cadet's one—that had been automatic because of my mother's accomplishments. Still, I couldn't help wondering. Did I deserve to be here? Would Ironsides ever have kicked *me* out of cadet training? The son of Algernon and Jeshua Weight? I'd tried my best, done everything I knew how to do. But if I hadn't, I would probably still be standing here, my whole life laid out before me, predetermined just like my uniform.

"How does it feel to finally make full pilot?" my father asked.

This too had a right answer. "It feels great," I said. I glanced back at the now-empty medal stands and allowed myself this one admission: "Not that I'll be flying for long."

My mother's lips set into a line. "Thank the stars you won't have to."

I'd been told before I started flight school that I'd only fly active duty for six months. I should be grateful for that, but I wasn't. I wondered if FM would get to keep flying, or if our whole flight had been trained—using DDF resources, all the focus we'd put into it, the lives of my friends—for nothing.

I knew better than to say that aloud. I didn't need the lecture about how every sacrifice was part of a greater goal. I knew it by heart. I'd occasionally given it myself.

I could never say my mother didn't understand—she understood better than anyone. She was a decorated pilot. She'd lost friends, flightleaders, wingmates. I could see the heaviness in her eyes, the burden she carried. She pushed on, doing everything she could for our people, because she believed in the cause—because we had to survive.

I was afraid I would never have the stomach for it, that I was soft and weak and would never be able to harden myself to do what needed to be done.

But if I was being honest with myself, I was equally afraid that I would.

1

Seven months later

Enough.

I stood in the landing bay on Wandering Leaf, staring through the windows at the exploding Superiority ship as the wreckage spiraled out into the blackness of space. The eerie blue shield of Detritus loomed in the distance. My flight stood around me, all watching the remains of the explosion, the tomb that had claimed my parents and half of our National Assembly.

We were supposed to have saved them. We were supposed to have won. Instead we'd barely gotten ourselves out alive.

I could have died in there. I almost did. I should thank Alanik for pulling me out, but I felt frozen, like something inside of me had died after all.

"Did Gran-Gran—" Rig asked.

"She escaped," Alanik said. "So did Cobb. I saw them." I could feel her reaching out through the nowhere, searching for them. "But . . . I don't know where they are."

"At least they weren't here," FM said. She put a hand on my shoulder, but I shook her off.

"Boom," Boomslug said mournfully, looking at the wreckage. I didn't know what to do with his sympathy, let alone everyone else's. They were all staring at me, waiting to see what I was going to do. This was the moment a good commander should give an inspiring speech. Maintain morale. Treat this as a setback.

It wasn't a setback. It was a scudding *disaster*. I didn't have anything inspiring to say. I wasn't even sure how I was staying on my feet.

I had to though. They were all looking to me. Or *at* me. I couldn't really tell.

I wasn't going to fall apart. Not here, not where my entire flight could see.

Fragments of the ship spun out into space, while others careened toward the planet. One hit the shield around Detritus and bounced off.

In my mind, my mother looked directly at me.

Do better than we did, she said.

Enough.

In the distance, the Superiority station that monitored Detritus blinked out of existence, hyperjumping away.

They wouldn't even give us the dignity of revenge. They'd run like cowards. There was no one left for us to attack, just the terrible wreckage floating ever outward, a monument to our diplomatic failures.

"We're going down to Platform Prime," I said. Out of the corner of my eye I could see the others looking at each other, not sure what to make of that.

"Okay," FM said. "But I think you need to stop for a minute—"

No. I couldn't stop. This wasn't about me. It wasn't even about my parents. It was about what we were going to do for Detritus.

"*Now*," I said.

The UrDail were expecting us back to finalize our alliance. That was more important now than ever. The war went on, and we were losing badly. We had to get back on track, and the only way to do that was to find Admiral Cobb and return power to the DDF.

The assembly'd had their chance. We were looking at the remains of it.

"I'm sorry, Alanik," I said. "We'll be a little late returning to Re-Dawn. There are some things we need to take care of first."

"Jorgen," FM said, "I think you should sit down for a minute."

I *couldn't*. "Put Gill in the hyperdrive," I said to FM, mostly so she'd have to stop talking. "I'll give him instructions to take us into the airspace beneath Platform Prime."

FM hesitated long enough that I looked back at her.

It was a mistake. She was watching me with so much concern that I wanted to shout at her. Scream at the sky. Break things.

But I was the flightleader. It was my job to stay in control, at least until Cobb was back. He'd probably try to send me on leave then.

I'd tell him I didn't want to go. We needed every person to face what was coming. Maybe Cobb would see that. Maybe he'd let me stay.

"Do it, FM," Arturo said.

"Yeah, okay," she said. She headed to the control room, and Rig went with her.

I turned to Alanik. "I need to know where Cobb is," I said. "Where did Gran-Gran take them?"

"I don't know," Alanik said. "I'm looking for them, but I can't find them." I closed my eyes, reaching out toward the planet. It would make sense for Gran-Gran to take them somewhere beneath the surface—to her home maybe—but I couldn't sense her mind. Not on Platform Prime, not on the surface, not in the caverns below.

"Keep trying," I said. "Once you find Gran-Gran, we can go pick them up."

I strode toward my ship, turning my back on the glowing wreckage. I didn't need to see it again. The spiraling shape was already fixed in my mind, expanding outward forever.

"Boom," Boomslug said.

"Boom," I agreed with him.

"Jorgen," FM called. "We're ready."

I reached out to Gill, giving him a clear impression of the air-space below Platform Prime. Wandering Leaf was an abandoned battle platform with hyperdrive technology, and its autofire could tear other platforms to pieces, so we'd need to park it far enough down in the upper atmosphere that the other platforms would be out of range.

Go, I told him.

And then I floated beneath the vast starscape of white eyes. They didn't focus on me—we were invisible to them as long as we used the slugs to hyperjump. But I didn't like the eyes any better when they couldn't see me. I always felt as if they could see *through* me, like I was made of something flimsy and superficial with nothing substantial underneath. This time though, I felt something different, something new.

I *hated* them.

It was irrational; they weren't the ones who'd spent the last eighty years raining down death on my people. They hadn't trapped my parents in a ship and blown the thing to pieces. I didn't know if they were responsible for these strange powers I had neither asked for nor wanted. As far as I knew, they weren't even responsible for taking Spensa away. She'd done that herself.

But I still couldn't smother the sudden startling feeling that at its core, everything bad that had happened to us was *all their fault*.

Wandering Leaf emerged far below the vast metal underside of Platform Prime, the current DDF headquarters. "Flight," I said, "take your ships up to the landing bay."

"What are you going to do?" Nedd asked.

The raw hatred I'd felt for the eyes was still hot in my veins. It felt *good*, better than the icy chill of shock or the raging terror of grief.

"I'm going to make sure no one else does anything stupid until Cobb gets back," I said. I climbed into my ship. I'd already given my orders to the flight, so I left my radio off.

"Cobb gets back," Snuggles said, settling on the floor of the cockpit by the side of my seat.

"Let's hope it happens soon," I said. And then I directed Snuggles to hyperjump my ship out of Wandering Leaf and up to the landing bay of Platform Prime.

The ground crew looked shocked when we appeared. They wouldn't have been able to see the explosion from here, not with the platforms forming the shield above them.

But word spread fast when half your government was annihilated.

I left the slugs in my ship as I disembarked. "We're under orders to arrest you for desertion," Dobsi, one of the ground crew members, said. She looked at me uncertainly, like she didn't want to be the one to carry out that particular arrest.

A good call on her part. "Admiral Cobb gave us orders to leave," I said. "He'll clear everything up when he returns."

Dobsi hesitated. "Where did he go?"

"It's classified," I said. It wasn't a great answer, but it was the only one I had.

My flight hyperjumped into the hangar, their ships all connected by light-lances. FM and Alanik jumped out first, and the ground crew looked suspiciously at Alanik like she might be the cause of all the trouble.

Alanik stared them down, but she did move quickly over to me. FM looked at me with that terrible sympathy in her eyes again.

Before she could open her mouth, I turned on my heels and headed toward the command center. There wasn't time to stop, not now. I had to make sure that my flight wasn't going to be scudding arrested. The assembly's plan had blown up in all of our faces—literally.

We were going to do this Cobb's way now, whether they liked it or not.

I walked in, Alanik and FM on my heels and the rest of the flight trailing behind, to find the command center in shambles.

380

Cobb's aides were all staring at monitors and talking over the radio to various DDF departments on the platform and on the ground. Commander Ulan and Ziming from Engineering were having an argument near the hypercomm, while Rikolfr from the admiral's staff kept trying to page Cobb, but to no avail.

They couldn't find him either. Without him, the explosion of the Superiority ship had sent the staff into disarray.

Enough.

"Admiral Cobb is alive," I said loudly. Most of the room turned to look at me. "The person who's been giving you orders since last night was a Superiority plant using a holographic disguise."

Not how I would have started, Alanik said in my mind. *You don't have proof of that, do you?*

"Anyone who doesn't believe me," I said, "is invited to find Cobb so he can confirm. He was kidnapped and taken to the Superiority ship."

"The one that *blew up*?" Commander Ulan said.

"That's the one," I said. "He and Mrs. Becca Nightshade escaped together. They'll be making their way here soon, and until they get here, *no one else* is going to do *anything stupid*. Do you think you can all handle that?"

"You're back," a voice said from behind me, and I turned to see Vice Admiral Stoff striding toward me. He was one of three vice admirals who served under Cobb. My flightmates stepped aside to let him pass. Rig followed behind him. He hadn't had a ship, so he'd probably asked Drape to hyperjump him to the slugs' home location in Engineering. "Flightleader Weight, you're under arrest for—"

Not this again. I wasn't going to sit in the brig and watch while more people I cared about got hurt.

"The charges were a sham," I said. "Either they were issued by my mother—who didn't have the authority—or they were given by the false Admiral Cobb, who was actually an alien wearing a hologram."

Vice Admiral Stoff blinked at me. This was definitely not the attitude I was supposed to take with my superior officer. On a normal day, I would have been horrified with myself.

Today I had met my capacity to experience horror. I wasn't looking forward to the moment it all caught up to me.

"An alien wearing a hologram," Stoff repeated.

"Yes!" I said. "You know, the hologram the Superiority learned how to construct by disassembling the remains of Spensa's starship—the one we *handed* to them?"

Stoff looked around the room, but no one spoke. "How do we know that's true if Cobb's no longer here?"

"It's true," Alanik said.

Stoff sighed. "We'll take you to the debriefing room," he allowed, like he was doing me a great service. "We can make a determination about the court-martial proceedings after—"

"No," I said.

Stoff stared at me. "What was that?"

"*No,*" I said. "We have an alliance to formalize with the UrDail on ReDawn, and my flight and I are expected to be there." Stars, I didn't know how I was going to get through that kind of political meeting. I lacked diplomatic finesse at the best of times. Just look at how *this* was going.

"Flightleader," Stoff said, "that alliance hasn't been authorized by the assembly—"

"The *assembly* got blown to bits!" I said. "Do you have footage on the monitors? Should we replay it for you?"

"I'm aware," Stoff said. "But you don't have the authority to—"

Saints, if we were going to talk about authority, I could talk about authority. "Section 1809 of the DDF Command Protocol says that the chain of command can be temporarily interrupted in the event that the commanding officers are unaware of intelligence that would change their orders beyond reasonable doubt if they *were* aware."

"In this case," Stoff said, "there is no such intelligence."

"You have been taking orders from a Superiority plant!" I shouted at him. "You couldn't tell the difference between Admiral Cobb and the *alien* who took his place. And he wasn't even *all that good at pretending.*"

Vice Admiral Stoff's mouth opened like he wanted to defend himself, but then he shut it again.

"Meanwhile," I said, "my flight and I have been off on *another planet* trying to secure an alliance so that *all of you* might live to see another day. Cobb ordered us to find allies, and we did. We have a military full of UrDail fighters ready to challenge the Superiority with us. Meanwhile, you all were trying to bargain with them. How did that turn out?"

Stoff stared at me with his mouth hanging open. I was only a flightleader, but because of my parents everyone in the DDF knew who I was. Despite the recent charges, I still had a reputation for being a rule follower. This outburst was the last thing he expected from me.

"You know what?" I said before he could respond. "Maybe we should call my mother and ask her."

Stoff looked up at the ceiling. I waited for him to cuff me and take me to the brig, but instead he nodded. "We need to have that debriefing."

"Stars, yes, we do," I said. "But in the meantime, *no one* is doing *anything* until Admiral Cobb is back."

"Technically, sir," Rikolfr said, "Vice Admiral Stoff is in charge in Cobb's absence—"

"He would be in command if Cobb was indisposed," I said. "But Cobb *isn't* indisposed. He will be back soon. And my flight and I are the last people to whom he gave orders and direction before he was kidnapped." I didn't technically know if that was true, but none of them could contradict me, given that they hadn't even realized Cobb had been replaced. "If Cobb were here, he would agree with me because you people are a mess without him. If you want proof, *look* at what happened to the delegation you sent!"

"Fine," Stoff said. "Until we can get all the information to the assembly—"

"*No*," I said. "No more talking to the assembly."

Stoff stuttered at me.

You should point out that their peace deal turned out to be a sham, Alanik said in my head. *They have no hope of securing an alliance with my people without you, and they desperately need one.*

Good point, I said to her. "All hope of securing a treaty with the Superiority is dead. Our only path forward is to ally ourselves with the other peoples the Superiority is trying to oppress. And you're going to need cytonics for that. Unless the assembly has found a way to get themselves across the expanse of space without us."

"We'll see what Admiral Cobb has to say when he returns," Stoff said, and then he spun and strode out of the room again, with the air of a man who had lost an argument but didn't want to admit it.

I reminded myself to breathe. Stoff wasn't going to let me get away with this forever. He was giving me some leeway because I had information he didn't, and more because of what had happened to my parents.

"We need to find Cobb immediately," I said, mostly to myself.

"Where is the admiral now?" Rikolfr asked.

I looked over to Alanik, and she shook her head. I couldn't pull off telling this crowd it was classified. A lot of them had security clearance higher than mine. "We don't know exactly where he went, but he'll be back soon."

He'd better. There was only so long I'd be able to hold things together in his name before people started questioning why they should listen to me.

I was questioning it already.

"Sir?" Ashwin from the Communications Corps held a radio out to me. "National Assembly Leader Winter is on the radio. She wants to talk to you."

To *me*? I wondered if any of what I'd just said had been broadcast over the radio. There were several people who'd been in the middle of conversations when I'd walked in, and it wasn't a complicated procedure to switch from headset to ambient reception.

I wondered if NAL Winter wanted to yell at me for what I'd said to Stoff, or give her condolences about my parents.

Either way, I didn't want to hear it. And while I had some things to say about what I thought of the assembly, none of them would be productive. "Take a message," I said.

"Sir?" Ashwin said. "Under the circumstances—"

"Take. A. Message," I said. "In detail. And then tell her that according to Section 57 of the DDF Communications Policy, the DDF has three days to respond."

Ashwin blinked at me. "Three days, sir?"

"*Yes*," I said. This fiasco had been the assembly's idea. All of it. It was *their fault*, and I wasn't going to listen to a word they had to say even one second before I had to. "And then make yourself a memo to remind us two days and twenty-three and a half hours from now that we need to draft a response. Or better yet, make a note to tell *Cobb* to do it, because *he* will be back by then. Is that clear?"

"Um, yes, sir," Ashwin said.

"Good."

I turned around and found FM watching me nervously. "Are you going to tell me I should talk to the assembly?" I asked.

"No way," FM said. "Not a chance. You're absolutely right. That disaster was their fault. Being made to wait is the least of what they deserve. But Jorgen, you need to talk about what happened—"

"You want to talk about something?" I said to FM. "Let's talk about how we're going to find Cobb."

We both looked at Alanik, who held up her hands. "I'm trying," she said. "It's a big universe, Jorgen, and I don't know where Gran-Gran tried to take them."

"She'd never been off this planet, had she?" FM asked. "Where else would she go?"

"She was born on the *Defiant*," Rig said. "She used to travel the stars as a little girl, but she said she didn't remember much about it. I can't imagine she'd try to take them anywhere else."

"They aren't here," Alanik said. "I'm sure of that."

FM looked to me for confirmation. I closed my eyes, reaching down beneath the surface of the planet again. There were more slugs down there—I could feel their vibrations.

But no cytonic people, and definitely no Gran-Gran.

"I think she's right," I said. "But Spensa managed to contact me from the *nowhere*. If she could do that, we should be able to find Gran-Gran wherever she is, right?"

"I'll keep trying," Alanik said.

Arturo stood behind her in the doorway. "Come on," he said. "I'll find you someplace quiet where you can concentrate."

Alanik nodded and turned to follow Arturo out.

I was being too hard on her, probably. It wasn't her fault Cobb disappeared.

I'd apologize after we found him.

"Jorgen," FM said. I knew what she was going to say. She'd said it several times.

"What I need," I said, "is to find Cobb. Are any of the slugs familiar enough with the admiral to hyperjump to him?"

"I don't know," FM said. "We haven't tried to get them to recognize him, but some of them might . . ." She looked like she was going to go back to arguing that I should sit down and stop for a minute, but I didn't want to stop. I was outrunning the storm right now, and I was going to keep running as long as I could.

"Find out," I said. "Get Rig on it too." I turned and strode down the hall into Cobb's office, closing the door behind me.

I didn't know what to say to any of them, not about what happened, not about what had to happen now. Cobb would know what to do with all of this.

But he wasn't the one I missed most at the moment. In my mind, I watched the Superiority ship explode over and over again. Some of that image must have leaked into the nowhere, because Snuggles and Boomslug appeared on my shoulders, and Boomslug slid down my arm into the crook of my elbow and softly trilled, "Boom."

"Can you find Cobb?" I asked Snuggles.

She responded by nuzzling my ear, but she didn't take us anywhere. I pressed my back against the door, closing my eyes.

More than anything, I wished Spensa were here.

2

Two days later, we still hadn't heard a word from Cobb. Alanik tried her best, but no matter where she looked she couldn't find Gran-Gran. They'd simply disappeared, she said.

At this point, I was the only cytonic from Detritus who *hadn't* mysteriously disappeared. Spensa was stuck in the nowhere, but she'd at least managed to get in contact with me twice. It had been several days now, and I was anxious to hear from her again.

But from Cobb and Gran-Gran, there was only silence.

I sat at a conference table with Alanik, FM, and Minister Cuna, the dissenter Superiority bureaucrat. Boomslug and Snuggles snuffled around under my chair like they expected someone to have spilled some caviar down there, though the floor was swept twice a day as per Mandate 27 of the Facilities Regulations. Alanik had just returned from ReDawn with half the flight—I'd sent Arturo, Nedd, and Kimmalyn to finish solidifying the alliance.

"Rinakin is prepared to send a flight of ships to Detritus as a symbolic gesture," Alanik said. "And more, certainly, if there's a need for them here."

I struggled to focus on what she was saying. I'd barely been sleeping—every time I closed my eyes, that ship exploded in the darkness. In my dreams, I watched my mother mouth those words at me through the glass: *Do better than we did*. The ship tore to pieces before my eyes, sometimes while I watched from the platform—sometimes with me still inside it, somehow conscious of everything as it shredded me.

In the very worst nightmares, it was Spensa on the other side of the glass.

"ReDawn is more vulnerable," I said. "We have the planetary shield to protect us. We should be sending flights to defend *you*."

"The taynix will help with that," FM said.

We'd given Rinakin a single taynix of each type, and we already had people from the ground crews scouring the caverns of Detritus for more. We'd lost many in the trap set by the Superiority, and we were going to need all the hyperdrives we could find in the coming days.

"Do you think Stoff will let us take flights to ReDawn if the Superiority attacks again?" FM asked.

"Maybe," I said. I'd stayed behind while the others went to ReDawn, because I'd wanted to be here to keep an eye on things until we found Cobb. "He's been weirdly receptive to my suggestions."

"Do you think it's because he agrees with you?" FM asked. "Or because he sees an opportunity to escape blame if all this goes wrong?"

"It's the second," I said. Once Stoff got over the idea of me challenging him, he'd become almost *too* accommodating. If things went well, I fully expected him to take credit for all of it. If we crashed and burned, he was going to pin it all on me. "But I don't think Cobb is going to reprimand me for trying to protect our people in his absence."

FM looked concerned. She was still doing that a lot in my direction. She'd mostly stopped trying to corner me to get me to talk, which was good. I didn't need to talk. I needed to stay focused, move forward. My refusal to let her talk to me also meant we still hadn't addressed the fight we'd had on ReDawn. Her words still rang in my mind: *You're not my flightleader.*

I understood why she'd said that—she'd been rightly worried about the taynix being turned over to the Superiority—but it still stung. We were all trained to follow orders, to do as we were told. How bad must I be at this if a member of my own team—and a friend, I'd thought—could disavow me so easily?

"Winzik will not take the defeat on ReDawn well," Cuna said. "Detritus might be the more difficult target, but he will only see that as a challenge to his authority. He is probably mobilizing more ships even now. He will gather enough force to break through Detritus's shield eventually, even with the cytonic inhibitor in place."

That was true, but I didn't know what to do about it. I didn't think Stoff did either. "We need to find Cobb," I said. "He'll know what to do."

FM looked doubtful about that, but she didn't voice it.

"About Cobb and Mrs. Nightshade," Cuna said. A pin on their collar translated their words, which were spoken in an alien language. "If Mrs. Nightshade merely took them to another room on the Superiority ship, they might still have been caught in the explosion."

"No," Alanik said. "I scanned the ship after they left, and there weren't any cytonics on it except for me and Jorgen."

"It's possible they were in an accident returning to the planet," Cuna said. "If they hyperjumped into a dangerous position, they might have been killed on return. That would explain your inability to find them, would it not?"

"Don't say that," I said. "They aren't dead."

Alanik and FM exchanged a look.

"We have no *evidence* that they are dead," I corrected myself. "We aren't going to assume that they are without evidence."

"Stoff isn't going to hold off on replacing Cobb forever," FM said. "Even if he thinks he can use you as a scapegoat, at some point they're going to need to name a new admiral. They're only taking your word for it that Cobb didn't die on that ship."

Alanik looked personally offended. "We are witnesses, so taking our word for it makes perfect sense."

"Maybe," I said. "But FM is right. They aren't going to let this go on forever." It wouldn't necessarily be Stoff who took Cobb's place—there were two other vice admirals of equal rank, though they were both planetside at the moment, trying to deal with the fallout of the Superiority broadcasting the deaths of half the assembly to the citizens of Detritus.

I didn't think Stoff wanted control of the DDF, or he would have seen Cobb's absence as an opportunity instead of a burden he was mostly trying to shift to me. "I'm not sure what options we have though," I said. "Our military is too small and ill-equipped to take on the Superiority once they get their forces mustered. The Ur-Dail pilots are well trained but inexperienced, and the Superiority's technology outpaces us all. And that's assuming they don't try to send another delver after us. Spensa said the Superiority was trying to make a deal with them."

"We need to continue to reach out and form other alliances," Cuna said. "There will be many peoples who don't approve of Winzik's methods."

I wasn't sure that Cuna entirely approved of *our* methods. They still seemed to find us aggressive and barbaric, even though our tactics had saved them from capture on Sunreach.

"It may be only lesser species in the beginning," they continued. "But as time goes on, I'm sure the more advanced species will also begin to turn on Winzik."

"Those *lesser species* saved your life," Alanik muttered.

"Twice now," FM added under her breath.

"Of course!" Cuna said, as if this didn't contradict what they'd said previously at all. "All species have something wonderful to add to the Superiority—"

"This isn't the Superiority," I said. "We're not trying to join them." Cuna wanted us to see the Superiority as a diverse group of peoples, and I'm sure they were, given the thousands of planets that were apparently under their control. But. "The Superiority has been killing our people since long before Winzik took over, and we're not making an alliance with any part of it. Not again."

Cuna looked like they might argue, but I wasn't going to hear it. Alanik had been right about the Superiority. My parents had tried to reason with them, and look where that got them.

"Boom," Boomslug muttered from down by my feet, where he'd curled around the leg of my chair.

I reached for him and scritched him between his spines. He nuzzled his body against my hand.

"Cobb ordered us to find allies though," I said, before Cuna could make any more defenses of the Superiority. "So if we reach out to others, we're still following his orders."

"Technically," FM said, "he ordered us to make allies of the UrDail."

"Technically they weren't orders at all," Alanik added. "They were not-orders."

"That's beside the point," I insisted. "If we're making alliances, then we're doing what Cobb would do. And if our superior officers know we're doing it, and they don't order us not to, then we're still operating within the current chain of command."

"Do you know anyone we can reach out to with the hyper-comm?" FM asked Cuna. "Other species we could make an alliance with?"

Cuna shook their head, laying their hands flat on the conference table. "I have tried to reach my contacts, but some have gone underground. Others might side with Winzik, so I have to be careful whom I reach out to. Your hypercomm does not have the data banks that mine did, and without the coordinates to reach the others—"

"We don't know their radio frequencies, basically," I said.

"Precisely," Cuna said. "I have allies among the figments, if we can reach them."

"We might be able to do that cytonically," Alanik said. "Though if we try to reach out to the wrong people, we might set ourselves up to walk into another Superiority trap."

I nodded. We couldn't approach other cytonics indiscriminately. "You can monitor hypercommunication though, can't you?" I asked Alanik. I hadn't been able to figure out how to do that yet, but Alanik seemed to do it easily. "You could see if you can find any anti-Superiority communication, and we could try to pinpoint the frequencies of the people who are sending them and contact them as potential allies."

"Most of those who oppose Winzik won't be using hyper-comms," Cuna said. "The lesser species don't have access to them, and those who do will be afraid of being overheard."

Alanik looked like she might punch Cuna if they called her "lesser" one more time.

"If it's the only idea we have," FM said, "then it's still worth a try."

"I agree," I said. "And we don't have to ask Stoff for resources to try it, so that's even better." I turned to Alanik. "I'd like to help canvass for hypersignals," I said. "You'll have to teach me, but I've caught on quicker to the communication skills than hyperjumping."

"Of course," Alanik said. "I'd be happy to have your assistance."

I hoped I would *be* of assistance, but we were getting desperate, and until we found Gran-Gran I was the only other cytonic we had.

Rig knocked on the doorframe to the conference room. His yellow hyperslug, Drape, peered over his shoulder from his perch in one of the new backpacks Engineering had devised. A boomslug—as everyone had begun calling them, even though technically it was Boomslug's name—peered over his other shoulder.

"Are you carrying one of those around now?" I asked. That was strange. We'd mostly left the boomslugs alone, except for Boomslug. Everyone else was too worried about triggering the mindblades.

Rig shrugged, and the slugs bobbed along with the gesture.

"Boomslug saved my life back on Wandering Leaf, so I thought we should try to keep more of these guys around. For purely experimental purposes, of course. I'm definitely not carrying a slug as a bodyguard."

I couldn't blame him if he was.

FM smiled at Rig. The two of them were scudding adorable, which lately made me want to punch things. Spensa's influence, probably. "He named this one Squeeze."

Of course. FM had taken glee in naming my hyperslug Snuggles before she assigned her to me. If I hadn't already bonded with Boomslug, they no doubt would have tried to push Squeeze on me as well.

Cobb would tell me I should have more of a sense of humor about myself. He was usually right.

"Did you need something?" I asked Rig.

"Just wondering if FM was available to run drills with the slugs," he said. "We've got Stardragon Flight ready to practice with the new keywords."

The other flights had been less than thrilled when FM stole some of their taynix, but she was largely forgiven now that the assembly had lost most of the other taynix to the Superiority. We hadn't secured enough new slugs to outfit all the flights yet, and any new ones we found in the caverns would have to start their training from scratch.

Which meant I shouldn't keep them from it. If she was busy, FM had less time to worry in my general direction. "Yeah, we're done here," I said. "How is the platform exploration going?"

"The team is still working on it," Rig said. They were looking for more platform control rooms like the one on Wandering Leaf. It was similar enough to the platforms on Detritus that it seemed likely we might have some with similar capabilities. More platforms that could hyperjump or fire hyperweapons would be a valuable asset. "There is a lot of junk in the debris belt, and a lot of platforms to search."

"I understand," I said. "Let me know if you find anything."

"Will do," Rig said as FM pushed her chair away from the table and moved to join him. Rig didn't report to me officially, but we were all in a holding pattern until Cobb returned, so sharing information only made sense.

"Are you ready to look for signals now?" I asked Alanik.

"Yes," she said. "But not here. These chairs are too square. It's distracting."

I didn't have a chance to ask what she meant, because Alanik had already stood up from her . . . *square* chair and marched out of the conference room.

I scooped up Snuggles and Boomslug and followed Alanik, as she seemed to know where she was going. I hoped I'd be able to help. I had to do *something*, because if I didn't, the tragedies we'd suffered would only be the beginning.

3

Alanik brought me to one of the small meeting rooms. At the head of the square table sat the weirdest chair I had ever seen. It looked as if it was made entirely from tree branches, sanded and polished and warped into twisting shapes that stretched up the back in a spiraling pattern. As I got closer I could see that it was a continuous carving from a single large piece of wood.

"Did you *bring* that here?" I asked.

"Yes," Alanik said. "It was Arturo's suggestion. I was saying that I find your furniture strangely square, and he said that if I was going to spend hours searching for Gran-Gran and Cobb in the negative realm, I might as well bring myself back a comfortable place to sit. It's my favorite from my own home."

The seat was polished wood rather than a cushion, and Alanik folded herself onto it with her legs tucked under her.

There was another chair in here—which did look squarish beside hers, but it had cushions covered in a plain brown fabric, and looked much more comfortable to me. I wondered if Arturo had been using it. They seemed to be spending a lot of time together.

I sank into the chair. "I don't know if I'm going to be any help at this."

"If you're willing to try," Alanik said, "it can't hurt."

I leaned back in the chair and closed my eyes. As I reached out with my cytonic senses, I could feel Alanik on the chair beside me, and Boomslug and Snuggles settling on my lap. I widened my focus and found the other slugs across the platform, and—dimly—the vibrations that indicated there were still more taynix down on the planet that we hadn't been able to locate.

I should probably be down there looking for them myself, since I could sense them and the ground crews couldn't. Maybe Cobb would use that as an excuse to send me away for a while once he returned. It would be better than bereavement leave. At least I'd have something to focus on, something to *do*.

"Okay," Alanik said. "We're going to reach away from Detritus. The universe is like a giant map, and we can examine places up close or at a distance. Do you know what I mean?"

"Not really," I said. "I can focus in on one person's mind, or sense the cytonic . . . vibration of a group. But I don't see locations, only people."

"People!" Snuggles announced. I thought she liked being included.

"Hmm," Alanik said. "This is why you have a hard time hyperjumping, probably."

"I can visualize a physical place in my mind," I said. "Like I can imagine the trees of ReDawn, because I've seen them, and send that picture to Snuggles."

"Snuggles," Boomslug said affectionately.

"Forget about the places then," Alanik said. "I think our experience of them is different. Instead, try reaching for people, but instead of looking for them, *listen*."

That sounded just as nonsensical, but at least it didn't require me to look for things I couldn't see.

"When you say 'listen,' do you mean for things you hear? Or the way Spensa heard the stars, the way I heard the slugs. Like, the vibration of the universe?"

"Neither," Alanik said. "Like when I speak in your mind. Listen for the voices of others. You can intercept their communications, whether it's hypercomm or mind-to-mind. It all passes through the negative realm, and if you are passing through it at the same time . . ."

Okay. That made sense. "Thank you for explaining," I said. "When Gran-Gran taught me this stuff, she mostly made me knead bread and told me to listen to the stars. It helped, weirdly, but it wasn't exactly intuitive."

"That's not as bad a tactic as you might think," Alanik said. "My training was similar. I can try to explain things to you, but in the end your intuition is the only way you will learn."

I hated that. I liked things that could be explained, preferably with proven pedagogical techniques, written reference materials, and lots of concrete examples. Cytonics was the opposite of that in every way, and I couldn't help but feel that whatever force was handing these powers out had given them to the wrong person when they picked me.

Spensa seized her powers and made use of them. I was floundering around in the dark.

Beside me I could feel Alanik's mind as she expanded her senses, reaching out into the void. I tried to do the same, at first looking for other minds, then listening for voices.

I wondered if I could find Spensa that way, the way she'd reached out to me from the nowhere. My mind was passing through it, and if she was in there it made sense that I would be able to find her again. I hoped every day, and even more since the explosion, that I'd hear from her. I wanted evidence she was all right, news that she was finding a way to return.

But more than anything, I desperately wanted to hear her voice again.

I expanded my mind, listening.

And then, just barely, I heard a snatch of something. A voice in the nothingness. —*solar flares on the*—*avoid the area*—

"I heard something!" I said. "Something about a solar flare."

"It's a weather report," Alanik said. "I found that one. It's a Superiority broadcast among their hyperjumping ships, warning them about hazards as they navigate the galaxy."

Of course Alanik had already heard it. But that didn't change the fact that *I'd* found it. I'd given up hope that I would be able to hyperjump, but Alanik said every cytonic should technically have access to all cytonic powers, even if various ones could be harder for some than for others.

Maybe I wasn't completely hopeless. Maybe I could still master this, or at least gain some passable skills.

I continued listening. The sounds were tiny blips in a vast area, like a taynix hiding among all the caverns of Detritus. I found another broadcast giving what sounded like navigational coordinates, and a ship captain complaining about some of his subordinates to his commander. These were all hypercomm signals—they didn't originate in the nowhere. But if Spensa was in here, there had to be a way to reach her. *Spensa*, I thought. *Are you there? Can you hear me?*

"Stop that," Alanik said. "You're drowning everything else out."

My face flushed. Oh. Right. Of course Alanik could hear that. She was sitting right next to me, literally searching for cytonic signals.

I can hear all of that too, Alanik said. *It would be wonderful if we could find Spensa in here and find a way to bring her home, but perhaps we could focus on one matter at a time?*

"Of course," I said. "Sorry."

I sat and listened to the echoing void of the universe, trying not to radiate any thoughts that would overpower Alanik's search. I still wished I could search for Spensa, instead of combing through mundane hypercomm communications on the off chance someone might be sending anti-Superiority messages through the nowhere. The more I thought about this, the more it seemed like the odds of finding such a communication at the precise moment it was being sent would be one in a million. And it was frustrating to hear the

Superiority using this technology like it was basic radio—they had made hypercommunication part of their civilization, while the rest of us were only now clawing our way out of the dark ages.

Spensa would be angry about that. She probably *was* angry about it. I wished she were here; she'd be better at this than I was. Spensa would probably—

Spensa!

I opened my eyes, blinking rapidly. That hadn't been Alanik's voice, or the slugs'.

Had I imagined it? After everything that had happened, was I losing my mind?

I reached out again, focusing on the voice. *—please respond.*

And then it started again. *Spensa, human of Detritus—*

"I found something," I said.

Where? Alanik asked. I could feel her mind reaching out for mine, following me into the nothingness.

—return them! Please—

"I hear it," Alanik said. She focused on the words as they repeated again—it was an ongoing signal being broadcast on a loop. As we listened, the words became more and more clear.

Spensa, human of Detritus! the message said. *This is the* Swims Upstream! *We have your humans and would like to return them! Please respond.*

"They have our humans and would like to *return* them?" I said.

"That's what they said." Alanik frowned. "Do they mean Cobb and Gran-Gran?"

"Or other humans," I said. "We don't know if there are other prison planets like ours, or if we're the only ones left."

"If they found an entire planet of humans, would they really be contacting Spensa to *return* them?"

"I don't know," I said. "I don't know what '*Swims Upstream*' is. I don't have any idea who's trying to reach us." The Superiority knew about Spensa, and that she was connected to our planet. They knew she'd disappeared, and they were no doubt trying to find her. This might be an attempt to bait her into the open, the way they did to my parents.

I supposed there was some comfort in knowing that if she was stuck in the nowhere, she couldn't fall into that trap.

"I can pinpoint the coordinates," Alanik said. "I could give them to the taynix in your hypercomm, so you could respond."

"*Should* we respond?" I asked.

"It's a lead," Alanik said. "The only one we have. And if they do have Cobb and Gran-Gran . . ."

I reached out for the message, listening to it play again. "Can you teach me how to pinpoint the message?" I asked. "Can we respond directly?"

"You said you weren't sure you should respond. Don't you want to run this by your commanders? I thought that was your answer for everything."

Alanik had me figured out. "Yes," I said. "But I want to know what's possible. These are skills I need to learn, even if I don't know if we should answer this particular message."

"Listen then," Alanik said. "You know how you can tell which mind is mine in the negative realm? You don't try to speak to me and accidentally reach the taynix. You can even tell the individual slugs apart, can't you?"

"Yes," I said. "At first I got them confused, but now I can tell one from another, as long as I'm familiar with them."

"Places are like that too. They each have their own individual . . . feeling. And even if you can't see the whole of the universe, you should be able to recognize the difference in sensation."

"Like the vibrations," I said. And . . . now that she said it, I *did* feel a distinct vibration coming from the message.

Could I use that to communicate with it? Could I speak to the recording as if it were a person? "If I tried to talk to it, would anyone hear me?" I asked. "It's a hypercomm, not another cytonic."

"It depends on whether there's a person listening on the other end," Alanik said. "But you could try."

She was right that we should loop Stoff in on this. I wanted to keep an eye on things, make sure no one came up with any new terrible ideas in Cobb's absence. But I couldn't leave either the DDF or the National Assembly in the dark completely. I might be stretching the limits of my authority lately, but if I started keeping secrets from my superiors I'd be breaking them entirely.

Still, none of them were cytonics. Even if I looped in Stoff, Alanik and I would still be the only ones who could communicate with these people.

I focused on the vibration of the recording, trying to treat it as if it were the mind of another cytonic, or one of the taynix. *Can you hear me?* I asked.

The recording stopped abruptly, right in the middle of a sentence.

Hello? a voice said on the other end.

Scud. They'd heard me. The voice felt different than a full cytonic mind, but I was able to target the vibration.

Is this the human planet Detritus?

If I told them they'd reached us, would that give anything away? The Superiority already knew where we were. *It is*, I said, but I left it at that.

The message changed. *Human!* it said. *This is Kauri of the kitsen, captain of the* Swims Upstream*! Can you put me in touch with Spensa?*

"Interesting," Alanik said.

"What's interesting?" I asked.

"That they're a kitsen," she said. "Or they claim to be one. They're another of the species the Superiority believes to be *lesser*. They're small furry creatures, not unlike tree squirrels, but they're as intelligent as UrDail. I've never met one, but I've seen a picture. They look . . . adorable."

So I was either talking to a Superiority trap, or a tree squirrel that knew Spensa. I wasn't sure which was more disturbing. "Okay," I said. "You're right that we should bring this to the attention of

402

Command. This is too sensitive to handle on our own. We need to go to the comms people with this, and let Stoff know."

"If you're sure that's wise," Alanik said.

I wasn't sure it was, but I also wasn't ready to strike out entirely on my own. I was merely watching over the DDF for Cobb until we could find him.

Let me speak with my superiors and get back to you, I said.

We eagerly await your return! the voice said.

"If they *are* a squirrel, they're a very enthusiastic one," Alanik said.

"True." I focused one more time on the vibration of the transmission. Alanik said she could give it to Fine in the hypercomm, but I wanted to learn to do this too. I waited until the vibration felt familiar, the way I could find Alanik's mind quickly now that I knew her. And then I pulled my mind back to Detritus, where I could feel the buzz of the taynix all around, and then toward the room where I could feel Alanik sitting next to me.

As I drew inward, passing by the minds of the taynix on the platform, the area around me suddenly felt . . . denser. *Bumpier*, like it was filled with a hundred raised ridges in the otherwise empty space. They were there, and then as I focused on them, spontaneously absent.

"Did you feel that?" I asked.

"Feel what?" Alanik said.

"That . . . texture. Like there was suddenly something else in the nowhere with us."

"Something *in* the nowhere? Like the eyes?"

"No, I don't think so," I said. Scud, I *hoped* what I'd felt wasn't some sign of an impending delver attack. "Maybe it wasn't *in* the nowhere exactly. More like I could feel something *through* the nowhere, all around us. Not more cytonics, but—"

Alanik stared at me, shaking her head. "I didn't notice anything. I don't feel anything here but you and the slugs."

"Maybe I imagined it then." The idea that I was losing my mind was somehow less scary than the thought of some *other* new thing emerging from the nowhere to haunt us. "I need to talk to Cuna and Stoff, to figure out what we're going to do next. If the kitsen are really reaching out to us, we have to follow up on it."

Whatever Stoff's motives, I hoped he continued to be accommodating.

4

Alanik followed me up to talk to Stoff, and I didn't stop her. Stoff had the entire DDF behind him, and I wanted a little strength in numbers of my own. I would have called in the whole flight if I'd thought it would help.

Stoff was sitting in his office—he'd left the admiral's office empty in Cobb's absence, which I took as another sign he wasn't looking to usurp Cobb's position.

"We've found a transmission from a hypercomm, sir," I said. "Someone called Kauri looking for Spensa."

"Is it the Superiority?" Stoff asked.

"It could be," I said. "But they claim to be a kitsen. We have the coordinates for the message, so we can try to reach whoever it is by hypercomm. The message said they have our humans and they'd like to return them. It could be Cobb and Mrs. Nightshade, but we don't know for sure."

"Thank you," Stoff said. "If you get the hypercomm set up, I'll speak with them."

"I'd like to talk to them, sir," I said. "Alanik and I made the initial contact, and if they really are a kitsen, that might be another group we could approach about an alliance. Cobb put us in charge of making alliances, so we should have the clearance to do so."

I knew that was a stretch, but I tried not to show it. Stoff sighed and gave me an appraising look. I was pretty sure he was weighing how much rope he could give me to hang myself without looking like he was part of the problem when Cobb returned.

But there wouldn't *be* a problem when Cobb returned, because we were doing what Cobb wanted in the first place.

"All right," he said. "Your team has the most experience dealing with aliens, so you may take point."

Alanik raised an eyebrow at him. I didn't think she appreciated our efforts with her people being reduced to "dealing with aliens," but at least he hadn't called them lesser.

"I'd like to brief Cuna on the interaction as well," I said. "They might have some insight about who we're dealing with."

"Agreed," Stoff said. "I'll call the team to the command room in thirty minutes."

"Thank you, sir," I said.

Stoff nodded. I was dismissed.

I found Cuna sitting in their living quarters with the other diones we'd rescued from Sunreach. "We've intercepted a message from someone looking for Spensa," I said. "They claim to be a kitsen named Kauri."

"Oh, that's wonderful!" Cuna said. "The kitsen are among the most advanced of the lesser species when it comes to their nonaggression. It's their outdated monarchy that has kept them from ascending to full citizenship."

"I'm not sure if this really *is* a kitsen," I said. "I'm concerned it might be a ploy—Winzik or his people trying to capture Spensa by pretending to be her allies."

"Spensa worked with a group of kitsen when she was training on Starsight," Cuna said. "So the claim is plausible! I interacted mostly with Hesho, their former monarch. His people could be powerful allies. They've had a long military history to overcome as they've worked to be ready for inclusion among the higher species."

I stared at Cuna. "*Our* people have a long military history," I said. "And that's the only reason we were able to rescue you from Winzik in the first place."

"Twice," Alanik said.

"Of course," Cuna said, though I wasn't sure they'd understood my point. "And your people have a distant connection with the kitsen. They have some of the best records of cytonic history, despite having produced no cytonics for centuries."

"We're going to talk to them over the hypercomm in a few minutes, if you'd like to join us. I need to make sure the hypercomm is ready."

"I would love to join you," Cuna said.

"Thank you," I said, and went off to get Finc into the hypercomm.

Stoff only invited a small number of people to the meeting. He and three people from the Communications Corps sat around the conference table. Cuna and Alanik entered and took two of the remaining chairs while I used the frequency impression I'd learned earlier to ask Fine to open communication with Kauri.

I spoke into the hypercomm's microphone. "Kauri," I said experimentally. "Can you hear me?"

"Human," the voice said. "We are trying to reach Spensa, who once called herself by the name Alanik. Do you know where we might find her?"

"Spensa is away on a mission," I said. It was true, even if it wasn't complete. "We would like to speak to you though. What did you mean when you said you had our humans?"

"Two humans hyperjumped to our planet a few days ago," the voice said. "We believe they might have arrived here by accident. We would have contacted you sooner, but we had to commandeer a hypercomm to do so."

"You stole a Superiority hypercomm?" I asked.

"We did!"

"Kitsen are known for their bravery," Cuna said. "It is a good quality, if it can be divorced from violence."

I was certain violence was going to be necessary before all this was over, so I didn't see that as a downside.

Alanik opened her eyes. "I'm searching the area near their broadcast point, but I'm not able to find Becca Nightshade. I don't think she's there."

Kauri could be lying. Or these humans might have nothing to do with us. "Kauri," I said. "What method did the humans use to hyperjump to your planet?"

"I don't know," she said. "I assume one of them is a cytonic."

Alanik shook her head, speaking quietly so the microphone wouldn't pick her up. "I'm not sensing any cytonics in that area."

"Would you be able to tell from this distance?" Stoff asked.

"Yes," Alanik said, in a tone that said she didn't like being questioned by someone who had no idea what they were talking about. "I have used the location of the hypercomm signal to pinpoint the area. I am quite reliable, especially when it comes to reaching a cytonic I'm familiar with."

"If one of them is a cytonic," I said, "they should be able to reach out to us, shouldn't they? Why would you need to steal a hypercomm?"

"Well," Kauri said, "something must have gone wrong during the hyperjump. Your humans are unconscious."

I looked at Alanik, and she shook her head. She should still be able to sense an unconscious cytonic.

"If your cytonic died on arrival," Cuna said, "you would no longer be able to sense her. Hyperjumps can be dangerous, and—"

"Are you certain they're alive?" I asked Kauri.

"Yes," Kauri said. "They are breathing, and their bodies are warm. We are not experts in human health, but we believe this means they are living."

Two living humans could be anyone, from anywhere. "Can you describe the humans to me?" I asked.

"One of them is quite wrinkly," Kauri said. "The male's body is rather mottled and purple."

"He's purple?" I asked.

"Cobb was injured," Alanik said. "When I saw him on the Superiority ship, he looked like he'd been in a fight."

"Yes. The large gentleman with the hairy face has some wounds we're trying to attend to, but we don't know much about human physiology."

"I still need someone to explain that lip hair to me," Alanik said. "It seems problematic."

"We would like to return your humans to you for medical attention!" Kauri said. "We have been to the location of your planet, but we don't have a hyperdrive to reach you! We were able to stow away on a carrier ship to return home from Starsight, but stealing a ship of that size is beyond our abilities. Do *you* have access to a hyperdrive?"

Alanik and I exchanged a look. Winzik already *knew* we had hyperdrives, so giving that away wouldn't be terrible.

"We have transportation," I said.

"That is most fortuitous!" Kauri said. "We look forward to making your acquaintance. Though Spensa deceived us, we found her to be a most honorable and formidable warrior, and we look forward to meeting with her peers, if indeed she has any."

I wasn't sure if I should be offended by that or not.

"Are we going to go?" Alanik asked quietly. "I still think it's suspicious that I can't find Gran-Gran on their planet."

I hesitated. We hadn't said we would go, but if they had Gran-Gran and Cobb, we had to do everything in our power to retrieve them. It was a risk, but without taking risks we'd never be able to find more allies.

I muted the microphone. "Sir," I said to Stoff, "I would like to send a small group to investigate. If we control the destination of our hyperjump, we should be able to scan the area for Superiority presence before we're spotted. According to Section 14 of the DDF Statutes on Prisoners of War, if a commander is missing behind enemy lines, it should be considered an implied order to rescue

409

that commander if it does not directly interfere with the current mission. In this case, I'd say the section applies."

"I agree," Stoff said. "I think you should accompany your flight and investigate the situation."

I blinked at him. I wanted to go—I never wanted to send my flight anywhere without me. Even staying behind when they returned to ReDawn had been difficult.

Stoff knew that. Did he want me to go because he knew I was watching him? Alanik and I were the DDF's only cytonics. They needed us, so they should be reticent to send us both away at once.

But old prejudices ran deep. They were still *afraid* of us. So sending us away on a mission—one they could either take credit for if it was a success or scapegoat us for if it was a failure—probably seemed like a convenient excuse to get us out of the way.

If it meant we'd get Cobb back though, it worked in our favor.

"Yes, sir," I said. "I'll get my team ready."

Stoff nodded. "Better tell them you're coming, then."

"I think it would be better if we don't," I said. "If it is a trap, they'll have less time to prepare."

"All right," Stoff said. "But you'll want to hurry. If Cobb and Mrs. Nightshade need medical attention, we'll want to get it to them sooner rather than later."

"Agreed." I unmuted the microphone. "We will try to make arrangements to retrieve our people," I told Kauri. "We thank you for your patience."

"We look forward to making your acquaintance, human," Kauri said. "May the stars guide you."

"And you," I said.

I hoped Cuna was right that the kitsen would make excellent allies.

But at the moment, I would settle for having Cobb back, healthy and well.

5

When my flight hyperjumped near the coordinates we'd gotten from the hypercomm, we appeared in space around a large, bluish-white planet. A blinding star illuminated most of this side of it—far away, but still much larger and closer than I'd ever seen a star before. The planet was *huge*, even from this far out, and the whitish parts of it were moving across the surface, bubbling and roiling.

Clouds, I realized. Collections of moisture that would rain down periodically. I'd read about them, but I'd never imagined them looking so . . . fluffy. They looked almost *soft*, like cotton. Not like water at all.

"Oooh, that's pretty," Sadie said.

"Gorgeous," Kimmalyn said. "And I'm reasonably certain at first glance it isn't going to eat us."

The rest of the flight detached and separated into wingmate pairs, with the medical transport ship sticking close to me. The flight adopted a wedge formation around us, with Arturo and Nedd taking point, FM and Sadie on one side, T-Stall and Catnip on the other, and the rest following.

"Can we fly through all of that?" I asked. Our starfighters were airtight of course, but I still wouldn't expect all the systems to function perfectly underwater.

This water wasn't solid though. It was more like steam rising from a boiling pot. Did that mean it would be scalding to touch? "Our ships can handle extremes in temperatures," I said. "So even if they're hot—"

"The clouds are not hot," Cuna said, sounding amused. They were riding with FM in the Dulo. We'd brought them along to help with diplomacy. "The atmospheric pressure allows the water to remain in its gaseous state at a low temperature."

Huh. Okay.

"I think it should be fine," Alanik said. "Your ships handled the miasma, didn't they? It's just a different type of gas."

Right. That made sense. "Still," I said, "I think we should try to fly through the gaps between them." Visibility would be limited in the clouds, and who knew what might be lurking within them. They shouldn't be too difficult to avoid. Large swaths of the atmosphere were clear, showing through to a brilliant blue-green surface.

More water. An *ocean.* Stars, I'd read about those too, but I'd never been able to quite picture *so much water.* It sounded terrifying to live on a planet covered in that much water. How could you be sure it wasn't going to wash over everything and swallow it?

I zoomed my proximity monitors way out, searching for other spacecraft or aircraft, but I couldn't find any around the planet. If there were ships, they must be much closer to the planet's surface. So far this didn't seem like a Superiority trap, given the lack of cytonic inhibitors and enormous battleships, but we couldn't rule out that they might have changed their tactics.

A signal came through the comms—a local radio transmission trying to reach me. I switched over. "This is Skyward One, callsign: Jerkface," I said.

"Human!" a tiny voice said. It sounded like Kauri, though I wasn't confident I'd be able to tell kitsen voices apart. "Welcome to the Den of Everlasting Light Which Laps Gently upon the Shores of Time. We will send you a heading to meet us on the Burrow from Which Spring Dreams Both Sweet and Sorrowful!"

"Um," I said.

"Um," Boomslug repeated.

"Thank you," I said. "We look forward to . . . making your acquaintance." Scud, I'd listened to enough political pleasantries in my life. Why could I never remember them when I needed them?

Kauri gave us the coordinates, and I instructed the flight to head toward them in formation. We flew down into the atmosphere of the planet and through a large gap in the clouds.

As we neared the enormous blue-green expanse, I began to be able to pick out landmasses—large islands of broken land that looked almost like crumbled pie crusts at this distance. The coordinates led us to one particularly large island, and we flew over some rock formations weathered into bulbous pillars, the stone worn into the same geometric shapes over and over like a castle made out of sand.

The coordinates marked a spot on the far side of the island where one edge of the land met the ocean. The water below us was moving, the blue-green edged with white sea foam where it met the beach.

Waves. I remembered learning about those—they were caused by wind and something to do with a moon, I thought, though I didn't see one of those at the moment. The sky was a wide swath of blue from down here, dotted with clouds, the sun too bright to look at without squinting.

A ship slightly larger than our fighters waited for us on the beach. I reached out to Alanik, who flew in front of me. *Do you sense any inhibitors?*

No, she said. *Still no cytonics either, though I think that ship has a taynix.*

That would make sense, if they had a hypercomm. These aliens

413

had managed to steal a Superiority taynix, which was impressive. It also showed initiative, a good trait in allies. We couldn't be expected to protect every species in the galaxy when we could barely protect ourselves.

We cruised in for a landing on the sand, and I used my ship's air quality monitor to check the levels of oxygen in the atmosphere. The air appeared to be breathable, and there were no alerts about any noxious gases like the miasma on ReDawn.

I landed my ship within sight of the other vessel, and the rest of my flight landed around me. I waited until we were all on the ground before opening my canopy.

The ocean, I discovered, was scudding *loud*, like it was being run by a starfighter engine. The water rushed toward us, the peaks of the waves rising and then receding, like an arm reaching for something it couldn't quite grasp. I didn't understand how it *moved* like that, as if it were alive, and it made me wish I'd paid more attention when they'd taught us about Old Earth.

I climbed out of my ship, and the members of my flight joined me one by one. Though we should have been focused on the ship, and watching for ambushes over the strange, layered sandstone cliffs that lined the beach, I noticed mine weren't the only eyes on sthe ocean.

I turned toward a flurry of motion over by the kitsen ship, shielding my eyes from the blinding sun. A group of rodents was moving toward us, the one in front floating on a disk about the size of a dinner plate—a small acclivity-stone craft, I was guessing. Most of the rodents were wearing flightsuits, but the floating one wore a red and gold uniform and had a furry head with a set of enormous ears that looked something like the pictures of foxes from Old Earth, though I thought foxes were bigger. These creatures were around twenty centimeters tall.

But they were coming toward me from a starship, standing on two legs, and wearing clothes, so . . .

I turned around, looking for Alanik. She was already walking up behind me. The sand seemed to slip from under her feet as she walked, making the trip laborious.

"These are kitsen?" I asked her.

"Yes," she said. "I've never met one, but I learned about the species before I left for Starsight. They have a dynastic culture, I believe."

Dynastic. That seemed so primitive, like something out of Spensa's stories.

Farther back on the sand, I could see Cuna and FM climbing out of the Dulo, which had landed next to the medical transport ship we'd brought along for Cobb and Gran-Gran.

The kitsen were growing closer now, and the robed one on the floating platform raised a paw clenched into a fist, like they were angry with me.

I wasn't the most qualified person to establish diplomatic relations, but I had been the one talking to Kauri over the radio.

"Hello," I called. "Are you . . . Kauri?"

"Yes, human!" the kitsen said. She had a translator pin affixed to the front of her uniform like a brooch. "I am Kauri." She floated up in front of us on her dinner plate while the rest of her crew clambered over the sand behind her. "I am the captain of the *Swims Against the Current in a Stream Reflecting the Sun*, and I welcome you to our planet."

"All their names are like that," Alanik said quietly beside me. "The Superiority shortens the name of their planet to Evershore."

The kitsen's ears twitched, and I wondered if this was an offensive term given to them by their oppressors.

"That is very astute, Alanik!" Kauri said. "Indeed, you may call it that if you wish."

"Evershore," I said, glancing at the ocean again. "That seems fitting." Though Alanik seemed somewhat alarmed that the kitsen knew her by name.

"Thank you, human," Kauri said.

"You're . . . a friend of Spensa's?" I asked. "But you knew her as Alanik."

Alanik seemed to relax a bit. It was probably disconcerting to meet people who felt they knew you, but didn't quite.

FM and Cuna trudged up beside us. I was glad—I could use their help.

"Yes, I know Spensa," Kauri said. "I was hoping to see her again after her disappearance from Starsight. Is she well?"

I didn't know if Spensa was well, but I had to believe she was. "She's on a mission to learn more about the delvers."

"Ah yes," Kauri said. "We were there when Winzik summoned the delver. A nasty decision, and one I fear he intends to repeat."

FM and I exchanged a look. If this ship—stars, it would be a whole battleship to them, given their comparative size—was there in the battle with the delver, then the kitsen had been fighting on the other side.

"Which one of you is the human Jerkface?" Kauri asked.

Scud, I'd forgotten to introduce us. "Sorry," I said. "That's me. I'm flightleader Jorgen Weight. This is Alanik of the UrDail. And this is Minister Cuna."

"It's a pleasure to meet you," Cuna said. "Your people are quite advanced for a lesser species, and have been very close to acceptance into the Superiority. I hope that we will be able to help you continue to advance, as we consider what is best for all of your species." Cuna raised their fist in the air with this pronouncement, in a similar greeting to the one Kauri had given me, though Kauri did not look impressed.

Alanik shot me a look. Cuna really had to stop announcing that they found every species we met to be beneath them. We'd brought them along to help with diplomacy, but I didn't want it to seem like they spoke for all of us.

"And this is FM," I said. "She's our . . . diplomatic specialist."

FM's mouth fell open. I raised an eyebrow at her, questioning whether she was going to argue with me. I probably should have put her in charge of this interaction to begin with. I'd been too busy avoiding her to think of it, which meant I was letting my own personal feelings get in the way of my job. That had to stop.

"Thank you for the invitation to your beautiful planet," FM said. "That rock formation we passed over on our way in—was that a city?"

Cuna bared their teeth in one of their strange smiles, which I thought meant they were okay with FM taking the lead.

Whether they were okay with it or not, it was clearly necessary.

"Yes!" Kauri said. "The Burrow from Which Spring Dreams Both Sweet and Sorrowful! You may call it Dreamspring, if you wish."

"Dreamspring," FM said. "That's beautiful. I would love to see more of it."

"And I would love to share it with you," Kauri said. "But we must be careful. Not all of my people will welcome your—oh, how unfortunate."

She looked up at something in the sky over my shoulder, and I turned to see another starship approaching. This one had a startling number of guns mounted on the front, far too many to be tactically effective.

"Humans!" said a kitsen voice through a loudspeaker on the ship. "Your invasion stops here! You shall not step one more foot into the beauty of the Burrow from Which Spring Dreams Both Sweet and Sorrowful! We will cut you down where you stand."

Scud. I took a step backward, taking shelter against my ship, and FM and Alanik joined me. If that ship let loose its destructors we were dead, all of us. The rest of the flight scattered, ducking beneath wings and jumping back into ships.

"It's all right!" Kauri said. "That's Goro. I will speak with him."

"He said he was going to cut us down," I said. "I don't think that implies a lot of talking."

"Yes," Kauri said. "And he wonders why the Superiority thinks we're primitive."

The other ship didn't fire, but instead began to lower itself onto the sand. Bits of grit blew in our direction, and I shielded my eyes.

A host of kitsen poured out of the ship, all of them wearing tiny suits of power armor and carrying guns no longer than my hand. That made them *enormous* to a kitsen though, and they all wore tiny metal helmets with a visor over their eyes and holes cut out for their ears.

That seemed somewhat impractical—I wondered if they used their ears to regulate their temperature like some animals did back on Old Earth. Or perhaps their ears grew back and were therefore seen as expendable.

In the air above them, riding on another dinner-plate-size platform, was a large kitsen wearing richly ornamented plate armor that looked like something out of another century entirely. His helmet had curved horns jutting out of it, so large that they almost reached the tips of his ears.

Oh, Spensa would *really* have loved *this*.

"Scudballs," I heard Arturo say.

"Oh dear," Cuna said. "Such aggression."

I couldn't argue with that. The kitsen swiftly marched across the sand. More of my flightmates climbed back into their ships. Since we were currently being flanked by what amounted to rats with rifles, I didn't blame them. I supposed I should give orders to my flight, but I didn't have any better idea what to do in this situation than they did.

FM stayed by my side, Alanik and Cuna a step behind.

Kauri rotated her platform to float between us and the oncoming kitsen, though her other people mostly seemed to be getting out of the way. Since they were both unarmed and unarmored, I didn't blame them either.

"Goro," Kauri said. "What are you doing?"

"We intercepted your transmission, traitor!" Goro said. "You invited these treacherous giants onto our planet. Bad enough that any of their kind are being permitted to sully our sands. We should have blown them out of the sky when they first appeared."

"No one is getting blown out of the sky!" Kauri said. "These are friends of a friend." She looked over her shoulder at me. "Aren't you?"

"Um, yes," I said.

"Other kitsen!" FM said. "I am a diplomatic representative from our people." I barely heard her add "apparently" under her breath. "We're here to collect our lost friends and discuss an alliance. We're not . . . invading anything, and we don't mean to . . . sully your sands."

"This is heresy!" Goro shouted, pointing a furry finger at me. He had quite a loud voice for such a small creature. "We will not be fooled by your gilded words! The Den of Everlasting Light Which Laps Gently upon the Shores of Time has seen the last of your tyranny and we will not suffer it again!"

"I'm sorry about him," said a voice near my feet, and I looked down to see that one of Kauri's people had scurried over to join us. "Goro has . . . a tendency toward the dramatic."

"It's understandable," Cuna said. "Your culture is not yet advanced enough to move beyond these aggressions."

FM sighed and ignored Cuna, addressing the kitsen at my feet. She had little white tufts at the ends of her ears and a brownish one at the end of her bushy white tail. "What's your name?" she asked.

"Hana," the kitsen said.

"Hi, Hana," FM said. "I'm FM. Your people have interacted with humans before?"

"When the first wave of humans conquered the galaxy, they started with us," Hana told her. "Our ancestors fought bravely, but they were no match for human technology. And it didn't help that at first they welcomed the humans to our shores—the kindly giants straight out of legend! The tales of our early interactions through the nowhere had been passed down for generations."

Goro's soldiers had stopped about three meters from Kauri, but their tiny kitsen leader floated his platform up until he stood toe to toe with her. "I demand that you step aside," he said.

"I will not," Kauri said. "I contacted the humans so they could collect their lost people. They aren't invading, and there is no need for all of . . . *this*." She gestured at the kitsen soldiers, whose power armor hummed ominously. The kitsen hummed with it. It was probably meant to seem intimidating.

It was working.

"Very well," Goro said. "If they claim to come in peace, they must prove it by the sword."

A sword? I supposed that might be preferable to being shot at by many tiny rifles, but . . . *why?*

"Send forth one of your people," Goro continued, "and they may duel my champion in honorable combat."

"Champion?" I said.

A single warrior stepped out of the mass of kitsen. Her power armor was decorated by a tiny skirt, and her helmet curved into two wicked points underneath her chin. She was carrying a sword slightly longer than a dinner knife, which made it taller than she was.

I looked at FM, but she was staring at the kitsen champion. Cuna was watching us all with wide eyes, like they couldn't believe they had deigned to be present for so much barbarity.

On this particular point I had to agree, though it wasn't the barbarity that alarmed me so much as the practical concerns.

A *sword? Really?* "We're not fighting that," I said. "No way."

"I'll fight it!" Nedd called from behind me, and FM shot him a withering look.

"We don't want to fight anyone!" FM said. "We're here on a mission of peace. Our people have also been oppressed by the Superiority, and—"

A chortling sound came from the kitsen. Stars, were they laughing?

"You call it oppression?" Goro said. "When you leveled the great city of Defies the Void with Mighty Heart and Endless Perseverance, that was oppression! When you burned the forest of Rain Falls from Clear Skies, that was oppression! When you—"

"That's enough," Kauri said. "They get the point."

"When it happened to you," Goro added with a menacing growl, "it was *justice*."

"Our people weren't even involved in the last human war," I said. "We were a traveling fleet of ships. It was only when the war was over that we were captured and contained by the Superiority. Also, that was a century ago, and—"

"It doesn't matter," Goro said. "All humans are the same." He pointed at Kauri. "You returned from Starsight spouting ideals of democracy and claiming we could make decisions together without our esteemed One Who Was Not King! But then you skirt the will of the senate, and seek to ally yourself with the enemies of the Den of Everlasting—"

"You're right!" Kauri shouted. "You're right. We should have had a vote about it first. But *you* have marched your clan in here and challenged the humans to a fight without bringing your grievance before the senate, even though your clan's representatives agreed that they would abide by senate decisions."

Goro looked somewhat disgruntled at this point. "This is correct. But the invaders must be stopped immediately, so there is no time for—"

"We're not invading!" FM reminded them.

"Right," Kauri said. "There is still time to consult the senate and see if they are willing to hear the human offer of peace, or if they would prefer that your clan be permitted to prove them in trial by combat."

Kauri seemed to find this as ridiculous as I did, so maybe it wasn't a kitsen thing so much as a Goro thing. Kauri's ship, after all, had only an average number of destructors.

"I didn't agree to any trial," I said. "By combat or otherwise."

"Hush," FM said. "She said they're going to vote on it. We could at least wait to see how the vote turns out."

Given the disaster that had resulted from the DDF trying to work with our own assembly, I wasn't eager to meet with another group of politicians. But we were looking for alliances, so we'd have to work within the kitsen governmental framework at any rate.

"Fine," I said.

"Very well," Goro said. "First we will prepare a feast, and all may partake. Then, after the vote of the senate, we will see who is right."

"A feast?" FM said to the kitsen at my feet. "That's good, right? Unless they mean to poison us—"

Goro's disk shot to the side, and he glared at FM. "Never would my clan participate in something so dishonorable!" he shouted. "Before you die, you will be staring down the glinting metal of my champion's blade!"

"Um," FM said. Even she was starting to look unnerved.

With that final outburst, Goro and his people marched back to their ship, their power armor leaving rows of tiny footprints in the sand. Kauri hunched a bit, clutching her hands together like she was trying very hard not to tell Goro exactly what she thought of him.

"The feast is not a good thing," Cuna said. "Their tradition is to dine first with those they wish to fight to the death. Over the meal, each will try to determine the weakness of the other. They consider it . . . honorable."

I didn't like the implications of that. "We're *not* going to *fight* them—"

"Hopefully you won't have to," Kauri said. She flew her platform over while Goro and his people piled into their miniature battleship. "I think the senate will see reason."

"I'd like to see Cobb," I said. "And Gran-Gran. The humans you found."

"I can arrange that," Kauri said. "If you will follow the *Swims Upstream*, we will take you to see your people."

"Thank you," I said. Hana raised her fist to us, and Kauri and her people traveled across the sands again to their ship.

"That was surreal," FM said.

I nodded. "Not the welcome I expected to receive."

But they were taking us to Cobb, and none of my people had yet found themselves on the wrong end of a kitsen blade, glinting or otherwise.

I supposed that meant we were doing okay.

6

We flew along the shoreline and landed beside the *Swims Upstream* on another beach below the cliffs that sheltered the towering city of Dreamspring. The stone cliffs had clearly been worn over time into fins and ridges by the wind, the sandstone striped with hundreds of red-orange layers. I directed the flight to leave their taynix in the boxes in their ships—the kitsen knew about hyperdrives, but I still didn't want to advertise that we had so many of them. I left Snuggles and Boomslug out of their box, but gave them a stern instruction to stay. I wanted at least one hyperdrive we could access in a hurry if things went wrong, so it was worth the risk that they'd disobey.

I joined Kauri, and my flight and the medtechs followed after us around a bend in the cliffside. The beach down the way was covered in kitsen who appeared to be playing in the surf and relaxing on the sand, at least until they spotted us. We *were* giants to them, and I watched carefully where I stepped, not wanting to flatten any picnic spots.

These kitsen were enjoying themselves, completely oblivious to the war with the Superiority. We were interlopers, bringing the conflict with us.

It was coming for them regardless, but it still felt tragic to disturb the peace. I wondered what it was like to live that way, in a place where taking a trip to the beach to sit and enjoy yourself was an option on any given afternoon.

The concept seemed alien, but stars, it must be nice.

The kitsen gathered together, watching us. Some appeared frightened, others curious, but none attacked us. Kauri floated out in front, waving both paws at the other kitsen. I wasn't sure exactly what that meant, but they seemed to believe she had us under control, because no one else came after us demanding that we duel their champion to the death.

We walked up a narrow path toward the city—no, it was a wide road to them. The path was lined with small mound-shaped structures cut into the rock or formed out of intricately worked sandstone. The structures had arched doorways with tiny stone or metal doors affixed to them. Some had signs in a language I couldn't read, while others had little pots of flowers sitting on the doorsteps or in boxes hanging from circular windows.

"Saints and stars," Sadie said somewhere behind me. "This is so *cute*!"

She wasn't wrong. It reminded me of a story my mother had told me when I was a child, about a man named Gulliver who traveled to a land full of little people who were wary of him because of his size. He befriended them, but was later kicked out when he doused a fire in the palace by peeing on it.

As a child I'd found that part of the story hilarious. Now I thought maybe the little people had a point.

I shielded my eyes from the sun and looked up the hill at the mountainous city. As the road ascended, the little burrow structures began to pile up, dug into the walls of the cliff or sculpted one on top of another into tiny hills with doors on all sides and at all levels. I wondered if they opened into tiny multi-floored houses, or if each entrance went to a separate room isolated from the others. As we walked, little kitsen hovercars pulled over to the side of the road to allow us to pass. They chattered at each other, some too far away or faint for the pin to translate, though I did catch a few words.

"—humans returned!—"

"—don't look threatening—"

"—can't trust them, look how they—"

"—dione with them, does that mean—"

I glanced back and found that Kimmalyn had stopped, bent down beside what looked like a landscaping shop with barrels and stacks of bricks and groundcovers, all organized by type. A kitsen waited out front while two others used a large metal winch to load a huge decorative rock into the back of a hovertruck.

I couldn't hear what Kimmalyn said—she didn't have a translator pin, so she wouldn't have been understood anyway. But then the kitsen stepped back and Kimmalyn lifted the rock—which was only half the size of her palm, but still enormous for the tiny creatures—and set it in the rear of the truck.

One of them tipped its nose up at her, and I hoped that was a gesture of thanks. We didn't need to be accused of property damage or delivering insults. The kitsen we'd met so far didn't seem like they'd appreciate being condescended to.

"Do you think she should be doing that?" I asked FM.

"She's not hurting anything," FM said.

Cuna walked up behind us. "Compassion is universal," they said. "It's seen in all cultures, though it is communicated differently."

FM sighed. "I suppose there might be some cultural norm we're not aware of, but any of us could break one of those at any time and cause an interstellar incident."

"Scud, our lives have gotten weird," I said.

"That's the truth," Arturo said, following us up the road. "It was simpler when we were fighting the Krell."

Simpler, but also stagnant. Our people had spent eighty years fighting for our lives, which meant we had very specialized skills. We were a well-oiled survival machine, but we lacked something these people had. It wasn't happiness exactly. We had that, even if it was tempered by pain and fear.

Prosperity maybe. Peace. I wondered if this was what we would have seen on ReDawn, if we'd spent any time in their cities.

Kauri had drifted ahead of us a bit, and she hovered back, watching us. "Do you need to stop and rest?" she asked. "I'm sorry if I'm outpacing your human endurance." Her shipmates were walking up the path on foot, and they seemed fine. They ran many steps to our one, but they didn't seem to be tiring.

"No, we're fine," I said. "Just appreciating your beautiful city."

"This used to be the home of Hesho, the Most Honorable and Magnificent One Who Was Not King. He died in the battle with the delver at your planet." She gave a little sigh. "We miss him. The Superiority insisted that we needed to transition to a democracy in order to advance to primary citizenship, and I think that change was good for us. But I wish Lord Hesho had remained here with us to see the initiative of his people. He and his ancestors before him served us well for centuries."

Kauri continued to lead us up the path, and the pinnacles of the city of Dreamspring came into view. The cliff had been split into little vertical ridges, the effect uneven enough to be natural rather than kitsen-made. The rock was full of holes and walkways so the kitsen could duck from tunnel to tunnel all across the cliff face of the upper city. The city only rose in height along the cliff face; in front it opened into a sprawling urban landscape that filled the stone area between the sheer cliff and the sand of the beach.

Here along the wall, our faces were even with the higher stories of pathways and tunnels. Scud, we wouldn't fit in their buildings. We couldn't sit down in their homes with them or enter their shops. I imagined what we would feel like on Detritus if ships full of sixty-foot giants suddenly arrived. They'd be unable to fit in our elevators, unable to visit our caverns.

We'd be terrified. It was a miracle that the kitsen had welcomed the humans in the past. And those humans had taken advantage of their trust—that wasn't our fault, but we were responsible for overcoming that history now.

"Kauri," I said, "I know you need to speak to your senate, but where will we even be able to meet with them?"

"Our senate meets in a large auditorium," Kauri said. "We can welcome you there, but you'll have to remain on the floor. I'm afraid we don't have any chairs that will accommodate you. We destroyed all the humans' dwellings after they were expelled from our planet in the Second Human War. Perhaps we could find some sturdy tables for you to sit on."

I worried about our ability to sit on even the sturdiest of kitsen tables. Like FM said, we didn't want to cause any interstellar incidents. "We can sit on the ground," I said. "If there's room."

"As long as that wouldn't be too much of an insult," Kauri said. "We wish to meet with you as equals, but we do not know your customs."

"No," I said. "No insult. Where exactly are Cobb and Gran-Gran?" They wouldn't have fit inside these buildings either. And if they were unconscious—stars, they wouldn't fit inside a kitsen hospital.

"Our feasting grounds are just beyond the turn of the cliff, and the tent with your people is beyond those," Kauri said. "We might be able to put up another tent large enough to shade you while you eat, but the first one took us quite a bit of effort to construct."

"It's not necessary," I said. "Please, take us to Cobb and Gran-Gran."

We took a narrow road across the clearing in front of the cliffs, the roads continuing to empty as we passed through. When we reached the other side of the city, the road turned toward the beach again, and Kauri presented the feasting grounds, which were basically a wide stretch of sand with stone tables and small gazebos set against the cliff. Some of Goro's people—I recognized them by their armor—were filleting fish as big as they were and loading them onto conveyers that rolled into ovens carved out of the cliff face.

"Scud, I don't know if we can eat the food here," I said.

"What are those things?" Alanik said, staring at the fish. "They look . . . slimy."

Huh. They wouldn't have fish on ReDawn, I supposed. We had some that we raised in vats, and a few that lived wild in underground lakes.

"Those are fish," Cuna said. "They pull them from the ocean and eat them. You will be better off trying the fruit." They gestured to the bowls and platters being laid out on the banquet tables. "It should be palatable to your people."

Alanik did not look thrilled, though she'd been polite about the food we'd given her on Detritus, despite most of it being made out of algae.

"If you want to leave some of your people here you may," Kauri said. "The tent near the hospital is up ahead."

"That sounds good," I said. I waved to Kel and Winnow—our medtechs—to join us.

I looked over at Alanik. The kitsen seemed to react better to her, since she wasn't human. "Come with me?"

"Of course," she said.

"Do you want me to come?" FM asked.

"No," I said. "Stay here and maybe do some diplomacy?"

FM gave me a withering look.

Cuna wandered over to the kitsen, observing their cooking. I lowered my voice. "Try to make sure Cuna doesn't insult them too much," I said. "And that Nedd doesn't volunteer to duel creatures one-tenth his size, all right?"

"I can try to make sure he doesn't volunteer *again*," FM said.

"Good. I do not need that on my conscience."

FM turned to the others and directed them out onto the beach. The burrow that Kauri said held the hospital was enormous, towering up into the air. There were many small doors into the complex itself, none of which an adult human could fit through. The kitsen only needed a small fraction of the head clearance humans did.

Kauri led us to a tent that had been erected out front. It looked like many smaller tents had all been affixed together on long poles, creating a structure perhaps three meters long by two meters wide. The roof was about the height of my shoulders, so when Kauri maneuvered her platform near the entrance and pulled back the tent flap, I had to stoop to look inside.

There, on two platforms so low to the ground that I thought they might originally have been kitsen banquet tables, lay Cobb and Gran-Gran. Their bodies had been covered with many blankets layered over each limb and across their torsos.

Kel and Winnow both ducked inside, and Kauri continued to hold the tent flap open as they examined Gran-Gran and Cobb. They were both breathing, I was relieved to see, but their eyes were closed, and one side of Cobb's face was covered in bruises. Some medical equipment was attached to the side of the tables, and kitsen wearing little white robes and hats were surveying it. One stood on a ladder that reached to about the height of my knee, changing out the tiny bottle on what looked like a makeshift IV pole.

At least they were alive and had already received medical attention. "You'll want to get them home to your people, I imagine," Kauri said.

"Yes," I said. "We brought a medical transport ship, and our medtechs will supervise the transfer."

Alanik was watching them both with concern on her face, and she shook her head. "I'm still not sure that's Becca Nightshade."

I blinked. The person in the bed looked like Spensa's grandmother. "Why do you say that?"

"Because she isn't cytonic," Alanik said.

I reached out, trying to sense the vibration I always felt near another cytonic. I could feel waves of it rolling off Alanik.

But she was right. Nothing from Gran-Gran. Farther out, I could feel our taynix still in our ships, but no other cytonics.

But there was something, a vibration coming from the cliffs behind us. Not the concentrated frequency of a cytonic mind, but more like a . . . cloud of something.

"Do you feel that?" I asked. "The strange buzzing from behind the cliffs?"

Alanik frowned. "No," she said. "I'm not finding any cytonic presence here."

That was odd, and I had no idea what it meant. I moved past Winnow to Gran-Gran's bed and brushed the blanket off her hand on one side and then the other, checking for hologram bracelets.

There weren't any. And if the Superiority were trying to trick us, where was the spring for the trap? I reached up and brushed Gran-Gran's hair with my hand. It moved exactly as I expected it to.

"I think that's her," I said. "But you're right, her cytonic abilities seem to be gone. What *happened* to them? And why did they end up *here*?"

"Gran-Gran was behaving strangely before she hyperjumped," Alanik said. "She told me she could tell where Cobb was on the ship, which doesn't make sense. He's not cytonic, so she shouldn't have been able to find him through the negative realm."

That was strange. "But you knew it was her then," I said. "Because you were familiar with her mind. So was I. She wasn't a Superiority fake."

"She also said she was hearing voices calling to her, asking her for help," Alanik said. "She asked if they were my people."

I narrowed my eyes. That could have been the Superiority interfering with her cytonics. Like what happened to Spensa's father.

I looked at the medtechs. "What is their condition?"

"They seem stable," Kel said.

"We've focused on keeping them nourished and hydrated," Kauri added. "Our lorekeepers have some records of what nutrients your people need."

"Cuna said that your people don't have cytonics," I said, "but that you still have information about them."

"Yes," Kauri said. "Our lorekeepers have preserved the records, and they study and understand them, but we have not had kitsen cytonics for centuries. Some of my people believe it's a curse, that we haven't proven ourselves worthy to regain the powers."

That was unfortunate. Still, detailed records of cytonic powers would be useful. "We would love to speak to your lorekeepers," I said.

"Of course," Kauri said. "I will send a message saying that you've requested an audience with them."

"In the meantime, we can load Cobb and Gran-Gran into the transport ship." Something strange was happening with Gran-Gran, possibly with both of them, and they needed better medical care than our medtechs could give here in the field.

"I think you should meet with our senators first," Kauri said. "If you remove your people from the planet before the meeting, Goro may try to use that as evidence that you're trying to sneak away, or that you're preparing to attack."

I hesitated, looking to Winnow.

"I don't think a few hours are going to make a difference," Winnow said. "Unless their conditions worsen."

That was fair. I looked at Cobb one more time. His face was pale, but he was breathing. He was alive.

We'd wake him up. We had to.

He had to find us a way out of this mess.

7

When we returned to the feast area, we found FM sitting cross-legged at one of the tables, rolling melons the size of her head through a machine with many coordinated blades that cut them into precise slices. Nedd and Arturo sat behind her, loading citrus fruits onto small spindles that spun around a sharp blade, which removed the peel in a long, thin strip. Nedd deposited the peels into very small waste canisters, which two kitsen replaced with empty canisters and then scurried away to offer the full canisters to a pen filled with miniature goats, about the right size for a kitsen to ride as a mount. Kimmalyn and Sadie were seasoning fish with very small seasoning shakers, while Catnip and T-Stall knelt next to the ovens, using handheld controls to remove the fish from the conveyors with acclivity-empowered spatulas.

"I'm sorry," Kauri said to me. "You are our guests. Your people shouldn't have been asked to prepare the food."

Hana ran up, sitting at my feet. "We didn't ask them," she said. "They volunteered. In fact, FM *insisted*."

FM raised her eyebrows at me from across the sandy pavilion.

"We take no offense," I said. "Thank you for allowing us to serve you."

FM smiled.

This was kind of brilliant of her. We were trying to convince them that we weren't invaders. I bet the humans who'd marched in and declared them a colony didn't offer to help them with food preparation.

"What can I do to help?" I asked.

Alanik and I were brought to rotating spits where squashes roasted over a fire. We were instructed to use miniscule spray bottles to hydrate the turning vegetables with a brownish liquid that smelled both sweet and spicy.

I sprayed a bit on my finger and tasted it. Stars, it was delicious.

Not long after, Goro arrived. His champion rode on the saucer beside him, her sword tucked into a sheath and strapped across her back.

Goro didn't look happy to see us all helping prepare the food. He gave me an especially affronted glare. I was supposed to be the enemy, the invader he was here to defeat.

Putting FM in charge of diplomacy had clearly been the right decision.

When we finished the food preparation, several kitsen carried away the remaining waste and cooking implements, and Kauri returned with another kitsen riding a second, smaller saucer.

"This is Juno," she told me. "One of our lorekeepers. He has offered to dine with you, though he will wait until after the senate meeting to impart knowledge."

"I am sorry this is necessary," Juno said, "but there are some among us who find our lorekeeping to be superfluous or even threatening. It was only the will and continued patronage of the Most Honored One Who Was Not King that sustained our order. We do not wish to go against the will of the senate or attract the ire of—"

"Humans!" Goro bellowed from the head of one of the large tables. "It is time to begin to feast. I will not offer you welcome! You come as invaders, and so we give you the greeting fit for those who dare think to conquer the Den of Everlasting Light Which Laps

Gently upon the Shores of Time! A full belly to make you sluggish, so that my champion may more easily pierce you with the sword!"

"Well that's disturbing," FM muttered beside me.

"At least he's upfront about it," Alanik added.

"Let us feast!" Goro shouted, and the kitsen all echoed these last words with their fists raised in the air.

I was beginning to wonder if I'd made a grave tactical error by dining with these creatures. I thought we were doing the right thing by being diplomatic and trying to prove we weren't here to conquer them. But now I worried they would discover some weakness they might use against us.

"Juno," I said as one of the kitsen brought me a small plate—it must have been an oversized serving platter to them—piled high with fish and nuts. "I know you don't want to share your knowledge with us until the senate agrees to it, but may I ask if any of this food is poisonous to humans?"

"Certainly," Juno said. "The photophores of the flatfish are mildly venomous, but those have been removed. Our records show that humans ate most of our foods, and indeed put a great strain on our resources, trying to export some of our most prized delicacies for their own gain. To answer your question, the only foods we eat that would be poisonous to you are a few varieties of berry and some of our summer shellfish, and none of those have been offered to you this day. Make no mistake, Goro means to kill you, but he will only do so with senate permission and in the way that is most advantageous to him."

Over at Goro's table, I heard him comparing his fish to a worthy foe slain in battle. That seemed like a stretch to me, but I'd once heard Spensa muttering something that sounded a lot like "fear the wrath of my very soft socks" on requisition day, so she probably would have approved. I wasn't sure how fighting one of us with a sword could be advantageous to him, but clearly he had some kind of endgame in mind.

FM poked at her own fish, then took a bite. "This is delicious."

"Eh," Nedd said, settling down cross-legged on the sand by Kimmalyn. "It's a little fishy."

FM blinked at him. "It is literally fish."

"Right," Nedd said. "But . . . *fishy* fish."

"Totally," Catnip said. "I hate it when my food adjectives its own noun."

"Exactly," Nedd said.

"It's like the Saint says," Kimmalyn added. "You are what you eat."

"Hey, look!" Sadie said. "There are boats out there!" She pointed out onto the water, beyond the waves. The noise from the ocean was fainter this far up on the beach. And out on the blue-green expanse that seemed to go on and on forever until it melded with the sky . . . scud, she was right. There were ships out there. Sailing vessels that couldn't have been much longer than a meter or two, bobbing up and down in the waves.

"I understand the basics of how boats work," I said. "But how do they do that? How do they *sail* out there on all that water, without worrying that it's going to swallow them up?"

"Sometimes it does," Juno said. "The water is dangerous, especially for sailors who are caught in a sudden storm. As for how they brave it—how do you fly into the blackness of space? It seems just as unknowable to me, and a great deal more vast."

That . . . was a really good point.

"I don't know," Arturo said. "You can't drown in space."

"But you can asphyxiate," Nedd said. "Which sounds just as unpleasant."

The food suddenly felt heavy in my mouth. I set down my fork, which might have originally been some sort of gardening implement.

"Or freeze to death," Catnip added. "It's cold in space."

"The ocean can be cold," Juno said. "Depending on the currents and the time of year."

"You don't depressurize if you jump into the ocean though," Nedd said. "Scud, that sounds nasty. Did you know it can make your saliva boil in your mouth?"

"Ew, Nedd," FM said. "We're eating."

The Superiority ship exploded before my eyes. The bodies of my parents were flung into space, fluids voiding, their eyeballs boiling.

I shook my head and set down my plate. That hadn't happened. They'd been torn apart by the mindblades first.

Hadn't they?

"The ocean does the opposite," Juno said. "The pressure in its depths is so great it can crush you."

"Whoa," Nedd said. "That's awesome."

Stars. Why did everything in the galaxy feel like it was trying to kill us? I had started this conversation, but now I had to get away from it. "Excuse me," I said, and I got up, leaving my food behind. I moved away from the city, down the beach toward the water.

A projectile shot over the ocean, and I flinched. Was the *water* attacking us now?

But no, it was a *bird*—a whole flock of them, wings tucked against their bodies as they shot like bullets into the waves, and then flapping to give them lift again, carrying them into the air with fish in their mouths.

Stars. I'd seen pictures of birds, but watching them glide over the water like so many starfighters . . .

It was incredible, but it didn't stop my hands from shaking.

I wiped cold sweat from my forehead. Scud, I'd walked away from the feast. Was I ruining our diplomatic relations? Offending the kitsen somehow? Would they perceive this as a threat?

It didn't matter. I couldn't go back. I couldn't *breathe*. As I stared out at the ocean, the whole of it pressed down on me, all the weight of what felt like millions of miles of water bearing down on my body.

It was too much.

"Jorgen?" FM said. I wheeled around to find her watching me with concern.

Scud, not concern. Anything but concern. I wished she'd look at me the way she had back on the platform on ReDawn, when she'd been pissed at me for telling her she shouldn't have liberated the slugs from Detritus. She'd been so angry at me, when I'd simply pointed out the obvious—she'd broken the chain of command, violated our orders, and put our comrades in danger.

You are not my flightleader, she'd said.

That had gutted me then, but I found it infinitely preferable to what I knew she was going to say now.

"Are you okay?"

"I'm fine," I said.

"Jorgen," FM said. "You aren't fine."

"Yes," I said. "I am."

"That's ridiculous. You can't be fine. Your parents—"

"This isn't the time!" I said. "We are in the middle of a diplomatic mission! We need to talk to the senate so we can get Cobb and Gran-Gran home."

Once we brought Cobb back though, Stoff was definitely going to declare him indisposed. There was no avoiding that. In fact, according to protocol, I should have already told Stoff that we'd found Cobb and he was indeed unconscious.

I . . . didn't want to. As soon as I did, Stoff would be fully within his rights to start acting as admiral. I had no idea what he would do, but whatever it was . . . I didn't trust it. Cobb knew what was best for the DDF, for our people, for Detritus. He should be the one in charge.

He would get us through this.

FM stared at me with her lips pressed together like she was trying to hold in all the things she wanted to say.

"This isn't about Cobb," she said finally. "It's not about Gran-Gran, and it's not about our diplomatic mission."

"Exactly," I said. "And those are the only things that matter right now."

"That's not true," she said. "*You* matter, Jorgen. What happened to you, it matters."

I balled my fists, turning away from her to look out at the sea. A particularly large wave washed up the beach, and I wished it would come all the way up and wash me out to sea and be done with it. I imagined the water pulling me down, crushing me the way Juno said it would, all that weight blocking out the questions, the demands, the *needs* of everyone else.

Moments ago all that water had seemed terrifying. Now it felt like release.

"Jorgen," FM said, "you need to talk to someone. It doesn't have to be me, but have you said *anything* about your parents? To anyone?"

I hadn't. I couldn't. Not until I knew everyone was safe.

"We need to be prepping for the senate meeting," I said. "Go ask Kauri what we can do to support her in convincing the senate we're here in peace."

"I don't think—"

"Do it, FM."

"Jorgen—"

"That's an *order.*"

I looked back at her, and she stared at me. There was some anger there now, and that was good. Much better than pity. For a moment I thought she was going to tell me off again, announce that I wasn't her flightleader and I couldn't tell her what to do. Say what we both knew: that I was only pretending to be in control, that I'd never known what I was doing, that I was incompetent to be in command, and that I was failing at everything—even this.

"Fine," FM said, and she spun around and marched back up the beach. Past her I could see that the rest of the flight had finished eating. Kauri escorted them down to the water, where Nedd and Kimmalyn took off their shoes and rolled up their jumpsuits, letting the water wash over their feet. Alanik and Arturo sat in the sand, laughing.

I couldn't remember what it felt like to laugh.

I wondered if that meant I had already drowned.

8

I was still on edge when Kauri led us to the senate assembly, held in an arena built into the cliffside. The arena was an enormous space for the kitsen, containing hundreds upon hundreds of small padded seats carved into the sandstone, ascending up to the ceiling at the back of the room. There was barely space for Alanik to stand, and I had to hunch my shoulders to avoid scraping my head.

The floor at the bottom of the seats provided enough space for a few of us to sit. The others stayed on the beach, while FM, Alanik, and I all tried to squeeze in together. We'd used the lack of space to leave Cuna out of the meeting, but in reality I was afraid of what they might say.

We had to sit with our knees tucked up to our chests to fit all three of us. A kitsen floated on a small platform with a raised wall around it, like a cup we might drink out of on Detritus. The cup had a microphone attached to the front of it like on a podium.

"I am Adi, director of the senate," the kitsen said. "It is my job to ensure that the proceedings progress in an orderly fashion. You will not speak unless you are asked a direct question."

"Will we be given an opportunity to plead our case?" I asked. "We're trying to retrieve our friends and offer an alliance, and if we aren't allowed to speak—"

"You may be called upon to speak if there are questions," Adi said. "Please do not speak out of turn."

We *may* be. Stars, I hoped Kauri had this under control.

The kitsen senators began to file in, all wearing silk robes of a similar style. The colors varied widely, and I wondered if they were based on personal preference, or if they indicated what region the kitsen was from. We'd landed on this island, but we'd passed over hundreds more. As the hall began to fill, I noticed physical differences in the kitsen as well. Some had longer ears and smaller snouts, while others had darker coloring to their fur. A pair in the back each had an ear notched as if ceremonially cut, and one that took a seat toward the front had a row of silver earrings pierced all the way up to the tip on one side.

"That's a lot of kitsen," FM whispered beside me. "Are you going to do the talking if there are questions?"

"I appointed you our diplomatic specialist," I said. "You should do it."

FM took a deep breath. "Okay. But if I say something wrong, I'm a little afraid Goro's champion is going to run me through with a sword. It's not easy to get in and out of here. We wouldn't be able to escape."

"I'll talk, if neither of you wants to," Alanik said.

"No," FM said. "I can do it. But . . ."

Goro arrived, riding on his disc with his champion beside him. He'd left the rest of his entourage outside. The champion's sword was still sheathed, and I hoped it would remain so.

Goro lowered his platform to be even with the bottom row of chairs, presumably so he wouldn't block the view of any of the senators. This put him alarmingly close to Alanik's knees, but she didn't seem intimidated by him.

It was hard to be intimidated by something so small, but that didn't mean I wanted his champion charging our ankles with a sword. Diplomatic disaster or not, someone could get seriously hurt, and it could be one of us.

441

Adi called the meeting to order. Only about a third of the senate seats were filled, but I imagined there were probably senators who were away, or who hadn't been able to gather on such short notice. A lot of the kitsen were watching us suspiciously, but none of them were advancing on us with weapons drawn, so this was still an improvement.

Until they started to speak.

Adi gave both Goro and Kauri the floor, which surprised me. I'd sat through enough boring assembly speeches that I expected this meeting to be much the same. But instead, Goro and Kauri entered into a sort of debate.

"These human invaders," Goro said, "must be dealt with. Given our long and violent history with them, we know what language the giants speak. They must receive the only communication they understand—a swift and violent lesson by combat. Their kind has brought only ruin upon our shores, and it is up to us to visit vengeance upon all our enemies."

FM leaned over and whispered to me. "He says violence is the only language *we* speak, but he's the one who keeps trying to attack us."

That was an interesting argument. I wanted to hear more, but it was apparently Kauri's turn.

"The humans *aren't* our enemies," Kauri said. "They have come by my invitation to collect their friends who arrived here by accident, and who are even now receiving medical treatment. They also bring with them a promise of an alliance, which they have already established with the UrDail."

Most of the audience eyed Alanik, and Alanik stared back at them, stone faced.

She wasn't any better with people than I was, but at least she didn't go around referring to them as lesser. She leaned over to me. "You could just fight him," Alanik said. "He is literally asking for it. Any of us could beat him in combat."

"If we do that," FM said, "we'll only solidify their image of us

442

as dangerous, violent, and aggressive. All the things we're trying to prove we aren't."

Besides, the kitsen were fast and trained in dueling. I wouldn't put it past them to get a good blow in on one of us and seriously injure us. I doubted they'd manage to kill us, but I didn't want any of it on my conscience.

If Spensa were here, she would have seen it differently. She would have dueled the kitsen and probably won spectacularly, and would have somehow spun that victory into an alliance. But she wasn't here, and I was doing the best I could.

"Of course they *say* they come in peace," Goro said. "But we all know what humans are like."

"I don't think we do!" Kauri said. "Humans invaded us in the past, but *these* humans have a common enemy in the Superiority. I was there when Winzik summoned a delver to destroy the humans."

"It was in that battle that we lost our most Honored and Revered One Who Was Not King!" Goro said. "If we had not meddled in interstellar affairs, he would be with us even now."

"It was Lord Hesho's decision to answer the Superiority's call," Kauri said. "Do you question his will?"

Goro sputtered. "No, but—"

Kauri continued as if Goro hadn't interrupted her. "The delver immediately turned on Winzik's own people, but still he persists. He offered us a path to primary citizenship, but we were only pawns meant to enact his violence for him. If we don't begin to forge alliances, we will stand alone when the destruction comes."

"This is fearmongering," Goro said. "The humans are the real threat."

Kauri replied and the two of them went on, arguing back and forth.

Juno, the kitsen lorekeeper, sat in the front row near my feet. I leaned forward and whispered to him. "Is it always like this?"

Juno leaned toward me. "No," he said. "Our senate is young.

Before we lost our king he made the decisions, instructing our people how to vote. It was easier then for us to arrive at decisions. Our wills were aligned, and we had unity."

Alanik bristled a little at the wording, but I saw his point. That was the way the DDF worked. Our admiral made the decisions, and the rest of us carried them out. We could act quickly that way, and decisively.

But it also meant we could swiftly make the wrong decision, if the person at the top made the wrong call.

I thought about what Arturo said, that our lives were easier when we could think about things simply. We had to kill the Krell because they were trying to kill us. There was no moral ambiguity, no diplomacy to navigate. I supposed after a fashion my parents had been doing something brave, trying to pioneer a new way.

In other circumstances, they might have been heroes.

Goro looked ruffled, like he felt he was starting to lose the argument. "We must settle this matter decisively," he said. "Allow my champion to fight a champion of the humans' choosing. Our might will decide the victor."

He seemed to have only that one argument, and I noticed no one in the senate had brought a champion with a sword. We hadn't seen anyone else dressed like Goro in the city either. He was the only one insisting that a trial by combat was a reasonable course of action.

"The humans have already said they mean us no harm," Kauri said. "They don't want to fight with us. A physical fight between kitsen and giant would only cause unnecessary pain."

"To them maybe!" Goro said. "My champion will fell the giant like our heroes of old! They will not stand before the blades of—"

Yeah, his argument was starting to reach the fever pitch of someone who knew they were losing. But the senate members hadn't given their opinions yet, so why would he be?

Goro looked over at me and seemed . . . confused.

Was he trying to *bait* us into fighting him? That would certainly make his argument easier.

Kauri followed his gaze and I raised a hand, indicating that I wanted to speak.

"For my next argument," Kauri announced, "I would like to introduce the witness testimony of Flightleader Weight."

Goro hunched a bit, looking disgruntled.

"Jorgen?" FM whispered. "What are you doing?"

"Trying something," I said.

"This is preposterous," Goro mumbled. "A human should not speak to the senate."

"Kauri is allowed to enter the testimony of another to make her argument for her," Adi said imperiously. "Flightleader Weight, you may speak."

Stars, I wished I was more prepared for this. I'd have preferred to have FM do it, but there wasn't time. She was right. If we gave even the slightest indication that we would participate in Goro's duel, we solidified their already terrible preconceptions of us. "On behalf of my people," I said, "I'm sorry for what you've suffered at human hands. But we aren't interested in fighting you."

"They arrived with destructors on their ships," Goro said, "and they expect us to believe—"

"You will wait your turn," Adi admonished him, and Goro snarled a bit but shut his mouth.

"Our destructors are used in defense," I said. "Of ourselves and of our allies. And we would very much like you to *be* our allies."

Goro's furry little brow bunched, and his champion leaned over and whispered something to him, though Goro waved her off.

Kauri gave a triumphant little smile. "I rest," she said. And she nodded to me.

Goro *had* been trying to bait us into something. And if we'd risen to the bait and fought his champion, we would have proven everyone right about us. Goro clearly wanted that. Was it because our presence weakened his power, or did he think he was doing his people a favor by trying to reveal our true intentions?

"Very well," Adi said. "The argument is over. We will now hear from the senate."

Kauri turned around and raised her fist at me, in a gesture I was coming to recognize as both a greeting and approval.

Goro floated closer, his champion standing beside him with her gauntleted arms crossed. "I don't know what your game is, human," he grumbled.

"I don't have a game," I said. "Except to bring our people home, make peace with you, and coordinate a resistance against the Superiority."

Goro narrowed his beady little eyes at me. "Your people never looked at us as allies before."

"And I'm sorry for that," I told him. "But we aren't them. We're concerned about your welfare, and the welfare of all the species the Superiority claims are lesser."

I looked over at FM and she nodded her approval. Stars, maybe I was getting some of this right at least.

"Hmph," Goro said, crossing his arms to mirror his champion. "Well, we will see."

Paws waved in the air all around the room, and Adi floated her microphone over to them, allowing the senators to speak.

The first few senators focused on Goro's argument—his right to challenge newcomers to a trial by combat. Several felt there was no harm in granting his request—though they all seemed to regard it as odd—and suggested we should be obliged to appoint a champion or leave the planet in disgrace. The kitsen with the rings in his ears said that Goro had no authority over Dreamspring or the surrounding island, so his challenge was invalid. Goro would need to wait and reissue it if one of us set foot on his island, which had another long name I didn't quite follow.

Stars, it was getting hot in here. We were inside the rock, where

446

it should have been cooler, but the heat of so many bodies in one place was starting to make the room humid and stuffy.

I looked over at FM, who was listening to the kitsen speak with obvious and growing concern. "This isn't going well," she said to me.

She was right. Instead of focusing on what I'd said about peace, the conversation was getting bogged down in the disputed legality of Goro's request. And in between, senators began to comment on the bigger issue—dare they defy the Superiority by working with us? That would mean throwing away all their progress toward primary citizenship. They gave up their *monarchy* for that, which they all seemed to consider a great sacrifice.

"Lord Hesho gave his life to try to further our cause with the Superiority," one of the kitsen with a notched ear said. "How can we dishonor his sacrifice by abandoning his quest?"

Kauri squirmed like she dearly wanted to argue with that, but both she and Goro remained silent, which I gathered was the rule.

We had not been given permission to speak again, and we hadn't interrupted. I simultaneously wished someone would ask our opinion and was unsure of what I would say.

If Spensa were here, she'd say *something*. She wouldn't be able to sit here and listen to this without telling them how wrong they were. She wouldn't worry about finding the right words—she'd trample forward on moxie alone, and it would *work*, because Spensa was amazing like that.

And somehow she had confidence in *me*. Stars, I could have used a little of that confidence right now. I let my mind slip into the nowhere, searching for her. Alanik was sitting right here, and while I didn't hear her in the nowhere, I also didn't want her to open her mind and hear me, so I stayed quiet, looking, listening.

The kitsen senators continued to argue, but I caught only snatches.

"—Superiority has the power. Who are these humans, that they think they can win—"

The nowhere was quiet as ever, devoid even of that strange raised texture I'd encountered on Platform Prime.

There was *something* though, there in the emptiness. Not Spensa, but . . . an *image* of her. She was . . . cleaning a part from a starfighter. I couldn't see the area around her, but I could see *her*, and could sense . . . her loneliness. And a feeling of concern for her that wasn't mine. It came from the image, from the nowhere.

Stars, was the *nowhere* concerned about Spensa? It was only a strange place, it couldn't think or feel—

Could it?

The kitsen went on, the arguments getting more heated as they went.

"—threaten our way of life. We shouldn't be working with any of them, unless we want—"

The image of Spensa faded. It hadn't seemed like it came from Spensa herself, but I had no idea where—or who—it had come from. It was gone now, and I couldn't find it again.

"—destruction for us and all our kin. If we aren't careful—"

An image welled up in my mind—the Superiority ship where my parents died, cut to ribbons and expanding ever outward against the blackness of space.

I shoved it down, reaching through the nowhere again. Spensa was in here somewhere. I'd found that image, I should be able to find *her*. Even if we couldn't talk, I wanted to *know* she was *there*—

That vibration I'd felt before grew stronger, a cytonic resonance from somewhere on the island. And then, loud in my mind, a voice cried, *HELP US!* and I visibly startled.

Other than Juno, who looked up at me in alarm, the other kitsen didn't seem to notice. Both FM and Alanik did though, and they turned to me.

Are you okay? Alanik asked.

Fine, I said. I drew back into myself. That voice—it had come from the nowhere, but it wasn't Spensa. I didn't know *who* it was.

Maybe Gran-Gran? But she was here on Evershore, not in the no-where.

Scud, why was it so *hot* in here? The sandstone walls felt like they were closing in on me. I wanted to escape, but I couldn't slip out. I'd have to crawl through the scudding doorway on my hands and knees again. What kind of message would that send?

I tried to focus on the words of the senator who was speaking, a very large kitsen with brown tufts at the ends of his ears.

"—if our most Honored One Who Was Not King were here, he would surely agree that—"

"Do not profane the name of the One Who Was Not King!" another interrupted. "In his wisdom, he would surely have said—"

Stars, they all seemed to have an opinion of what their not-king would do if he hadn't died in the battle with the delver. Did *we* kill him? We very well might have.

And when they invoked his name, they sounded uncomfortably like *me* trying to convince Vice Admiral Stoff of what Cobb would do if he were here.

Stars, was this what I sounded like? Like I was merely trying to win a scudding argument, making the specter of Cobb agree with whatever I said?

Jorgen, Alanik said again, *are you okay?*

I'm fine, I said, and I cringed, glad FM couldn't hear me.

You aren't fine, she'd said. *You can't be fine.*

She knew. Stars, everyone probably knew. I was trying to hold everything together, but it was all slipping through my fingers and—

Help us! the voice in the nowhere said again.

Stars. It didn't *sound* like Gran-Gran. Who *was* that? Didn't they know I couldn't help anyone, not my flight, not even my parents?

"Our lives are stable here," a greying kitsen said. His skin was loose around his face, and he carried a small cane that he leaned on while he sat. "Why would we risk angering the Superiority?

We should be working with them, or we will end up hunted like the humans have been, and we will have no one to blame but ourselves."

Damn it. The kitsen might have easier lives than we did. They might be able to choose to go play on the beach in the afternoon, or have feasts, or duel each other needlessly because they were squabbling and bored, but if it drove them to that kind of thinking then it was a luxury that bred carelessness. My parents had wanted that kind of luxury for me, for *us*, and they'd reached for it—and that was why they were dead.

I saw my mother's face behind the glass, resigned to her fate.

Do better than we did.

But we weren't doing better. We were having the same damn argument *again*.

Help us! the voice said from the nowhere. No, *voices*. There were many of them. Maybe they weren't real. Maybe it was my own mind conjuring up all the people I was failing—Cobb and my flight and all the people on Detritus who were going to die because *I* didn't know what I was doing.

I can't do better, I thought to my mother. She couldn't hear me. She wasn't here with us. She wasn't in the nowhere. She wasn't anywhere. She was *gone*, and soon the rest of us would be too and it would be all my fault.

I tried to take a deep breath, but I couldn't. The room was stifling, and the walls were closing in, and that Superiority ship exploded and contracted again and again in my mind, the bits of debris flying outward into the void. There was a hollowness in my chest where my soul used to be, where the part of me that loved my parents—that cared and felt—had been kept. Now it was nothing but emptiness, and for the first time I was glad Spensa wasn't here. I didn't want her to know. I didn't want her to see. The shame of it all coiled inside me and then exploded outward like the Superiority ship—

Boom.

Bits of the nowhere ripped through my mind, coalescing into physical waves and bursting out like shrapnel from a bomb. The explosion caught the platforms on which Kauri and Goro were hovering and pitched them to the side, dumping the kitsen to the floor. Adi's cup tilted wildly, bits of the sides chipping off. The force of it knocked several of the kitsen in the front rows back in their seats.

Alanik grabbed me by the arm. She seemed unharmed but—

What just happened?

Snuggles and Boomslug suddenly appeared at my feet. "Boom!" Boomslug said. The senators were all staring at me, and many of them began to talk at once. The pin couldn't parse what they were all saying, but I gathered that not one of them was happy with me.

"What the scud was that?" FM asked.

"Mindblades," Alanik said. "Jorgen, how did you—"

"I didn't mean to," I said. "I didn't mean to." Saints and stars, I'd just been talking about peace and now I did *this* in the middle of a diplomatic meeting?

"Boom," Boomslug said again, and he started to nuzzle my ankle as if in sympathy.

He hadn't done this. He and Snuggles had felt it through the nowhere and had come to *comfort* me. I'd somehow manifested mindblades in the middle of a room full of scudding diplomats and now—

"Order!" Adi called. "The house will come to order!"

Goro regarded me with satisfaction. "Now you see!" he bellowed from the floor, close enough that the pin managed to pick him up. "The humans speak only the language of violence! It is the only means they'll respond to!"

I couldn't catch all of it, but several of the kitsen raised their fists in that gesture of solidarity.

Stars, I'd ruined everything. "That's not true!" I said. It came out louder than I wanted it to, my voice overpowering Adi's as she called for order.

"That's not true," I said again, and the senators began to quiet.

Several of them had scrambled over the backs of their seats to use them as shields. "We're not here to hurt you," I said. "We only want you to understand that we have tools to fight the Superiority. It is possible for us to beat them, but only if we work together."

That was a lie on two fronts. I *hadn't* done that on purpose as a display of power and I *didn't* know if we really had the power to defeat the Superiority, even together.

But Saints and stars, I was in it now. "I understand. It's a lot to ask for you to side against the Superiority. I know they have better ships and better technology. But that's been true since long before I was born, and my people have been successfully resisting them for eighty years! We don't know anything about you or your culture, but we know about *them*, because we have fought them and we have *survived*. We don't want what happened to us to happen to anyone else. We don't want anyone else to be hunted, to have to live in hiding, to be killed in droves every time you so much as stick your heads out of the ground."

The kitsen's eyes widened as they watched me, and several of them laid their ears back in what I thought might be fear. I didn't know if it was still me they were afraid of, or the Superiority, but I'd made this mess. I'd insisted on coming here. I'd scudding lost control in the middle of the most important diplomatic meeting I'd ever been in, and stars, I had to fix it.

"You may feel like you have peace and prosperity here, but Kauri is right. The Superiority is trying to make a deal with the delvers, and they're going to come for anyone who opposes them. This might be our *last chance* to resist before they have the power they need to control every planet in the galaxy. How long do you think your planet will last without allies?"

FM put a hand on my arm, and I startled. Scud, was I messing this up? But beside me, she smiled and nodded.

Keep going, Alanik said in my mind. *You have to convince them.*

The kitsen watched me in shock, but not one of them had complained yet that I was speaking out of turn.

I didn't know if I *could* convince them, especially after what I'd just done—stars, what had I done?—but I had to try.

"We tried to reason with the Superiority," I said. "They offered us a treaty, and we sent a delegation to sign the deal." My throat closed, but I spoke through it. "The Superiority offered us peace and then locked our leaders up in a ship and blew it to pieces. Half our government is gone. I *will not* fight you, because I have had enough of senseless violence and death. If you want, we will collect our people and go. But before we do, I want to offer you the opportunity to join us. The UrDail already have! The Superiority made a deal with the UrDail—and then visited their planet with a battleship bent on destroying them. This new Superiority government, that's what they do. And if you try to reason with them, they're going to come for you, too. And I don't want to see it happen again. Not what happened to—"

My voice broke.

"—to my people."

To my parents.

The room was so hot, but my hands felt cold. My vision blurred. I couldn't stay here anymore. I had to get out.

"Thank you," I said. And I stood, my neck bent to avoid hitting my head on the ceiling, then moved in a crouch down the aisle and got down on my hands and knees to crawl through the double doors out of the chamber.

The cool air hit my face, and I squinted against the bright sunlight.

I turned toward the beach, careful not to step on anyone or anything, and ran away as quickly as I dared.

9

I made it almost to the water before FM caught up to me. My calves burned from moving so quickly across the sand, though I'd been out of breath since before I left the senate.

"Jorgen," she said.

I didn't turn around.

"Jorgen!" She caught me by the shoulder, spinning me around. My thoughts raced, and I felt like I could just keep spinning.

What the *scud* had I just done?

I'd shot a bunch of *mindblades* at a group of politicians. I'd sat in so many of those kinds of meetings growing up. I knew how to behave, how to hold everything in, how to present a calm front no matter what was going on inside.

Why did I have to go and do *that*?

"Jorgen," FM said, "this has to stop."

She was right, though I wasn't sure which "this" she meant. The part where I faked being in control, though I didn't have any idea what I was doing? This charade where we pretended we could put together alliances and fight the Superiority? Even if these people did agree to join us, what did we have to offer them? Was there any victory over an enemy this powerful? The best we could say was

454

that so far we hadn't been exterminated completely—though until very recently I didn't think the Superiority had really been trying.

"Say something," FM said. I didn't see Alanik behind her. I wondered if she'd gone to tell the others what happened, or stayed to try to reason with the kitsen some more. She couldn't possibly do a *worse* job than I'd done—

I swore, scrubbing my hands over my face.

"Okay," FM said. "That's a good start."

I wanted to order her to go away again. I wanted to tell her I had no desire to talk about it.

But I also . . . *didn't*. I was drowning, and I'd brought my whole flight with me, and—

A large wave crashed onto the sand, and I jumped.

"Scud, Jorgen," FM said. "Sit *down*."

That was the only thing I thought myself capable of, so I did.

FM sat next to me and set Boomslug and Snuggles into the sand next to her.

"I messed that up," I said. Stars, I was the flightleader. I wasn't supposed to admit weakness. If I had to, I was supposed to go to my superior officer so my flight wouldn't lose respect for me.

But FM had lost respect for me a long time ago, so I guessed there wasn't much to lose.

"Actually," FM said, "I think what you said *improved* the meeting. I mean, I wouldn't have suggested that you start throwing around random cytonic powers—"

"I didn't do that on purpose," I said.

"I know. But you got their attention, and then you gave them the speech they needed. And now they're going to have to make a decision. And if they choose to side with the Superiority . . ." she sighed. "Sometimes people are going to make bad choices, and there's nothing we can do about it."

"That sucks," I said.

"It's the worst!" FM said. "But it's not your fault."

Scud. "We're talking about my parents now," I said.

"Yes, we're talking about your parents!" FM said. "And don't even try to order me not to because I'm not going to listen to you this time. You are holding everything in so tightly that it *literally* exploded. We are doing this now, whether you like it or not."

I expected to feel angry, but instead I felt . . . relief. Like I'd been holding up something very heavy and someone else finally saw through my assurances that I had it and took some of the weight.

That didn't make any sense though. "Talking about it isn't going to change anything," I said. "Nothing can change it."

"That's true," FM said. "And trust me, I don't like talking about these things any more than you do. But it helps, I promise. It doesn't change what happened, but it changes *you*."

I looked over at her. "You know this from experience?"

FM nodded. "Rig taught me that. Sometimes he has to *make* me talk, but every time I'm glad I did."

"You guys are really good together," I said. I would never have guessed it before they got together, but they seemed to balance each other out.

FM smiled. "Rig is my safe place," she said. "But we're not talking about me. We're talking about you, and the fact that you need to talk or you're going to explode. Again."

I ran my hands through the sand. The grains were so tiny, and some of them stuck to my fingers. "I don't even know what to say," I said.

"Okay," FM said. "I'll go first. I was terrified when that Superiority ship exploded. I thought you had died in there. That's the second time in a couple of weeks that we all thought you'd died, and it was *horrible* both times. So I would appreciate it if you'd stop doing that."

I hadn't thought about what that was like for the flight, waiting in their ships. They'd known there was a bomb. Alanik had pulled Rig in to try to disarm it.

Oh scud. "Is Rig okay?" I asked. "He knows that it wasn't his fault, right?"

FM held out a hand and wobbled it back and forth. "I mean, logically he knows. He is not an expert at defusing explosives. But he still blames himself."

I should have said something to him. I was the officer in charge of that operation, and it was my responsibility to—

"We're not talking about Rig either," FM said. "The question is, do *you* blame yourself?"

"Yes," I said. I didn't even have to think about it.

"But you know it isn't your fault, right?"

I stared out at the ocean. The sun was starting to get lower in the sky, the light over the whole landscape turning an orangey-yellow.

I didn't answer, and FM sighed. "What happened on the ship? Before the explosion."

I closed my eyes. My memories felt fractured, slowed down and sped up all at once. "We split up," I said. "I was taking fake Cobb to my parents to out him. Alanik went to release Gran-Gran. She was able to communicate with Gran-Gran, and Gran-Gran said she could sense Cobb, like, cytonically, even though she shouldn't have been able to do that."

"So something strange was going on with Gran-Gran even before they hyperjumped," FM said.

"Yeah, I guess so. Alanik also said Gran-Gran was talking about hearing voices."

Voices asking for help.

Oh *scud.*

Whatever had gone wrong with her, was it happening to me too? She'd somehow lost her powers because of it, and if I did the same—

"There's more," I said. "Those people in the tent are Gran-Gran and Cobb—at least, best as we can tell—but Gran-Gran doesn't appear to be cytonic."

"What does that mean?" FM asked.

"It means her mind isn't . . . visible to us in the nowhere any-more. She's lost her . . . vibration, I guess."

"I'll take your word for it," FM said. "That's bad, Jorgen."

"Yeah," I said. "She was fleeing a Superiority ship. Maybe it was a trap they left for anyone trying to hyperjump away? But Alanik and I didn't get caught in it."

Not yet anyway.

I remembered the strange *things* I'd felt when Alanik and I were looking for Gran-Gran and Cobb in the nowhere—the texture, like there were hundreds of beings around me, there one moment and gone the next.

There was something out there in the nowhere. Maybe it wasn't the Superiority at all. "I wonder if it's *them*," I said. "The delvers. The voices didn't sound like I would imagine a delver—"

"Wait," FM said. "You've heard them? The voices that asked for help?"

Scud. "Yeah," I said, rubbing my hands on my knees, trying to wipe off the sand. The stuff seemed to cling to everything. I wondered if we'd ever be free of it. "I heard them in the meeting. Right before I . . . Right before."

"That's not good," FM said. "There's something really weird going on, and you're all caught up in it."

"I know," I said.

"And that's the only reason I've let us get sidetracked for this long. You were telling me about what happened on the ship. You told me all about what happened to Alanik . . ."

"I went to find my parents," I said. "It took me a while, be-cause the ship was big and I took some wrong turns. Eventually fake Cobb got away from me and ran off. He seemed really eager to get out of there, though I didn't know why until Alanik told me about the bomb."

"Right," FM said.

"By the time I found my parents, they were trapped in this room in the center of the ship. I could see them through the glass but it wouldn't break, and all the doors were sealed shut."

I saw my father's face through the glass, his resignation when the Superiority announced they were going to be exterminated. My mother yelling at me to leave them, to escape, to save myself.

"The Superiority announced they were going to kill them," I said. "Alanik and I tried to find a way to get them out, but there wasn't one."

"That's not your fault," FM said. "You had minutes at best, like Rig. You weren't prepared for that and it isn't your fault. The Superiority did this, not you."

"My mother told me to go, but I didn't. I wouldn't listen to Alanik either. And right before Alanik pulled me out, my mother spoke to me through the glass—she said to do better than they did."

"Stars," FM said. "No wonder you feel pressure to stay in control of everything."

I didn't want to be in control. I just wanted to make sure the DDF was in the hands of someone who would keep our people safe.

"I didn't want to leave them," I said. "If Alanik hadn't pulled me out, I would have died there."

FM closed her eyes. "Thank the stars for Alanik then."

I couldn't say this next part. I couldn't bring myself to form the words, especially not to FM.

Maybe it would have been easier if I had died there.

I looked out over the ocean.

I couldn't think like that. My flight needed me. *Cobb* needed me. We had to figure out how to reverse whatever the Superiority or the delvers had done to him and get him back in charge of the DDF.

FM was right. My parents' deaths weren't my fault. But all the ways I was failing everyone now, falling apart when I should have been leading—

That was squarely on my head.

I stood up and brushed sand off my flight suit.

"You aren't done talking," FM said.

"Yes," I said. "I am." I couldn't sit here being useless. Maybe FM was right. Maybe talking could change how I felt, but it didn't do anything to help everyone else.

I couldn't indulge in that. I couldn't be useless. I'd already lost Spensa, lost my parents.

I couldn't let it happen again, not to anyone else.

"Maybe for *now*," FM said. "We'll talk more later."

Scud. I'd answered her questions. Wasn't that enough?

I was almost glad to see Alanik headed my way with Nedd and Arturo. Juno floated along farther behind them. I didn't want to answer their questions either, but at least they weren't going to probe me about my feelings, especially in front of the kitsen.

"Dude," Nedd said when they drew near. "Did you seriously *explode*?"

"Shut up, Nedd," Arturo said. "But, did you?"

"I already told you what happened," Alanik said, looking annoyed. "You didn't believe me?"

"We believe you," Nedd said. "We're just incredulous."

"That word literally means 'unable to believe,' " Alanik said. "Is there a translation error, or are you making fun of me?"

"Neither," FM said. "They're just idiots."

"Yeah, it's true," I said.

"That they're idiots?" Alanik asked.

"Sometimes," I said. "But I did . . . explode."

"That is *awesome*," Nedd said. "I mean, not the part where you threw around deadly mind weapons at a political summit. That seems bad."

"Bad" didn't begin to cover it, but there was also something off about it. Juno finally caught up to us, which was good, because I wanted his opinion on this.

"Why didn't I hurt anyone?" I asked. "When I startled Boom-slug, he cut me up."

460

"Your mindblades are ill-formed," Juno said. "You need training to make them sharper, stronger."

"I don't *want* them to be sharper," I said. "I could have killed somebody."

I waited for one of them to tell me I was being overdramatic.

They didn't.

"When Kauri said you wanted to learn about the shadow-walkers," Juno said, "she didn't tell me you *were* one. I have spent my life studying their texts, their lore, their ancient wisdom. You have strength, but you need control, and I can teach you if you will consent to be taught."

"What about your senate?" I asked. "Will they allow it?"

"The senate has taken a recess," Alanik said. "They want to think about the things you said, and then they're going to convene in the morning to make a decision. In the meantime, they say we're free to transport Cobb and Gran-Gran home to Detritus."

"Okay," I said. "We need to take care of that first."

"I can handle the transport," Alanik said. "You can go with Juno, as long as you promise to fill me in on what you've learned later."

"Okay," I said. "You hyperjump Gran-Gran and Cobb to Platform Prime with the medical crew." Hopefully Cobb and Gran-Gran would recover faster with our medical resources at home. Then they could tell us what had happened to Gran-Gran's powers. I turned to Arturo and Nedd. "You two help her get them there safely."

"Of course," Arturo said. "We've got this." And they all headed toward the hospital tent.

"I'll go check on the others," FM said. "And see what kind of accommodations we can find for the night. We may have to sleep in our starships, but I guess Spensa did that for most of flight school, so it can't be too bad."

She walked away, leaving me alone on the beach with Juno, who hovered up until he was at eye level with me.

"I have studied mindblades all my life," Juno said, "but I had never seen them before today. Tell me, human. What you did, was it a stunt? A display of power? Were you trying to intimidate them?"

"No," I said. "I just . . . lost control."

"If I may ask," Juno said, "control of *what*?"

I blinked at him. "Of myself," I said. "Of . . ."

Of this unstoppable, unknowable force that wanted to rip its way out of me. I'd been taught all my life to feel shame for the defect, never to speak of it. I'd spent so long wishing I could keep up with Spensa, with Alanik, wishing I wasn't so hopeless at using my powers—wishing I could harness them to protect the people I loved.

But somehow I'd still never made this connection: I was *dangerous*.

"I want to learn how to control them," I said.

"Good, then," Juno said. "Come with me, and we'll see what we can do."

10

"**B**reathe in, breathe out," Juno said. "You are now completely relaxed."

I was far from completely relaxed. I sat cross-legged on top of the cliff above Dreamspring while Juno hovered on his platform in front of me, reading from a book that he said contained the ancient exercises used by kitsen cytonics. He'd changed into a set of power armor that covered every part of him except his ears, his eyes, and his nose. The terrain up here was rough and rocky, the orange stone warm beneath me. We'd chosen this location because the tops of the cliffs were unpopulated; if I managed to produce a mindblade, there was no one around to be hurt by it but Juno, and he swore it was his sacred responsibility to put himself into the line of fire.

I didn't know how much his armor would help against a mindblade, but he'd insisted on wearing it anyway.

And it did look badass, I'd give him that.

"I thought this was supposed to focus on mindblades," I said. "Not breathing."

"Patience," Juno said. "According to the wisdom of the ancients, in order to achieve control, you must first accept that you have none by bringing yourself into alignment with the will of the universe."

"I can't both achieve control *and* have none. That's ridiculous."

"It is the way of the shadow-walkers," Juno said. "It is the way the ancients channeled their power, and the way that you must channel yours."

I sighed, interrupting the "continuous breathing" that Juno insisted I try. That didn't make sense to me either—I was pretty sure every creature with lungs used "continuous breathing" to stay alive, so why was that something I needed to practice? Spensa had figured out how to hyperjump and Alanik could do it with ease, and I was pretty sure extra "continuous breathing" had not been involved.

Then again, it wasn't any *more* ridiculous than making bread with my eyes closed, and that had been oddly helpful.

It changes you, FM had said. I still wasn't sure I'd done a great job of talking, but maybe I could be better at this. Breathing was easy, so what did I have to complain about?

"Let's begin again," Juno said. "Close your eyes." And instead of telling him this was a waste of my time, I did.

"See yourself walking along a beach," Juno said. "With each breath, the waves wash in, and the waves wash out."

Less than a day ago, I would have had no idea what Juno was talking about. But now I *could* picture myself on the beach. I could practically hear the churning of the ocean, the strangely mechanical white noise produced by so much water moving at once.

"Feel the wind on your skin," Juno said. "The heat of the sun as it burns down from above. Hear the sounds of the waves as they lap upon the shore. Smell the salt in the air and the rotting of the seaweed washed up on the beach as it slowly decays."

"That's disgusting," I said.

"Yes," Juno said. "But it is the method of the ancients. And you're not supposed to speak during the exercise."

"Sorry," I said.

"You walk forward and stand in the ocean. Feel the water as

464

it washes against your feet. The temperature is pleasant, not too warm, and not too cool."

If Spensa were listening to this, she would embellish on it.

I laughed.

"Is something funny?"

"No," I said. "Just imagining the ocean running red with the blood of my enemies."

Juno sounded startled. "Is that some kind of . . . cytonic premonition?"

"Nope," I said. "A memory of my girlfriend. Never mind. Go on."

"The waves wash against your legs once . . . twice . . . three times. Feel the pull of the ocean current as it tugs on your feet. Your mind is the ocean, flowing from this realm to the next, drawing close and then away again. Let your mind slip outward like the tide, into the vast ocean of nothingness that surrounds you."

Scud, my mind did slip into the nowhere as easily as he said. In and out, like the tide. The longer I pictured it, the easier it was to do.

I didn't want to be in the nowhere. That was where the voices came from, and that strange texture, the presence that felt like so many beings all crowding in on me. Either or both could be the eyes, but they *felt* different. Not as menacing. Friendly even—

"As the wave of your mind washes into this dimension, it carries with it a bit of the nowhere. Shards of nothing ride atop the wave, washing into the somewhere, each of them *becoming* only for a moment, then fading away."

I could feel them. The fragments of nowhere, the little bits of nothing following my mind into the somewhere. They had to take form—everything in this world had form, while that world was the absence of it.

A presence pressed in on my mind—Alanik working with the medtechs to transport Cobb and Gran-Gran. She might return with orders from Stoff calling us back to Detritus, so I needed to concentrate and learn while I still could.

"Observe the fragments as they emerge. Notice their shape and their texture. Draw them forth from your memory."

The fragments *did* have a shape. My mind skipped over the nowhere like a stone on a pond, and each time it made contact the fragments of nothing broke off. They were shaped like crystals, oblong with crisp, faceted sides. I couldn't hold them so much as *glimpse* them.

"Picture their shapes in your mind, and begin to mold them. Will them to alter their form little by little, growing sharper, larger, stronger. The fragments are you, and you are the fragments. They bend to your will, as you bend your will to the vibrations of the universe."

I didn't know what it meant that I *was* the fragments, but I focused on them, trying to change their shape. And they *did* change, as if they weren't bits of nothing at all, but pieces of my mind—energy that was scattering and dissipating while I made contact with the nowhere. My whole body tensed as the fragments got sharper.

"When you are ready, bring your mind into alignment with them. Feel their rhythm; align your vibration to theirs. You are them, and they are you. You are as one—neither exerting control over the other—of one mind, one will, and one spirit."

"What am I supposed to do?" I said.

Juno cleared his throat. "Do you want me to read it again?"

"Okay." Though I wasn't sure I was going to understand it any better the second time.

"I will admit, when I imagined having the opportunity to guide the meditations of a shadow-walker, I had not envisioned quite so many interruptions."

"Sorry," I said.

As Juno read, I tried to focus on the vibration of the fragments— were they really my own mind?—flying out of the nowhere. I worried about what they might do if I tried to move them, especially since I didn't have any idea how to align my *will* with them.

But I needed to try. I touched the fragments lightly, and—*Oh*. I opened my eyes, sensing a fragment flying off over the cliff, cutting through the breeze before it dissipated. "I think I did it," I said.

The sky above us was turning a deep shade of indigo, but over the water it was a bright yellow, which faded into orange and then pink. A sunset. I'd seen paintings of those, but they'd failed to capture the beauty. And here I had been keeping my eyes closed.

I hoped the rest of my flight was watching it at least.

"We came up here because you would not harm anything if you succeeded in manifesting the blades," Juno said. "Now I see the folly in it. We cannot tell if you've manifested them, because there is nothing for you to manipulate but me."

That wasn't entirely true.

"Hang on," I said, and I turned around—scud, now I was facing *away* from the sunset. But if this worked, it would be worth it.

"Read to me again," I said. "The part about the continuous breathing."

Juno started the meditation over, and I closed my eyes and tried to focus on my surroundings, to skim the surface of the nowhere with my mind, until I could feel the fragments appearing and scattering. I focused on them, molding them into tiny points, like blades of grass I'd seen in paintings of Old Earth. I reached out, touching the fragments lightly with my mind.

And then I pushed them down, shoving them out away from my feet.

A sound, like marbles hitting sandstone.

I opened my eyes.

Scud, I'd *scratched* the stone in front of me, leaving gouges in it.

"Shadow-walker," Juno said. "It seems the meditation has worked."

It seemed it had. "Let me try that again," I said.

Juno read to me from his meditations, and each time I aimed

with the strange shards of nowhere the grooves in the sandstone grew deeper, until I was cutting deep gashes no wider than my index finger.

"Do you have more of those meditations in your books?" I asked.

"Many more," Juno said. "Entire volumes, in fact."

If Stoff decided to pull us home, maybe I could use that knowledge as an excuse to stay, at least until Alanik and I could learn more about how to use our powers. We were the best weapons the DDF had right now, but we needed more training. A lot more.

"Thank you, Juno," I said.

"It has been my pleasure, shadow-walker."

It was strange for him to call me that, since I didn't *walk* anywhere. I wondered if he had a meditation in his book that could teach me to hyperjump.

"Let's try it again," I said, walking over to a fresh section of the cliff. "I want to see how deep I can make the shards—"

I slipped into the nowhere, and immediately a voice entered my mind. *We hear you,* it said.

Scud. Was that the delvers? It didn't *feel* terrifying, but—

Help us! it said. *We* hear *you.*

They didn't sound menacing. They sounded . . . desperate. Scared.

I don't know how to help you, I said.

"Is something wrong?" Juno asked.

"I can hear someone," I said. "Someone asking for my help."

Jorgen? a voice said. I recognized that one.

Gran-Gran! Was she awake now? *You have your powers back?*

I . . . What?

Your powers, I said. *Are you awake? Did they disappear while you were asleep somehow?*

Not a lot of time, Gran-Gran said. *Hard to concentrate, but you need to . . . help us . . .*

Her voice faded, and while I called her name again into the nowhere, she didn't respond.

Jorgen, Alanik said. *We need you at the medical tent. You need to see this.*

She sounded urgent, so I didn't ask questions. "Excuse me," I said to Juno. "I want to learn more, but my people need me."

"Of course," Juno said.

I called to Snuggles, who was waiting again in my ship. She appeared in my arms. "Take me to Alanik," I said, sending Snuggles a picture.

"Alanik!" Snuggles said.

Juno, the cliff, and the melting remains of the sunset all disappeared.

11

Snuggles and I passed by the eyes and jumped to the front of the medical tent, where the medtechs had loaded Cobb and Gran-Gran onto stretchers. Nedd and Arturo each stood at the foot of one of the stretchers, with Kel and Winnow at the heads. I sent Snuggles immediately back to Boomslug in my ship.

"What's wrong?" I asked Alanik.

"We started moving them over to the ship," Winnow said, indicating to where the transport shuttle was waiting down by the water. "But as we took them farther from the tent, they started to deteriorate."

"What do you mean?" I asked.

"Blood pressure dropped," Kel said. "Heart rates became irregular. What's strange is that it happened to *both* of them at more or less the same time."

"Why would that happen?" I asked.

"I can't explain it," Kel said. "Even weirder is they stabilized as soon as we brought them back here."

"It's like they don't want to be away from here," Winnow said. "We wanted to load them in the ship first so we wouldn't jostle them when we hyperjump—"

"If their condition is linked to this place then we definitely can't hyperjump them," I said. "But why would it matter if they're *here*?"

"Your guess is as good as mine," Winnow said. "But my professional judgment is that we don't move a patient if moving changes their condition for the worse."

"Can you treat them here?"

Winnow nodded. "We may need to go home for some equipment. But for the moment we can get them comfortable."

"Thank you," I said.

Arturo stepped up beside me. "What do you think is going on?" he asked.

"I don't know," I said. I slipped into the nowhere, listening, but the only cytonic I felt nearby was Alanik. "Gran-Gran's powers still seem to be gone. But I *heard* her in the nowhere."

"Really?" Alanik asked.

"Yeah. Hang on. Let me—"

I focused, returning to the imaginary ocean from the meditation. Instead of focusing on the fragments—which I now realized splintered off every time I touched the nowhere—I listened, trying to hear her again.

Gran-Gran?

No response. I tried to push farther, listening closer . . .

And then I felt the texture again, the strange sensation of *bumps*, hundreds of them—maybe thousands—all over and around the island. One minute Alanik and I were alone, and then there were so *many* of them.

What *were* those?

I shook myself, dropping my link to the nowhere. "Do you *feel* that?" I asked Alanik. "Those . . . weird ridges?"

"No," Alanik said. "And I don't hear Gran-Gran either. You're sure it was her?"

I was sure. If this Gran-Gran didn't have powers, but *another* Gran-Gran was talking to me from the nowhere, did that mean she was lost in there like Spensa somehow? I'd assumed Spensa's body had gone with her when she left, but I hadn't asked, and maybe she wouldn't even know.

Juno had finally caught up to me, his disc floating toward us from the cliff face.

"Juno," I called to him. "Do you know anything about shadow-walkers projecting their spirits into the nowhere without their bodies?"

"The soul is made up of the body and the mind," Juno said. "Your mind enters the nowhere whenever you interact with it. Only when you hyperjump does your body follow."

"Sure," I said. "But can the mind end up *stuck* in the nowhere without the body to follow it?"

"I have not read of it happening," Juno said. "Not in all the books of lore."

"It wouldn't explain this anyway," Alanik said. "When your mind goes into the negative realm, your body remains and continues to resonate cytonically. Otherwise we would stop being able to sense each other every time we communicated through the negative realm. Why would your body stop resonating if your mind was stuck?"

"I don't know," I said. "But I wonder if it has something to do with the voices Gran-Gran was hearing before she hyperjumped." The voices I was hearing now. Scud, I did not want to end up in a mysterious coma. "Something went wrong in the jump, and it's still possible that she's stuck somehow." Though I didn't know why she would have stopped talking to me. She said it was difficult somehow . . .

"Juno," I said. "Can you show me where Cobb and Gran-Gran first came through the nowhere?"

"Of course," Juno said. "They were found in the burrow that once belonged to our master shadow-walkers. Now it is our library, the home of our lore."

In a *library*? That seemed . . . unhelpful. But still . . . "I'd like to see it," I said. "Alanik, will you come with us?"

472

"Of course," Alanik said. She seemed confused about why I'd want to see it, but she didn't argue.

"FM said we're camping on the beach tonight," Nedd said. "Because there are no kitsen buildings big enough to hold all of us. We'll go see about setting up camp."

The sky was rapidly growing dark now that the last sliver of the sun had finished setting. The horizon over the ocean had turned a rosy shade of pink, but over the cliffs I could make out the first of the stars.

"Thank you," I said to Nedd, and I followed Juno as he led Alanik and me toward the library.

Unlike the elevated burrows of the rest of Dreamspring, the library was set down in a kind of crater, deep beneath the sandstone cliff. We descended a set of tiny stairs, and Alanik and I pressed our hands against the sandstone walls, resting our feet on three or four steps at a time, using them more for traction than as stairs. As we moved I felt that cytonic resonance I'd detected earlier growing stronger. We were heading toward something important.

We descended far enough down that if the waves were to lap this far, they'd surely fill the basin. But they must not ever reach this part of the island if the library had remained intact for so long.

We had to crawl through the ornate arched doorway after Juno, but the library itself was several levels tall, which allowed Alanik and me to stand with a meter of headroom to spare. The room was filled with tables barely above ankle height, and I was careful where I stepped, so as not to disturb any of the cushions set around them or the carts covered in books and scrolls.

Along three of the walls were shelves covered in books, all of them smaller than the palm of my hand. Ladders scaled the walls, which were lined with railed walkways for perusing the rows of shelves, though several of the acclivity stone platforms also waited at the entrance of the room to provide ease of access.

It was the fourth wall though that caught my attention.

It was a stone wall, smooth and polished, with rows and rows of lines carved into it in a strange, almost technological design. The wall radiated a power that was undeniably cytonic, and something about it felt familiar.

"This is where you found them?" I asked Juno.

"Yes," Juno said, hovering in the doorway on his platform. "Over there, by the scroll case. They appeared lying side-by-side on top of some tables."

Alanik picked her way across the room and examined the wall, which stretched all the way to the relatively high ceiling. She pressed her hand to the lines on the wall. "I've never seen anything like this," she said.

Neither had I, but I swore I'd heard of a wall like this.

Oh, *scud*.

Now I remembered where.

"Alanik, step away from the wall," I said.

She looked over her shoulder at me like I was crazy, but she did as I asked, working her way past the rows of tables littered with books.

"What is it?" she asked.

"I think . . . I think it's a portal," I said. "An entrance to the nowhere. Spensa told me there's one in the caverns of Detritus. She said we should search for it—but that we needed to be careful, because a cytonic could fall through and get stuck there like she did." We had teams looking for it, but I hadn't heard if they'd found anything.

Alanik suddenly looked alarmed. "What does that mean?" she asked. "If Gran-Gran hyperjumped, she shouldn't have had to use a physical portal. There wasn't one like this on the Superiority ship."

"I don't know what it means," I said. "But Gran-Gran heard voices asking for help before she jumped, right? And I've been hearing them too."

Alanik squinted at me. "Voices from the negative realm?"

"Maybe," I said. I concentrated, listening for them again. "Juno, you said this used to be the burrow where your master cytonics lived. What happened to them?"

"They met in a great summit to compile the vast knowledge of our people," Juno said. "During the summit, they simply disappeared, leaving behind only these strange symbols." He gestured to the wall. "Beyond that we don't know, as there was no one left to write down the history."

There wouldn't be, if they all disappeared at once. My people had lost knowledge the same way. After the crash of the Defiant fleet, the first lifebuster bomb dropped by the Superiority had killed all the officers, the entire command staff—everyone who knew what had happened and why. We were left to make up our own stories about the "Krell."

Thanks to Spensa though, I had a hunch as to what might have happened. "They left this wall behind," I said, "because the summit was here? In this room?"

"Yes," Juno said. "This city has been our capital for centuries, so it was a natural meeting place."

"If they decided to try out their knowledge," I said, "they might have figured out how to create this portal into the nowhere and then gotten trapped inside."

"If that is so," Juno said, "I'm afraid they should have died many years ago."

That was true, but I'd heard *something* in the nowhere. I focused on the portal. I couldn't hear the voices at the moment—not Gran-Gran's or the others.

They were asking for help. Gran-Gran had heard them—she'd spent so many years trapped on Detritus, listening to the stars. If anyone could have honed their skills at detecting signals in the nowhere no one else could hear, it was her.

"Did Spensa tell you how to open it?" Alanik asked.

"No," I said. "And I haven't been able to reach her again these last few days, so I can't ask." I turned to Juno. "Are there legends of what happened to the cytonics?" If there was any truth in them, there might be some clue as to how to reach the kitsen cytonics—and Gran-Gran, who had been lost chasing after them.

"Oh, many," Juno said. "Most of them are children's tales. My favorite involves a band of space pirates who flew through the skies on the back of an enormous turtle."

"Space pirates stole your cytonics?"

"Almost certainly not," Juno said. "I said it was my favorite, not the most accurate."

"Which would you say is the most accurate?" I asked.

"It's impossible to say for certain, of course," Juno said. "But I've always given credence to the theories of Ito, who wrote that—"

"Jorgen!" Arturo's voice came from the handheld radio clipped to my belt.

"Yes?" I responded.

"Superiority carrier ship," Arturo said. "There are fighters headed this way."

Scud. The Superiority. I'd hoped they hadn't heard Kauri's signal and didn't realize we were here.

Apparently I was wrong. "We have to go," I told Alanik.

"If you are going to use your new skills against the enemy," Juno said, "perhaps I could accompany you."

I didn't know if I was ready for that, but a kitsen wouldn't take up much space in my cockpit. Even less than the slugs, though I hoped he didn't want to cuddle as close. "Okay," I said. I called to Snuggles, and she appeared instantly on my shoulder with Boomslug in tow, because she couldn't seem to go anywhere without him anymore.

I put one hand on Alanik's shoulder and one on Juno's platform and asked Snuggles to hyperjump us all to the beach.

12

The carrier ship loomed in the sky above Dreamspring, illuminated by the ivory-colored moon peeking over the horizon. The ship sat directly above the city, ringed by puffs of clouds. It looked out of place over the idyllic landscape.

"They are here for you?" Juno asked. He didn't sound like he blamed us. He was simply gathering the facts.

"Probably," I said. We'd brought this down on the kitsen. It was our responsibility to do what we could to protect them.

I didn't have to give the order for my flight to get to their ships. They were already running. I kept my hands on Alanik's shoulder and Juno's platform and directed Snuggles to hyperjump us to FM's fighter. "We need to release the taynix," I said. "We might need them to retrieve the others." I raised FM's canopy and released Gill, and then Alanik and I raced between the ships, opening the boxes. When we finished, I had Snuggles hyperjump Juno and me straight to my cockpit.

Alanik ran for her ship, while Juno took up position right behind my seat. We lifted off as four enemy ships swooped in overhead.

The rest of the flight were still running. We needed to provide air support or they were going to get gunned down before they got into the air.

Cover me, I said to Alanik.

Got it, Alanik responded.

I flew straight at the enemy ships, opening fire so they had to scatter or lose their shields. Juno gave a little squeak of surprise, like he hadn't expected the fighter to . . . what? Fight?

Alanik got a few good shots on the ships as they rolled, and then followed on my wing as I pursued the ships long enough to draw their fire and lead them out over the ocean away from the beach.

"Well, that was exciting," Juno said. He seemed to have affixed the boots of his power armor to his hovering disc so he wouldn't go flying off as I accelerated.

"You haven't seen anything." *Circle around and cover the others*, I told Alanik, and she peeled away and shot at one of the enemy ships, which had also turned back.

For all Alanik's talk about proving yourself in combat, she fit effortlessly into the flight and never argued when I gave her orders.

"Jerkface," Arturo said over the radio, "the others are getting in their ships now, but Quirk and Sentry are pinned down over by where we had that feast."

"Got it," I said. "Angel, cover the others until they get in their ships, then back me up." I darted off down the beach, immediately spotting the ship Arturo was talking about. It was peppering the rock with destructor fire, and I hoped Kimmalyn and Sadie had found good cover. I opened fire, getting in one good hit before the ship went into a bank, then rolled and returned fire. I flew beneath the ship, forcing it to turn again and keep its attention on me. Once I had it, I threw my ship into a wave sequence, evading its fire, leading that ship out over the ocean again.

I caught the attention of two more tails. Arturo and Nedd were both in their ships now, circling over the area where Kimmalyn and Sadie had been pinned down.

"Amphi," I said, "how are Quirk and Sentry?"

"Climbing out of an oven, it looks like," Arturo said.

"How clever," Juno said behind me.

"They're coated in soot," Arturo said. "We can cover them to their ships."

"I've got it," I said. Kimmalyn and Sadie couldn't call to their slugs, but I could let the slugs know where they were. I sent Cheeky and Happy a mental image of the oven area. I felt the slugs hyper-jump to the ovens, and then to the ships.

"They're here!" FM said. "Very dirty, but they appear to be fine."

"Good," I said. "Everyone sound off when you're in the air."

My three tails were trying to catch me in their crossfire, and I darted through another defensive sequence while the flight sounded off. Instinct took over while I kept mental track, making sure no one was missing.

"Is someone helping Jerkface?" Kimmalyn asked over the radio.

"I've got it," I said. My tails were right behind me, all three targeting me at once, though I still had my shield and they were firing wildly.

"This might be a good time to try a meditative exercise," Juno said.

"How do you figure?" I asked, going into a barrel roll. Juno's platform tipped to the side, and he let out a little squeak that sounded suspiciously like a *whoop*.

The others were all in their ships now, so I didn't have to worry about leading the enemy away. I didn't want to encourage the enemy to fire on the kitsen city, but I also didn't want to leave the city alone for too long and have it get blasted in our absence. I didn't know what the Superiority's orders were, so we had to plan for anything.

"Remember the fragments," Juno said. "Your breathing."

"I'm busy," I said.

Juno continued as if he hadn't heard me. "Breathe in, breathe out. You are now completely relaxed."

479

I was not at all relaxed. I'd seen the biofeedback reports, tests where the DDF tracked our vitals even on routine flights. We functioned on pure adrenaline up here. "Juno," I said. "I don't think—"

"You are a stone, skipping on the sea," he said, and I remembered that sensation, the skimming across the nowhere. The vibration I felt along the boundary between this world and the nowhere was not unlike the vibration of my ship as it cut through the sky.

"I can't manifest mindblades inside my ship," I said. "I could cut the ship to pieces." Slices of metal curling outward, flying away from each other in a giant burst.

"Boom," Boomslug said.

"Right," I said. "No booms. Not here."

"Not here," Boomslug agreed.

The enemy ships were still on my tail, and I evaded their fire and swung around parallel to the beach. If I brought them back, I could—

"Jerkface, you okay?" Arturo asked.

"Fine," I said. "Get the rest of the flight in offensive formation." I couldn't get a good view of the battlefield without giving an opening to my tails, so Arturo would have to manage it. He was capable. He could handle it without me.

"Ah, here it is," Juno said, flipping through the pages of the book. "Return to the ocean. Stand with your feet in the water. You are a part of it, as it is a part of you."

I could hear Arturo over the radio, giving instructions to the rest of the flight. He had Nedd supporting Kimmalyn while he and Alanik came after me. "Juno," I said. "I really don't think—"

"As the wave of your mind washes into this dimension, it carries with it shards of the nowhere. Feel them fly from the surface of the ocean of nothing. The shards are far from you, farther than your reach. They are not shards at all, but birds, growing wings, flying far, reaching into the beyond, cutting everything in their path with their razor-sharp beaks."

Scud, I could see them, the shards, the *birds*. They flew along the edge of the nowhere like the ones I'd seen dodging over the waves earlier. I jogged my ship to the side to avoid a blast of destructor fire and completed my loop, heading for the beach. "You know if I mess this up, we're going to fall out of the sky, right?" Snuggles could hyperjump us out, but I'd lose my ship and this was not the moment for that.

"Feel the birds fly away from you, the flock sailing toward your enemies, their beaks sharp and ready."

Scud, was he going to keep reading this until I tried it? On my proximity sensors I could see more ships reaching the beach, engaging the rest of my flight. We couldn't call for backup immediately. Either Alanik or I would have to go to Detritus to retrieve them, so we needed to exhaust our other options first.

"All right," I said. "Fine. I'll deploy the birds."

I shot upward toward a low-flying cloud. Alanik said these things would be fine to fly into, and we'd been watching them pass over all day without incident, so I didn't think there was anything nefarious hiding within. Using the cloud for cover, I executed an Ahlstrom loop and then watched on my proximity monitor for the ships to enter after me. They kept chasing me, but I used the cover to shake them off, coming out the bottom and banking hard toward the beach.

Arturo and Alanik caught up, showering my tails with fire.

"Amphi, Angel, back off," I said. "I'm going to try something."

I didn't want to close my eyes, not in the air. But I let my mind disconnect, flying by instinct. It was dangerous to do with three tails and with my backup dropping away like I'd asked them to. I might not have more than a moment, but I reached into the ocean of the nowhere and caught those fragments, forming them into birds that flew forward like missiles, their wings tucked against their bodies, their beaks sharp and ready.

One of the enemy fighters got a hit on my shield, and then another. I launched into a twin-scissor to avoid the fire, still trying to split my mind, to focus on the fragments.

"You are the birds, and the birds are you," Juno read. "You and the birds are one. You are one with the nowhere, and with yourself."

I zipped away, my tails still following me. "Everybody stay back," I said, and I slowed, nearly letting the enemy catch me.

My shield took one more hit and disappeared. I reached out for my flock of projectile birds.

And like tiny ships, I flew them into the enemies behind me.

The pilots didn't dodge. They never saw it coming. The mindblades tore through their wings and hulls, ignoring their shields, taking them apart. In my mind the fragments scattered and dissipated. The chunks of ship fell over the ocean, pieces of metal cleanly cut apart from each other.

Over the radio, Arturo swore.

"What was *that*?" Nedd said.

"Mindblades," FM said. "By the stars, Jerkface, that was incredible!"

My own ship was fine. I was almost surprised.

"I can't believe that worked," I said to Juno.

Juno made a self-satisfied little noise. "The lore of the ancients contains much wisdom."

Apparently it did.

"Fine," Alanik said over the radio. "You were right. You don't need to fly out front to prove yourself."

"Listen to her, Jerkface," Nedd said. "Fall back and leave some for the rest of us."

"Gladly," I said. I took cover by the cliffs while I reignited my shield. Kimmalyn hovered above me, watching my back. While I waited I extended my sensors, taking stock of the enemy ships as the others engaged them. There were many of them, but not *overwhelmingly* many, and they seemed to be firing only on us, not the kitsen.

At least so far. I expected that meant they had come looking to eliminate us, not necessarily to destroy the kitsen for harboring us.

That could turn very quickly, but I imagined that convincing the kitsen to help us if we were the only ones under attack was going to be—

Two ships bore down on us, and Kimmalyn tipped her nose in their direction—

The ships soared over our heads, and a new voice shouted over the radio. "Invaders!" it said, the words translated out of the sharp kitsen language by my pin. "Do you think to mar our beautiful home with your vulgar presence? We will cut you down where you stand, and you will regret the day you set foot on the Den of Everlasting Light Which Laps Gently upon the Shores of Time!"

Was that— "Goro?"

"Human," Goro said. "I offer you a temporary reprieve from my challenge."

At least that tirade wasn't aimed at us then.

"I don't have one of those pin things," Catnip said. "Anyone want to translate for the fox-dude?"

"He's offering to let Jerkface out of fighting him," FM said. "Not that he agreed to fight him in the first place."

I hoped this wasn't another trap. Goro could offer to help us, only to turn around and use the fact that we'd fired at the Superiority as evidence of our savagery. "We are *defending ourselves*," I said over the radio.

"Of course!" Goro went on. "You have proven yourself a coward in one-on-one combat, but many who are cowardly with the sword show their courage when they step into a ship!"

Stars. "I'm not a *coward* because I refuse to kick around someone one-tenth of my—"

"If you were to face my champion in combat you would bleed like the Red Rivers That Lead to the Empty Sea!"

"You shouldn't let him bait you," Juno said. "I think at this point he's doing it for sport."

I was glad one of us was enjoying it. "Goro," I said, "we're defending ourselves, and your people as well. The Superiority were willing to turn on the UrDail for harboring us, and they'll do the same to you."

I winced. That might not have been the best thing to say— that we'd knowingly put them in danger by coming here. But we couldn't go *anywhere* without putting people in danger, and we needed to—

"This is your opportunity to prove yourself, human," Goro said. "If you are defending the sacred cliffs of Dreamspring, then you are already our allies. Our ship might not be as fast as yours, but she is no less fierce. We will fight by your side as equals."

Oh. That sounded more like an . . . opportunity. If we flew together, fought together, he might begin to believe that we truly intended to be their allies and not their conquerors. FM continued to translate for the others, catching most of the gist. Our response was up to me.

"Excellent," I said to Goro. "We are pleased to fight by your side."

"Jerkface," Arturo said. "Another large group of fighters has left the carrier ship, headed this way."

"*Jerkface?*" Goro said. "My shipboard translator interprets that as—"

"It's not what it sounds like," Alanik said. "Just go with it."

"Goro," I said, "are there other ships that could fight with us?" I widened my sensors to get a look at the incoming ships. Scud. "We're badly outnumbered."

"We're here!" Kauri said, cutting in over the radio. "And there's a small airfield on the other side of the island. The Air Force That Does Not Belong to He Who Was Not King should be joining us soon."

Stars. "Your names are so long," I said to Juno. "Aren't your people ever in a hurry?"

"We shorten them often," Juno said. "We use the full names when we want to impress or intimidate."

Ah, okay. That made more sense. And an influx of kitsen ships could only be a good thing.

"Skyward Flight, let's push the ships away from the city. FM, Sentry, you two take up the rearguard. We don't know what the enemy target is, and I don't want civilians getting hit while our backs are turned."

"Copy, Jerkface," FM said.

I didn't command the kitsen, and I couldn't act like I did. "Goro and Kauri, if you fly with us, we'll protect your gunships while you shoot down the incoming enemy. Is that strategy acceptable to you?"

"The enemy's faces will glisten with tears as they know the honor of being defeated by the *Ever-Glorious Crashing Waves of Time*!"

I took that as a yes.

"Is that . . . the name of your ship?" Kimmalyn asked.

"Yes, treacherous human," Goro said.

So he hadn't entirely given up on baiting us.

"I'm calling you *Crashing Wave*," I said. "Unless that offends you?"

"If I am calling you Jerkface, I believe the offense is to you, human."

"Yeah, probably," I said. My parents had been on me to change my callsign ever since I finished flight school. I should probably do it now out of respect. If I said that was why, no one would question it.

But the real reason I'd kept it wasn't because I wanted to defy my parents. I *liked* my callsign. Spensa had given it to me, and it reminded me of her. I wasn't going to change it.

Especially not now.

My flight pushed toward the new ships and I flew out to join them, watching their approach. The Superiority forces were inconsistently trained, and this batch looked like they hadn't been in ships for long. Some of the Superiority groups seemed to have flightleaders, but these weren't following any specific formation. If they had leaders, they didn't know what they were doing.

My flight divided into three groups—a rearguard over the city, and then a two-pronged offense that came at the enemy ships from either side. The tactic was designed to break up a formation—and since a formation was already lacking, it sent the enemy ships into chaos. Goro and Kauri split up, one at the center of each prong, and Kauri especially seemed to understand our maneuvers and complement them.

Kimmalyn was ordinarily my wingmate, but I'd assigned her and Nedd to support each other. Nedd was usually Arturo's wingmate, but Arturo had taken it upon himself to get Alanik up to speed to fly with us. I wasn't sure how necessary that had been—she'd taught us as much as we'd taught her in terms of maneuvers—but I also hadn't seen a reason yet to break it up.

A group of nearly a dozen ships slipped away from the rest of our flight and headed for the city.

"FM, Sentry," I said. "We have incoming."

"We see them," FM said.

"Protect the city," I said. "We don't know their exact target, but—"

Scud. All of those ships seemed to be headed directly for *me.*

"I think we know what their target is," FM said. "They saw what you did earlier."

"Would you like me to read the meditation again?" Juno asked.

"No," I said. "I think I've got it. Unless you have one in there about getting your birds to fly better."

"Fly better!" Snuggles said.

"Let me see," Juno said, flipping through his book.

The ships were rapidly incoming. I didn't have time to wait for Juno.

"Cover me," I said to FM and Sentry. "But keep your distance."

"Done," FM said.

Instead of turning and making the ships tail me, I flew directly at them. I pictured those birds over the ocean again, finding the rhythm of the waves, the way the nowhere pushed against my mind and my mind against it.

The ships scattered as I approached, all firing on me wildly. They didn't want me to get too close.

I had an idea. "All ships, keep your distance."

"Jerkface?" Arturo said. "What are you doing?"

"Something Spensa would try," I said. If this worked, I would wish she were here to see it. If it didn't, she was going to hear about it anyway. "Hold on, Juno," I said. And I reached out in my mind for that flock of birds, raising them from the waves of the ocean so they skimmed along outside my ship, following me, flying with me.

I chased after the fleeing ships, dodging fire. I hit overburn on my boosters and cut a path up through the battle, ships scattering in front of me. I sent my mindblades out in clustered flocks, catching this ship and that one, cleaving off wings and tail fins and noses while my flight shot down the others as they ran. A few of the braver pilots tried to charge in after me, and pieces of their ships rained down over the ocean, torn to ribbons.

"*Damn*, Jerkface," Arturo said.

"It seems you were correct," Juno said. "You didn't need a meditation."

"Boom," Boomslug said from his spot below my seat.

I gripped the edge of my panel to keep my hands from shaking. I *shouldn't* be able to do this. It felt . . . unnatural.

"Supernatural" might be a better word. Why was it so much easier to watch Spensa do things like this than it was to do them myself?

"The enemy is headed toward the city," FM said. "Sentry and I are on them."

Sure enough, the enemy ships were fleeing in the direction of Dreamspring. I'd scared them, but instead of retreating to their carrier ship they were going to hit us where it hurt.

I didn't think the kitsen's dwellings were going to stand up well to destructor fire, and Cobb and Gran-Gran had no more cover than a scudding *tent*.

"Skyward Flight, shoot down those fighters," I said. "Don't let them fire on the city."

Gunning them down over Dreamspring would cause damage, but not as much as if we let the ships attack. I hadn't seen any carrying lifebusters—they had come looking for us, not to destroy the kitsen city.

But that didn't mean they couldn't do a hell of a lot of damage if we let them run wild.

"Amphi," I said, "where is Cuna?"

"They ran for the city to find shelter," Nedd said. "I gave them a radio to stay in touch."

"I am here," Cuna said over the radio. "I took shelter in the senate building."

The medtechs should be with Cobb and Gran-Gran, but they were all exposed. "I need you to go to the medical tent and help the medtechs move Cobb and Gran-Gran."

"We can't move them," Alanik said. "Remember?"

We couldn't leave them in a tent during an aerial raid. "They appeared in the library," I said. "And our medical transport was in the other direction. Maybe moving them in the toward the library will be okay."

"I'll give the medical personnel your instructions," Cuna said.

"Let me know how it goes," I told them.

The flight chased after the ships as they cruised toward the city, while I watched our six, making sure it wasn't a ploy to let another group of fighters from the carrier fall into flanking position. No more ships came from that direction. Yet.

"We've got incoming," Arturo said, and sure enough from the

other direction, over the cliff above Dreamspring, more ships were joining the fight. Kitsen fighters, two dozen of them, all engaging the remaining ships as they reached the city.

"Welcome, kinsmen!" Goro shouted over the radio. "Now we'll show these humans how it's done!"

The enemy ships turned their destructors on the new arrivals, sparing the city a bit, and my flight flanked the enemy, shattering shields and bringing down ships. One of the ships careened toward the city, and Alanik caught it with her light hook, dragging it toward the beach and dropping it on the sand where it wouldn't destroy the buildings. Nedd did the same with a ship Kimmalyn shot down right over the middle of the city, dragging the fuselage up and dropping it on the cliffs. Some debris was pelting the city, but hopefully damage would be minimal.

"Jerkface," Alanik said. "The enemy is going to fall back."

She'd barely finished saying it when the enemy ships turned almost as one and accelerated out over the ocean again, angling up to the carrier ship waiting in the clouds.

"Do we follow them?" Nedd asked.

"Wait," I said. I didn't know what their game was, and I didn't want to leave the city vulnerable to another attack.

The fighters slid into the clouds near the carrier ship, which was half hidden now as the cloud cover moved overhead. They were still up there, beyond the clouds—I could see them on my proximity monitor. The only reason for them to pull back like that was if they thought they had more of an advantage at that fallback position, or—

"Angel," I said. "You heard a transmission?"

"Yes," she said. "They were given orders over the hypercomm to retreat and wait. They've reported that the kitsen are fighting alongside us, so they want a larger force to beat down the resistance."

Saints, that was not a good sign. "Amphi," I said, "I'm giving you temporary command of the flight."

"Jerkface?" Arturo said. "What are you doing now?"

489

"I'm going to go for help," I said. We had a few moments here, so this was the best chance I was going to get. I couldn't rely on the mindblades for everything. They were an effective tool, but I'd seen some of the monstrous weapons the Superiority had on their side and I wouldn't be able to stop them all—not even with the rest of the flight watching my back. "They're waiting for backup, so we need it too. I'll try to get Stoff to let me take the platform." I was tempted to tell him, rather than ask him, but I wasn't sure how much longer that would work. It had only worked the first time because the command staff was reeling from the loss of Cobb and half the assembly, and because no one wanted to argue with me after what had happened to my parents.

I needed to feel out the situation, and I needed to do it quickly. "FM, I want you to come with me. Sentry can team up with Quirk and Nedder for the moment. We'll land our ships and leave Snuggles in mine so we can return quickly and get back in the air."

I hoped it would be quick, anyway. I didn't know how long we'd have before the Superiority forces would arrive. "Alanik can keep me posted. Contact me immediately if you need us. Everyone clear?"

"Yes, sir," Arturo said.

"Say hi to Stoff for us," Nedd added.

I landed my ship against the cliff where it would be partially sheltered from view. FM's came down beside me.

I looked over my shoulder at Juno. "Do you want to stay here?" I asked. "I can't guarantee you'll be safe in the ship."

"I'd like to come with you," Juno said. "Clearly my presence has been helpful."

"It has," I said. "I'm not going to use mindblades on Detritus though."

"A shadow-walker travels the path at all times," Juno said. "Not only when violence is required."

I didn't really know what that meant, but I also didn't want to have to explain Juno's presence to Stoff. "Actually," I said, "the most helpful thing you could do is stay here and teach that medita-tion to Alanik." She might not have a lot of time to learn, but she didn't know how to use mindblades, and if she could pick up any skill at all . . .

"I can see the wisdom in that," Juno said. "I never dreamed I'd work with a single cytonic, let alone have the privilege of directing *two*."

"It's your lucky day then." I flipped on my radio. "Angel, if you want to come pick up Juno, he can run you through some exercises while I'm gone."

"If his exercises taught you to do *that*," Alanik said, "then I'll be right there."

"She'll probably complain less than I did," I said to Juno. I showed him how to work the radio in case he ran into trouble before Alanik arrived, and then I lifted the canopy of my ship.

My taynix needed to remain on Evershore so Gill would have a target he recognized to bring us right to our ship. "Stay here," I said to Snuggles and Boomslug. Not that Boomslug could go far, but he tended to go wherever Snuggles went.

"Here!" Snuggles said.

I didn't know if she understood, but it had to be good enough. I climbed out of my ship and met FM and Gill out on the sand.

"Ready?" she asked.

"Yeah," I said. "Let's make it fast."

"All right," she said, putting a hand on my shoulder. "Gill, take us home."

13

It was even later on Detritus than it was on Evershore, but when we emerged in the taynix room on Platform Prime, we found Rig still at his desk in Engineering. Rig smiled when he saw FM, but then his smile immediately dropped.

"If you came without the rest of the flight, I'm guessing this isn't good," he said.

"It's not," I said. "We need to talk to Stoff."

"I'm sure he's gone to bed," Rig said. "Almost everyone has."

"Except for you," FM said.

"Yeah," Rig said. "I've been looking at some of the reports on the other platforms from the exploration crews. They found one a few hundred klicks from here with some similarities to Wandering Leaf. We think it might have a control room, and I'm charting us a good way to get in and take a look without getting hit by the autofire."

That could be useful. I wondered if Stoff would let me take a few of the platforms to defend Evershore. Our planetary shield filled in the gaps between the platforms that had been wrecked, so I was pretty sure we could take a few without leaving ourselves entirely open, but Stoff wasn't much of a risk-taker.

I could probably bring Wandering Leaf, because it technically belonged to the UrDail and not to the DDF, and I hoped he'd send a few extra flights. It might help if I reminded him that the Superiority hadn't attacked our planet since we'd put up the shield, and that we could hyperjump back in a hurry the moment anything changed. Though I'd have to spin it in a way that allowed him to cover his ass later if I had any hope of convincing him extra firepower was necessary.

"How are things with the kitsen?" Rig said.

"Precarious," FM said. "Come on. I'll explain on the way to wake Stoff."

Dragging the man out of bed probably wasn't going to endear us to him, but we didn't have a choice. I doubted those Superiority ships were going to wait until morning, and even if they did we'd better have reinforcements in place long before that.

While FM filled Rig in, I reached out to Alanik. *Status?*

Still waiting, she replied. *I don't like it.*

Neither did I. The Superiority had both cytonics and hyperdrives—they could bring vast resources to bear in an instant. If they were hesitating, it was because they were calling up their people wherever they were stationed—and it could be nearly anywhere in the galaxy. We'd taken out their planetary cannon on ReDawn, but I doubted it was their only one.

And Juno? I asked.

He keeps telling me I am relaxed. I am not.

Yeah, I said. *I wasn't either. It worked anyway though.*

That is encouraging, Alanik said. *Thank you.*

Keep me informed, I said, and I felt her agreement although she didn't respond in words.

When I tuned back in, FM was in the middle of telling Rig about me taking out the Superiority ships with the mindblades.

"That sounds dangerous," Rig said.

"It was amazing," FM said, and she sounded like she meant it.

"Sure. Amazing, but dangerous."

"It was kind of surreal," I said. "But it worked well in that fight.

It won't be enough in the long term though. Now that the Superiority knows we're working with the kitsen, they'll gather more ships to bring against us. We need help."

We reached the corridor with Stoff's quarters. At the end of the hall a guard stood watch by his door—Kelin, who'd been assigned to watch Cobb since he became admiral.

That seemed like a bad sign.

She saluted as we approached. "I need you to wake Vice Admiral Stoff," I said. "We have urgent information."

Kelin nodded—I had higher clearance than she did, so she didn't ask me for the information. She stepped inside, and then came out a few minutes later with Stoff, who wore a dressing gown.

"Oh good," Stoff said. "You're back. How are Cobb and Mrs. Nightshade? Are they in the infirmary? What is their condition?"

Oh, scud. Of course we had to start there. "The medical team was unable to move them without destabilizing them," I said. Hopefully Cuna was able to move them into the library—I'd left before I'd found out the outcome. No need to get into the strange details of that. Stoff would only want answers I didn't have. "The team wants to keep them there until we understand more about their condition."

"Okay," Stoff said. "I hardly think I needed that report in the middle of the night."

"We have a bigger problem," I said. "The Superiority found us on Evershore. They must have heard Kauri's transmission and came looking for us. They attacked, and we defended ourselves and the nearby city, but then the Superiority withdrew. We heard over the hypercomm that they're waiting for reinforcements."

"Well," Stoff said. "That does sound like a problem."

At least we agreed on that. If he'd tried to convince me this wasn't *our* problem, I would have worried about exploding in mindblades again.

"Sir," I said. "We need to take Wandering Leaf to defend against whatever the Superiority is planning."

"Fine," Stoff said. "You didn't need to wake me for that either."

Didn't I? It surprised me that Stoff wasn't trying to claim DDF ownership over the thing since we were the ones who had retrieved it from ReDawn and figured out how it worked. It was a good thing—both for our current situation and our relationship with the UrDail—if he didn't. But . . .

"We also need DDF support," I told Stoff. "A few more flights at least. The more you can spare, the better."

Now Stoff looked skeptical. "Detritus isn't under attack," I said. "We have the shield to protect us even if the Superiority were to return, and with the hyperdrives we could be here at a moment's notice. We can spare the ships, not only to protect Cobb and Mrs. Nightshade, but to show solidarity with the kitsen."

Stoff watched me carefully, and then looked over at Kelin. "Excuse us," he said.

"Yes, sir," Kelin said, and she paced off down the hall.

Stoff glanced at Rig, as if considering whether to send him away as well, but seemed to decide it wasn't necessary. "Okay," he said.

Um. "Okay, sir?"

"Okay, take the flights. How many do you need?"

"How many will you—"

"Never mind," Stoff said. "Don't tell me. I'll radio over to Command that I've authorized you to call up flights to support you on Evershore. You can call them up yourself."

I could? "Sir?" I said.

Stoff sighed, and I felt like I was missing something. I looked sideways at FM, but she didn't seem to be any clearer on what was happening than I was.

"Your orders came directly from the admiral, didn't they?" Stoff said. "I wouldn't dream of overruling him."

Out of the corner of my eye, I saw FM and Rig exchange a look.

I didn't really know what to say to that. I didn't want to argue— I'd been worried that Stoff was going to take away what limited autonomy I had now that he knew Cobb was in fact incapacitated.

DDF protocol was clear that he had the right—even the responsibility—to do just that.

"I can decide how many flights to call to Evershore," I said. I didn't want to belabor this too much—it was good news really, and Skyward Flight needed us to take care of this quickly and bring them help.

But this felt more like a trap.

"Yes," Stoff said. "You've been very clear on what Cobb ordered you to do. If this is your mission, then you should have the autonomy to complete it, don't you think?"

Ah. I saw what he was doing. On paper I was a renegade. I'd taken my flight and our starfighters to ReDawn, officially against orders. I'd then returned and demanded that we cut the assembly out of the loop and that we work with the kitsen to retrieve Cobb. There were plenty of people who would testify to my insubordination—everyone but Cobb would consider that case open and shut.

Stoff hadn't arrested me when we returned, but he'd been watching me ever since. He'd been giving me a lot of leeway in case my actions might be in Detritus's best interest, but he'd never quite committed to attaching his name to anything I'd done in case it blew up like the scudding Superiority ship.

If Stoff kept this up, he could still take credit for anything Skyward Flight accomplished—if he *wanted* the credit. If we failed he'd be able to wash his hands of it. Say I acted on my own, say he didn't really understand what was happening while I was offworld.

Did Stoff really not care about anything but keeping his head down and avoiding responsibility for whatever came next?

"Sir," I said. "Forgive me for questioning, but that's a lot of autonomy."

"It's no more than the admiral saw fit to give you," Stoff said. "Isn't that right?"

Stars. Maybe that *was* all he cared about. This was in fact a *lot* more autonomy than the admiral had seen fit to give me. I didn't want to push Stoff too hard though. I only wanted to understand his motives, not change his mind.

"This is important," I said to him. "We're protected for now, but it isn't going to last. The Superiority's resources are as vast as the galaxy. They're trying to convince the *delvers* to be on their side. If we don't find a way to resist them . . ."

Stoff cringed, his shoulders hunching forward. "You don't have to tell me." I saw genuine fear in his eyes. He was *terrified*. "If you think you can do something to better our situation, then you scudding well had better do it."

He closed the door in my face.

"Did he seriously just do that?" FM asked.

"Dump responsibility for everything on us?" Rig asked. "Yeah, I think he did."

Not on us. On *me*. I was an easy mark. My parents were gone, so I couldn't depend on them to cover for me. I was isolated. Politically speaking, I was *expendable*.

Stoff seemed sincere about wanting us to succeed. He knew how desperate our situation was. But he wasn't going to do anything about it. He was a vice admiral; with Cobb out of commission it was his job to step up and lead.

But he was hiding like a coward because he was too afraid to deal with it.

"Jorgen?" FM said.

"Hang on," I said. "I need to check on the others."

I leaned against the wall next to Stoff's door, reaching into the nowhere. *Alanik?* I said.

Still nothing, she said. *This rodent keeps talking to me about birds. There are no birds living in my mind, Jorgen, and I don't know what he means about the waves either.*

Huh. That had made sense to me, but . . . *That's about how I feel when you talk about finding locations in the nowhere*, I said. *Maybe mindblades aren't your thing?*

I felt annoyance from her. Alanik didn't like to think herself incapable of things other people could do.

I understood. I didn't like it either.

I can keep trying, she said, *but I worry about leaving those ships alone in the sky. We could go up there and try to take them out if you want. Fewer to fight later.*

If there was the option to wait or to act, Alanik was like Spensa—she always leaned toward acting. More than leaned; she ran toward it at full speed. This time she had a point, but I still didn't think it was the right move. *No,* I told her. *Protect the city.*

There are a lot of cities, Jorgen, Alanik said. *A whole planet's worth. How are we going to protect them all?*

She was right. Evershore didn't have a shield, or even the cover of platforms and debris. They were so *exposed.* At least we'd only had to protect Alta. The kitsen were spread out over the entire *planet.*

How did people survive this way? How were we going to protect them?

Could we?

I'm working on it, I said, as if I had a clue about what I was doing. *Focus on Dreamspring for now.*

"Jorgen?" FM said. "Should we head over to Command?"

The command center was staffed all night. The vice admiral had probably already put in the call and gone back to sleep, leaving the rest of it to us.

We did need to head over to Command, but if Stoff was really going to let me have whatever I wanted . . .

"Rig," I said. "How long would it take you to get people over to the control room the exploration team found on that platform?"

"We can get there quickly," Rig said. "Whether or not we can get it to work—"

"It's worth a try," I said. If Stoff was giving me free rein . . . scud, he expected this to blow up in my face, and he might be right. "At least get a team over there to look at it."

"I'll start knocking on doors," Rig said.

I closed my eyes. I was pulling Rig into this. Again. He'd take the fall with me if we failed at this. "I can't order you to do that," I said. I didn't have the authority for that.

"Jorgen," Rig said, "I jumped on the going-rogue train with you all when I left with you for ReDawn. It's a little late to reconsider now." He squeezed FM's hand, and then he took off down the corridor toward the dormitories.

We were all on that train, and it was my scudding fault. The corridor walls seemed to squeeze in on me, and I closed my eyes.

"Jorgen," FM said.

I didn't respond.

"Say something so I know you're not about to cut the platform apart from the inside."

"I'm not," I said. I could control it. I *would* control it.

"He's setting us up," she said.

"Yes."

"He's going to try to make *you* look like this rogue who doesn't care about orders. *There's* a piece of irony."

I wasn't the only person who saw it. That was comforting. "Only if it goes wrong."

"Of course," FM says. "If we succeed, he'll probably try to take credit."

That was exactly what he would do.

"So," FM said, "are we going to call up the flights?"

That was what I should be doing. The others needed us.

But I couldn't move. I knew I should be acting, but was this really what I was doing now? Running off on another set of not-orders toward—what? Did I really think we could take down the entire Superiority air force with a couple of flights and one platform? Even if Rig got a few other platforms to move, did we stand a chance? We'd won on ReDawn, but that could have been a fluke. A bit of false hope that preceded total destruction. I could be leading everyone I cared about to their deaths, and it was *my* call, *my* idea, *my* decision—

I couldn't watch anyone else I loved die like that.

In my mind, I watched the Superiority ship explode again.

Boom.

FM grabbed me by the arm, and I startled.

"*Jorgen,*" she said. "Talk to me. You're starting to freak out again, and I *really* do not want to be diced up by your mindblades."

Stars, was she afraid of me? "I'm sorry," I said.

"Don't be sorry. You aren't alone in this. I know you think you are, but you're not."

"He's making me make the call," I said. "But is this the right one? I *think* it's what Cobb would do. But I don't really know, do I? And if I'm wrong . . ."

"This isn't all on you," FM insisted.

"It is."

"You still believe in the chain of command, right?"

"Yes," I said. "And we're operating way outside of it." By orders. Sort of. Two separate commanders had *sort of* ordered me to do this, and the "sort of" part felt like it was going to break my brain.

"It's a chain for a reason," she said. "It's not one person at the top all alone doing everything. Yeah, ultimately you make the decisions. And you are doing a scudding good job of that, okay? But we're all here to support you. The only piece you have to do on your own is the final word."

"I know," I said. "But at the end of the day, it's my call that saves people or gets people killed." Maybe both. Stars, why was it always both?

"That's true," FM said. "But we're all here supporting you because we trust your judgment."

"You question my judgment all the time!" I said. "On Sunreach, I was going to make the call to leave the flight behind. And maybe we could have gone back for them, but maybe we couldn't have, and who knows how many of them would have died in the meantime. *You* figured out how to save their lives. Not me."

"Okay," FM said. "But what about ReDawn? You made the call

to stay and take out that Superiority ship. We could have cut and run after the cytonic inhibitors were taken out, but *you* risked all of our lives to destroy that battleship and protect the people of ReDawn, and that was clearly the right thing to do."

"What about when I chewed you out for stealing the taynix and bringing them to Wandering Leaf?" I asked. "You didn't think I was doing the right thing then."

FM closed her eyes. We'd been avoiding this conversation ever since that happened. I didn't want to have it now—or ever—but I also wasn't going to let her pretend that she always agreed with me.

"I was angry with you," she said quietly. "And I was scudding *scared*. I said things I didn't mean. And I'm sorry I said those things, I really am, because they aren't true. You are my flightleader, and you're scudding *good* at it, Jorgen."

"It doesn't feel that way." It felt like I was failing them all.

FM shook her head. "Do you think we all follow you because of the chain of command? The things we have done lately are scudding *insane*. There is not an officer in all of the DDF who would condemn us for refusing to go along with it."

That was probably true. Stars, I'd justified a lot of things I shouldn't have, by the book at least.

"We're all here," FM continued, "because we believe in what we're doing. And we all trust you with our lives because we know that at the end of the day, Jorgen Weight is going to do the right thing. Sometimes you lose sight of that. Sometimes you get so bogged down in the *rules* that you lose track of what's right for a minute. But when it comes down to the decisions you make with our lives, you do the right thing every time."

I wasn't so sure. That was why I tried to follow the rules, because if I was going to make a mistake, I wanted it to be one that couldn't have been avoided. If I erred in following protocol, at least I always had the protocol to blame.

"You think I should call up the flights," I said.

"Honestly?" FM said. "I don't know. Maybe we should pull

back; maybe the Superiority would leave the kitsen alone. Or more likely they'd do some damage and there would be lives lost, but maybe it would be fewer lives than if we goad them into a full-scale attack that we're not sure we can defend against. It's a risky move, Jorgen, and I don't know what the right answer is."

I gritted my teeth, dragging my hands over my hair. If I could see the future, know which would be the right choice for the most people—for *our* people—I'd do it.

Why was it so scudding hard to know what that was?

"But," FM said, "one of our goals on Evershore is to make an alliance. And the calls you made on ReDawn are the reason we have an alliance with the UrDail. Because of *you*."

I shrugged. "I was ordered to make that alliance."

"Right. And everyone always succeeds at everything they're ordered to do, right? Having an order makes it easy! Basically done for you. So you barely get credit for it, because you were simply following orders. Is that it?"

"Um," I said. That sounded about right, but from her tone I could tell that it shouldn't.

"Meanwhile, if you don't succeed, *that* is entirely your fault. No one else could possibly be to blame, because Jorgen Weight is all powerful and if anything goes wrong it's always on him."

"I think that's a little hyperbolic."

"You think?" FM said. "Tell me that's not how you feel. Go ahead."

"Um," I said again.

"You can't have it both ways. You can't be powerless and totally at fault. Which is it?"

I thought about that. "It's neither."

"Right," FM said. "Some things are under your control, and others aren't. You do the best you can with what you have to work with. And *that* is what sets you apart—what you do with it."

I sighed. "Fine. You've made your point."

"So, what are we doing? What are your priorities here?"

"Cobb's life." That was a clear priority, clean and by the book. "And we can't pull him out." But stars, even if it would save kitsen lives, we couldn't *leave* him there.

"Okay," FM said.

"Also the lives of our flightmates," I added.

"And all the kitsen lives in danger right now? What about them?"

"They aren't our people. But Cobb ordered us to—"

"Forget for a minute about what Cobb ordered you to do," FM said. "What do you think is the *right* thing to do?"

I didn't know which call would turn out to be the best one, but for the moment I tried to set that aside. Maybe the right call was the one that hoped for the most good for the most people, even if the outcome wasn't totally assured.

Things seemed clearer when I looked at them that way. "Save lives," I said. "Defend the kitsen, defend Cobb, secure the alliance. Work together against the people who are trying to kill us all." It sounded so simple when I said it like that. It had a ring of truth to it.

"That sounds right to me too," FM said.

I nodded. "What Stoff is doing is a trap, but it's a political one. We can save lives first and politic later." I would have preferred to politic *never*, but if there was an order to this, that was it.

FM watched me, waiting. She was doing what she'd said—talking me through it, but then waiting for me to make the decision.

I could recall my flight and leave the kitsen to deal with the Superiority. If Stoff could hide behind the chain of command so could I, and no one in the DDF could blame me for it. I could pin the whole thing right back on Stoff, and he wouldn't have a renegade on whom to shuffle off the responsibility.

But I already knew I could never live with myself if I did that.

"Enough standing around," I said. "Let's call up the flights and get that platform."

FM grinned at me. "Yes, sir," she said.

And together we took off running down the corridor.

14

No one questioned me when I said I wanted three flights readied for hyperjump as soon as possible, and all pilots on standby in case we needed more. If we were committing to protecting Cobb, Gran-Gran, and the kitsen, then we had to be all in.

We'd left a taynix on Wandering Leaf—Bob the commslug, named by Nedd—so the other slugs could take us back and forth. Gill transported us to the taynix control room on the plat-form, a room with a wide control panel and rows of boxes to hold taynix in the various defense and weapons systems.

Everyone on the platform was asleep—some of the UrDail In-dependence pilots had chosen to stay here, probably to ensure that our military didn't adopt Wandering Leaf as their own asset.

FM tucked Gill into the hyperdrive box. I intended to direct the hyperjump to Evershore from this control room. I could send the instructions to the pilots' slugs from here, so long as each flight had at least one hyperdrive on board. Then I could hyperjump Wan-dering Leaf into the airspace over Dreamspring, coordinating with Alanik to ensure none of our people ended up close enough to get shot by Wandering Leaf's defenses.

Rig appeared in front of the control panel beside FM, and she jumped. No matter how many times we hyperjumped, it was still hard to get used to people appearing out of nowhere. It reminded me of the times as a child when I used to jump out from behind furniture and startle my mother. It always worked no matter how many times I did it, much to my mother's chagrin.

Sometimes it wasn't what happened that surprised you. It was when.

"I'm about to fly out to that platform that resembles Wandering Leaf," Rig said. "But I'm worried we won't be able to figure out how to move any platforms quickly enough. I'm equally worried that we will and we'll leave Detritus open to attack."

"There are already holes in the platforms around the planet," I said. "The shield stretches between them. It would continue to fill in the gaps if we only took a few platforms, wouldn't it?"

"I hope so," Rig said.

"If it doesn't, we'll return them," I said. "Maybe we won't even be able to figure out how to move them, but I think we need to explore all of our options."

"Of course," Rig said. "I'll have Drape with me, so if you need to communicate you can hyperjump in and back out again. I'll also see if there's a hypercomm there that we can get working." He looked nervously from me to FM, and FM threw her arms around him.

"Be safe," he said.

I hoped we would be, but stars, none of us could promise that.

Rig gave Drape the command to take him home, and he blinked out to meet with the engineers. FM looked shaken.

"You okay?" I asked.

"No," FM said. "But this isn't the time to talk about it."

"We have to wait for the signal from the other flights that they're ready to hyperjump," I said. "They've just been roused from their beds, so we have a few minutes."

FM squeezed her eyes shut. "Saints and stars, Jorgen. It's a lot easier to make you talk than to do it myself."

"I could call Rig back," I said. "But I think he needs to get moving with the other engineers."

"I don't want to talk to Rig about it anyway," she mumbled.

That surprised me. "I thought you said you liked that he made you talk."

"I said it was good for me. But I hate it. And I realize that if I don't talk to you right now, you're going to use that as an excuse to shut down and probably explode again."

I hoped that wasn't true. But I didn't deny it.

FM sighed. "So yes, it sucks, okay? I hate leaving Rig, knowing I may not be coming back. I know what it does to him and how much worse it'll be if something happens to me, and I feel terrible about it. I wonder if I ever should have started things between us, if that was really fair to him. *And* I wonder how much longer he's going to want to put up with this before he decides that I'm not worth the stress. Okay? Are you happy now?"

"No," I said. "But I'm glad you told me."

FM fiddled with one of the console buttons, looking at me out of the corner of her eye. "Do you ever feel like maybe you shouldn't have started things with Spensa?"

"I didn't start it," I said. "She did. But . . ." It surprised me how easily the answer came. "No. I've never regretted it. I could never regret one minute with her, no matter how it all turns out." The strength of my conviction startled me. I meant every word.

FM's shoulders relaxed.

"You don't regret it either," I said. "You're just scared."

FM pressed her lips together, and she nodded. "I don't think it's fair to him. But if you can handle Spensa running off into literally nowhere . . ."

Rig dropped out of flight school after his first time in the air, but he'd come with us into battle on ReDawn anyway, and he hadn't flinched. "He knows why you're doing this. He's making the same call."

"Yeah," FM said. "And I hate him being in danger too. I almost hope he can't get the platforms to move, because then he'll be here and he'll be safer."

If the platforms didn't move, we'd all have far fewer resources to deal with whatever the Superiority brought against us. But I didn't point out her bad logic. I understood.

"I'm going to go wake the UrDail pilots," FM said. "So they aren't frightened when the platform moves, and so they can decide to stay here if that's what they want."

"Good idea," I said. Alanik's brother and the others had fought beside us on ReDawn, but this wasn't their fight. They deserved the opportunity to decide for themselves.

"Jerkface," a voice said over my radio. "This is Robin from Stardragon Flight. We were told to contact you as soon as we were in the air."

Last time I talked to Robin over the radio, her flight had been called up to keep Skyward Flight from escaping to ReDawn. "Copy, Robin," I said. "Do you have a hyperdrive?"

"We've got one of them in our flight," Robin said. "Ivy and Victory Flights have a couple more each."

"Good," I said. "Connect all your ships with light-lances. Don't leave anyone behind. Signal me when you're ready, and we'll bring everyone with us to Evershore."

"Jerkface?" Robin said. "What the scud are we doing?"

"Defending potential new allies," I said. "They're under attack because the Superiority got wind of our presence there. We'll be joining their air force in defending their planet. I'll give you specific formations when we arrive."

"Yes, sir," Robin said.

I blinked. I wasn't technically Robin's superior, and I was giving her orders anyway. Stoff had given me leave to do that, but . . .

I didn't correct her. I was going to need them all to listen to me, so this was a *good* sign even if it wasn't exactly right.

Jorgen? Alanik said in my mind. *Another carrier ship has arrived.*

We're on our way, I told her.

I made sure Gill was ready while FM alerted the UrDail pilots.

"We're ready to go," Robin told me over the radio. "My flight wants to know where exactly we're heading?"

Had I not told them? "Evershore," I said. "It's a planet inhabited by small fox aliens."

There was a pause. "Okay," Robin said. "Thanks for filling us in."

I sighed. Answering all their questions would take time we didn't have. "You'll see soon enough. All flights, prepare for hyperjump."

FM returned to the doorway of the control room. "Gilaf and the others are getting ready. They're in."

"Good," I said. "We're going to need them."

I'm ready to hyperjump, I said to Alanik. *Get someone high enough in the air that the platform won't fire on the planet when we arrive.*

There was a long pause.

Arturo's up high enough, Alanik said. *The space around him is clear. Go.*

I reached out to the other flights, finding the minds of their taynix, and gave them instructions to go to Alanik's slug, Snide, down near Dreamspring. Then I reached for Gill in the box and instructed him to take the platform to Naga. I wanted us to emerge in the air, not drop the platform on top of the beach where the autoturrets would fire on the city.

We slipped beneath the unseeing eyes and appeared beneath the black sky, marred grey by periodic clouds. I could see the carrier ships Alanik was talking about up above the clouds, pieces of their large boxy shapes visible behind the fluffy obstructions. Arturo hovered right above the platform's surface, close enough that he wouldn't be hit by the autocannons.

"Scud, Jerkface," Arturo said. "That thing popping out of nowhere is terrifying."

The platform shook as the guns fired at some enemy ships that had been waiting right inside the clouds. They scattered and retreated.

"Welcome back," Kimmalyn said over the radio.

"Thanks," I said. "I'm going to do something about those carrier ships. Everyone else steer clear of the platform and defend the city."

"We've got more kitsen ships on our side now," Arturo said. "They're gathering over Dreamspring."

"And we will feast on the souls of all who dare to harm our beloved city," Goro said.

"I sure hope that's metaphorical," FM muttered, then turned to me. "Gilaf will contact you over the radio when he and the other UrDail pilots are ready to jump out to help. I'm going to take Gill to my ship."

"Do it," I said. "Amphi, I want you to command the flight. It's too hard for me to keep track of you all while I'm working the platform." Last time I'd had Rig to handle this, and all I'd had to do was command Boomslug to shoot the hyperweapon. This was going to be more complicated.

"Copy, Jerkface. What is our strategy?"

Scud, we needed one of those. Not only for our flight, but for everyone. "Protect the city," I said. "Victory Flight, make sure the city itself doesn't take fire. Keep the enemy distracted." I paused. "Amphi, have we heard from Cuna?"

"They're working with the medical people to get Cobb and Gran-Gran moved to the library. Going toward the cliffs doesn't seem to be causing their vitals to drop."

It all had something to do with that portal, but I didn't understand what. "Good," I said. "They'll have better cover there. But we still need to protect the city. Stardragon and Ivy Flights, intercept the enemy ships before they reach the city. Your goal is to make sure Victory sees no action."

"Copy, Jerkface," Robin said.

"Skyward Flight will take point. All flights stay at least five klicks from the platform to avoid the autofire. Our objective is to convince them we aren't worth it and pull their ships back. If you have a hyperdrive and need to be pulled out of the heat, let me know. Otherwise, Amphi will give you specific formation instructions."

"Okay," Arturo said. He probably wasn't prepared to do that for multiple flights, but he started doing it anyway.

Which left me free to focus on the new carrier ships in the sky. I wasn't going to sit here and wait for them to pour out their fighters to bombard the city.

I was going to take them out first.

"Jerkface," Alanik said, "your sidekick wants to join you again. I think he's given up on me."

"Send him over with Snide," I said.

Snide and Juno appeared a moment later, both riding on Juno's platform. A moment later Alanik called Snide back, and the slug disappeared again.

"I did not give up on her," Juno said. "I simply said she appeared to have less aptitude for mindblades than you do. It wasn't a qualitative judgment."

"To Alanik it probably felt like one," I said.

"Is there some particular meditation you would like to try?" Juno asked. "I don't have all my books, but I could—"

"Not right now," I said. I called to Snuggles, who appeared in my arms with Boomslug. I tucked Snuggles into the taynix box where Gill had been. "Maybe later. Right now I need to concentrate."

"The purpose of meditation is to help your concentration—"

I tuned him out, loading Boomslug into the platform's hyperweapon. Then I focused on the airspace near the carrier ship and sent Snuggles the instruction to go.

We slid beneath the eyes and then Wandering Leaf reappeared beneath the carrier ship. Our inhibitor field encompassed the enemy ship, preventing it from hyperjumping while the autoturrets fired, weakening the shield, piercing through it in a few places to punch holes in the hull. The hangar doors opened and ships poured out, trying to escape. The big guns couldn't possibly hit all those targets. The sensors showed that my people were still flying low—I didn't need to worry about clipping them yet.

Go, I said to Boomslug, focusing on the area right outside the hangar.

I felt the edge of the nowhere ripping apart as the hyperweapon fired, mindblades flying out at the escaping ships, bypassing the shields, cleaving their hulls in two. Debris rained down out of the sky. The pilots didn't even get a chance to eject.

I couldn't afford to feel sorry for them. I leaned toward the window, spotting the next carrier ship halfway behind a nearby tower of clouds.

Go, I said to Snuggles, and suddenly we were in front of it, the platform shaking with autoturret fire.

"We're ready," Alanik's brother, Gilaf, said over the radio. "But we'd rather not jump out right here, if it's all the same to you."

"Sorry for the short notice," I said. "We didn't get much more ourselves. I'll jump you down closer to the planet."

"Hell of a way to wake up," Gilaf said.

I contacted the taynix in Gilaf's ship and sent him and the other UrDail pilots down to the place where we'd first brought the platform in.

This carrier ship seemed mostly empty, but I still told Boomslug to fire, aiming the hyperweapon at the hull of the ship. It diced into chunks, bits of it blowing out into the sky and then falling.

"Did you do that?" Juno asked, watching through the window.

"I did," I said. Stars, this thing was powerful. This tactic could be less effective against a battleship, which might be equipped with an inhibitor, but we were putting a serious amount of metal into the ocean from these carrier ships. Bits were going to wash up on the beach for years.

What could we do if we were able to move more of the other platforms from their orbit around Detritus?

The third carrier ship belched forth more fighters. I could feel the distinct vibration of a cytonic among them, and I reached out, listening for any cytonic communications, to see what we could learn about their plans.

Instead I felt something else. A thrumming against the nowhere, a rhythmic knocking like someone tapping their nails against the boundary between that world and ours.

The enemy cytonic sliced across the battlefield, headed directly for Alanik. The thrumming followed them, and as I focused I could feel small projectiles swarming around them, like pointed shards of glass made out of bits of the nowhere.

Oh, *scud.*

"Angel, get out of there," I said. "That incoming ship has—"

The shards of nowhere flew out around the enemy pilot's ship in a swirling melee, clipping wings and piercing hulls. Two ships went down—one from Ivy Flight and one from Stardragon—as the ship neared Alanik.

Alanik's ship blinked out of existence and reappeared farther down toward the city, where Victory Flight was chasing off the fighters that had pierced through our other forces. The enemy ship sailed right past the place where she'd been, toward Kimmalyn and Nedd, who darted away. The ship pursued Kimmalyn. Before I could say anything, Arturo was yelling at her over the radio to go into a dive, get out of there.

She dove, but the enemy ship followed her, slicing her ship into three even pieces. The wreckage fell to the ground. She didn't eject, but she wouldn't have needed to. I searched for her taynix in the falling wreckage, but I couldn't find him. I hoped he'd hyper-jumped her out.

"All flights," I said, "that pilot has mindblades. Take them down."

"We can't get close enough to use the IMP," Amphi said. "Quirk's our best shot and she's down."

"Nedder," FM said. "Did Quirk make it out?"

"I don't know," Nedd said. He sounded shaken. The cytonic with the mindblades dove again, this time taking off after Catnip.

I found Catnip's slug, Whiskers, and instructed it to jump down closer to the city, below Victory Flight. Catnip disappeared. Our ships flew loosely around the enemy cytonic, all trying to peg the ship with destructor fire without getting close enough to be torn apart by the mindblades, but the enemy ship rolled and dodged, evading their fire.

I couldn't let this continue. I could get in my own ship and try to go after the cytonic, but I imagined they had a lot more practice with those mindblades than I had, and possibly a lot more reach.

"All flights," I said, "pull up."

All across the battlefield, ships shot up into the clouds, clashing with the Superiority ships that had made it out of their carriers. Not all the kitsen flights obeyed, but those that didn't were far enough away from the cytonic that they should be safe from the autofire above and below.

Go, I told Snuggles.

And I hyperjumped the platform directly below the cytonic pilot.

The cytonic pilot immediately pulled up, accelerating to get out of the inhibitor field.

Go, I said to Boomslug.

Boomslug fired the hyperweapon in the direction of the pilot, but they reached the edge of the inhibitor field and hyperjumped away. I searched for them across the sky—

And found them high above the planet, farther even than the carrier ships. Most of our forces were between me and them, but I could follow in an instant, if I could only see where they'd gone. I looked up through the window at the clouds—

And was blinded by a blast of blue energy that poured down from the sky, striking the shield around Wandering Leaf, which sputtered and crackled.

I squinted against the light. When it faded, I stared up at a large, newly arrived ship with an enormous cannon on the front of it.

Scud.

Scud.

"What is that?" Juno asked.

"It's a planetary weapon," I said.

"A weapon for planets," Juno said. "It seems wrong to invent such a thing."

"No argument here," I said. It looked just like the one we'd destroyed on ReDawn. It made sense that it hadn't been unique. They must have had the thing charged before they hyperjumped it in, which made a sick, reckless kind of sense.

We could *not* let that thing fire on the planet. I didn't know how many kitsen that ship could destroy in one blast, and I didn't want to find out.

"Jerkface—" Arturo said over the radio.

"I see it," I said. "All flights, clear the space around the cannon." The flights split, going into evasive maneuvers and leading the enemy ships away from the cannon, which was fixed squarely on Wandering Leaf.

They'd take out the platform and then Dreamspring. I had to destroy the cannon before that happened.

The airspace between me and the cannon was clear. I still didn't know for certain if Kimmalyn was okay, or if any of my friends had been caught in that energy beam, but there were going to be a lot of other casualties if I didn't act quickly. I focused on the space just below the cannon and hyperjumped the platform up.

The autoturrets fired immediately, pummeling the cannon and the ship around it. *Scud*, this thing was terrifying from this close. Last time it was Rig who'd had to stare one of these down. I hadn't given him enough credit for it. The blue light was building again. I focused on the cannon, ready to tell Boomslug to fire—

And suddenly the vibration of the universe went dead. I could no longer feel the cytonic inside the enemy ship, or the minds of Boomslug and Snuggles so nearby in the boxes. Scud, the enemy cytonics had put up an inhibitor, and I'd brought the platform right into range. It was the same thing I'd done to the mindblade cytonic, but they had a ship with an engine, and Wandering Leaf moved only by hyperjump.

I was stuck here.

"This seems bad!" Juno said, his voice almost a squeak.

The blue light glowed brighter and brighter, and then the beam pummeled my shields again. The shield crackled and then blinked out, leaving the platform vulnerable to the next attack. I couldn't hyperjump out. I couldn't use the hyperweapon. I didn't have a starfighter on board, and Alanik couldn't come in to get me.

I stared up into the mouth of the cannon as it once again began to glow with an eerie blue light.

15

The autoturret continued to pound at the cannon. It was doing damage, but it wasn't going to disable the thing fast enough. I was going to get blown to pieces on this platform the moment it finished charging.

"Amphi," I said over the radio. "I have to get out of here. The autoturrets are distracted. Can any of you dodge the fire and fly in to pick me up?"

"Nedder's closest," Arturo said.

"On it," Nedd said.

"Follow me," I said to Juno. I scooped Snuggles, Boomslug, Bob the commslug, and the inhibitor taynix out of their boxes and took off at a full run toward the hangar.

When I arrived, I watched through the windows as Nedd pulled a barrel roll past the autofire. The turrets were focused on the ship with the cannons and were doing some impressive damage to the ship *around* it. Maybe they *would* be able to disable the thing before—

The blue light grew even more blinding. Nedd used his light-lance to flip around one of the turrets and landed on the platform right outside the hangar.

Juno's floating platform zipped along behind me as we ran up to

Nedd's cockpit just as he lifted the canopy. The noise of the autofire was deafening, and I dove into the cockpit behind Nedd, straddling the back of his seat and holding on with both hands. Juno hovered beside Nedd's seat, and the four slugs flattened their bodies against me.

Nedd pulled down the canopy and didn't even have time for a wisecrack before he took off again. The turrets were so focused on the planetary weapon that they didn't fire on us, but when we got far enough away that the vibrations returned, I had Snuggles hyperjump us several kilometers farther just to be certain.

The world flared blue as the cannon fired, the blast rocketing through Wandering Leaf, tearing it apart. The autocannons had taken out a good half of the Superiority ship, and the cannon's light faded, no longer powering. We'd gotten rid of the weapon.

But we'd lost the platform in the process.

"Jerkface," FM said, "did the UrDail pilots all make it out?"

"They did," I said. "No casualties. Just catastrophic damage."

"Dude, I saved your life," Nedd said. "The least you could do is stop squeezing my pecs."

I dropped my arms from around Nedd's chair. I hadn't realized I was holding on so tight or so . . . awkwardly. "Sorry," I said. "Hang on, I'm going to transport us to my ship." My whole body was squeezed into a space so tight I wasn't sure how I was managing to fit. I'd only gotten in here on pure adrenaline.

I directed Snuggles to jump Nedd's ship to the beach next to mine, still sheltered under the cliff, then I held on to her and had her hyperjump me, Juno, and Boomslug out of the cockpit. We landed in the sand outside my ship.

There standing in front of it was Kimmalyn, with Happy tucked into a sling across her chest. "Thank the stars you're okay," I said.

"Happy teleported me to the other side of the beach," Kimmalyn said. "I was thinking about stealing your ship, but I guess you need it."

"I do," I said. I didn't think for a minute that the cytonic with the mindblades had been killed in that blast. They would still be out there, and I wasn't going to let them wreak havoc on our forces. "If you take Happy home, you can get another ship and then hyperjump to Naga," I said. "That'll get you back in the fight."

"On it," Kimmalyn said. "Just . . . be careful."

Scud, she'd been shot out of the sky. It was only Happy that had saved her. "If you're too shaken up—"

"I'm fine," Kimmalyn said. Her hands were shaking, but she gave me a very forced smile. "I would feel much worse knowing you all were still up there without me. Happy, let's go home."

Kimmalyn disappeared, and I climbed into my cockpit, Juno floating in behind me before I closed the canopy.

My radio was going nuts.

"Jerkface!" FM said over the radio. "Are you okay?"

"He got out," Alanik said. "He's down on the beach."

"I'm here," I said. I lifted my ship a couple of meters, using my sensors to take stock of the battle. The planetary weapon was high enough in the atmosphere that it wasn't falling immediately to the ground, though the cannon was obviously destroyed.

Jorgen, Alanik said in my head. *Watch out—*

With a great crunching of metal and shattering of glass, my ship ripped apart around me. A pair of mindblades sliced down into the dash, obliterating the canopy. I slammed down the altitude control and jumped out through the torn metal, pulling my slugs with me out onto the sand.

I could feel the enemy cytonic over on the beach. They'd hyperjumped after me. Juno slid out through the broken glass and hid beside me, the ship between us and the enemy cytonic.

It wasn't going to last for long. I felt more mindblades forming around the enemy cytonic, another volley about to rip through the ship to get at me.

"Now would be a good time for that meditation," I said to Juno.

"You are completely relaxed!" Juno said.

I reached for the nowhere, skimming my mind over the surface.

My birds formed again, little shards of death and nothingness, and I flew them with all my might over the ship toward the enemy cytonic. More blades flew at us, and I pulled Juno's platform down as I flattened myself against the ground. The enemy's mindblades dug into the ship, and I twisted mine around, jabbing at the enemy cytonic where I could see them in my mind.

The enemy's mindblades vanished. We'd had cover but they hadn't, and when I peered over the ship I found the body of a dione with bright red skin lying bleeding on the ground.

Scud. I'd never killed someone at such close range before. I'd never had to stare at their bleeding body, knowing I caused that. The sand beneath the dione turned a strange dark blue color. The body didn't so much as twitch.

My ship was thrashed, but the radio still worked. "Jerkface, you okay?" Arturo asked.

"Fine," I said. "But I lost my ship."

"We've got more company." I looked up and found another carrier ship arriving. The Superiority had to be mustering their ships as they went, or else they'd underestimated what size force it would take to defeat us.

But they were going to keep coming until they'd accomplished it. We were going to need to bring a lot more fire to this fight.

"Amphi," I said, "you're in command. Protect the city. I'm going to go check on Rig, see if we can bring more platforms."

"Copy, Jerkface," Arturo said.

I picked up my slugs again, letting Boomslug ride on my shoulder, and placed a hand on Juno's platform.

"You want to come with me?" I asked Juno.

"Where you will go, I will go," Juno replied.

I would give the kitsen this—they were some of the bravest beings I'd ever met. "Take me to Drape," I said to Snuggles.

"Drape," Snuggles said.

Evershore and all of the ships above it disappeared. We passed beneath the eyes, and then suddenly I stood in a small room much

519

like the one on Wandering Leaf. The window looked out at the stars, over half a broken platform drifting next to the one where we'd landed, a large defunct autoturret jutting up beyond it. The walls were lined with boxes.

Scud, there were so *many* of them. Taynix boxes from floor to ceiling, enough to house maybe a hundred taynix.

"Jorgen," Rig said. "How are—"

"We lost Wandering Leaf," I said. "Planetary weapon destroyed it."

Rig's eyes widened. "Is—"

"FM is fine," I said. I probably should have led with that. If it had been Spensa, that was the first thing I'd want to hear. "But Winzik sent more reinforcements, and they may not be the last. We need to get more platforms over there."

"Yeah, about that," Rig said. "We have a small problem." He gestured around him. "We don't know what any of these boxes do, much less where we would get enough slugs to power them. I sent the transport ship back to collect the taynix on the base, but most of those belong to the remaining pilots. I'm not sure they're going to part with them, not without a direct order from Stoff."

Stoff might give such an order, but the more I involved him the more he'd feel he had to question me, which we did not have time for. The flights on Evershore could be dead by the time he made a decision. We'd also need the taynix with those pilots if we had to bring in more reinforcements.

I looked around at the boxes again. We'd sent expeditions down to the caverns to look for more slugs, but it was taking them time and I understood why. The slugs tended to hide in the less inhabited areas, and I'd been too busy to go down myself.

Scud. "Do you need to use all the boxes?" I asked Rig. "Can we figure out which one is the hyperdrive, then take the platform over and use the autocannons?"

"Maybe," Rig said. "Even figuring out which is the hyperdrive is going to take time though. The boxes aren't well labeled."

Rig looked around, wringing his hands. I was putting a lot of pressure on him and demanding instant results. Just because we'd been able to pull ourselves out of some tight spots in the past didn't mean he could produce miracles on demand.

"I know you're doing your best," I said. "I know you don't have enough time or resources. You're doing amazing work for us, and you've saved all our lives several times now. If you can't figure this out it isn't your fault, but I need you to try."

"Of course," Rig said. "We're just not prepared for this."

"What can I do?"

"Finding me more slugs would be nice."

"Okay, let me see what I can do." I moved out into the corridor. In the rooms along the hall, other engineers were calling to each other about the contents of each one. I peered through the nearest doorway.

Scud. More taynix boxes.

We were going to need a lot of help. Rig's team had done so much for us. Now it was time for me to come through for them.

I found a bench in the corridor and sat down, Juno hovering over my shoulder next to Boomslug.

"Do you have a meditation for searching?" I asked Juno.

"Not in this book," Juno said, "though most of them begin the same: 'Breathe in, breathe out. You are now completely relaxed.'"

I wasn't, but I tried anyway. I reached out over the planet, searching for that vibration, the one I'd heard in my dreams. The one that had called Spensa's great-grandmother to Detritus to begin with—the reason we'd arrived here.

It was still there, that resonance. We'd found some taynix, pulled them up from their mushroom-infested caves and brought them to live with us. But there were more down there, maybe a lot more.

Help, I called to them. *We need help.* It was hard to pinpoint the individual minds of the slugs—it always was, before I became famil-iar with them, and when there were so many together. I could feel them listening to me though. They were interested, but unmoved.

"Hey!" Rig said. "Get back here!"

I looked through the doorway to see Fine, our original comms slug, wriggling out of his grasp.

"Hey!" Fine shrieked at him. "Get back here!"

Snuggles disappeared from the crook of my arm and reappeared on the floor by Fine, and then picked him up and brought him to me.

"I'm trying to concentrate," I said.

"Sorry," Rig said. "I think I figured out which box is the hypercomm, but when I tried to test it he went crazy."

"Crazy!" Fine shouted.

Rig looked at him. Fine wasn't usually this agitated . . .

"Leave him," I said. "Try again in a minute when he calms down."

"Okay," Rig said. "Sure."

I reached down and petted Fine on his spines. This slug—in conjunction with Gill—had saved us on Sunreach. The least I could do was give him a little breathing room.

I reached toward the planet again, down toward the vibrations that were actually taynix. Many of them, beneath the surface, in caves we hadn't yet discovered. As I did I felt that texture again, the strange bumps in the nowhere—little ridges, all packed together in clumps below the surface of the planet. They weren't taynix—they didn't vibrate with energy. Instead they felt hollow, like little vessels waiting to be filled. The way they grouped together, thousands upon thousands of them, was familiar somehow. The shape of the gatherings. The pattern.

Scud. Those were the Defiant caverns. They were filled with thousands of *somethings*. They couldn't be delvers, could they? No, they were something else. Maybe—

Stars, were they *people*?

I focused on one little raised vessel, drawing close to it, examining it. It was . . . *thinking*. Its mother had set it here, and told it not to move until it was ready to apologize for hitting its brother. But it would never be ready to apologize, because its brother had really, really deserved it.

My mouth fell open. I wasn't supposed to be able to do that, was I? Find the minds of non-cytonics?

Listen to them?

"Juno," I said. "In your books, are there meditations for communicating with other people? People who don't have cytonic powers?"

"You communicate with them all the time," Juno said. "You use words."

"This is not the time to be pedantic!" I said. "Could your cytonics talk to other people mind-to-mind?"

Juno's little brow furrowed. "I have read that a few achieved it. But if there are meditations for that, I have not read them. As you are just learning, it seems like it might be wiser to try to stick to the more general skills, and not rely on those only a few were ever able to achieve."

That did seem wiser. And I hadn't *communicated* with that little kid, only listened to his thoughts. That could *also* be useful—scud, the espionage possibilities were endless.

Now though, we had cities under attack on Evershore and a room full of empty taynix boxes. I searched for the slugs in the areas around the caverns. I felt the vibrations, concentrated in the caverns away from people. Minds that were smaller yet *louder*, projecting themselves into the nowhere instead of remaining self-contained.

I could figure out what to do with the rest of it later. For now I needed to focus on the taynix. I didn't know how many of them would come to me—they hadn't jumped on it the first time I asked, but maybe I could convince them.

We need your help, I said. *Please.*

Someone else reached for me, so near that I startled. Another cytonic mind joined my plea, and with it came an image.

Mushrooms. Caviar. Friends. Family. *Danger*. The fear was so strong, though the mind that sent it was small. I saw all of us crowded together on Sunreach, holding on to each other while Gill took us home.

Help. It wasn't a word so much as a feeling.

Fine was helping me. He was making a *case* for me, though not in so many words. Telling the other taynix he was happy here. That he liked us, that we treated him well and were good to him, that he *cared* about us.

We care about you too, I thought at him. FM cared most of all. I knew she thought I was heartless sometimes, but I didn't want anything terrible to happen to them if I could prevent it.

I didn't want anything terrible to happen to *anyone.*

Maybe when I was speaking to the taynix I should focus less on the words. Everything was translated to thoughts through the nowhere anyway—that was how Alanik and I could understand each other.

I focused on the idea of home—my home, and what it meant to me. The danger the Superiority posed to this planet we all shared. The power we had to stop it, but only with *help.*

It was more hope than I truly felt, but it was the message they needed and it wasn't a lie. It was simply a different way to tell the story.

Do better than we did.

"Scud!" Rig shouted, and I opened my eyes as hundreds of taynix all appeared in the corridor at once. They spilled into the various control rooms, all wriggling on top of one another. They were bunched together in groups, taynix of many colors all rolling and sliding away from the hyperslugs they'd been huddled around.

The ones who could hyperjump had answered me, and they'd brought friends.

There were so *many* of them. Commslugs, and mindblade slugs, and the hyperslugs too, of course. Also the blue and green kind we'd found on Wandering Leaf, the ones that powered inhibitors.

It made sense there were some on Detritus—there had to be a few somewhere, enabling our cytonic inhibitor.

But there were more still. Wrinkled grey ones with black and white spines, several with spines that faded between the many colors of the rainbow, and a strange set of mostly blackish ones that shone an iridescent blue under the control room lights. Some of the slugs were significantly smaller than the others, teal colored with pink spines. Were those babies, or a smaller variety?

The other humans and I all stared at the slugs dumbly. While we did, Boomslug, Fine, and Snuggles jumped into action. Snuggles teleported Boomslug right into the middle of the taynix. Snuggles started touching slugs and hyperjumping them into the control rooms, gathering them in front of the boxes, while Boomslug herded groups of them together with the light touch of a blunt mindblade. The other slugs slithered out of his way, heading in the directions he sent them. Through the nowhere I could feel Fine sending them all feelings and images. Danger. Help. Hurry.

"Um," Rig said. "I know I asked you for more slugs, but I really don't know which boxes to put them in. I have no idea what some of these slugs would *do*, even if we did figure out where to put them."

"Do your best," I said. "They came to help, and we need all the help we can get."

16

Rig and the engineers started working on where to put the slugs. We'd only need a few to move our platforms, but I wasn't going to complain about having access to extras. Meanwhile, I reached toward Evershore to contact Alanik.

Report? I asked her.

We're managing, Alanik said. *But there were a lot of ships in that last carrier. I don't think we can handle another without reinforcements. Will Rig be able to move the platforms?*

We've summoned help, I said, watching the slugs writhing about in the control rooms. *But it's going to take some time. I can send over another few flights, but I'm worried that the enemy is going to keep coming. Do you think Rinakin would send some of your people to help?*

I can make a case for it, Alanik said. *It would be best if I went in person.*

Ask Arturo if he can spare you, I said. *I'll send in reinforcements as soon as I can.*

Will do, Alanik said.

Help! a voice said. It came from near Alanik, somewhere on Evershore—the voices I'd heard before. *Help!*

I didn't have time to help voices I didn't know. Enough corporeal people were in danger.

We know, the voices said. *We want to help!*

Who are you? I asked, but the voices faded again.

I didn't have time to figure out where they were coming from. Gran-Gran had heard voices calling for help before she'd had what appeared to be a hyperjumping accident. I still couldn't rule out a Superiority trap, so I needed to focus on the help I knew I could trust.

I used my radio to put in a call to Command, asking them to get another three flights in the air. They agreed immediately—apparently Stoff hadn't rethought the length of the rope he'd given me to hang myself with. The other flights had all been put on alert, so it wouldn't take long for them to get in their ships, but I couldn't return to Evershore without them.

While I was still here—

"Rig," I said. "I don't want to scare you, but I'm going to try something."

Rig poked his head out of the command room. "Something more scary than dumping hundreds of unknown taynix at our feet?"

"Potentially," I said. "Or maybe nothing will happen. I don't know."

"So either you're going to scare me or nothing will happen."

"Right," I said. "You can keep working. I just wanted to warn you."

"About potentially nothing."

Stars, I shouldn't have said anything. It would have taken less time. "Exactly. Sorry, I didn't mean to interrupt."

Rig gave me a very confused look and went back to examining the taynix boxes. I closed my eyes and focused on the now-overwhelming cytonic resonance all around me. The times I'd felt the strange ridges, I'd been listening to the nowhere the way Gran-Gran taught me.

"Can I assist you, shadow-walker?" Juno asked.

It was only then that I realized that Juno hadn't remarked on the sudden arrival of a horde of gastropods, most of them bigger than he was. He didn't seem shocked by much of anything, taking it all in quietly through that eye slit in his armor.

"I don't know," I said. "I'm trying that advanced thing you said wasn't wise."

"You've done a great many things I thought were unwise," Juno said. "But it seems to be working for you so far."

I hoped the trend continued. I focused on the vibrations. I located Boomslug and Snuggles, and they seemed to sense that I was reaching for them, because they returned to my shoulders. They each had their own type of hum that was distinct, the way every human has a slightly different voice. It was almost like FM's music, harmonious in its own subtle way.

I stretched my mind, trying to push past the vibrations, and searched for those ridges again, the ones that were so still and quiet. I gripped the edge of the bench in frustration—I'd done it when I wasn't meaning to. I should be able to do it on purpose.

I remembered what Alanik had told me back on ReDawn. *Try, Jorgen,* she'd said. *Stop focusing so much on what you aren't able to do, and try.*

"Hey, Juno?" I said. "Can you read me one of those meditations again?"

"Of course," Juno said. "Breathe in, breathe out . . ."

I did that all day, every day of my life, but this time I tried to really focus on it. I tried to let go of everything I wished I could do, all the ways I could solve our problems if I were only better, stronger, smarter.

Do better than we did, my mother said.

For the moment I tried to let go of whether I could. I listened to the slugs, to their vibrations, to their hums.

"See yourself walking along a beach," Juno said. "With each breath, the waves wash in, and the waves wash out."

I tried to hear the ocean, to really be there, be present and let go of the frustration of everything I couldn't yet do.

In order to achieve control, Juno had said, *you must first accept that you have none.*

I have none, I told myself. And for the first time, instead of terror and frustration accompanying that thought, I felt relief.

"Feel the wind on your skin," Juno said. "The heat of the sun as it burns down from above."

"Above!" Snuggles said.

And then, all at once, the ridges appeared around me. Not nearly so many as I'd felt down beneath the surface. Only half a dozen moving about the platform. Minds, so quiet but no less real. I approached the one in the room nearest me and listened. This mind was working through a complex calculation, trying to figure out which of the wires from the taynix boxes went into which of the many holoprojectors labeled along the wall. *Why couldn't someone have labeled these effectively?* they were thinking. *Did the labels disintegrate maybe? Surely they had to have—*

Rig? I asked.

The thought stuttered to a stop.

Jorgen? Rig said. *Are you* inside *my mind?*

Apparently, I said.

Okay, yeah, Rig said. *This is deeply terrifying.* He paused. *Is this what it's like for you and Alanik all the time?*

I laughed and let the link drop. Rig appeared in the doorway. "Jorgen," he said. "What the scud did you do?"

"I think I did something really advanced," I said. "Something Juno didn't think I should try."

"Hmph," Juno said. "I never said you *shouldn't* do it. I only said I thought there were better exercises to try first."

This one, though, seemed like it could be an asset at the moment.

I radioed Command. "How are those flights coming?"

"They're in the air," the Command staffer replied. "Working on the light-lance connections before they give the go-ahead to hyper-jump."

"Excellent."

I closed my eyes again, trying to see if I could still find the ridges. They were faint but they were there, easier to recall now that I'd brought them up once.

Help! A faint whisper, calling to me through the nowhere. *Help us*, the voices said again. *We want to help.*

I sighed. I had no idea where those voices were coming from, much less if I should respond—

Listen, boy, another voice said.

Scud. That was—*Gran-Gran?*

She didn't answer, but an image formed in my mind, clear as anything.

A picture of the portal in the library, the strange wall with the lines, the gateway into the nowhere.

Gran-Gran, I said. *What happened when you appeared near the portal? Where are you?*

She didn't—or couldn't—answer.

"Jerkface," Steadman from Command said over my radio. "The flights are ready for hyperjump."

"Good," I said. *Rig, how much longer do you think it will take you to figure out if we can move the platforms?*

We're going to need time, Rig said. *I can't tell you how much, but I can keep you posted.*

And he could do it without a hypercomm now.

Okay, I said. *I'll check in.*

I put a hand on Juno's platform, and instructed Snuggles to take us to the beach on Evershore near the wreckage of my starfighter. We passed beneath the eyes, and then the sand of Evershore formed beneath my feet, the roaring of the ocean loud in my ears.

I reached toward Platform Prime, finding the taynix belonging to those flights. Corgi was among them, I thought, though I couldn't remember the rest of their names. FM would know. She knew them all.

I gave the taynix a clear image of Snuggles. And a moment later three flights of ships—light-lanced together in three distinct groups—appeared over the sand, some of them extending out over the waves.

"Amphi," I said over my radio, "I brought backup."

"Platforms?"

"Not yet," I said. "Three flights of ships. Can you get them up to speed?"

"Copy, Jerkface," Arturo said.

My proximity sensors had been busted when the cytonic slashed their mindblades through my dash. I looked up at the dark sky, trying to read what was going on with the battle.

Scud, there were a lot of ships up there. Our side seemed to be holding their own, but we needed the backup badly.

Alanik, I said, *status?*

Rinakin is sending ships to support us. He says the kitsen alliance is worth the risk. I told him you were going to bring platforms from Detritus. Did I lie to him?

Rig is working on it, I said. *Can you come support Arturo?*

I'm on my way, Alanik said. *I'll come back for the flights after they've had a few minutes to prepare.*

Good, I said. *Keep me updated.*

"Should we have brought you a new ship?" Juno asked.

"I'll get one later," I said. "Right now I need to have a look at that portal in your library."

17

"The portal?" Juno said. "This seems like an odd time—"

"I know," I said. "But I think it's important." My mindblades could help in the battle, but we needed more than that. We needed Cobb's command expertise. We had to get him back in charge of this battle, of the war.

The medtechs would be crowded into the library with Gran-Gran and Cobb, and I didn't want Snuggles to accidentally land us on top of one of the stretchers. Instead I put a hand on Juno's platform and had Snuggles hyperjump us to a foothold I could see at the top of the cliffs. From this vantage I could see the staircase that led to the library, and I had Snuggles make a second jump to land us outside the domed doors.

I reached down below my knees for the handle, but found the door locked.

I knocked, and there was a scuffling inside.

A moment later the door cracked open. On the other side Cuna stooped down, looking out at us, and then opened the door the rest of the way. "I didn't think that Winzik would knock," they said. "But one can never be sure."

"Not Winzik," I said, crawling into the room.

Kel and Winnow knelt between the long tables, which had been scooted together so the stretchers holding Cobb and Gran-Gran could rest on top. Several of the kitsen doctors sat on the stretchers, helping the medtechs monitor Cobb and Gran-Gran, while their transport pilot, callsign: Zing, listened to the radio that was perched on a glass case filled with very small books. I could hear Arturo giving orders to the new flights. Hopefully the additional ships would help us hold out a while longer while Rig figured out the platform.

"How are they doing?" I asked Winnow.

"Stable," she said. "You were right—moving them didn't cause them to deteriorate this time. It's possible we could put them in a ship now."

"I don't want to move them while we're under attack," I said. "And I don't think it's the time that made the difference. I think it was the direction. Farther from that." I indicated the wall, and the medtechs only looked more confused.

"What is that?" Cuna asked.

"A portal to the nowhere," I said. "I think."

I was becoming increasingly sure that Gran-Gran—or her spirit? her soul?—was behind this wall. I hoped Cobb was there with her, that non-cytonics could even exist in that strange place. We'd learned from the datanets that the Superiority had mines in the nowhere and ran entire operations to get acclivity stone. They probably used people who weren't cytonic on those missions.

Of course, those people probably had *bodies*, so it wasn't a perfect comparison. Still, I suspected the kitsen cytonics were lost in there too. I didn't know how they could have survived all this time, but it seemed likely those were the voices I was hearing.

I looked up at the portal, at the strange mass of interconnected lines running all over the wall. I could feel the vibrations of the nowhere, but not Gran-Gran's distinct signature.

"Quiet, please," Juno said to the others. "The shadow-walker must concentrate."

Zing turned off the radio, and everyone else was silent. That was helpful, if a little presumptuous of Juno. Usually *he* was the one chattering and distracting me.

I considered the portal. Spensa said if I got too close I might fall in. There was a draw to that—the idea that if I got lost in the nowhere I could see Spensa again. But I had no idea if I would be able to find her, and I couldn't leave while Evershore was in peril, my friends in jeopardy.

Instead I reached out to the wall with my mind, inspecting it.

Are you there? I asked.

The answer was immediate. *We're here. We want to help.*

The kitsen cytonics had been gone for centuries, Juno said. Cytonic powers were genetic, so if the kitsen cytonics had all been lost somehow, it made sense no more had been born. Though . . . Spensa had said she thought living near a portal could change some people into cytonics; why hadn't that happened to any of the lorekeepers?

An image struck me. Voices calling out of the portal for years and years, but there was no one left on the other side who could hear. Eventually they stopped calling.

Stars, was I imagining that? Or . . . *reading* it somehow? I needed to reach them, but I didn't want to get lost in there. If I could find Spensa, could she find them in the nowhere and help me somehow? Together maybe we could find a way to get them all out at once.

I reached across the nowhere, searching for Spensa. I'd found her before, even if our connection was strange and distant.

Something reached back. It was another image of Spensa cleaning a piece of a ship, a different one from the last time. I'd been too distracted before to think about the significance of that. We had ground crews for that, but Spin didn't have those in the nowhere. Did she have a ship? I thought she'd lost M-Bot on Starsight, and that was how the Superiority got hold of his holographic projector.

The image was hazy, but the *feeling* that went with it was unmistakable. Loneliness. Loss. A fog of forgetfulness, like the stupor of coming out of an illness and not really being sure how many days had passed. It was so un-Spensa-like that it floored me.

When I talked to Spensa before, she was right there, face-to-face with me. This was so much more distant, almost like a memory.

As if it came from someone else, someone watching her from the outside.

Who is this? I asked.

I felt a tingle of . . . amusement maybe? And then an image came into my mind of a hyperslug sitting on the control panel of my starfighter. "Jerkface!" it cried at me.

Doomslug? I asked.

The tingle of amusement grew stronger.

Huh. I'd apparently found Doomslug in the nowhere. It made sense that she'd left with Spensa, but the fact that I could contact her and not Spensa herself was more than a little concerning.

Is Spensa okay? I asked.

The amusement faded, replaced by a sadness, a loneliness.

Saints. *What can I do?* I asked.

A trickle of doubt. Doomslug didn't know.

I sent a picture of the portal in front of me. *Do you know how to open it?* I asked her.

I heard nothing in response, except maybe a tiny bit of confusion. Either she didn't understand, or she didn't know.

"Are you learning anything from staring at the portal?" Juno asked. "I don't mean to interrupt a shadow-walker at work, but—"

"Oh," I said, shaking myself. "I was listening."

"To the silence?" Winnow asked.

"No," I said. "To a taynix. But I don't think she's going to help us here." Though if I could figure out how to open the portal, I still might be able to use it to get Spensa and Doomslug home.

"Did you want to try another meditation?" Juno asked.

"Do you have any meditations for traveling to the nowhere?" I asked.

"There are many meditations for hyperjumps," Juno said. "I could select one of my favorites."

Learning to hyperjump without a taynix would be useful, but

it wasn't what I was after here. "Hyperjumping is moving *through* the nowhere," I said. "I need to be able to move *into* it. And ideally back out again." That was the important part, really.

Juno paused. " 'In and back out again' sounds indistinguishable from 'through.' "

I blinked at him. I supposed it did. "When we hyperjump, we pass beneath the eyes, but there's no one else there. This time I want to *stop* while I'm in there and help my people escape—and the kitsen cytonics too."

Cuna and the medtechs all looked at each other. The medtechs, at least, seemed to think I had lost my mind. I was the scudding commander of this battle, and here I was staring at walls and claiming to hear things while everyone else was fighting. I would have thought the same thing in their place, and maybe they were right. If anyone got hurt up there while I was chasing shadows, it would be my fault. I'd never forgive myself.

"You really believe that our shadow-walkers still live, trapped on the other side of this portal."

"Yes," I said.

Help us, they called.

I picked up Snuggles, and she nuzzled my wrist.

Juno steered his platform over to the glass case filled with books and opened it, extracting a volume. The thing was as thick as three of my fingers together, but no larger than the palm of my hand. It still looked enormous in Juno's paws. "Let me find one of those meditations."

I wasn't sure a meditation was what I needed, not for this. Instead I took a step closer to the portal.

"Shadow-walker?" Juno said. "Are you sure you wish to get closer? If you truly believe it to be a portal into the nowhere—"

"Spensa said a cytonic could fall through it," I said. "And maybe that's what happened to your people long ago. But if I don't at least try to interact with it, how can I reach them?"

I walked between the stretchers holding Gran-Gran and Cobb

and moved up to the portal, careful not to step on any of the tiny tables or chairs or carts covered in books. I walked within arm's length of the portal and examined it.

I *could* feel them. Kitsen, many of them. I felt their sorrow and their frustration, trapped behind the portal. Generations of them, some born behind the portal and unable to ever leave. Some had died, while others had learned to extend their lives. They'd been sucked in and trapped, leaving no one on the other side who could hear them, their planet devoid of cytonics for centuries.

Until now, one of them whispered. I could feel their hope, and their disbelief.

And then suddenly a familiar voice filled my mind. *It's about scudding time you listened*, Spensa's grandmother said. *I am too old to be trapped in here for eternity with gerbils, and too set in my ways to live to be two hundred, even if I could figure out what in the stars they're talking about.*

Scud. *Gran-Gran*, I said. *Are you in there? We found your body and Cobb's. How did you—*

I was trying to follow the voices, Gran-Gran said. *And I followed them all right. Right into the same scudding trap. Never listen to a rodent who asks for your help. Let that be a lesson.*

I supposed I had volunteered to help rodents, but I didn't regret it.

Is Cobb okay? I asked.

He's here, Gran-Gran said. *Growing grumpier by the hour. The kitsen say they're not sure our bodies could have survived out there. They say we might be dead.*

You're not dead, I said. *But* why *did this happen?*

I couldn't figure out how to pinpoint a location to hyperjump to, Gran-Gran said. *But I could hear the voices calling to me. So I tried to go to them instead.*

Oh, stars. *I haven't been able to figure out how to do that either*, I said. *It doesn't make sense when Alanik describes it. That was clever, trying to move toward the voices instead.*

It would have been, Gran-Gran said. *Except when we got here, our bodies were gone.*

They're trapped outside the portal, I said. This was why we had to hyperjump to places we knew, or places we could see. Gran-Gran had tried to go somewhere unfamiliar, somewhere she couldn't physically hyperjump to—and it had only partially worked. *I think trying to hyperjump through the portal severed your soul in half.*

Sounds like the sort of thing that could kill a person, Gran-Gran said.

That it did, though it hadn't killed them yet. But scud, how long could they survive like this, half in and half out of the nowhere? I wouldn't have thought such a thing was possible.

I could see the other side of the portal in my mind now. It looked like Evershore, a sandy island in an ocean of nothing. It looked . . . oddly corporeal for a place called the nowhere.

I understood. "They accidentally closed the door behind them," I said. "They were trapped, with no one left on this side to let them through." They'd remained there, huddled together, for so many years.

Scud. That was incredible. The *knowledge* these kitsen must have.

Through the portal, I could feel the despair of the kitsen as their kinsmen died, their fear that they would all perish behind the portal, that their long life would run out, that they didn't have enough people to breed and sustain their numbers. That the line of kitsen cytonics would come to an end, long after the rest of their people had supposed it had. They'd been searching for help for so long, and now they were weary. So weary. Gran-Gran was among them, and they were afraid her end would come even faster, separated from her body as she was.

Juno had piled several books onto his platform, so many that he barely fit in the center in his suit of power armor. He held one of the new books open in his gauntleted paws, floating over to me.

"The waves of the ocean wash upon you," Juno said.

"I thought you didn't have a meditation for this," I said.

"I don't," he said. "But the last one seemed to help you even though it was not specific. This is a meditation for the ages. One that is meant to sharpen your mind and your focus, to bring out your best potential. I don't have the answer for you, but you may find the answer for yourself."

Huh.

"Should I go on?" Juno asked.

I didn't see what it could hurt. "Yes," I said.

"The waves of the ocean wash upon you, but they have no power to drag you away. You are one with the waves, and you are one with yourself. You are eternal, relentless as the rising sun. Your heart beats with the rhythm of the stars."

I still wasn't relaxed—when was the last scudding time I had been relaxed?—but I could hear it, the rhythm Juno was talking about. The vibration of the stars. The heartbeat of the universe. I could hear it in the taynix, and in the battle above. I could feel it from the portal, brimming with power.

I felt a nudge at the edge of my mind. It was that image of Spensa again, lost and alone. No, not alone. Doomslug was with her, and M-Bot, though I didn't know how that worked if M-Bot's ship had been dismantled by the Superiority. I couldn't help Spensa, couldn't reach her. I didn't know how to do anything except—

Take care of her, I said to Doomslug.

And then something shifted, and Doomslug teased a thread out of Spensa's thoughts and passed it on to me, clear and powerful as anything.

Stars, it was her memory of *me*. She was forgetting herself, her friends, her family, everything, but she still remembered *me*. She *cared* about me, deeply and with a ferocity that was totally and uniquely Spin.

That made me incredibly lucky. More so than I'd ever be able to express.

I felt a swell of agreement from Doomslug; she would take care of Spensa. But it was accompanied by gratitude that I already was.

Thank you, I said. I tried to hold on to that snatch of memory, to cling to what little I had left of Spensa, not sure if I'd ever see her again. But it was slipping away along with Doomslug, back into the nowhere.

Doomslug faded, but the portal remained, pulsing with power, with a rhythm all its own—a rhythm that felt familiar somehow, like a melody I'd heard before.

"You yield to the universe," Juno went on, though I'd missed some of what he said, "not because of its power, but because of your wisdom. You yield power over all things, and in doing so become one with the stars—"

I felt the impenetrability of the portal, the lock that kept me from pushing through. I didn't know if I could fall through, or if it prevented entry from both sides.

I couldn't open the portal, I realized, because I lacked the key. Similar to the impression that let us use our powers inside a cytonic inhibitor, there was some kind of cytonic vibration that would open the portal, letting the kitsen pass through.

"Juno," I said. "Do your people have any kind of recordings from the days before the kitsen cytonics disappeared? Some kind of database, or digital records?"

"We do not," Juno said. "We lost much when we were colonized, and more in the War of Liberation."

Stars. I didn't even know if such a recording had ever existed. The kitsen had become stuck, after all. They might never have been fully capable of traveling in and out. I didn't know how to get in and out of a portal, and since Alanik hadn't recognized it, she wouldn't know either. She hadn't even been able to *hear* the kitsen.

I could feel the sense of failure pushing in around the edges, the sense that I never had enough to give, never had the right pieces at the right moments to really come through for the people I cared about. FM was right though. Sometimes I did. But the failures loomed so much larger than the successes that it was easy to forget.

"You are completely relaxed," Juno said.

I *tried* to relax. I didn't need to solve all the problems on my own. I was supposed to lean on the people around me for help, and while no one on this side of the portal had the information I needed . . .

I want to help you, I said. *But I don't know how to open this portal.*

I felt despair from the other side. Weariness. The burden of centuries spent watching, wondering, hoping and then losing hope, and struggling to find it again and again. A picture formed in my mind—a wrinkled kitsen watching her friends and loved ones die, knowing others were dying on the other side of the portal as time passed, knowing she would never see them again. The occasional glimpse of a cytonic nearby—probably Superiority ships visiting the planet. But they never heard, and they never came to help.

Then a voice, far away. A woman who had spent her lifetime listening finally heard them.

And now she was trapped somehow, strangely separated from her body. Regret, a sense that reaching out was selfish, because she and Cobb had now suffered their same fate.

"The stars shine upon you, an ancient light in the darkness," Juno continued. "The darkness widens to swallow them, but they shine endlessly on."

We're going to get you out, I said. It was a promise I didn't know I could keep, more a message of determination than of certainty. *How did you get* in *there?*

What followed wasn't words so much as images. A summit. A room full of kitsen, each bringing their unique talents, knowledge, and abilities. They meditated together, sharing their knowledge, their scribes writing furiously to contain it all.

They toyed with the threads of the universe, the barrier between our world and the nowhere. I could feel the memories now, not only from the old kitsen but embedded in the portal itself, as if it were *made* of experiences.

Together the kitsen had picked at the boundary, separated the threads. They'd meant only to figure out how to visit that realm for a time, the way the legends said their people did when they first met humans. But instead they opened the gaping maw of nothingness and it swallowed them all, along with a large chunk of their world.

Stars, the chasm this library was built in. It was formed when the kitsen left the somewhere, taking the stone of the cliffs *with* them.

"You look up at their lights," Juno said, "letting their vibrations wash over you. You too are eternal like the stars, a piece of the endless *something* that makes space for the *nothing*, but never yields to it."

I didn't know what that meant, but I tried not to focus too hard on it. I concentrated instead on the threads that made up the border, infused with memory, vibrating so strongly as if the nowhere wanted to burst out of the portal. I didn't want it to swallow Dreamspring, didn't want to open the entire thing.

Just enough for those trapped on the other side to come through.

I could feel Gran-Gran listening, noticing what I was doing as I began to manipulate the threads. The way Alanik described the boundary—it was like listening to a description of an ocean when I was young. I never really understood until I saw it for myself. But I could *feel* the boundary between the realms. I might not be able to carry myself through, but here I had power.

I tried to give you the story you needed, Gran-Gran said. *I told you to imagine yourself flying among the stars.*

I remembered Gran-Gran's story, about how disobeying orders could be the right thing to do.

Wait until you hear what I've done, I said.

I can see it, she said. *I tried to give you the story you needed, but perhaps you've found your own story after all.*

Had I? I could feel the way the threads of the boundary wove together, sealing the portal. I didn't know how to move them, but I focused on them the way I had the birds. That image wasn't quite right for this, so I tried vines all woven together, creating a wall between us and them. I didn't want to cut the vines down, only move a few aside, forming a small area where the kitsen could return, where Gran-Gran and Cobb could slip through.

"You are the light and the darkness," Juno said. "You are the place where the two worlds meet. The intersection of what is, and what could be."

Spensa flies among the stars, Gran-Gran said. *But you build things up from the ground. She is a warrior, and you are a defender. It's a different kind of story.*

I can't protect them all, I said.

You can't, Gran-Gran said. *We all have our own burdens, even if we carry them differently.*

I thought about the way I'd lost it in the senate meeting. *I'm not carrying mine well*, I said.

Ah, Gran-Gran said. *Well, you're not alone in that.*

I hated it. I wanted to get it right, to get everything right. But maybe sometimes there *was* no right. There was only the best I could do.

I pictured the vines and touched them each in turn, trying to see which would shift and which held fast. I was able to bring one to the side, creating the smallest part in the jungle of them, but there were more vines on the other side, ones I couldn't reach.

I couldn't do this alone. I needed help.

I reached out to the old kitsen on the other side of the portal, trying to show her what I saw. Her mind seemed to receive it, as if she also knew the barrier well, had been over these same vines thousands of times. I showed her the ones I could move, and I felt her study them.

And then the ones on the other side began to shift.

I focused on the vines I could control, feeling the vibrations, holding fast the ones that supported the entire structure while manipulating those that only supported tiny bits of it.

"You are completely relaxed," Juno said.

I breathed in rhythm with the vibrations. I wasn't relaxed, but I was calm. I was at peace. I *was* the power.

And then all at once, the smooth surface of the portal cracked open, and a kitsen hobbled through. Her fur was greying and her skin was so wrinkled it folded down over her eyes. She pushed it back and looked up at us.

And then a dozen more followed.

18

More kitsen crowded into the area in front of the portal, all blinking at each other and at us. Several of them hummed with a cytonic vibration, though some of the younger-looking ones didn't. Non-cytonics who'd been born on the other side of the portal, who'd lived their whole lives there.

Juno nearly fell off his platform. He bumped his stack of books and had to snatch at them to keep them from sliding over the edge. He started fumbling through his book, like perhaps he needed a meditation to calm himself.

"Human!" the one with the wrinkled skin said to me. "Are you the one who released us?"

"Yes," I said. "I can't believe . . . I can't believe that worked."

I looked down at Cobb and Gran-Gran, but they lay still with their eyes closed. Scud, had it *not* worked for them?

No. Wait. I could feel something, a signature emanating from Gran-Gran.

That had to mean . . .

Cobb stirred, and then he coughed. Kel bent over the screen that showed his vitals.

"Is he okay?" I asked.

"He's improving," Kel said.

"Will he wake up?"

"I don't know. But if he does, he'll be in no condition to help. We should get them home to Detritus."

Stars. Of course he wouldn't be in any condition to lead. He'd spent the last *two days* with his mind disconnected from his body.

A loud boom sounded through the walls of the library, as if the stone above us had been struck—probably by a falling starfighter.

Zing turned the radio back on, and the airwaves were a mess of talking.

I didn't want to take the time to sort that out. *Alanik*, I said, *how's it going with those reinforcements?*

The UrDail flights have joined the battle, she said. *What are you doing down there?*

Found us some more backup, I said. Cuna had bent down to the level of some of the kitsen cytonics and was conversing with them quietly. I hoped to all the stars in the sky they weren't calling them "lesser."

That's good, because we need help.

Scud. *Sitrep?*

Three more carrier ships. No planetary weapons yet, but Arturo is worried. Something about a bomb.

Oh no. *What bomb?*

He said he spotted a ship with a strange flight pattern.

My whole body went cold. I focused, widening my reach—

And I found the impressions again, the minds of the pilots, all flying around in what felt like disarray.

No, there was a method to it. Arturo had them divided into flanking groups and the flights were working together, though I couldn't pinpoint the strategy at a glance. If Arturo had seen what I thought he'd seen, I didn't have time to consider it. I found his mind flying near Alanik. As I drew closer I could feel his focus, his determination.

And his *terror*. He didn't know where I was, wasn't sure what they should do. He spotted that ship again, moving slowly in a familiar pattern he'd never wanted to see again—I could see it in his mind. We'd fought a lot of those ships in our days as cadets, though we hadn't seen one since we'd driven the Krell away from the surface of Detritus.

It looked like a lifebuster.

Amphi? I said.

I felt Arturo startle.

Jerkface? he said. *Are you in my scudding head?*

Apparently, I said. *You saw a lifebuster?*

Yeah. It's moving slowly like they do, but it's headed toward Dreamspring. Kimmalyn and Nedd are keeping an eye on it.

I closed my eyes. A bomb of that size could take out the whole island, maybe more. Such an impact would have been big enough to cave in the caverns below the surface of Detritus—I didn't want to see what it would do to the kitsen city, how far the devastation would reach.

We'd have to be very careful taking that down.

When I opened my eyes again, several of the kitsen cytonics had disappeared and the others were moving toward the exit. Juno had landed his platform and was powering up some of the floating disks that would let them reach the top library shelves, and the kitsen cytonics were boarding them.

They were going to help, but if we let a bomb hit the city that wouldn't be enough to stop it.

I turned to the medtechs and Cuna. "Stay here," I said. "Get Cobb on the radio the *minute* he's awake."

"Yes, sir," Kel and Winnow said. They didn't tell me again that he needed more rest. We all needed a lot of things we weren't getting tonight. Survival took priority.

Juno climbed back onto his platform and hovered up to my shoulder.

"You could stay here," I said. "It would be safer."

"You are the Restorer of Lost Souls," Juno said solemnly. "He Who Hearkens unto Silent Voices, Opener of Locked Doors. Where you go, I will go, shadow-walker." He still had his platform piled high with books, and I wanted to tell him I didn't think those would be helpful to bring, but they'd done all right for us so far.

"Okay," I said. "Let's go." I put a hand on Juno's platform and asked Snuggles to take us to my ship on the beach. I wanted to get a better picture of what was happening.

We appeared next to the wreckage of my starship, and I tried not to focus on the body that must still be lying on the sand somewhere behind me. Several kitsen ships flew down the beach, fleeing the city. None of them looked like fighters, and one was nothing more than a water tank bolted to a floating pedestal. It didn't move as fast as the others, but it was carrying five kitsen all packed together inside. If the bomb hit, I hoped they could get far enough away, but I wasn't sure there was any place far enough, not on this island.

The sky above the city was full of ships—Superiority, human, UrDail, and kitsen. I could feel some of the kitsen cytonics—those who could hyperjump—already moving around in the gunships above, and one shot forth a flurry of mindblades, cutting an enemy fighter to pieces. Another disappeared and then reappeared on the other side of the battlefield, catching an enemy ship with its shield down in a barrage of destructor fire. The wreckage fell from the sky.

This was good. The contributions of the kitsen cytonics would give my flight some time to deal with the lifebuster without losing ground to the Superiority. I wanted to return to Detritus for a ship, but every second counted. I leaned against the damaged fuselage as I reached out to Arturo again. *How far out is that ship?*

Too close, Arturo said. *Hard to say without Command to run numbers, but if we bring it down I can't guarantee it won't destroy the city.*

It must not have reached optimal placement yet, because they were still bringing it closer before detonating. I had no idea how much time we had, but if we couldn't shoot the ship down without the risk of destroying Dreamspring, we had better work fast.

Have Nedder engage his IMP, I told him. *Then Quirk can shoot the ship down and someone can grab the bomb with a light-lance. The safest place to take it will be out of the atmosphere.*

Spensa had managed to carry one off once and survive, but it was dangerous. If the bomb was on a timer and that person didn't get out before it exploded, they'd be gone.

Arturo didn't like that idea. He knew that was what had to be done, he was just terrified to do it. *I'll take the bomb,* he said.

No, I told him. *You're in command. You have to give it to someone else.*

The hell I do, Arturo said. *If someone needs to risk their life like that, I'll do it.*

No, I told him. *You won't. That's an order.*

Arturo cussed me out, and I understood. It was terrible telling your friends they had to be the ones to do it. Any of them would though. In a heartbeat.

Have Alanik carry the bomb, I said. *She doesn't have to use a hyperdrive to get out. Might save her the half second of communication time.*

Scud, Arturo hated that even more. He was . . . oh, he was *attached* to Alanik. Nothing was going on between them yet, but he hoped for it.

I'm sorry, I told him. Spensa didn't need me to order her to get into trouble, but it hadn't been easy flying with her, knowing I might be the one to give her the order that got her killed. *I get it.*

I know you do, Arturo said. *I'll take care of it.*

I pulled back, away from Arturo's fear and pain. I tuned my handheld radio to our general channel—I wanted everyone to hear this next part, and that was the fastest way to talk to all of them at once.

"Kauri," I said, "do you copy?"

"Copy, Jerkface," Kauri said. "We've called in as many ships as we can. We have more, but they aren't fighters."

If we sent civilian ships, we'd be needlessly throwing away lives. "Are you in contact with your senate?"

"I am," she said. "They have taken shelter, but they have encouraged us to defend the planet. They fear if we surrender, the Superiority will destroy us anyway."

The ivory moonlight glinted off the shards of the canopy on my broken ship. "That's exactly what will happen," I said. "I want you to extend them an offer of evacuation. We can grant your leaders safe harbor. Detritus has a shield. It's protected. We could get your senate out. Their families. *Your* family. Maybe some civilians from Dreamspring. We will continue to fight here, but I don't know if we'll be able to save the city, and at least this way your government will survive. Some of your people will make it out."

We could fit a lot of kitsen on a human transport ship. We had the one we'd brought to carry Cobb and Gran-Gran. I could go get another or send someone else to get one. With a hyperdrive we might be able to get some of the kitsen out before the lifebuster arrived.

"I will send word to the senate of your offer," Kauri said. "Thank you for your generosity."

I believed her gratitude was genuine, but her voice sounded frightened. I didn't blame her.

"Tell them to hurry," I said. "I'll have a transport ship meet them at the senate meeting hall."

"Thank you," Kauri said.

I looked up at the sky again. Wreckage smashed against the cliff maybe half a klick from me. I thought it was UrDail, but I couldn't be sure.

"Jerkface?" Arturo said. "What can we do to support the evacuation?"

"I want FM and Sentry to land and orchestrate the evacuation effort," I said. "Can you spare them?"

"Yes," Arturo said.

"Good. FM, Sentry, get as many kitsen leaders on board the medical transport ship as you can. Alanik or I will jump them out as soon as the ship is full. We're going to need plenty of cover over Dreamspring while we evacuate. Everyone you can spare."

"I'll tell them," Arturo said.

"Are we planning to pull back?" FM asked.

"No," I said. "But if that bomb hits the island, I want to have saved as many people as possible."

"Copy, Jerkface," FM said. "We're on it."

I saw FM's and Sadie's ships soaring down out of the sky above the city to land near the senate building. If anyone would do their best to save literally everyone they could, it was FM.

I reached out. *Alanik,* I said. *Status?*

We're coming up on the bomb, she said. *Shield is down. Kimmalyn— she hit the ship!*

Alanik dropped off, probably swooping in with her light hook, and I reached out to the minds around her, finding Arturo.

Scud, his whole mind was lit up with fear. I watched through his eyes as Alanik caught the lifebuster with her light hook and disappeared, taking it up into the vacuum.

She's got it, Arturo said. He was wound tight, and I almost asked Juno to read him a meditation.

It wouldn't help. Not in a situation like this. I could feel the others, I realized. Kimmalyn, Nedd, T-Stall, Catnip—all of us holding our breath. They wouldn't relax until—

I felt Alanik emerge on the other side of the battlefield. *She's back,* I said.

The lifebuster flashed across the sky with its three distinct explosions. I felt profound relief, not only from Arturo but from all of us. We could do this now. We should still load that ship for evac just in case, but without that bomb—

Oh, *scud.*

I watched in horror as the Superiority ships began to scatter, spreading out away from the island. There were more carrier ships in the sky now, belching forth more fighters, but they were all fanning out, moving away from Dreamspring. What the hell were they doing?

They're spreading us thin, Arturo said. *They know they don't have to defeat us to win. We're protecting Dreamspring, so they're going to take their vengeance elsewhere.*

It would work, too. They outnumbered us. If we split up, we lost our position. If the battle spread everywhere, they could circle around and fire on Dreamspring while we were out trying to protect the other cities. There weren't enough of us. The damage would be immeasurable.

The Superiority didn't care who they hurt, as long as they got what they wanted. We'd escaped them too many times. Now they were going to teach us a lesson.

And the kitsen were going to pay the price.

19

Arturo had our flights concentrated over Dreamspring, focusing on the ships that remained here. But it wouldn't help the kitsen on the surrounding islands. Some of the kitsen cytonics had hyperjumped their ships after the enemy—I saw one with mindblades trying to take down a ship, another using what felt like concussion bolts to stun a flight of enemy starfighters. They were fighting valiantly, but there were so many of the enemy, and maybe more yet to arrive.

We weren't going to be able to save everyone.

I looked up at the sky, at the relatively fewer number of ships. This wasn't a good thing. The Superiority would destroy the outer islands and then return for Dreamspring when they were done. I couldn't stop it.

The words of Juno's mantra came into my mind again, although the kitsen was silent beside me.

In order to achieve control, you must first accept that you have none.

I wanted control though. I wanted to put a stop to everything terrible that was happening, to save my people, to rescue Spensa, to pull her out of the nowhere and have her with me again safe.

I wanted to go back and save my parents. They'd died because they'd made a desperate gambit in hopes that they could control our fate, make a better world for me, for all of us.

They failed. They couldn't control it. And neither could I.

I closed my eyes. In my mind, the Superiority ship exploded over and over.

Do better than we did.

We weren't though, were we? We were trying, but failing all the same.

"Boom," Boomslug said.

"Boom," I answered him.

A wave of helplessness washed over me. I couldn't stop what was coming. It would be like trying to stop a wave in the ocean. I couldn't stop it, but I could let it wash over me and I could remain standing after it passed.

My radio flashed. Arturo's private channel. "Amphi?" I said.

"Jerkface. What . . . what are we going to do?"

We needed more help, but at this point I wasn't sure what else we *could* do. Against any other enemy it made sense for us to withdraw, to hope that they would have mercy on the kitsen. But I was never going to count on the Superiority's mercy.

"Protect the city," I said. "Send Quirk and Nedder to Detritus for more transport ships. Ask Angel if she can bring in any UrDail transport ships to evacuate other cities. We need to get as many people as we can off this planet before the Superiority musters up another one of those planetary weapons."

"Copy," Arturo said. He sounded as hollow as I felt. We both knew what we were about to watch. It would be the worst atrocity either of us had ever seen.

The general channel flashed. "Jerkface?" FM said. "The kitsen are boarding the transport ship. Should we send them out?"

"Is the ship full?" I asked.

"It will be soon. But . . . we can see the closest island, off to the dawnward side." She'd picked up that term from Alanik, and it was helpful, I had to give the UrDail that. "The ships are firing on the island. Shouldn't we . . . *help* them?"

There was pain in her voice, not unlike Kauri's. FM had a gift for that—feeling what other people were feeling.

Today it might as well be a curse, but at least I'd been able to give her the job of saving the people we could.

"Take the ship out," I said. "I'm going to check on Rig. We'll try to save them, but . . . I don't . . ."

"It's okay," FM said. "I know you're doing your best."

That was what I was afraid of. That this was my best.

And it was never, ever good enough.

"Juno," I said, "I'm going to take you to safety."

Juno looked down at his platform, at the piles of books stacked at his feet. "I should have brought more," he said. "The books are digitized—the knowledge will not be lost, but these are the originals. It is a tragedy to lose them, but that's even more true of my kinsmen."

My throat closed up. All their knowledge. We needed that, and the Superiority would do their best to destroy it.

Stars.

In my mind, I reached for Detritus, searching for Rig. I felt his adrenaline before I'd even found him. He and his team were worn out trying to get the platform up and running, but they were still there doing the best they could.

Report? I asked him.

We've got lots of slugs in lots of boxes, Rig said. *And we* think *these rooms are connected to several platforms. That's the only reason we can see that you'd need so many. But Jorgen, we don't even know what some of these systems do.*

Alanik's words to me on ReDawn echoed in my mind: *Focus on what you have.* If we could get even a few of those platforms here, we might be able to protect more cities while we evacuated them. There were hundreds upon hundreds of kitsen cities. The death toll would still be horrible. But . . . it would be something.

I'm coming, I said. *Whatever you've got, we need to try it now.*

Okay, Rig said.

I looked up at the sky. I could see what FM was talking about now—the flashes of light over the water, the Superiority firing on that island. FM should be pulling the transport ship out, but that was one tiny group of kitsen among so many.

It was going to take a miracle to get us out of this. Spensa taught me never to count a miracle out, and I hoped that held true even if she wasn't here to work one for us this time.

"What are you going to do?" Juno asked. He stood with a book open, resting it on his forearm. In his paw, he held a small stick poised over the page.

A *pen*, I realized.

"What are *you* doing?" I asked.

"I'm making a record," Juno said. "An original account of the actions of a shadow-walker."

"No one's going to want to read about anything I've done," I said. I immediately realized it wasn't true. He might be chronicling the end of civilization on Evershore. That depended not on me, but on how far the Superiority wanted to take their vengeance.

"I have waited all my life to witness the deeds of a shadow-walker," Juno said. "And if this day is the last for my home, it will be my honor to record that it was not because your people left us to suffer alone."

Scud. Wouldn't we, though? We could evacuate *some* kitsen, but if we couldn't turn the battle in our favor I was going to have to pull my people out. I couldn't let them all die for nothing.

Do better than we did, my mother said.

I closed my eyes. I didn't know if I could, but I was going to keep trying until I knew the answer. I rested my hand on Juno's platform.

"Snuggles," I said, "take us to Drape."

We appeared in the room with the boxes and a lot fewer roaming slugs, most of which had been corralled into corners by the engineers.

Rig spun around from one of the control panels on the walls. "Jorgen," he said.

"FM is fine," I said. "She's working on the evacuation effort. But the Superiority is fanning out over the planet, bombing civilians." I didn't know how they justified this to themselves. I didn't know how they justified anything, but we had to put a stop to it. "We need to get these platforms over there. As many as we can move, as quickly as we can."

The hum of all the slugs around us was overwhelming, and it was difficult for me to pick them out one from another. I tried to focus on the hyperdrive slugs, but I couldn't because there were so many. I didn't want to give a blanket instruction to all of them, since we didn't know what many of them could do.

"Where's Fine?" I asked.

"Hypercomm box, I hope," Rig said. He moved down the row of boxes. "Over here."

I found Fine before he did—one of the few signatures I knew in this cacophony. *Fine,* I said. *Can you tell them to take* these *platforms to Evershore?* I showed him an image of the slugs he knew—Naga, Happy, Chubs, Whiskers—all flying around the planet, and then some of the platforms appearing in a ring beneath the clouds, where they could fire on enemy ships.

Go? Fine said to me.

Go, I responded.

He hesitated for a moment—conversing, I thought, with the other slugs. And then I felt us slip into the nowhere, the surface of it rippling around us like rings on a pond. We passed beneath the eyes—scud, this was working. We'd be able to support the flights, and at least reduce the damage the ships were able to do to the islands of Evershore.

As we reemerged, I looked out the control room window, expecting to see the stars above.

Instead I saw the planet itself, an enormous ball of water, punctuated by sand-colored islands. Scud. The platform was way too high up, and we were facing the opposite of the direction I'd expected. I could see the backside of several of the Superiority carrier ships. They might be in range of our hyperweapons, but—

One of the engineers swore. "Flightleader Weight," she said, "you're going to want to see this."

She indicated the proximity monitors, which showed the planet of Detritus and all the platforms moving around us—the entire belt of them.

They were *still there*.

Scud. The control room had worked, but it hadn't only moved some platforms. It had moved the whole damn *planet*.

Go, I heard Fine say through the nowhere.

And all around me, the nowhere began to ripple, tear, and explode.

20

Bits of the nowhere ripped apart, exploding outward toward nearby Superiority carrier ships. Scud, there were more of them. It was kind of gratifying, seeing how much force Winzik felt he had to bring in order to take us down.

But he hadn't done it yet. Hyperweapons I didn't know we had erupted from the surfaces of the platforms, ripping up enemy ships. Ships swarmed below us, mostly centered over the island of Dreamspring. They weren't much more than dots, but through the nowhere I could feel the minds of the pilots—UrDail, kitsen, and human alike—all fighting together.

We were pretty high up, maybe even out of the atmosphere, so many of the enemy ships were out of range. I didn't feel like we should move the whole planet on a whim, though scud, did we need to move it farther away? What were two planets this large going to do to each other?

Jorgen, Alanik said. *What did you—*

We brought company, I told her. *All of it.*

Apparently, she answered.

My view of the planet below began to shift, and I realized the platform was drifting *away* from Detritus.

"Rig," I said, "are we *moving*?"

"Oh, scud," Rig said. "Is *that* what that navigation system does?"

Rig called to the other engineers, and several of them joined him at the panel. "Here," he said. "These are navigation controls like the ones on Platform Prime, but because there are no engine systems I could never figure out what they're for. But now—I think these inputs here are for coordinates, and then the system tells the hyperslugs where to go."

"Jerkface!" Kauri said over the radio. "I don't know what's going on up there, but our tidal authority would like you to know that your planet is going to pull on our oceans, gathering all the water on that side, causing an *even worse* wave to engulf our islands. Wait—oh, they say it will do that *if* one of our planets doesn't rip the other one apart first."

"They're right," Rig said. "But it should have happened already." He scanned the monitors, looking for something. "I don't know why it hasn't, but my best guess is that the planet itself has some kind of gravitational capacitor—almost as if it was intended to be a traveling space station, so it has systems to counteract the gravitational forces for the surrounding bodies—"

"The *planet*," I said, "has *GravCaps*?"

"Yeah," Rig said, shaking his head. "Apparently it does."

"Negative, Kauri," I said over the radio. "Detritus has systems to prevent damage to Evershore."

"If so, they aren't working perfectly," Kauri said. "The tidal authority is seeing a rise in the water, though not nearly as bad as they'd expect."

"We're too close," Rig said. "GravCaps have limits, and running them at this strength has to be depleting their power source quickly. We need to move the planet farther off."

"Let's do it," I said. "Before that though, can you send the platforms out to the kitsen islands to defend them?"

"I need to find the coordinates," Rig said, tapping at his console, using the platform sensors to pinpoint the coordinates of the various islands.

"Kauri," I said. "Does your tidal authority know how far out Detritus needs to be to keep you safe?"

"They're working up some coordinates now," Kauri said.

"Okay," Rig said. "Here goes."

The platforms around us began to move, this one jumping to that island, that one to another, the hyperweapons firing on the Superiority ships caught in the air above the islands. We hadn't sent our forces out that far, so they wouldn't be caught in the blasts.

"We can't move all of them," I said. "We don't want to leave Detritus exposed. But let's unload as many as we can and then I'm going to instruct the slugs to move the planet again."

"This is Commander Ulan," a voice said over the platform radio. "What the *scud* is going on up there?"

Oh stars. I couldn't explain this, not now. "Defense protocol to protect the kitsen planet, sir," I said. "I'll give you a full briefing when the sequence is complete."

"You're calling this a *protocol*?" Ulan said.

I was stretching the definition of the word, that was for sure.

Rig reached over and turned down the volume on the radio. "Gerrig, help me enter these," he said, and one of the other engineers stepped up beside him, assisting Rig in getting more coordinates into the system.

"Jerkface," Kauri said. "The tidal authority says the water levels are still rising. Even if you move the planet, this is going to cause a tidal wave to hit Dreamspring. They've put out a warning to the city for everyone to get to high ground. The other nearby islands are doing the same."

Moving everyone to high ground would make them easy targets for the Superiority, but if they were to drown anyway, what choice did they have? "I'll send my people on the ground to help," I said to Kauri, and then I switched to the medtechs' channel. "Cuna,

Zing," I said. "There's a tidal wave coming. Go into the city and help the kitsen get to high ground."

"Copy, Jerkface," Zing said.

I turned to Juno. "Will the cliffs be high enough to protect the library?"

"It has stood for centuries," Juno said, "and we have faced tsunamis before."

This one might be bigger. It depended on forces I didn't fully understand. "Kel and Winnow," I said over the radio, "Keep an eye on the water. If it looks like you'll be overwhelmed, we'll get you all out with a hyperdrive."

"Copy," Zing said again.

"I'm working on it," I said. "Make sure your people are still headed for high ground." I turned to Rig. "We need to move fast so that wave doesn't get worse."

"We've got platforms moving toward the islands that are under attack. Shield still operational. Ready when you are."

I reached out to Fine, expressing our need for the slugs' help again, showing him an image of the planets tearing each other apart and an approximation of how far out I'd like them to move Detritus.

Go, Fine said.

Go, I agreed.

And in a blink we passed beneath the distracted eyes and stared out at Evershore, which was much smaller than it had been. Beside me Rig swore.

"Kauri," I said, "is that far enough?"

"They're watching the tidal levels," Kauri said. "They say they would like advance notice before your planet decides to visit again."

"Tell them we'll call first next time," I said. "And let me know if we need to move again. We can keep trying until we get it right."

Jorgen, Alanik said, *we could use some help down here.*

I expanded my senses outward, taking in the whole of the battlefield. Our people were fighting, but they were scared. The appearance of Detritus and the scattering platforms both encouraged and confused them. Arturo was doing a good job with our people, but a lot of the UrDail and kitsen couldn't understand him, and they lacked our organization and discipline. They were struggling.

I felt the kitsen cytonics wielding mindblades, hyperjumping their ships into better positions. I felt their joy at being reunited with their kinsmen and their terror that this day could be the last for their home. Down on the planet, I could feel the kitsen civilians huddling, frightened. And one mind listening carefully, with rapt attention and a fair amount of confusion.

Was that—

Cobb? I asked.

Son, he said, *I don't know what you've done up there, but for the North Star's sake don't stop now.*

I closed my eyes. There were people all around, fighting and dying because of me. I'd worked so hard to find Cobb, but now I realized I was *afraid* to find him, afraid of what he'd think of what we'd done.

All this, all the resources we'd expended, moving the scudding *planet*, that was on me—

You WHAT? Cobb said.

Oh. He could hear me. Scud.

Sir, we—

Never mind, Cobb said. *Focus. You've got a battle to win.*

I felt like I should stop and give a full report, find out what my commander's orders were. But I was pretty sure he'd *given* me an order, so . . .

Over by the control panel, Rig was fiddling with a radio, finding the flight's channel. We knew he'd found it when Arturo swore loudly. "Is that *Detritus* up there?"

"Yes, it is," Rig said. "If we couldn't bring you home, we thought we'd bring home to you."

"Saints and stars," Sadie said.

I waited for Nedd's wisecrack, but it didn't come and my heart dropped.

"Amphi," I said, "why don't I hear Nedder?"

"Because he's speechless for once," Sadie said.

"Like the Saint says," Kimmalyn said, "if you don't have anything to say, you might scare your flightleader into thinking you're dead."

"I'm here," Nedd said. "Just . . . wow."

"Orders, Jerkface?" Arturo said.

"The enemy ships are scattering away from the platforms," I said. The platforms were taking care of the area far above Dreamspring now, but even with their mobility they weren't versatile enough to do all the work. "All flights, intercept those fighters and chase as many as you can in the direction of the platforms. We have the advantage now. Let's use it."

Arturo started giving orders, but I could already see what the problem was going to be. We had three different species of pilots in the air, and only some of them had translators in their ships. Defending a city was a more contained effort. Trying to catch and herd the enemy ships was going to take an enormous coordinated effort. We needed precision, but we had different training, and some of the kitsen ships probably had no training at all in working with a group this large. Communicating with them all was going to be impossible.

Unless.

Scud, I had an idea. I reached for Fine's box and opened it, pulling him out into my arms.

Thank you for your help, I said. *Mind lending me some more?*

"Fine!" Snuggles said.

"Fine!" Fine said.

"Fine," I said. And I focused on the battle again, on the many minds now scattering out over the planet. I felt Fine following me, his mind scanning over all the fighter pilots, a few of them winking out of existence, others blind with terror about what would become of them. Some determined. Fighting. Focused mostly on staying alive.

I could see the shape of the battle. I could see the patterns in the chaos, the places where we needed to push forward and those where we needed to pull back to manipulate the enemy. To stop their destruction and get them where we wanted them.

"Ready?" I said to Fine.

"Ready," Fine said.

And I pushed outward toward their minds, sending them all the vision, helping them see what I could see. Not a mass of individual fighters, but a military so brave and strong and *powerful* that even the almighty Superiority was afraid of it.

This was it, I realized. The thing the Superiority feared the most. The power of all of us working together.

I could feel other commslugs joining us, amplifying the signal to my allies below. I could sense their minds responding. I couldn't pick out individual voices, only this *feeling*. We were in this together, and in that we had hope.

I focused on the different fronts, directing our flights, pushing this one here, that one there. Pulling back some of our forces and urging others to retreat to the city, to cover the hospital area and the homes of the civilians. They all understood me, because in our minds there were no languages, no barriers. Around me Rig's team continued to direct the platforms into place. Piece by piece the platforms were extending their shield across Evershore, trapping the enemy inside where my fighters hunted them mercilessly, driving them up into the fire of the platforms.

So many pieces, but I could see the larger pattern and I did my best to express it. Our fighters began to fly better, more precisely, taking more and more control of the skies—

And then I heard a whisper from the nowhere. One word, the sweetest of all.

Retreat.

The Superiority ships began to race for the edges of the shield, the fighters pouring into their remaining carrier ships, which blinked out of existence. Some of the fighters turned and ran without a ship to go back to, flying with blind terror, and my people picked them off one by one.

In my mind, one feeling resonated above all others.

Relief.

They were leaving.

We'd won.

It was only one battle, one raincloud from the oncoming storm. But we were going to hold out. We were going to keep fighting.

From now on, we'd do it together.

21

When the battle was over, I hyperjumped with Juno down to the cliff above Dreamspring. The tidal wave had hit the lower city while I'd been gone, and there was considerable flooding, though the upper city remained intact and the water hadn't reached the cliffs by the library. A few of the buildings had taken damage from falling ships or destructor fire, and bits of wreckage were scattered over the fins and ridges of the city.

"I'm sorry this happened," I said to Juno.

"So am I," Juno said. "But my people leave today richer, despite the setbacks."

"You have your cytonics back," I said.

"It is more than that," Juno said. "We are no longer isolated."

There was still so much to figure out, so much work to do. The ever-present political squabbling would continue on.

But Juno was right. We weren't alone anymore. We were still fighting for our lives, but at least now we could fight side by side.

I squinted up at Detritus, which hung in the sky like a second moon, a bright sphere of metal and glinting shield. Stars, I didn't know how long we should leave it here, but I was going to let Cobb make that call. And all the calls from here on out, just as soon as I explained everything to him.

A transport ship hyperjumped into the middle of the road below the cliff face, probably carried by one of the taynix from Platform Prime. I squinted, watching as the ship's cabin lights illuminated a man in a vice admiral's uniform.

Stoff climbed out of the ship and moved toward the library. The medtechs were just pulling Cobb and Gran-Gran down the stairs, still on their stretchers. They left Cobb at the top and carried Gran-Gran, who protested loudly all the way down to the transport ship.

"I have to go talk to my superiors," I said to Juno. "It's better if you don't come with me this time."

"That's all right, shadow-walker," Juno said, lifting his book. "I have a great many things to record."

"Snuggles," I said, and I urged her to hyperjump us to the roadway beside the ship. When we arrived, I could hear Gran-Gran yelling at the medtechs.

"I can walk!" she said. "I may be old and blind, but I'm not infirm!"

I stepped aside as the medtechs persisted in carrying her to the transport ship. "It's okay, Gran-Gran," I said. "No one thinks you're incapable."

"They'd better not," Gran-Gran said. "Or I'll show them."

I was sure she would.

Stoff had already made it to Cobb's side. FM came up next to me—I saw her ship parked up the road now, by Sadie's.

"Sir," Stoff said. "We are so thrilled you're back. We've made some great strides in securing alliances with the UrDail and the kitsen."

"That's good," Cobb said. He looked over to me, like he was waiting for me to say something. His face was still bruised, his left eye partially swollen shut.

"It's true, sir," I said. "We have made progress." I knew Stoff was going to take credit for everything now that it had panned out, and I didn't want to start a war with him. I was too tired from the one we'd just fought. We'd saved lives and made alliances. That was what mattered, not the petty politics of who ordered what.

I glanced at FM, thinking she'd be glad I wasn't picking this battle.

"Stoff had nothing to do with it," she said.

"Excuse me?" Stoff said.

Cobb looked over at her.

"Permission to speak freely, sir?" she asked.

"I think you've already started doing that," Cobb said, his voice hoarse. "So go on."

"Stoff had nothing to do with the alliance with the kitsen," FM said. "He refused to make the call to send the flights to help them. He dumped all the responsibility onto Jorgen so that if it was the wrong choice, Jorgen would take the fall for it."

Stoff's mouth fell open.

"Is that true, son?" Cobb asked.

"Yes," I said. "Though in Stoff's defense, I did come in swinging."

FM gave me a sharp look, like she didn't understand why I was speaking in Stoff's defense, but it was the truth.

"I told him we were already authorized by you to make alliances," I continued, "and we weren't going to hear anything more from the assembly about talking to the Superiority." I was pretty sure I'd implied we weren't going to hear anything more from the assembly *ever*, but that was obviously not a long-term solution.

"Before we knew of your whereabouts," Stoff said, "we felt it was best to follow your last orders."

"Who is we?" Cobb asked. "Last I checked, in the absence of the admiral the vice admiral's job isn't done by committee."

Stoff stammered.

"If he hadn't listened to me," I said, "we might never have found you and Mrs. Nightshade. I don't know how long your bodies would have lasted with your spirits in the portal, but I can't imagine it would have been long."

Cobb gave me a look that said I wasn't helping myself, but it was true. Stoff was a coward, but he'd stayed out of my way when it mattered.

"The point is," FM said, "Jorgen is the one who found Kauri's transmission, which led us to you on Evershore. He made the call to travel here to find you, and to try to follow your last orders to us and make alliances for Detritus. And when everything went wrong, Jorgen is the one who made the call to pull in more flights, to put Rig and his team on moving the platforms, and to ultimately make the discovery together with them that we could move the planet."

Cobb looked at me. I couldn't deny anything she'd said. Those were the facts. "That's true, sir. Though she did leave out the part where I manifested mindblades in a meeting full of alien politicians. So it wasn't all good."

"Yes, well," Cobb said, "you seem to have overcome that misstep all right."

"Sir," Stoff said. "I'm sure you understand that I was only trying to do what was best for the people of Detritus. Clearly you had put your trust in Flightleader Weight, and so I—"

"That's enough," Cobb said. "Stoff, take a walk."

Stoff's jaw dropped again. "Sir?" he said.

"*Take* a *walk*," Cobb repeated.

Stoff blinked at him, and then he turned around and left.

"It really was a good thing he listened to me," I said. "If he hadn't let me make the decisions, we could have lost the whole kitsen planet."

"That may be," Cobb said. "But a commander who shuffles off the hard choices is no commander at all." He looked at me like he was considering something. He bent over for a moment, coughing, and FM and I looked at each other in alarm.

I had no idea what being half-stuck behind that portal had done to Cobb's body, but he seemed to be weathering it poorly.

"Sir?" I said.

"FM, would you excuse us?" Cobb said when he could speak again.

My heart dropped. Here it was. He was going to chew me out for taking control. The decisions I'd made were far above my pay grade. I shouldn't have done the things I did, even though they'd saved lives.

Stoff would have painted me as a renegade if things had gone poorly, but that wouldn't have taken a very broad brush.

FM gave me one worried look, and then she nodded and turned to leave. Cobb sat up in bed, glancing with irritation at the medical devices still strapped to his arm.

"I'm sorry I acted rashly, sir," I said. "I can brief you on everything, get you up to speed."

"I heard quite a bit over the radio there at the end," Cobb said, his voice still strained. He looked up at me like he was struggling to focus. "And that thing you did, speaking directly to everyone's minds. That's cytonic, isn't it? You haven't manifested some other ungodly power I need to know about?"

"No sir," I said. "It's cytonic. How . . . how long were you listening over the radio? I told them to call in as soon as you were awake—"

"And I told them to keep their mouths shut and let you work," Cobb said. "It was clear you had things well in hand."

That . . . seemed like an overstatement.

"We may not have done everything exactly by the book," I said, "but we've made progress on the alliance, and we have a lot more knowledge of how our own technology functions. I think you're going to be really pleased about what we have to work with. There were some rough patches, sir, but we pulled through them. And now that you're back—"

"You've taken on an incredible amount of responsibility," Cobb continued.

"I'm sorry, sir," I said. "I was doing the best I could with the resources I had. And I think my judgment was a little impaired by what happened to my parents—"

"I'm sorry about what happened to them," Cobb said. "The med team filled me in. They were lost in the explosion?"

"Yes," I said.

Cobb shook his head. "We disagreed, but they didn't deserve for it to end like that."

My eyes started to burn, but I blinked it away.

"None of that changes the incredible work you've done here," Cobb said. "If this is what you do when your judgment is 'impaired,' I'd like to see what you do when you're thinking clearly."

"I was simply trying to do what I thought you would do if you were here," I said.

Cobb gave me a look, and I stuttered.

"I may not have predicted that perfectly," I added.

"In this case, that only seems like a good thing." He looked up at the clouds and shook his head again. "You have things so well in hand that I'm going to promote you to vice admiral."

Stars. *Vice admiral?* That was skipping a lot of ranks. Though I did like the idea of getting to advise Cobb directly, what with everything we'd done and learned since he was replaced by that Superiority plant.

"Thank you, sir," I said.

"As soon as that's taken care of," Cobb said, coughing again, "I think it's clear that I'm in no condition to lead, especially when we're now hopping our entire *planet* around the galaxy." He eased himself back on his stretcher, staring up at the sky. "So I'm going to need to relieve myself from duty, until such a time that I'm fit for command."

I blinked at him, trying to make those words mean something other than what I thought they meant. "Which of the vice admirals do you intend to give operational command to, sir?"

"I know subtlety isn't your strong point," Cobb said, "but if you can figure out how to move an entire planet, I think you can answer that question yourself."

Saints and stars. "You can't be serious. You have so much more experience—"

"With all of *this*?" He waved his arm, taking in the kitsen city, the ships above us, Detritus shining in the sky like it had always been there. He winced, holding his side, and then let his arm fall again. "No, Admiral, I would say you and your flight are the only ones with *any* experience dealing with all of this. Both our military and a coalition of alien races are ready to follow you into battle against a foe so powerful they probably shouldn't have any hope of survival, much less victory. But they *do*. They're chattering about it over the radio, all of us resisting together."

"I didn't mean to take control," I said. "I was only trying to hold out until you returned. I never wanted—"

One corner of Cobb's mouth turned up. "No," he said. "The good ones never do."

I stared at him. "You're serious."

"I am. I don't intend to abandon you. There's a whole lot of paperwork surrounding the position, and it'll be good for you to have someone to help keep that out of your way. But clearly you're best suited to be in strategic command. The Saint knows you're better suited to it than I am." Cobb raised an eyebrow at me, and his mustache twitched. "Unless you mean to turn down the promotion."

He watched me carefully, waiting for my answer.

I looked up at the sky, at the gleaming moon of Evershore and Detritus hanging up there with it. I'd brought us this far on the hope that Cobb would relieve me of the responsibility to pull us through this—if not unscathed, then at least *alive*. I'd thought there was an end, a point at which I could unload everything that rested on my shoulders.

If I said yes, that might never end. But if I refused, I'd only be shuffling it off to someone else. There was no one besides Cobb that I'd trust to lead us as we faced what was coming. I'd pushed us this far so we could have the benefit of his judgment again.

And if this was what he thought was best, then so be it. "No, sir," I said. "I'll accept it."

"Good." Cobb put a hand on my arm. "I wish your parents could see what you've accomplished. They would be so proud of you."

Something inside me cracked.

In my time in the Defiant Defense Force, I'd felt lost and inadequate. I'd felt undermined and humiliated in front of both my flightmates and my superiors. I'd made calls no human being should ever have to make, had been both right and wrong about them, and had to live with both. I'd stayed in control through it all, because that was what I had been raised to do.

But at that moment, the veneer of my composure shattered like a damaged canopy. In front of my superior officer—*scud*, was he still my superior?—I started to cry.

"You're going to be all right, son," Cobb said, squeezing my arm. "If you need my help, you can now contact me no matter where I am. Which is a little disturbing, by the way. If you're going to make a habit of it, find some way to give me warning. It's going to take some getting used to."

"I'll try, sir," I said.

Cobb shook his head at me. "You can do what you want with Stoff," he said. "It's your decision."

"I don't think he should be in command anymore," I said. "But I don't want to punish him either. He really could have made things a lot more difficult and gotten a lot more people killed."

"That seems like a good decision," Cobb said. "Not your first."

"Thank you, sir."

"Now if you don't mind," Cobb said, "I'm going to close my eyes for a minute."

"Of course, sir," I said.

"And Jorgen?"

"Yes, sir?"

Cobb sighed. "You're going to have to stop calling me sir."

EPILOGUE

I left Cobb with the medtechs and stumbled up the road toward the city. I found Cuna standing outside the senate building. It appeared to be filled with kitsen, all packed in together. Goro hovered by Cuna's shoulder, still in his ceremonial armor.

"How did the evacuation go?" I asked.

"Very well," Cuna said. "We opened the buildings in the upper city so that the kitsen in the lower areas had somewhere to take shelter. I believe most of them made it out."

"Thank you for your help," I said.

"I'm glad I could be of service," Cuna said. "And that we could save the people here." They looked back into the senate chamber, packed with so many kitsen I could hardly tell one from another.

Cuna cared about these people, I realized. They spoke like they thought themself superior, but they were trying to save lives. I could work with that.

"I'm sorry about the flooding," I said to Goro.

Goro looked out at the city somberly, and I expected him to announce that we were enemies once again, for all the destruction we'd brought in our wake. "Tell me, human," he said. "Now that you have fought on our shores and won, do you consider us your conquest?"

"No," I said. "But I'm hoping we can call you our allies."

Goro narrowed his eyes at me. "Cuna says you've brought back our shadow-walkers, who we thought lost forever. You command the tides themselves, moving celestial bodies in the firmament. But you don't mean to rule us?"

"If I commanded the tides," I said, pointing toward the lower city, "I wouldn't have told them to do *that*. We humans have enough trouble ruling over ourselves. We only want an alliance, I swear to you. No one is going to invade."

Goro snorted. "Fair enough, human. It's not my decision, but I will speak for you if you need my support."

"Thank you," I said. Though at this moment, what I needed most was to get away. I excused myself and strode down the road, past the crowds of kitsen who were leaving the buildings of the upper city to survey the damage.

I found FM at the end of the road, where the water now flooded the lower levels of the city. Ships hovered over it, pilots lifting their canopies, looking up at the platforms surrounding the planet. Some of the platforms disappeared and reappeared again in different positions—Rig was obviously still working out their optimal spacing for generating the shield.

Stars, the things we'd accomplished, and yet there was still so much work to do. We had to seize on this—the way we'd worked together, the potential we had as a group. Someone was going to have to keep that momentum going . . . and scud, that was *me*.

Do better than we did.

I was . . . *excited* to get started.

"How did it go?" FM asked.

"Cobb made me vice admiral," I said. "And then he stepped down and put me officially in charge."

Her mouth fell open. "What?"

"You heard me."

"Jorgen," she said, "that's wonderful."

"Is it?"

"*Yes*! I mean—" She shook her head. "You'll be so great at it."

FM knew my weaknesses as a leader as well as anyone, so her confidence meant something.

"Scud," she said, "that means you won't be our flightleader anymore." She sounded sad, which was also significant.

"Yeah," I said. "That's right."

I looked up at the sky. The clouds had thinned, and stars peeked through the blackness, so clear it felt like we were out in space.

"You could take over the flight, you know," I said. "You'd be good at it."

"I don't want it," FM said. "I've never wanted to be in charge."

"I know," I said. "I think I'm going to leave it to Arturo."

"You should. He'll do a good job."

"He will." FM would too, but I understood why she didn't want it. Besides, I needed her somewhere else. "How would you feel about leaving the flight?"

FM looked at me. "What?"

"You were right," I said. "We don't have diplomats, and we need them. The assembly is a mess, but we do need to work with them. The DDF needs a diplomatic program to work with our *own* scudding people in addition to our allies. We've got to get everyone on the same page, and we can't do it by ordering them there. I'm going to need someone in charge who cares about more than the chain of command."

"*You* care about more than that," FM said.

"I do," I said. "And that's why I want to put you in charge of our diplomatic program. We need your empathy. *I* need you to help me figure out how to handle all of this—the politics, and the foreign relationships. You're so good at seeing through the rules and the orders and the scudding red tape and getting right at what needs to be done for the people involved. I know you don't want to be in command. But there's nobody better to be in charge of *this*."

I took a deep breath. I could order her to do it. I had the authority now, but I didn't want to do that to FM. She was my friend.

She'd already gone above and beyond for our people. She didn't have to take this on if she didn't want it. "It's your choice though. I understand if you want to stay with the flight."

FM stared up at the sky, the stars reflecting in her eyes. "I'll do it."

"Really?"

She nodded. "I hate the idea of the flight going out without me. I hate that I won't be there to protect them."

"You'd be protecting them in a different way," I said.

"I know. And that's why I'll do it. I never wanted to fight, you know. I only wanted to do what was best for the people who don't have a voice. The people the DDF ignores."

I nodded. "And I don't want to get so caught up in the military structure that I forget why we're doing this. I need your help."

FM nodded. "You're going to regret having said that when I start disagreeing with you."

I laughed. "Probably. But that's what I need you for."

"I'll be sure to remind you of that often."

"I wouldn't expect anything less."

FM continued to stare at the sky with a troubled expression.

"Are you sure this is what you want?" I asked. "If you need to think about it—"

"I'm sure," FM said. "I feel relieved, and I hate myself for it."

"I don't think you need to."

She looked sideways at me. "Does that ever stop you?"

Um. "No. But if it makes you feel better, flying is probably a whole lot easier than getting people to communicate with each other."

"Probably," FM said. "And it's not like our lives won't still be in danger. But it's not the same."

"No," I said. "It isn't." I'd already made calls that put my friends in danger. I was going to have to do it again and again and again. I wasn't sure how to feel good about that.

Maybe I never would.

Maybe that was because I shouldn't.

"I'm going to go tell Rig," FM said.

I wondered if she was agreeing to leave the flight because of him, but I didn't ask. I wouldn't judge her for it if she did.

FM looked at me. "If you need to talk more—"

"We'll do that later," I said. "You can go."

I did need to talk more, I realized. I couldn't do this alone, so it was a good thing I didn't have to. Right now though . . .

I wished I could talk to Spensa. I missed her so much I ached. I wanted to know what she thought of all this.

She would believe in me. I was sure of that much. She *always* believed in me, even when I drove her crazy. The same way I believed in her, even though I hated how far away she was, hated that I didn't know if she'd make it home.

I reached out, searching for her, and I found that presence again. Doomslug. She was worried about Spensa. I could feel it. So was I.

I'd done some impossible things tonight, things I couldn't explain. I usually thought of Spensa as the one who pulled off impossible tasks, but apparently she wasn't the only one.

I wasn't going to give up on her. I'd keep learning, I'd keep trying, and I'd find a way to help her if I could.

But if not, I would at least make sure she had a home to come back to.

DELETED SCENES FROM *SKYWARD*

WITH COMMENTARY FROM BRANDON SANDERSON

Commentary

One of the most common revisions I make to books is tweaking the beginning of stories. I find that only after I've written the entire book do I know the best place to start it. This makes sense—once you can view the entire arc of a character or plot in its completed form, you find that the first things you tried with it are rough compared to the final flourishes you made.

I don't usually get bothered by this in early drafts. If the opening is weak, that's all right—because I will know better after the book is done how to tweak it. I do this a lot, but *Skyward* happens to be an extreme example, where I tried several very different beginnings before I settled on the final one. So here, enjoy the first of these attempts, and I'll explain more after the fact!

1

Deleted

Twelve years later, I hung from the ceiling hundreds of feet above the underground city of Igneous, seriously questioning my life decisions.

Not that I minded dangling there. Who wouldn't want to get a view of the entire city, which glowed a brilliant orange-red from its lava flows. Thousands of buildings, huddled in clustered neighborhoods, shaped like cubes growing out of one another. Metallic walkways, made from the steel of cooled magma, pounded flat and polished. It couldn't compete with the sight of the sky up above, but it certainly had its own charm.

But man, I was thirsty. I was two hours into my climb, and I had only just realized that I'd forgotten to refill my water bottle. What I wouldn't do for something to drink. A some fresh water from the springs, a little JAM from the bottling plant, or—in a pinch—an overturned skull filled to the brim with the tears of my enemies.

Turns out, weird little girls tend to grow up into weird young women.

I wiped my brow, then chalked my hands with the bag I wore at my waist. I dangled by my knees from a large, staple-shaped hook in the ceiling of the large cavern. Those were set into the rock in rows, so workers could get up here to scrub away soot or check ventilation shafts.

They were also useful if one wanted to deliver a very important, very secret, payload to the roof of the city. I hauled myself up by one arm, inspected the next hook, then reached out and grabbed it. I swung over, ignoring my increasingly aching muscles. I was almost in position. Good thing, too. The backpack I was lugging was *heavy*.

I kept going, pausing occasionally to wipe my brow and re-chalk my hands. Other than the oversized backpack, I wore my standard exploration gear: work pants, a pair of good—if second hand—boots, buttoning shirt, a vest my mother had sewn with a billion pockets in it. Sturdy clothing, workmanlike and functional. Who cared if it had a few patches here and there? The great warriors of the past wouldn't have worn the newest, stylish trends. And if people laughed at *them* for looking poor . . . well, laughter tended to end when you buried a battle-axe in someone's sternum.

Not that I *had* a battle-axe. I really needed to look into that.

I swung to the next "staple," then hit a snag. The next one in this line was missing. I could see the holes in the ceiling, where it had been, but something had happened to it. I glanced down at the people walking silvery walkways along magma veins—which were walled off from touch by thick glass barriers. The temperature in the cavern was a comfortable warm—even hot, though I usually didn't notice that unless I was just coming back from a trip to the surface.

I liked being up here, higher than everyone else. Why hadn't I ever thought of this before? Unfortunately, I couldn't stay forever. I had a mission to complete. Eventually, the wrong people were going to spot the random girl hanging from the ceiling, and ask themselves, "Did *I* give her a permit for that?"

Permits were, of course, the bane of any reputable warrior's existence. (Well, that and blisters.)

So, I activated my father's light-line and attached it to the ceiling here. I gave it maybe ten feet of slack, eyed the distance to the next hook beyond—which was well out of reach—then added another couple of feet of slack. Then I returned to the hook I'd just left, pulled back until the line of glowing light was tense, and pushed off.

I swung in a nice little arc, like a pendulum—though I didn't smash into the ceiling on the other side, like I'd been expecting. I just barely got close enough to snatch the next handle in the line.

Niiiiice, I thought. Not a bad move. Had those little people below seen that?

I climbed maybe four more hooks before I judged myself to be in position. Right, then. Time to deliver the payload. I used the light-line to stick myself to the ceiling, letting me work with both hands, and dangled there as I pulled off the backpack.

It was almost as big as I was, which—to be honest—wasn't saying much. I could claim to be five feet tall if I wore my boots, but even that was stretching it by an inch or so. I always told myself that was better for a fighter pilot. Surely the smaller you were, the better you fit into a cockpit.

I kept my hair cut at about shoulder-length, in an A-line—long at the sides, but shorter in back. Like wings. It was getting long enough now that I'd want Mom to cut it. I didn't want too much hair, because of the inevitable day when I'd get to wear a pilot's helmet.

I kept it dyed a deep purple, with my natural black showing through in places. I used to tell people that I did it that way because it was the color of bruises, but that always sounded better in my head than when I said it out loud. Truth is, I just like the color.

I pulled a couple of ropes from the backpack and tied one onto the hook above me, then I pushed on my light-line and swung over to the next one, where I hung on long enough to tie the other rope from my backpack.

Payload delivered. Task at long last finished, I swung back, then took a deep breath. Finally, I let the slack out on my light-line, dropping me slowly toward the ground below. As I did, the two ropes inside my backpack pulled out—and the force deployed the long piece of thin cloth I'd stuffed inside.

I rode the light-line all the way down to the ground. It could get long—hundreds of feet long, as evidenced by the fact that I made it down safely. I had to be close to hook it to something, though.

The wide cloth ribbon I'd hooked to the ceiling ran out about a quarter of the way through my descent. I looked up as I, finally, hit the ground on a walkway between several buildings designed like metal boxes sprouting other, smaller boxes. I looked up and grinned—the cloth I'd attached to the ceiling hung down like a banner. It looked a lot smaller from down here than I'd hoped, but I could make out the letters I'd painted on it, after pinching it from the recycling station several nights ago.

(It wasn't actually stealing because it would just end up back at the recycling station—so it was just extending the use of the cloth before it got reclaimed.)

It read, simply, RATS—and had an arrow pointing right down. I'd gotten the location mostly right, as I was only two streets off from our family food cart which sold real meat.

Rat meat, granted. But anything was better than algae paste. I hurried off to see just how big a crowd my stunt had caused.

Commentary

So, what is wrong with this beginning? It is bombastic, has Spensa being her crazy self, and is in many ways a good introduction to the story. It sets up the extreme lengths she'll go to, as well as the desperate nature of her people and her family in particular.

Problem is, I felt it was a little *too* over the top. There was a comedic bent to what she was doing here—it felt like the kind of exaggerated stunt you'd see in a sitcom, with a character pulling off something they probably never should have been able to.

It was a tone issue, then. Yes, it set up Spensa. But the feeling was off—making a poor contrast to the melancholy prologue, with the loss of her father. I wanted something a little more grounded to start the story.

Next comes the second chapter, which I wrote immediately after this first one and which follows it chronologically. But you can also consider it as another attempt at introducing Spensa and her current life.

2

Deleted

On my way to our cart, I passed groups of men and women trudging along the walkway, heading home from work. Third shift was done. I could read their jobs on their clothing—vaguely greenish-brown stains for the vat workers, who stirred and maintained the algae. Soot and burn marks for those who worked the forges, turning magma or recycled metal into usable bars. Oil and grease on the jumpsuits of those who worked the factories, assembling munitions or starfighter parts for the war effort.

No pilots, of course. Those lived up in Alta.

Our cart had in a prime position next to the Fallen Ships monument, a big bronze statue in the shape of a multitude of ships taking flight, each one a copy of the others, and interjected artfully by lines and geometric patterns. I looked, eager to see how many people my advertising stunt had drawn to our stand.

None so far. The food cart sat in the shadow of the massive statue, like a spare bolt that had fallen off a wing somewhere and been left on the ground. A tall (but hunched over) young man sat on a stool beside it, his face buried in a large textbook.

I stalked over. "Rigmarole? What are you *doing*?"

Rigmarole—Rodge McCaffrey—looked up and blinked at me.

"You're wasting profitable opportunities," I said, waving at the people walking back and forth past the statue, and therefore the cart. "Commerce is a *fight*. You've got to face it on your *feet*, with gun in hand! Or . . . in this case . . . a ratmeat sandwitch in hand. Whatever."

I hauled him to his feet, which was hard because he was approximately a hundred feet taller than I was. Why had he grown when I hadn't? He didn't even stretch.

"Come on, Rig. Look confident! Sell it, don't just sit around and wait for it to get sold!" I waved my hand out. "Rats!" I shouted. "Rats for sale! Juicy rats! Come on, you guys *know* you want a rat!"

Rigmarole just smiled, then looked upward. "Hey! You actually *did* it?"

"Of course I did," I said, looking upward, feeling—admittedly—a bit gleeful how surprised he was. The banner had wrapped upon itself a little in the cavern's ventilation breeze, but you could still mostly make it out.

I grabbed a drink—finally—from a canteen I'd stowed in the cart, then hopped up on Rig's stool and continued shouting at the crowd. "You know what's great after a day of stirring stinky algae paste? A Rat! Come get your Rat!"

"You know," Rig said, "You're being a little . . . um . . . you today, Spensa. Even for you. I mean . . . ." He glanced up again. "You *sure* you're not nervous about the tests?"

"Of course I'm not nervous. Why would I be nervous? I got this *down*."

"Not sure I do," Rig said, glancing at his textbook.

"Rigmarole . . ." I said.

"You should probably just call me Rodge. I mean, we don't have callsigns yet. Not unless we pass the tests."

It was still stupid to me that pilots were chosen based on

a *sit down, pen and paper* test. What could you tell about a future warrior from their essay questions?

Still, we *had* this. "Five basic turn maneuvers?" I asked.

"The Reverse Switchback," he said immediately, "Alhstrom Loop, the twin shuffle, overwing twist, and the Imban Turn."

"Average seconds to blackout at five pulls?"

"Fifteen and a half."

"Engine type on a Pico Interceptor?"

"Which design?"

"Current interceptor."

"AG-113-2."

"You *got* this, Rig!" I said. "We got this. No need to be nervous." *No need to be anxious, or find things to fill your time and distract you while you wait for the tests . . .*

Still like four hours left. Scrud. Maybe I could go hang another banner?

"Rats!" I shouted. "Yes, the banner doesn't lie! We got rats right here for—"

Customer!

A man in a mechanic's jumpsuit walked up, looking over the prices posted in requisition chip denominations.

"Hey! Welcome!" I said. "What can I get you?" I stirred the sauce, a thick red paste with rat meat cut into it. We would stick a glob onto a bun made from pressed and dried algae paste.

Yes, I'd read about times when people ate better than this. But there's only so much you can do when living under ground, cultivating crops engineered to need heat—instead of sunlight—to grow. And rat isn't that bad. They might not eat it up in fancy Alta, but down here, protein was protein.

I looked at the customer hopefully.

"How do I know," he said, "that it's real rat."

"How do you . . ." I gaped at him.

"I mean, it could be anything in that mush."

"What are you worried about?" I said. "That we've substituted the rat for like beef or something? You're afraid you will *accidentally* get meat that is worth ten times as much?"

"I just like to get what I pay for," he said, but coughed up a few requisition chips and walked away with a sandwich. We did a brisk business, actually, over the next half hour or so—and I'd like to think my banner was the reason, though to be honest, we always sold well during shift changes. There weren't a lot of stands that sold actual meat. We had a secret weapon.

Me.

By the time mom arrived, we'd actually sold through almost all of our rat. Rig pointed her out to me, which was remarkable, as he'd spent the entire time with his nose in the textbook instead of helping me sell rat. Yes, he threw the occasional question to me to help me prepare, but I'd expected more enthusiasm from him. It wasn't every day that he got the privilege of being roped into helping his best friend with her family business—even if it was his one day off from his normal job in the precision electronics department.

He nudged me with the book and pointed down the road, to where Mom was limping along on her crutches, a large basket on her back. I cursed softly and ran to help, lifting the basket off of her back. Mom isn't terribly tall, but the injuries make her seem even smaller.

We'd long since passed the point where we pretended she would walk normally again. I smiled as she thanked me for my help, but inside I seethed, remembering a day some five years ago when I'd been told—while minding the cart—that my mother had been attacked. The officers said it was a random act of violence, but I'd gone to the scene myself, and found the words, *Death to Traitors and Cowards* scrawled on the wall where they'd found her.

I helped mom over to the stool and took her crutches. She frowned then looked up at the banner. It had twisted more on itself, and now looked like it read PTS. "Marigold told me that she saw someone climbing the *ceiling.* Someone who had a light-line?"

"It totally worked," I said.

"It kinda worked," Rig said from where he sat on the rim of the statue nearby.

"We sold out of rat."

"Don't you sell out almost every day?" he added.

I ignored him and showed mother the requisition chips. Together, it was almost half what we'd have made working a regular job at the vats or in a factory—an amount that was, for us, practically a fortune.

Mom smiled.

I loved it when she did that. It seemed so . . . rare these days. I'd happily wear worn-out clothing, work a job nobody else wanted, and bear the scorn of the others. As long as I could see her smile once in a while.

"Thank you," she said, holding my hand. "For what you do."

"I shouldn't *have* to do it," I said. "You shouldn't *have* to pay rent when we can barely eat. We—"

"Spensa."

"—should be taken care of by the pilot's foundation, like any other widow or widower."

They wouldn't pay for the families of a man who had been stripped of rank.

"Spensa," Mom repeated, but I pulled my hand out of her grip and turned away. Man . . . what had set me off? Hadn't I just been smiling?

"Hey," Rig said from his seat, "Spin? Did we study advanced flight formations? I don't remember studying advanced flight formations? I think I'm going to fail!"

Dear, oblivious Rodge. "You rattled them off to me yesterday," I said, turning to him. "In order, alphabetized. Starting with Abrupt-wingout?"

"Oh, oh right." He took a deep breath.

"Don't you two have lessons today?" Mom asked. "Shouldn't you be going?" I didn't have a regular job, like most of the other students, but I was allowed to sit-in on lessons for educational purposes, so long as I helped sew clothing.

I made it on time at *least* half the days.

"Lessons are canceled today," Rodge said, "so we can have a little extra time to study for the tests tonight."

"Then you should be studying, not covering for me at the cart!" Mom said. She reached into her basket and began getting out plates of algae cubes, which she stir fried and sold most of the time. The rat was a more special kind of deal, when I had managed to hunt a few up on the surface.

"Mom," I said. "We got it. We're good."

"I don't know if *I've* got it," Rig noted. "I'm not really even sure what *it* is . . ."

I helped mom set out the algae cubes, clean up some rat-paste stains, and change the signs. *One more day of this,* I thought, *and she can move to Alta and live in comfort.* One more day, and we'd have a pilot in the family again.

One more day, and I would cleared our name. Ace the tests, get into flight school, and people wouldn't *dare* speak of Father the way they did now.

I just had to pass the tests.

Scrud, I needed something to do to occupy myself. If I sat around thinking about this, I'd just get more nervous. "Maybe I'll do a quick run up to the surface and see if I can find us a rat or three to—"

"No you don't!" Rig said, standing up abruptly. "The testing is in *under* four hours."

"I can get up and back by then. No problem."

"No," Rig said. "Spin, I know what you're going to do. You're going to vanish, and then I'm going to sit there and worry about you until—at the last minute—you burst through the door."

"So, I'll make it."

"And I'll sit there having a heart attack waiting and worrying! Don't do this. I think I'd die if you missed it. Wingmates, right?" He held up a fist.

I reluctantly bumped it. "Wingmates."

"Oh, look!" mother said. "Isn't that your teacher? Maybe she wants some algae cubes."

Rig and I turned together, mirrored looks of dread on our faces. Indeed, a small family was walking down the silvery walkway—a woman in a skirt and a mustached man in a brown suit, with a daughter who had golden hair. They looked distinctly out of place compared to the many groups of workers walking home from shifts.

"Mrs. Vamber," I muttered. Delightful. I had hoped, with class canceled today I wouldn't have to see her—or more specifically, her daughter, Dia.

My first instinct was to walk off, so I didn't have to talk to her, but I was *no coward.* That wasn't the warrior's way. So as they approached the stand, I started toward them.

Rig caught my arm. "Spensa," he whispered, "you *do* remember what Dia's father does, right?"

I frowned. Had she talked about that?

"City inspector," Rig said, then nodded to the man, who was pointing with his fancy cane up toward my improvised banner.

Great.

"Quite an interesting project," the man said to my mother. He had an overblown voice, like someone who was afraid nobody would pay attention to them, so they made sure to overdo every little word. "Did you get a permit for that advertisement?"

"I . . . ." Mom said. "It was just . . . ." She deflated. Ever since the attack, she just didn't have the grit she'd once shown.

"I did it," I said, stepping around the side of the cart. "I just wanted . . ." I trailed off, pausing. "Is that a *cadet's pin*?"

The man lowered his cane and puffed out his chest. Pinned to the lapel of his jacket was a sparkling silvery pin, a blue sphere with a red starship. The pin of someone who had been accepted as a cadet in flight school.

It wasn't a pilot's pin, like my father's—which I kept pinned to the inside of my sleeve. It meant this man had passed the tests and gotten into flight school, though he'd eventually not made it to full pilot. It was still impressive. No wonder he had a cushy job.

"Made it all the way to the last cut!" he said proudly. "Eventually was forced out because of my eyesight, but with full honors! But about that banner, young woman. We have to discuss what you've done here!"

"She's always doing stuff like that, Dad," Dia said. The blonde girl had walked over to sit beneath the statue, just to the right of our cart. "Best not ask why the Spaz is Spastic. Half the time, she doesn't even show up for lessons, because she's off climbing somewhere."

"Yes, well, that's not an *excuse,*" he said. "Half the people in this district showed up at the offices, complaining that some fool was climbing across the ceiling!" He squinted. "What does that even *say*? 'Pets?'"

The man's wife—Mrs. Vamber, who often taught our lessons— was an overdressed woman in floral prints and too much makeup. I didn't actually mind her, as her voice was nice, and she didn't chide me too badly when I was late. But she also *rarely* talked about the important things. If I was going to be a pilot, why did it matter if I knew how to find the area of a parallelogram?

Her husband blustered about my advertisement, and I stood my ground, though I needed a box or something so I could look him straight in the eyes. Mrs. Vamber, however, quieted him and nodded toward my mother.

"Right, right," the man said. "We were here to talk to the mother, weren't we? A moment, child. We'll deal with your infraction in a moment. For now, excuse us."

A moment? Excuse them? For what? Why would my teacher need to speak with my mom?

Former teacher, I thought pointedly. *Lessons are done. Tests are tonight.*

I stood my ground until mother quietly asked me to step away. And . . . well, even though she was quiet, I couldn't ignore when she spoke to me. So I retreated over to the rim around the statue, near Dia, who was more and more turning into a copy of her mother. Right down to the floral dress.

Mrs. Vamber leaned in and began speaking quietly to my mother. Rodge waved to me and nodded toward his home. We'd meet at the testing.

"So, Dia," I said, sitting stiffly next to the perfumed young woman. "Not cramming in some last minute studying?"

"I've gotten a job as an inspector," she said primly. "Assistant to my father."

"Jobs aren't given out until after the tests," I said.

Dia rolled her eyes.

"You should still try," I said. "You should see how you place. What if you get in. What if you could become a pilot?"

"You really don't know, do you?" Dia asked. "You really haven't guessed, after all these years?"

I frowned. "Guessed what?"

"The tests are fake, they don't determine anything," Dia said. "The people who are going to be made pilots have already been chosen. It's all a game to make us feel better."

I laughed. Like, laughed out loud, because the concept was

so ridiculous I was *sure* she was joking. Unfortunately, Dia wasn't exactly the joking type. She just rolled her eyes—again—and dug some lipstick from her purse.

"Whatever," she said. "I'm just glad that *I* have something secure lined up. You do realize they'll never let the daughter of a coward fly, right? Even if the tests meant something, *you* wouldn't be allowed to pass."

I stood up abruptly, and she jumped. Good. She feared me.

I pointed at her, finger fraction of an inch from her nose. *"Don't,"* I said. "Don't *taunt me."*

"What are you going to do? Punch me? Honestly, Spaz, that might be for the best. Hit me. Get tossed into the detention, miss the tests. That would be better for you than embarrassing yourself by showing up tonight."

I felt the heat rise inside of me. My face going cold, like it did—strangely—when I got angry. I felt my fingers pulling into a fist, and I swear, I almost *did* punch her. That face of hers could use a good clock, right across the cheek.

[The chapter ends the same way as it does in the final book, except Spensa's job offer is working at the algae vats.]

Commentary

So, here we have another attempt. This is more realistic, though it keeps some of the same themes. I tried out some things, like her mother's infirmity, that I didn't end up liking. (I felt like it was too on the nose, indicating that she wasn't going to be able to help Spensa in this.)

Spensa's personality is coalescing here; she feels more like the version I went with. At this point, I went ahead and kept writing the rest of the book. But looking at it again later, I wasn't yet pleased with this version of the opening. In contrast to the previous one, it was too mundane. I wanted more action, a more interesting situation, to start her off in. Something visually or at least thematically dynamic.

So, on to attempt number three.

1

Deleted

Nine years later, at age sixteen, I hung inside the tunnel-like tube of an ancient ventilation shaft, seriously questioning my life decisions.

Not that I minded the experience. I liked a good adventure, even if I was strapped a little too safely into my harness. An enormous fan lay far beneath me, at the bottom of the tunnel. It wasn't moving at the moment, but wind would periodically blow in from side tunnels and ruffle my shoulder-length hair.

A wall panel hung open to my right, exposing wires, circuits, and other mechanical doo-dads. I knew how important this sort of job was, logically. We lived in caverns beneath the surface—without ventilation like this, we'd all suffocate.

It was just that, fixing ventilation machines didn't *feel* like work for a warrior. I was going to be a great pilot, so why did I need to train on reading service diagrams and practice doing mundane repairs?

"Fifteen minutes, Spensa!" Instructor Dagny yelled into the shaft, echoing against the metallic sides.

It's just another test, Spensa, I thought, dangling from

my harness and setting to work *Your life is full of tests.* Everyone tested the daughter of a coward.

Well, I'd show them. I wielded my screwdriver like the ancient sword Naegling, deftly spearing screws like they were the eye-sockets of my enemies.

Turns out, weird little girls tend to grow up into weird young women.

I worked quickly, repairing the machinery as best I could from my memory of the week's lessons. I *had* paid attention to these ones. A pilot had to know how to repair her ship in a pinch, right? In case she was shot down in a distant locale, and her emergency radio transponder broke?

I got the wires screwed back in what I hoped was the right order. But something was missing. I dangled in my harness, fishing in my pocket for the little diagram of the mechanism I'd been given. I held my flashlight in my teeth, holding up the diagram beside the machinery.

There was a part missing, a little flat piece of metal about the size of my palm, something that other wires connected to. Huh. I searched around inside the panel, then turned my flashlight downward.

Yup, there it is, I thought, noting the piece of metal laying near one of the enormous fan blades. Well, this little training exercise was about to get way more interesting. I quickly unstrapped from my harness, dangling from it by one arm as I rolled up the right sleeve of my standard-issue student jumpsuit.

Underneath, always on me but kept carefully out of sight, was my father's light-line. Everyone assumed it had been destroyed when my father's ship exploded, and nobody had ever asked me about it. I intended the secret to stay that way, but at the moment, I wasn't being watched.

So, I carefully activated the device, and the bracelet

601

began to glow with a soft orange-red light. The light-line wasn't actually the bracelet, though—that was just the housing. The light-line itself was a glowing rope of energy that could be stretched hundreds of feet. It contained its own ancient power source, and was a piece of technology as old as the Apparatus that kept the caverns running.

On the bottom of the bracelet, two ends of light protruded from holes near the palm of my hand. I pulled one of the cords out—it was only a little thicker than the wires in the contraption I'd been fixing earlier—and stuck it to the wall. It stretched from the bracelet easily, and adhered where I put it. From there, it was easy to slip out of my harness and—carefully controlling the release mechanism with two fingers on my left hand—lower myself down toward the fan below.

Easy. Descending into the monster's den, just like an ancient warrior from my Gramma's stories. I landed on the fan, then reached across its blades for the piece of metal. In doing so, however, I noticed for the first time that I could see down through the gaps in the large fan.

The entire cavern of Igneous spread before me; I was provided with a stunning view from the very top of the cavern. I could see the many box-like apartments, built together like cubes splitting off one another, that made up neighborhoods.

Towering over them were the housings of the Apparatus—ancient forges and refineries that turned molten rock drawn up from below into usable metal parts. Heat rose through around me; Igneous was a suffocating place, always hot and humid, with all those refineries, factories, and algae vats. It was painted a red-orange, most light provided as a side effect of heated metal and tubes of molten rock.

I was above it all, like I was flying in the cockpit of a fighter, soaring above the cavern city.

"Five minutes, Spensa!" Instructor Dagny called down.

Right. The test. I snatched the part, then engaged my

lightline, which retreated into its housing and pulled me back up into the air. I didn't bother with the harness for the moment, instead scrambling to pull out my screwdriver and get the part back into its slot. I didn't have time to consult the diagram; I worked by memory, getting it screwed into place.

"Time's up!" They started hauling my harness back up by its ropes. I snatched it and shoved my arm through, and—as I was pulled up to join the class—I got my sleeve back up and covering the light line.

I was soon pulled up through a panel in the floor of an ancient metal room, where the other seven students in my current class were waiting with Instructor Dagny and several men from the Ventilation Repair corps. I let go of the harness as they pulled me through, then grabbed the sides of the hole and hauled myself up.

"Spensa!" Dagny said. "You undid your harness?"

I shrugged, settling down on the floor, only now realizing how much I was sweating. That might not have been *true* warrior's work, but I was surprised by how much I'd enjoyed it.

One of the men from the ventilation corps suited up in the harness next, then lowered himself down to inspect my handiwork. Instructor Dagny folded her arms and watched me with a critical eye. She was a severe woman, slender but forceful. She wore a simple worker's jumpsuit, instead of the more fashionable clothing some of my teachers picked.

I liked her. I could imagine her brandishing a pitchfork in one of Granna's stories, defending the town while the menfolk were away sailing longboats.

She scowled at me, but I was used to treatment like that, even from the teachers who weren't as bad as the others. The daughter of Chaser, the Coward of Alta, wasn't someone you treated with anything but contempt. As was my habit, I met her glare straight on, and lifted my chin.

It would take a few minutes to get a report on how I'd

done, so I stood up and walked toward the other students. Behind Instructor Dagny walked over and spoke to the overseer in a hushed tone. I heard the words, "Brash" and "aggressive."

That was unfair. It had been *at least* two months since I'd gotten into a fist-fight with one of the other students. Granted, they did kind of shy away from me as I walked over. All except for Rodge, of course. He sat on the floor by the wall, his lanky form hunched over, his nose buried in the instruction manual for ventilation repairs.

"Rodge!" I said. "Rigmarole!"

His nickname—the callsign we'd chosen for him when he became a pilot—made him finally look up. "Hey!" he said. "Done already?" He raised his hand, and I hauled him to his feet—which was hard because he was approximately a hundred feet taller than I was. Why had he grown when I hadn't? He didn't even do stretches every morning, like I did.

"I'm next, aren't I?" he asked. "What was it like? Did the harness hurt? What if I get the wires wrong?"

"Eh, don't stress it," I said. "This sort of thing doesn't matter. We're going to be *pilots*."

"And what if this is on the pilot's tryout test?"

"Ventilation schematics? On the *pilot's test*? Don't be ridiculous."

"Of course I'm not nervous. Why would I be nervous? I got this *down*."

"Not sure I do," Rig said, glancing at his textbook.

"Rigmarole . . ." I said.

"You should probably just call me Rodge. I mean, we don't have callsigns yet. Not unless we pass the test."

It was still stupid to me that pilots were chosen based on a *sit down, pen and paper* test. What could you tell about a future warrior from their essay questions?

Still, we *had* this. "Five basic turn maneuvers?" I asked.

[Their conversation is the same, and then the draft skips ahead a little.]

The other man from the ventilation corps—their overseer—wrote down on his clipboard. "Well, Student," he said to me. "I have to mark you down for ignoring proper safety protocol. Anyone who applies to be in the ventilation corps needs to understand the importance of following instructions. We provide a vital function for the city."

The sanitation crews from last week had said much the same thing. And the algae-vat workers from the week before. And the factory workers from the week before that. They all had practically the same speech—something about society being a machine, and each person an essential screw or cog.

"Every job in the cavern is a vital part of the machine that keeps us alive," he explained, speaking not just to me, but to the other seven students in the room. "But without ventilation, everyone would die of suffocation."

It's essential, I thought, anticipating what he was going to say, *that you learn your place, and do your job well. Follow the manual. Be precise.*

"To join us, you have to be able to follow instructions," the man said. "You have to be willing to do your part, no matter how small it may seem. We survive the krell attacks through absolute precision and dedication."

Obedience is defiance.

"Obedience," he said, *"is—"*

"Hey, Aulfr!" a voice called up from the shaft below. "Check the connections for me, would you?"

The overseer paused his speech, then went to the wall and checked on some lights there. Readouts for the status of the fans below.

Commentary

This is the best of the three failures, as it is more dynamic and interesting a scene—yet I felt it was adhering too much to what I'd tried before.

The final published version has Spensa hunting in the caverns, isolated from everyone else. A loner, imagining herself on some grand hunt. The key was doing that—pulling her away from the situation entirely, and letting her be part of her own adventure. Both to highlight where the book would go (giving promises of tone and theme) but also to reinforce that Spensa is only part of the main structure of society in specific ways. She's mostly an outsider.

In the end, that was the problem with all of these. Except the first, they had her playing too much by society's rules, which didn't give the right tone.

Next are some deleted scenes from later in the book—where I was working on Spensa and Jorgen's romance.

43

Deleted

[Chapter 41 in the final book. Spensa confronts Jorgen after learning that Arturo's parents have pulled him from flight school because of the danger.]

"You realize the only ones who died on our team were the common ones," I snapped. "Bim, Morningtide, Hurl. Not a single deep caverner among them!"

"They were my friends too, Spin."

"You, Arturo, Nedd, FM. All alive," I poked him in the chest with each name. "You had training ahead of time. A leg up, to keep you alive, until your coward families could stick some medals on you and parade you around as proof that you're so much better than the rest of us!"

He grabbed my arms to stop me from poking him, but wasn't mad at *him*. In fact, I could see in his eyes a frustration equal to my own. He hated that he was boxed in like this.

I shook out of his grip, then took hold of him, pulling my head against his chest squeezing my eyes shut. Another one of us was gone. I knew, deep down, that was the *real* source of my anger. The fear of losing more friends.

And right then, I needed something to hold onto.

Jorgen tensed, probably expecting me to attack him again.

Fool girl. But I held on, and finally, he folded his arms around me and rested his head against mine.

"I only just got to be part of the flight," I whispered, "and it's being ripped apart *again*. Part of me is glad he's safe, and will stay safe, but part of me is angry. Why couldn't Hurl have been kept safe, or Bim?"

Jorgen didn't respond.

"Cobb told us, on that first day, that only one or two of us would make it," I said. "Who dies next? Me? You? Why, after decades, don't we even know *what* we're fighting or *why* we're doing it?"

"We know why, Spensa," he said softly. "It's for Igneous, and Alta. For civilization. And you're right, the way we do things isn't fair. But these are the rules we play by. They're the only rules I know."

"Why is everything about rules, to you?" I asked, head still pressed against his chest, the scent of his clean flight suit close, the quick thumping of his heart in my ears. "What about emotion, what about feelings?"

"I feel."

"What do you feel now?"

"Like . . . I never want to let go."

I squeezed my eyes shut tighter and held on. I thought about the DDF, about Alta and Igneous, and about the fact that I just didn't have anything to defy any longer. I'd spent my life fighting against the things they said about my father.

But now . . . now I knew they were right.

About him. About me.

Finally, I looked up at Jorgen. Looked him right in the eyes, and we were very close. I drew closer, going up on my toes . . . and . . .

And he started blushing.

Jerkface, blushing?

"You realize," he said, face inches from mine, "we are

very close to getting kicked out early for breaking inter-flight liaison rules."

I held on for a moment, then released him. "Yeah, well. You grabbed me first."

"You were attacking me!"

"Lightly tapping your chest for emphasis." I turned and glanced around, realizing that if I were going to try to kiss my flightleader, I *probably* shouldn't do it in the middle of the main launchpad walkway.

Was that what I was doing? Trying to kiss him? Where had *that* come from?

It hit me like a thunderclap, though. It had been building ever since I'd seen him trying so hard in the simulation to protect Bim and Morningtide. So subtle, I hadn't seen it.

And suddenly, something that had always been there in the flight seemed strange, new. Possibly wonderful.

FM stood just inside the doorway into the building, arms crossed and a smile on her face, watching us. Jorgen was *still* blushing, which was . . . well . . .

Huh. It was attractive.

He blushed further, then spun and walked into the building past FM.

"Making moves?" FM whispered to me as I walked in after him. "I approve."

"It wasn't that kind of hug," I said.

"Sure," she said. "And it wasn't 'that kind' of kiss, either."

"That was *not* a kiss!"

FM just smiled. We walked to our new classroom, which only had five holo-projector seats, reconfigurable for a variety of different ship dashboard layouts. We settled down to listen to Cobb, but I couldn't keep myself from looking at Jorgen—then looking away when he looked toward me. Then looking back.

Finally, I leaned my head forward against my console and closed my eyes, listening with only half an ear to Cobb. Five weeks until graduation, and I wasn't sure I even deserved to be a pilot. My father's treason, loosing Arturo, Hurl's death, M-Bot, and . . . and now this.

Scud, this was getting complicated.

Commentary

I've got a good friend in my writing group, Kaylynn, who is much better at romance than I am. She made some suggestions to tweak the Jorgen/Spensa romance and give it more time to grow. My initial pitch to myself on her sequence here was "She falls in love with the Draco Malfoy of the book and finds out he's not such a bad guy."

Kaylynn said that, contrary to my expectations, going too quickly would be adverse to the romance working. So this change, and the next one, are following her advice in this regard. I just thought it would be fun for you to see the "what could have been" of the book.

I hope you enjoyed this glimpse into the rough draft!

—Brandon

46

Deleted

[Chapter 44 in the final book. Spensa goes to talk to Jorgen in the garage.]

I pulled off my helmet and handed it to my ground crew-member, then hopped onto the ladder and skidded down. FM waved to me, and I waved back, but jogged past her ship. Sure enough, Jorgen was already making for the garage where he kept his hovercar these days. He'd given up on trying to hide it outside, and had asked for a small hangar near the launchpad.

I debated for only a moment, then took off after him. Right now, there were a lot of things in my life that didn't make sense. What I'd seen my father do, what the DDF *continued* to do in monitoring my brain, the strange starfield of eyes that had appeared in the cockpit. M-bot, powering down and leaving me.

On top of that, I wasn't sure I could trust my own emotions or judgment. I seemed to be losing control of everything. Or maybe I'd never had any control in the first place. It was frustrating.

No, it was *terrifying*.

My sudden but profound attraction to Jorgen was just an-other thing on the list. But it *was* something I could seize, something I could try to understand. At that moment, I needed *something* about myself that I could control.

I followed him into the small hangar with his car. He took his jacket off a peg on the wall and pulled it on, then turned back toward his car and saw me in the doorway. He froze.

I felt a momentary panic. What if I was wrong, and he *wasn't* attracted to me back? What if I'd read *way* too much into our interactions on the launchpad that day, and he'd simply been suffering me? He could be so hard to read sometimes.

"Oh," he said. "Hey, Spin. What are you going to do with your leave? Go tinker on that secret—"

"Don't go all casual on me, Jorgen," I said. "It's time for answers. I need to know how you feel about me. Are you avoiding being with me on purpose? Do you think I'm crazy? Do you think I'm interesting? Both?"

"Now might not be a good time to—"

"Don't dodge my questions, Jorgen Weight!" I said. "I will have answers. I have made my stand, raised my banner, and sounded the call to battle! I will *die upon this hill!*"

He put the heel of his hand to his forehead. "You are so weird sometimes."

"At least I tell people what I'm thinking!"

He sighed, then walked deliberately over and shut the door—but not before peeking out to see if anyone was watching. The garage was lit by a few red emergency lights along the floor. He turned back. His face was so stern, with his lips drawn to a line. Scud, he was *tall*. I glanced around, looking for a box or something to stand on.

"Spensa," he said, "if something were to happen—between us, I mean—my parents would protect me. Cadet relationships are forbidden, but I'm too important to get kicked out of the DDF for something that simple. I can't offer *you* that same protection. So we have to stay distant. Is that really so hard?"

"That depends," I said. "Do you *want* to stay distant?"

"I . . ." He took a deep breath. "Do you?"

"You're dodging my questions again." Stars, he was frustrating!

"And you're dodging mine!"

I strode up and poked him in the chest. "You're the one who has been treating me strange this week. You've been overly stiff with me, barely meeting my eyes."

"Again with the chest poking?" he asked.

"Well," I said. "Last time, it made you grab me. So . . ." What was it that was so fun about making him blush? "Are you interested or not? I need to know."

He looked down at me, and blushed further. It was a deep, rosy red, beneath his brown skin. He stepped closer to me, and inside, my heart fluttered.

Soul of a warrior, I thought at myself. *Don't back down. Meet the charge head on.*

"You," he said, "drive me crazy. Everything about my life has been planned out. Careful. It makes sense. I understand it. Then there's you. You ignore my authority. You insult me. You talk like some valkyrie from a scudding ballad. I should hate you. And yet . . ." He stepped closer, leaning down over me. "And yet, when you fly . . . And when you look so eager, so passionate, about what we do . . ."

"What?" I whispered.

"Fire. When everyone else is calm, you're a flame. A burning bonfire—passionate, gorgeous, incredible. You ruin all my plans, make me want to toss them into the fire and ignore what is *supposed* to happen. So yes, I am interested. I was interested that first day! *But this is not time.*"

I felt a deep warmth rising inside me, washing away my panic. "Gorgeous?" I said, feeling a little dizzy. *"Gorgeous? Really?"*

"Gorgeous like a newly forged blade."

I would take that. That was kind of wonderful, actually. "From the first day? What about . . . when I punched you?"

"Well," he said, still standing stiff, with hands clenched at his sides, "I didn't particularly like *that* part. Nor the time when you collided with my ship. Nor, in fact, when you named me Jerkface. Do you have any idea how frustrating it was to keep trying to impress you, only to have you seem to hate me more each time?"

"Impress me?"

He nodded.

"You really didn't do a good job of it . . ."

He put his palm against his forehead again, sighing.

"Sorry," I said. "I didn't mean that to be an insult."

"It's all right. I can be . . . stiff, sometimes. And I'm your flightleader, so a relationship would be doubly inappropriate. I had to be *extra* careful. Keep you at arm's length. Try to, anyway. You're *very hard* to pin down, Spensa."

Wow. With everything going so wrong lately, I realized I'd come in here *expecting* this to blow up into another disaster. Somehow, it wasn't. Somehow . . . somehow it was working.

I went up on my tiptoes, reaching my lips toward his.

"We should wait," he said.

"'No country has ever benefitted from a protracted war,'" I whispered. "Sun Tzu."

I kissed him. It *felt* like fire. Inside me, running all the way from my lips down to my toes.

Yes, my life was in chaos. I'd lost M-Bot, I'd lost my friends. I'd even lost, to an extent, my will to fight.

Yet I'd found this at the same time. *Fire.*

He leaned into me, *melted* into me, like molten steel. Two heats, enflaming one another. A long, unhurried, *passionate* kiss.

Then he pulled back, breathing heavily. "Two weeks," he said. "We graduate in two weeks. After that, the rules against cadet romances won't apply to us."

Slowly, I nodded. I suppose I could accept first blood in lieu of a complete victory.

"Would you like to join me," he said, "for the party my parents are throwing the night of graduation?"

I leaned back against his car, smiling. "I'm sure they'd *love* that. You, showing up at their fancy party with the daughter of a coward?"

"I've been talking about you to them," he said. "I think . . . I think my mother has figured out that I'm a little obsessed. They think it's good that Chaser's daughter should redeem her family. It's an object lesson that no matter how lowly their status, anyone can rise to serve the Defiant cause."

"I'm not sure I like being an object lesson," I said. "Besides, approving of me 'redeeming' my family is one thing. Dating their perfect, destined-for-politics son is something else, I'm sure."

"Yeah," he agreed. "Though, considering how persistent you are, I have a feeling they might not have a choice. But really, I *do* need to get going. They're expecting me for my graduation uniform fitting, and I'm already late."

I smiled and stepped back, barely preventing myself from melting into a pool on the floor. That had been a *really* good kiss. And it was incredibly satisfying to see him looking so flustered as he failed twice to get his door open.

He finally got into the machine and sat down. He glanced at me, then blushed. "I'll see you tomorrow."

I leaned on the door of his topless car. "When you'll go back to pretending I'm just another flightmate?"

He rubbed his eyes. "Please don't say the word 'mate.'"

I grinned wickedly—just long enough for him to crack an

eye, blush again—then turn his face forward in a determined way. "You realize there's a *reason* for those rules. What happens if I get so distracted staring at you that I fly into a mountain or something."

"Blah blah," I said, then leaned in and kissed him on the cheek. Finally, I backed up and let him push a button to raise the bay door and drive out. When he glanced at me though, he was smiling. A wide, joyful, and *un-Jerkfacey* smile.

I strolled to the mess for lunch, and tried to hold onto that warmth, that fire. But it was cold out in the land of reality. As I ate my sandwich, I couldn't help thinking about how *impossible* it would be for something to ever happen between me and Jorgen. More likely we'd graduate, be put into different flights, and just kind of . . . never see one another again.

That was how most romances went in the real world. A transfer, a move, a change of circumstances. He and I didn't even have a relationship, really. He was the only guy who'd survived our flight, and I was one of two girls. How much about it was simple proximity?

His parents would kill this spark. Or society would kill it. The admiral was probably still hunting for a way to make sure I didn't graduate. And so, while I clung to a tiny ember of warmth, I found myself feeling cold as I finished my meal.

I fetched my pack from my room and started walking. But where was I going? To M-Bot's cave, where he sat lifeless? I couldn't face that. But what else was I going to do with leave?

The answer seemed obvious.

It was past time for me to return to my family.

ACKNOWLEDGMENTS

My huge thanks go to Janci Patterson, who did the heavy lifting on this book. Your touch has brought these characters to life in such a fantastic way.

To everyone on my team at Dragonsteel Entertainment, thank you as always. Emily Sanderson, Peter Ahlstrom, Karen Ahlstrom, Isaac Stewart, Kara Stewart, Adam Horne, and everyone else, thank you for everything you've done on all of the Skyward Flight novellas.

Once more, thank you to Isaac Stewart, our art director, and Charlie Bowater, our cover artist, for their work on the beautiful cover art. And again, thank you to Karen Ahlstrom, our continuity editor, and to Kristina Kugler for her editorial services on the line and copy edits. You guys were great.

A special thank-you, as always, to Max and the Mainframe team for their great work on each of the audiobooks. For this Delacorte edition, my thanks go to Krista Marino, Beverly Horowitz, Lydia Gregovic, Tom Marquet, and the ebook production folks, Jeff Griggs and Andrew Wheatley. My agents at JABberwocky, Eddie Schneider and Joshua Bilmes, facilitated it.

Finally, once again, thank you to the fans of this series. I hope you have enjoyed this look at Skyward Flight.

—Brandon

I am so grateful to the fantastic teams at Dragonsteel and Mainframe for helping make this book a reality, and to the team at JABberwocky for being such consistent supporters of me and my work. Special thanks to Peter Ahlstrom for helping us iron out some plot issues on a tight schedule, and thanks especially to Max Epstein for putting up with my neuroses, and even occasionally finding them amusing.

Thanks to Cortana Olds (callsign: Halo) for stealing my copies of *Skyward* and *Starsight* because she heard her mom was anxious to talk to her about a book. Cori was my outline sounding board and my first reader on my first draft, so she saw the book in a worse state than anyone else and loved it anyway. (And wasn't afraid to point out my terrible metaphors.)

Thanks to Megan Walker, who listened to a lot of whining about the state of various drafts and still brought me motivation cookies, and also read an early draft. Thanks to my writing group Accidental Erotica of Whatever We're Called Now for jumping into the early chapters of this with absolutely no context and still managing to make some helpful comments. And thanks in particular to James Goldberg, who read an early draft of *Sunreach* and offered feedback.

Many thanks are due to the Dragonsteel beta team: Darci Cole (callsign: Blue), Liliana Klein (callsign: Slip), Alice Arneson (callsign: Wetlander), Paige Phillips (callsign: Artisan), Jennifer Neal (callsign: Vibes), Spencer White (callsign: Elder), Mark Lindberg (callsign: Megalodon), Deanna Covel Whitney (callsign: Braid), Joy Allen (callsign: Joyspren), Suzanne Musin (callsign: Oracle), Paige Vest (callsign: Blade), Jayden King (callsign: Tripod), and Linnea Lindstrom (callsign: Pixie). Special thanks to Jayden for his flying expertise and for being generally awesome and to Linnea for her fan art and enthusiasm.

Thanks to Kristina Kugler for her *truly fantastic* edits on these books. Kristy did amazing work on these books on a very tight and demanding schedule, and I'm forever grateful to her for it. Also, Kristy, I love you fifty million billion.

A huge thank-you is due to Darci Cole, who listened to more whining than anybody and did a serious amount of cheerleading as I worked through the drafts of this book. Darci, you are amazing. Thank you for your optimism and your friendship. I would have lost my mind without you.

Thank you to my husband, Drew Olds, for his infinite patience with me and my work, and for always believing I can do it, even when I lose faith.

Thanks most of all to Brandon, who has believed in my work longer than almost anybody. Thank you for trusting me with your characters (and giving me a hand up out of my own deep plot holes). It's an honor and a privilege to tell these stories with you.

—Janci

Thank you to Brandon and Janci for such amazing Skyward Flight novellas. It was a wonderful experience working with you both on each one. A special thank-you is also due to our incredible narrator, Suzy Jackson, for giving her voice to these amazing characters that Brandon and Janci have created.

Thanks are also due to Joshua Bilmes, Eddie Schneider, and everyone at JABberwocky Literary Agency, Samara and the team at Brickshop Audio, as well as everyone at Listening Library, Penguin Random House Audio, and Delacorte Press.

And, as always, thank you to everyone at Mainframe involved in this project, especially Juliana Fernandes, Julian Mann, Will Newell, and Craig Shields.

—Max

Many thanks to this book's gamma reader team: Brian T. Hill (callsign: El Guapo), Chris McGrath (callsign: Gunner), Kalyani Poluri (callsign: Henna), Sean VanBuskirk (callsign: Vanguard), Joy Allen (callsign: Joyspren), Philip Vorwaller (callsign: Vanadium), Sam Baskin (callsign: Turtle), Evgeni Kirilov (callsign: Argent), Joshua Harkey (callsign: Jofwu), Ian McNatt (callsign: Weiry), Jayden King (callsign: Tripod), Jessica Ashcraft (callsign: Gesh), Gary Singer (callsign: DVE), Ted Herman (callsign: Cavalry), Rob West (callsign: Larkspur), Megan Kanne (callsign: Sparrow), Jessie Lake (callsign: Lady), Dr. Kathleen Holland (callsign: Shockwave), Jennifer Neal (callsign: Vibes), Eliyahu Berelowitz Levin, Frankie Jerome (callsign: Wulfe), Erika Kuta Marler (callsign: Leviathan), Suzanne Musin (callsign: Oracle), Paige Vest (callsign: Blade), Glen Vogelaar (callsign: Ways), Tim Challener (callsign: Antaeus), Deana Covel Whitney, Joe Deardeuff (callsign: Traveler), Zaya Clinger (callsign: Z), Heather Clinger (callsign: Nightingale), and William Juan (callsign: aber). You are the eyes that see all, but not like the delvers! Also, Betsey Ahlstrom did a ton of work on the proofread. Thank you!

—Peter

ABOUT THE AUTHORS

Brandon Sanderson is the author of the #1 *New York Times* best-selling Reckoners series: *Steelheart, Firefight,* and *Calamity* and the e-original *Mitosis;* the #1 *New York Times* bestselling Skyward series: *Skyward, Starsight,* and *Cytonic;* the internationally bestselling Mistborn trilogy; and the Stormlight Archive. He was chosen to complete Robert Jordan's The Wheel of Time series. His books have been published in more than thirty-five languages and have sold millions of copies worldwide. Brandon lives and writes in Utah.

brandonsanderson.com

Janci Patterson's first book, *Chasing the Skip,* was published by Henry Holt in 2012. After publishing several contemporary YA novels as well as the YA paranormal A Thousand Faces trilogy, Janci discovered a love of collaboration and has written books with Megan Walker, Lauren Janes, James Goldberg, and Brandon Sanderson.

Janci lives in Utah with her mini-painting husband, Drew Olds, and their two awesome kids. She has an MA in creative writing from Brigham Young University. When she's not writing, Janci enjoys turn-based RPGs, miniatures board games, Barbie repaints, and playing with her border collie.

jancipatterson.com

Don't miss the rest of the Skyward series!

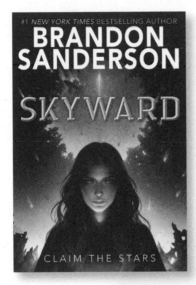

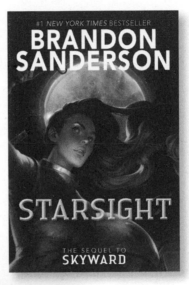